WHERE THE SEA USED TO BE

RICK BASS

WHERE THE SEA USED TO BE

HOUGHTON MIFFLIN COMPANY

BOSTON · NEW YORK   1998

For information about permission to reproduce selections from
this book, write to Permissions, Houghton Mifflin Company,
215 Park Avenue South, New York, New York 10003.

Library of Congress Cataloging-in-Publication Data
Bass, Rick, date.
Where the sea used to be / Rick Bass.
p. cm.
ISBN 0-395-77015-7
I. Title.
PS3552.A8213W47   1998
813'.54 — dc21
98-12842   CIP

Printed in the United States of America

QUM 10 9 8 7 6 5 4 3 2 1

This book is printed on recycled paper.

This novel is a work of fiction. Names, characters, places, and
incidents are either the product of the author's imagination or
are used fictitiously, and any resemblance to actual persons,
living or dead, events, or locales is entirely coincidental.

The author wishes to acknowledge the use of various entries from
Alexander Winchell's 1886 *Walks and Talks in the Geological Field*,
from which many of the "lectures" in this book were adapted.
The author is also grateful to have quoted from *Black Elk Speaks:
Being the Life Story of a Holy Man of the Oglala Sioux*,
by John G. Neihardt.

The photographs on the title and part-title pages are
by Stuart D. Klipper.

For my editors —
Harry Foster,
Dorothy Henderson,
and Camille Hykes

The Wolverine, Carcajou, or Glutton

This Species of animals is very numerous in the Rocky Mountains and very mischievous and annoying to Hunters. They often get into the traps setting for Beaver or searching out the deposits of meat which the weary hunter has made during a toilsome days hunt among mountains too rugged and remote for him to bear the reward of his labors to the place of Encampment, and when finding these deposits the Carcajou carries off all or as much of the contents as he is able secreting it in different places among the snow rocks or bushes in such a manner that it is very difficult for man or beast to find it. The avaricious disposition of this animal has given rise to the name of Glutton by Naturalists who suppose that it devours so much at a time as to render it stupid and incapable of moving or running about but I have never seen an instance of this Kind on the contrary I have seen them quite expert and nimble immediately after having carreyd away 4 or 5 times their weight in meat. I have good reason to believe that the Carcajou's appetite is easily satisfied upon meat freshly killed but after it becomes putrid it may become more Voracious but I never saw one myself or a person who had seen one in a stupid dormant state caused by Gluttony altho I have often wished it were the case . . .

— Osborne Russell, *Journal of a Trapper, 1834–1843*

BOOK ONE

H E HAD BEEN EATING THE WHOLE WORLD FOR THE SEVENTY years of his life; and for the last twenty, he had been trying to eat the valley. It was where he, Old Dudley, sent his young men to look for the oil he told them he was sure was there, but which they had never found.

He preferred to chew through his geologists one at a time, so that he could focus the brunt of his force upon them without dilution. In his fifty years of searching for oil and gas, he had burned out over a dozen good geologists, burning them to a crisp like an autumn-dry piece of grass lit by a match, though other times crushing them to dust by manipulating their own desires against them: by allowing them full access to their urge to search the earth below.

He allowed them to drill wherever they wanted, and as often as they wished; and after they had burned to ash or been crushed to dust, it was as if the wind blew even those traces away. He never saw them again. And he would go out hunting for a new geologist to train, teach, and control.

Old Dudley avoided searching for them in the schools. In Dudley's mind, by the time a geologist had been through a university, he or she was ruined. And he chose only young men, knowing full well that the women would be harder to crush — more enduring, and able to outlast him. Dudley knew also that his own brittleness within — the tautness of his aged but still-intact libidinal desires — would end up burning or crushing him, rather than the other way around. He knew that with a woman geologist, he would be creeping around the office, forever wanting to crawl under her table as she mapped — wanting to sniff beneath her dress, wanting to lick her calves. He would look at a woman geologist and see only sex: he would not, could not, see the universe below.

So he chose only men, boys, really: eighteen, nineteen, twenty years old, nearing their physical peak, and still operating fully on passion rather than technique or intellect. He had to catch them before someone got to them and taught them to believe in borders and limitations. Once they got that into their heads, it was very hard to coax them into flaming out or smashing themselves to dust. And once they'd been taught or lectured by another, they might question his vision of how it was in the netherworld — the comings and goings of things below.

He had to get to them first. He had to let them be born into the world and go about their own business of growing up — he couldn't just put them in a pen and farm them, nor did he exactly go cruising the streets at night looking for young men about to ignite — but he was always alert, ever aware of the possibility of encountering such a recruit.

Old Dudley could tell in a glance whether one of them had those coals within. He could see it in the shape of the young man's shoulders and in his posture. He could smell it, and he could see it in the young man's eyes. He could gauge it in every manner — sensing the internal temperatures and possibilities and heat of that young man as if holding his hands in front of a campfire to warm them.

It was never a blind allegiance that Dudley was looking for — that would have made it too easy, and in the end that geologist would never be able to become any better than Old Dudley himself. Old Dudley was more sporting than that. The best, the absolute best, was when the geologist, after a long time, came to understand Dudley for the monster he was — the manipulator, the domineer — but also understood that it was too late to turn back, that only with Old Dudley could the geologist keep drilling his wells when and where and however he wished — as long as they were not dry holes.

That was when the geologist finally began to crumble, or to smolder: when he became aware of the trap Dudley had laid for him from the beginning.

It was very strange. This was also when Dudley began to take pity on his geologist, and even feel love for him, or a thing as close to love as he could achieve.

The struggle of the geologist between his two masters — the young geologist's bondage to Old Dudley's horrific nature, and the young geologist's pure desire to reach, again and again, those craggy lands below — so unattainable, possibly even invisible, to other geologists, as to perhaps seem maddening to the seer who knew of them — reminded Old Dudley of some model of the very workings that so fascinated him: the earth's volcanic strainings and belchings, as one continental plate drifted over another like massive fire-breathing animals procreating: fissures and clefts channeling magma to the surface and giving birth to islands, new stone, then soil, then life.

Huge chunks of continent were forever falling back into the magma and lava — melting back into the mixture, caught and shredded between the gearworks far below, with the earth's brute physical desires at the center; mountains rising only to be sanded down in the blink of an eye, to then be redistributed in layers of wind-whipped sediment on the other side of the globe, even as new mountains were swelling like waves at sea rising to loom over and then crash down onto those earlier sediments, leaving no trace, not even a memory . . .

To go down into that battleground and find the oil — to travel into those lands — to avoid being crushed by those falling mountains, or drowned within those swamps and seas — this was as close to love as Dudley could get, and once his geologist found himself imprisoned by the knowledge that Dudley was his master — that was when Dudley felt a small warmth, and sorrow.

The sorrow fulfilled a space and a need within him. It helped him achieve his fit in the world. Perhaps it helped keep the gearworks, and perhaps the world itself, turning. The sorrow, however, was insignificant to the warmth Dudley felt watching the geologist flee deeper into those subterranean lands — the geologist trying, in that manner, to escape his bondage to Old Dudley, and in so doing, bruising himself against those rocks.

Whereas before in the young geologist there had been the grace of innocence, an absence of self-knowledge, there were now sparks of friction as the geologist tumbled among those gearworks like a falling bird with an injured wing.

Old Dudley was not a pleasant man to look at. Though ancient, he appeared to be no older than his early sixties, and he had the build of an ex-athlete who had labored to keep himself firm and steady. His eyes were a shade of gray that somehow — whether he wished this or not — gave others the illusion of deceit. His thinning hair, cut close, was silver. He carried, at all times, an air of roughness, no matter how dapper his dress. Something about the build of his frame — his musculature, his stance and carriage — made it easier to imagine him doing some physical violence to someone — swinging a wooden club — than being sedate and civil. The disparity between his fine dress and the awkwardness of his posture only made him seem more unpredictable — as if he were trapped, and as such, always within only a stone's throw of rage or harm-making.

Further unsettling, to anyone who knew the specifics, was his nearly immeasurable wealth — the hundreds of oil and gas fields that he had discovered, lying at varying depths all around the country: billions of dollars of reserves.

More troubling still was the fact that he capitalized very little on his great riches; whatever money was gained from the production of his oil and gas fields went always and unceasingly into the drilling of more, so that his operation was always expanding, oil flowing up his discovery wells to fuel the downward drilling of new wells elsewhere. The effect was that of a relentless sewing machine; but instead of stitching anything back together, he was forever piercing the earth, jabbing more holes into it, so that his company was more like some sharp-toothed beast eating the world, the lower jaws forever rising and gulping, the upper jaws simultaneously clamping down; and growing ever larger as it fed.

But it was Old Dudley's tong marks that caused the greatest unpleasantness in his appearance. There was a matched set of indentations on either side of his skull, dark creases like shadows that did not change or wane even when he stepped into the light: an ancient birthmark, the signature of forceps. It gave him an alien, reptilian look, and there was no way to view the tong marks without understanding that to come into the world, he had to have been pulled, kicking and screaming, from his mother — not wanting to leave that aqueous, other world, and not wanting to ascend to this one, either.

He had a way of seeing straight into the heart and weakness of a person, in the moment that any of them saw him for the first time. During the brief nakedness of that first startled moment, as they viewed his tong marks, he could see — for a few seconds — all the way into and through a person.

He would not have traded this gift, this power, for anything in the world.

Of late, Dudley had been running with two geologists rather than just one, which was invigorating to him: an older, experienced one, already knee-deep in the rubble and flame, Matthew, and a newer one, Wallis, whom he had found in the Texas hill country, and had been unable to pass up.

Wallis had been working behind a store counter in a country grocery store, reading a book on a slow breezy blue October Saturday, and this had reminded Old Dudley somehow of his only daughter, his only child: the way the young clerk fell out of this world and into whatever lay below.

In Old Dudley's view, book-reading was usually the kiss of death for the kind of geologist he was searching for. He needed someone more likely or willing to make that leap across those jagged chasms — more willing to attempt to convert the imagined to the real, the physical. Book-readers, he knew, didn't want to make that leap — wanted instead to keep everything nice and safe and comfortable, all imagined, at arm's length. Better to hire a plow horse or a mule than a book-reader. But Wallis seemed somehow different — not like a practiced book-reader, but a crude one. He had undeniably the scent, the potential, and Dudley could not resist him.

Could Dudley handle two geologists at once? He didn't know, but now when one burned or was crushed out, the other would only be hitting his stride. There wouldn't be the long waiting period of transition in which Old Dudley had to start over from scratch, molding a new one from loose clay. When Dudley had been younger, that had been part of the pleasure. But now such patience was not in him.

He didn't know how the two would work together — Matthew and Wallis. They might waste too much time and energy chewing each other up: there might be friction expended that would detract from their seamless plunges into the lands below. He didn't know. But he knew he had to choose Wallis: knew it even before he saw Wallis look up slowly from his book; knew it even before he saw Wallis's blue eyes, rimmed red from grief, grief that could come from only one thing — the loss of a loved one.

Dudley didn't need to ask a word. He could read scents and gestures as other men and women might read a newspaper. He could follow these scents straight into their seams of weakness — the soft places. He might not know the specifics of Wallis's grief — that for fifteen years Wallis had lived with his girlfriend and her old grandfather and their horses along a creek, and that she, Susan, had died six months ago, and that weeks later, with his old heart broken, her grandfather had followed her in death. Dudley could not read the specifics of how their life had been, there along that creek amidst the live oaks and beneath the half-domes of granite that the Indians used to call holy — domes of polished granite looming all around them, smooth and pink as muscles, glinting with reflected star- and moonlight. He could not know the sounds the creek made — different at night, then different in the day, and different in all the seasons, too — but Dudley could know the flavor of these things, and knew that Wallis had lost these and more — that Wallis had lost everything — and hungry, he rushed in to snatch up Wallis. Perhaps in his old age and his haste he was making a mistake, but he didn't think so, book-reader or not. Wallis reminded him so much of Mel.

And to Wallis, dwelling in that land of grief, it had seemed at the time as if he were being rescued. He had followed Old Dudley down to Houston, had put away his books, and had begun learning to read the stories below him: not a few inches below, and not a hundred or two hundred feet down, but instead, almost all the way down — almost to the core — losing himself in lands where no one had ever been, or seen, or even imagined; and where certainly there was no such thing as grief.

It was like an adoption, or absorption, the way Dudley took these men and molded them into creatures better able to dive into those precipices and chasms: the way he bent their weaknesses in that direction. They thought they were simply becoming his disciples. They did not understand — until it was too late — that the oil beneath the ground, the oil in which they trafficked — the combined molecules of hydrogen and carbon, reassembled from old life into the sour vat of death — was like the old steaming blood of the earth, and that it bound them — Old Dudley and his geologists — with at least as much fidelity as did any blood of humans.

They did not understand, never understood, until it was too late and they were crumbling or afire, that they had come into his family; nor could they conceive — again, not in time — of a beast who ate his family.

A year later Dudley cast this second son, Wallis, into the valley. He sent Wallis north with only the crudest of maps, a series of lines sketched on a brown scrap of paper, telling him the name of the valley, the Swan, and the approximate location of it, in northern Montana. They — Old Dudley and Matthew — told him that Dudley's daughter, Mel, was living up there in the snow with the wolves — it was November — and that it was the valley where Matthew had been born. Mel had met Matthew in Montana, and they had become lovers, and still were, of sorts, though for the most part, Old Dudley had succeeded in stealing him from her, so that now Matthew lived year-round with Dudley in Houston, along the Buffalo Bayou, where buffalo had been gone for over a hundred years.

Dudley and Matthew told Wallis that there were two Swan Valleys, up in the northwest corner of the state, and that it was the second, hidden one, where he was supposed to go: that it was the one nobody knew about, the one the century had not yet been able to reach. They said that the second Swan Valley was like a shadow of the first. They told him that Mel would meet him on the valley's summit on a certain date — there was only one road leading in and out of the valley — and that he had to cross over into Canada and then loop south, crossing back over the U.S. line again, in order to get there.

They told him that he would probably fall in love with Mel, and that she might even fall in love with him, but that none of that would matter — it wouldn't last.

Old Dudley was a falconer — less ardent about it than he had been in his youth, though he still kept a couple of falcons tethered on perches in the back yard of his townhouse overlooking the bayou. From time to time he would hunt his falcons on the pigeons that lived under the bridges of the interstate, and would even take them downtown with him to hunt there. Old Dudley instructed Wallis to try to find the oil that neither Dudley nor Matthew had been able to find, and to then return. He gave Wallis a set of instructions, in this regard, as specific as the DNA coding of a cell.

Wallis had lived on the bayou with them for that last year and had watched Old Dudley work the falcons enough to know what Dudley meant: that the falcon would starve without the falconer. A falcon could live either all wild, or wholly captive — but a hunting falcon, one which had been trained to be somewhere between the two — always crossing back and forth between those two lands, hunting whenever the falconer unleashed him, but then sitting idle for two or three days, too weak to fly hard enough to kill, and having to be fed pigeon breasts in order to get its strength up enough to fly and hunt again — that kind of bird could not survive without the falconer.

The penalty — nature's penalty — for failing to learn such a lesson was always death.

They told him all of these things, not so much like predictions, but as if they were seeing them so clearly that it was as if they could see into the future as well as the past: as if the future were just another version of the past, obscured beneath something, but that they could chart and map and manipulate that, too: that nothing could remain hidden from them.

"She's mine," said Matthew.

"She's probably nobody's," Wallis said. The two men were not as close as brothers, but perhaps cousins. There was no rivalry; there was only the hunt, which they both loved dearly.

Dudley had never had a geologist last as long beneath his tutelage as had Matthew. Sometimes Old Dudley would wake in the night and have the fearful thought that this one, Matthew, might outlast him — that the scent of metal-against-metal sparks Dudley was smelling this time was coming not from his disciple, but from himself. He would fear for a moment that the sound of loose rubble sliding down the mountain came not from some safely removed distance, but for the first time, from himself. Because such a thing had never happened before, how- ever, Dudley could not imagine it or believe or accept it, and he would label it for what it was, a nightmare, and would get up in the night and go fix a drink and sit at his drafting table beneath the lone overhead lamp, a pool of yellow light in the depth of the blackness all around him, and he would stare with fondness at whatever map lay on the table — the elegance of the map's contours, the feminine curves of buried earth.

"Leave her alone. She's mine," Matthew said again, as Wallis was leaving.

He fled Texas, driving in an old jeep north and west, following no map, knowing only that not until he neared the end of his journey would he need the little scrap of map Dudley and Matthew had sketched for him, though perhaps he would not even need it then. He felt a pull, a tug, and a snatch upon his heart as he crossed over the hill country where Susan was buried, and he slowed, felt her with him as strongly as if she were clawing up out of the ground to be with him, or as if he were being drawn down into that place to be with her. He hesitated, but then thought not so much of the falconer, to whom he had no overbearing allegiance, but of the thing itself that had given his life surge again, the oil, and he kept going, continuing north and west.

Across the dry gold grass of the plains, then — mid-November — beneath swollen, purple winter skies the color of bruises; through sleet, leaving north Texas, and up into the piñon hills of New Mexico, with the smell of smoke in the wood stoves, and magpies flying through the falling snow.

The hawks from the north were in the midst of their autumn migration, and every day, all day, through clearing patches of sky, he would see them heading south, sometimes drifting and soaring, other times flying, but always heading south, so that it gave him a strange feeling to be pushing so resolutely north. One night he camped in a pale arroyo beneath an old railroad trestle that smelled strongly of creosote, but which provided shadow against the relentless moonlight. He awoke in the night to feel the ground trembling and thought at first a flash flood was coming, but then he heard the wail of a train and looked up to see its huge black mass go roaring past twenty feet above him. The sparks from the steel wheels showered down upon him, and long after the train had passed, his heart was still pounding with the excitement and beauty of it — the speed and force with which it had passed.

There was no heater in his jeep, and the farther north he got, the more often he had to stop and warm himself: in a restaurant or service station, or, increasingly, by building a fire of sage and juniper, and then, higher, farther north, with fires of fir and spruce. He slept beneath the jeep when snow fell and listened to the snapping of the fire. When he slept sometimes she would come up from behind him, from out of Texas, as if to capture and pull him back down with her — and often he would not sleep but would lie in his sleeping bag watching the fire; and sometimes it would feel as if the world beneath him was still moving, still drawing him north and west, so that his own desires seemed to have no say in the matter: that too much of it was already decided as if by some alignment or movements of the constellations above, or by forces below. He knew this was not the way Old Dudley or Matthew moved through the world — he knew they pinned it down as if with their paws and told the world what to do and how to behave — but Wallis liked watching the fire and letting the earth keep moving along beneath him, with him riding on it.

In southern Colorado the snow was coming down so hard that he had to slow to a creep. He drove along at five and ten miles an hour. Deer and elk were coming down out of the mountains, moving down into their winter range, and often they walked alongside him, on either side of his creeping jeep as if in a parade, coming down off the high pass and onto the back side of the Divide. Snow collected on their backs in thick coats. They wore their antlers like kings.

He turned west and drifted up and across Utah. He saw almost no one. There was a lure, a pull, now, that turned him north again: up through Idaho, like a salmon. He crawled beneath the jeep, tried to get to sleep quickly, absorbing the last remnants of warmth from the engine, and it kept snowing, burying the winking red coals of the fire he'd built, and then there was the huge silence as the night's new layer of snow settled onto the world, burying everything that had happened during the day, burying all the days. It was possible now, as he drew nearer to the Swan — not like an arrow fired from a bow, but again, like some fish working upstream — to believe that he would have found or been directed toward this place, this rhythm, without instructions — without having been directed toward it by the falconer.

He stayed north — did not cross back over the Divide, where he could feel the sea of grass behind him and to the east. Instead he turned west, traveling farther into the deep timber: up through the Bitterroot and then farther, where the trees were taller, the mountains higher, and it stopped snowing, as if all that was below him now. The whole world had turned white, save for the deep blue of the sky, a depth of blue he had never seen, and there was so much silence that it seemed to be a sound of its own. The sun was bright but there was no warmth. He wanted to build a fire but wanted also to keep going.

He passed only two other vehicles all day: immense snowy logging trucks, tires swathed in clanking chains, slapping sparks behind in roostertails — the trucks' long trailers loaded-to-groaning with the giant trees, the first trailer carrying only five trees to fill its load, and the next trailer, six; and they left behind the thick, sweet scent of fresh-crushed boughs.

Wallis began to consider consulting his map, but decided against it, in a way that he knew would displease the falconer. He felt a stillness entering his heart, a peace, not unlike the one he felt when mapping the lost lands that were twenty thousand feet and two hundred million years below. Could he have found, or imagined, such a place without Old Dudley's — and Matthew's — instructions? He felt a gratitude toward them, and confusion too, as his heart grew still calmer. If this place did exert a pull on him — if it did have a desire for him — why had he never felt it before? What crust had overlain?

Shortly before noon on the last day he rolled through the little town called Swan — a wide spot in a river valley with a few snowy pastures, buck-and-rail fences, and old cabins with smoke rising straight from their chimneys. He stopped at the only store and bought gas and asked the lady what lay farther north.

"Nothing," she said, and laughed. "Trees and clear-cuts," she said. "Then the clear-cuts end — just trees, the woods they haven't gotten to yet — and savages." At first Wallis thought she was saying the people taking the trees out were savages, but then he understood that she meant the people who lived back in the woods.

"The other Swan," she said. "The second Swan." She lit a cigarette, looked out at the bright day: seemed trapped by the beauty that was too cold to go out into. "I've never been up there," she said. "It's mostly dope addicts and hippies," she said. "Criminals. It's right on the Canadian line. Part of it goes over into Canada. They say there are about twenty or so people living up there. Dark, wet — way back in the woods. A ghost town. They get a lot of wolves up there." She drew on her cigarette. The odor of it stung Wallis's face, but he could tell that his own days'-traveling smell was none too fragrant to her. "You can shower back there for a dollar, if you want," she said, pointing to the bathroom behind the poker machines.

"No thanks," he said, and then, "That other place, the one that has the same name — how far is it?"

"You go to the end of the world," she said. "Go til you begin to hear wolves, til you see their big pawprints in the snow along the road. Go until the road stops." Another puff of cigarette. "Go til you see all the dead deer and the flocks of ravens, from where the wolves have been." One more puff. "We had the name first."

And he had not traveled another twenty miles before he began to see the wolves, or what he thought at first were wolves, gathered on the sides of the road gnawing on the frozen red carcasses of deer, their faces masked red, with vapor clouds drifting from their mouths as if they were speaking, and eagles soaring overhead, waiting for a chance to join in on the feast.

They were only coyotes — shadows of wolves — but they were larger than any coyotes he had seen in Texas, so that they might as well have been wolves: and there were so many of them, and the woman was right, the ravens, flocks of them, were always in attendance, like black flies over spoiled fruit — though this meat was not spoiled, this meat had been living earlier that very day.

He reached the Canadian line — a small green and white sign said, simply, "Canada" — and opened the iron gate that spanned the road (only a lane, now, where a snowplow had tunneled through) — and he passed through it as if driving in to visit someone's home. He stopped and closed the gate behind him.

It was dusk now and he followed the winding icy road as if on a toboggan run. The stars began to appear through the forest and cast themselves brightly about him in a multitude, and the temperature fell away in the sun's absence, falling like a thing tumbling from a cliff edge. Twenty-five, thirty below by the time he reached the summit, which he knew was the summit because he could go no farther. The snow had not been plowed on the back side, so that the valley beyond and below him was sealed in.

Wallis was not sure when he had crossed back over out of Canada, but he could see the faint shape, the dark bowl of the second valley. He got out and looked at his watch — he was six hours late — but could tell that Mel had not been there yet, because of the absence of tracks in the snow.

He could smell the forest even more strongly — could breathe deep into him the scent of things, the names of which he did not yet know.

There were only two lights in the distant valley that he could see — lantern light, he knew, or bulbs powered by generators. He had been told that there was no electricity in the valley, and only one pay phone — a strange jury-rigged system that combined a shortwave radio with various ephemeral satellite links — the satellite passing the valley's side of the earth only every second day — so that as often as not the valley lay in near-total isolation, save for that one slender road leading in.

Wallis gathered green fir branches and built a fire in the middle of the road. He took a hatchet from the jeep's tool box and chopped down a small tree and burned it, branch by branch and length by length. With each flare he could see a short distance into the woods around him, and could feel brief heat, but then the flare would fall away to tiny, insignificant flames; though through the night, as Wallis kept diligently adding limbs — breaking snow trails into the woods and snapping off branches like some hungry creature browsing — the fire built enough coals to melt the snow around it to bubbling, boiling water, and steam.

He was able to bank the coals around the jeep — a glowing orange ring of quickly cooling fire around him — and in that manner, in that brief breath of heat, he was able to fall asleep at ten thousand feet, looking up not at the stars but at the meandering pipes of his jeep's underbelly. In the half-land before sleep, he rolled, in his mind, so that he was not looking up, but down — twenty thousand feet below these ten thousand feet — looking for black oil in a world void of other colors.

If the falconer said it was down there, it was, though how much of it, he could not be sure. Across the thousand square miles of the little valley, and at any depth below, in one of an infinite number of seams, there might be only a ribbon of oil: only enough to fill one bucket, enough oil or gas to burn one candle, one lamp, for one night.

Wallis wondered if Mel would be like her father, or if she would be his opposite, as often happened: as if blood, as it runs through a person, spirals and twists — bright and glittering one moment, and then shrunken and opaque, between generations.

Isolated from the world as she was, she might have been shaped not so much by her blood lineage as by the land itself — though from the brief, starlit glimpse of the bowl of dark valley below, Wallis would not have been able to guess what kind of a person that landscape might scribe.

He dived deeper in his sleep: vertical now, so that it was not like swimming, but like a falcon in its stoop, though without the falcon's speed. He descended to the safest place in the world.

And while he was twenty thousand feet below, did the rest of him which he had left behind — the skin or husk of his body curled there atop the snow — drink in and absorb the scent of spruce and smoke? Did it absorb the faint light of the stars? Did the movement of the stars, in this new place, carve new messages across him, even as he slept: wrapping him in those new thin scribings?

The coals of his fire froze and the steam went away. The jeep itself began to freeze, contracting in the cold and making groaning sounds like an animal; and in his descent, Wallis, if he heard or felt the sound at all, imagined that it was the sound of the world below: the risings and fallings of things — secret passageways becoming open and available for a moment — chasms appearing, then being quickly filled — peaks and crags, whole mountains wavering like flowers in a breeze.

The oil inside the jeep turned thick as licorice, but the blood inside him was still hot, still flowing — sparkling like the stars, as he slept — running strong, while above, the stars kept writing their faint messages across him, as well as all around him — hemming him in, whether he realized it or not: or hemming in, rather, that part of him that he had left behind in his descent.

As he slept — as his body slept, while the rest of him dived, gaining speed and depth now — an owl hooted, but he did not hear it, could not hear it.

Snowshoe hares, the color of the white world, edged around him, made curious by the dying fire. Snowmelt from the fire's perimeter froze into twisted, grotesque, translucent shapes — resculpted from snow's smoothness into clutching, clawing shapes all around the jeep and flecked with charcoal and bits of wood.

From above it would have looked craterlike; and it would have looked too as if Wallis was frozen in the grip of that ice. It would have looked as if, as he slept, the ice had crept toward him in waves and begun wrapping itself around him.

A WOMAN'S VOICE SAID, "I THOUGHT YOU WERE DEAD." Wallis opened his eyes to stunning brightness. His own breath was so cloudy that at first he could see nothing; but as the cloud faded, he saw the woman who was speaking. He struggled to lean up on one elbow, beneath the jeep, but his blankets and sleeping bag were frozen in the ice. She laughed as he struggled to free himself.

Her hair was long, and not so much white as it was the color of frost — as if her rhime-breath, or the winter, had colored it — and her face was long and narrow. She was a big woman — tall, with rounded shoulders, and a strong neck. Her eyes were green, and they held Wallis now with a steady, curious look of amusement. She was hunkered down, leaning in to peer at him in a way that made him think of the phrase *sitting on her haunches*. "Mel," she said, introducing herself. She took her glove off and reached her hand in under the jeep. Holding onto his hand, she pulled him free of the curls of ice that had gripped him, and she laughed again, once he was out, as if she had caught a fish.

"You don't have skis or snowshoes," she said.

"No. I wouldn't know how to use them anyway."

"You sure made a mess." She was still hunkered over her heels. Charcoal and ash-flecked gnarls of rutted ice stretched everywhere. Wallis couldn't remember when he'd seen someone so cheerful and full of life. *Healthy* was the word; robust. Her vigor reminded him of the energy possessed of a man or woman deep in love. It did not seem possible that that kind of energy could come from within: that there was not some other, external source helping support it.

"You're the geologist," she said, and studied his face as one might examine the skull of some extinct species, vaguely hominoid — marveling and wondering at what shared similarities there might be, despite the presence of some immense gulf of time, and evolution.

"I'm learning," he said. "They sent me up here to find oil. They told me you might not be too happy about it."

She smiled. "What else did they tell you?"

Wallis blushed. He couldn't tell if she was beautiful or not. He thought she was, but her force, her strength, was so overriding that that was the main impression he got, looking at her. Her beauty — if it could be called that — was not so noticeable, not any singular thing. If he watched her eyes, he would not be able to pay attention to the shape of her mouth. Her lips were pale from the cold. Her eyebrows and eyelashes, already sand-colored, were also rhimed with frost. She had a ski cap on.

The valley below gleamed in the sunlight — the velvet uncut forest cupped within it. A few gray threads of smoke rose from the chimneys of a handful of cabins that he could not see. A river cut through the middle of the small valley, sometimes straight and other times winding, and he read it quickly, like an x-ray technician, imagining already the fault structuring that had given birth and shape to such a river.

The valley was ringed by high white mountains, jagged, stony. The night before, the dim shape of the valley had looked like a sump, a depression — a trap one could stagger into, with no way out — but in the morning, in that bright cold sunlight, it looked like a haven.

"They didn't tell me much else," he said, and she studied him less like a specimen now — less interested in cranial content — and more like a living human; as if interested in his specific secrets.

"Uh huh," she said. "I'll bet they didn't." Another laugh — a sharp breath of ice — and now he studied her teeth, square and white, as if she ate nothing but snow.

When they stood, he saw that she was leaner than he had first thought — wide-boned, but loose-fleshed — and she saw that he was leaner, too. She had imagined — in the little she had thought of it beforehand — that he would be shaped like Matthew: as if that was how the earth sculpted geologists — wide, short, and muscular; as if even the body desired to move boulder and earth.

Wallis, she saw, wasn't much of anything. Plain old brown hair, with a glint or two of red in it. She wondered if each geologist Dudley sent, after Matthew, would be more and more diminished, like waves thinning as they slide into shore.

"You'll be here until the spring?" she said.

They both knew it would be the summer at least, and probably into the fall: that the snows would not melt, revealing the surface rocks for him to map, until April or May. Wallis wasn't sure why Old Dudley had sent him into the valley so early, unless it had something to do with the way Dudley hunted his falcons and hawks: the "waiting on" period being nearly as dramatic as the dive itself: the hawk hovering so high as to be sometimes out of sight — suspended, like desire drawn taut, waiting for the quarry to flush — waiting forever, it might seem. Waiting to see if there even was a quarry.

"Climb on my back," she said. "You can come get the jeep in the spring."

"They won't plow the road until then?"

Mel shrugged. "Maybe. Sometimes we try to keep it open, so a supply truck can make it in. But a lot of years we can't. It may open up one more time, around Christmas. People like to leave a car or truck up here so they can get out, if they have to. You can just leave your keys in it. Come on," she said.

"I'll walk," Wallis said. "How far is it?"

"Almost ten miles," Mel said. "You wouldn't get there today. Come on."

They went fast, down the iced-over tracks of her ascent, and faster yet with his added weight. It was far too quick for Wallis — a hurdling, a falling — and he held on for dear life. He was amazed by her strength. She skied in a tucked crouch, her knees bent. Her back was broad, and he stayed in close against it, his head turned to one side, watching the scenery flash past. Her hair blew back in his face and swirled in his eyes. He could feel the strength of each muscle in her flexing, working with each curve in the road. It was not like riding a horse. It was not like sex. There was nothing to compare it to that he knew of. It was like being locked leg-in-leg and arm-in-arm with someone falling from the sky.

When she made her turns — sinking even lower into a crouch to do so — roostertails of sunlit ice shavings sprayed them both. The wind from their speed was cold. They dropped lower down the mountain, descending, corkscrewing, as if into its interior. He could feel the pleasure coming straight through her — could feel it like heat conducted, as if it were his.

They raced lower into the valley. The trees were immense, and the sunlight fell upon them in shafts. A rock wall appeared on their right. Snow-covered, it followed the road in a crooked, wandering weave, and seemed to Wallis to make the scenery not more bucolic, but wilder, as if they were going back in time, back to some time before true fences. The wall reminded him of the crude territorial boundaries of some feudal warlord. It was waist-high and constructed almost as if without seams, and he watched it, nearly hypnotized, instead of watching the woods.

He tried to imagine such a seam of rock wall running underground, but couldn't; the piston risings and fallings, the fracturings and grindings would in no way allow such a thing to travel that far uninterrupted, nor so gracefully.

They skied across a wooden bridge. Dark water rushed beneath them, with steam rising where it passed into the sun. Snow and ice lacework fringed its edges, closing in on the stream from both sides.

The rock wall passed through the stream — enormous rocks, now, to withstand ice floes and jams — and behind the wall, upstream, the water had backed into a pond of black water ringed by white bare-limbed aspen trees. The dark water behind the wall had not frozen yet, but something about the appearance of it made Wallis think that it was about to any day, any moment.

He caught a glimpse of movement in the pond as they thundered across the bridge. Their sudden appearance had caused some great dark creature at the back of the pond to lift its head. It was a moose, chocolate-brown, with a mantle of snow on his head and wide antlers, his back freighted with snow. With water dripping from his muzzle, he watched the skiers, and Wallis wanted to stop and watch him. Standing knee-deep, serene amidst all that snow around him, the moose seemed somehow wise — his head huge as an anchor. But then they were past him, and there was only more forest, and rock wall, and they raced on, past more and more of it, as if it would never end.

Around one corner, Mel tipped too far forward and hit a small bump — her eyes blurry with icicle tears from her speed — and they became airborne. There was an alarming moment when Wallis could feel her strength leave her, as she lost contact with the ground — it was as if he had his arms and legs wrapped around just any old person, rather than someone of such strength — and they cartwheeled wildly when they landed; and when they finally skidded to a stop, it seemed to both of them as if he had pursued and caught her, had tackled her, like some predator pulling down its prey. But she was the first one up, dusting herself off and then helping him up. No injuries. The buffering, the forgiveness, of snow.

He climbed up on her back again, and they skied on. The snow crusted their faces like masks from where they had fallen, and caked their clothes: and doubled up as they were, humpbacked, they looked like some strange creature born from out of the snow.

The road pitched and dropped. Wallis could see the river now through the trees, and was surprised at the size of it, for such a small valley. Again, he tried to imagine what story lay beneath it — whether the strike of the formations, the outcrops, was canted left or right — a reverse, normal, thrust, or slip-fault. He scanned the snowy mountains for clues, but it was impossible to say. He wondered again why Dudley had sent him up here in the winter, and what he would do during the long months to keep his skills sharp, when instead he still could have been down on the Gulf Coast finding oil. Wallis wondered if it were a kind of punishment for his not finding enough oil. He thought he had been doing a pretty good job: not finding as much as Matthew, but finding a lot; and he was still learning. Matthew had peaked. Matthew was definitely finished with learning.

Mel was skating now. They came around a corner and into town, still following the stone wall. Wallis saw buildings that he had not been able to see from the summit: a store on one side of the street and a bar on the other. A couple of dusty-windowed outbuildings, already snowed in for winter.

There were horses, cars, and trucks parked on both sides of the street. Wallis glanced back and saw that two coyotes were running along behind them, but the coyotes turned back when they reached the edge of town and skittered into the woods.

There were people standing out in the street in the sunlight, and there were long food-covered tables set out. Men, women, children, and dogs surrounded the tables. Steam rose from a turkey carcass as a huge man with a big black beard carved it. The children played bare-headed, threw snowballs, chased each other in circles. People stood in small groups, drinking hot coffee and cider, with steam rising from their cups.

Mel skated up to the bar's wood-rail porch and unloaded Wallis like a sack of mail — as if he were the one who was tired.

A few faces turned to look at Wallis, briefly, but most stayed focused on the long tables of food. There was a roast pig, glaze-glistening with the apple still in his mouth, legs outstretched as if in flight. There was a little fire burning off to one side, and children roasted marshmallows on it. Wallis caught the scent of pumpkin pie. Mel and Wallis brushed the snow from their clothes and went into the bar.

A roar came from the men and women gathered around the table as a gust of icy wind blew a funnel of loose snow down the lengths of the tables and swirled cyclone snow-devils off the roofs of the buildings.

For a moment, all visibility faded — there was nothing but blowing snow, drifts and drifts of it — but then the wind paused, and the world filled with sunlight again, and the men and women and children resumed filling their plates.

They brushed the windblown snow from the turkey carcass and brushed it from the pig's head. The snow steamed from where it had landed on his hot back. They cut into him with silver knives. Steam rose from the ribs. Those gathered around the pig made small gasping and groaning sounds of pleasure as they tasted the meal, and their cries of approval brought others. More gusts of ground snow blew back in, obscuring their dark shapes: but Wallis could hear them, down there by the pig, as they fell upon the feast with what seemed like neither mercy nor thanks, only hunger.

D ANNY WAS THE OWNER OF THE BAR — THE RED DOG. IN one corner, a huge wood stove cast a ferocious heat. Dogs napped next to it, their fur steaming, and there were various articles of clothing hung on racks next to it to dry, and boots and more clothes scattered on the floor, also steaming, as if the bodies they housed had disappeared or been consumed from within. The heads of moose, wolf, coyote, lynx, bobcat, marten, fisher, elk, deer, caribou, bighorn, mountain goat, black bear, grizzly, whitetail, mule deer, mountain lion, badger, and wolverine stared down from the walls in such an assemblage of fang and horn that in viewing them a person felt neither awe nor a sense of majesty, but instead only a relief that the animals could do no harm, would forever be poised at the edge of no longer being able to do harm. And from that relief — the feeling that one was safe, and alive — came a feeling of security, if not comfort.

Some of the dusty, patchy heads of the animals looked as if they had hung up there, straining to bite, for perhaps a hundred years. And the heads of the prey, especially the deer and elk, looked different to Wallis — like different species or subspecies brought back from some distant continent — a red deer, rather than an elk — so that he wondered if that short stretch of time, a hundred years, had been able to produce some kind of speciation — isolating some traits in one population while gathering certain others, so that, while no one had been noticing it — death by death, and life by life — various new species, or subspecies, had been crafted, while old ones had fallen away.

The thought of it made Wallis dizzy, as might a blasphemy to the ears of the devout. Wallis was so used to dealing in chunks of a hundred million years at a time — the birth and then total erasure (grain by grain) of entire mountain ranges — that the notion that anything of significance could occur in only a hundred years seemed to threaten who he was; or rather, who he had become.

There were pictures of Matthew all over the walls too — and pictures of Mel, and Old Dudley, and Danny — and Wallis noticed that all of the pictures were old — the youngest of them from twenty years ago, it seemed.

Was it his imagination, or were the smiles, the laughter, from those times more boisterous, more complete? He shook the thought away. These were the kind of thoughts that would impede his ability to dive into the boulder fields — to track the old paths of mountains as they moved across the landscape of the past like dunes of sand.

Danny was bringing them drinks, and pouring one for himself. He kept shaking Wallis's hand and patting him on the shoulder, touching him, saying how glad he was to have him in the valley, and asking about Matthew and Old Dudley. The feeling Wallis got from Danny's enthusiasm was that Old Dudley and Matthew could do no harm, nor Mel either — and, by extension, neither could Wallis, now that he was among them. But Wallis also had the feeling — irrational, unprovable — that it was as if he, Wallis, had become trapped — coming in over the pass like that, just as the valley was being sealed in by winter's snow — and that Danny's pleasure was partly that of the trapper who, upon approaching his set, finds that he has been successful.

"How's Matthew doing? Is he finding lots of oil? Are he and Dudley getting along? When are they coming back?" Danny was in his early fifties, flat-bellied, childlike. "Tell me about yourself," he said. His eyes were pale blue, a shade that Wallis couldn't remember having ever seen in a human before — almost like a Siberian husky's, he thought — and Wallis wondered if, as with the heads of some of those animals, the color of Danny's eyes was a color left over from the century before: like someone's grandfather's eyes, or even further back than that.

"You'll be staying out at Matthew's cabin?" Danny asked, with a glance at Mel. He gestured to the bar. "You're welcome to stay here, if you'd rather — I've got an extra room in the back." Mel smiled, shook her head, and said, "Relax, Danny, he's not going to *ravage* me; I'm still Matthew's girl." Danny looked relieved, even hopeful, but said, "That's not what I meant — I just meant, if he needed a place to work and concentrate, you know, be alone . . ."

Mel smiled again. "I think it'll be quieter for him out in the woods. Anyway, I won't ever be home, except at night, when I get in from tracking. It'll be fine," she said. She laughed. "He's not going to find anything, anyway. No offense," she said, speaking to Wallis now, "but you're not."

Wallis shrugged. "I didn't come up here to fail."

Mel shook her head. "He sent you up here to train you and to play you against Matthew. The whole time you're up here, looking for oil in places where Matthew couldn't find it, Matthew will be worrying about that, and working harder, down in Texas." There was less cheer in her voice now: more matter-of-fact. "He's doing this to see what you've got — to see if maybe you can figure out something new about this valley — but mostly to lash Matthew to work even harder. To try to melt him down. My father has a real problem tolerating strength, beauty, or grace."

"Well," said Wallis, "I guess I've seen a little of that about him. But he can find oil," he said. "And that's what I'm here for. I don't know about any of that other stuff."

Danny interrupted. "Mel doesn't want there to be any oil or gas here," he said. "Me, I guess I'd kind of like to see it — just a little bit of it. I don't see how a little would hurt anything. It wouldn't be much different from cutting a load or two of firewood, or shooting a deer, or planting a garden."

Mel walked away from him, went over to one of the bar's two small windows. Wallis wondered if she ran from all arguments. The dim light was blue on the side of her face, making it look as if she were submerged.

A roar went up from the crowd outside, and Wallis and Danny went over to the other window. It had gotten darker as they had talked.

They saw that a deer, a whitetail buck, was bounding down the center of the street, its head a crown of antlers. The deer kicked up tufts of snow as it ran, running right through the middle of the crowd but touching no one.

People were diving out of the way, ducking under the dinner tables and rolling to the side. One man tried to tackle the deer and was bounced backward several yards. Mel sucked in her breath. The heavy man with the big black beard, who was carving on the turkey again, hurled his butcher knife at the deer, end over end, as it ran past; he missed, but almost got a woman standing on the other side of the street.

Now Danny was running to the cash register, where he pulled out a pistol, and he ran out onto the porch and fired twice as the deer ran past, and the deer leapt and humped up its back and then skidded to a stop, still as a rock, and Wallis was struck by how quickly the snow was already piling up on him, from the very beginning: big flakes, now, already trying to bury him.

Blood seeped from the deer's nostrils and mouth. He lifted his head once, grunted, then died — died twice, it seemed.

The snow was so silent. The two shots seemed never to have happened. Already it was as if the deer had befallen some accident — a visiting king or emissary, now, struck down in the town, his antlers rising high above him, like branches trying to catch the snow. The tips of them were stained red from where he had been fighting another deer. He was in rut and his neck was swollen with muscle, and they could smell his sex and musk, and now his blood. Danny had hit him in the jaw with the first shot and the shoulder with the second.

People walked through the falling snow toward the deer, then stopped a few yards away, because it was Danny's deer, and he was the one who should touch it first, and also because it was possible that the deer was not yet dead, but was merely resting at the edge of death, ready to make one more run.

"Jeez, Danny," Mel said, "you really know how to sneak up on 'em," and Danny laughed and said, "What can I say? The deer *came* to me. My Eskimo friends have a saying: Sometimes the animal wishes to lead me on a long chase, and sometimes it only wishes to lead me on a short chase."

"Your Eskimo friends, my ass," said Mel.

Danny had a hunting knife in a holster on his pocket, which Wallis had dismissed as a kind of belt-buckle braggadocio, but now as Danny unholstered it and walked down the porch steps, Wallis saw that it had a purpose.

Danny stopped when he was within three feet of the deer and admired it, remembering the kill. This was the last time, the last moment, that he would be able to look at it as a trophy — studying the high antlers, and remembering the strength and speed of the deer, and the beauty of the moment as it had run. As soon as he began cutting it with the knife, it would cease being a deer, a thing of beauty, and would become meat.

Danny stepped forward with the knife: took the deer's antlers in one hand and lifted the head from the snow. Blood dripped from the wet black nose. The deer had long eyelashes, like a lady. Danny put the point of the knife to the buck's throat and pressed in to make the cut, to bleed the deer right there in front of the bar.

The deer's eyes fluttered open, as if the point of the blade had resurrected it. For half a second, the deer studied things. Danny saw what was happening and made a quick slash with the knife, but he didn't cut deeply enough, and the deer leapt to its feet, throwing Danny backward, and the deer galloped off, a red stain spreading from its throat. It ran into the forest. Several people began chasing it, and others turned their dogs onto the trail.

For a moment, Wallis saw it all with clarity, as with a sudden gust of wind that brings new scents — an understanding, where before there had not even been a question. He saw how the long, sleepy moments of things lie in calm stretches, eddies, which we continue to believe are peaceful, serene moments — nothing more than slow passages of time — but which are really only a coiling and deepening in preparation for the sudden, near-frantic weaves and pursuits — the lusts. He saw how in the hunt, it all falls into place — how all the elements that seemed previously to be meaningless become now spurred into action: how every element, every atom, has meaning — and how this is the perfect desire of nature, the moment toward which all waiting, which is not really waiting, moves.

The deer led the chase, and all the men, women, children, and dogs pivoted, and whether to watch or to chase, made no difference: the deer, and its blood collar, were a lever to the universe, whose flight swung into focus all sets of eyes, all attentions. Now it all mattered: snow depth, wind direction, temperature, light remaining in the day, sense of smell, creeks to cross, ridges to run, forests, open meadow. The deer's flight was the lever to it all. The earth herself was but a fulcrum.

Charlie, the pig's cook — surprisingly fast for such a big man — was in the lead. It seemed that his desire propelled him close behind the deer, rather than any athleticism, but that it was almost enough. Two black and white scruffy dogs ran alongside him, barking, and then three or four more men and then a young boy, and then a woman. Then two more women, then some more men and then more children. An old lady trotted behind all of them waving a spatula.

As Danny, Wallis, and Mel watched, a cold wind blew the snow past in a slant, whipping the vinyl red and white checkered tablecloths over on themselves. One old man remained standing at a table with plate in hand. A haze was spreading across the sun, burnishing it, and the northern sky was a wall of gray, coming in over the beautiful day like some huge freighter from sea. The old man picked at the turkey carcass. A raven appeared and flew in a circle over the abandoned feast, eyeing the leftovers, then seemed to grow excited — picking up the hints, the echoes, of the chase. It gave two barking *caws!* and then was off in the direction the deer and the people had gone, flying with hard, fast wing-beats.

"If they wouldn't chase him, he'd run a hundred yards, lie down, and die," Danny said. "They know that — they should know that. Fuck," he said, "if it was their deer, they'd leave it alone — they wouldn't push it like that. Shit," he said. He walked alongside the tracks for a short ways, being careful never to step in one, and Wallis and Mel followed. Some of the tracks had blood in them, and the heat of what life the deer had left had melted the snow into clear ice, from where he had passed, and Mel said, "Well, easy tracking anyway, unless he stops bleeding or runs out of blood." Streamers of mare's tails were stretching overhead now — and in the wind, the first few snowflakes were tumbling like tiny shavings of pure white wood — not really falling, but floating.

"If he runs out of blood, he'll die, and we'll find him," Danny said.

Mel shook her head. "You'd think so," she said. "But sometimes they keep going. I don't know how," she said. "But they do — they just keep going."

"Forever?" Danny asked, like a child.

"No," Mel said, "but farther than you can go — so far that you can never find him. It'll be easy tracking at first, but then you'll have to hurry," Mel said, turning her face up to the falling snow, "because then it'll be no tracking." She looked at Danny, as if having just suspected something in his hesitancy. "You *do* have to find him, you know."

"Oh, I will," Danny said. He shrugged. His words came in breath-smoke. "I don't like to lose meat. If I *did,* it wouldn't matter — the coyotes and wolves and ravens would have a feast. But I want that meat, too," he said. "I'll find it."

"You have to," Mel said. "You saw that the knife was still stuck in the deer's throat?"

"No," said Danny, "I didn't see that." He shrugged again. "I can always find another knife," he said.

"No," said Mel — as if she were talking to a child, instructing him — and Wallis saw that Danny noticed this too, and was not pleased by it — "You have to go get that knife. You have to find that deer. There'll be blood on the blade. The coyotes and wolves will lick it, and cut their tongues. The taste of their own blood will excite them and they'll bite harder. They'll cut their tongues off, in their frenzy. There'll be blood everywhere," she said. "They'll be attacking each other. They could all eat each other up, just because of that one knife blade. Go get it. Better hurry."

"They wouldn't do that," Danny said.

Mel said nothing; scuffed a covering of snow off of one of the tracks. "In the spring, the bears would find the carcass," she said. "They'd come gnaw on it and get all cut up. Their mouths might get infected, so that they couldn't eat. They'd die, too. Shit, Danny," she said, "you could wipe out the whole upper part of the food chain single-handedly."

She was not angry, and Wallis could see there was some bond between them that allowed her to talk this way; some strange respect he had for her, and she for him. Danny nodded and said, "All right. Let me go get another knife to clean him with, when I find him."

People were returning from the woods now, walking, snow-wet and tired. One old woman was walking with her head down, as doleful as if she had lost a mate. The men were coming back, too. Wallis sensed that they wanted to avoid Mel, though finally a couple of them came over and told her, "That deer wasn't hurt; we tracked him for two miles and he was still running as strong as ever," which Wallis knew was bullshit, because they had only been gone for fifteen minutes; and now the children were coming back, and even the cook, Charlie, with his cleaver, and the old woman who'd run after them with her spatula. Returning without it, having lost it in the snow.

"I'll go look for him," Danny said. "You go on home and get Wallis settled into his room," he said. The snow was beginning to come down steadily, and Danny began dressing — an old coat, a ski cap, gaiters, snowshoes, a pack, a lantern. "I'll bet he didn't go a hundred yards past where everyone else turned back," he said.

"Better hurry," Mel said. "You're going to lose his tracks." She snapped on her skis. "Do you need help?"

Danny shook his head. "You all aren't dressed for it. You go get Wallis settled in." He checked his pack for matches, primed and tested the lantern, lit it: it made a tiny roar, then settled to a hiss. "There's no rush," he said. "It's a big deer. I'll find it."

"Climb up," Mel said, and Wallis, a little embarrassed, did so, from the front porch of the bar, as if climbing onto a horse.

The feast was over; men and women were gathering their plates and dishes and carrying the chairs and long tables back up to the bar; folding the checkered tablecloths in the falling snow. One man tied the carcass of the pig to the side of his saddle and rode off toward his cabin along the river.

Others headed north on foot, walking or riding on the road down which Wallis and Mel had skied. They disappeared quickly, as if being swallowed by the dark forest and the blowing snow, and Wallis had the feeling that he might not see any of them again until spring.

Mel was skiing strong — stronger, it seemed, now that they were headed home. "I'd carry you for a while," he said, "if I knew how to ski."

"You'll have to learn," she said.

It seemed though almost as if he were learning, in part, by holding onto her: by feeling the movements and rhythms of her body. His head was turned sideways again to watch the woods pass, and her hair was in his face once more — he could smell the faintest bit of wood smoke, as if it came not from her hair, which the cold wind had scrubbed clean, but from the roots, from her skin — and he closed his eyes and tried to imagine that he was skiing, and that he was as strong as she was.

It felt to him as if they were moving away from a place he needed to be, a way of being, in order to do his work — that it was almost as if he were being lured far away — but the rhythm of her body was hypnotic, as was the sensation of traveling so fast, so easily, across the surface.

He wondered if Old Dudley thought he was a fool — if that was why he had sent him up here. He wondered if he was a decoy — fodder, emotional fuel, for the legend of Matthew — the one geologist Old Dudley hadn't yet been able to burn up.

They skied south, and back into the forest. The river fell away below them. The snow was swallowing everything. Wallis could feel Mel's body warming and then perspiring through her wool. She labored, going up the small hills; they sped, sailing down the back sides of the hills. The road was a narrow lane through tall trees and rich scents, a path of white through darkness.

They followed the road for several miles — Mel skiing hard, but saying nothing, and her back growing wet beneath Wallis, and the back of her neck sweating, then icing over. They turned and went down a narrower road, barely a trail — a wide truck could not have fit.

There were no more tracks. No cars or trucks had been down either the main road or this one since the snow had started.

They skied a mile down the trail, to the place where it ended, and they slipped through a slot in the bushes and started skiing up a footpath, through old cedars and larch, and then into country slightly more open, with aspen trees — a relief to Wallis, after the darkness of the forest. He had not yet decided whether the dense woods were claustrophobic or soothing.

Farther up the hill was a snowy clearing, and halfway up that clearing, a small dark cabin with a porch. Home, Wallis thought, though he knew that he had only come here for a while.

Wallis's arms were asleep from having held onto Mel's back for so long. His arms had been wrapped around her for so long that he felt he knew her body as well as a lover, and felt strange, disassociated from not having the emotional bond to go with that intimate knowledge.

They half-toppled onto the porch, stumbling over one another as Mel let him down, and only now did she show that she was in the least bit tired. She sat there with her legs stretched out and rubbed her knees for a moment, and breathed carefully, and waited to cool down. They listened to the snow fall.

Finally Mel's breath began to send out whisper-clouds again, mists of fog, and when she moved, stiff-legged and stiff-backed, Wallis could hear ice crack from where her sweat had cooled and frozen against her body.

She gave him a hand up and they went inside. It occurred to Wallis that there should be some ritual or ceremony for first entering another's home — he thought of how it was before he began a map — of how it was before he prepared to enter those lands below, each time — and he thought it was interesting how freely people take one another in and out of their homes. A home to him, and going into it, seemed as special as a person's body, yet the entry into it carried none of the ritual or ceremony involved with going into another's body. Mel was as unselfconscious as anyone, or more so, walking straight in ahead of him and lighting first a propane lantern by the fireplace, and then one in the kitchen. She didn't say anything: just walked right in as if she and Wallis had been coming here every day of their lives.

The cabin smelled strongly of wood smoke: almost twenty years' worth of fires. It was cold and drafty — as if they had crawled into an ice cave — and Wallis went over to the stone chimney and felt the cold rocks over the fireplace.

There were dried flowers hanging from all the walls, dulled and subtle splashes of sun-faded blues, old yellows, pinks, and fading reds. There were cloves of garlic hanging in the kitchen, and in the living area there were pelts and furs: snowshoe hare, coyote, beaver, wolverine. There was a patch of some kind of fur over a bookshelf, a dark patch that looked pubic — Wallis would find out later that it was buffalo — and next to it was a ball of white hair that Wallis felt sure was wolf.

There were books everywhere: books on the shelves, which lined all of the walls except the south wall, where there was a big plate glass window — Wallis could see the snow driving sideways against the glass and piling in drifts — and there were books stacked along the walls, and below the big window, and a trail of stacked books that wandered crookedly into the kitchen.

Mel was building a fire in the wood stove: splintering kindling, pieces that were half-split already and had some twist in them, so that she could pull them apart with her hands. Wallis looked at her bookshelves — at the books themselves, and at the objects that surrounded them — feathers, stones, dried bundles of sweetgrass, more old flowers, an arrowhead, a piece of driftwood in the shape of a face, and an old fly-fishing reel, and some dry flies, scattered loose like fluff from cottonwoods in the summer.

He heard Mel tear apart a green-sounding piece of wood and then she said "*Shit*," and Wallis turned and saw that she had gotten a splinter stuck up in under the back of her hand — into a vein, it seemed, for bright red blood squirted as she pulled the splinter out. It had gone in nearly two inches. As she removed it it seemed to keep coming forever, but finally it was all out, and the blood came in a stream. She lifted her hand to her mouth and sucked for a moment, then wiped the blood on her jeans and kept splitting wood. She lit the fire and opened one of the stove's doors for it to draw air, and Wallis listened to the fire snap and then roar. Mel passed him, sucking on her hand once more, and went down the narrow hallway to go doctor her hand.

He walked over to her desk, to the corner by the stone fireplace. It was immaculate: papers stacked neatly, technical papers about juvenile dispersal of wolves in Labrador, and her field notes, sketches of tracks with gait measurements. He noticed there were no photographs at her desk — that there were none anywhere in the cabin. There were maps all over her walls, but even they seemed to speak of the future: diagrams of where she believed the wolves would go next, rather than where they had been. Wallis knew little of their cycles, and did not yet understand that wherever wolves had been was also where they would return.

Mel came back out with a bandage over her hand. The cabin dimmed; the propane lamps sputtered as the temperature outside grew colder, deeper into dusk, as if the whole cabin, or the world, were sliding down a funnel into darkness.

"Come here," Mel said. Her bandage glowed pale in the cabin's orange-hued dimness. "Look at this," she said, opening her propane refrigerator. The yellow battery light glowed when she opened the door.

The refrigerator was about four feet tall, old and bare and white. Inside, there were only a few items on the side door — eggs, mayonnaise, mustard — but in the center, where all the wire racks had been taken out, there was a huge gleaming fish, a silver sockeye salmon so large that it had been doubled over to fit. The effect was that it appeared to have been surprised in mid-leap. The curved, toothy, underslung jaw; the wild eyes; the torpedo-shaped head — and that silver, with the black speckles and red dorsal line down the side of the fish — it was all as shocking to Wallis as if a human body had been hanging in the refrigerator.

"Matthew sent it to me," she said. "I haven't had time to eat any of it yet. I'm anxious to eat it, but I also like looking at it. Isn't it wonderful? Smell it," she said. "Touch it. Look." She leaned in and sniffed the fish's flanks.

The water rattled in the pot on the stove. Mel left the refrigerator door open and went over to the stove and took the lid off, then poured tea. They moved over to the window to sit in chairs and watch the snow come down in the last bit of light. They said nothing, just watched the snow come down harder, piling higher. It was difficult for Wallis to not be panicked by this. He was used to doing the diving himself; he was not used to being buried by the earth.

He relaxed and let it come. But as he relaxed, it seemed to snow harder.

The refrigerator door was still open. The light shone on the bright salmon. The salmon watched them with its toothed grin, as if it had them right where it wanted them.

Mel continued to watch the snow. She held her tea glass in her cupped hands, so that the steam seemed to be coming from her hands.

The fire popped. They watched the light go away, watched the night come in from out of the woods: watched the tea cups stop steaming, watched the snow turn bright in the night and the woods turn black; and even when they could no longer see the snow falling, could see only white shiftings, they sat there and felt the compression of it — felt autumn leaving.

Mel went to the refrigerator and with a large knife cut some meat from the side of the great fish. She placed the small offering on two small china plates, bone-colored with a faded blue floral pattern, and handed one to Wallis.

They ate in a darkness that was broken only by the orange firelight. The fish did not taste salty, as he had imagined it would, though he could taste the smoke of the alder in which it had been cooked. He could taste other things in it, too, things he knew nothing about.

They drank more tea, staring out at the paleness of the swirling snow. When Wallis could no longer stay awake, he lay down on the couch and pulled an elk hide over him for warmth.

Sometime in the night Mel got up and added wood to the stove, then returned to her seat by the window, where she lit a candle and read. At some point she got up and rinsed the fish's residue and odor from the plates and put them away, but Wallis dreamed of the ocean nonetheless. The earth desires life — this was the last thing he remembered thinking before he fell asleep beneath the elk's skin, and with the beginning of winter trying to bury everything on earth below.

He dreamed of the ocean, dreamed of the forests that had yielded the years of firewood that had been burned in the cabin to give it its smell. He slept long and hard, moving from dream to dream — dreaming of Susan, and then of Matthew, and then of the falconer — dreaming like an elk moving through a snowy meadow, pawing beneath the snow for green grass.

In the morning the snow had stopped, and the day was bright and cold. They skied back to town to see if Danny had found his deer. Mel had an extra pair of skis that belonged to Matthew, and she gave Wallis some of Matthew's clothes to wear. The clothes were too large, but warm. They moved slowly, Wallis following in Mel's tracks as he tried to learn how to use the skis. He fell often, but it was not a thing that was beyond his ability to learn.

Coyotes came to both sides of the road and stood on top of snowy logs and watched them pass. Here and there would be a stump where a woodcutter had felled a tree for firewood.

The deer had been moving at dawn — trying to adjust to the cold, and to find the browse that was now hidden. Their trails wandered delicately through the woods like sentences trying to describe something great and wonderful just ahead, though Mel and Wallis saw none of the deer themselves, only the signs of their passage, and it made Wallis feel as if he were late for something.

"Yesterday was Thanksgiving, wasn't it?" he said.

"I think so," said Mel. "I think that's what all the food was about."

A band of ravens followed them, curious about their procession and intent. From time to time the ravens would call out to one another in their odd croaks, then would fly ahead in a sprint, doing barrel rolls and spins; but after a while they disappeared, though for some time Wallis and Mel would still hear their shouts in the woods ahead — a sound almost like human voices.

When they got to town, they went around to the back of the bar and peered into Danny's window, where they saw him sleeping on his bunk, mouth open, snoring, swaddled in a mass of hides and blankets. There was no sign of the deer. Mel said that if he'd found it, it would be hanging from the rafters in whole or part. Danny's lantern and pack were on the porch. She took the hatchet and bone saw from his pack, examined them, found no blood or hair.

"Let's go look for his deer," she said.

They entered the woods where the deer, and his pursuers, had entered. It had snowed several inches, but the path of the pursuers' passage was still visible under the soft swells of snow. They followed it until it ended, only a few hundred yards into the woods.

From that point, they followed the faint snow-muted trace of Danny's lone passage — trusting that he had been on the deer's tracks, that he was not leading them astray. Sometimes his tracks were hard to find, and Mel would have to brush away the snow to find his footprints in the compressed ice beneath the new snow. Occasionally when she did this she would find bits of frozen blood, and would point it out to Wallis, who told her he was color-blind, that he couldn't see red, nor red and green in combination. This surprised her so much that she stopped skiing for a moment. "Oh," she said. "So is Matthew."

She wanted to keep thinking about this, to ask if it were coincidence, or if it were a thing Old Dudley sought in his geologists, but she knew these thoughts would get her off the focus of finding the deer, and so she let them fall away unconsidered, as if to be buried by falling snow. Wallis didn't remind her of Matthew, but perhaps she was missing something.

They followed the faint scallops of the deer's trail. They came to the place where Danny had given up and turned back, and now the tracking became harder. At one point Mel stopped and showed him a blood-mark against a spruce, where the deer had brushed against the tree. There were coarse brown and white hairs caught in the bark.

Wallis found Danny's knife: skied right over it and felt it clink against his pole. He stopped and dug it out, picked it up. It was a nice knife.

"You're good at finding things," Mel said.

Wallis shrugged. He was enjoying the outing, but was impatient to begin his job. He felt as if he were betraying himself, letting his talent slip away from him, by his traveling horizontally, rather than straight down.

"Danny won't believe it," Mel said. "He'll be very pleased."

The tracks disappeared beneath velvet mounds of snow, but Wallis saw that Mel knew deer so well, and had already in tracking this one learned its rhythms well enough, that she could tell what the deer was going to do in response to the landscape. She stopped and began clawing at a mound of snow; she uncovered a red-smeared depression, an ice-cast of where the deer had lain.

"Spruce and pine trees have a physical quality," Mel said. "Cedar is a tree of spiritual qualities. This deer's not ready to die yet. He'll stay in the spruce and pines for as long as he can. Only when he knows he's going to die will he go down into the cedars. But that's where he's headed," she said. "I think he knows already." She lifted her hand to her throat. "If the snow hadn't fallen, you could see all the blood," she said. "It would look like a forest of blood. I can smell it, even beneath the snow.

"It would have died here," Mel said, pointing, "if folks from town hadn't kept pushing it. It would have laid down under this cedar and rested, and gotten ready to die. But they must have been right behind it, at this point. Closer than they realized.

"I've seen them get shot and fall down in a stand of fir or spruce or pine, then get up and crawl a hundred yards or farther to die under the cedars," she explained. "Scientists will give you some mumbo-jumbo about physiological responses, that the cedars are darker and cooler. They'll talk about thermal regulation and reduced fucking phototropism. The truth is simpler. The deer are leaving this layer of earth and are going to the next kingdom, and the cedars are a bridge between those two worlds.

"Science has never been all the way right about anything," she said.

They traveled now with great anticipation through a tangle of old cedars. There was a silence and stillness, a compression of space and time, which they felt as a ringing in their ears. They slowed, then stopped, knowing the deer was nearby, but that they just were not seeing it.

"There," Mel said, and Wallis saw the deer curled up, as if only resting. It was beneath the shelter of cedar fronds. A light dusting of snow had filtered down onto its back. The antlers rose sweeping into the branches, so that it seemed the antlers had become the branches. The deer's back was to them, so that it appeared he was not dead but instead only looking off in the other direction, ever vigilant.

They cleaned and boned and quartered him and loaded him into their packs, along with the hide and antlers. They cleaned him with the knife Wallis had found in the snow, the bone-handled knife that had helped kill him. Before leaving, Mel rearranged the bare bones and hooves into a running position beneath the tree. The blood from where they had cleaned the deer, though no longer warm, had soaked down through the snow, where it would stain the ground until spring: soaking down into the soil an inch or two, but then no farther.

The packs were heavy. Mel carried most of the weight. They followed their own tracks back out. When they reached the part of the trail where Danny had still been tracking — closer to town — Mel pointed to a grove of trees whose trunks were coated with ice. She had noticed the grove on the way in but hadn't commented on it, wanting to see if Wallis would notice it.

"Danny stopped here to rest for a while," she said. "It was night by that time. The heat from his lantern melted the snow in the trees and it ran down the tree trunks. Then when he moved on, it got cold and froze again."

The trees glittered. Now the path was easy to follow — a winding path through the woods, the injured deer always choosing the easiest route, and the trees shimmering in their ice coats, as if in some beautiful hallway. Mel and Wallis knew that the proof of the deer's passage, the blood and the tracks, lay just beneath them, beneath the snow.

By the time they neared town, they were drenched with sweat and discolored by some of the deer's blood that had leaked from their packs. Though it was only mid-afternoon, the sun had peaked and was in fast descent. They stopped to drink water from a trickling creek: took off their packs and crouched in the snow and lapped the water straight from the creek, to avoid wetting their hands.

They skied back into town and left their skis stuck in the snow in front of the bar. The sweat and blood had started to freeze on them again, but now in the heat of the bar it melted quickly, running down them in a sheen. They said nothing but unloaded their packs, laying the mahogany antlers on the floor and stretching the furred hide out. Danny came over, grinning, and gave Mel a hug. He shook Wallis's hand enthusiastically — and when Mel said to Wallis, "Go on, show him what you found," and Wallis handed Danny his knife, they thought Danny was going to explode out of his skin. Danny whirled in dervish circles and bounced up and down like a man on a pogo stick, holding the knife in both hands — Wallis thought at first he had been drinking, but Mel told him later that no, that was just the way he was — and Danny hugged them both now, almost lancing Wallis with the knife as he did so, and rang the cowbell at the bar's counter, announcing free drinks for all. Then he dropped to one knee and ran his hands through the deer's hide, admiring it, and found the four holes — two entries, two exits — of the bullets; found them hidden beneath the thick fur, and examined each one with his fingers.

And while Artie, the bartender, was pouring drinks, Danny took the antlers and went over to one corner of the bar and with hammer and nails tacked them to the wall, with the fur still fresh upon the skull-plate. Wallis felt dizzy from the heat and weakened from the rigor of packing the deer out, and from the shock of his drink, a rum and Coke. He imagined what those antlers would look like twenty years hence, and how the story behind them would be told — perhaps altered slightly, its boundaries compressed here or expanded there, as if the story itself were a thing that was still moving across the landscape, along with the cultures and lives of the humans who carried it . . . and Wallis wasn't sure he liked that feeling. Part of him was proud to be accepted into this — what? village? clan? pack? — so soon, even if in a small way — but another part of him wanted to take the antlers down and have the story, and the day, slide away into darkness.

But it was too late. Danny was packing the meat into his propane freezer, wrapping it and labeling each cut of it, and Charlie — the big man with the black beard and the cleaver, from the day before — was searing some of the meat in a skillet on the big wood stove, salting and peppering it as he cooked, and passing out samples to everyone; and the story, the moment, was alive and well on its own, beyond Wallis's control.

Wallis began looking at some of the old photos on the wall. There were so many of them, and yet he understood that this was almost all there was: that this valley was still so new to the world, so recently wrested free of glaciers, and inhabited marginally by humans, that this was it — there was almost nothing else beyond what was on the walls. The Indians had hunted the high valley in the autumns, but had never settled there. It had been even colder then, so close to the time of glaciers, and before the earth had begun its slow warming, like a face turning slowly toward the sun.

Charlie threw more wood in the stove — big logs, each seeming as long as a small canoe. His face shone with sweat, and he grinned, as if he loved only those two things in the world — cooking and sweating: as if he could not get close enough to the fire. He was wearing only a T-shirt and jeans; he did not own a coat.

There were so many photos of Matthew, and of Matthew and Mel together — so young, already so long ago. Wallis found it hard to believe this was the same man he had shared an office with: a volatile man whose sole focus was diving and striking at the oil, and who did so with eerie, overwhelming success.

In some of the photos, he was just a boy with a rifle — a brace of grouse set before him, a dog, a picture of the boy in snow, on snowshoes — and a young clear-eyed man standing next to an elk, and in another photo, a monstrous deer.

Photos of Matthew lounging in a hammock with Mel — eighteen, nineteen years old? (Wallis had never seen Matthew sleep before, except when he occasionally fell asleep at the drafting table late at night, and lay there with his head down for a while, as if listening to the map he had just drawn) — and photos of Mel and Matthew ice-fishing, and photos of them canoeing in summer. Mel in a straw hat. All black and white photos; all ancient, it seemed. Wallis stared, tried to remember being young with Susan. He had saved nothing from that life. He couldn't believe Mel's and Matthew's youth. Twenty years had never seemed so long to him.

There were older photos, too: from fifty, sixty, seventy years ago. He peered closer. The men and women from back then definitely looked different, as did the country, in some slight way.

Danny came over to where Wallis was studying the photos — studying them as if for a test — and he, in his exuberance, was wrapped in the deer hide. He clapped a hand on Wallis's shoulder, squeezed the muscles between his neck and shoulder, and called back to Mel, "With all that sweat and blood on him, except for being a little on the puny side, he even kind of looks like Matthew."

"I shape them that way," Mel said, laughing. She had finished her drink.

"Old Dudley shapes them that way," Danny said.

Wallis went back to sit with Mel, and to have a drink. It seemed important to have only one, or possibly two. He imagined how easy it would be, in the midst of all the snow — but secure and warm in the bar — to start drinking and not stop until the days grew bright and long again.

He had been away from his work for a week: the longest ever. One more drink. Mel looked at him and smiled, remembering the simplicity of the day: hauling meat.

The door opened and with it came a blast of cold air, made colder to those inside by their having become accustomed to the warmth, and in the doorway stood a tiny old woman, tottery not from the cold or the wind, but from age. She had wild thinning white hair, and there was snow on her back and shoulders — a blizzard was coming, the season's first big storm — and someone shouted, "Close the door, Helen!"

She was wearing old wooden snowshoes, and she clumped across the floor in them, sat down at Mel's and Wallis's table, and began unbuckling the leather straps, glaring first at Mel and then at Wallis in a way that told Wallis the old woman was a fan of Matthew's.

Mel introduced them. "Wallis, this is Helen — Matthew's mother. Helen, this is Wallis — Old Dudley's other geologist."

Wallis stood and reached out his hand to shake. Helen didn't want to take it, but had to. "Where are you staying?" Helen asked.

"In Matthew's cabin," Wallis said, and she scowled.

"Helen runs the mercantile across the street," Mel said. "We couldn't get along without her." She patted Helen's arm, and there was some immediate softening. She looked like she was a hundred years old. "Helen raised Matthew since he was four years old," Mel said. "She didn't take delivery of him til she was forty-two."

Wallis didn't want the second drink, but the first one was gone. Artie came over and sat at the table with them, bringing everyone a new round, and there were still stories to be told.

"By took delivery of, she means adopted," Helen explained. "His real mother got pneumonia. She fell through the river while she was deer hunting. Matthew's father pulled her out and rescued her, but she got pneumonia and died. Matthew was three. She'd been pregnant again, but of course the baby didn't get born. Matthew's father died a year after that. He just quit living. You ever see anybody do that?" Helen asked Wallis, and he looked away, didn't answer.

"Grandma Helen," Artie said — not a salutation or a question, simply a statement, a naming. "You raised a good boy." Artie stared down for a moment, then turned to Wallis. "What does he *do* down there?" he asked, and for a moment Wallis thought he meant, What is it like, beneath twenty thousand feet of stone? But then he understood that Artie meant only Texas, and the Gulf Coast — and that furthermore, "down there" or "out there" could just as easily be anywhere in the world, as long as it was on the other side of these mountains.

"He's happy," Wallis said, a little defensively. "He loves it more than anything." A glance at Mel to see if it hurt her, and he saw that it hadn't.

"Yeah, but I mean, what does he *do?*"

"Well, he sits at his drafting table and makes maps," Wallis said.

"*Maps,*" Artie said. He looked around the bar and seemed on the verge of a philosophy lecture, but in the end only took another drink and shook his head.

Now the stories came rolling in like waves — Matthew this and Matthew that — and Wallis wondered if they could be talking about the same man he worked with. He was still physically strong, and in some ways reckless — though to Wallis it seemed as if the recklessness had been transformed, under Old Dudley's guidance, into more of a gluttony — and Wallis had the strange feeling that they were talking about someone from another lifetime, even another century.

If Matthew still had the strength — the flamboyant strength they were talking about — then Wallis had not seen it. He was a great geologist, but all that myth lore — if Matthew was still that way, it must be only underground now, in his dives.

Wallis listened to stories of Matthew performing feats of strength — carrying propane refrigerators on his back, even as a boy — and of unbounded energy, as if in eternal adolescence, eternal growth — stripping naked in the summer and covering himself with a film of gasoline, then lighting himself on fire and leaping out of the bushes and into the river, into the back eddy where the swans used to rest, back when there had still been swans in the valley, thirty years ago.

"I saw him do it a couple times," Artie said. "He'd go ass-busting out there, all lit-up, and splash down right in the middle of all those swans. The swans wouldn't make a sound — they don't utter a peep until the day they die. I guess that's why he was fucking with them, trying to see if he could get them to croak, or peep, or make *some* damn sound — and sometimes he'd even grab one by the wing, or brush against it as he went into the river, and that swan would get a little gasoline on it, and for a few moments, while it was rising into the air and then flying, part of the swan would be on fire. I tell you what," Artie said, "it was a thing to see. Matthew would bob up to the surface and float there, and just laugh. It was always just a film of gas that would get on the swans — the flame would burn out before it did any damage to the feathers, or to the bird itself — but it was a sight to see. You could be working in town and look up and see seven or eight swans flying past, over the tops of the trees, with one of them on fire, and you'd know he was down there fucking with those birds."

"He was such a sweet boy," Helen said. "Such a fun boy. I was always having to run behind him to be sure he didn't hurt himself. I was an old woman, even then." She touched her weathered face and laughed. "My God, he aged me. He wore me out," she said. "In the summer, you could see burnt bushes all up and down the river from where he'd hidden, lit himself, and then gone running through the brush. He tried to get farther from the river each time. It looked like otter-slides, up and down the river. Sometimes I'd get to the river and find some bushes still burning, and the swans would be gone, and I wouldn't see any Matthew, wouldn't know where he was. I'd call and call for him, and he wouldn't come in til late that night, or sometimes even the next day; said he'd gone *exploring*, had gone up into the mountains."

Helen pressed her hand to her heart, which Wallis imagined to be about the size of a pea or a raisin, now.

Stories of his endurance. "That dang wall," Artie said.

Helen smiled, and explained to Wallis, "He started building it when he was seven. Just started hauling rocks in from the mountains and stacking them. Then when he began driving his jeep, he hauled them in that."

Wallis had seen those pictures, also yellowed and ancient, in the hallway that led to the bar's restrooms. In those photos, not just Matthew, but all manners of men, women, and children had been carrying and stacking the big square rocks. "I thought they were miners," Wallis said, "or workers in some quarry somewhere."

Helen shook her head. "Matthew started it, but by the time he was sixteen, the thing was twenty miles long, and so beautiful that the rest of us started helping him with it — working on it whenever we pleased, like a hobby." Helen reached in her coat for a pack of cigarettes, tried to light one. Wallis watched the hypnotic snap of her lighter, which finally took flame. Helen's hand shook afterward, just from that simple exertion.

"I was out back, bringing wood from the shed to the porch," she said, motioning to her snowshoes.

Mel said, "Oh shit, Helen, I'm sorry, I forgot," and Helen shrugged, clearly pleased with her martyrdom. "We'll haul some in for you tonight," Mel said. She told Wallis, "I always help Helen bring her wood in. Matthew used to do it before he went away, but now I do it every autumn. It's already cut and in the woodshed, curing. I just need to bring it to the back porch."

It was strange, Wallis thought, the way they kept talking about Matthew: as if believing he were going to come back someday.

"Why did he build the wall?" Wallis asked, and Helen shrugged, drew on her cigarette. She seemed to be falling away, dreamy-eyed. "Does anyone still work on it?" he asked.

"Not so much, anymore," Artie said. "Sometimes a little. But not like before."

"It's real pretty," Mel said. "You'll have to see it in the summertime."

"But it doesn't serve any purpose?" Wallis asked.

"No," said Mel.

Wallis and Mel said their good-nights and went to the door. Danny called out, "Wait a minute!" as they were leaving — they didn't hear him — and produced from behind the counter a bulky camera, and snapped off a quick crooked photo of the two of them going out together, with snowflakes swirling in through the door.

They crossed the street and hauled firewood in silence, glad to be out in the cold fresh air, carrying one armload after another from the shed to the back porch, wearing down a packed trail through the knee-deep snow. Helen's firewood was fresh-split larch, dry but heavy, and Wallis enjoyed the smell of it. He scented, too, the deer blood still on him as his body warmed.

Tired and tipsy — four drinks for Wallis, but only one for Mel — they skied home, following the snow-covered wall. At one point where the road crossed a small creek Mel said, "Come here," and skied a short distance into the woods, following the creek.

Stars glimmered broken in the riffles. Mel was crouched next to a mound of snow. She laid her head against the ground. "Listen," she said.

At first Wallis heard nothing — his face right next to Mel's, his eyes watching hers. She watched him back, but she was listening to the ground below.

"What?" he said, but she only held a finger to her lips, and kept listening, watching Wallis as if willing him to hear it, and then he did. He had to reach deeper to hear it, and when he did, it was like a background sound he had already been hearing but hadn't paid attention to. It was a kind of humming.

"This is where he sleeps every year," Mel said, and for a moment Wallis thought she was talking about Matthew again. "An old black bear," she said. "He must weigh five hundred pounds by now. This is his creek," she said. "He dens here below the cliff every November and lets the snow cover him." She pointed to a small hole in the snow-mound. "He's breathing only about once a minute. His blood is right at thirty-two degrees. But his breath is still warm. It melts the snow for these blowholes." Mel smiled. "Do you think he hears us?" she asked. "Do you think he hears us, and is dreaming about us?"

"I don't know," said Wallis.

"I think he does," said Mel.

They lay there over the sleeping ice-hump as if trying to give him extra warmth, and listened. They could hear the creek gurgling.

"When will he come out?" Wallis asked.

"Mid-April," Mel said. "When he hears the leaf-buds opening. When the creek sounds different, and when the sun starts to strike the ice cave again — when it starts to glow inside. He'll get up and stir a few times in the winter — will stick his head out, may even walk around in a circle, as if confused, just checking things out — but then he'll go back into hibernation."

"Have you ever seen them do that, in winter?" Wallis asked. "Come out of their den?" He tried to imagine it: the big black bear wandering across the snow, moving like a sleepwalker, just going in circles, and almost everything else in the woods silent.

"No," said Mel. "Sometimes I'll come across their tracks, and I'll know that I've missed them by a day, or even hours — but I've never actually seen it. It may be one of those things you don't see," she said. "It may be one of those things you're not supposed to see."

"Like what else?" Wallis asked.

Mel shrugged. "I don't know. Some kind of forbidden thing. Come on," she said, "let's get home."

Once back at the cabin, they hauled water from the creek. "It's been a long time since I haven't carried it all by myself," Mel said. They began heating the water on the wood stove for a bath. There was a water closet, too, with an overhead reservoir and a chain attached to it, which, when pulled, released the water from the box and down a pipe, to flush the toilet. Wallis filled that, and, as was the cabin's rule, left a backup bucket by the toilet's side, so that the next person did not have to go out in the middle of the night.

The cabin warmed quickly. "How old is it?" Wallis asked.

"Nineteen-forty-seven," Mel said. "Matthew's parents were teenagers when they built it. The valley had only been settled by whites for about thirty years."

"It's so new," Wallis said, "to seem so old," and Mel laughed. "Everything is the same age up here," she said. "Everything is ten thousand years old, and that's that. The last glacier went away, and the northern forest filled in. Hunters came down into this country after the ice left, killed the last mastodons and mammoths, but other than that, things are still pretty much the same. Fourteen-ninety-two, seventeen-seventy-six, eighteen-sixty-three, nineteen-forty-seven — it doesn't matter. It's all the same age. It's not an old country. It just feels that way."

It bothered Wallis that Mel thought ten thousand years was a long time. He looked out into the night — at the flakes falling past the window and brushing up against it. "What's the oldest a tree gets to be, up here?" he asked.

"The cedars down in Ross Creek are over a thousand."

"So there have only been nine or ten generations of cedars, since the ice left?"

She stared at him, understanding for a moment — seeing things the way he saw them — but she caught herself — righted herself, is what it felt like to her — and she shook her head and said, "You're just like my father — you city guys. You forget how long time can be — four seasons, for instance. You like to compress things, rather than drawing them out. *Attenuating* them." But she smiled.

"Is Matthew a city guy?" Wallis asked. He couldn't picture him being anything but: had never seen him, on a weekday, in anything but a suit.

"He is now," Mel said.

They took turns bathing in three inches of water, but were glad to have it. The salt of their sweat mixed with the steam, and the blood on them melted once more and slid from their bodies, viscous, like afterbirth, then rough and clean as each toweled off. It was not yet ten o'clock. Mel said that in the winter she usually went to bed around eight.

They were too tired to eat. "I don't have your room made up," Mel said. "I didn't really think you were coming. You can sleep in here by the fire tonight. It's a mess in that other room — backpacks, tents, sleeping bags, snowshoes, lanterns." She laid a pallet out for him — elk and deer hides — and exhausted, he lay there beneath them, with the hides feeling heavy as stone. Mel lay down on the pallet not that far from him — less than arm's length — and propped her head up on one hand.

"What are you thinking?" she asked.

"Nothing," he said.

"What's Matthew like down there?" she asked. "Is he really happy?"

Wallis lay there with his hands behind his head. "I don't know," he said. "I mean, he'll laugh at something, if it's funny. It's not like he's really *tormented*, or anything. But I wouldn't say he has a deep peace."

"Do you?" Mel asked.

"I'm not looking for it," Wallis said. "I'm just looking to drill ahead."

"Like a machine," Mel said. "Like Old Dudley teaches you to be."

Wallis shook his head. "I think of it as being more like an animal that has to do only one thing — that spends all its waking and dreaming moments thinking of only one thing: the next thing."

"I only know of one kind of animal like that," Mel said.

"He's not *un*happy," Wallis said. "Not like he'd be if he wasn't doing it."

"I know that," Mel said. "I've known that part for a long time." She rolled over on her back. "Thanks," she said. "It's good to hear it again," and Wallis was reminded strangely, sadly, of a child who is told an old familiar story again and again: who needs the repetition of it for solace — and no matter whether it is a happy story, or a terrible one — only that it is the familiar story, and therefore the one that makes sense.

They lay there and listened to the fire die, and when the fire was soon silent, they moved with peace into that half-land between waking and sleeping — both of them beneath the spread of the hides, yet separate. Mel imagined that she was slipping into the fit of her steady stride across the snowy landscape, looking for tracks, while Wallis imagined that, finally, he was descending, as if down a mine shaft — *only one possibility;* and the last conscious thought he had was a new one to him, one that might have come from Mel's perspective: a thought so strange that for a moment he opened his eyes and felt the urge to right himself, to catch his balance.

His thought was, How fast a single day goes by, but how much you can fill it with, which in turn seems to slow it down so — but then he was gone, unconscious, and listening with his body but not his mind to the old echoes and stories and days of the elk above him; and farther above, to the sound, the pressure, of the snow landing on the roof and pressing down, sealing them into a place for a little while, even as in their dreams they strived to keep traveling.

Their breath rose in twin trails, slow rivers of warmth from their sleeping lungs, while the rest of their world, canted now away from the sun, cooled and sank, as time — their time — fell away and below, like a thing shed.

IN THE MORNING, AT GRAY LIGHT — NINE O'CLOCK, AND snowing harder than ever — Wallis woke to find that she was gone. When he went out onto the porch, her tracks were already buried; he had no clue of which direction she might have traveled, or when she would be back.

He went back inside, built the fire up, and scavenged for food, of which there was not much: a small bag of oats, some dried mushrooms, and tea bags; some stale bread and purple jam. The salmon. A bag of potatoes. He felt a wave of shame at not having considered the weight of his existence in her life — the simple weight of his appetite — much less her own need for space, solitude. He understood that it was Matthew's cabin, or had been, but certainly it seemed to be hers now. Matthew and Old Dudley only got out here two or three times a year now, though sometimes Matthew came alone, on an occasional impulsive vacation, when Matthew might decide to head north for a weekend.

Matthew still talked about Mel occasionally, in the office — still called her his girl — but the word when he spoke it had a strange dissonance to it, as if she were in some lightless prison four continents away and might never be seen again.

Wallis had a piece of toast with jam and a cup of tea and a plate of cold salmon, then went into the spare bedroom to see if he could find the maps that Matthew had said would be there. After an hour of rooting, he found them folded in plain brown envelopes, unlabeled as to even which direction was north, and he spread them out in the hallway. He found a carton of core samples, too, and a box of loose rocks and dust — again, no labels as to what part of the valley they came from, or what depth — but it was good to be working with rock again, good to be smelling it, and he examined the chips and chunks of rock and the plugs of core samples. He spent most of the morning arranging and rearranging them in various positions on top of the blank map in such a manner as to possibly conspire to tell some story or make some sense: as if he could construct them (as if the world below were his to construct) into structures and formations that would channel the oil into one sure and certain place, and then trap it.

Basalt, rhyolite, shale, slate; a quartzite, totally impermeable, totally hopeless for oil. A tight dolomite, but no limestone, no sandstone: nothing that he was used to.

He knew the rocks were old; just by holding them and smelling them, he could tell they were far older than anything he'd ever worked with. Some of them had to be close to a billion years old — they had no echo of life, no scent — while others had a few crude fossils. It was almost hopeless; but still, it was comforting to be handling the rock.

It was dark in the hallway, even in midday. He lit lanterns, and wondered what Mel did for money: if Matthew helped her out, or her father. Wallis didn't have much — Old Dudley scarcely paid his geologists, saying that a geologist should hunt for the oil, not the money — though he would buy them almost anything of reason they asked for.

Wallis turned off the lanterns later in the day and lit candles. He envied Mel's neat workplace: her clean desk, her own set of maps and journals. He kept rearranging the plugs of rock all through the day, acquainting himself with them — these tiny samples of the whole — and did not grow frustrated. He tried to keep his confidence up, though in that dimness, he could not help but start to wonder if Old Dudley had gone mad, sending him up here in November.

How to map a land that cannot be seen? The snow in the high country would not be gone for another seven months. Wallis knew Old Dudley had been near the far end of eccentric, when he'd hired Wallis over a year ago; but now he wondered if the old man were not unraveling, like the earth herself turning away from the sun in winter, shunning warmth. There was no law that said that just because Dudley was a great and cunning geologist he could not also go mad.

The cabin grew chilled — Wallis had let the fire go out. He built it back up, then fixed more tea. The sun had gone down behind the trees, though there was still the gloomy blue winter light of the forest outside; he guessed it was still daytime. He studied the pelts and skulls and antlers and bones hanging from the rafters directly above him. The long orange teeth of a beaver, like tusks, or fangs: a depth and beauty of orange he had never seen before. The cinnamon red of a marten's pelt. Even the color black was different, up here — more glossy, and more absolute, in the bear's pelt, and in the feathers from a raven. Wallis shook his head as if to clear it of these distractions of color — distractions which could threaten to unravel toward longing.

Reaching for the kettle to pour his tea, he burned the side of his hand on the stovepipe: seared it, a quick crescent-moon welt of pain, as if he were being punished for something total and unforgivable. He gasped, then went to the sink and plunged his hand in a bucket of water. He felt oafish, incapable of inhabiting the surface of the earth: unable to even move around doing simple or mundane tasks without bumping into things or doing them clumsily, incorrectly.

In one of the wooden boxes in the storeroom there had been some musty old books and journals — Old Dudley's textbooks and notebooks from the early part of the century, when he'd gone to a reform school in San Antonio. Wallis wondered if, perhaps at that age, Old Dudley had been relatively normal. Perhaps his eccentricity, or madness, was a deterioration in which the closer back to the source one got, the less distinguishable it became. Perhaps at the age of sixteen and seventeen Dudley would not yet have revealed a clue of his coming estrangement from — what? The surface of things?

But then again, perhaps not. Wallis picked up one of the old madman's journals and began reading its handwritten, child's-scrawl pages, and was surprised, almost alarmed, for even then, it was already the voice of an old man. Perhaps he had been *born* old.

Wallis's hand throbbed, but his blood chilled, as he read the ancient, loopy ramblings of the precocious teenager.

> *This work attempts to hold a position between textbooks and books of light reading. The formal textbook would not suit the class of readers addressed: future citizens of great intellectual vigor. The style of light reading would have been unworthy of the theme, and would not have supplied the substantial information here intended.*
>
> *My method of treatment is simple. The reader begins with the familiar objects at his very door. His observations are extended to the field, the lake, the valley, and the mountain. They widen over the continent until all the striking phenomena of the surface have been surveyed. The course of observation and reasoning then penetrates beneath the surface.*

The various geologic formations and their fossils are described, first in descending order, then to the oldest. We find here indications of heat which stimulate speculation and bring out the grounds of a nebular theory of world-origin.

Wallis thumbed ahead.

Facts; Or, The Record Given Us to Read Among the Rocks.
I. The Geology at Our Doors.
Surface Materials
    Geology is the story of the earth and of earth's populations. It is more than a story told by some narrator to whom we must listen. We ourselves shall weave the story. Perhaps we will ask the world to tell its own story; but we must try to possess the skill to understand the narrative. The world is vocal with instruction for those who know how to listen, and it is telling many secrets about its hoary past which are not suspected by those who have not learned to listen.

    We shall travel all over the world. We shall climb over mountain-cliffs and descend into deep mines. We shall go down under the sea and make the acquaintance of creatures that dwell in the dark and slimy abysses. We shall split the solid rocks and find where the gold, the silver, the iron, and the oil are hidden. We shall open the stony tombs of the world's mute populations.

    We shall plunge through thousands of ages into the past, and shall sit on a pinnacle and see this planet bathed in the primitive ocean; boiled in the seething water; roasted in ancient fires; distorted, upheaved, moulded, and reshaped again and again, in its long process of preparation to become fit for us, the deserving, to dwell upon it.

    We shall see a long procession of strange creatures coming into view and disappearing — such a menagerie of curious beasts and crawling and creeping and flying things as never yet marched through the streets of any town. And what is most wonderful of all, we shall plunge through thousands of ages of coming events, into the future, with our knowledge, and sit on our pinnacle and see the world grow old — all its human populations vanished — its oceans dried up — its sun darkened, and silence at midnight and Winter reigning through the entire province in which a sisterhood of planets at present basks in the warmth and light of a central and paternal sun.

These are themes which arouse the profoundest curiosity in an intelligent soul. I fancy a masculine reader is impatient to begin.

But we must begin at the beginning. Those who go on long and pleasant journeys have to start from their own doorsteps. Geology tells all about this *world. The world is here — under our feet. It is in the garden and along the roadside, and in the field, and on the shore where the summer ripples sing lullabies to the sleepy crags, and winter storms tear them from their resting-places. No summer ripples or wintry storms are here, but the solid land is here. Let us walk up this hill-slope and sit where we may get an outlook over a little piece of the world's surface.*

Wallis squinted, trying to read the crude lettering by the wavering candlelight. He felt somehow that he should not be reading the journal, and yet that he was also getting a naked glimpse at a thing: and he felt that these crude imaginings of how to find oil — Dudley would have been seventeen, at the time he wrote the notebooks — could help Wallis learn new ways of moving through the underground, if he dared approach so close to what seemed like madness.

Wallis had to force himself to read further: tempted, yet repulsed.

The houses and the herds, the wheat fields, towns and gardens, schools and nunneries: these are accessories. But the dark, beetle-browed ridge which skirts the horizon — that is nature's. The green forest which glides down to the field borders; the stream which winds across the landscape, and rises and falls with the rains; the low swells and the valleys between; the outcropping ledge in the field, and the loose stone by the roadside — these belong to nature. There, in the distance, flies the train of steam-cars, its iron-bound way has been cut through hill and rock mass, and opens to our view something of the hidden material which goes to form the world.

How charming is all this scenery! How many times, imbued with the love of nature, we have strolled on the borders of this quiet lakelet, or lounged on the green slope, which seemed set, like an amphitheater, to accommodate the visitor who loves to look upon the scene.

Perhaps, as urchins straying from school, or getting the most out of a Saturday holiday, we have angled along this brook, or paddled our skiff over this pond. Perhaps in wonderment we have seen the artist from the city, with easel and brush reproducing on canvas the beauty of this simple landscape, thinking to win a prize in the Academy of Art, or at least to afford the pent-up dwellers in the dusty town the luxury of knowing how lavishly the beauties of nature are strewn before the gaze of those who dwell here in this agricultural vale — in this quiet hamlet which Providence has made our home.

This is all geology. We are in the midst of it. We have been enchanted by it before we knew its name.

Wallis closed the old leather journal; bits of dust fell from its binding as he did so, and he wondered how much longer the book would be in the world. It would not last long. He might be the last person to read it.

He returned the journals to their fraying wooden box and set them back in the storeroom. He left the rocks scattered like toys in the hallway. He put more wood in the stove and was wondering at the increased cost of that, as well, due to his presence — wood that Mel would not have been burning — when he heard her come up onto the porch and knock the snow from her boots. He hadn't heard any approach before that; her skis had been soundless.

She came through the door in good cheer, taking her ski cap off and brushing the snow from her hair, smiling to see him, but then frowned when she realized he was still in the same clothes he'd worn the night before, and that they were not snow-damp.

"You didn't go outside today?" she asked.

"No," he said. "I stayed inside and worked, and read. It was nice."

"Oh, you've got to get outside," Mel said, and he thought she meant in the future, but she meant that night. "You've got to get out and move around," she said, "or you'll get depressed. You'll go crazy. The winter will get in your blood. Everyone knows that. We'll go after supper — we'll go put that salmon carcass in the creek. You've got to get outside for at least a little bit, every day."

"Fine," Wallis said, though he did not believe her.

They had salmon and bread for supper. They peeled from the bones the flesh they couldn't finish and put it in containers to keep in the refrigerator. Wallis asked if Mel had seen any wolves that day and she laughed and said she hadn't seen any wolves in over two years. "Sometimes I see their tracks," she said, "but I haven't even seen those in two weeks. It's hard, when it's snowing like this. You've got to be real lucky. You've got to be almost right on top of them."

They had Graham crackers for dessert. Wallis put on one of Matthew's old coats and heavy boots, and they went back outside, wading through the snow. Mel carried the salmon's skeleton in both hands. Wallis looked back at the cabin and could see only the faintest glow from one lantern.

The creek flowed through a lane of cedars. The snow was coming down in swirls now, twisting in whirls away from them. Mel put the skeleton into the creek and held it there in the current, her hands and wrists bare, sweater rolled up to her elbows.

"The salmon used to be here," she said. "And the country's still good for them. They just can't get here anymore," she said. "Only five hundred miles to the ocean, but five hundred dams between here and there." She stirred the fish gently, made it undulate as it had when it was alive. "They'll be able to smell this one," she said. "They'll taste it, out in the ocean, and they'll see it in their dreams. And maybe they'll come looking for it. And maybe they'll get here. Maybe they'll make it back somehow."

She stepped back, clapped the water from her hands — for a moment, Wallis thought she was admonishing the salmon to leave — and for a moment, too, with the current rippling across the ghost-bones beneath the dark water, it looked as if the fish were obeying, was already beginning to swim back to where it had come from.

She crossed her arms, tucked her hands under her armpits. "Come on, I'll show you the smokehouse," she said. The snow was coming down so hard that Wallis could no longer see the lantern's glow from the cabin.

The dark outline, the bulk, of the smokehouse appeared. When they got to the doorway, Mel kicked away a drift of snow and opened the door by slamming her body against it shoulder-first.

Inside it was just as cold, but it was a relief to be out of the snow. Wallis recognized instantly the ancient smell of horses and old hay. The snow's reflected light barely made it in through the dusty windows.

Gradually he became aware of other presences. His eyes become more balanced with the darkness, and he began to see shapes hanging from the rafters. He could smell meat.

Mel went over to the wall, found a box of matches, and lit one. Wallis saw the flare of the match lighting her austere face — the cheekbones large, even muscular, but not unattractive — and she was working over a lantern, trying to light it. As the match dwindled she got the lantern roused into sputtering light; and as the light blossomed around her, he saw the figures hanging from ropes and chains, brilliant and glazed in the lantern's broad light, and it was like coming into a new world, with new beings and citizens all around them: elk, deer, trout, and grouse. Juniper bushes, with their autumn berries still blushing blue-green on them, hung like tobacco sheaves.

Mel's arms glistened as she held the lantern up to better illuminate a giant bull elk. There had been ice on her arms from where she had turned the salmon loose, and now those thin plates of ice were slipping from her and falling to the smokehouse floor and melting into steaming puddles. Her breath leapt in clouds. The lantern hissed and sputtered, coughed, as if protesting the necessary stir of atoms, the reluctant call to flame.

The elk was skinned, and his legs below his knees had been cut off, so that he was hoofless — but he still had his head and antlers attached, and the antlers rose into the high rafters. He rode the air in chains, as if flying — one set looped around his chest, another around haunches and hams, so that he seemed still to be galloping. A rope fastened around his head, tipping his antlers slightly back, and it looked as if he were about to bugle his autumn war-cry.

Only one steak had been cut from his left ham: all the rest of him was perfect and intact, powerful. Wallis walked around him, admiring the way he had been made for the mountains — the way he and his kind had made themselves fit the mountains — admiring every muscle and cross-muscle, every ligament, every woven tendon leading to movement and desire. Mel followed him with the lantern. The meat was deep red, and in places contained an iridescence that gave it a purple sheen. The muscles were frozen: tiny ice crystals were locked in the clefts between muscles, and before the dull heat of the lantern they melted and then fell, as if the meat were weeping.

Wallis walked around to the other side — beneath the dull blue marble eyes, the polished antlers, the black and tan cape. There was a small hole behind one shoulder where the bullet had gone in, and on the other side, a larger hole where the bullet had torn itself out, as if seeking freedom after its bloody passage through the elk's heart and lungs. Damage to all that it touched, and then a yearning for sky again. The elk hung there motionless, suspended, as if all this were only an inconvenience.

"Matthew got him on Halloween afternoon, up on Boyd Mountain," Mel said. She reached out to the elk's bare muscle, the frozen slab of it, and rested her hand on it as she would a horse. "Boy, that was a happy day."

"Matthew was here — that recently?" Wallis asked. He tried to think back to Halloween. If Matthew had come up here, he hadn't mentioned where he had gone.

"Just for a day and a half." Mel tucked her free hand in against her chest once more, warming it. "He always comes and gets my year's meat," she said. "He's always done that." She brightened, remembering the day. "We built a sled and skidded it to a cliff — lowered it down to the Bull River — built a raft, and rode, and swam with it, out to an old logging road. Loaded it into the jeep and drove home."

They walked over to the other of Matthew's bounty: a giant mule deer, not yet skinned, also hanging parallel to, but above the ground, like a ghost ship. "Matthew got him that next day, at daylight, just before he left, on the mountain behind the house," Mel said, remembering the details with what seemed like the intensity of hunger. "I went out with him. There'd been a light snow that night. The deer was browsing kinnikinnick leaves. He had one stuck between his teeth and was standing there with his head pointed straight up, trying to dislodge it with his teeth. The sun was behind us. You could hear snow melting all over the mountain. When Matthew shot, this old boy went down like his legs were knocked out from beneath him.

"He was dreaming the sleep of angels even before the sound of the shot reached him," Mel said. "While we were cleaning him, a grizzly came over the top of the ridge and sat and watched us. They're starting to learn that when they hear a rifle in the fall, it usually means a gut pile to feed on. Sometimes they run the hunters off and eat the whole deer. Sometimes the wolves and ravens and coyotes and other creatures also come to the sound of the shot. But this day there was just that one big bear, and he didn't bother us. We had blood up to our elbows, but he just sat there and watched us. We left the heart and liver for him. A big boar grizzly.

"He could have gotten us if he'd wanted. What a day," she said.

They toured the rest of the smokehouse. All three of the valley's species of grouse — ruffed, spruce, and blue — hung with heads and wings folded, feet dangling. Some were plucked; others still had their feathers. It was like being in a delicatessen, and Wallis hoped he would get a chance to eat them. He wondered what they tasted like. They were the size of small chickens, but as beautiful as pheasants: some rust and russet, gray and black, others dusky blue, with tiger bars across their tails, and short, sturdy beaks.

"Is Matthew a good shot?" he asked.

"Yes," said Mel.

There were fish hanging, too, skillet-sized trout and whitefish, belly-swooped from the gorging of summer, and the fish had absorbed the smokehouse's odors, apple and cherry wood, and some alder. Wallis sniffed the side of one trout, a two-pounder — "Go ahead," Mel said, "take a bite" — and he did. It was delicious.

"Do you ever use mesquite?" he asked. "Do you ever have Matthew or your father send it up from Texas?"

Mel shook her head. "No," she said. "I don't ask for it, if it's not from the valley. I try not to bring in anything alien, anything foreign," she said. "If Matthew sends it, I'll use it — but I don't ask." She looked to the back of the smokehouse, to her stack of wood, as if Texas, and mesquite, were in that direction.

"Apples and cherries grow up here?" he asked.

Mel smiled. "Yes," she said. "At the school, and behind Helen's house, behind the mercantile, down low, along the river. Helen's trees don't blossom, and they don't bear fruit, but they grow," she said. "They're real big, and real old." She shrugged. "Maybe one year they will."

"How old are they?" Wallis asked.

"Helen planted them when she was a little girl. Seventy, eighty years ago. I don't know."

"And they *never* blossomed?" Wallis asked.

Mel shook her head. "They just grow," she said, a little defensively.

There were more fish, pickled in jars, and other fish packed in last spring's ice in cedar crates, resting on sawdust. They gleamed before the light of the lantern, as Mel showed them to him, case after case, like a proud grocer.

She lifted the lantern, and now he saw that there were iron bars in front of the windows, and his first thought was that she truly believed these creatures of the woods might still somehow by desire alone make it back into the woods, and that she was trying to prevent their escape.

"The bears try to come in sometimes," she said. "And wolverines. There are old tooth marks and claw marks all over this building," she said, "beginning from when Matthew's parents first built and home-steaded this place, on up to this year." Mel laughed. "Sometimes in the spring, before they've had their greens — when their gums are still weak — they'll bite at the sides of the building, and their teeth will come out and get stuck in the wood. The wolverines are the worst; they won't run from you. They'll sit up on the roof for two or three days, trying to come down the chimney, and just snarl at you. I've thrown snowballs at them, shot the rifle over their head, *everything,* but they won't run off. Ravens and coyotes try to get in, and eagles, too. Some mornings in the fall there'll be a pair of golden eagles sitting on the roof.

"My father used to hunt with eagles," she said quietly. "He went over to Russia and bought one of those big Asian golden eagles. He spent a month over there using it to hunt deer, wolves, and even bears. They used to use them in battle, to hunt men." She was speaking calmly, with no trace of revulsion or wonder — just a quietness, as if she were unsure of even her own family's past. As if even events of the past could not be trusted if the tracks or other proof of them were not before her, lying somewhere out into the future.

"It was before I was born," she said. "I've heard him talk about it. The authorities wouldn't let him keep the eagle."

Mel was silent then, thinking of how Matthew and Old Dudley had twined together — of the way she could no longer think of one without the other, so that it was as if she had had them both taken from her — and she stepped in next to Wallis and tucked her head down. Her weight was hard and dense against him, though he could tell, too, that she was holding something in reserve: that always, she would be doing that, with anyone. He would never have guessed she was lonely. She had too much to do, it seemed, and the days were too short. Never in a million years would he have guessed that.

The light cast a glow around their frozen feet and steam rose from their boots. All the animals hung silent, motionless, as if respecting Mel's sadness; mouths gaping, hearts cut out, and eyes blue-blind, but still seeing, and feeling: all pointing skyward and rising, but with part of them lingering too, communicating with her — speaking some intermediary language that rested between man and the stars.

Mel and Wallis stood there like horses in a stable, their ankles steaming from the lantern heat, for a long while, just listening to the snow fall, and to the hiss of the lantern. When the lantern spent its fuel and died with a sputter, the smoke drew back into a genie's bottle, and as the light went away it drew with it the final, fading images of the moon-eyed elk, the giant-racked deer, and the sleepy grouse, their heads hung, and the brilliant brook trout, the ascending silver rainbow trout and the blood-bright cutthroats.

In the last wisp of gold light, Wallis saw a dark pile of potatoes in one corner, the pile assuming the shape of a bear as the light fled, and in the gathered darkness the fish and ascending game were turned into silhouetted angels.

Now there was just the sound of the snow burying Wallis and Mel. Wallis put his arms around Mel and held on as if they were going down together.

Mel steadied and took a step back. She said nothing of the moment. Wallis thought how to her it must have seemed as natural as holding a hand up for help, had she slipped and gone down on the ice; and because it was cold, so cold now that it hurt their lungs to breathe, and because they were shivering, they left the smokehouse.

When they stepped outside into the night, the sound was fresher.

The light from their cabin was gone — either burned out, or, more likely, obscured by the blizzard. Mel stood shoulder to shoulder with him, pausing for only a moment after she had shut and barred the smokehouse door behind her. She looked up the hill in the direction where her instinct and memory told her the cabin was.

If the cabin's lantern were out, and if she veered off her heart's course by a degree or two in the beginning, they would never reach the cabin. They might miss it, in their errant arc, by twenty yards, or by a few inches — their groping hands catching only feathery, falling snow.

And that is how they would die — two strangers, only beginning to know anything about each other. They would travel past their home, would feel the jungle brushing against their faces, and know they'd overshot the tiny sanctuary of the cabin.

"Hold onto me," Mel said, looking up the hill with resolve, almost anger — as if the cabin were hiding from her — and she started up the hill, wading through the deep snow fast, without a trace of hesitation or caution.

It seemed to Wallis that they walked for a long time, and then he was certain that they had walked for a long time, and still they had not yet come to the cabin.

He held onto Mel's coat as he would the tail of a horse. She stopped when it seemed sure that they had gone too far. He moved in close, heard her grunt a curse, but he did not hear fear in her voice. Was it too late, he wondered, to hunker down — to burrow into the snow like a bear or a grouse; to let it cover them until it was warm as a blanket, and then to come back out when it stopped snowing, if it ever stopped?

Mel turned and began moving hard to the right — almost a lunge — and Wallis nearly lost his grasp on her. She traveled another ten steps and then stopped again. They stood there in the blizzard like ghosts.

Mel was looking hard in one direction, her stare fixed at nothing. Wallis watched too. It was as if she were listening to something, though all of the senses were gone, rendered unintelligible, meaningless. There was only the weight and pull of gravity beneath their feet.

Her tenseness eased. Her breathing steadied. She continued to watch in the one direction, as a hunter watches a meadow. Wallis could see it, then — or thought he could see it. A paleness in the storm disappeared when he looked at it, but when he tried to look away, it came back again: not a glow, by any stretch of the imagination — not the thing they were looking for — but a lessening, a gauziness, which was inviting. It tempted them to step through it.

Wallis wanted to move toward it immediately. Pants cuffs frozen solid. Shaking and rattling, shivering like a sack of bones. Mel held her ground: watched that different patch of storm as if challenging it.

It began to storm harder, and the patch, the place of nothing they were looking at, disappeared. Mel took a full step toward it, and then another, and then she began moving toward it quickly. It reappeared, and now it had the faintest yellow color to it, and then more, until it was a glow, and it was exactly the opposite of how the light had gone back into the lantern.

Inside, the boards beneath their feet. The familiar objects on her shelves, when they stepped inside: feathers, stones, shells, and the sprawl of closed, silent books — each one of them swimming with millions of hieroglyphics that were designed, upon being scanned, to ignite into light and knowledge, into images and scents and sounds.

The pine planking of her floor. The dishes from their meal, the cold stone fireplace, and the cold air in the cabin, the lantern's bright light, and the snow not yet melting from their boots, for already the cabin had grown so cold. Only a degree or two — the tiniest bit of correction to the angle of their arc, in the beginning — separated them from all the snow beyond, and so much cold — too much cold, even for Mel.

They knew better than to talk about it, or to joke about it.

Wallis got the fire going again. Mel crouched next to him and warmed her hands before the flames. When she had feeling in them once more, she stood and walked once around the inside of her cabin, examining things — handling this river stone, or that piece of obsidian — and when she went past her desk, she paused and looked at her notes spread out there. She tapped the open notebook once, as if trying to remember all that lay beneath that open page, and she completed her lap by coming back to the fireplace, where Wallis was still adding kindling.

It was a cold fire. That was one of the things that amazed him most about the valley: how sometimes it would be so frigid that he could see a fire's flames, could smell them, could hear the wood snapping, but could still feel no warmth. He could pass his bare hands right through the flames and be shivering all the while.

Wallis slept on the floor in front of the fire, wrapped in elk hides again. Mel touched his arm, then went down the hallway to her bedroom. The flames threw light all around the cabin, but gradually grew lower as Wallis dreamed his way toward darkness. When the fire had gone completely out, he woke once and got it lit again, then went back to sleep. It was so cold that his head hurt. He wondered if the trees felt pain, or sensed it, before they cracked open in the night. He could hear them splitting.

He dreamed about the subterranean lands he would endeavor to enter in the summer or fall, and of the distant lands he had entered elsewhere, and broken apart. He dreamed of the mineralization that binds sand grains together — sometimes calcareous, other times friable and porous, easily crushed. It was hard for him to imagine the specific processes that had given rise to those individual cementings below: hard to imagine the specific processes that had held an ancient land in place; but that night, in his dreams, he imagined that perhaps those old lands were held in place by a quietness and enduringness — a smoothness of fit. The way rain falls, the way snow falls. The way birds sleep. The way lichens grow in red and blue mosaics across damp boulders and old stone walls. The way a log rots.

The slow moths that emerge from the log's orange rot.

If wolves howled that night, he didn't hear them. The snow absorbed everything.

NOW THE WOLVES TOOK HER AS SURELY AS IF THEY HAD come in the cabin and seized her in their jaws. Each morning long before daylight Wallis would awaken to the glow of coals from where he had let the fire burn down and would see Mel in the kitchen working by candlelight to avoid waking him. She would already be bundled in her parka, breathing frost, making a little fire in the kitchen's wood stove to boil water for tea, and fixing a slab of toast, over which she would spread thick butter and jam.

She would eat in silence, standing on the other side of the cabin, watching him, and then she would dust the crumbs from her hands, dab a towel at the corner of her mouth, and go out the door quickly.

And the geology, the old earth, took Wallis, just as surely as if he had died and was now only some ghost wandering the surface, trying to get back to the time when he had felt most alive, and not noticing the paradox: that in his rigorous efforts to return to that past, he was becoming more alive.

As if he could be both numb and aware. As if a man could be both awake and asleep, or both good and evil.

Some days he was so hungry for a taste and feel of the soil, some sighting of rock, that he would wander out into the yard, or into the woods beyond, and would begin digging in the snow with his gloved hands, or with a shovel: digging like a madman or a searcher looking for something dropped, until the shoveltip clinked against the frozen soil. He would chip away at the soil, sparks skittering sometimes as steel struck flint — that acrid odor — and then he would scrape up the small tracings of soil and study them. He would look at the towering, snow-clad mountains above, and he would want to howl at the gulf of knowledge. He would feel trapped, that for all of his laborings he could only get a few inches into the recent glacial moraine. He would feel bereft of intimacy.

His despair would broaden from that. He would believe that Old Dudley had sent him up here to abandon him: that Dudley had found another geologist to train, and that Dudley and Matthew and that third geologist were busy cracking open old anticlines like streamside raccoons cracking freshwater mussels to suck out the meat, and him not included in any of the fun.

The caw of a lone raven, overhead: cold blue skies, and the stillness of the north: and then after the raven's echo was gone, only silence. He could not get to where he wanted.

And when Mel came home in the evenings, she would sometimes notice the small mounds from where he had been digging — a faint sprinkling of black earth atop the snow — but said nothing, glad only that he was getting outside.

Some days the coyotes would hear his labors and would appear at the edge of the woods to watch him as he worked. They could smell the blood from his barehanded labors as he tried to pluck polished moraine from frozen earth, and Wallis would not notice them until — as if to mimic him — the coyotes would begin digging also, tunneling at the snow, digging fast and furious.

Wallis would hear the roostertails of snow swooshing up and landing in clumps and patters behind the coyotes as they dug, and he would pause in his own digging, sheened with sweat, and would watch; and after a short time, one of the coyotes would appear with a mouse in its jaws gotten from beneath the snow. At that point the other coyotes would chase the one with the mouse, all the coyotes flowing lightly across the top of the snow, dodging and feinting not like individuals but like one swirling organism — and then after a while whichever coyote had ended up with the mouse would tease both the mouse and the other coyotes by tossing it high into the air and then catching it again. Finally one of them would eat the tattered mouse, and Wallis would go back to digging, and the coyotes would sit on their haunches and watch him a bit longer, and when Wallis looked up again, they would have vanished, though later in the day he would hear them laughing and howling and yipping back in the woods, chasing something.

He despaired. In the evenings, when Mel came home, she could see that he had despaired, could read the landscape of his frustration by the dozens of half-finished diggings that surrounded her cabin — dustings of frozen black crumbs of earth resting atop the snow — but still she said nothing, though she was sad, believing that in no way could this one be as enduring as Matthew — believing for certain that Dudley would consume him soon.

And perhaps for this reason — believing that Wallis would soon be crushed and buried — she did not volunteer things, did not teach him the things she knew. She found reasons to stay out later, and traveled farther, tracking and mapping the wolves. When she came home in the evenings, she isolated herself from him. She read, or worked quietly in her journals. And though the romance between her and Matthew was all but over, worn smooth — Old Dudley owned him completely, now

— she nonetheless found herself trying to keep track of the days and dates, knowing Matthew and Dudley would be coming up for Christmas. She thought of her own entrapments — her memories of Matthew of when he had been free. He had loved her; he had loved hunting the oil. Matthew had once said that if he remained with her in the valley and did not follow Old Dudley down to Texas, some part of him would always feel trapped, and would resent her for that. So she had turned him free — he had turned himself free — and now had gone and gotten trapped anyway. All to naught.

So almost as if blaming Wallis — as if Wallis were some residue of her father — she shunned him now without being rude about it. She simply distanced herself from him, as many animals are said to do when one of their number becomes injured. It was only the wolves who would wait with one of their injured, and tend to it until it recovered. All the other social animals vanished when one of their kind went down — knowing that the crippled one would rob valuable resources, would disrupt delicate rhythms, and, worst of all, would summon predators.

Wallis could feel the winter sickness coming on. Knowing the name of it, however, did nothing to ease his despair. The waning days, waning light, and his isolation from the world: he felt his power draining from him as if from a wound, and felt old grief rising. He suspected the nature of what Old Dudley was doing to him, why he had banished him to this place. Wallis knew he was being stripped from the secure world of data and facts, stripped of the assurances of reality he'd come not only to depend upon, but to which he had become addicted. He understood that Old Dudley was jerking his head around, forcing him, like a dog whose leash is tugged sharply, to become a creature of the imagination, rather than fact.

He could only imagine what lay beneath the snow. It was as if Old Dudley — or the land itself — was bending Wallis's mind, forcing it to alter shape and capability completely. Wallis could feel his mind threatening to crack, under that pressure — swelling, bucking, and folding. Some days out in the snow fields Wallis would sink to his knees and then lie down on the snow, face down. The falling snow would cover him.

But as it covered him, he would calm, as if healed, and would sit up, ready to try again, not knowing whether it was his will — some spark within — which had lifted him back up, or the land itself, or even some thing buried beneath the land.

And each night, upon returning home, Mel would wander around her cabin before going inside — reading clearly Wallis's story of that day's despair. To her the signs of floundering — the weary snow angels — were not even so much like the etchings or scribings of Wallis's despair as they were evidences — the tracks, the prints — of Old Dudley's awful domineering: as if the beast of Dudley himself had passed through there earlier in the day; and Mel would shiver, and, half-believing that he had, would be glad that she had not been there.

Mel had survived beneath his thumb for eighteen years — though because his blood was hers, she sometimes did not stop counting from the day she left home, but was still counting, at thirty-eight.

Matthew had survived nineteen years of it, thus far. Mel stood in the snow some nights before going inside and wondered what Matthew might look like when he was an old man — if he managed to survive — but she knew what the answer was, even as she considered it. She could take her gloves off and touch the side of her face — the place where the lines were coming — and know the answer to that sculpting. It was the same answer for her. Old Dudley was carving one of them with his blood and the other with his hands.

Occasionally, at her desk — listening to Wallis roll the rocks around in the hallway, positioning and repositioning them on that blank map like some demented child — she would feel pity for him; other times, sorrow, and other times, a shared bond. But still she kept her distance; and likewise Wallis told himself not to pursue Mel. To struggle to dive deep, rather than traveling far.

H E WAS LEARNING NOTHING. THE SUN HAD GONE TO the other side of the world. Cold rolled onto the land as if venturing from cracks and fissures in the earth. Trees exploded all night, every night, filling the woods with the sounds of their cannonade. As they fell, the creaky, twisted splintering sounds — the muffled *thumps* — drummed the earth so soundly that surely it was awakening, even if briefly, the bears sleeping like astronauts frozen in the earth. The smell of the trees' crushed green limbs permeated the woods.

The snow robbed all other sounds — took away even the silence, so that there was now a thing even more absolute than silence. One lone raven could break the day open. Three feet, four feet, five feet of snow. Wallis stayed inside and read.

In Dudley's late adolescent scrawl, his young man's scrawl, Wallis read the words that had been written as if beneath a fever. He marveled at the insane arrogance: as if the writer had truly traveled to and seen these places, rather than imagining them, and was describing them from ancient memory.

Introduction to the Rocks
Kinds of Minerals and Stones

It is not entirely satisfactory to roam over the fields with bowlders lying on the right and left, but without any knowledge of their natures. True, we shall experience much satisfaction in feeling that we know something of their origin and their history. We may walk up to the side of one of these way-worn rock-travelers and say: "Old Hard Head, when did you arrive in this country, and where did you originate from?" Old Hard Head will lie sullenly and answer never a word. But he is written all over with inscriptions which we can begin to decipher. So we look on the rounded and weather-beaten form and say to ourselves: "This immigrant rock came from a northern country. He left his mother rock, and most of his kindred, in the woods, or up in the mountains. A large number of his kindred came with him. He rode part of the way on the back of a glacier. By and by he fell off, or got into a hole; and after that he had a severe squeezing. He got crushed and rubbed and rolled and pushed for some thousands of years.

But every year he made some progress. By and by there was a great change of weather. The ice carriage melted away from him, and fine weather returned, and lo! he found himself, one spring, in this field. That was long enough before Adam and Eve set up business in gardening and other such fuckery. But here old Hard Head has been lying ever since. And now, we are the very first persons who ever stopped to pay him a moment's attention, and make his acquaintance.

If old Hard Head thinks, he is revolving some handsome compliments on our intelligence. Whatever old Hard Head may think, we are sure the ability to learn something of the method of the world was given

us to be exercised. If we go stupidly through the world without exercis-
ing that ability, we do no better than an ox. But if we seek to gain an
insight into the method and history of the world, we honor the Author of
the world; we read His thoughts. Knowing some of His thoughts, we
come into more intimate relations with Him. The study of science is a
virtue. Attention to geology is a human duty.

To complete our introduction to old Hard Head we must know his
name. To call him old Hard Head is like calling a man "Old Russian" or
"Old Englishman." He has, besides, his personal name. Now, there is
a way of finding out the particular name of each rock. Like a dog with
his name on his collar, each mute rock displays a name written on its
exterior.

Do you see that nearly all these bowlders appear to be mixtures of
different colors and kinds of rocks? See one rock with round pebbles
imbedded in a mass of smaller grains. See another rock, less coarse, with
silvery scales. Now, all these differently colored constituents of the rocks
are so many different minerals. *Rocks are composed of minerals. Some*
rocks have two minerals; some, three; some, four. The particular name of
a rock depends on the minerals in it. As soon as we know the minerals,
we can call the name of the rock: can shout it to both the heavens and
hell. Now, sit down and take a lesson in minerals.

Do you see this white flint rock, composed throughout of one kind of
mineral? That mineral is quartz. *It is the hardest of all the common*
minerals. Try to scratch it. You see the point of steel makes no impression
on it. But it leaves a black mark. The quartz wears away the steel.
When one of these bowlders is thus composed entirely of quartz, its
name is quartzite. *There are many quartzites, as there are many Smiths*
and Joneses. Let us learn the other part of the name. Look at these
uniformly colored quartzites — white and gray. You see one is com-
posed of distinct grains; this is a granular *quartzite. One contains peb-*
bles; this is a conglomeratic *quartzite, or simply a* conglomerate. *None*
of it is worth a good gott-damn for holding oil, but once eroded back
into sandstones of sufficient porosities, can again be of use in the service
of possessing petroleum. In fact, quartz is the most abundant of all
minerals . . .

Wallis skimmed ahead. He knew about conglomerates: knew how
two things were forced to become one. He was more interested in
learning about the workings of Old Dudley's — young Dudley's —

fevered mind. What percentage had been fact, and what percentage imagination, back then? When he described a sound, did he really hear it in his mind? What did it take to succeed — to find oil — as Old Dudley and Matthew were finding it?

The winter silence, or absence of silence, deepened; the snow fell more soundlessly than ever, compressing everything, as Wallis read:

The sharp clacking collision of transported rock fragments accompanies the loud roaring of the impetuous stream. The white streamlet, always rapid, has been swollen to a furious torrent by a recent cloudburst. The torrent in its rage has rent all barriers and courses over adjacent lands. Stones, up to several tons in weight, hurl right and left, in the same fashion as an autumn wind disperses the leaves of maples along the street. Hundreds of acres lay buried beneath sand and mud, cobblestones and massive rocks. The rough and rocky slope receives her deposits; the last goat pasture lies concealed beneath a bed of stones, and the grassy flat lies hidden by a blanket of gravel and slime.

Observe the power of sorting exerted by moving water. The heavier rocks are left where the most precipitous hillside graduates into the sharp slope. Here is the first abatement of the force of the stream. It drops what can no longer be moved by the diminished power of the torrent.

The smaller rocks lay next in order. Where the slope passes into a gentler grade, the still waning force of the maddened stream becomes insufficient to bear them on.

Still farther, on the lower levels, the flood is widened, its velocity slackened, and its transportative power so abated that the average-sized cobblestones have to be left.

Still travels on the gravel, finds pause only on the pastures where domestic animals have been grazing.

But the sand is borne to the lower level and spreads itself out over many an arable field and fragrant meadow; while the fine alluvial mud floats with the tired waters, which seek out sheltered nooks and depressions in which to rest, searching the swamps and bayous and peat bogs.

This was yesterday. This morning the lesson lies before us. Here are effects of a geological cause on whose action the startled peasant yesterday gazed despairingly. He needs no theory to convince him of the nature and mode of action of the forces which devasted his fields.

Not far from the home of my boyhood was the mill pond, dear to every schoolward trudging urchin who had to pass it, and a Saturday

resort for many others who lived in the adjoining "district." Here we
bathed; here we fished; here we risked our lives in shaky skiffs, and
astride of unmanageable logs. The water was deep and clear. Last sum-
mer I visited the old pond. Like the anxious parents who shared with
mill pond the affections of which boyish hearts are susceptible, the scene
of so much truant enjoyment was changed almost beyond recognition.
The deep, clear water was silted up, and logs were thrusting their brown
noses up in the sites where I used to swim in summer and skate in winter.
Sedges fringed the borders; bulrushes, to their knees in water, were
holding possession of land that was expected to be, and their encroaching
march threatened to corner the anxious perches and sunfishes in the last
lingering bowl of clear water close by the decrepit old dam. This, I
thought, is a picture of the history of the world. How long, I queried,
before this mill pond will be a swamp? Is this the impending fate of all
our ponds and lakelets? Johnny, do you think your favorite skating place
will ever come to this?

.

Perhaps Old Dudley had always had an old soul, Wallis thought. He
was pretty certain Dudley had never had any damn skates, much less a
mill pond. In the year that Wallis had lived and worked with him down
in Houston, Wallis had had the notion that Old Dudley had been
growing older, like some doddering old man who was watching his
fortune, his capital, grow and multiply at some vast and unstoppable
pace, regardless of his attention or inattention: that things were out of
control, and that his fortune was recklessness, with his two geologists
finding oil and gas as easily as sunlight finds the earth — unable to
miss, in rhythm and in groove.

What if, however, Old Dudley was growing younger and less horrible? What if — pathetic as he was, unlovely as he was — he was, in his
advancing years, finally aware of his horridness, and was trying to put
on the brakes — trying not to waste or spurn love and friendship,
trying not to consume so wantonly?

If this were so — if he were really trying not to be an asshole — it
would seem to make his wanton consumption seem somehow even
more horrible.

Stranded up in the valley, Wallis imagined all sorts of awful things.
He imagined, and then had dreams, of Old Dudley clawing up from
great depth beneath a rubble of stone, emerging monstrous and earth-

dripping; and then, deeper into winter, the dreams worsened, so that it was Wallis himself who was buried and gasping for air and light, but finding only earth, soil, stone. His lungs filling with dirt, his body turning into dirt. Some fire within him blinking out.

Mel heard him cry out in his sleep some nights and shook her head, felt herself soften and fill with sorrow as she would upon hearing the sounds of a wounded animal that she knew was not going to make it. She would grow angry with Dudley for continuing to eat the young men, and angry with Wallis and Matthew for allowing themselves to be eaten. Angry with herself for even listening, much less responding, to Wallis's groans and whimpers, and angry at herself for her inability to tear fully away from either her father or Matthew.

She would get up and put a piece of wood on the fire. She would study her maps by firelight: the tiny stipplings, the dots and dashes, of the pack's comings and goings in the river bottoms and side canyons. The dates and locations of their kills. A different map for each month. The position of the moon and stars overhead, as if the wolves (and the deer they followed and chased) were but a gearworks of their own devising, with blood and gristle as the lubricant. She didn't even know for sure how many wolves there were. Sometimes she thought four; other times, three, and on other occasions, five. She saw them so rarely. Except for the raw carnage of their passage — the jaw-crunched bones, the hide and hair, and the piles of shit, and the tracks of their huge feet (each larger than her outstretched hand) — a person could easily believe that they were not really there.

To give the wolves space, and respect, she tracked them backward, hoping to avoid giving them the feeling that she was chasing them. She worked backward along their trail, working always two or three days into the past. The maps would look the same anyway; as long as she could find the tracks, the story would get told. And as seen from the air the map would look identical, whether she mapped them forward or backward.

She would read her maps by firelight for a while, then go back to bed. She would put the pillow over her head to block out the sounds of Wallis's bad dreams, and would try to get another hour or two of sleep before it was time to go out again.

She didn't think Wallis could possibly last through the winter.

She knew she needed to sleep: especially in the winter. But it wasn't as it had been when she was younger. She no longer fell into sleep as if diving deep, plunging, only to emerge, shimmering and cleansed, eight hours later. It was as if she had become a little clumsier, now, even in her sleep — grasping, even stumbling. Awakening every few hours, as if trying to recall a thing she was missing. Not a child, or a husband, or a lover, but something — as if she were missing out on, or had misplaced, something.

Once out in the woods, following the tracks backward, those doubts and feelings would fade — but lying still and alone in bed each night, she felt them moving in closer, where before she had not even known they existed.

Helen came skiing up one day, pulling a sled behind her. It was a sunny day — the temperature nearly up to freezing — and Wallis was wrapped in an elk hide, sitting in a slash of sunlight, drinking hot coffee and watching the stark mountain to the south — watching the snowy wall of it, and the way the sun was striking it, as if hoping or believing that the purity of his need might make the snow slide from those rock cliffs, like the unclothing of some beloved.

Helen skied up to the porch. Wallis rose to greet her. "Are you hurt?" she asked.

"No," said Wallis.

"Then why are you just sitting there?"

"I was thinking."

Helen stared at him not only as if he were ignorant, but worse — as if he were some infiltrator sent into the valley from the outside world to weaken things, to dilute hidden strength, and foment discord.

"You've got to keep moving, in winter," she said. "Especially this early into it. You'll go down for sure if you don't keep moving. Your blood will pool. Part of you will rot. The other parts will stiffen." She waved her hands. "What's the word?"

"Lithify," he said. He could feel it already. He didn't need her to tell him. It was a feeling like giving up. He had felt it before.

"What are your designs on Mel?" Helen asked, unclipping the skis and coming up onto the porch.

"Designs," he said.

"She still belongs to Matthew," said Helen. "She will always belong to him."

Wallis sat back down and pulled the elk hide tighter around him and stared out at the wall of mountain again. He knew there would be cross-bedding planes visible, formations laid down atop one another visible even to the naked eye. He knew he could sit on the porch in the summer and study the direction and depositional history of them through a telescope; and that he could also climb the cliffs' crevices, could climb like a spider and with his rock hammer could chip the real and physical samples from the cliff walls — ancient petrified oceans frozen to stone and lifted high into the sky so that the world — erosion, weathering, wind, and the clutch of plant-roots — could begin eating at them.

He was afraid he might go mad if he kept staring at that wall, not knowing which way the formations ran.

"Say it," Helen said. "You're in love with her." She peered at him closely. "I think he's going to come back soon. Maybe in a year or two. I think he misses the valley. I'm pretty sure he's coming back. And Mel will still be here, waiting for him. Does he ever talk like that?" Helen asked. "Does he ever mention quitting?"

Wallis looked away from the snowy cliffs: studied Helen as if he had forgotten the difference between the animate and the inanimate. "Can I fix you some coffee?" he asked.

"Tea, please," Helen said. They rose to step inside to warmth, though lingered, in the doorway, reluctant to leave the rare bright light.

"I'm not in love with her," Wallis said. "I just want to find oil."

"It's not here," Helen said. "If it was, Matthew would have found it." Wallis smiled, built the fire up in the kitchen's wood stove to heat more water.

"What's in the sled?" he asked.

"Grapefruit," Helen said. "A Christmas present from Matthew. He had the grapefruit brought in over the pass on a snowmobile."

"Are they still coming for Christmas?" Wallis asked.

"Of course," Helen said.

"How long?"

"They never stay long. Just a couple of days."

"No," said Wallis, "I mean how long before Christmas?"

"A week," said Helen.

"How will they get here?" Wallis asked.

Helen shrugged. "Sometimes snowmobiles, sometimes helicopter. Some years, dog sled. They always get here." She studied Wallis.

"You're really not in love with her, are you? You really want them to come up here." She paused. "Who do you miss more, Old Dudley or Matthew?"

"I don't think of them individually," Wallis said.

Helen frowned. "They're not at all alike! Matthew's a lot different —"

"I know. But I think of how they are together. The two parts of them combining."

Helen was silent for a while. Wallis handed her the tea.

"How come you and Mel never come into town?" she asked.

Wallis shrugged. "She's always out tracking. I . . ." He shrugged, gestured to the books on the shelves, and to the woods. Did not have the nerve to tell her the truth, that he was simply too tired: that it was too far.

"Do you mind if I stay this evening, to watch and be sure?" Helen asked.

"To be sure of what?"

"That you're not in love with her."

Wallis smiled. There was no way in hell Matthew would be coming back, but he could not say that to the old lady. Her own entrapment was like anyone else's, like everyone else's, even here in the center of this free valley. He thought of the freedom he found at twenty thousand feet, and would find one day again.

When Mel got home, she went out to the smokehouse and gathered several grouse for dinner, which pleased Helen; it was her favorite food. They basted the birds with butter and salt and pepper and roasted them in the wood stove until the scent filled the cabin fully.

Once again the coyotes appeared — Wallis could see their moonlit shadows moving around in the blue woods at a distance — and one coyote suddenly appeared at the picture window as if he had been hiding beneath the sill, and had leapt up solely with the purpose of startling them, which he did.

The coyote had a large gray ruffed grouse in his jaws — its wings were still flapping furiously — and the coyote stood there in front of the window, his mouth full of struggling grouse. They could see terror in the grouse's eyes as it flapped. Loose feathers floated in all directions. Then the coyote disappeared, taking the grouse with it.

It was hard not to believe that the coyote had performed some magic — that it had transformed one of the autumn-dead birds in the smokehouse back into the living — and Mel had to go down and be sure she had closed and barred the door.

They sat down to dinner at the long table. The flames of the candles reflected themselves against the bronzed, bare breasts of the grouse.

They ate until only bones remained: no bread, no vegetables, only grouse. For dessert they tried to peel the grapefruit Matthew had shipped in, but the rinds were frozen. They ended up peeling them with pocketknives, as if carving wood, and spooning out the frozen pulp, which was still sweet.

"How many wells?" Wallis asked. "How many have they drilled so far?"

Mel thought for a moment. Helen and Wallis leaned back in their chairs, sated. "Seventeen?" she said. "Eighteen, maybe?" She got up and went over to her desk, pulled down some old hide-wrapped journals, scanned through the pages; then she unrolled a hide map and spread it out on the floor.

It was the most beautiful map Wallis had ever seen, tanned nearly as thin as the linen on which he drew his own maps. The hide was cream-colored and bore the charcoal smudges of age on it. It was as large as a rug and had the valley shown on it four different times: a map for each season. The four maps showed the paths of the wolves, and other landmarks: kill sites, dens, and places where Mel had glimpsed the wolves: places where the wolves had allowed themselves to be seen by her.

Mel counted the well symbols, which she had marked with tiny skulls and crossbones. Wallis touched the hide, the well locations, with his hands. "How deep was this one?" he asked — a location along the river. "And this one?" — farther up in the mountains.

Mel was still counting. "Hell, I don't know," she said. "I don't care about any of that. What does it matter? They drilled them," she said. "They were dry holes, they went away, but they'll come back."

"Nineteen," she said, when she had finished. She sat back and touched the hide: followed, with her long fingers, some of the wolves' passages from the winter of that year. There were more data on that map; less on the summer map, when it was so hard to find their tracks. Usually she had to follow them in summer and fall by mapping the flocks, the calls and gatherings, of the ravens above, who followed the wolves from kill to kill; the ravens riding above the paths of the wolves.

Helen hunkered down on all fours and also touched the map, so that all three of them had their hands on it. "Is this the deer that Matthew shot up on Waper Ridge last year?" she asked.

"It is," said Mel.

They could all smell the smoke in the hide: the way it had absorbed the odor of wood burned in the fireplace. "Where's my store?" Helen asked, trying to orient herself.

Wallis wanted to know more about the wells, but Mel said Old Dudley had told her not to let Wallis know anything about the wells: which, said Mel, was one of the reasons she was showing him.

"Do you have the logs?" Wallis asked. "The electrical logs, the well logs — the paper printouts, the drill rates, anything?" Mel shook her head, looked back at the map. Her fingers rested at the site of a moose kill dated September twenty-fifth.

"The drill cuttings — the ground-up chips of rock," Wallis said. "Where are they?"

Mel studied him a moment. Did he think she was as willing and eager to help him find oil as he was to discover it?

"Take, take, take," she said. "What do you have to give?"

At first he thought she meant a trade, a price for the information, but then he understood what she meant: that desire, even ravening hunger, was permissible in her home, but not to cross over into the territory of greed. To rein in, if he could at all help it.

"Some they sent down the river," Mel said. "They pumped the slurry straight into the river. Others, they buried in big pits. It was all mixed up and gooey with mud — you wouldn't be able to make anything of it anyway," she said. "It would drive you crazy."

"I need that old data," Wallis said. "The old well logs."

Mel shrugged. "That's your business. But my guess is that if Old Dudley wanted you to have those things, he would have sent them up here with you."

Mel folded her map and stored it in a cedar chest. Helen rose and went over to one of the bookshelves and began touching the spines of the books. "If you've read all these books, you're one smart cookie," she said.

"I've read them," Mel said. "Most of them I read a long time ago, but I read them." She went over and stood next to Helen and stared at the books as if they were both watching animals in some meadow: deer, perhaps, or elk. "It's not so much as if I've quit reading," she said. "It's more like now I'm reading stories out on the land — stories tucked under the snow, stories running from me, just around the next bend. It still feels like I'm reading," she said. "I just don't get to open a book much anymore."

"That's a little like how it is for me," Wallis said.

"That's what it was like for Matthew, too," Mel said.

Helen watched them, satisfied they weren't in love.

"How can you not fall in love with her?" she asked Wallis. Mel blushed slightly. "She is like a daughter," Helen said, taking Mel's arm in her hand.

Mel shook her head, patted Helen's old hand. "I'm a fanatic, Helen," she said. "One-dimensional. It's like I'm always falling," she said, "tumbling down some deep chasm. Falling forever." She shrugged. "Who wants to go down with someone like that?"

Helen's eyes were large and worried, behind her thick glasses.

"Why, shoot," she said, "almost anyone would, honey. Men don't care about any of that. They'll fall in love with almost anything, when the time is right for them."

Mel laughed.

She opened the bottom drawer of her desk and pulled out another deerskin, tanned and folded neatly. There were holes in it — tooth marks — and only a few data in the winter quadrant: that year's map, still in progress.

"This is a deer the wolves killed," she said. "I went in after they'd been eating on it and saved the hide before they ate that, too. I don't know if it was right or not, but it was a thing I'd been wanting to do for a long time. Isn't it strange," she said, pointing to her ink marks — the black dashes and dots of the tiny pawprints she'd pricked, like tattoos, into the hide, "to think that the wolves are still traveling across this deer's back, while the rest of the deer has been consumed by them, and has become a wolf?" She touched the soft hide as if for balance, or solace. "It's as if everything else cancels out, and this is all that's left," she said, studying those ink tracks. "The story of it."

IT WAS SNOWING IN THE MORNING. WHEN WALLIS AWOKE, there was so little light, and with such odd blue cast to it, that he wondered if up in this part of the world daylight was like some animal that traveled a short distance on some days, and farther distances on other days.

There were no leftovers. He made toast. He listened to the snow fall, and to the crackling of the fire. He stared out the window, trying to gauge when Mel and Helen might have left, but their tracks were already buried.

He watched the yard for the sight of some animal — a deer, coyote, raven, anything — that might hold his interest — but there was nothing, no movement, only the snow falling.

He read:

> When I was a young boy, I hied away from authority for a while and rode on the deck of a steamer between Kansas City and St. Louis, and higher up that valley. All are merged together; but we can be sure that, if upstream, the water and the mud from our own village — our own farms — are there with the rest. The stream moves on — it never rests — and it grows as it moves. It courses across a state; it marks a boundary between states. Men had made it a vehicle for floating logs; a highway for skiffs and barges. Now, the more pompous stream styles itself a river. It hastens to join the Ohio and share in the dignity of floating steamboats and carrying on the commerce of a populous valley. The Ohio has even surpassed the tributary by which we have been led, in taking on its cargo of mud. We stand in the middle of the suspension bridge at Cincinnati and look down on the yellow surface of the great stream. There go the contributions from half a dozen states. There goes the soil filched from our garden or torn from our new-made road, two hundred miles away. We know it is there.
>
> Look on the map and notice how many rivers are bringing their sediments to the Ohio. Trace these tributaries to their sources. Notice that the Ohio carries its burden to the Mississippi. Look again upon the map and see how many other great rivers bring the mud from other far-off regions to concentrate it all in the mighty Father of Waters. Here in this restless tide floats the identical soil which was washed from Farmer Jones's potato field.
>
> In this view, consider the great Missouri. It pours its yellow stream into the clearer tide of the Mississippi a few miles above St. Louis. I have

stood on the deck of a steamer between Alton and St. Louis and looked down on the Missouri's turbid volume pushing far into the Mississippi, and retaining for miles a distinct boundary between the waters of the two rivers. It appears that the contributions from the far northwest exceed all those from the east.

Follow the whirling tide of the Missouri farther upward toward its sources.

There stand great cities of men, some good and some evil, on its alluvial banks. The crumbling bluffs slide into the river. Above the limits of city populations the river is already gathering in the mud destined to journey to the Gulf of Mexico — mud which has already been floated from some remoter region and deposited here at times of overflow.

Here comes the Niobara, with slime from the prairies of Nebraska; the Cheyenne, with washings from the mining camps in the Black Hills; the Little Missouri, Platte, and Yellowstone, with sands worn from the Big Horn, the Wind River, and the Snowy Mountains; here, on a grassy plain, unite the Jefferson, Madison, and Gallatin tributaries, which bring the dust of the continent from the high watershed of the Red Rock Mountains, which parts the continental drainage to opposite points of the compass.

It is a bewildering breadth and complexity of operations! Over every foot of this wasting expanse the land is yielding to the corrosive actions of rivers and rains and frosts. The proud mountain domes and pinnacles are coming to acknowledge the supremacy of its powers of domination. The Rocky Mountains have begun their journey to the Gulf of Mexico. Cubic miles of their granitic substance are buried in the delta of Louisiana and the bar of the Mississippi.

Every river, in its search for a resting place, has cut a way of even grade across the inequalities of the land, and the rubbish has been dumped somewhere.

We have not seen how any of these works began; but we see them in progress; and we feel bound in reason to infer that the rivers have worked in the distant past as they are working before our eyes. But when one thing dies, another must live. Observe a wall of mountains, a ridge of stone. We have not detected Nature anywhere raising such a wall in the night, as we sleep. Such mountains must instead be remnants of distant, buried civilizations of stone; once stretching far away north and west. The forces of erosion have worn away the formation on both sides, *creating the wall, exposing a basilica of relief in the same fashion as the statue emerges from the block of stone under the chisel of the sculptor.*

Across this country, and buried in all places beneath us, are great formations and walls such as these, like the boundaries around civilizations which never existed, or have yet to exist. For the most part these formations have been carried away, save here and there the isolated remnants which lie like islands in the midst of geology of an entirely different matter.

We shall have other occasion and opportunity to talk about these savage places of remnancy and the powers they retain; for they are burial places of the brute populations which held possession of America before the advent of man.

The two great processes, erosion and sedimentation, must be vividly and simultaneously appreciated. The whole history of the land has consisted chiefly of upbuilding and destruction, rebuilding and disintegration, by the action of forces which have left gigantic monuments of their former power, and are even in our time worked on a scale large enough to illustrate how the foundations of the land were laid and how the face of the earth has been carved into the fashion it presents to interested eyes.

In another walk we must follow the sediments under the sea, and try to learn what goes on in the mysterious abysses through which no highway has opened.

There wasn't a damn thing Wallis could do. He wanted to dive, but there was nowhere to dive to. He put on his coat and coveralls — Matthew's coat and coveralls — and skied to town, to consort with people, as if taking medicine. As he had been instructed to do each day, he first went down to the smokehouse and checked to be sure the door was barred. He peered in through the window. There was enough food in there for an army, it seemed — though also, he suspected, with the amount of country Mel ranged over, following the wolves (or rather, moving away from them), it would be just barely enough.

Wallis checked in on the giant salmon skeleton, too, before leaving — as if examining the boundaries of his compressed territory before traveling to some other place of dubious security — and he watched, and was comforted by, the cold waters passing over the salmon's hollow ribs and skull. The salmon seemed to be waiting patiently for some signal, perhaps still hoping to begin its migration. The illusion of the ripples over its back made it look once again as if its tail were moving back and forth, steadying its position in the current.

He traveled to town, tense at first, but loosening as the snow kept coming down. He said Susan's name out loud once and felt better for it. He watched the dark spruce woods all around him receiving their snow, and yet in the same moment he recalled sitting with Susan on the porch in the hill country in the yellow summer twilight, watching bats flitter over the thin-trickling creek and feeling the reflected heat of the pink-polished granite boulders all around them finally beginning to cool slightly — and it was strange, like having some kind of double vision, or a mild schizophrenia, to be carrying two such disparate images at once within him: reality, and yet, just as strongly, the echo of reality.

The snow was so soft and deep that even on his skis he sank into it up past his ankles. It was mesmerizing to watch it pile up around him like surf as he plowed through it, encountering no more resistance than as if in a dream.

Out on the main road, which was a tunnel of untouched white beneath the giant trees — a road to nowhere, he thought — he turned toward town as if it were his home.

Along the way he passed deer standing beneath the great tamaracks, feeding on the mosses still attached to fallen branches. Wallis stopped and watched for a while, resting — hot as a firebrick amid that falling snow — and as he watched, he saw how the heavy snow accumulated on the moss-covered branches, causing them to snap; and while he stood there, several branches broke free from high up and came floating slowly down — falling not much faster than the curtain of snow. The branches' descents were buoyed by the long airy trellises and streamers of the black moss, and though the branches fell soundlessly, the deer would look up and wait for them, would watch them fall, and then would converge wherever the branch landed and begin pawing at it, tearing and chewing. From time to time they would look up with long black beards hanging from their mouths, so that it looked as if they were wearing costume mustaches: a comedy made more poignant by the fact that they were standing belly-deep in snow and soon on their way to starving to death.

The bucks still had their heavy antlers — antlers that were easily twice the size of any Wallis had seen before — though when one group of them turned and ran, made uneasy by his staring, a buck's antler fell off, tumbled from his head like a man having his hat knocked off, and Wallis knew all the antlers would be falling off in the next several days, like brown leaves in the autumn, or like the mossy branches that were falling and drifting down from the trees.

Wallis watched as the bucks floundered, thrashing through powder, stumbling and lunging — up past their shoulders in snow sometimes. Seen from a distance, they appeared like swimmers navigating a turbulent ocean, though the waves were frozen, and it was only the deer that were moving, not the waves.

In town, Wallis was greeted like a long-lost resident — like some hermit who had not been seen in years — and the afternoon's gathering at the bar fell upon him with great hunger and friendliness. He saw Danny, and black-bearded Charlie, and Artie, the bartender; but there were others, too, their faces as unfamiliar to him as the words of a foreign language, and Wallis felt awkward, not just as if unknowledgeable about the local customs of this place, but worse: as if he were incapable, and even undesirous, of learning. As if he had been asleep for twenty years.

"You look a little shaggier than when you got here," Danny said, grinning, and Artie handed him a bourbon, which was the color of dark honey. Wallis wondered what would happen if the bar ran out of whiskey: if there was, one year, not enough to make it through the winter.

"What've you been up to?" Artie asked. "Is Mel teaching you anything?"

Wallis smiled and said, "She hasn't wanted to have much to do with me lately," and Danny and Artie laughed, seeming relieved.

"Finding any oil?" Charlie asked.

Wallis grimaced, shrugged. "How?" he asked, waving out at the dim blue portals of window light. The whiskey was hot. He felt as if he had traveled farther than seven miles.

The men laughed. "Welcome to the winter, buddy," Danny said, clapping a hand on his shoulder. "Welcome to the winter."

A woman and her child sat at one of the tables, the woman drinking beer steadily from a mug, and the child, a boy, staring off at some distant but intriguing nothingness. The boy looked to be about twelve or thirteen; the woman, a few years on either side of forty, though not in any way that reminded Wallis of Mel. This woman looked if not used up, then close to it. She looked cautious; as if, in addition to having all of her chores set out before her, she knew also precisely how much energy she had remaining to accomplish those tasks, and that the tasks and the energy required were rarely to either the debit or excess of one another; that she had to be prudent and frugal, even cunning, to get things done each day and still be upright, come day's end.

It was not at all the way Mel did things, Wallis thought. She planned nothing, calculated nothing, gave nothing her forbearance. She simply pinned her ears back and went.

Now Wallis saw that the woman was older: forty-five, perhaps. He knew he had no basis for such imagining, but it seemed to him that she had run out of steam only recently. Even watching her, he could feel his own energy draining.

"That's Amy," Danny said, "and her boy, Colter. Her husband, Zeke, died last spring. He went through the ice," Danny said. "He was a trapper. You can still see him down there," he said, and at first Wallis thought Danny meant you could see Zeke's likeness in the face of the boy. "He's only about twenty feet down," Danny said, speaking quietly beneath the noise of the bar. "The water is as clear as gin, cold as hell. Everything's still the same on him, same as it was the day he went in. He's got his arms raised up like this" — Danny demonstrated, as if signaling a touchdown — "and his hair is still waving in the current, black as his over there" — he pointed to Colter — "only longer. It kept growing after he died."

Artie got up and brought more drinks for the two men. It was amazing, Wallis thought, sipping his second, how one drink, one fire in the stove, one story, could keep the whole awful weight of winter at bay. He felt badly for not having come down to the bar earlier: a hermit, even in a valley of hermits; an island, even among islands.

"He should have known better," Danny said. "He should have crossed on thicker ice, or farther upstream, where there wasn't any ice, but where he could have waded. It must have been late, right at dark. He must have been in a hurry to get home to his family. His traps must have weighed him down."

"We guess he's still down there," Artie said. "Least he was a couple of weeks ago, before the river started to freeze up. We won't know til spring, now. But he was still there, last we saw of him."

"Why didn't they pull him out and bury him in the ground?" Wallis asked.

Artie shrugged. He had a loud, clear voice, as if unaware of its timbre. "Said she liked to still be able to see him now and again. Said she didn't want her or the boy to forget what he looked like."

"They've built a kind of a cairn down there," Danny said. "They've put it at the edge of the river, with stones and skulls and antlers and feathers and things — but there's one in the river, too. They toss in rocks and antlers to pile up next to him. His old traps. Stuff like that. A lot of time the river sweeps those things away, but he's still there. Or was. Got his boot tangled in the crotch of a sunken cottonwood limb."

"You can see the white marks on the bark, where he tried to cut free with his knife," Artie said.

"He ran out of time," Danny said.

They went over to sit with Amy and Colter, and to introduce Wallis. Amy was not drunk, nor was she drinking as if in sorrow; but nonetheless, she was putting the beer away, despite not being very large. Artie went to get her another pitcher, and Wallis saw that it was more like a meal for her than grieving. She wanted to be around people, and that was what one did in a bar: drank.

He saw too that the boy, Colter, had some interior shine — saw it perhaps the way Old Dudley had seen it in Wallis. Wallis and Colter stared at each other for a moment after being introduced, and Wallis saw the hunger in Colter's eyes then, saw the boy's loneliness at being trapped, stranded, unable to get to his father.

"You're living with Mel," Amy said.

"I'm staying in her cabin," Wallis said.

"Did you used to go to a church, down in Texas?" Amy asked. She had a small, quiet, kind voice, and Wallis had trouble picturing her as a trapper's wife; though he was not sure, either, what he would have imagined.

Wallis thought for a moment. "My parents did," he said, "a long time ago. But they died — Mom first, and then my father. He stopped going when I was still young."

Wallis paused, perilously close to the old debris of story that was of no use to him anymore: moving in with Susan and her old grandfather. A new love, a new life back then — like climbing up out of some horrible pit.

"Amy used to want to get a church going up here," Danny explained.

"Were you a missionary?" Wallis asked.

"No," Amy said, twisting her beer mug. "I just wanted a church."

"It didn't work out," Artie said. "No one would come. Everyone was always out hunting, or cutting wood, or gardening, or something."

"Do you mind my asking," Wallis said, "what —"

"I tan hides," Amy said. "The hides Mel uses for her maps." She looked under the table, nodded at the moccasins Danny was wearing, and at some of the jackets hanging on hooks by the door. "Those shoes, those shirts — when people kill a deer or elk, I tan and sew the hides for them." Her voice, despite the beer, was clear and calm. As if it were she who was passing across ice of unknown or suspect thickness. "He looks for antlers," she said, nodding to Colter. "We box them up and ship them to stores. We get by," she said, "just as good as we did when he was still living."

"You're a tailor," Wallis said.

"Yes," Amy said, after thinking for a moment, "that's a nice word. I hadn't thought of it that way."

A third bourbon for Wallis. The winter fell back further. He saw Helen come in, heard the rouse and chorus of greetings.

"I used to be in the choir, in Pennsylvania," Amy was saying. "We sang on Sundays. We practiced three times a week."

"You can't bring that with you," Artie counseled. "You can't bring anything with you. Everything's new, up here. You've go to start all over."

Amy nodded. Wallis felt winter creep in a few feet closer in the silence.

Another bourbon. "How long have you been up here?" Wallis asked.

"Twenty-five years," Amy said. "Sometimes it seems like yesterday; other days, like another lifetime." She reached over and touched her son's face. "I'm glad he's getting a chance to grow up here," she said. "He's everything," she said, "everything, now."

Charlie was cooking more venison on the stove: they could smell it. A strange somber blue wave seemed to have passed through the bar while Amy had been speaking, and for a little while the bar was hushed, as if waiting for the wave to pass over; but now with the scent of venison people's spirits surged again, and they began wandering over to the stove to pick tidbits from the iron skillet, the meat disappearing quickly in this manner, all mouths chewing, and when Wallis asked Danny how much of his deer was left, Danny said that was almost the last of it.

Wallis took a drink over to the wall of photos and looked at them again, in closer detail. The photos were mostly of Matthew-this and Matthew-that — Matthew around seventeen or eighteen, he guessed, holding a giant sturgeon from the river, the fish longer than Matthew was tall; and an even younger picture — sixteen? — holding up three enormous swans — and another of Matthew younger yet: thirteen or fourteen, working on that rock wall, wrestling squarish ice-cracked boulders into place like a prisoner on work detail.

Wallis studied these pictures briefly, then moved on to others: dusty, grainy photos of the whole valley carrying stones up and down the road, and of men shirtless in overalls with straw hats to block the sun, busting boulders with chisel and sledge to make them fit just right.

A photo of the bar itself, looking no different then than now. In that photo, a recently killed bull elk hung from the porch rafters, and snow was falling. The men had mustaches, and though it was a black and white photo, they appeared to have that tone or color of hazel eyes that is rarely seen anymore. Someone's dog — thirty years gone, now — sat young and proud, staring expectantly at the camera.

And where were the photos of the photographer, Wallis wondered — of Matthew's father? There were none. You would have to look at Matthew to catch a glimpse of him, in certain lights and at certain times. That was all that was left. Wallis thought back to his own father — liver cirrhosis when Wallis was fourteen — and to his mother, whose heart stopped, stopping like a clock that one day does not get wound, when he was eight — a child's memories of her, instead of a man's — and Wallis wondered how he would have been different if he'd grown up in this part of the world.

Wallis wondered if he would have participated just as deeply in the seasonal hunting and gathering — the killing, the taking — as well as in the fragmenting of stone. The men (and there were some women in the photos; women hauling stones, women pushing wheelbarrows full of stones) seeming — in those photographs, at least — to possess a peace and steadiness, which, like those strange hazel eyes, was not seen much anymore.

How much of a man, or a woman, was shaped by his blood, and how much by a place: the blood forming the infant but then the land beginning its own carving at child's birth?

And how much do we carve at and upon each other? Certainly Old

Dudley had, in only twenty years, very nearly finished what could almost be considered a clone of his awful self, from the raw material of Matthew: seizing upon the similarities and chiseling away all differences . . .

Wallis walked farther down the hall, his glass empty. Pictures of Helen as a young woman in a canoe on the river — the trees behind her looking only slightly smaller and younger.

This was a little what it was like, looking for oil and gas. Going down, farther down and back — sheets of time falling away in layers, with the newest resting atop the oldest. His affinity for this kind of searching must always have resided in his blood. No man, and no landscape, could have instructed him in that pleasure. It was too deep, too certain. Surely he had brought that pleasure with him into the world.

Helen came over to where he was standing. Wallis was swaying slightly, but Helen had another drink for him, and she steadied him.

"He loved that camera," she said, speaking of Matthew's father. "He and his wife never had any money to spare. He always wanted to take lots of pictures, but he only allowed himself one a week. Sometimes, on special occasions, two. He'd send the roll of film off to Helena to get it developed. Everyone in the valley would have to wait a couple of weeks for the photos to come back — him checking the mail every day, having been sleepless all night, he said — and when the pictures came, he'd lay them out on the floor of the bar and study them for what seemed like forever.

"And when he died, I gave the camera to Danny, who now takes only three or four pictures a year." Helen's voice was hoarse and gravelly. She moved down the hall, squinting in the dim light through her thick glasses. A lit cigarette dangled from her mouth. "Here," she said, "here, I think, is where Buster left off and Danny picked up."

Buster's last photo, a close-up, had been of a pattern of lichens on gray stone, up in the high country. There were tufts of alpine bracken clinging to the rocks, and some fresh blown snow. "He was out on Robinson Mountain, in October," Helen said. She pointed to the snow in the picture. "A storm came in that afternoon, and he got wet and caught the pneumonia that killed him. He could have beaten it, but he just quit." She drew hard on her cigarette, frowned, trying her best to remember something important. Released the blue smoke from her mouth and then from both nostrils. "I can't remember if he ever saw this picture or not," she said. "Seems like maybe he didn't." She shook her head, surprised by the memory of the sadness she had felt back then — so distant and without substance, now. As if she had somehow not been justified in feeling it so deeply, for it to all be gone now.

"How old was Matthew?" Wallis asked.

"Little," Helen said. "Four."

"It's amazing," Wallis said. "You really can't tell where one left off and the other picked up."

Helen laughed, stubbed out her cigarette. "It's a good camera," she said. "Cost a pretty penny, even then."

Wallis headed back to his table, bumping one table with his hips, and then another. Made it back to his chair just in time, before his legs went out: all power draining from him, except for that required to lift another glass to his lips.

"The caribou," Colter said, and Wallis thought he meant something that was cooking on the stove — but everyone was rising and moving over toward the windows. Wallis followed them to the front door, still unsteady.

The caribou had their faces pressed against the glass of the windows — big bulging eyes, with long white manes and beards that made them look like circus creatures. As they tried to peer in, the windows would fog, then clear, then fog, then clear, with each breath, so that the caribou's faces were visible only in shuttered pulses, like the awkward frames from an old motion picture. Everyone went out onto the porch to marvel at their strange and magnificent antlers.

"They come down from Canada sometimes," Helen said. "You hardly ever see them anymore. They're damn near extinct. Woodland caribou," she said. "The kids are all certain they're reindeer."

Wallis counted twelve of them. They milled around like horses bunched together for warmth. There was snow on their backs, and when one caribou's antlers brushed against another's, there was a dull clacking sound like the music of rocks tumbling downstream under heavy water. "We just see them in the snowiest winters," Helen said. "I guess it's going to be a corker."

"Do they always come here?" Wallis asked. "To the bar?" It seemed to him that they were like strangers checking into town.

"Always," said Helen. "They're so damn tame. We may or may not see them again this year. I think they just come by to check in on things, and to let us know they're around. They'll disappear after this. Look," she said, and pointed to Colter, who was feeding one of them an apple. "It's an omen," said Helen.

"Of what?" Wallis asked.

"I don't know," said Helen. "But it's an omen."

The caribou — a bull — finished his apple, and all the caribou stared at the people a little longer, and the people stared at the caribou, and then the caribou turned, as if having heard some unspoken command, and headed back up the road. They soon disappeared into the falling snow.

"They'll go to the peaks of the mountains," Helen said. "The more snow, the better. They've got those big feet, so that they just float on top of the snow. They reach up and eat lichens from the tops of trees. They need all the snow in the world."

When the caribou were gone, everyone turned and went inside. Already, in that brief time, their hats and backs and shoulders were covered with snow. Colter put on his coat and told Amy that he was going to follow the caribou on his skis for a short while.

"He's like a little Indian," Amy said, after he was gone. "He's like his father."

The cold had sobered everyone — or made them believe, for a moment, that they were sober — and so more drinks were ordered. Now Wallis felt himself wobbling, felt his interior self diving, and was relaxed: this was sometimes how it was, at depth, mapping. A free fall, with no struggling against one's plummet.

Mel came in the bar, snowy and steaming. She shook the snow from her hair and clothes, knocked it from her boots, and began unpeeling. She too was greeted with great joy and warmth, and it was some time before she could separate herself from conversations and come over to Wallis's table, where, upon seeing his condition — lights out — she asked him how many drinks he'd had.

He barely heard her telling him — instructing him, almost commanding him — to never again have more than one drink in winter.

"Your blood's too sluggish, and your brain shrinks, same as it does for bears in hibernation. If you drink even two, then it's all over — you can't stop. Two's the same as five or six, seven or eight. How many did you have?"

Wallis made a dim attempt at answering. Artie and Danny tried to cut him some slack — they weren't in much better shape themselves — but were silenced by Mel's glare, and they made excuses to leave the table and find other things that needed doing. Mel frowned, nodded at Amy's empty pitcher and Helen's near-empty shot glass. "Y'all know how it is up here, in winter — he doesn't. That wasn't fair," she said.

"He's a grown-up," Helen said, but Amy agreed with Mel and said, "You're right, we should have taken better care of him."

Helen was annoyed. "Since when is it your job to take care of him — and why can't he take care of himself?"

"He's my guest," Mel said. "I have to live with him. I don't want him coming down here every night like some runaway hound." She picked Wallis up — he was unconscious now — and folded him over her shoulder like a bag of feed. "He doesn't know any better yet," she said. She headed back out the door, Wallis's head bobbing behind her, upside down, like a gutted deer.

Chastened, Danny followed her outside and gave her a lantern to take with her on the ski home. She thanked him and took off down the road without using her poles: holding Wallis in place with one arm, the lantern and poles in the other. The lantern cast a small yellow globe of light in front of her: a mesmerizing light filled with millions of falling snowflakes, as if she, too, were descending. Wallis's body was warm against Mel's back and shoulders. She was not angry at him, and told herself that he was not so much drunk as only sleeping.

He awoke with his head clear, but with his muscles feeling poisoned. Mel was gone — a note on the chopping block in the kitchen, next to a new-baked loaf of bread, said "Back after dark," and he fixed toast and tea, then stripped and went down and sat in the creek, and then lay down in it to bathe. It was still snowing.

Wading out, he rolled in the snow, ran back up to the cabin, and dried off and dressed by the fire, shivering. Later in the afternoon, still trying to shake the poison from his muscles, he went out to the woodshed and split kindling.

At dusk — still snowing — he fixed more toast and tea, and pulled down the old journals, as the short day slipped away, like all the ones before it.

A Walk Under the Sea
What Goes on in the Ocean Depths

"The sea! The sea!" shouted the companions of Balboa, as they caught the first glimpse of the Pacific from the heights of the American Isthmus. The sea has always inspired the wonder — often the veneration — of mankind. Its vastness and power overwhelm the imagination. Its permanence, its antiquity, form a bewildering conception. The same "far-sounding sea" roared in the hearing of the mariners of the remotest past. The same ocean floated the ships of the Tyrians and Carthaginians. Its mysterious depths aroused the superstitions of the ancients the same as they excite the intelligent curiosity of modern science. A "glorious mirror," as Byron conceived it,

> "Where the Almighty's form
> Glasses itself in tempests,
> Boundless, endless, and sublime,
> The image of eternity — the throne
> Of the invisible."

Let us stand on some bold headland and look out over the Atlantic. Let us plant ourselves on Sankaty Head, the eastern promontory of Nantucket, itself the "ultima Thule" of New England. The breakers roar along the beach. Across the billowy blue, thought wanders to the European shore. Underneath the ruffled surface, imagination pictures a world of curious and wonderful existences. There lie the skeletons of noble ships — there moulder the dead sailors of all nations — there rot invaluable cargoes — there sleep the mysteries of steamers which sailed out of sight of land and never returned — there swarm the sharks that desecrate the sacred forms of humanity which sank into their silent empire. Shall we venture among the dangers of the underworld? Yes, we invoke the magic protection which has made warriors invulnerable, and shielded adventurers upon the waters of Styx, and the fiery waves of Phlegethon.

We go down like bathers in the sea. We pass the margin where

> "The dreary back seaweed lolls and wags."

We traverse the borders where the brown, belted kelp sways to and fro in graceful curves. We get beyond the slope of stony bottom to the smooth sand. We come to the gardens of the rosy-tinted sea mosses — the

Dasya, *the* Grinnellia, *the* Callithamnion; *and startle the bluefish and halibut in their safe seclusion. A moonlight gleam is here, and the water also takes on the chill of evening. We attain a depth of half a mile. Our feet press into the finer sediments derived from the land — the dust of other "continents to be." The twilight has faded into a deep shade. The creatures of the sea swarm curiously about us, then flee in terror from our presence. We feel the gentle movement of "a river in the ocean," but surface disturbances do not reach to this depth.*

A change of climate impresses itself on our sensations. The water where we started had a temperature of sixty degrees — here it is forty. But we are panopalied against harm; we press on. We descend to the depth of a mile. The species of the shallower water appear no more. Their home is the zone which now stretches above our heads. The green and rosy sea mosses never venture here. We are in total darkness. No chlorophyll tints the growths of the vegetable kingdom. Here are only stony, white calcareous algae and silicious diatoms of microscopic minuteness.

We pause to contemplate the awful stillness of the submarine realm, and feel our slimy path down to the deeper profound. Above us now float two miles of black sea. Any surface fish brought down here perishes from the effect of enormous pressure, if possessing an air bladder. If it have none, the fish becomes torpid, and finally dies.

We are here, probably miles from the shore — that varies with the steepness of the slope. The sediments which the rivers have brought to the ocean have mostly been. But here still are some of the finest particles contributed by the land — slime from Louisiana, from the Rocky Mountains, from our native town. Will these far-brought and commingled atoms ever see daylight again?

We are standing on the border of the vast abyss which extends over half the area of the earth. It is an undulating, silent desert. No diversity of mountain and valley, cliff and gorge exists. By a gentle grade the bottom descends to a depth of five miles. Over all this dread waste, no rocks rise above the bed of slime.

The pressure on us in this abysmal region is four or five tons to every square inch. The water is ice-cold everywhere. The darkness, absolute and palpable. A curdling revulsion of feeling and purpose seizes us. We halt and reflect. We turn our eyes upward with a painful longing for the "holy light, offspring of heaven first-born." Only the black ceiling appears. Two miles above us is the sunny sea, where all the blue of a genial sky beams down. Will we ever return? There float the ships in summer calm upon a "painted ocean," or tossed and rent by the winter tempest which inspires the waves with madness. But no summer and winter vicissitudes are here. No sunrise or noonday or sunset is ever known.

As it was when the Garden of Eden was first consecrated to man, so it has remained and must remain. Not even the crash of thunders or the roar of storms can be heard. Into this world, too, I can be master. The huge waves, crested with elemental fury, roll on, but make no stir in the stillness and stagnation of this abysmal realm.

When we crossed the borders of this dark and silent abyss, our feet sank in a white pasty slime which has been designated "Globigerina ooze." The dredges of the ship, the Albatross, *have been down here, hung by a piano wire over the stern of the vessel, and samples of this ooze have been studied. We find it composed chiefly of microscopic dead shells called* Fo-ram-i-nif'-e-ra, *together with others called* Pter'-o-pods. *The little creatures which formed the shells do not live here; they dwell in calm zones of water far above. When the conscious animal ceases to live, its tiny house sinks down into this dark world. And thus, as the ages roll by, the fine chalky rain of their deaths slowly accumulates upon the bottom. When this ooze is dried and hardened, it resembles the chalk of Europe; and when that is examined, we find in it the same little* Foraminifera. *These are important geological facts, which, though they come out of an abyss of darkness, throw a vivid light on equally dark chapters of the world's long-past history. Perhaps they will pool in their death to create my oil.*

We have groped our way down three and four miles beneath daylight. A sort of ooze still spreads over the bottom; but it is not the Globigerina *and* Pteropod *ooze. It is a fine rusty clay. But the white shells are not wanting because the tiny creatures which secrete them are not overhead. They swarm there as elsewhere, far from land with other pelagic forms. But the fragile matter of the shell is dissolved before it reaches this great depth. Only the aluminous and insoluble constituent reaches the bottom. This clay ooze possesses other interest. Disseminated through it are minute crystals of such minerals as escape through the throats of volcanoes into the upper air. Here are the dust particles which have imparted a ruddy glow to many a past sunset. Once the source of the roseate glory of the twilight hour, they lie now in impenetrable darkness and the repose of death. How changed the fortune of the little particle! It floated for months in the upper thin air — in the film of space* which separates earth from heaven — borne hither by the simoon, thither by the antitrades, hurled in the vortex of a cyclone and precipitated in mid-ocean by a down-falling mass of vapor. Then, perhaps, seized by the waves, and rocked and beaten at the surface till it reached a zone of calm, it began its silent descent into the dark world where it is destined to rest undisturbed for centuries.

Here too is cosmic dust. The seeds of worlds have been sprinkled through space, and some of them have been planted in the soil of this abyss. These minute globules of magnetic iron were sparks emitted from a burning meteor. The meteor was a small mass or particle of material stuff coursing swiftly through the cold interplanetary spaces. It pierced the atmosphere of the earth. The friction resulting ignited the meteor, and for a brief moment it painted a fiery streak in its flight, until it found, at last, a resting place in the cold bed of the Atlantic. What a reversal of fortune was here! The particle might have swept on through space, as many of its companions did, until it became part of a glowing comet. Perhaps it once shone in a star — now it is dead for a cycle of ages. It is an impressive thought that here, in this rayless night, we find the black ruins of a star.

We still stand wondering over the scene which surrounds us. How oppressive in this silence! How welcome would be the cheerful chirp of the sparrow! Even the piping of the hated mosquito would break the eternal monotony.

From age to age this reign of death persists. A chill which is more than icy pierces us to the marrow. Sometimes, as we grope through the gloom, we kick the bones of aquatic creatures which have perished in the water above us. Often their kind is still in existence; but sometimes their species are long extinct. Here are teeth of sharks and ear-bones of whales which have lain during geologic ages. Grand vicissitudes have passed by, which transformed the aspect of continents, but these relics lay here undisturbed — unburied — so slowly do the sediments accumulate.

But there is indeed life here. Sparse, quaint life; and the species are of archaic and embryonic forms; that is, they resemble creatures which lived in the earlier ages of the world, or creatures which have undergone but a part of their development — crude, uncouth, and alien to the modern world. Here are Crinoids, or Stone Lilies, which, in all other waters, have perished from the earth — save one species long known in the Caribbean Sea. But from deep waters off the coasts of Florida and Norway, comes up, with other forms, Rhiz-oó-ri-ns, a genus which *disappeared from shallow seas unknown millions of years ago; but here, where nothing changes, it has perpetuated its existence through half the history of the world. Between death and the changeless life which here reigns, the difference is slight.*

Still more startling in their grotesqueness are some of the fishes which lie here more than half buried in the mud. Here is one fashioned like a scoop net. The long, slender body is the handle, and the net is an enormous pouch under the chin, which would take in the whole of the body three times over. Another hangs like an open wide-mouthed meal bag. In this case, also, the bag hangs suspended from the part where the throat should be. The diminutive body is noticed as an appendage attached to the back side of the bag. It is known by the fins. Four of these bodies might be contained in one pouch. A different, but equally erratic form brandishes an attenuated body like a whiplash appended to an enormous head, exposing an eye which is nearly half its own diameter. Still again, we note a sharklike form, with enormous gape and horrid teeth, having a range of spines along each side of the slender body above and below, and, most curious of all, a long, threadlike organ depending from beneath the chin, with a tassel-like tentacle bearing structures for feeling.

But see! Somebody is here with a lantern. How sleepily the light gleams in the darkness. There is no fire in it. Something it is. An animated lantern. A lantern without a flame. It is another strange fish. It is phosphorescence which gleams from his shiny sides. Still another lantern-bearing fish. Here are luminous plates beneath the eyes; behind them, in a cavity, retinal tissue, as if these structures were planned for eyes; but they are not eyes. Real eyes are present: our own. We discover, then, faint relief from the palpable darkness in which we have groped.

But our task is done; our curiosity is gratified; we have glimpsed the underworld, and have gathered observations on which we shall ponder many a day. Let us now, like the heroes of epic song, ascend to the light of the upper world.

T WO DAYS BEFORE CHRISTMAS EVE, THERE STILL HAD BEEN no word from Old Dudley and Matthew. The summit had received more snow than ever for that time of year; but still, Mel believed they would make it, if only because they always had before.

Mel followed the wolves backward through the new snow, following their tracks until they disappeared beneath the night-before's snow, never knowing even the color of the animals she was following. She knew from the fur she would sometimes find tangled in the brush that some of the wolves were the color of smoke and that at least one of them was as black as a raven, but she could not match their prints to their fur; and though she knew both sexes were present — some urinations made from squatting positions, others with raised legs — again, she could not be sure of the numbers of each.

She had the suspicion that some days there were only four or five wolves that traveled up and down the river, while another wolf stayed at some distance, only to rejoin the others days later. She logged it all into her notebooks, to transcribe onto her maps, and tried to sort it out in her mind nightly, but she knew that she was not seeing the real thing: that instead she was applying a structure, an explanation and logic to their movements, which was constructed at least as much from her own imagination as from the wolves' desires and communications: and this gap, this failure, would sometimes cause Mel great sorrow, even in the midst of her pleasure of being out and amongst the wolves, or the day-before's echo of the wolves, and in their great country.

There were days when the wolves would leave the river bottom and travel inexplicably up into the mountains, where there was little if any game, and Mel would be filled suddenly — exhausted by the steep climbing and deeper snows, her legs aflame — with the knowledge that the wolves knew she was backtracking them and had gone up high only for the purpose of tiring her.

Or perhaps they simply liked the view of the valley from up high. Every sixth or seventh day, they would go up high; and every seventh or eighth day, she would follow them, would follow where they had been. She would rest up there, staring down at the narrow valley, and would sometimes hear their howls even in the middle of the day, many miles distant — as if they knew where she was and what she was doing at any given moment, and were calling specifically to remind her of the slight but real difference between wolves, and the tracks of wolves.

Sometimes the wolves would be silent for days, and in the falling snow, Mel would feel as if she had stepped into some dreamland, and that even though she was traveling backward, she would meet up with the pack at any moment.

Never had anything so invisible seemed so real. Her own hair became tangled in limbs and branches as she followed their passages through thickets, and in the spring, birds would line their nests not just with the warm insulating fur of the wolves but with Mel's hair, plucked from those thickets; and in the spring, when she would hear birdsong — Swainson's thrush, red-eyed vireo, Bohemian waxwing, siskadee — she would feel bound up in that, too — and rather than feeling trapped by this, it was a feeling like freedom. It might even have been the thing or essence of freedom itself: beyond the imagined sensation of it.

Though her thoughts were free and clear most of the time — twined only with the immediacy of the moment, measuring this track or that, this instep or that stride — she would occasionally think of the stranger who had come to live in her home, like some dim echo of Matthew.

Mel was still certain that Old Dudley would crush Wallis, as he had crushed or burned to ashes all of the others; but she felt also as if she was starting to have some sort of investment in Wallis — if not so much by the harboring and feeding of him, then by the fact that, bit by bit, the valley was attempting to absorb him, and Mel was so of-the-valley that there was little difference; it was as if she too were absorbing him.

And she had the thought that as Wallis was absorbed by the mass of the valley — gaining, in that initiation, access to some of its characteristics and values — it would be harder for Old Dudley to find or grasp him again; and harder, too, to crush him.

In this manner, every day that Wallis survived in the valley was to Wallis's advantage — strengthening him one day further — and it also allowed Mel, incrementally, to consider accepting him.

Not falling in love with him — not while still in the echo of Matthew — but not pushing him away at arm's length, either.

Back when she'd lived in the city, she had listened to the radio stations while driving, and she remembered how she had listened to the sappy, insipid love songs of both the pop and rock stations — the breathy vows of eternal love, the proclamations of gotta-have-it-now incandescent desires — and then as she grew older, she would hear the same songs and marvel at their brittleness and falsity. Clearly the songs themselves had not changed, only her own attitudes toward love, so that for a long time she had questioned her passion. Love was supposed to hit like a hurricane, according to the songs, but for her, desire —

when she felt it, on occasion — when she surfaced from the peace of her life — was like a light rain falling.

It had been more than fifteen years since she and a man had lived together for longer than two weeks. Matthew still came out on his various seasonal trips, but again, there could be no denying that though his body was real, as was hers, when they lay together warm and bare beneath the blankets and hides — as real as anything on this earth — they were nonetheless living on an echo, rather than the thing itself.

Sometimes the other kind of desire would surface or awaken — for a few hours at a time, or even a few days; and she would feel volatile, tormented — that old wonderful, intoxicating incandescence, where nothing in the world mattered, nothing in the world made sense beyond the desire for another — but just as surely those brief bouts, like fevers, would carry with them, like a hangover, the accompanying chill or near-frigidity — the carelessness for such things — that followed.

Best of all was when she was in neither of those yaws or pulls (which did not come often anyway, and seemed always beyond her control), but was instead drawn or summoned by the valley — following a thing, submissive to it, rather than trying to dominate and consume it. Gliding across the landscape in any season — on foot, or snowshoes, or skis — she would feel as steady and calm and full of peace as the waters of a deep lake far back in the woods.

No more scrambling, no more of the frantic erraticness that she feared was her true nature, her blood identity; instead, there was only the steadiness of the valley — its cycles and regularities as dependable as the tides, or gravity — and from that regularity, a great power and calmness.

She went out into the woods each day as if going to a meal. Some days Mel wondered if the wolves were not but an excuse to be drawn out across the landscape — to cast herself across it like a net, mapping its surface not so much with pen and paper as with her body, trying to stretch thin and taut across it, trying to embrace all of it — trying, even, in some strange way to consume it, or to consume the knowledge present in it.

She followed the tracks backward almost dreamily — almost as if consuming the wolves too, or the signs and proof of them — though she was cautious to avoid stepping in their tracks. The snow covered her, as if to erase even her. She remembered again what it had been like to be in love. She remembered what it had been like to be owned by love. The years mounting. That was its own kind of isolation, the love becoming habit more than thought — an isolation more severe in some ways than the one in which she now was immersed.

Mel remembered how — back then — she had had to love as well as be loved. It had been like a pulse, like a coming and going; it had had its own power.

Pushing forty years! Where had that old power gone — that youthful ardor? Was it spread thin across the landscape now, like scent scattered by the wind? She did not think that even in the midst of such peace she could sleep forever, and forever keep love at arm's distance, but certainly in no way could she imagine loving such a tame and odd specimen as Wallis.

She accidentally stepped on, and erased, a line of tracks, and cursed her awkwardness. She sat down to rest, and to clear her mind. She ate her lunch: an orange, a piece of cheese, frozen and crumbly, but warming in her mouth, releasing its taste, and two old biscuits with honey inside them, also frozen — crunchy and brittle — but they too melted in her mouth, and slowly released their flavors.

It was still snowing. She sat a while longer, letting it cover her, but worrying too that it would obscure the tracks of last night. After a while she stood up and skied on.

She traveled across the dens of sleeping bears. Sometimes she found their portholes, vapor-vents where the slow warm breath of their exhalations rose from their sleeping mounds below. When she encountered such a vent, she would lie down on top of the mound and put her ear to the vent and try to see if she could hear the faint sounds of the sleeping bear: the low hum, like the buzz of bees.

She continued on. She skied across their backs. She continued to use up her days like sticks of firewood, of which she had only so many, tossed on some fire that was providing light for no one other than herself, and keeping no one warm but herself.

A feeling, sometimes, as if she too, like the bears, might as well have been sleeping. Would Matthew never come back? He had told her that he wouldn't: not ever. She was about to believe him.

Mel wasn't sure that her calendar was accurate. She knew she was probably correct within a day or two, but stopped by the mercantile to check with Helen how many days until Christmas. Helen wasn't in, but clouds of blue cigarette smoke still hung in the high rafters of the old merc. Mel followed Helen's smoky scent trail outside and across the street to the little cemetery set back in the woods, where Helen was putting antlers on her husband's grave, and before approaching, Mel stopped and watched. He'd been gone forty years — longer than Mel had been alive. It seemed like a long time to be dead in the ground — bone dust down there, if even that — but did not seem like that long to be alive.

Mel certainly didn't feel old: not half as old as Helen looked, kneeling there in the snow, arranging antlers as a substitute for flowers. Helen was wearing a charcoal-colored coat, and the snow was still coming down hard.

Mel stepped forward, startling Helen. Mel apologized for frightening her, and after a moment, asked the date.

"The twenty-third," Helen said. "This is the day he died," she said. "We buried him Christmas afternoon."

Mel looked at the headstone and noticed for the first time that the stone had only the years of his birth and death, not the months or dates.

"It was too sad," Helen explained.

This bothered Mel — the lack of precise record-keeping — but she said nothing.

"So they might be here tomorrow," Mel said. "Christmas Eve."

Helen rose stiffly. Snow fell from her back. Mel could tell by the imprints of her kneeling that she'd been there a long time. Mel tried to imagine loving Matthew deeply after he'd been dead or gone for forty years.

"Do you think they've left Houston yet?" Mel asked. "Does it feel to you like they're on their way?"

Helen stared up at the falling snow. She lit a new cigarette and coughed. An owl answered. Dusk.

"I think so," Helen said, after a long time. "I can't feel it like I usually do — it's not as strong — but I think I can still feel it, a little. I *think* they're headed this way. I don't know," she said, looking down at her arms — her palms outstretched. "My blood's getting old and sluggish. I can feel the fizz going out of it, and there's not a damn thing I can do about it. It's just the way things are turning out."

"I can still feel my fizz," Mel said. She held her arms out, as if to catch radio signals, or simply more snow: as if each snowflake, if examined closely enough, would have locked within it the message of their coming, and of all else. Mel did not say what she suspected: that perhaps it was Matthew's blood, as much as Helen's, that was getting sluggish, and no longer able to be ascertained or felt, reflected among the stars.

The two women stood in the falling snow, feeling the peace and silence of the cemetery. After it had grown dark, Mel said, "I think I can feel them now — I think they're coming. I'm certain of it." Helen began to cough harder as the night settled into her lungs. They headed back to the mercantile.

"Do you need help getting a Christmas tree?" Mel asked, and Helen coughed again, shook her head no, and said she would get one to-morrow.

"Nonsense," said Mel. "You go sit down by the stove and fix a pot of tea and rest. I'll run down into the woods and get one. You just pull a hide up over you and rest."

Helen didn't argue, and seemed pleased by the attention. "Get a good one," she said. "Get one that Matthew will like."

Mel took a lantern and went down through the woods toward the river, amazed and a little irritated at where time went: how any free time inevitably filled in with duties, like sand pouring down a funnel. She was anxious to get home and begin decorating her own cabin — now that she could feel them coming for sure — but it was unthinkable that Helen not have a tree.

The snow made hisses of steam as it landed on her lantern. Steam followed her through the snowy woods. She found a beautiful little spruce — her favorite — but knew that Helen disliked the prickliness of them. She searched longer for a fir that the deer and moose had not winter-browsed, found one, cut it with the hatchet, and began dragging it back up to Helen's, relaxing again into the rhythm, the ritual, of the act. She stopped by a grove of big cedars and pulled down several boughs with which to make wreaths.

When she got back to the mercantile, Helen was asleep, her mouth wide open, snoring — her cup of tea only half finished. The cigarette had fallen from her hand and ignited the fur of the elk hide, which was burning in a small blazon when Mel walked in. Mel went over and put the flames out, and wrinkled her nose at the odor of burning hair. In her sleep, Helen did not notice.

For the next several hours Mel wove and hung the wreaths, popped corn, and strung it with needle and thread to hang around the tree. She put the tree up and decorated it. Then she turned out the lamps, put another hide over Helen, another log on the fire, and skied home, thinking of her own decorations. She did not get home until after midnight — Wallis was asleep — and, unable to sleep, she started to go back out into the woods to search for her own tree.

She thought how it would feel to Wallis when he woke up and saw the tree that he had missed out on gathering, and of how that might make him feel more like a guest than ever, and so she went in and woke him up and asked if he'd like to go with her. "Yes," he said, and dressed quickly.

They snowshoed a long way, looking for a perfect tree. They traveled for a couple of hours through curtains of snow, sheets and weaves of snow, until they came to the right one — a little large, but they could cut it off at the base — and Mel chopped for a while, her hair swinging wild, and snow sliding from the branches above and covering them both — and then Wallis finished chopping. The tree tilted crooked against the sky as it leaned and then fell. They tied a rope around it and hauled it home as if dragging an enormous animal. It was hard work, heating their muscles to a temperature that felt good. They could smell the tree as they dragged it.

"I think this is the best one ever," Mel said. She had her ski cap off to keep from overheating in the labor of hauling the big tree, and from time to time individual strands of her hair would continue to catch and snag on the branches she passed beneath — gossamer filaments leaving the thinnest trails behind her.

Her tiny trails across the surface of the landscape were as thin and imperceptible as the smoke trails of shooting stars that scorch nothing but air: the story of her life, her hermitage, a strand of her long white blond hair. What list, what chart, could show her accomplishments, or how she had changed or influenced anything significant in the world? Freedom was something she could nearly taste.

More popcorn, and the ornaments from her box in the attic: tiny antlers, feathers dangling from threads, freshwater pearls, a faded gold star that had been her mother's. She wept, trying to remember decorating the tree with her mother each year, but was able to remember only a love so unconditional as to be taken for granted. Of the kind of woman her mother might have been in the eyes of another adult, Mel could remember or guess nothing. Mel's gaze — her child's awareness — had been elsewhere, studying with wonder other sights of the world each day. Her mother had not been rare to her. There had never been any cause to believe she would not always be there.

Wallis tried to comfort her. Mel shook her head, her face in her hands: both hands wet with her tears. "You don't understand," she said. "Every image I have of her — everything I believe about her, and every memory — is suspect. I don't know what's real about her, and what's simply a thing I've imagined. And I'll never know."

Wallis was quiet for a while; he just held her, let her wind down; felt the tension drawing from her.

"Don't you know what I mean?" she said later. "You lost both of your parents pretty early on. Helen told me you talked of it in the bar. Wouldn't you like to be able to — I don't know, *look* at them now, or *study* them, to get kind of an idea about what works and what doesn't?"

"You mean like a model," Wallis said, and Mel shrugged.

"Not even so much a model," she said, "but just — oh hell, I don't know. Don't you *miss* them? Don't you sometimes feel like half of you's missing, and that you can't ever be as fully alive?"

Wallis nodded — thinking of his parents first, but then of Susan. Halving a half made a quarter. What would be next: an eighth? And then did one disappear, beyond that — did one become loose soil, for the next generations to arise out of?

"They say it's worse with divorce," he said.

"I don't know," Mel said, dry-eyed now. A year's worth, or more, of not-crying gone from her now: as cleansed as if she'd bathed in the river. "I can't believe she married my father. Was she at all like me? How could she have married such a person?"

Wallis laughed. "Maybe he was better then."

Mel's face darkened. "Oh no," she said — as if Wallis were her brother, and had forgotten, rather than having never known. How much to tell him? "He was worse then," she said carefully.

She watched him intently: waited for him to ask how much worse. Part of her wanted him to ask, and part of her wanted him to never get near the subject.

He saw this in her eyes and drew back, and the question fell away between them.

"The tree is beautiful," Wallis said.

"My mother's trees were beautiful," Mel said. "I can remember that. I guess we're the same, she and I, that way, at least."

They fell asleep on the couch in each other's arms. For Wallis, it felt strangely — before he fell asleep — as if he had captured her: as if for all his life she had been moving away from him, but that now she had grown weaker or had stumbled and he was with her; and he could feel that weakness within her so tangibly that night, that hollowness, that it could as well have been his own, as he rested with her.

But he could feel also her recovery: the strength she was getting just from the physical act of lying with, and touching, another human being.

Mel felt nothing. She fell almost forty years that night; but in the morning, before awakening, she climbed all the years back to the surface: confident, for once, and able to make that journey securely, while Wallis anchored her above.

They were awakened at dawn by Colter's raps on the window and sat up to see his face staring at them through frosted glass. They had both slept deeply, and the fire had gone out. They got up, untangling themselves from each other as if they had fallen from some height and landed that way, and let him in, then began building a new fire.

"I'm off to look for antlers," he said. "I wanted to look for the one you said you saw fall off that deer yesterday. If you weren't planning on looking for it," he conceded. He paused. "I can go show you where my father is buried." A trade.

"Go on," Mel said to Wallis. "It'll be good for you. You'll learn some things. I'm going to stay here today and cook and decorate, and do some paperwork, and wait for the guys."

"You really think they're coming?" Wallis asked.

"They always come," Mel said. "They'll come for me, and this year, they'll come for you, too."

"Come on," Colter said.

Wallis pulled on Matthew's coveralls, cut off a slab of bread, and went out onto the porch with Colter. Colter had a burlap bag in which there were already several antlers, and he showed them to Wallis as if they were fish he had caught. "I just keep the big ones. I leave the little ones for the squirrels and porcupines, and for the soil. The little ones aren't worth much anyway," he said, and shrugged. He could have been a farmer talking about his crop, Wallis thought, with the whole valley his farm: though acres of it he would never even be able to see in his lifetime.

"How much is this one worth?" Wallis asked, picking up the largest antler: a thick palmate antler with twelve points on one side. Colter had looked hard but hadn't been able to find its mate: he would have to return to the same area in the spring and look harder when the snow was gone.

"By itself like that, only about seventy-five, maybe a hundred bucks," he said. "But if I can find its match, a lot more." He studied the antler closer. "Maybe twelve hundred — maybe fifteen hundred. Maybe more." He pointed to his stash. "Was the one you saw fall off as big as any of these?"

Wallis wasn't sure. "Borderline," he said. "Maybe. It was a pretty long way off."

Colter's face fell. "This isn't a wild goose chase, is it?" he asked, and Wallis laughed at the boy's intensity. They set off on skis. As much snow seemed to be falling from the sky as was already resting on the ground, so that it sometimes felt as if they were swimming: as if the ground had been taken out from beneath them, ground inverted to sky, and as if there were nothing in the world but snow.

"I guess you can make a fair amount of money, in a good year," he said. "Do you have any plans —"

"Ma wants me to go to a Bible school," Colter said.

"But you don't want to?"

"Hell no," Colter said.

They skied on without speaking after that, their skis cutting fresh powder, and the antlers in the bag thrown over Colter's shoulder clunking together and rattling. Sometimes bucks who still had their antlers would hear the dull sound, and would suddenly appear a short distance from them, eyes bulging, nostrils flared, and they would stand there as if planning to stop the skiers' passage, wanting to fight: believing that the sounds they heard were the rattlings from two bucks fighting over a doe. The first rut had occurred a month ago, but now there was the secondary estrus, twenty-eight days later, and whenever the bucks that still had antlers would appear before them — just standing there, plumes of frost jetting from their nostrils — Colter and Wallis would have to stop and wait for the bucks' adrenaline to subside before they could pass safely.

Sometimes in the dense-falling snow the bucks would be unable to see clearly that Colter and Wallis were humans, and would walk closer, and Colter and Wallis would have to shout in order to break the deer's procreative trance.

Colter pointed to one large buck that was watching them from back in the forest. "I'll come back for that guy."

They followed the slender paths the deer had beaten and packed in the snow, their tiny hooves compressing the snow to blue ice. Those trails now lay beneath the night's new snows and would have to be cleared out again and again. They could see only faintly the old paths the deer had beaten down. The snow before them was rolling, like the slow rolls of waves at sea, as yet uncut by the day's passages; and as he skied, Colter probed with his poles as if wading, searching for clams in the surf, and occasionally struck the tip of a fallen antler with the end of his pole. He would crouch down, grope barehanded for the antler, and would dig it up and examine it briefly before usually tossing it back farther into the woods.

"The squirrels and porcupines chew on them in the spring for the minerals," he said, "which is when they need nutrients, because they're pregnant. But the hawks, owls, and eagles have their little ones to take care of then, too. They can't eat antlers the way a rodent can. So they pound on the squirrels and chipmunks, and get the antlers' minerals that way. When you stop to think about it, it's pretty wild," he said. "This spring when you see a hawk flying through the forest, it's going to have part of one of those antlers inside it." He picked up another small antler, which had been shed so recently — perhaps in the night — that it still had a ring of blood and damp flesh around its base. Colter tossed the antler into the woods. "Think of it," he said. "A flying ant-ler." He spoke not of his toss, but of the hawk carrying the rodent carrying the antler inside it.

"Did you think that up, or did your father tell you about it?" Wallis asked.

"You don't have to think it up," Colter said. "Hell, you look around and you can just *see* it."

Wallis wondered if Old Dudley would be drawn to Colter — if he would try to recruit him as well. He didn't think Colter would go willingly.

Wallis also thought Colter might be a little wild, a little too rank, for Old Dudley's use; though from what Wallis understood, that was how Matthew had been when Old Dudley had first swooped down on him, long ago.

They skied into the opening where Wallis had seen the deer lose its antler. The big trees all looked the same, and with the paths buried by the new snow, he couldn't be sure where it had been, but he stood and tried to remember — the landscape looking so different only two days later. He finally decided on one tree, then headed toward it. They circled that tree in wider and wider circles, plunging their poles into the soft snow, and finally Wallis came upon the antler, as if it were a ring or a set of keys he had dropped, and he was amazed by the pleasure he felt at having connected and found that for which he had been searching.

He handed it to Colter. Colter smiled, said thank you, and dropped it into his sack. They spent some more time searching for its mate, though they could not find it, and were not even sure if it had fallen off yet.

"Do you keep notes of where you find one antler, on any given day, so you can go back later in the spring and look for its match?" Wallis asked.

"No," Colter said. "I don't have any problem remembering it."

Colter took Wallis down into the woods toward the river. It was hard going on the skis, and they spent much time sidestepping and herringboning over fallen lodgepole; using deer trails when they could, but often creating their own; and whenever they looked back, they could sometimes see, through the swirling curtain of snow, one or two bucks still following the sound of them.

"The wolves lay trails like this, in winter, to trap the deer," Colter said. "They know the deer have to stay on these little paths — they can't venture off even a step to the left or the right or they'll sink to their necks in the snow, and the wolves, with their big feet, can run across the top of the snow and catch them at will — so when the wolves find a winter-range herd of deer they'll carve out a new trail that leads past a good ambush spot. The wolves will run up and down that new trail, packing it down good, so that the deer will be tempted into using it. The wolves will leave the area then. More and more deer will start using that trail, cutting it deeper into the snow — heading right past that ambush spot, just the way the wolves want it — and then *pow!* The wolves come back a week or so later, and they'll just have a *feast*. They'll kill and eat a deer off that trail two or three times a week, before the deer decide to get the hell out of there and go look for a new winter range; and the wolves kill the hell out of them then too, once the herd abandons the trail system and starts floundering into new territory, trying to cut new trails. The wolves follow them."

"Have you seen this?" Wallis asked. "Did you figure this out, too?"

"No," Colter said, "my father told me that part. But I've seen it."

Wallis wondered what in God's name he had to offer or teach Colter. He figured the lone antler might be all he had to give.

They were nearing the river — close enough that they could see the bright space ahead of them. They were still on one of the deer trails.

"By the end of winter, the trail will be six feet deep," Colter said. "It'll be like a tunnel. The lions can sit above these trails and wait for the deer to pass below. It's like the deer are trapped in ice burrows or something; like they've become a different kind of animal."

"A different species," Wallis said.

"Yeah," said Colter. "People think all animals are always the same. Hardly anyone understands how different they are, each month of the year."

They followed the trail into the willows. A grouse leapt into the air, wings beating furiously — it was gone in an instant — and Colter flinched, and Wallis understood they were nearing the spot where his father had drowned.

"You'd never know any of this was ever here — this trail system — in the spring, after the snow's gone," Colter said, and Wallis looked around and nodded, imagining how it must be: the ice highways, so unavoidably noticeable — you could travel nowhere else — melting and relaxing, sliding away into sheets of water, leaving nothing except perhaps a few strand lines of dropped antlers, and deer scat, and leftover bones from the wolf- and lion-kills — antlers and bones marking the old paths like the residue of seafoam from a recent tide.

"Have you been seeing those antlers in the trees above us?" Colter asked. Wallis stopped and looked up and at first saw nothing, but when Colter pointed it out to him, he saw a large antler wedged between the forks of a larch tree, about fifteen feet off the ground. The antler had been placed there so long ago that the cambium had grown clutching around the antler.

"Squirrels?" Wallis asked, and Colter smiled, said nothing. And they went farther down the trail, and Wallis kept staring up into the trees, and now he began seeing antlers up in the trees all along the trail. Often the antlers looked just like branches, but other times they were silhouetted against the snowy sky. A brace of elk antlers spanned the narrow trail in one place, twenty feet up, between two lodgepoles.

"Indians?" Wallis asked. Colter smiled and shook his head. "Matthew?" Wallis said, and Colter nodded.

"These ice trails were here in these same places, when he was a kid?" Wallis asked.

"More or less," Colter said. A hallway of antlers, is what it seemed like to Wallis, and he said, "Why'd he do that?"

"I don't know," Colter said. Something clinked in the snow beneath him, and he stopped and dug up another antler.

They came out into the brightness of the clearing at the river. The river lay sheeted with ice. A moose stood on the other side, watching them, snow piling up on its back.

"There," Colter said, pointing to a snowy mound of rocks at frozen river's edge: a cairn, about four feet high. They skied over to it and Colter set his bag of antlers down and with his gloved hands began brushing the snow from the stones. Strings of feathers began to appear — raven, eagle, snowy owl — as did the sightless skulls of martens and weasels, beaver and deer.

The tips of antlers bristled everywhere from beneath the rocks. Colter kept having to brush the snow back; no sooner had he cleared a glimpse of the cairn than the snow began covering it again.

He took several of the larger antlers out of his bag and began wedging them into the cairn. Wallis helped him. When they were finished, they looked back across the river. At first they thought the moose was gone, but then Colter's eyes picked out the shape of the moose's ears; it was lying down, bedded down for the storm's duration, watching.

"Would you like to see him?" Colter asked. "I'd like to see him once more, before winter closes him off."

They began gathering branches and limbs: snapping twigs, gathering dried black wisps of old-man's-beard, and soon had a fire crackling out on the ice above the river. They had scraped away three feet of new snow, down to the blue ice below, and beneath the ice they could hear the river running strong, and could feel the tremors of it. The ice was not yet thick, and they moved carefully, not desiring to join Zeke.

The smoke from the fire rose in sheets and twists, and the orange flames danced across the ice. And the river below seemed to run faster as the fire grew larger. They kept piling larger branches on it. They dragged a fallen larch tree over and laid it atop the fire. The ice began to grow smoky clear in the heat. Three-toed salamanders began to wriggle from out of one of the rotten logs. Colter gathered them as they exited and put them in his pocket to bury safely back beneath the snow at a later time. The salamanders were sluggish and awkward, as if not just chilled by the ice but drunk too on the wood smoke. A black-backed woodpecker crawled from one of the log's cavities and leapt into the air with a quick, pulsing flight — as if awakened from some rude dream — and shortly after that bats began to wriggle from out of the log and took erratic flight, looking strange in the daytime, and amidst so much snow — as if the rules for some sort of normalcy had been interrupted, and things and patterns were no longer as they had once been.

The fire wandered and wavered, extinguishing itself in some places, as sizzling, hissing snow-melt pinched it out, but enlarging in other places as they kept adding fuel. It crept across the ice like an animal turning round and round, looking for a place to bed.

They followed the fire's path, trying to peer down through the heat-seared, glassy ice, but could see nothing. Finally the ice began to thin and then crack, with dark waters appearing below, swallowing the coals and the flames instantly with quick burps and belches of steam. Colter and Wallis backed away and watched as the hole enlarged.

They watched the snow landing on the dark waters and thought their own thoughts. The moose kept watching them from across the river.

When the fire had burned completely out, they crept out on their bellies and peered down into the water.

Zeke was still down there, his arms still reaching up. It looked almost as if he could still be saved. They lay there a long time watching him — the falling snow cold on the backs of their necks — and then Wallis got up and went back to the cairn and waited.

When Colter finally stood and came back to the cairn, his tears were frozen on his eyelashes like little crystals. He brushed them from his face like crumbs.

Wallis had thought Colter would want to head home after that, but instead Colter stayed with him and they headed back toward Mel's. They did not travel on the road, but explored the woods, searching for, and finding, a few more antlers. The snow was finally beginning to let up, dispersing beneath a north wind as they neared the cabin at dusk.

They could smell Mel's cooking — pies and bread baking, and a venison ham. When they entered the cabin the scents deepened, and Colter paused for a moment, remembering previous Christmases. Mel, who had not heard them come up on the porch, was startled, then looked disappointed. "I don't guess you saw them," she said.

Wallis shook his head. "We went to see Zeke."

Outside, the wind, stronger than ever, shaped and swirled the new snow into powdery drifts. The snow made a sifting, tatting sound against the windows, like thrown sugar, or sand. They could see bright stars appearing above the rivers of snow, which were snaking southward.

"I hope they're not out in this," Wallis said.

Mel shook her head. "They'll be okay, if they don't panic. Matthew should be okay. If they get in trouble, they can just burrow in on the lee side of a big spruce, make a nest under all the snaggly branches, and light little fires all night. They might have to share the space with a couple of grouse or snowshoe hares, but they'll be okay." She smiled, thinking of Old Dudley being forced to take refuge in such a manner. "Was Zeke still there?" she asked.

Colter nodded, then turned away and went to the window to watch the wind redistributing the snow. Mel wet her thumb and rubbed at Wallis's cheek and forehead. "Y'all are both covered with smudge," she said. Throughout the day she had been thinking about how it had not been so bad sleeping in Wallis's arms on the couch, and she had been worrying that once she had taken such a small pleasure as that one, it might be as if a gate had been opened: that like some kind of glutton, she might begin to desire more from him. She was relieved, as she dabbed the smudge from his face, to realize it was not this way. Still, she was surprised to find that she wanted him to look presentable when Matthew and Old Dudley came.

"Here comes Ma," said Colter, still staring out the window. "She's got the carolers out with her tonight." Now they could hear, carried on the strong wind and leaking in through the cabin chinks, the sounds of children singing, and of adults' voices, too — among them Amy's voice, pure and perfect.

They could see lanterns held barely aloft above the shimmering snow rivers — and as the singers grew closer and clearer they saw that there were two great draft horses, each as large and dark as a moose, plowing the snow ahead of them, and that several of the smaller children rode atop the horses, safely above the flowing snow dunes, which were glowing now with the color of the stars. The temperature had fallen at least thirty degrees in the last hour. There was not even the warmth of a moon.

Mel and Wallis and Colter went out onto the porch to greet the carolers, expecting them to tumble into the cabin blue-lipped, exhausted, and frostbitten; but first the carolers had work to do. They had not come this far not to deliver that which they desired to give, and they sang "Silent Night" beautifully, though it seemed incongruous with the wind still blowing and the snow hurling itself against the cabin.

Wallis and Mel and Colter, without coats, and without the warmth of activity, found themselves wishing the song would move faster; and when it was finished, the children came inside, steaming like animals (Amy and Colter went and haltered the horses on the back side of the cabin, out of the wind), and they kept singing, filling the cabin with their sound: more people in the cabin than perhaps there had ever been at once, and so many of them singing.

The children finished that carol — "God Rest Ye Weary Gentlemen" — and began shedding their coats and boots. Clumps and mounds of snow lay everywhere.

Mel hesitated only slightly before bringing out the pies and the fresh-baked bread, still warm, which she sliced and spread with honey. The children sat down and fell to the feast as if they had not eaten in weeks and would not be eating again for some time. The boys smelled the venison and asked about it, and Mel brought it out for them — it was glazed with honey and sugar — and they fell upon it, too; the entire ham was gone in less than a minute after having been cut and served.

It was harder than usual for Mel to let go of the regret that Matthew and Old Dudley were not there to see and hear and enjoy the carolers, but she did. She had gotten good at living without regret, over the years, and she released this one as she had the others and stepped forward into the moment. She looked over at Wallis and smiled.

The wind had died down and a great cold and a silence had settled over the valley. When all the food was gone, Mel made hot chocolate, and they drank it by the fire, warming themselves for the journey home. They sang more carols before dressing again and stepping out onto the porch into a cold so brittle that it seemed the air around them would shatter to crystals just from the act of their walking through it.

Amy asked Colter if he wanted to go home with them — Mel's cabin had been their last stop of the evening, and now Amy would be returning the children to their homes — but Colter said that no, he wanted to stay there with Wallis, and that he would be home in the morning. Amy looked hurt, but only for an instant, and she studied Colter for a moment as if he were going on some journey or voyage.

Then she smiled and thanked Mel and Wallis and told them good night and Merry Christmas. She lifted the smaller children onto the warm backs of the draft horses, who were throwing so much heat that standing next to them was like standing next to a stove whose fire has only so recently gone out that it is still warm to the touch.

The children leaned their faces in against the horses' necks to feel that warmth, holding on tightly with mittened hands; and like icebreakers at sea, the horses set off into the starlit snow, which was now sanded as smooth as the surface of a calm lake.

Their old trail had been filled in by the wind, but they took the same route out, the horses pushing through snow up to their chests. They plowed resolutely through it not only as if unaware they were retracing the same path they had just carved out less than an hour ago, but as if enjoying the labor.

Wallis, Mel, and Colter stood on the porch and watched the glow of the lanterns, a dark procession, disappear into the woods; and even after the procession was gone, they remained there and listened to the singing.

They heard other singing, too — the wolves on the mountain behind them — and they listened to that for a while, and then Mel went back down to the smokehouse — running, because she was cold; running across the taut-frozen shell of snow as if it were a hardened cast of concrete, so quickly and deeply had the temperature dropped — and she came back quickly, carrying a goose and an elk shoulder. They went inside and shut the door against the cold, and Mel began cooking all over again, preparing once more for the visitors she was not even sure were coming.

As if in a parlor game, a thing to keep Colter entertained, Wallis pulled down one of Old Dudley's journals and read aloud to Colter, while Mel baked and breaded and basted.

Scenes from the Coal Period
How the Coal Beds Were Formed
 While the grisly monsters of the ancient deep were luxuriating in empire and blood, the premonitions of progress were felt. The world was not made for them, but only an age of the world.
 Behold, the tide bears out into the sea a floating log. Its exterior is marked by peculiar and significant impressions. They reveal the crest of a dynasty in the vegetal world. They are the seal of a Sigilla'ria. *It has*

floated from the shore of a low-lying and silent continent. There is a meager nursery there where nature is training vegetation for thriftier times. In this log is written the doom of the old placoderms which had stirred the Devonian mud of the sea bottom. It is a voice crying in the wilderness of waves. Prepare the way for new land, new forms, new sense, and new history. God almighty, Man is coming!

It was back then the beginning of the Carboniferous Age. The tremors incident to the upthrow of a new belt of land had strewn the submerged continental slope with the sandy ruins of older lands and left the bed to mark the beginning of a new system of strata. They were not outspread in a day. They were laid down only with the destiny to be torn up in the human age — to serve as foundation stones for our more elegant structures.

Meantime the waters deepened, and nature seemed to have forgotten her announcement. She had promised land and green forests; but instead she gave deep sea and an expansion of the empire of bony-scaled ganoids. She gave larger development to Brach'iopods. She dallied with the chambered shells and gave the world an improved type, which we have named Goniatites. She lingered lovingly over one of her ancient conceptions which we style crinoidal. She had had it in her repertory of beautiful thoughts since early Cambrian times — the pretty little stone lily. She had taken it up in every age, and had turned out yearly some improvements and some new decorations.

But now, during this waiting period for man, she seems to have returned with true devotion to one of her first ideas. She gave great attention to diversifying life, decorating it, and filling the sea with its delicate and graceful forms. All for only the Age — not for perpetuity; for it, while we stand on this verge of a grand epoch, we lift the veil which separates the one beyond, we find the crinoidal conception gradually falling into forgetfulness.

But then this dream of placid waters and teeming populations was broken as if within a dropped jar. Some long pressed crust of the earth was broken by the accumulated strain, and the mud of the sea was stirred from its prolonged repose, and floated over the fields where those crinoidal stone lilies had flourished, generation after generation.

Tenants of the sea, alarmed, retreated to deeper waters or perished in their homes, and received a Pompeiian burial. The ocean bottom had been lifted to a higher level! The scene was totally changed. The summer *sea became a stormy and turbid shore; and a broad belt was given to the land. The torn beach, crumbling before the waves, contributed coarse rubble for the foundations of new land in some future age.*

The vegetation promised for the impending epoch was crowding into possession of the ground. It flung its fragments into the deep in challenge to the conflict which now sent its murmur through the world. These chips from the bystanding forest were buried in the sands which loaded the sea bottom.

Everything was ready; the curtain was about to rise.

Now came the first charge in the conflict destined to alternate during an age. The land uprose by another notch; the bottom of the sea was lifted to the surface. The great "Carboniferous Conglomerate" was now first bathed in air and sunlight. The new territory included all the regions which had been selected as the sites of the capacious coal repositories for the use of civilization: Man! All this was being prepared lovingly for man.

It was not a dry upland. It was a broad and mighty marsh. Texas was not included in the common continental marsh, but stood apart for a special destiny.

Now, over all this breadth of bog and swale sprang up vegetable growths — trees and herbs, ferns and rushes, with the all-engrossing airs of those who come to hold possession. Whence these forms? Some, as I said, had been nursed on the older and contiguous land, and now entered upon a new possession because these patterns were already in existence. Some sprang from germs fresh planted by some unseen hand. What mean all these transformations? They mean progress. They mean man. They mean civilization. It is not change alone; it is improvement.

This luxuriant crop is sustained by the carbonic acid of the atmosphere. This, as is generally supposed, was in excess. It made the air irrespirable; no terrestrial creature could live. But terrestrial animals must constitute the next step of progress. Man must arise from the swamp.

The march of improvement had now gone as far as possible with water-breathing populations. The highest type of animals had been reached and its aquatic class had lived a striking career. Nature had now paused for the purification of the air for the next class. The plan of nature was blocked until this could be done. Man had to arise; man had to be summoned.

The power which had called matter and force into existence could have made other disposition of this difficulty. The carbonic acid could have been combined with lime and fixed in limestones. It could have been banished from the planet. But carbon is precious. It is the basis of all our combustion. It warms and blazes in coal and petroleum, peat and gas. The carbon must be preserved for future use. Man would discover its utilities, though in the age then passing had no use for it. Man was yet far off; but man was anticipated; man was involved in the plans of the world; man was prophesied in these preparations. The earth must receive her kings.

So vegetation was appointed to do the work and to conserve the material. This explains the presence of coal-making trees upon the shores of the preceding epoch. They came by appointment, they were to fulfill a plan; they stood waiting by the border of a domain which had been promised them for a possession. All the conditions favored. This was not fortuitous; it was a preparation. Unlimited supplies of aliment pervaded the atmosphere. The marshy situation exhaled the abundant vapor in which vegetation delights!

The earth, in its comparative newness, retained the warmth to stimulate the root. So tree fern and herbaceous fern, Calamite and Sigillaria, began work. Atom by atom, they selected the poison from the atmosphere, and, returning the oxygen, fixed the carbon in their tissues. Frond, stem, and root treasured up the fuel impelled by the force of sunlight. Every pound of vegetable answered to a given amount of solar force. The world was in balance! A rough work in progress.

Generations of plants succeeding each other fell prostrate and added their substance to the growing bed of peat. Standing water protected the peat from decomposition. Now the skies again were lowering, and forebodings of change trembled through the continent. A cataclysm was at hand! The wide expanse of marshy land again went down.

Old Ocean, which had roared and frothed in rage around the borders of the territory of which he had been dispossessed, came careering back to his old haunts.

Old Ocean brought a freight of mud and sand, and he spread it over the whole vast peat bed — as if to make sure of no renewal of the usurpation — like those who sow with salt the sites of ruined cities to make the ruin a finality.

But the salt sowed by resentful Old Ocean was in truth a packing away of something destined to be saved, not forgotten. It was part of a beneficent plan, and the anger of the ocean was made an instrument for

this accomplishment. Beds of clay and sand shut out from the atmos-
phere the sheet of peaty matter which was to consolidate to coal.

The dominion of the ocean was temporary. Apparent regress was in
truth a forward movement! Again the reeking sea bottom came up to
sunlight, and another scene of bright verdure was spread where late,
Old Ocean had celebrated a jubilee. It looked as if the former forest had
undergone a resurrection. Here stood again Lepidodendron *in its sum-*
mer hat, and Sigillaria *and the other established forms. But they were*
other species; and with them was an occasional newcomer among the
vegetable types. They understood for what purpose they had been sent,
and resumed the work of selecting the impurity from the air. Already,
some adventurous and hardy types of air-breathers had colonized the
jungle. They were sluggish and slimy creatures, with whom life passed
slowly, and respiration was a matter of comparative indifference. Yet
they enjoyed existence. They grazed on the humble herb; they seized the
dragonfly, alighted to rest his wing; they violated the home retreats of
the passive snails. They crawled out and sunned themselves on the ferny
bank. There were grosser and heavier forms, mail-clad and vociferous:
haunting the bayou; paddling for some eligible fishing station; bellowing
like oxen, when excited in pursuit; stirring up the mire of the stagnant
bay; resting their chins on the reeking bank to absorb the slanting
sun-warmth of the early morning, or lolling under the noonday shade of
some wide-spreading and umbrageous Lepidodendron.

Why prolong the tale? The land continued to oscillate as long as the
purification of the air was incomplete: working, slaving to make the
world clean for man. Again and again the forest resumed its work,
and bed after bed was stored away beneath ocean sediments, to await
the end.

When the beneficent work had been accomplished, the tired forces,
those which had endured with trembling and vibrations — the enor-
mous strain that had been accumulating under the prolonged contrac-
tion of the earth's interior — yielded with a tremendous collapse that
jarred the hemisphere like the finishing throes of some great rutting
thing.

Huge folds of massive crust uprose and were mashed together till
their crests pierced the clouds. This was the birth of both the Appalachi-
ans and the shining Stony Mountains. This event proclaimed the end of
the long Paleozoic Era.

Only the stumps of those folds remain today. Though crumbling, they

*stand as monuments of the mighty means through which the world was
prepared for man and civilization. Lo, I come!! Me — Dudley Estes.
Lo! I am here! The world was finally made ready for me!!*

•

Mel was still working in the kitchen, but had been listening and smiling
as she worked. When he was done reading, Wallis asked Colter what he
thought about all that — if that was the way they still taught it in
schools.

"I'd say that's one mixed-up lunatic nut case, is what I'd say," Colter
said, forgetting that he was talking about Mel's father.

But Mel took no offense. "He's out there all right," she said.

"Is he crazy?" Colter asked.

Mel thought about it for a moment. "Well, he's *functional,* if that's
what you mean," she said. "He's able to get by. And he's a great geologist."

"That's not what I mean," Colter said.

"No," Mel said, "he's not crazy."

Colter wasn't convinced. "He sounds like it." He thought for a moment and then asked, "Do you think that's what some of those people
at the Bible school are like?"

Mel shook her head. "Dudley's not a churchgoer. The only god or
church he believes in is the church of Himself."

She brought them each a cup of tea. It was two o'clock. The roof
and rafters were groaning and creaking, contracting in the deep cold as
if being clutched by it. "Cheers," Mel said, "Merry Christmas." She
patted Colter on the back.

They sat for a while watching the fire, and then Colter rose and said,
"I changed my mind. I'm going home now."

"Are you sure?" Mel asked. "It's so cold."

"Yes," Colter said, and they didn't try to talk him out of it, but felt
guilty that they hadn't been able to provide him with whatever it was he
was looking for. Wallis felt especially bad, believing that perhaps the
passage he had read from Old Dudley's journal had upset him.

Colter wouldn't take an extra coat with him, or matches, though he
did agree to take a lantern.

"I'll stay warm enough, walking," he said. He stepped out onto the
fierce crust of snow. "It'll be fun, walking across the top of it. It's like a
highway." He wished them good night and Merry Christmas, and set

off toward the woods. The wolves were still howling, and Mel wondered if they were frustrated that, this evening at least, their prey could run across the top of the snow rather than floundering.

Colter's lantern disappeared, following the trail of the carolers.

Mel and Wallis went back inside. They built the fires back up: stoked them full. They sat in the den — Mel at her desk, working in her notebooks, and Wallis sitting on the floor next to the fireplace, reading further into the old journals — and the clock ticked quietly, and all was as calm as if they were an old married couple.

At midnight Mel blew out her lamp, put more wood on the fire, said, "I feel marooned," and sat down next to Wallis.

"I do too," said Wallis.

They slept again in each other's arms — closer, this time — and, carefully — careful because there was still no love in it, only curiosity and loneliness — he kissed her, and just as carefully, she kissed him back once, slowly, and then they slept, both of them being extraordinarily cautious to avoid thinking of the future.

THE MASTER CAME CREEPING INTO THE VALLEY AFTER midnight, bringing with him his human captive as well as two hawks. He was anxious to check in on, and in some manner reclaim, even if invisibly, what was his: his daughter and his other geologist.

He had chilled the hawks — redtails — in the freezer at his townhouse in Houston, nearly to the point of freezing, and then had hooded them and wrapped them in newspaper for insulation and bound them with twine and duct tape before stuffing them into Matthew's duffel bag, hoping that airport security would not discover them, which they did not.

They had rented a car, a limousine used for dignitaries, in Helena, and had driven north, against Matthew's protests that no vehicle would be able to get into the valley: that they would need snowmobiles, or helicopters, or skis. Matthew had seen Old Dudley like this before — almost rut-crazed with obstinacy, so much so that it seemed as if even a small matter had become a struggle of life and death. When he got this way, it was as if there had been a slippage within Old Dudley, as if the tooth of some gear had been chipped — and Matthew, who had been

stalked by lions and charged by bears, was never so chilled or frightened — the hair on his neck rising — as when one of Old Dudley's
gears slipped and he fixed upon Matthew, or whomever the transgres-
sive party happened to be, that unblinking round-eyed stare of what
seemed to be nothing less than pure malevolence.

Old Dudley's tong marks would pulse and flex deeper, with a respiration of their own, as if two organisms, two beings, were inhabiting
Old Dudley — one controlled by the human beatings of his heart, like
any other man, and the other controlled by some awful, unknowable
rhythm or pulse behind those tong marks.

And always the offender would wilt and fall back, or turn away, and
Old Dudley would get his wish; and the issue in question would no
longer seem so important to his opponent, who would instead carry
within him or her for days the illogical but inescapable feeling that he or
she was fortunate simply to be alive.

If Matthew had stood firm and argued further against the limousine,
would the old man have flown at him, and tried, with his teeth, to rip
his neck out? The force behind Dudley's anger was such that it seemed
he would.

They had driven north in the long black car, through blinding snow,
slipping and fishtailing on wind-scoured ice, then plowing through
snow, while the hawks, still hooded, riding perched in the back seat,
warmed back into full life, shitting and hissing, with their strength
fading fast, and needing to kill soon. With each bend and slip in the
road, the hawks had clutched the leather seats tighter with their talons,
so that soon the upholstery was shredded.

As usual, the northern landscape began to arouse discomfort in Old
Dudley: the slashing snow, the tunnel of dark towering trees through
which they were speeding made it seem to him, always, as if they had
gone past some point of civility, past some point where things could be
relied upon to turn out all right. A place where man was not king. He
missed the steamy tropics of Houston — the heat and haze and sluggish, sweaty, fungal torpor; and to allay his nerves, he drank steadily
from a bottle of rum, and from time to time turned on the overhead
dome light to peer at the small photographs of nude women, cut from
the pages of skin magazines and glued to the backs of index cards,
which he carried with him on trips away from home for the purpose of
cheering himself up.

He studied one photo, his favorite, in particular.

"Man, I ever catch up with this one, I can't begin to tell you the things I'd like to do to her," he said.

Matthew rolled down the electric window, snatched the photo from Old Dudley, and tossed it outside. Dudley wailed, causing the hawks to screech and flail about on their jesses — wings beating and drumming against the roof — and then said, "Ah, that's all right, they're not the real thing" — and he stared out at the snow spiraling past as they climbed higher into the mountains. Dudley said, "Oh, I've got to stop thinking about it, got to get it out of my mind, or I'm lost," and he drank from the bottle and was silent then, settling down into some grim, lower place of torpor.

They drove into and then through the cold front, so that the snow was behind them and the stars burned fiercely above, so bright that the stabs and flashes of them welded and seared old memories in their minds, summoned things within them, old stories and histories they had not remembered in a long time, or had never known.

At the summit, the pass was snowed in, but the upper skin of snow was frozen so tight and polished so smooth by the wind that Old Dudley believed they could drive across it, and he forced Matthew to keep going.

They had extra clothes in their suitcases and duffel bags, but they were still wearing their black business suits and ties, and their slick-soled little black leather pointed-toe dress shoes, so that they looked like undertakers. If they got stuck, Matthew thought — if even one wheel punched through that crust, taut as stone but only a few inches thick — the car would be swallowed by snow, and they had no skis or snowshoes, nor even winter boots or sleeping bags, so that almost surely they would freeze.

Perhaps Matthew could build a few small fires with the limousine's cigarette lighter, and perhaps they could hunt a grouse or a hare with the hawks, but then one or both of the hawks would fly off and not come back. Matthew and Dudley would starve if they did not freeze first, for no one would be up in the high country to help them for months. There would perhaps be a mid-winter delivery by snow machine, but perhaps not. In any event, they would be buried beneath several feet of snow by then, and their frozen carcasses, and the car itself, would not be discovered until May or even June.

They raced across the ice shield, sliding crossways and backward sometimes, skating and spinning, with Old Dudley ranting at Matthew to "Push on, push on"; and they were in too deep, Matthew understood, to do anything but that. Sometimes in their spins the flanks of the long car grazed the trunks of trees. Matthew had no idea whether they were on the road itself. He knew they were near it, but it was also possible that in places they were driving over hundred-foot gorges filled with snow. Shooting stars tumbled from the sky like diving things taking shelter from the presence of the two men's horrid advance.

Dudley's adrenaline, his musk, was as dense as the odor of overripe fruit, so that Matthew had to roll the window down despite the great cold. The hawks chittered and shat more freely than ever. A snowy owl glided across the snow in front of them, carrying a still-struggling snowshoe hare: white on white on white, illumined in their headlights.

They almost made it. They found the road again — scattered the caribou herd like sheep before wild dogs — and passed through town without pausing. Matthew wanted to stop in and see Helen first, to wake her and tell her he was back in the valley, but Old Dudley said, "No way; push on," and so they kept driving. The heat of the car's engine began to melt the ice beneath them, so that their tires were beginning to sink as if in slush; and as they drove, they bogged deeper and deeper, the engine revving and racing harder than ever — a raw, roaring sound that could be heard all through the valley, and which troubled the dreams of all who heard it — and when the car finally sank up to the windows, they were less than a mile from Mel's cabin. They rolled the windows down and climbed out like escaping convicts and went hurrying across the frozen landscape, carrying nothing, only running, as if being pursued, or late to some important engagement: hurrying to get there before they froze. They each carried a hawk on one arm.

Matthew led; Old Dudley struggled to keep up. Not far from the cabin, Matthew cut across the tracks of the carolers, and the horses' hoofprints and turds, and read what had happened — but then closer to the cabin, he came across Colter's tracks, and paused, intrigued. The tracks, striking straight for the river, were about the size of Mel's, but Matthew couldn't tell from the gait and carriage of them whether they were masculine or feminine. They seemed to be both. He lay down on his stomach and sniffed them. He did not smell Mel's scent in them.

"What in the fuck are you doing?" Dudley asked.

Matthew sat up on his knees and stared off toward the river. He rose and hooded his hawk and tethered it to the low branch of a lodgepole, then took Dudley's hawk and did the same.

"What are you doing?" Dudley asked. "I thought Mel's cabin was that way." His voice rose as Matthew started off in the direction Colter's tracks had gone. "Why aren't you taking the hawks? Are you lost? Which direction is Mel's cabin?"

Matthew didn't answer. He was anxious to see Mel — anxious to see Wallis, too, and reclaim him — but the unknown tracks were too fresh, too mysterious, too tempting.

Old Dudley waited until Matthew was almost out of sight before running after him: tripping and stumbling as he ran, and glancing behind him often to be sure that some horrible predator — wolf, lion, bear, lynx, wolverine, or some fanged creature not yet known to man — wasn't following him. He hurried as fast as was possible for a seventy-year-old man, trying to keep the dark figure in front of him from disappearing.

They found Colter down by the river, collapsed and frozen, his face as blue as a robin's egg. He had had a small fire burning out on the river ice, but he'd curled up on the shore while the fire was still burning and had gone to sleep. If the river had opened briefly beneath the fire to reveal another glimpse of his father, it had done so as he slept, and now with the fire extinguished and the great cold and wind having swept through, the river was sealed off again for good.

As Colter slept — his heart having slowed to around thirty beats a minute — he was dimly aware of a force beneath the frozen ground, something still vital and alive, which — in his sleep — he was convinced was his father; and as Old Dudley and Matthew pulled him from the snow — kicking at the wind-curled ice clutches that had swept over him as he slept — Colter felt that force growing weaker with distance, and was convinced it was his father still down there, caught amongst those branches, holding steady; though as Old Dudley and Matthew carried him away, all he could hear was the river itself, faint but strong, riffling and murmuring beneath the vastness of the ice.

Carrying him was like portaging a pillar of ice, and despite their labor, they soon grew chilled, wearing only their thin silk suits. They moved through the woods like black-shimmering angels, or devils, their own feet and fingers turning numb — their faces paling to blue — and gasping, sweating, Old Dudley said, "The little fucker's already dead, or is going to be — let's leave him" — and in his ice-sleep, Colter heard him. Dudley released his share of the load and stood there panting, searching for a depth and ease of breath he could not find. Matthew then assumed all of the load, shifted the stiff-frozen boy across his back and draped both arms over him as if in a yoke, or as if carrying a crucifix; and once again, Old Dudley hurried to keep up with the dark figure ahead.

It was too cold. They couldn't make it, Matthew thought. Should they stop and make a quick fire to warm up — to gather enough brief warmth to enable them to rest and recover, and then push on?

He decided against it. They were so close, and it was so cold that he did not think a fire would matter. That had been Colter's mistake.

They reached the tree where Matthew had tethered and hooded the hawks. There were now only piles and tufts of feathers on the snow; two russet martens sat on the branch side by side, their eyes gleaming, holding the remains of the trapped hawks in their paws and crunching on the hawks' skulls. The hawks, weakened from not having hunted in so long, had been unable to pull free and escape.

Dudley wailed in anger and pain: his feet in agony, his fingers, his nose; he moaned and wept, but did not quit, and now they turned toward the cabin, less than a quarter of a mile away. Their shoes were wet from the snow and ice and had refrozen, picking up clumps of snow, so that it was as if they were treading in ice boots, which helped make the walking a little easier, though now they could feel nothing from their knees down.

In the cabin, wrapped in their sleep of warmth, Mel and Wallis awakened to the nearing sounds of the howls, and believed at first that it was the wolves. When they went to the porch, however, they recognized the pitch and tenor of the two men, and Mel cried, "They came! They made it!" and now they could see the strange silhouettes of Matthew carrying something, and the floundering, humpbacked figure of Old Dudley behind him.

They saw then that it was a human that Matthew had on his back, and they ran out onto the snow-crust in their stocking feet and took Colter from him, and hauled him inside.

Mel hugged Old Dudley and Matthew — Dudley was still whimpering like a pup, but was glad to see his daughter. He shook hands with Wallis, as did Matthew, and Wallis marveled at the iciness of their hands.

The men shed to their underwear in front of the fire and warmed their skin — it turned patchy and mottled, from blue to red, ugly as an old turkey gobbler's head and cockscomb — and then they dressed in some of Matthew's old coveralls.

As the two men were dressing, Wallis noticed that Dudley had a long purple scar, crescent-shaped, running across one side of his chest — that one nipple was missing, as if seared or scalded or melted into some new clastic shape, and he wondered if Dudley had received it when he received his tong marks. It looked as if he had been branded. The scar was a foot long.

Rocks — yellow ore — tumbled from the pockets and clattered to the floor as the two men pulled their coveralls on — rock specimens Matthew had gathered on his own missions long ago — and Wallis gathered them up as they rolled across the floor.

Colter lay by the fire like one prepared for burial.

The two men moaned and whimpered as life returned to their digits and limbs with a vengeance — Old Dudley fell to the ground and grabbed his bare feet with both hands and began rocking back and forth, keening like some deranged bear in a zoo — and now Colter began to murmur and groan as the pain of life returned to him, also.

Colter could no longer feel the river moving beneath him. He coughed up crystals of ice, his lungs practically frozen. His eyes fluttered.

"Guess I was wrong," Dudley admitted. "Guess he's going to make it after all."

Mel got more tea for him. Colter sat up, stunned, and though the blueness began to leave his skin, it was not replaced with the kind of ruddiness that had returned to Matthew and Old Dudley, but instead came as an ashy gray color. Mel got a towel and rubbed hard at his skin, trying to raise his blood from its depths, but it would not come to the surface. Colter still appeared dopey and loopy to them — he tried to say something, but then paused, unable to organize the words into complete sentences — and Mel frowned and rubbed harder, wondering what part of him had been left behind.

"Isn't there something that occurs like the bends, if they wake up too quickly?" Matthew asked. "The raptor of the deep?"

"I don't know," Mel said. "I never heard of it. But he doesn't look right."

"He has been to a faraway place," Dudley said, "that's all. He will be fine."

"He doesn't look right," Mel said. "He doesn't look like he used to."

Colter could hear and understand everything. It was true that the words he heard them speaking were processing themselves more slowly in his mind than usual, but that seemed to help him understand them with a greater depth and power. Again he opened his mouth to speak — intending to tell them about the faraway place he had visited — but still, no words would come.

"Good God almighty," Old Dudley said, horror-stricken.

Salamanders were crawling slowly from out of Colter's pockets. They were coming from beneath his coat, warmed by the fire, so that they seemed to be hatched from his chest. Black and silver, with electric green stripes running down their spines and purple hoodoo masks around their faces, they appeared from beneath his coat as if crawling out of a rotting log.

"A nasty savage," Old Dudley said, regaining his composure. "A pure-God, nasty little savage."

Colter's eyes, seemingly catatonic, stared straight at Dudley, and the salamanders kept climbing out from his coat and tumbling down the front of his coat, spilling to the floor and creeping away from the fire, traveling in Dudley's direction, wriggling and yawning with silent little roars. Mel gathered the salamanders and put them in a saucepan, and for a moment, Old Dudley thought she intended to cook them.

Steam rose from Colter — from his wild, ice-bent hair, and from the damp back of his neck — and it seemed more than ever that he was incubating those salamanders.

Mel covered Colter with more hides. Blood was slowly returning to his face; perhaps the salamanders were what had been the matter with him.

Now Old Dudley turned his attention to Wallis. "You've changed," he said, not entirely pleased with what he saw. It was the look Wallis had seen on the silly-ass businessmen sitting on park benches in downtown Houston on a fine spring day, legs crossed and the newspaper opened double-wide before them, held inches from their faces, as they squinted through their bifocals and tried to ascertain that day's stock listings — their little stockpiles — while overhead, the geese cried, heading back north against a blue sky.

"You're all *black*," Matthew said. "What have you been doing?"

Dudley felt the edges of alarm rise up in him: the suspicion that he might have picked the wrong one, or turned him free too soon. Things had been going so well in Houston: Wallis had been finding oil, and had been showing every sign of developing an addiction.

"I was helping Colter build a fire earlier this evening," Wallis explained.

"Well, my God, son," Dudley said, "don't you ever take a bath? You're not going native, are you?" He stepped forward, peered into Wallis's eyes — stepping over Colter to do so, ignoring him as if he were cordwood — and for a moment, as Dudley's fierce golden-green eyes held him, Wallis felt a hypnosis coming over him: a feeling he imagined to be very much like what Colter had felt as he curled up and lay down for a nap in the snow.

"Oh, son," Dudley said slowly, still staring into Wallis's eyes, "you've been spending too much time up on the surface."

There was an infinite sorrow in Dudley's voice: not so much at the fact that Wallis had failed, but that a pure potential had been squandered, or underutilized. It seemed to Wallis that it must have been like an extinction: a species vanishing, leaving behind only a niche unoccupied in the landscape. An echo; a loneliness. Other species eventually divide up the forfeited territory and move in slowly — but they are the generalists, and rarely in claiming such a territory do they possess the grace of fit, the authority, of their predecessors.

Finally Dudley broke eye contact with Wallis. He turned to Mel and said, "You have been corrupting him."

"I have done no such thing," Mel said, "but if I wanted to, it would be my own damn business. All I've done is fed and sheltered him for you for the last month, and you come up here saying I've *corrupted* him, like he's some piece of property you own, or like I am? If that's the way you're going to be, you can just march your sorry old ass right outside the door and head back home, and take your *boys* with you."

"Easy, easy, little filly," Dudley said, chuckling. He held his hands up, palms out. "Easy. No harm done. He's still salvageable. It's just that you've set me back a little, is all. You've undone some of the good at which I'd labored so long and hard —"

"Stop it!" Mel said. She slapped her father's still-outstretched hand. "Listen! This is my home and my valley you keep punching around in. I wish the whole lot of you would clear out and never come back. So stop the bullshit about how I'm causing you problems. And anyway," she said, "he's been working on a map. He's been reading your foolish old books" — Old Dudley's gaze flickered to the shelf, and a strange look passed between him and Mel — "and he's been working his ass off out there, clawing at the ground like some goddamn neurotic hound looking for a bone. So cut the shit."

Was it better to have a bad family, or no family at all? Mel went to her bedroom.

Everyone was still ignoring Colter, who nonetheless listened, processing the sentences, the anger of them, with that slow power, so that he seemed to know more about what was being said than the mere content of that which was being carried along on the surface, by the skin of the words and sentences themselves.

He felt as if the ice had cleaned his brain: as if he were watching and listening to two things at once. Part of him was hearing the argument, but the other part of him was imagining a place quieter and more peaceful than this one; a place farther north and west, even more isolated, raw and untouched. A place for which no map would be accurate.

He was tired. Absorbing the meaning of what people were feeling and what they really wanted — the direction and content of their sentences like a decoy, so that their true intents were buried below — was exhausting. He lay back down and went to sleep. Still no one paid any attention to him. The three men in the room reassembled now like one organism, and began to talk gingerly around the edges of their one goal.

"It must be her period," Old Dudley said primly, "or the stress of the holiday season. She was like that, growing up, too." A pause. "She really never finished growing up," he said. He shook his head and tsked. "If only her mother hadn't died so young, she would be normal," he said.

Matthew stared down the hallway: his old hallway, his old cabin. He knew he should go in after her and try to make amends for the brutishness of their arrival. He knew too he should ski back into town and let Helen know they had arrived safely.

"You mentioned a map," Old Dudley was saying. Wallis nodded and went to get it from the middle room, and Matthew knew Wallis would be staying.

Wallis spread the crude map out on the floor, proud and nervous. He had constructed it almost entirely from his imagination, and the only thing he knew for certain was accurate about it were the four directions.

It was the roughest of outlays. There were no strata delineated —

only the perimeters of the valley, with some of the rivers reflecting possible fault patterns going on below, and some educated guesses about angle and direction of dip.

Old Dudley studied the map for several minutes, implacable. Wallis waited.

"It's all wrong," Dudley said finally. He picked the map up, rolled it up, and fed it to the fire. "Start over," he said. "It's all wrong." The paper caught flame and lit the cabin briefly, brightly, with its burning, then was gone, blackened char, like Wallis's face. Matthew had a slight smile — almost a smirk.

"What parts of it were wrong?" Wallis asked. "What parts were right, so I can use them on the next map?"

"It was all wrong," Dudley said. "The whole fucking thing."

Matthew got up and went to the porch, retrieved another log, and brought it in for the fire.

"You're worrying about that damn car, aren't you?" Dudley asked Matthew. "We rented it in your name and now you're sitting there worrying about that, instead of the real matters of life, the only thing in life, the sole question, which is, *Where is that oil?*" Now he laid into Matthew as if beating a rented mule. "You don't worry about that car," he instructed. "Either that car will take care of itself or it won't. It's just a *thing*," he said. "If you live to get old and smart like me, you'll understand there are a lot of *things* in the world — that that's all there is up top, is *clutter*. Shit, that's why you couldn't find any oil up here, even with all the chances I gave you. You either had your head up your ass, walking around looking at all the pretty flowers, or you were so hooked up, engaged, *coupled* with her" — Old Dudley pointed down the hall — "that you couldn't have found oil in a service station."

"That's not true," Matthew said. "I worked my ass off. I generated —" he paused, counted on his fingers, trying to remember — "nineteen different prospects up here," he said. "All good ones — all prospects you yourself believed in at the time."

Dudley ignored this as he ignored anything he did not wish to hear. "All dry holes," he said. "Bone-dry. Blind, mindless, root-hog *probing*." He shook his head, then searched his memory. "Seventeen million dollars I spent on your soft-dicked *probing* up here," he said.

"I thought money was just a *thing*," Matthew said.

"It is an indicator," Dudley said primly, "and it indicated that you blew it. It's a small miracle you were ever able to find oil again — a small miracle you weren't ruined. I was able to resurrect you," he said, and sighed, "but it took effort."

"These rocks," Wallis said, hoping to break the tension between the two men. He fished some of the yellow ore from out of his pocket. "Tell me about them. Where did they come from? What do they mean? How old are they?"

Old Dudley looked at the rocks as if they were turds, and snorted. "Fuck *rocks,*" he said. "I'm talking about the oil *in* rocks." He snatched the rocks from Wallis, studied them briefly, then tossed them back in disgust. "They're just pretty little rocks he picked up off the ground and probably brought home to show his *sweetie.*"

Matthew took one of the rocks from Wallis, examined it, broke off a few grains, and rubbed them between his fingers. "Carnotite," he said. "It means —"

"Carno-*fuck,*" Old Dudley said. "I don't want to hear any of that shit. It's Christmas. Let's don't have any of that kind of talk."

Wallis gathered the rocks and put them in his cardboard box in the middle of the room. He also had half a dozen little bags of dirt — faint spoonfuls of topsoil — in his collection. What map could come from such thin supply?

He went over to the fireplace, where the two men were talking, having made their peace. They were sharing a flask — Matthew offered it to Wallis, who took a sip and then shuddered, thinking at first that it was oil — "Absinthe," Matthew said. Wallis asked Old Dudley how he got the scar.

For a moment Dudley bristled, and then was very still — thinking at first that Wallis was making reference to the tong marks, which no one had ever had the temerity to ask about — but then he remembered undressing by the fire, and that Wallis had seen the scar melted across his breast, which had been for so long a part of him and hidden to others that he did not think of it as a scar.

"When I was a child," Dudley said, "in East Texas, living in a cabin — a hovel, really, not unlike this one — there was nothing I loved more than pumpkin pie. By God, I could eat a whole one right now. But back then, I was even crazier for them than I am now. I *had* to have pumpkin pie, any time I saw it. Probably some vitamin deficiency or something, living in such squalor as I was.

"It was late on a Thanksgiving afternoon, and we were all sitting around in that dim light by the wood stove, just trying to stay warm. It had been raining for a week, so that it had turned that whole part of the country into a red sea of mud, and we had that wood stove rocking, just roaring fire-belch, as much as it could roar on that pissy green Southern yellow pine — *we could not get warm* — Ma, Pa, and me — and there was this pumpkin pie sitting there on top of the wood stove, a whole second pumpkin pie we hadn't even touched, left over from the big feast. I'd already eaten one whole pie and Ma had said I couldn't have any more til the next day, but she got up for a minute to go do something, and Pa was looking out the window at the damn rain or something, and so real quick I leaned over and reached for that pie.

"My chair slipped and my chest pressed in against that stove," he said. "I could feel it burning me, could smell the searing flesh — my God, it was hot: it hurt so bad. I felt like puking — but I still couldn't quite reach that pie, so I leaned across a little farther — *yow!* burned the rest of my right teat off — but I got that fucking pie, and I leaned back in my chair — tears running down my face — and sat there and ate that whole damn pie, and my old man just stared at me, with his mouth hanging open — my shirt had burned open in the shape of the scar, and was still smoldering — and when Ma came back in the room, she said, 'What's that smell?' Pa told her what he had just seen, and she looked at me funny, then sat down by the fire to warm herself and said, 'Serves you right. I told you not to get that pie.'"

Colter began to stir, as if awakened by the story. He sat up again and this time he looked and felt better, and the words he was hearing were passing through his mind at their usual pace — though in some strange way that he could not pinpoint, he missed the submerged, slower pulse of the way things had been earlier, and he tried in vain to hold onto the feeling of how it had been, as one tries upon awakening to hold onto the already disappearing clarity of a dream.

Dudley handed the flask to Colter, who took a sip, then coughed and spat it into the fire, where it flared orange and green.

"Good God, boy, you just spit out about a hundred dollars!" Dudley cried. "No more for you, little pup!"

Mel came back down the hall, silent in her socks. The outside cold was seeping in between the chinks in the cabin, and the rafters continued to make groaning, twisting sounds as they contracted.

"Greenhouse warming, my ass," Old Dudley said, and he finished the flask.

Mel sat down next to the fire. "You don't know what it's like, being your daughter," she said. "It's really, really hard." She laughed, though not with humor. "Even way out here, two thousand miles away, it's hard," she said.

"And even then I'll come looking for you," Dudley said, pleased at the show, the admission of weakness.

"Stirring things up," Mel said. "Rutting up the ground. Making chaos. You can't stand it, can you — that I'm away from you?"

Dudley smiled, looked down almost shyly, said nothing.

"If I left the valley, you'd probably stop drilling here, wouldn't you?" Mel asked, and again Dudley just smiled, shrugged. "You'd like to see me down in Houston, trapped by concrete and trapped in a marriage to a man" — a glance at Matthew — "who's buried beneath the ground almost twenty-four hours a day. *Why?* What have you got against someone being free?"

"You left out barefoot and pregnant," Dudley said. "That would be good, too. Have a boy-child, maybe — someone to carry on the carnage, after I'm gone."

"You won't ever be gone," Mel said. She turned to the others. "You all think he's joking. He's not. He's dead serious. He's not joking."

"Mel," Matthew said, "it's Christmas."

"The hell with Christmas. The hell with all of you. You, too," Mel said to Wallis, "this is what you bought into. I'm stuck with Pop by blood, but you chose him. God help you," she said, and went back down the hall.

This time Matthew went with her.

"Well, shit, boys," Dudley said. "I don't know what to say."

"She's been so calm," Wallis said.

"I guess she just doesn't like me," Dudley said.

"Would you stop drilling here if she didn't live here?" Wallis asked.

Dudley grimaced. "Oh, son. That's some bone-ass question. Son, son, son," he said, shaking his head. He dropped down to all fours, and at first Wallis and Colter thought he had fallen ill. Old Dudley began crawling forward, like an old lion, slinking.

"This is what I do to maintain my youthful figure," he said. "It's called *creeping*. It's an exercise I invented. It tones the arms and shoulders as well as the lower abdominal muscles used in fucking," he said. He was on the far side of the room now, his face flushed a violent red with the effort. His words were growing thicker, garbled, but he kept speaking as he crawled, wheezing through both nostrils like a horse swimming across a river; and they could hear, too, a rattling in his lungs. It seemed that he might not even make one full lap around the room.

"It stimulates the more primitive, powerful components of the brain," he said. He was nearing them now — prowling the perimeters. More red-faced than ever. Wallis wondered what woman could place herself beneath him, for the sex act. He would not have been surprised to see Old Dudley hoist a leg and begin peeing against one of the bookshelves.

By the time he reached them again, he was slick with sweat, and Colter and Wallis could smell a rankness coming from him: a dense, sharp odor, as if he had come in his pants. "I do this every night," he said. "Drunk or sober, fresh or tired — without fail. It's helped make me the man I am." He passed by them and began another lap, as if binding them with invisible ropes. "Fifteen minutes, every night," he said.

It was unsettling to watch Dudley crawling around down there at ankle-level, and Colter said, "I have to go home now, my mother will be worried" — it was 4 A.M. — and Wallis, also rattled by Old Dudley's behavior — by the nakedness of it — didn't try to counsel Colter otherwise, but instead primed the lantern for him and gave him an extra coat.

"Stay away from the river," Wallis said.

Colter buckled on a pair of Mel's snowshoes and took off across the starry, glassy crust. Soon he was trotting, and even after he was gone, Wallis could see the weave and wander of his lantern through the trees — the trail of light like the script of a sentence whose sole message was *homesick,* and Wallis allowed himself to remember his own Christmases past, both with his parents, and then later, with Susan and her grandfather — and it pleased him to see Colter hurrying home to where he belonged: pleased him to think of the joy of Colter seeing his mother's face.

Old Dudley crawled out onto the porch and rested there, still on all fours — sweatier than ever, steam rising from his back — and he watched the firefly trail of the lantern through the woods. He shouted out after him, "Go on, run, you little bastard — flee, you little cocksucker!" — and the sound was louder than Wallis imagined a voice could be. The sound bounced across the frozen skin of the earth like a stone skipping across water. And in the extraordinary stillness, the air was so thin and free of moisture that he could barely get enough of it into his lungs to breathe, even when he drew a double lungful.

Up on the mountain behind them, the wolves began to answer. "Holy shit, let's get inside quick," Dudley said, crawling back inside. "Lock that door," he ordered. He resumed his creeping. "Do you think they'll get that salamander-boy?" he asked.

Wallis didn't answer, but instead prepared an elk-hide pallet by the fire. He turned out the lamps, exhausted. He could feel the earth below him spinning in one rhythm, and at one speed — *winter* — while he above was moving much faster, in step with neither the time of year nor the place.

Old Dudley kept creeping. Wallis could tell where he was by the sounds of his huffing and puffing, and by the way the floor would creak whenever Dudley passed by, and by the damp, dank odor of him, like mushrooms in a shady forest — and after a while, he heard Dudley collapse in a heap at the base of the couch, then heard him climb up onto the couch, where there was the rustling of hides and blankets as he covered himself for sleep, like some creature crawling back into its burrow: though even then, in the quietness, there was still the rankness, the odor of him, which kept blossoming from him as he slept, like some flower blooming in the night. Wallis's last thought was of how someone as precise and understated — as *watchful* — as Mel could have come directly out of such a rutting old boar as Dudley.

Dudley was staring at Wallis when he awoke. It was daylight, mid-morning, and still snowing, and he was standing a few feet away, just watching him. The fire had gone out and the cabin was cold. The blossoming odor was gone.

"Listen," Dudley said, and pointed down the hall. "Do you think they're *coupled?*" he asked. "Do you think they're hooked up?"

"I'd rather not —" Wallis started to say, but then the sounds began, the sounds that had awakened Dudley. "*Listen,*" Dudley said. He crouched a bit, as one might crouch in the woods, listening to the approach of a deer. "Does it sound like mouth-fucking to you?" he asked. He started to say something else, something unguarded, but stopped and eyed Wallis differently.

"You're vile," Wallis said.

"Well, yes," Dudley said. "America is vile. These are vile, hungry times. People are hungry for my oil and gas without even knowing they're hungry for it. And you work for me, and you find it, so you're vile, too. We're all vile." He sat down, his feelings clearly hurt.

"Don't tell me you haven't been with her yourself," he said. "I can *smell* it on you."

Wallis went into the kitchen and busied himself lighting the wood stove.

Old Dudley followed him. "You've been with her, right?"

"No," Wallis said.

The headboard was bumping against the wall of the cabin now. Dudley grinned hugely.

"You're different than you were in Houston," Wallis said, and Dudley shook his head.

"I'm different from how you chose to view me," he said. "You just weren't seeing clearly. You didn't want to see. Anyway," he said, "how I am has nothing to do with below, does it?"

"No," Wallis admitted, "not really."

There were more rustlings in the bedroom.

"You wouldn't know where I can get me some, would you?" Dudley asked. Wallis pretended not to know what he was talking about. "No, I don't guess you would," he said. He left the kitchen then, as if to be alone in his disappointment, or as if Wallis's prudery were contagious. He went to the fireplace and tried to get a fire going. Wallis began mixing pancake batter, and watched him. He was doing it all wrong — stacking green chunky logs on top of each other without any kindling, and without any air, and he kept lighting matches and holding them against the big chunks of wood until the matches burned down. He singed his fingers and he cursed and flapped his hands, then tried again.

Dudley continued to curse, and, finally admitting failure, came back into the kitchen, where he moved in close to the wood stove. He proceeded to tell Wallis all of the things he intended to do when next he did find someone.

Now the sounds from the bedroom were coming in a different rhythm. Old Dudley cocked his head like the RCA dog and ventured back into the other room, to better formulate a theory — and Wallis wanted space, more space from this craziness, or if it wasn't craziness, from this hunger.

The sounds stopped, then — the musical rumba of the bed frame having finished things off — and Old Dudley leered at Wallis. He said, "Sometimes I forget he's not my son — sometimes he seems more my son than she does my daughter."

Though the odor of Dudley's creeping from the night before was gone, Wallis needed fresh air. He went down to the creek to haul water to heat for baths. When he came back, Mel and Matthew had joined Dudley at the table and things were calmer. Mel seemed willing, always willing, to give Dudley another chance — and as if playing cat-and-mouse, Dudley was willing to take it. It seemed to Wallis that if she were going to disown him, surely she would have done so by now.

She was wearing an old white terrycloth robe, her hair was brushed, and she was smiling. Wallis saw for the first time that she was not simply attractive, but beautiful, and marveled that in the depth of his funk or numbness he had missed it, after a month of living with her.

She thanked him for bringing the water in and began making pancakes for breakfast. Wallis went out for more water, again and again. Old Dudley and Matthew sat at the table and talked about oil and gas. Wallis wanted to listen — was crazy to listen, after so long a silence, a separation from it — but the water needed to be hauled. He wore his path deeper and deeper — a rut, a tunnel — with each passage. He wondered how many trips Matthew had made up and down this same path. He wondered where it had all gone: all the water Matthew had hauled, all the trails cut deep into the snow and ice, and all the love he'd had for Mel.

When he brought the last of the water in, everyone was seated at the table. Matthew and Mel were waiting for him to join them; Old Dudley had forged ahead, had spread maple syrup and huckleberry jam thick across his pancakes and was chowing down, making the most awful smacking noises. Matthew and Mel were holding hands but Wallis knew that there remained between them only the thinnest threads of a bond, that it was only an echo of what once had been.

As if reading this thought, Old Dudley finished one pancake, paused for a swig of milk (into which he'd poured a dollop of rum), and said to Wallis, "You've got to dive, boy — I'm telling you, you're going to jack around up here at the surface and get stranded — you've got to turn loose of, and ignore, all this bullshit." Dudley waved his hands at everything in the cabin — the books, the antlers, the fireplace, and lastly, Mel.

Mel stared at him for a moment but said nothing, having decided to let him stew in his own vapors. She would try to salvage what she could of the day and ignore him, though she knew that after a while it would be like trying to ignore a dog turd in the middle of the floor.

There was a tapping at the window: a small face appeared, cup-handed, and they thought it was Colter again, but saw then that it was Helen.

"Aww, shit," Matthew said, "are her feelings going to be hurt, or what?" He got up and hurried to the door to let her in. He hugged her and said, "Merry Christmas, Ma." She was holding an armload of wrapped presents — small, bright boxes she'd brought over in her pack — and she smiled uncertainly and stepped in, confused by the sight of a table-setting that did not include her. Mel jumped up and fixed a plate for her, poured her a cup of coffee in her one good china cup.

"I got up and looked out my window and saw the two of you drive through town," she said. "In that long black car, gliding across the snow. I thought it was a dream and I went back to sleep. But in the morning I saw the tracks. I waited for a while, thinking you'd be coming over for breakfast, but then I came on over. I saw where the car went through the snow. I guess that's why y'all couldn't get back over to the mercantile," she said, though she knew full well that Matthew, even the city-husk of him, could have skied or snowshoed back to town easily.

"We were just about to head over there," Matthew said. "Right after we finished breakfast, and right after we took our baths."

The silence following any lie, or half-truth.

"Here," Helen said, handing them each a gift. "Merry Christmas."

"Oh, Helen," Mel said, "you do this every year, and we ask you not to. We didn't get anything for anyone. We just eat, and visit, and hang out . . ."

"I don't want anything," Helen said. "I just wanted to give y'all a little something. If it's that uncomfortable for you, next year I can bring them over the day before Christmas, or the day after. But it makes me happy. You don't have to give me anything. Please open them."

They peeled off the hand-painted wrapping paper. Four tiny deer hide pouches, soft and thin, and smelling of wood smoke. Wallis's eyes stung with the pleasure of being included. They opened their draw-string pouches — each small enough to be held in the palm of a hand.

A river stone, smooth and polished as an agate, for Wallis.

A handful of porcupine quills for Mel, beautiful as ivory, each one nearly weightless and perfect for the duty for which it had been crafted: defense.

An eagle's talon, gnarled and dried but razor-sharp, for Old Dudley.

An old silver pocketwatch for Matthew. He held it, studied it, wanting to know — he looked inquiringly at Helen — and she said, "Yes, I *think* so."

Matthew held it to his face to smell the odor of it — tarnished silver, ancient silver — and to glean the echoes of any memories that might be emanating from it.

"I think so too," said Matthew. "How did you find it?"

"Amy found it, when she was going through some of Zeke's things," Helen said. "She remembered that Zeke's father used to hang out with your father a lot, when they were younger — they used to go bird hunting together a lot — and after Buster died, the watch must have somehow gone to Zeke's father, and after that, to Zeke. I guess after that it would have gone to Colter," Helen said. "It was awfully sweet of Amy to think of it."

"Amy," said Old Dudley, fingering the tips of the eagle's claws: the ankle as bright a yellow as an ear of corn. "She's the one with the nice bumcakes, right?"

They ignored him. Matthew pressed the smoothness of the watch to his face, and closed his eyes for a moment.

"It doesn't work anymore, of course," Helen said. "But maybe you could get it fixed somewhere."

Matthew opened his eyes, but she saw that he was not seeing her, or anyone, or anything. Helen wondered if after she was gone, he would ever hold anything of hers that tightly to him.

A thing like a scar, a crescent of pain, ran through her center, from her waist and across her chest. She flinched at the tightness of it — the illogical pain of sorrow amidst joy — and tried to relax, tried to tell herself that it didn't matter; that the good fortune was hers for having known and loved him, for having been able to raise him in his parents' stead. The fact that she might be forgotten, dust, the moment she stepped off the earth, did not matter.

Mel got up and hugged Helen, thanking her again. Old Dudley made a childish, clawing motion at the air with his eagle talon, of which he was clearly proud. "I'd get up and thank you," he said, "but I've got a king-sized boner, thinking about Amy. You wouldn't want to see it. It would shock and amaze you," he said.

"Thank you," Helen said. "Please stay seated."

Wallis fingered his river stone: worn and abraded smooth. It fit the palm of his hand, and the space below his ear, where his jaw hinged. He pressed it here and there, as Matthew had done with his father's watch, and said thank you to Helen.

"Let me see that old thing," Dudley said to Matthew, reaching across the table for the watch. Matthew handed it to him. "Careful," Matthew said, as if speaking to a child — but Old Dudley was reckless with it, opening the lid and shaking it and holding it to his ear, then shaking it again, rough as a primate. The watch slipped from his hands.

Wallis had been watching, anticipating; he dived for the falling watch, lunged from his chair, and caught it in one hand just before it hit the ground, while the rest of them sat petrified, waiting to hear the sound of its breaking. There was a nauseating silence, as all their adrenaline resettled, and Old Dudley chuckled, a *heh-heh* kind of chuckle, and said, "Good catch." Wallis handed the watch back to Matthew.

They went into town that afternoon, after they had all bathed, taking turns in only six inches of hot water in the big tub, changing the water each time; and when they went out on their skis, their hair was still damp, and it froze around their skulls like helmets, and their skin contracted, stretched tighter to take the wrinkles and crow's-feet from their faces, and made them all feel younger as they skied. They skied in single file, and when they passed the limousine they saw that it had sunk a little farther, as the temperatures had warmed slightly.

The breeze was at their backs now, from the south, and to the south they could see a high wall of purple clouds, another snowstorm coming in, squeezing in again over the same pass through which such storms had passed for thousands of years — coming through the notch of Gunsight Mountain — and then being channeled along the river, flanked between the high mountains on either side. Dumping snow every time as if to bury the valley, either because it was too beautiful to be seen by the world, or as if in punishment for some evil long-forgotten. Always the storms took the same path.

When they got to town, the Red Dog was full, overflowing; despite the cold, the door was open, and people lounged on the porch dressed in heavy quilted coveralls and wrapped in fur robes. Heat from the stove trickled out the door for a short distance like spilled water. A few horses were tied to the porch rail, where they stood with heads down, snow-matted, dreaming of, hungering toward, their next feeding of hay, while other horses wandered loose and milled around the porch, even took the first few tentative steps up onto it — feeling that warm air from the open door trickling around their ankles — and it seemed that they were considering going into the bar, and it seemed also from the degree of inebriation of those on the porch that the horses might be welcome to do so.

Old Dudley did not get into the valley often, and when he did, he delighted in buying drinks for the house, all day or all night — for however long he was in the bar. He enjoyed being around the savages, as he called them. For a few hundred dollars he could afford to buy them all drinks for days on end, if he wished — as if they were fish in an aquarium that had gathered for him to observe, as he fed them — and they in turn were delighted to be able to examine him. They found him more savage and fascinating than any creature in the woods, and their response to him was a strange mixture of respect and ridicule. He was clearly talented at what he did — how else could he have earned so much money? — and understood the subterranean workings of the earth far more intimately and in more specific detail than they could ever imagine. But of his oil-finding ability, all they knew was what they had seen, which was that he had thus far failed nineteen times in their valley. Some worried that he might soon stop coming to the valley if it didn't soon produce something for him. Such was their economy that he could spend two hundred dollars in an evening and six months later, a hundred and fifty of it would still be in the valley.

When the rigs came, there was very little money that went into the valley directly — the payments instead went to outside contractors, and the trucks involved in the hauling of equipment were run by out-siders, as were the crews involved in the drilling — but the spectacle of the operation, surreal and monstrous — the rig towering up with the trees; the clanging and hissing and roaring of motors — brought some entertainment to the valley, during the long, lazy two months of sum-mer; and occasionally, one of the rig workers would buy a pack of crackers or a can of sardines from the mercantile; and they patronized the bar as well, though not with the enthusiasm that might be expected, so tired were they from the day's or night's work. They lived in a squalid tent camp down by the river, when they came, and bathed in the river and killed deer out of season, does with fawns, and cooked them continuously over large sprawling ragged fires down by water's edge; and each spring, after they were gone, the high water of runoff scoured away their leavings.

As with anything of this nature, the valley was somewhat divided on the issue of whether the drilling was a good thing or a bad thing; but it was always a dry hole, and the rigs always went away, and the quiet, the peace, always returned, like vegetation growing back in over a scratched-bare spot, or like a scar knitting flesh back together.

So they welcomed Dudley as a pack of dogs welcome one of their own: everyone rising and coming up to touch him — to shake his hand or pat his back or grip his shoulder — and they welcomed Matthew with even greater zeal — as if he were some kind of prodigal, Wallis noted — and with some large measure of relief, too, as if there had been a collective fear among them that one day he would not come back.

And Wallis could feel it, as if he were already one of the locals: a settling or shifting of things — of the entire valley, is what it felt like — so that things seemed to fit once more as they had, and in a manner around which other things had been designed or adjusted.

Mel, Wallis, and Helen hung back, accepted a few greetings, filtered into the crowd. There were the usual odors of smoke, alcohol, sweat, and adrenaline; but mixed in with it were the buffering odors of fir and spruce sap, snow, and horses.

Dudley pulled out a wad of hundred-dollar bills, the stack of them as thick as a big hamburger, put two down on the counter, rang the cowbell to announce the free drinks, and a cheer went up.

People kept swarming around the two men, kept touching Matthew, as if to see if he were still real, after so long down in the city.

Wallis sat at a back table with Helen and Mel and watched the snow come down. The sight of it was utterly hypnotic. Wallis felt as if he were viewing the white noise in his own mind; that the snow was passing through his mind and cleansing it with its passage. It did not seem to matter that he was working for a buffoon.

"Remember," Mel said — her voice startled him — "one drink. Make it last."

Wallis smiled. "Maybe two, since it's Christmas."

"Not me," said Mel. "Just one for me."

Danny came over and joined them, as did Amy and Colter. Colter was wearing a new necklace of shining teeth on a deer hide thong, and everyone exclaimed over it: another find from Zeke's tanning shed. Mel leaned in and touched each tooth, named them as she touched them. Grizzly, coyote, wolf, beaver. The ivory eyeteeth, little hidden tusks, of elk. Lion. Badger.

"My word," Mel said, "I had no idea." She could barely speak. Her hand lingered on the necklace. "It's so beautiful." She was quiet for a long moment. "What does it feel like, to have it on your chest?"

"It feels good," Colter said. He started to take it off to let her try it on.

"No," said Mel, "it's yours — your father's."

"Well," said Colter, "it feels good."

"I imagine it does," said Mel.

Old Dudley had purchased a bottle of rum and had climbed up on the counter and was proclaiming loudly about something, they couldn't hear what — clearly using up air space to keep people from paying too much attention to Matthew. Gusts of snow blew in through the open doorway, but no one made a move to get up and shut the door.

Amy poured beer for everyone at their table except for Colter; emptied the pitcher. A look of pleasure, even contentment in her eyes, despite the recent loss of her husband. She smelled the empty pitcher and closed her eyes: remembered growing up in Pennsylvania, her father and six brothers drinking beer at lunch, at supper: remembered them drinking it like water as they plowed and broke the black soil. When a horse went lame or needed resting, one of the brothers, each over six feet tall and weighing more than three hundred pounds, would step into the traces and pull until the horse healed.

"Were you born here," Wallis asked Danny, "or did you come from someplace else?" It seemed to him that hardly anyone — Helen, Matthew, and maybe a couple of others — had been born here. As if it were instead only a place to come to.

Danny smiled sadly, realizing for the first time that Wallis could not possibly know his circumstances: that it had not been gotten by osmosis.

"I came here in grief," he said. "A place to start over. From Florida. I was a bronc rider." He peered at Wallis sidelong. "Do you want to know the specifics?"

It seemed rude to say no; it seemed salacious to say yes.

"People around me were getting sick," Danny said. "My wife, my old parents — my wife's kids from an earlier marriage. She was pregnant with our first.

"They started dying — some fast, like my old man, with his heart attack — but others, real slow. Cancers and such. Right before my wife died — the baby was never born — her old mother told me it was my fault, that it was a curse — that I was not living a path of righteousness, that I was being cursed for being away from home too much. No offense," Danny said, with a glance at Amy, "but she was a big church- · goer." He shook his head, though how many times in the twenty years since had he told the story? Laying it down each time like a foundation, like steppingstones across some dark river.

"She even got my wife thinking that way, before she died," Danny said. "Funny thing was, it probably *was* my fault, unintentionally; there was probably some damn nuclear waste in the soil, or invisible night fumes from some refinery that settled where we were living. People in that neighborhood were always getting sick, and I couldn't afford to move us to a better location; or I didn't think I could. And we had a good time," he said. "We had a good life. But after that, I lost it. After the funeral — five of them in two years — her old momma kept hounding me, kept after me like some little dickey bird chasing an owl. I was drinking and doing drugs, and one day she came over there to yap in my face — damn near crazy herself — and I hit her." Danny looked Wallis straight in the face. "I hit her hard. I went ape-shit. They had to put her in the hospital. I've never been sorrier for anything in my life.

"I did my three years, then came out here. I didn't even know 'out here' was here; I just headed this way, and stopped when I realized this was where I needed to be.

"The day I got out of jail, her old husband — Lucinda's stepfather — was waiting for me with a gun — a little pissant Saturday night special. I got off the bus in town and he was waiting there for me, and shot me with it, but the pistol blew up in his hand," Danny said. "Some of the bullet went into me — went right through my ribs — and some of the gun shrapnel cut up his hand. There was a lot of blood.

"I didn't say a damn thing," Danny said. "I took off my shirt and wrapped up what was left of his hand in it, took him down the street to a doctor's office, checked him in — blood was coming out of my ribs at a pretty good clip — and I just kept on going. I knew the battery in my old truck would be dead, so I bought a new one, and walked home with it. It was August, about a hundred degrees, and the heat and blood loss was making me dizzy. I got home, drank about a gallon of water straight from the garden hose — swapped batteries, hosed myself off in the front yard, slept til dusk beneath a shade tree, then woke up and got in my truck and headed out.

"I still don't feel like I paid my dues or debts," Danny said, staring at his hands. "It's not like I feel *absolved* or anything. I guess it just feels like that was then and this is now."

Wallis held the story for a while. "Were you a good bronco rider?" he asked, finally.

"Naw," Danny said, "that's the hell of it. I wasn't worth a damn, really. I just enjoyed it, was all."

"Do you think back to it much?" Wallis asked.

"Nah. Probably no more than once or twice a day now. Not like what I used to."

Up on the counter, Old Dudley had rung the bell again and had rolled up a piece of posterboard to form a sort of megaphone. He was braying about his hawks and eagles, shouting their story so loudly that there was no way anyone else could have told another story anyway.

He was talking about when he had first started looking for oil and gas — when he and his wife and Mel, just a baby, had been living out in West Texas. They rented a little one-bedroom, one-bath adobe house for thirty-five dollars a month. There were hawks and eagles all around the house — the newspapers on the floor had to be changed daily — and when Old Dudley went out into the oil fields, he would take his hawks with him, to train, while the rig drilled almost ceaselessly deeper. It was long, slow work, waiting for the well to reach its final destination. All the craft had been expended in preparing the prospect for drilling — in creating the map — and then it would be expended again, interpreting the results once the well was finished — taking the data and altering and revising those maps — but during the in-between time there was just a lot of straight-ahead drilling, and it was Dudley's job back then to simply be within rough shouting distance should something occur.

As he lectured, his voice boomed across the bar. No one could do anything but listen.

"I remember being out dawn til dusk some days," he was saying. "I'd hunt six birds in a day. I'd keep 'em hot and fresh. And when I wasn't hunting the old one, I'd be training the young ones. I was a good trainer. You have to start when the birds are little. They're too wild at first — they don't want to do what you ask of them — they kill, but by nature they don't want to bring back what they kill and hand it over to you — and so you have to forge this bond. You have to alter their nature.

"The simplest way, when you've got 'em young like that, is to just wear the fuckers out," he said. "You keep 'em awake — you stay awake, too, with them — for however long it takes to wear them out: three, four, five days in a row, day and night.

"Every time the bird tries to rest, you wake it back up — sometimes you even devil it a bit — and it flies at you in a rage, screeching and clawing. You have to wear a leather suit, like armor — and you let it wear itself out like that, until the wildness goes away, and its will becomes instead your will.

"It was a long time ago," he said, "when I was raising all those young hawks and falcons — but I was good at it." Dudley laughed. "They'd be all over the house — each on a different perch, and out in the garage. They stole the baby's toys" — he glanced out at Mel, in the audience, almost as if not realizing she had been that baby — "and Madelyn, my wife, was always afraid they'd snatch the baby up — that they'd mistake her for prey while she was crawling around beneath them." He studied Mel now as if for signs of scars from almost forty years ago. "They never did though," he said. "I told her they wouldn't, and they didn't. There were some places where they wouldn't hunt, simply because I didn't want them to. Their will was my will," he said again.

He was shouting now, like a preacher. "I made those birds. God made them and then I took them from God and turned them around in the other direction and made them into something else.

"There is this lightness the bird gets when it is on your arm, and when it is finally exhausted — when it finally gives up," Old Dudley sang. "When it gets to that point — when you have won — you can actually feel something leaving the bird, and can feel it getting lighter as a result, until it is almost weightless. God, it's sweet when that happens," he said. "Usually sometime around the fourth or fifth day. You'd think they'd fight longer. Considering I own them forever, once this happens."

Colter's face had grown more serious throughout the recitation, so that now it was in sharp contrast to all the other faces around him, who were enjoying the entertainment. Colter leaned across the table to speak to Wallis, though Mel and the others at the table could hear him too.

"I don't like him," he said, and then sat back in his chair, brooding.

Old Dudley raved on. He was shouting now about the best bird he'd ever had — the giant Asian eagle, the *berkutsk*. Dudley said that the Arabian princes who gave him the bird told him it had killed giant cranes, and even leopards and tigers; that it had killed a hundred wolves in Russia, each time by diving and batting its great wings about the wolf, blinding it, and then driving its talons through the wolf's head. He said they told him it had even killed men before, always unpredictably — killing its own masters, sometimes, out of boredom — falling upon them from out of the sky — and that you could even still see the stains of that human blood on its feathered shanks; that the stain of it would not wash out. Dudley was talking about how he'd always had to keep the bird out of direct sunlight, which had been a problem in West Texas — how their blood ran hot, usually around 111 degrees Fahrenheit, so that sometimes before hunting he'd had to trickle cold water over the eagle's head and wings, because the bird's heart would get to pumping so hard that he'd heat up just *thinking* about the hunt.

"It was in the days before air conditioners," Dudley said. "Driving out into the desert with him, at dusk, with him in the truck on the seat next to me, was like having this *magma* or something in there with me. God, what a beast," Dudley said. "His fucking legs were six inches around. In the winter, when a cold front would blow through, I'd take him outside on my arm, and the steam would just roll off of him, when he ruffled his feathers: him so hot, and the sky so cold. God," he said, "I remember everything about those days."

"I was a big bad motherfucker," Dudley went on — the chemical release of the bonds in his brain perhaps finally beginning to occur, yielding to the alcohol's inevitable will. "I was as big as him," he said, gesturing to Matthew, who was coming back with two bottles of wine. "Carrying that big fucker around on one arm — it was like holding a whole set of encyclopedias out on your arm — and you owned the fucker, owned him in every way ..."

Snow continued to blow in through the open door. Dudley shivered, got up, and walked along the counter like a circus high-wire performer — at least one of his steps had a looseness, or a trace of drunkenness to it, but only barely — and he hopped down and shut the door, then climbed back up on the counter to finish his story.

Mel interrupted him.

"Oh, what a catastrophe for man," she called out, quoting D. H. Lawrence, "when he cut himself off from the rhythm of the year, from his unison with the sun and the earth. Oh, what a catastrophe, what a maiming of love when it was made a personal, merely personal feeling, taken away from the rising and setting of the sun, and cut off from the magical connection of the solstice and equinox. This is what is wrong with us. We are bleeding at the roots —"

"Hey," Old Dudley said, "cut that shit out. Stop it," he said. Mel smiled. Dudley rang the bell, rummaged in his pockets for more money.

Dudley picked up his megaphone again. "There are two theories why the falcon returns to the falconer," he bellowed, as if preparing his listeners for an exam to be given later. "One is that the falcon is conditioned to its hunger pains: that it has learned to associate its master with food. But the other theory is that the falcon truly loves the falconer, and returns solely out of love."

"Which do you think it is?" Mel asked.

Matthew was listening intently.

"Both," said Old Dudley. "I think we manipulate them coming and going. I think the poor creatures are born with exquisitely pure souls which only through superior association with beings such as myself are able to be bent and retrained. I think we teach them to confuse hunger with love, and love with hunger. I think we mix it all together, and that only when they're way the fuck up there, half a mile above, can they draw things back out pure and separate once more: a distillation of how it was when they came into the world, and how they are really supposed to be.

"But it's too late. They are owned by another. They have lost their ancient selves. They are but feathered ghosts.

"Shit," he said, "it's a miracle they can still hunt, when we get through with them."

He climbed down from the counter, flush-faced — looking like an old man, and a little rusty, but still vigorous, and in some way that Wallis could not pinpoint, dangerous: as if some wild, unpredictable animal — a wolverine, perhaps — were in the bar among them. Not currently threatening them, but imminently capable of doing so. Dudley's tong marks were pulsing violent red, throbbing, as if he had just been pulled up from the sea.

The day had slid completely away from them, passing from afternoon to dusk so quickly and unremittingly that it seemed there had been some mistake: that two or three hours were missing. Wallis was matching Amy beer for beer, and Mel leaned across and whispered in his ear, "You have no restraint. You are like him." Wallis — a little drunk now — lurched back in alarm, believing her to have said something cutting, but she was only cautioning him, and was joking.

Other men joined Dudley at their table. Matthew, who had been sitting up front during Dudley's storytelling — sitting beneath the counter looking up at him like a child in story hour — also pulled up a chair and sat with them. More beer. Mel drank water, as did Danny. Helen sipped bourbon and stared fondly at Matthew. She could count on two hands the number of days she got to see him in the valley each year. The years hurtling by as if they had no end.

Mel coiled her hair as if it were a rope, lifted the ends of it to her face to take its scent — to ascertain the amount of cigarette smoke it had absorbed. She thought of the wolves, and of how sometimes they would backtrack her as she was backtracking them. "I'm going outside for a minute," she said, touching Matthew's arm. She lingered for a moment, as if believing or imagining that he might go with her — but Matthew and Dudley were explaining to Danny about how developing an oil field in the valley would not harm anything, and how it could even be of benefit to wildlife.

Wallis rose and went out the door with Mel. They brushed away the snow that had blown in on one of the benches and sat down and watched the snow slanting past, and felt the cold's embrace. Wallis could not remember the heat of the sun, and, surprisingly, did not care to. The snow that had been melting and dripping from the roof where the door had been open earlier in the day had already frozen into long shining teeth that hung down like glassine bars.

"I don't remember him being like this in Houston," Wallis said. "Maybe I was a little blind to it, because I had the maps to work on, but I don't think so. He was eccentric and opinionated, but not like this," Wallis said. "Not out of control. Not crashing."

"He's not crashing," Mel said. "He's riding hard. He's riding you and Matthew. Those kinds of performances cost him nothing. That's not out of control. You don't know out of control." She reached up and broke off one of the icicles. "I don't know how to explain it, but it's like he's got you and Matthew down in the mud and is standing with one foot on each of you. Like he's *blossoming* out of you." She sucked on a tip of the icicle. "He's worse around the solstices, it's true." She shook her head. "God knows what's in his blood."

They were quiet for a while, letting the snow and wind carry away the words that had passed between them. Mel splayed her fingers through her hair, helping the wind and the cold to scrub the scent from her. Where did odors go when they disappeared? Where did words go, once spoken? She tugged at a tangle of hairs, and a couple pulled free; she tossed them into the wind for the wrens to find and build nests with in the spring, or for mice to line their beds with.

"Why don't you leave him?" Wallis asked.

"It's not that easy," she said. She held out her arm as if to offer one for the donating of blood. "Besides," she said, "I have to be better than him. When he's bad, I have to be good. It's not any conscious decision on my part. I can just feel the balance of things that way — like when you're on a seesaw. And also," she said, "he and Matthew are insepara-ble. They're becoming one. They've already become one."

"Why don't you drop Matthew, too?" Wallis asked.

Mel was silent for a long time, and Wallis did not know how much he had offended her.

"It's like he's becoming my brother, more than my lover," Mel said finally. "It's very sad."

Matthew came out onto the porch, having torn himself away from Dudley long enough to look for them. Helen followed him, and they sat on a bench next to Mel.

To the three younger people, the cold was invigorating, but to Helen it was brutal. Still she could not break loose from the sight of her son. She knew from many years of experience that when he and Old Dudley decided to leave, they did so quickly, like the flash of a fish turning broadside in the current: silver for a moment, then gone.

It was snowing so hard that they could not see her store across the street. Helen leaned in against Matthew for warmth, as did Mel, and Wallis had the thought, You two are leaning against a rotting building. He felt a strange strength and calm in his isolation.

"They say everything happens twice," Helen said, staring out at the snow, and none of them had any idea what she was talking about. Mel thought she might be thinking of some long-past companion, or even a lover. Matthew wondered if she meant some weather pattern. Wallis, who had been thinking about Dudley's puzzling exhibitions, wondered if she meant another Dudley might be coming, or created. That Matthew might be the one.

"At *least* twice," Helen said. "If you live long enough, you see everything happen once, and then you start to see it happen a second time."

Helen was shivering. "Let's go back inside," Mel said — wanting to sit and stare at the beauty of the storm, mesmerized, but taking pity on her — and they went in to the noise and heat of the bar. Charlie was arm-wrestling all comers two at a time. Old Dudley was deep in conversation with Colter. Amy had gotten up and left the table.

Dudley carried with him sample vials of oil he'd found — carried the tiny glass bottles like talismans clinking in his pockets — and he opened one now to show Colter what it was like when it came straight out of the ground, unrefined. "Hidalgo County, 1937," Dudley said, and Wallis laughed at the expression on Colter's face: at the way he clearly thought that was ancient.

The oil had been discovered and brought to earth's surface sixty years ago. But it had been in the world, resting below, fully formed and waiting, for four hundred million.

Did some of the power lying in the gap between that disparity go to the man who discovered it? Even if there were but a tiny transference of that enormous distance, Wallis figured, the accrual would be immense.

When a trapper trapped and took the life of a wild and free creature — say, a marten or a wolverine — did a transference of force — even a tiny one — also occur there? The sum of all of the days of the wolverine's passage over mountains and through valleys, in all manners of seasons, ending up with the snap of the trap, or the crack of a rifle: and did the taker assume then even an echo of all that which had previously been possessed by the other?

Dudley was unscrewing the lid to one of the vials and inviting Colter to take a sniff of it, to dip his finger in it. The oil glistened in the dim light, reflected lanterns and light bulbs — darker than blood, black as licorice, shiny as obsidian, it seemed not to be anything as potent as the raw fuel of man's commerce as something simpler and more elemental: like a stone, an antler, or a piece of wood — its properties and characteristics not yet manipulated in one direction or the other.

"Go ahead," Dudley urged Colter. "Dip your little finger in it. Feel how slick it is." Colter did so, tentatively; sniffed it. It had a sweet odor, not quite like anything he had smelled in this world. Old Dudley winked at him. "It's especially fine for applying to your bony member," he said, "when you're trying to fit it into crevices and orifices which will not normally accommodate your bulk —"

"*Pop!*" Mel said, and Old Dudley jumped, not having noticed their return. Colter wiped his finger off on a napkin hurriedly as Amy came back from the restroom. Old Dudley stared at her for long moments with depthless, predatory eyes — becalmed, it seemed, finally, just to be considering her.

"There is no man who is not born into a trap, and yet all labor to climb out," he said, and at first they thought he was reciting poetry. "But what man has the courage to embrace his trap, and not fight against it, but dwell wholly within it?"

He leaned forward to take the scent from behind Amy's ear — to inhale deeply, and imagine himself already within her — but pitched forward, finally drunk, and passed out on the floor.

"He is excited from his travels," Matthew said. "He hardly ever passes out. He is excited to see you," he told Mel.

"Bullshit," Mel said. "He's old and drunk."

They sat him up in his chair — his head lolled like a pumpkin — and wrapped him in a blanket. Colter went across the road and rummaged in one of Helen's ancient outbuildings for a sled. He came back carrying the sled and a bleached buffalo skull. "What's this?" he asked Helen.

"Just an old thing I got somewhere — someone left it at the store a long time ago. Do you want it?"

"Hell yes," Colter said. Amy was aghast. "I mean, heck yes. Yes ma'am," he said.

They loaded Dudley onto the sled, folded him into it like a child going for a ride. His arms hung over the sides and his head was tipped back, his face upturned, his open mouth gathering snow. His legs were splayed out in front of him, so that they had to lash them to the side of the sled. Everyone gathered out on the porch to see them off.

Wallis and Matthew pulled the sled behind them like horses; Helen and Mel skied along behind Dudley, flanking him, so that as they skied off into the storm, it looked not as if they were transporting a passed-out old drunkard, but were escorting, with regal bearing, a fallen dignitary of exceptional prominence, one who still had something vital or worthy to offer the world.

As they skied, the snow piled thicker and higher atop Old Dudley, until he was buried beneath it, and the sled grew heavier from its weight. In helping load him into the sled, Wallis had been amazed at how heavy Dudley was — at the density of him. Though Dudley was not a large man, it had felt like loading stacks of iron. Wallis had wondered how the hell the old man even moved around — how he could move his own weight forward. He would have guessed Old Dudley to weigh about a hundred and fifty, just looking at him; but after lifting him, and then hauling him, he wouldn't have been surprised if someone told him he weighed three hundred — as if his blood was made of mercury.

They skied past a herd of elk that had bedded down at the edge of the road beneath a large fir. They passed within yards of the elk, and were puzzled, because they could smell the elk distinctly — like a stable of horses — but could not see them — but then Mel saw the branched antlers of the bulls rising from out of the snow, and she saw the twin plumes of breath from each of the elk, like the smoke from a hundred tiny fires, rising all along the road.

The elk watched them pass, and Mel and the others kept waiting for even one of them to panic and leap up in a cascade of loose snow, causing the rest of the herd to then bolt in similar fashion — half-a-hundred elk erupting from beneath the cover of snow, as if born not from any mother's belly but straight from the earth — but the elk stayed motionless, save for their chimney breaths, believing they were hidden.

At one point Old Dudley stirred and leaned his head over the side of the sled to vomit, but he did so quietly, still unconscious, and Matthew and Wallis kept on skiing, pulling him along as he retched, and Mel and Helen skied up to the front to escape both the sound and the odor.

The coyotes that had been following them, shadowing them unknown, fell in quickly behind them now and began tasting the vomit, laboring to eat the sweet-sour entrail juices before the leavings were covered by the snow; and the snow kept coming down, coming so relentlessly that it seemed it was endeavoring to cover everything in the world, regardless of whether a thing was moving or standing still, and regardless of whether it was dead or alive: as if, in winter, the distinction between the two thinned to almost nothing.

At one point farther into their journey, Old Dudley woke briefly and began wailing, believing that he had been given up for dead and buried alive. He fought the ropes that had him lashed to the sled and leapt to his feet, throwing off the heavy layers of snow that had blanketed him — he had been choking on snow, riding with his mouth gaping open, and his eyes were crusted with it, so that he could not see — and with the sled still lashed to his legs and arms, he ran blindly toward the woods, the sled on his back looking like a tortoise's shell. Such was the panic and strength of his flight that he pulled Matthew and Wallis along behind him for a short distance, until he ran headfirst into a tree and was knocked backward, stone-cold unconscious again, at which point they untangled themselves and righted his sled, with him still lashed to it, and began pulling once more without comment.

"He has never been at peace with the world," was all Helen had to say.

They stopped at the last creek before the trail up to the cabin and dipped Dudley's head in it upside down to clean him off, and to awaken him. But still he kept sleeping, as if drowned at the bottom of the sea, and now the water from the creek froze over his head and face like a mask, or shield, so that he looked like some horrible alien, all the more surreal for the dapper business suit he was still wearing.

At the cabin, Mel wanted to chip nostril-holes in his ice helmet for him to breathe through and then put him out on the porch until he awakened, but Matthew said it was still too cold, and that he would freeze; so they untied him from the sled and brought him inside, laid him in front of the fire, and watched with some interest, even fascination, as the ice mask polished itself bright before the heat and then slowly melted, so that like a chrysalis a normal human face emerged again: a face which, compared to what it had been moments ago, was — despite the tong marks — almost a thing of beauty.

Old Dudley kept sleeping through it all, and Mel made more pallets for Helen and Wallis, and everyone went to sleep; though at some point in the middle of the night, Wallis awakened and heard him creeping once more, crawling around and around the cabin's perimeter, and saw his silhouette, each time he crawled past the fire; and Christmas slid past them, was pulled into the vault of the past along with all the other days, as if it — that day, and all days — were a thing, a test, they had somehow failed, and that they would not be allowed to move fully and confidently into the future until they had somehow addressed that failure.

In their dreams, they all felt it, and Mel felt it most strongly of all: that the end of failure would yet someday be revealed to them by the presence — when it finally arrived — of an unquestioned, almost un-noticed, grace.

She moaned in her sleep. They all did, off and on, through the night, so that to anyone listening from outside, it would have sounded as if the cabin were full of suffering — as if it were some ship, some ancient wooden ark, drifting lost and full of curses: though for what reason of punishment, the tenor of the groans gave no indication, nor did, in their restless slumber, the dreamers know.

I N THE MORNING, THEY DRANK TEA AROUND THE TABLE AND admired the sunlight. They could see the frost crystals glittering, hanging suspended in the blue sky. Helen asked Matthew point-blank when he would be coming back to the valley to live.

"Well," Matthew said, glancing at Old Dudley, "it may be a while yet."

"He means not while he's alive," Mel said.

"Oh, he'll come back," Helen said. "He will. After he's found enough oil — after he's had his fill. And he'll be a better person because of it."

Old Dudley brayed.

"He will," Helen said. "You don't think he will. You'll see. Every-thing happens twice."

"Everything happens a hundred times," Dudley corrected her, "or ten thousand — but you won't see him in this valley again." He nodded toward Mel. "Like she says, not in our lifetimes, anyway. I own him, and I say *no*."

"No one owns me," Matthew said.

They sat and watched the sunlight some more. Already, each of them could feel Dudley's itchiness to be leaving. Matthew stared un-blinking not at the sunlight outside, but at the window pane of the stove.

"Listen to this," Mel said, and she got up and went over to a book-shelf and pulled down John Niehardt's transcription of *Black Elk Speaks*. She sat down with her back to the fire to read to them, and Old Dudley groaned.

"Oh, fuck," he said, "poetry."

Mel read: "He said that Crazy Horse dreamed and went into the world where there is nothing but the spirits of all things. That is the real world that is behind this one, and everything we see here is something like a shadow from that world. He was on his horse in that world, and the horse and himself on it and the trees and the grass and the stones and everything were made of spirit, and nothing was hard, and everything seemed to float. His horse was standing still there, and yet it danced around like a horse made only of shadow, and that is how he got his name, which does not mean that his horse was crazy or wild, but that in his vision it danced around in that queer way."

"Oh, God," Dudley said, "worse than poetry. *Indian* shit," he said, but then was seized by a sudden pain in his chest so sharp that he spilled his tea. The pain passed almost immediately — just a cramp — and Mel nodded and said, "You see, God was punishing you."

"Bah," Dudley said. "It's just that my procreative system is backing up and toxifying my blood. It needs *spillage.*"

"Stop it," Mel said.

They went out that afternoon to play the coyote game. Mel packed a lunch of apples and peanut-butter-and-jelly sandwiches — bright red strawberry jam spread across the chunky, crumbly slabs of her bread. She put a bottle of beer in each of the packs.

"A picnic," Dudley said. "A picnic at forty fucking below."

"We haven't played it in a long time," Mel said, rolling up five deer hides and putting them in a couple of larger backpacks.

"Not since —" Helen paused, barely able, or not wanting, to count the years. She looked at Matthew and then at Mel, and for a moment saw them as they had been almost twenty years ago, when they had played the game often, and when she had played it with them.

"Come on," Mel said.

"Is it going to hurt?" Old Dudley asked, but he would not be shamed into holding back, or asking more questions. "The coyote game," he muttered, as if he were long familiar with it.

They crossed the creek single-file on snowshoes, with the sky blue above them and the woods shrouded with the night's snow, illumined in gold winter light.

They climbed steadily in switchbacks up the side of the mountain through old fir and spruce, hemlocks and cedars, with Mel breaking trail and Matthew behind her, then Wallis, then Helen. Old Dudley and Helen had to stop often, but they did their best to stay with them. A rattling, fluttering sound came from Helen's chest whenever she caught up, and when Mel asked her if she was all right, Helen couldn't even speak, but waved approval with her hands, told them to go on, go on. Even Dudley, for all his creeping, was huffing and puffing, rivers of sweat coursing down his neck and the tong marks pulsing as hot as anvils.

Mel went higher up the slope, then stopped ahead of them and waited for the hearts of the others to stop fluttering. Old Dudley hawked phlegm and spat. His glasses were fogged over and he wiped them clean. Helen's rattley lungs, the catch and clatter of them, was a sound above all others, but gradually, the rattling slowed, then stopped. The sweat began to chill on them again, and they pushed on.

Another fifteen minutes and now Helen, unable to speak again, was holding on to the back of Matthew's belt, being pulled by him; another fifteen minutes after that, and he was carrying her.

She rode in his arms with dignity. Her thick glasses, always opaque from their sheer density, were even misty from the steam of her efforts.

They reached a meadow after another half-hour of climbing. It was a small, sloping meadow that led to the edge of a short cliff. Mel took a bottle out of her pack and began dousing their ankles with doe urine. Old Dudley started to howl in protest, but Mel told him to *ssshh*. She pulled the hides out of her pack and handed them each one. She hung her pack in a tree. Their breath was coming from their mouths and nostrils in milky clouds. Wallis imagined he saw a reddish tinge to Helen's clouds.

Below them the valley lay flat. The river wound slowly in some places, while in other places it ran straight and fast. They could see the smoke coming from each chimney — they counted thirteen fires — though they couldn't see the chimneys themselves.

It did not seem they could get there again, from where they were. They watched the valley for some time without speaking. It glittered beneath its frost.

"None of you have to be anywhere in a hurry, do you?" Mel asked. She took Dudley's and Wallis's hand and led them into the center of the meadow; Helen and Matthew spread out on their own. "Just make yourself comfortable," Mel said. "Lie down in the snow and carve out a little burrow. Lie down on your stomachs, on all fours, so that only your head's sticking up."

Wallis and Dudley began tunneling into the snow as if they were old hands at it. In less than a minute they had burrowed beneath it. "Okay," Mel whispered. She threw the deer hides over them as if putting children to bed. "Only your eyes showing," she said. She got down in the snow between them and pulled her hide over her.

She didn't do anything for a long time. She let them get settled — she let the silence, and the cold, and the world, seal itself back in over them. There was nothing to do, nothing to hear or feel, other than snow. The tops of their faces were cold where they squinted out at the meadow, but the rest of them was warm. It was not so much a silence, down there in all that snow, as it was the sound of quietness. There were pulses going on — waves, like the beats of a heart — but they were muffled.

Wallis could feel the snow filled with the day's yellow light. He could feel himself resting on that light — the sun's rays penetrating dully two feet below the surface of the snow.

Softly, Mel began to blow on her deer call — a length of what Wallis realized was a deer's esophageal tube. She'd put a flat piece of cedar in it to imitate the deer's tongue. The sound that came out when she blew was a gentle grunting.

They waited. The snow, and the hides above them, trapped and held all of their heat. Wallis felt that he could float there forever. There was yellow light all around him, and icy, subterranean blue light farther below. He wanted to lay his head down and go to sleep and listen to those slow pulsings.

After what might have been fifteen minutes, Mel blew again. Immediately, Wallis heard a tiptoeing through the snow — a snow-crunching sound. A coyote's legs passed in front of him, not five yards away. The coyote circled them twice.

A raven called once from above them — a warning, it seemed, though perhaps it was calling the coyotes to dinner: to the strange, injured deer lying below.

The coyote peered down so that its eyes were level with Wallis's. Wallis could see their amber light, could see the frost on its whiskers. It sniffed once, backed away, then shied over to Mel. The coyote seized Mel's deer hide by the ears, gently at first, and pulled on it, but Mel had hold of the hide with both hands and wouldn't let go. The coyote growled and shook his head, like a puppy. Wallis heard Mel trying to stifle a laugh; heard her blow on her grunt tube again.

Now Helen and Matthew began swimming through the snow toward them, coming up from behind, drawing abreast, and Wallis saw more coyote legs, four and then eight and then twelve, edging in — not entirely sure of their prey, but confident they could take it. Wallis saw their long bushy tails floating behind them, heard them yip with puzzlement and excitement.

One of the coyotes pulled at Wallis's hide and dug furiously at the snow beneath him. Mel snorted with laughter, then cried "Shit!" as one of the coyotes got her hair tangled in its jaws and backed away with a mouthful of her hair.

The coyotes scattered in four directions when she shouted, and Wallis saw that one of them had pulled Helen's hide off and was running with it, dragging it like a kite that would not quite get airborne.

Mel jumped up in a spray of snow, and Matthew did too, throwing back his hide, and Old Dudley and Wallis did the same. They floundered up out of their lairs, and now the coyotes were more terrified than ever — as if, in pulling Helen's hide off, they had pulled some terrible ripcord that had given birth to the humans, and the coyotes tucked their tails and galloped away looking back over their shoulders, streaking back into the woods. It was cruel, Wallis supposed, but he had to laugh at what must have been going through their minds: wondering if that was where humans came from — if they came up through some vent in the earth.

They laughed and shook the snow from their chests and shoulders. Dudley's eyes were bright. "Damn, I liked that," he said. "That was all right." He knocked the snow from his arms. His face was a healthy winter-cheeked red. The pulsings of his tong marks seemed pale and very far away — as if they would never pulse again, and were only old scars. Even Helen's cough was better. She patted her chest, gave one tiny hawking-clear of her throat, but that was it.

"They came right in," Mel said, glancing at the sun. "Sometimes you have to wait a couple of hours, or half a day, or even longer. Sometimes you have to *live* down there, take a canteen and sandwich with you down there, and wait until the ravens land and start hopping around, before the coyotes will get bold enough to come right in," she said. "It's especially nice if it's snowing. The snow mounds up over you."

"Remember the time Matthew and I got Danny?" Helen asked. "We'd been lying there for three hours during hunting season, and had about a foot of snow over us. Danny was out hunting and walked right over us," Helen said. "We stood up and roared. He thought he'd stepped on a bear that had just gone into hibernation," she said.

"Shit his britches, as I remember," Matthew said. "He couldn't speak for a couple of hours."

"I remember," said Mel.

"That was a long time ago," Helen said.

They spread the hides out and sat down on them. Mel handed out sandwiches, and they opened their beers and drank. The clouds were stained with light, a luminous purple and pink and rose red and gold to the east — a bank of them resting on the mountains — and the valley below was illuminated with a slanting shaft of light, so that where the beam landed in the valley's center was gold, while all the woods around that blaze of light were already touched blue with the deepening shadows.

Gray smoke still rose straight from the chimneys below, and they knew that they could go down into any of those cabins and be invited in with warmth, and to food — to whatever food there was.

Mel's hair caught a little of that sun, the last angle of it, and there was an incandescence to it, as when a filament is ignited with electricity. She ate her sandwich thoughtfully. The oddness of that jaw, giving her an almost horsey look, except for her eyes — the steadiness and depth of them, and the greenness — an electrical greenness, almost. Wallis felt pretty sure she was considering the wolves.

Dudley's eyes still had that clearness, an unguardedness to them. He didn't look like Dudley.

They sat and watched the light fade from the valley. When blue dusk had slid down off the hills and covered the valley below with cool shadow, they rose and folded their hides into the pack and buckled on their snowshoes and started back down the mountain in the dimming light. The first stars were out by the time they reached the cabin.

There was no turkey, but Mel went down to the smokehouse and selected the five largest spruce grouse. She sprinkled salt, pepper, and thyme on them, draped bacon over their breasts, and placed them in the wood stove over a pan of water. The cabin had gotten cold while they had been gone. Old Dudley poured Helen a glass of brandy, and she smiled and thanked him. Wallis and Matthew went down to the creek to begin hauling more water for baths.

The creek gurgled into the metal buckets as they lowered them into the cold dark waters. The sudden, frightening suck and surge of the buckets as they quickly filled was a feeling like falling through the bottom of something: ice, perhaps.

A star melted from the sky — sparkled as it fell.

The cabin warmed slowly; the rafters and beams groaned, accepting the heat. Matthew and Wallis stripped to their long underwear shirts and jeans. Old Dudley and Helen sat by the fire, wearing their coats. The first round of water was heated enough for a bath, so Helen went first. She had begun to shiver and cough, even sitting next to the fire, and Matthew had gone and poured the water into the tub for her. Steam billowed out of the bathroom and down the cold hallway as he poured it; Mel gave Helen an elk hide to use for a robe. Dudley filled her brandy glass again and told her to sit in the tub and sip that and she'd never cough again. It was the longest she had been without a cigarette since she was a girl.

Matthew went into the kitchen to be with Mel as she cooked and Wallis found himself alone with Old Dudley, with Dudley's strange gaze fixed upon him.

And as if Old Dudley could see Wallis's thoughts right then, as the deer is said to see the puffs of vapor coming from the cougar's nostrils as the cougar hides in ambush, Old Dudley began to speak to Wallis as if taunting him: speaking about eyes, and about the different ways of seeing. He was talking about his falconry days again — a sure sign, Mel had said, that he was relaxed.

"Curious bastards," he said. "They were always fucking with the neighborhood cats and dogs," he said. "Mel's mother and Mel and I were living out in Odessa — dust bowl country. I was running jug lines for Texaco, for five bucks an hour. Every day when I left for work, this old redtail I had —" Dudley faltered for half a second, started to give them the bird's name, then smiled at the momentary impulse toward sentimentality — "would be sitting on the sidewalk in front of one of the neighbors' houses, on top of some dead heap of fur. Cats, usually, but sometimes small dogs. It would be tearing at the fur and tufts of it would be blowing straight away in that horizontal Odessa wind that was always blowing, morning, noon, and night. I remember that it would put me in a certain frame of *mind*," he said, "driving to work each day, driving to the field, after having seen such a thing."

Mel and Matthew had finished in the kitchen. The food was ready and kept warm on the stove; they were waiting only for Helen, but would not rush her — soon enough, her bath water would grow chilly, and she'd come out — and Mel broke into Old Dudley's story.

"Yeah, and I was the one who had to clean up those damn cats and dogs before the neighbors found them," Mel said. "And sometimes they found out anyway, and would shriek at me. I was the one always taking your heat."

"There were rumors, weren't there?" Dudley murmured, half to himself — rubbing his temple with one hand.

Mel scowled, knowing she was being baited.

"They said we ate them," she told us.

"We were poor, I have to say that," Dudley agreed. "I can see how they might surmise . . ."

"I was not a class favorite," Mel said. "We kept having to move farther and farther out of town to distance ourselves from our neighbors and their supply of cats and dogs. Finally it was just us and the hawks and rabbits living out in the desert — big manic jackrabbits. And dust, and wind."

"Curious bastards," Old Dudley said again. "They've got those huge eyes, set in their tiny heads," he said. "Now you can't quote me on this, but I've always had the notion that they've really got nothing in their brains — and that all their impulses are wired straight from their eyes to their body."

Dudley was leaning forward, setting the bottle of brandy aside and pouring a glass of rum. The years were fading from him; he seemed not a day over fifty, there in the shadows of the fire.

"This I do know for a fact," he said. "What I *do* know for a fact," he explained, "is that they've got these two kinds of eyes, each one of them." He set his drink down, rolled up his sleeves. He pointed to one of his eyes and then the other.

"I don't remember if it's the left eye for one and the right eye for another — I don't remember how it goes," he said. "But one eye they use strictly for hunting — for searching — looking for shit. That eye is totally in command of searching for game. And then the other eye is wired only for the kill. They fly around all their lives like this — two sets of live hot wires leading into their body. They look at *everything* through those two eyes. And when those two wires cross — when they get you in their sights, so that you're suddenly in the focus — then *pow!*" — Dudley smacked his fist in his palm — "it doesn't matter who or what you are, they've got your ass, and you won't be able to get away."

He sat back, pleased with himself, and he allowed himself a tiny sip of rum, as if afraid that too much of it too soon after his story would chase away the warmth that he was feeling.

"Why did you stop?" Wallis asked.

He cocked his head sideways. "Because they couldn't bring me enough," he said. "They'd get tired of killing after only a few flights each day."

Mel rose to begin putting food on the table. "Oh, bullshit, Pop," she said. "He got rich. He stopped walking in the fields after work each evening with his hawks and instead stayed home, and up late at night, mapping his own prospects. Saved his pennies to buy the leases, then went out and sold deals while he was still working for Texaco, quit his job the day they spudded his well, and the rest, as they say, is history. He got enough, all right."

"Did you creep then?" Wallis asked, and perhaps it was some shift of firelight — coals from a log crackled, and a piece of wood fell like a burning bridge — because Dudley looked older again. He looked down at his drink and smiled a bit, as if amused that he was telling the truth. He said, "No, I ran then — like a hound," and finished his drink.

"How many birds did you lose?" Wallis asked.

He grimaced. "Ahh," he said, rubbing his temples and looking around for the bottle, "a shitload. The new ones were always flying away. Sometimes I'd only have one for a few days. They were always leaving," he said. "I couldn't hold on to one for shit. And worst was when I had a good one. I had one, an old bullet-headed goshawk, that I'd had for over a year. I took eight rabbits in an afternoon with that hawk. He was insatiable. But then he left. They all leave," Dudley said, with some surprise, as if he had only now realized it; as if all this time he had been thinking of each leave-taking as coincidental, not connected to any pattern or law or certainty.

He cleared his reverie then — shook his head as a bull might after having been foiled by some false pass at a red flag, and now he was his age once more; and where he had come from, and all that past, was far below once more — so far as to seem to have no bearing on the here and now, on this cold night-after-Christmas. "That's all over now, anyway," he said, and rose, looking for a new bottle.

"Supper," Mel said. She was smiling, and Wallis suspected that with the exception of a very few, perhaps, it was possible she had everyone she cared about corralled into her cabin that night, with the great shell of winter acting as a barrier for her — almost as if she'd herded or trapped them.

"The water's got to be getting cold by now," Matthew said. "Maybe you should go check on Helen?"

"I hate to rush her," Mel said. "We'll wait just a minute more."

They sat in silence and listened for the slightest noise that might give them a clue she was finishing. The swollen moon out the window looked injured — flattened by some distortion of the cold night air. It rose through the tops of the fir trees on the south ridge — chasing the winter-short sun — and they watched it for a while, smelled the food, listened to their stomachs grumble, waited on Helen, and anticipated the meal.

In the new, crooked light of the moon, they saw the large dark shape of an animal moving around in the yard.

They rose and went to the window. It was a moose drifting slowly by — not feeding, only passing through, just beyond where the weak yellow window light fell on the snow.

Something sparkled in the moonlight — something in the moose's ribs moved up and down with the moose's movements. It was long and metallic. As his eyes adjusted to the night, Wallis thought it looked like a knitting needle, but then understood that it was an aluminum arrow.

"That's an old one," Mel said. "See how there's no blood on its side, and no steam coming from the wound? I've been seeing her for four years now. The arrow must have hit a rib and gotten bent in there sideways, maybe just inches from her heart. And now all this scar tissue's built up around it and holds the arrow into place. She's as good as new. The scar tissue's probably stronger than the muscle it cut. I see her every year," she said. "I'm glad she's still okay."

The moose walked off into the trees — disappeared into the branchy whispers of fir, pine, and spruce, fitting back into the woods like an arrow passing between two ribs. A mist of snow trickled from one of the branches where the moose had gone — it caught the moonlight and glittered as it fell — and then there was no sign. The woods sealed back in around her.

"Helen must be asleep," Mel said. "I'll fix her some coffee. Then we'll eat."

Mel put the food back on the stove to heat again. The grouse sweated beads of fat-juice. Wallis was so hungry that if no one else had been in the room, he would have started gnawing on the bird.

Mel took a cup of coffee in to Helen.

They heard Mel knock on the door; heard her open it and ease inside. There was a long silence, and then they heard Helen hack and cough, a sound like a generator being started up — and then there were the quiet, unintelligible murmurs of the two women — an exclamation of surprise and a thank you — more hacking, as Helen came slowly back into the world — and Wallis wondered then, and marveled at, the fine line between living and dying — and at what point the process began.

Mel went to the kitchen and got the food to put on the table, and the others followed her. Wallis was a little surprised by the pleasure she took in the ceremony and ritual of tradition. She lit more candles, arranged the plates, straightened a placemat. The bone-handled knives glinted in the candlelight.

"She was sound asleep," Mel said, in quiet wonder. "She was dozing with just her head above water, and there was a skim of ice, the littlest bit of it, forming around the edges of the tub."

"She must really have needed to sleep," Matthew said.

"Careful what you ask for," Mel said.

Helen came into the room, dressed and wrapped in the elk hide, her face the blue-white color of someone who'd drowned. She stood by the fire for only a few seconds before Mel shepherded her and the others to the table. They took their seats, and Wallis thought for a moment that Mel was going to say a prayer. She bowed her head but didn't speak, and then Matthew reached across the table for a grouse.

Crumbs from the fresh-baked rolls fell to the floor; knives and forks clashed like swords. They drank wine, finished bottle after bottle until it was gone, and then Old Dudley stood up and said that they had to leave.

A look like anger crossed Mel's face but she said nothing. Helen said, "Please, no," but Dudley gave no sign of having heard her.

They dressed warmly and Matthew hugged Helen good-bye. Helen was too tired and cold to follow them into town. She stayed in the cabin while the four of them skied off to find people to help them dig out the limousine.

They gathered several recruits from the bar — Amy among them — and went knocking door to door as well, passing from cabin to cabin, reasoning that those who had not been in the bar drinking all day might be more stout of back. It was a little after ten o'clock when the procession, with lanterns and torches, arrived at the spot where the limousine had sunk through the snow. The moon seemed to be pouring down a coldness upon the land and the skin of the snow had stretched taut enough again so that it was possible, though not probable, that they might be able to drive out again. Their old tracks had already vanished. Wallis didn't think they could do it.

They'd brought shovels and saws and chains and horses and come-alongs, and they built fires to warm their hands. Matthew began digging at the snow; soon he carved out a tunnel that went beneath the car. He disappeared beneath the ice and others handed flat rocks down to him to place beneath the wheels, rocks gotten from the disassembling of his wall. Other workers were busy cutting poles and laying them beneath the wheels.

Dudley stood wrapped in a fur robe, watching it all. They kept laying flat rocks, disassembling a section of Matthew's wall, trying to build a small road up from out of the snow pit and back up onto the frozen ice. The light from the lanterns, and from the warming fires, cast a pulsing light on Dudley, so that he seemed to somehow be a part of the flames, as the light of those fires washed across him.

Old Dudley noticed Amy on the other side of the road and crossed over to see her. She began moving away from him, and he followed. She began walking in large circles around the car, not wishing to talk to him, but still he followed, until soon she was trotting, and he was running after her. Colter had not come with her — he was back at their cabin, skinning the pelts of the martens he'd caught that day. After a while Amy slowed to a walk, tired from running, and Dudley slowed to a walk also, still following her around and around; but finally she stopped, and Dudley stopped next to her.

Amy was breathing hard, like a deer chased by hounds. Bright silver plumes of crystalline breath rose from her nostrils. He said something to her that no one could hear and she turned from him and started walking away again, almost trotting once more; and once again, he followed.

Matthew managed to get deeper beneath the car, and he finally got the jack from the car's trunk beneath one of the wheels. He began winding it up, but the car wouldn't rise high enough to crack out of its ice shell. Mel borrowed one of the chain saws and began cutting slabs of ice away from the sides. Sparks flew from the guide bar as the chain brushed metal from time to time, friction that flowered into orange light and scattered across the snow like stars spilled. The woods were dense with the smell of smoke from the chain saws, busy with the noise of the workers.

Men began hitching their horses to the bumper as Mel cleared enough space in the snow for them to do so — in his eagerness, one man stepped in too close as Mel was turning away, so that the still-revving blade of her saw caught his pants leg up around the thigh and tore a quick rip in it, exposing bare skin — "Careful!" Mel cried — and the lookers-on standing by the fires passed around a bottle and offered advice to the diggers.

The horses were hooked to their chains and ropes and turned to look back at the load they would be pulling. Only the roof of the limousine was visible. It seemed to Wallis that the horses were eyeing the burden with dispassionate confidence.

Mel was on top of the entombed car, cutting the ice and snow cakes from it with her saw. Chips of ice sprayed her and the others in a firelit shower, caked against their faces and brows. From time to time Mel would straighten up to rest her back, with the saw still idling, and would brush her hair back from her face. When she bent back down to address the ice, the tip of the blade occasionally caught the submerged roof of the car and threw brilliant glowing embers of burning metal into the sky.

Matthew emerged from beneath the ground like a snow ghost and announced that he thought it was as ready as it would ever be. Old Dudley left Amy then — "Until the spring, adieu!" he cried — and came over and stood at the edge of the crevice and looked down upon the car. Backlit by the fire and shrouded in the heavy robe like a trench coat, he looked as if he were presiding over a burial, not a birth, and yet a burial for which there was good cheer.

Old Dudley and Matthew shook hands with Wallis. "You should come with us," Dudley said. "I've changed my mind about your staying."

Wallis studied him for a moment, then surprised himself by saying no — and Dudley, also surprised, squinted to look into Wallis's eyes to read him — but in the dim light, he could not be sure what he saw. "You should come with us," Dudley said again, but again Wallis said no, and Dudley smiled then and pretended that he wasn't bothered by it. He reached out and shook Wallis's hand again.

Mel shut the chain saw off, and she set it down and hugged Matthew a long time, but did not kiss him good-bye — only leaned into him — and then she held Dudley for a moment as well, circled her arms around him as if trying to cast a child's spell over him, some futile spell, to make him stop being the way he was.

She turned to Matthew again, who was still shrouded in snow. She took her gloves off and with her thumbs wiped the crust away from his eyebrows, then his cheeks and mouth, as if sculpting him back into who he was, or had been. Now finally she kissed him, leaned forward and took his face in both hands and kissed him as if releasing him forever. Matthew glanced back at Wallis one more time, and then he and Old Dudley climbed down into the snow crevice and in through the open windows, rolled the windows up, and started the car.

The limousine was still down in a hole, but the way out was now clear. Everyone gathered around and began to push, and Matthew, driving, revved the engine — the tires spun uselessly on their ice peels — but the horses, pulling from the other end, in combination with the shoves of the people, finally got the car moving. It groaned up from out of the pit and cracked free of its ice grip with a sound like a plate of glass breaking. The horses dragged it, skidding and bumping, sliding sideways, up onto the makeshift rock road that had been built, where the wheels found purchase; but still the horses kept pulling, breaking into a gallop now, in the spirit of the challenge, and the people kept pushing too, running down the road as if hurling the car from them.

They muscled the car all the way out to the main road in this manner — from time to time Matthew would gun the accelerator, but for the most part it was the pushing of the people and the pulling of the animals that kept the car going — he and Old Dudley were pitching around inside like tourists in a barrel going over some falls — and finally when the laborers had reached the main road, panting and sweating, covered with snow, they unhitched the horses. Matthew and Old Dudley drove away, drove north across the frozen snow, once more only guessing where the road lay beneath them — driving fast, slipping and sliding, knowing that they had to be out of the valley before the sun rose and softened the snow.

The crowd watched the taillights recede into the heart of winter.

Everyone trudged back in silence to where the fire had burned to low coals and was hissing in the puddling water, and where the abandoned lanterns cast melting scallop-shapes in the snow around them. The maw where the car had been looked like the gap left when a tooth is pulled. They all felt as if Dudley had somehow gotten away with something of theirs, but could not pin the feeling down with any specificity.

People gathered their lanterns and dogs, then soothed and haltered their sweating horses. They headed home quietly — sleepy and calm: holding the memory already of their night's work. They walked home together, still a community — and the woods absorbed it all, and slid back in over the people's night passage. Wallis, for one, could already feel things healing — the events of the night — almost as soon as he was aware that there had been injury, or disturbance.

Mel picked up the chain saw. She studied the wall where they had dissembled it to patch the road. In a single night, it had been worn down to ground level — twenty years of history laid flat.

She and Wallis snapped on their skis and headed home.

Now Mel would be going back to the wolves. Where else was there? She skied hard, even going uphill, kicking the tails of her skis out in her speed.

Exhausted when they arrived at the cabin, yet filthy again, Wallis hauled more water for baths. It had begun to snow lightly, and Wallis wondered what it must be like for Dudley and Matthew to be driving together through the roadless landscape, across so much snow, and with more of it coming down.

Mel bathed first. Wallis sat by the icy creek down by the smokehouse and let the snow cover him for a while. He looked back up at the cabin, and against the steamed yellow glow of the bathroom window's lantern light, he could see the silhouette of Mel drying off. The snow landed on his face and in the creek, disappearing when it landed in the water. He could feel the smokehouse's groaning cold behind him — the grouse and trout laid out in a line like soldiers, a regiment waiting to be consumed. He watched Mel dry her hair — elbows everywhere, shapeless form in the window light, floating in the woods on the side of the mountain. He saw her leave the bathroom then, and he waited for her to dress, then went up the hill with another bucket of water in each hand. Blue smoke streamed from the twin chimneys, rising to join the falling snow, and trees in the forest began to explode again, filling the night with the scent of fresh sap. Despite the beauty, he felt that he had been above ground far too long, and that it was time to dive again.

Before daylight, the icicles hanging from their roof lengthened as the escaping heat from the cabin melted them into drips, which froze again in the night. The icicles had been a foot long in November, then stretched to two feet; now they completed their descent, dripping all the way to the ground before freezing again, so that Wallis and Mel were imprisoned as if within an ice tomb.

The full moon appeared over Waper Ridge and struck their ice cage, the icicles as thick as a man's wrist, so that the ice was filled and then illuminated with that moon, as if they were in a glowing womb. Wallis and Mel, each in their separate rooms, awakened, feeling something different about the cabin, and they looked out at that blue light but felt no sense of alarm, only wonder, and in the morning, at dawn, after the moon had passed on, but with the stars still burning, they went out onto the porch and with ax and maul smashed their way through those ice bars and back into the cold winter air.

THEY FELL IN LOVE THE WAY ROUGHLY HALF THE WORLD does: not all at once, as if through a trap door, but gradually, through the incremental doings-of-things both together and alone — fitting and reshaping, settling into a newer place; and in their caution and deliberation, it could not be argued that they did not know what they were doing. There was not the excuse of innocence. Even though they understood what was happening, they would have been — and were — the last ones to call it love. They understood that it was the direction they were heading, but they told themselves they were not even ankle-deep in it; and then only ankle-deep, and then only calf-deep. As if it were a way of being that they could step back out of at any time.

Mel continued to do what she had set out to do twenty years ago with enthusiasm: to gather and accumulate the data — the paths and trails of the wolves — and to weave that data together; or rather, to uncover the pattern that was already weaving itself. Some days it was a wonderful feeling, though other days she longed for the time when there had been more mystery — when she had been unencumbered by the knowledge of where the wolves were likely to be — what they would be hunting, and even — from a sense she could now pick up from the woods themselves — what the pack's mood might be, on a certain day.

Still, the wolves amazed her now, even as she entered trail after trail into her journal, and layer after layer onto the maps of years. The generations of them stayed almost invariably the same — ever playful, ever fierce and determined, ferocious when need be, with enough unpredictability to always force her to never assume anything, despite the increasing burden of her knowledge. One day she found where they had somehow caught and killed and eaten a raven, who was supposed to be their partner in the hunt — their co-navigator toward distant game downwind, and the caller of alarms when danger approached: a thing as close to a friend as was possible, outside the confines of the pack.

Another time, for an entire year, there was an individual within the pack who hunted with them, but who always stayed on the other side of the river — following the rest of the pack and vocalizing with them, and hazing game toward them, but who, to the best of Mel's knowledge, remained always across the river from them, trailing them like a shadow, but never joining in on the feast afterward. Mel never saw this wolf; she never found its body. Perhaps it drowned, trying to cross the river one day — or perhaps it was simply an outcast for that one year, and rejoined the pack in subsequent years.

Mostly, it was her own self that was ceasing to amaze her. It was her own habits and continuity that she knew increasingly too well. Some nights she wanted to shriek.

She knew, or believed, she was going to follow the wolves backward until she died. And then either someone would take her place, and her sixty years of data, and add their own sixty years to it, or not. If her work were abandoned, her own studies would become isolated, and would dissolve, or be buried and forgotten, or never known.

And the wolves would keep hunting. As long as there was wild country in which they could travel great distances, they would keep being wolves, whether people knew their habits or not.

They needed wild country; they needed deer, elk, moose. And the forest needed them. Perhaps it was that simple. Maybe nothing else was required but a largeness of the country. There were too many days now when Mel doubted her work — not its integrity, but its value. What did it matter to anyone but herself how the wolves worked, or even how the woods worked?

It was a feeling like being buried alive: the insignificance of her work.

What about teaching? she wondered. There's a thing that matters. Maybe I should try and become a teacher.

She dreamed of being buried alive: the taste of the loose dirt in her mouth, dirt filling her lungs, and her sinking into the earth. Her moans awakening Wallis.

The wolves had moved to the far corner of the valley, but some nights their howls could be heard, even from that distance: and so faint, so far away, were the howls that they did not sound like howls, but like breathing sounds, or tiny groans from the next room; and sometimes Wallis would have to lie still and hold his breath to be sure they were howls, and not the heavy pulsings of his own blood: imagined sounds just outside the range of hearing. He would often be unable to sleep, wondering whether he was hearing them or not, and he would go out on the porch and wrap himself in hides and look up at the stars and listen, so that he could hear them more clearly, though they were still distant, as if it were the stars themselves that were howling.

He hauled wood and water for Mel while she was gone to those far corners. In the evenings she cooked for him — enjoyed having someone to cook for. She watched him inflating with muscle from the wood splitting and water carrying, and from all the good meat — watched him as if he were in some steady metamorphosis: returning, it seemed, the body or form of Matthew to the valley, though surely not his person or personality. Wallis was as deliberate, as precise, as an old man.

They discussed books. Mel could remember the specific passages from all the books she'd read. Wallis could remember only the varying degrees of pleasure each book gave him, and consistently forgot the details — though still, they managed to converse at length about books they had both read, or which only one of them had read, so that in all ways it was as if they were speaking two slightly different languages. But it brought them closer to each other, even in the midst of all that caution. Great expanses of time substituted for intensity. As if they had nothing but time.

She began reading to him at night after she had bathed, and as he lay in the shallow tub of new hot water: reading to him from the other side of the door, trying to catch him up on a lifetime's worth of her favorite poems, essays, stories, novels. She read to him deep into the night. Sometimes he would lie there until the water grew cold, and the pleasure was hers as much as it was his. They grew used to the sounds of each other's voices, and to each other's silences.

Wallis started over with the maps, too isolated to feel shamed by his failure. And in the beginning, what had he had to work with, anyway — a piece of paper, a pencil, and a few handfuls of dirt?

He took the rocks that had spilled from the pockets of Matthew's coveralls and studied them, dreamed stories for them. He studied anew the perceived slants and casts of the snow-clad mountain walls, but understood now that had nothing to do with the way things were structured at depth.

He constructed and reconstructed the lands below solely from his imagination: paying no attention to the snowy landscape on the surface. He pretended that he was right, and then he believed it. In the end he knew he might as well be mapping the contours of his own brain.

He mapped at five-hundred-foot intervals: starting a few hundred feet below the surface, and then descending — spending several days on each map. He kept the maps, when he was finished with them, rolled tightly within each other, like layers of onionskin. The paper was thin, so that when he held the maps up to the window in daylight, one map placed atop another placed atop another, he could see the transformations of time — the landscapes melting and reforming in places; could see certain features — ridges and knolls and mountains — shifting and sagging across the map, as if they had become fluid.

The knowledge was itself a kind of creation. It stirred chemicals in his blood, made his blood sparkle: almost carbonated. Wallis didn't mind the winter-short days, nor was he consciously aware of their subtle attenuation, now that the solstice had passed.

He kept carving away old rock, old dirt — brushing it away from each new surface like the leavings of eraser crumbs, and he could understand how a lifetime of such work — ten million worlds drawn, crafted, discovered, built — could either make a man exceedingly humble, or could make him believe he was nothing less than God. It seemed like an awful temptation to place in the hands of a man or woman; but he could not turn away. Even in his dreams — while Mel sleep-moaned in the next room — Wallis's hand was moving across the paper, half the time discovering secrets, half the time creating them.

He read more in the boy Dudley's journal:

Gaseous Sunlight
Natural Gas — Its Wonders, Its Geology
  The history of the search for native oil is romantic. Known for ages, it remained for a long time a mere curiosity. Even in America, where popular intelligence of a superior nature is supposed to utilize every possible advantage, petroleum rose only to the importance of a quack remedy for aches and other evils. But suddenly it assumed the scepter of king. It ruled the plans and lives of thousands; it sent men, many of them the most utter of numbnuts, blindly and stupidly in herds to the forks of streams in search of imaginary "ranges" and fanciful "oil belts." The smell of petroleum was a craze.
  Men pursued it with the sound and fury of dogs on the track of their prey. They lost their power of reasoning on the subject. They could not be convinced that mineral oil is a geological product, fixed in its relations to the earth and to the strata as unchangeably and intelligibly as iron or salt. They would not listen to the counsel of science. Every man was confident in his self-wisdom, and never inquired of true experts on what grounds he believed and acted as he did.
  Repudiating the advice of those whose special business it was to know something on the subject, they preferred the dictates of their own ignorance. They went by the scent of the stuff; they were led by the nose; they put their money in the ground with the assurance of infallibility — and many of them have lost it there, as the souvenir of a happy intoxication. There was oil — millions of barrels of it; and many investors were fortunate if not wise; and many, though wise, were not fortunate.
  It was a new situation. It must be confessed that geologists took up the subject as novices. Many, however, who advertised themselves as geologists, were pretenders and quacks. Recognized by the undiscriminating as geologists, possessing equal authority with scientific men who had earned reputations among their peers, these geological quacks

brought discredit on science, and justified, to some extent, the contempt of practical men such as myself, who appreciate certain conclusions, but spurn the illogical reasoning that leads to them.

Now, some of the scientific principles which must hold true without any regard to the particular causes and conditions of oil accumulation, are such as these:

1. Oil is not a direct deposit from the sea; it is the product of some changes in substances that became trapped in the ocean's sediments.

2. Being composed of carbon, hydrogen, and oxygen, it must have originated from organic substances.

3. Being lighter than water, it must tend to rise through the water that saturates almost all rocks, instead of sinking. The source of the oil, therefore, can never be in any formation situated at a higher level than the place of the oil. This is a principle which the crazy crowd can never be taught.

4. A good "surface show" is not favorable, since it is only caused by the escape and waste of the oil; while the thing wanted is an accumulation or retention of oil — that is, an absence of surface show. This the contemners of scientific guidance could not understand.

5. There must consequently be an overlying stratum that is impervious to oil, to prevent the product from rising to the surface, to be wasted in a "surface show." If a fissure even passes through this, the oil will escape. A bed of clay or compact shale might serve as such a cover. Compact limestone might serve; but most limestones are too shattered. Indeed, shattered limestones, in some cases, serve as reservoirs for the accumulation.

6. The accumulation of oil must be determined, among other things, by the attitudes of the strata. The trends of "oil territory" must conform to the trends of underground formations. But the situations of creeks at the surface might have no bearing on the underground distribution of petroleum. The junction of two streams and the location of a sand flat might sustain no relation whatsoever to strata three or four hundred feet farther below.

All of these principles have been disregarded by a majority of the "oil prospectors." Some men under pay from capitalists even resorted to the witch-hazel fork in quest of knowledge on which capital might venture investment.

It is generally admitted that the porous stratum in which oil accumulates must have an arched or anticlinal form. Otherwise the oil will spread laterally to an indefinite distance, and no local accumulation will take place. On the contrary, the oil will somewhere find an outlet to the surface, and be lost. It must be trapped and controlled by the earth to retain its power.

The escape of burning gas from the earth has been observed for ages. It has long been utilized in some mines where it escapes through crevices. In a similar way, it enters coal mines, and is known to miners as fire damp, since, mixed with a certain proportion of atmospheric air, it becomes violently explosive. The Chinese have for centuries employed natural gas for lighting and heating. In Kentucky, gas accumulates in underground reservoirs, and the elastic pressure is sometimes attended by explosions, constituting earthquakes of local extent and lending some plausibility to the ancient theory of those phenomena. At Fredonia, New York, are gas emissions that have attracted attention for many years, and have long been utilized for lighting and heating. A gas spring was discovered there in 1821. The gas at that time accumulated was used for lighting a mill and several stores. It was also introduced into a few public buildings, and was brought to the attention of General Lafayette when he passed through the village in 1824. Subsequently, a shaft was sunk, and sufficient gas concentrated to supply thirty burners. In 1858, two thousand cubic feet of gas were delivered daily through the village. But in 1860, the entire village blew up.

In my seventeenth year, during my frequent and unexcused absences from "The Home," I traveled to New York by rail to hie into the wilderness and search for traces and remnants of this spectacle. Imagine my pleasure, to a large degree almost sexual, when I discovered not only scraps of that decimated village, but that in the near vicinity there was still ongoing drilling activity, only sixty years later, as if the workings and desires of man were as mindless as those of ants: laborers probing still to reach into the same reservoirs that had so resolutely destroyed their predecessors.

I stayed there two weeks during the drilling of one of these wells. Other pump jacks were already in activity all around the reconstructed village, which had foolishly been given the same name as the previous hamlet.

During the drilling of the well — accomplished via a great pounding and sledging of the earth, which made the very skin of the ground tremble, and which excited me greatly — a stream of salty brine was *intercepted at about six hundred feet, and then another immense reservoir of gas was struck. The gas ejected the old ocean with great violence.*

It was harsh winter-time, and the water soon covered the derrick with ice, forming a glistening frozen chimney sixty feet in height. Through this the water was thrown, at intervals of about one minute, to double that height. After that came another great rush of gas, which continued until the pressure below was relieved, when the water once more began to accumulate, and was again ejected. When the derrick was covered with ice, the gas escaping from the well was frequently ignited, and the effect, especially at night, of this fountain of mingled fire and water, shooting up to the height of one hundred and twenty feet, through a great transparent and illuminated ice chimney, was indescribably magnificent.

I next visited the site in 1917. A two-inch gas pipe had been fixed in the orifice of the well, and the gas was still escaping with a power and volume that were startling. The sound could be heard for a mile. The pressure was two hundred and sixty-two pounds to the square inch, as reported by Mr. Peter Neff. The ignited jet formed a flame twenty feet in length, as large around as a hogshead. The supply of gas here was sufficient to illuminate a large city. Imagine a volcano.

Ten years afterward, personal information from Mr. Neff assured me that these wells continued to "blow," and from the gas he was manufacturing a refined quality of lampblack.

More wells were drilled; more subterranean writhings, resistance, turmoil encountered. In 1918 a well eight miles southeast of the new village, at the depth of one hundred and fifty feet, reached confined gas which threw tools into the air. It is said that much sand escaped, and a stone weighting "several" pounds was thrown over a barn "forty rods distant." That well was subsequently filled with cement, after the high pressure of the gas had subsided.

In 1919, at a place five miles northeast of the same doomed village, a well bored one hundred feet deep secured a supply of gas which was used thereafter for many years for illuminating purposes, rendering a quaint gaslight appearance upon the whole community of an evening. Subsequent powerful explosions south of the village however revealed the uncovering of other uncontrollable gas reservoirs in 1920. Religious proctors believed that hell had opened up and that the end of the world was two days nigh.

After burning wild for two years and scorching everything in a half-

mile radius to pure black, the earth's internal hell fire subsided enough that two relief wells were able to be probed at its flanks, though now the pernicious flames leapt uncontrolled from those fissures as well, so that the united illumination rendered newspaper print visible at night in town, even at the distance of three miles.

Eventually the wells began to hurl fresh water rather than fire into the sky, and in this manner extinguished themselves, converting the surrounding landscape to a horrific sodden paste of ash and mud, though two years later there grew across that mile's expanse the most vibrant field of emerald-colored grass, calm and level and serene, obscuring completely all traces of the terror of the year before, save for the slightest hint of sulphur.

Four miles west of town, in a copse known as Crab Orchard, a burning spring later appeared, unsolicited and unsummoned. This fresh-water spring is in a constant state of ebullition from the escape of its gas. The water is sweet to drink but the odor of the gas riding above the water's surface is hot and fetid, like the tongue-breath of some horrid monster hovering hidden over the source of the spring.

"Regularly every day," reported the late J. F. Henry, "between four and five o'clock in the afternoon, the spring overflows; a large quantity of gas is liberated, and, as if struck by the sparks of friction of some revolving gear- and cog-works below, self-ignites, with the resultant flames spewing merrily and untended for between four and five hours, on into the night, before fading. In winter, wild animals — deer and rabbits — sometimes gather around the flames for warmth, where hunters will hide in wait and then ambush them as these denizens warm themselves before the fires. Many such hunter encampments are situated around the burning spring, and the hunters will clean the animals and cook them over the very flames which moments before had provided pleasure and warmth."

Year and year again I returned to New Fredonia, learning what I could of the earth's trade. Standing on one prominent ridge top, I could see, on a dark night, the lights from all the various wells being flared, in addition to the burning spring, as well as the rogue fire-tongues of explosions where the earth was splitting and rupturing open unbidden. Well after well, roarers and gushers — elegant tongues of flame throughout the forest, and patchy brush fires burning here and there, so that I very much could have been gazing, from safe vantage, down into one of the suffering villages of hell.

One well in particular, visible to the south, was the most remarkable. It furnished light and fuel to all the vicinity, including the adjacent village of Saint Joe. It was situated in a valley surrounded by high mountains, which reflected and concentrated the light of the ignited gas flares. Many conduits started from the well; one led the gas directly to the cylinder of a strong motor, which, by its pressure, acquired a prodigious velocity. Another pipe fed a flame capable of reducing, it is said, as much iron ore as half the furnaces of Pittsburgh. This motor however drove nothing, merely spun and roared as if for exhibition, or like a caged animal trapped above earth's surface.

Fire to steel! I wanted into this power as much as I have ever wanted to foist between any woman's two legs.

I perceive that the world will split open in the coming years because of this: that mankind will blossom like some wonderful scented rose. It is not possible to imagine how sated our desires may be fulfilled with this luxury, nor the consequences to our character: only that good times, and peace, and a deeper and further integrity await us.

Unfortunately, Fredonia is no more. There were for a while ten iron and steel mills in the vicinity using the gas in their puddling furnaces and under their boilers; a dozen more were making arrangements for its introduction, and many other manufacturing firms had begun laying lines into the fissure. There were six glass-blowing factories in the vicinity, and every brewer in the county was tied in to the lines. Two of the largest hotels used it exclusively for cooking purposes. For general purposes, the town of Fredonia, until it burned and vanished to char and reek, had no rival for cheapness, cleanliness, modernity, and convenience of application.

Once more however the reservoirs, once cracked into, ruptured openly thereafter and swallowed in fire all traces of the town. A wilderness stands there now: tangles of briar and maple, jack pine and currant bush. Peace atop, though bilious gas even now lurks beneath its skin.

Until this golden dawn at which we now stand, our modern forests have been the chief producers of fuel in human times, via firewood. Now another tree need never be cut, save for an occasional home, should our country desire to expand, each according to our own biological imperatives to breed.

The sea supports a vast amount of vegetation; but we have not learned how to apply it to the production of heat. Strange as it seems, the

sea weeds that waved their graceful fronds in the oceans of millions of
years ago are smelting the iron for the pipes destined to bring their
transformed constituents to the sites of gigantic industries and warming
the dwellings of the populations which conduct them. Seaweed to iron;
man to God.

Will these marvelous supplies hold out? That is the question which
the owners of the millions invested are anxiously asking. Probably, as
had been proved with petroleum, particular wells will gradually dimin-
ish in supply; many will cease to yield; some will continue indefinitely.
But probably also new supplies will be discovered, and increasing de-
mands will be met for many years in the future. I, and a few others like
me, will not be denied.

•

Once again Wallis was troubled by the difficulty he had separating the
knowledge he was gaining of the buried earth, in reading the old journals, from the knowledge he was gaining about Old Dudley. "What
'home?'" he asked Mel one night. "It says here he was in a 'home.' I
thought he grew up with his parents."

"Well, there was some trouble when he was a little older," Mel said.

"At what age?" Wallis asked. "Fourteen, fifteen? Wait, let me guess
— when his testicles dropped?"

Mel smiled, but only slightly. "It wasn't real good." That was all she
would say.

They weren't sleeping with each other, weren't touching each other —
but they were traveling nonetheless into that country, as if laying down
stones for the crossing of a shallow river. Mel thought ahead to the days
when they might be across that river, and holding each other, and
loving. She was in no real hurry to get there, and she kept looking
back, too — but in her mind, sometimes she was already in the shallows with Wallis, the two of them laying down flat rocks for a crossing
— working seemingly without purpose or goal: working only in the
moment, is how Mel imagined it, with the sun warm on their backs, and
the sound of riffling water, and the lulling sound of stones clacking
together.

She followed the wolves backward — continuing to try to keep her
heart light, and to resurrect wonder each day; and each time, once she

was in the woods, the wonder returned. It was only in the winter stillness in bed at night that she questioned her worth, her life. Some nights she would wonder if the dissettlement was about children versus no children; but she had come to the conclusion that that wasn't the source; that it was deeper, simpler: that the brightness of her solitude was simply losing its luster. That the distance between being alone versus lonely was narrowing. That the line might even have already been crossed somewhere further back, unbeknownst to her.

The alpha male and female were pair bonding — beginning their preliminary courtship. She examined their scent markings. There was not yet blood in the female's urine, but the weave of their trails was beginning to travel closer together.

Some afternoons she would tire of following the tracks — following them in the wrong direction, is what it felt like, and knowing so well the story she would find at day's end: the tangled, picked-clean bones of yet another deer — and instead she would sit for hours at a time, sometimes making small wreaths from the wind-broken boughs and branches of fir, cedar, hemlock, and spruce — spending a whole afternoon weaving such a creation, only to hang it in a tree twenty miles from the nearest human. Other times she would sit and rest as if waiting for a thing to catch up, though she would feel confused, not knowing for certain whether that thing was behind her, or in front.

Never before had she been unsure of anything in the woods.

They went to the bar together more often, as winter sank deeper and the snows piled higher. People noticed their new comfort with each other — the friendship — but only Helen was made wary by it. The others seemed to accept the change as they would another cycle of the seasons. Those who bothered to consider the friendship understood that even if romance blossomed, Matthew would return, and he would win Mel back when he came.

Most of them, however, gave it no thought. Matthew was in Houston, as incapable of being betrayed as story or legend.

Wallis was settling in, however, as if building a nest. He studied the pictures on the wall, in the bar; he listened, asked questions. He felt the grain of forest growing slowly around him, even in winter. He listened to stories being told, and when he went back home, it felt as if those stories were walls — that a structure was being built with them — a thing which might contain him, then alter him.

One late night — New Year's Eve, though Mel and Wallis hadn't known that when they set out on skis for the bar — long after most everyone had gone home or had passed out in front of the stove, curled up with elk and deer hides wrapped around them — Wallis asked Artie how he ended up in the valley.

Artie looked surprised, then slightly confused. Though he was only in his late forties, it had been so long ago that he viewed that other time as he would another person or another life — as if it were in no way any longer connected to him.

"I had a good job in Oklahoma, as a sheriff's deputy, but then my wife left me — went off with another man — a fella I had arrested on a number of occasions. They took my two kids with 'em, took my car, money, dogs. I figured I was going to go crazy — that I'd either turn to drinking, or drugs, or some kind of lowlife — and so I just ran." He smiled sadly. "Man, I was angry," he said, shaking his head. "You can't believe how angry I was. I just took off running, to keep from hurting myself or anyone else.

"I came over the pass here in late August. It was like some kind of religious experience. I felt everything else just fall away." Artie's eyes teared now, and he brushed at his eyes, surprised by the emotion. "I don't know why. Man, it felt good." He stared at his beer glass. "That was a long time ago," he said.

"You drink now," Wallis noted — as if Artie were perhaps not aware of it — and Artie smiled.

"Yeah, I drink a *lot*. But I drink because I'm happy," he said. "Not because I'm sad or angry, or because I have to. I could quit at any time."

There was a silence after that, in which they could all hear the ragged chorus of snores, dog and human, coming from near the stove. The fire shifted, collapsed on itself within, then flamed anew, nourished by the stir of oxygen.

"I didn't know you had any children," Mel said.

"It was a long time ago," Artie said. "I haven't seen them since last I heard they were living in Kansas. Their mama moved back to Georgia to be with her folks. Shit, I guess she's getting pretty close to being an old woman now. Her old mama and daddy might not even be alive anymore."

"How old are your children?" Mel asked.

Artie looked up at the ceiling and tried to do the math. "Twenty-five? No, close to thirty, I guess. Still kids, anyway," he said.

"What about you, Charlie?" Wallis asked. The big man had been sitting quietly, his pale, hammy arms crossed over his chest, listening.

He shrugged. "It was different for me," he said. "I just came. But it was like Artie says: the minute I saw the valley, I felt something different. It was like something stopped inside me and got real still." And that was all he had to say on it.

Party favors — tinsel hats, noisemakers, confetti — lay scattered on the floor. Mel had had her one beer early in the evening, but then had allowed herself a glass of champagne, which rested before her half-full, though void of fizz.

Amy had been knitting all evening — sitting quietly during the music and dancing, knitting ceaselessly on a baby blanket, though no babies were known to be expected or imminent — but now she said to Mel, "He says that he is going to join the church — that he wants to join my church."

At first Mel did not know who Amy was talking about — she thought perhaps she meant Charlie — but then she understood.

"Oh, Amy," she said, "I don't think so." She almost reached out to pat Amy's hand. "Sometimes he just says things like that. Mother wanted him to go to church when I was growing up, and he never would. He —" Mel paused. "I don't think I'd count on it."

Amy picked up her knitting again. "I'm going to hold him to it," she said calmly.

"What lies to the north?" Colter asked Mel. He had fallen asleep during the adults' discussions, but was awake now. He asked it like a riddle. "What's over the mountains?" he asked her. "How far north and west would you have to go to see salmon again?"

Mel considered this, much as Artie had tried to recall the ages of his children. "Several hundred miles," she said. "Five, maybe six hundred. Are you thinking of taking a trip?"

"I want to see salmon," Colter said. "They were here when my father was my age. I'd like to see them."

Time versus distance, Mel thought. Did thirty years equal five hundred miles?

"Swans, too," Colter said. "The tundra swans. I want to see them."

She started to tell him he should be grateful for what was still here — the wolves and grizzlies, eagles and wolverines. The caribou and owls.

"I know it's nice here," Colter said, "but it's too tame. I want to see a place that's like what this place was like when my father was my age."

"It hasn't changed much," Helen said. "It's probably changed less than any other place in the States."

"The swans and salmon are gone," Colter said.

Helen shrugged. "They're not everything."

"I want to see them," Colter said. "I want to see what kind of country they live in."

"You'd have to go north and west to catch up with them now," Mel said. "Way on up into Canada, and almost to the ocean — to the Pacific."

"Do you think I could do it on foot?" Colter asked.

"Yes," said Mel, after some hesitation, and a glance at Amy, who kept knitting.

"The Lord be with you," Amy said.

"That's my goal," Colter said.

Wallis thought of a glacier, receding — warming, shrinking, leaving polished piles of rubble at its ever-diminishing perimeters. He imagined Colter clambering over those boulder fields: down into one valley, up and over the mountains, then down into the next, and so on — traveling across them as if crossing sluggish waves at sea.

"When?" Wallis asked.

"This year," Colter said. "As soon as the snow's gone."

"Will you come back?" Mel asked. Another glance at Amy.

"Well, sure," said Colter. "I mean, I think so."

Amy kept knitting: didn't miss a stitch. "Zeke was that way," she said, and seemed comforted by this statement.

It was two in the morning. Snow was falling again. Helen, fatigued by the hour, had a strange, momentary impulse of recognition that this was a conversation like one from long ago — when Matthew was a little boy — but when she looked around the room, she saw that none of the principals from that time were present, and so it could not have been.

She kept waiting for someone to ask how she had arrived here, but knew that the question would not be forthcoming. Everyone understood that she had been born here — had had no choice in the matter; and that night she had the curious loneliness known only to those who fall in love with their invaders, or who find that their culture has been sanded down and assimilated by a thing, which, if no longer bold and unique and fitted to a place, is at least more comfortable and ultimately familiar.

Colter made plans to go out antler hunting with Wallis again the next afternoon. Everyone rose and said their good nights, wished each other a happy new year. Danny was asleep on the counter, laid out like a corpse. Artie placed a blanket over him, but saw no need to lift him down from the counter.

They each went their separate ways then, skiing deeper into the falling snow. To Wallis it seemed that he was already descending, even by standing still.

As ever, they bathed to rid themselves of the scent of the bar: the beer, and Helen's cigarettes, and the human company. They told each other good night and went to their separate rooms, as if to caves beneath the snow.

They were going through the supplies three times as fast as planned, for Wallis ate twice as much as she did. It was hard to judge whether the meat would hold out, but there was a lot of it. Of the firewood, there was less bounty, and he was burning it all day long, while Mel was out in the woods, and then all night as they slept. It was all Matthew's, and Wallis consumed it without a shred of guilt. It was fuel for his dream, fuel for the imagination of his map which surely this time would rotate into place like lock and key. He wore Matthew's baggy clothes, like the husks of a man who was no longer living. As Wallis dived deeper into his maps, he grew bolder and more confident. It was like feeding a monster. Whatever the cost, it would be worth it.

Emboldened in appetite, he ate more, and burned more wood, raised the temperature of the cabin five degrees above its usual chill. The scar of the absence of Susan lingered, but even that was hardening beneath his new life. It all seemed to be fuel for this one map, and he hadn't yet seen a single inch of the valley beneath its blankets of snow: but by now he understood that he did not have to.

He descended, as ecstatic as an opium diver. He grew even fonder of his and Mel's lazy time together in the evenings.

They would eat supper together — the grain of wild meat from the forest entering their bodies as they ate in silence. By now Wallis knew the story of how each of the animals had been taken, as they ate on it. Then they would visit for a little while — fifteen, twenty, sometimes even thirty minutes — talking about their childhoods usually, but then, once the bonds of intimacy strengthened, venturing further, moving closer to the present by talking about their lives as adults: moving perilously close to the present.

Mel was always the one who would break it off. She would rise to go work on her map — to enter in that day's data, scoring still deeper her understanding of what was the wolves' central territory at different times of the year. And willingly, Wallis would take a cup of tea into the middle room and work on his own map.

He continued to work in ecstasy. Sometimes it would occur to him that they were somehow working together: she, in the next room, contouring the same movements and flows of patterns of the wolves through the years on a horizontal plane, while he, with far less precision, more recklessness, mapped vertical cross sections, all imagined, but also based on the repetition of patterns — one initial contour influencing forever all those contours that would follow — and, as they worked, there would be a density of silence in the cabin that made it seem to him as if they were creating something almost tangible, like two weavers on a loom; and later into the night, nearing fatigue, he would imagine that there might be no difference — that they were drawing the same lines, and that his hand was hers.

He would work all morning, not daring to believe that what he was envisioning was anything less than accurate this time. Then he would read Dudley's old journals in the early afternoon, and would split and haul wood from the woodshed up to the front porch. After that, he would go by the school yard to wait for Colter, and then the two of them would go into the woods looking for antlers.

One evening their searching took them over one of the ridges south of town — following one of Matthew's old antler paths, with the racks occasionally visible up in the snowy forks of trees — and, as they often did, they stayed out until dusk. "Come on," Colter said, "I'll show you something."

Wallis could smell wood smoke. They descended the ridge, passing by immense larch trees in the blue snowlight. The antlers rattled on their backs. Wallis saw at the bottom of the ridge a small unlit cabin — though smoke curled from the chimney — and behind the cabin, next to the river, a large barn, well lit by yellow lanterns. A canoe rested by the shore, tethered to a tree limb. There was no road. A huge black horse stood motionless beneath one of the old larch trees, waiting for spring.

"This is a guy you've probably never met before," Colter whispered. "He builds coffins."

Now they could hear, over the murmur of the river, the quiet, steady sounds of the sawing, and then, after a silence, hammering. More silence, and then a sound like sanding. They stepped in closer to peer through the window. The horse observed them but remained still.

There were fantastic, brightly painted, animal-shaped coffins stacked on sawhorses throughout the barn. The man, who was working in a heavy coat but bare-handed, had moved over to the little pot-bellied stove in the barn's center to warm himself: he stood draped over it like a vulture spreading its wings to dry in the morning sun, but could not seem to get warm; he shivered, and his breath came in white bursts, as if he were talking to himself.

There was a stack of wood by his feet, and he loaded more into the stove, then crouched before it, holding his hands almost directly in the dancing flames. The snow on the barn's roof was melting due to the escaping heat, dripping like spring rain. A cake of ice lost its clutch on the barn's roof and slid like a raft out over the edge and crashed to the ground in thousands of small explosions, and the horse, whom the slabs had narrowly missed, tried to dance away, but it was hobbled with chains and could only make short lunging hops. The sound of the prisoner's chains rattling had an oddly musical quality to it.

Wallis turned his attention to the coffins. He saw now that some hung suspended by heavy ropes in the loft, in the likeness of giant birds — golden eagles, bald eagles, and ravens, all with wings outstretched — and that their colors gleamed lifelike above the glow of the lanterns.

Down below were coffins both painted and unpainted, some rough and others sanded. Loose boards lay everywhere — Wallis could smell the delicious odor of fresh-worked wood — and there were fuselages, wings, and all manners of huge carved and painted pieces — the ears of bears, the feet of wolves, the beaks of herons — waiting to be assembled onto various boxes, though neither Wallis nor Colter could imagine how the builder kept each part straight in his mind.

"Come on in," Colter said. "Let's go see him and warm up. He's okay. He's a nice guy. He doesn't like to come into town, but he's nice. Sometimes I give him antlers to put on his coffins."

They rapped at the window, then went around to the door. The man — Joshua — let them in without a word, as if he had been awaiting their arrival.

The floor was heel-deep in sawdust and the bright yellow curlings of shavings. Joshua gathered up a handful and tossed them in the open door of the stove: they bloomed into fierce light and brief heat, and for a moment they felt the pleasure of that warmth. "Come on," Joshua said, "it's too cold to work anymore. Let's go inside."

He put on another coat, a ski hat, and gloves, then went out, unhobbled the horse, and led the horse into the barn. The horse, a stallion, was muscular, black as obsidian, and accepted the barn's warmth with relief — he nickered with gratitude. The horse moved next to the stove and stood near it. His hooves shone bright as the ice around them melted. There were coffins in the forms of elk and moose, as well as bear, and the horse stood among them looking like one of Joshua's creations, who, having come to life, was now unwilling to leave the shop.

"It's a lot warmer with him in here," Joshua said, petting the horse, "but I can't work with him watching over my shoulder."

He carried the lantern out with him and shut the barn door, sealing the horse behind into blackness, save for the pinprickings of stars through the windows, the dull orange glow of the stove's steel, and the tiny whispers of light creaking and flickering through the stove's door seams.

Inside, Joshua fixed them hot tea. His cabin was tiny, cramped with the three of them. The bones of various animals were fastened to the cabin walls in all their proper assemblages and articulations: the skeletons of deer, moose, and bear prowling the cabin's walls and the rigid pale bones of eagles, owls, and herons hanging from the rafters above them: the structures around which Joshua would model his work.

"The giant birds he can hang from a big tree," Colter explained, and Wallis understood that he meant with the customer inside, like some ride at an amusement park — a county fair, perhaps. "Or he'll bury them, or put them way up in the mountains, in caves, or just resting out in the open."

"The ones in the open, sometimes the animals tip over and crack open like walnuts, to get at the meat inside," Joshua said. "I hate to see that. They really mess up the work. But I guess that's part of it."

"Or he can turn them into boats," Colter said, "and send them down the river. Swans, usually."

"Do many people —" Wallis searched for the word — "purchase these?" he asked.

"They're not for sale," Joshua answered. "They're just for people here in the valley."

"Which one would you choose?" Colter asked.

"Mmm," said Wallis, "they're all so amazing . . ."

"Let me know," Colter said. "Then if something happens to you, you'll be taken care of."

"Most people up here are shy," said Joshua. "Most of them go underground, when it's over."

"It's better if you pick," Colter said, "rather than someone picking for you."

"I'll be glad when spring gets here," Joshua said. He flexed his old hands before the fire, tool-curled and scarred from a thousand slips of the knife. A trapper's hands, Wallis thought. Trapping things right up until the very end, and then beyond. "It's hard to work out in the barn, once it gets too far below zero, and I can't do any painting, either, til the temperature warms up. The paint freezes before it dries." He shook his head. "I love working with the wood, but in the winter I start dreaming about color, and can't wait for March and April to come, and then summer, when I can start painting."

"Which one do you want?" Colter asked the old man.

"Oh, the swan," he said, laughing. "A nice long boat ride in the belly of the swan."

Colter and Wallis finished their tea. The evening was still young, though the darkness had already settled profoundly. They said good-bye and thanked Joshua, then stepped out into the night. Joshua stood in the doorway of his little cabin briefly, framed by light, waving good-bye to them, but then quickly shut the door, before too much heat could escape.

Colter and Wallis trudged up the hill, snowshoes squeaking on the crisp snow, burlap sacks on their backs. Stars melted, fell from the sky before them in sizzling streaks, and they stopped at the top of the ridge to watch the shower of them.

•

Imagine! To heat the world with the unending fires from below! Not simply by the geothermal phenomena of hotsprings and geysers limited to those drifting fissures of earth where one formation slides so rudely

upon another, truncating past processes and interrupting logic — vent-
ing foul gases to the surface like some awful dinner guest — but to heat
the world via the ignition of the natural gas, the gaseous sunlight,
trapped below like lakes and rivers.

How to get to this explosiveness, this life-giving-ness? The forms of
the earth above conspire to deceive — they strive to lure us to purposes
of no account. All seeks to be erased into a stubborn silence. Notice how
symmetrically the contour of summits sweeps from the upper to the
lower stretches, seeking to conceal all secrets below. How gracefully
these mountain swellings dissolve in the green ground of the landscape
beneath.

Look at our feet. The naked rock lies cracked by the frosts of unnum-
bered winters. The chips of the mountain strew the valley below. There
the mountain firs, shrinking from the weather, begin to appear, but only
as prostrate, crawling, and stunted shrubs. These rocks are Cenozoic.
How hard and crystalline and stubborn they look. These black crystals
are pyroxene; *the dark, dusky ones are a species of feldspar called* labra-
dorite. *The mixture forms a rock known as* Norite.

It is not an easy matter to travel down the slope of this summit. There
is too much rock-rubbish, too dense an undergrowth. But the geologist
must ascertain by some means. How arduous are the labors by which the
investigator works out the geology of a wild region.

While men labor brute to warm themselves with chunks of coal and
grovel like low lemmings for scraps of wood, a few such as myself possess
the knowledge to feed them, to deliver them from bondage: to give birth
to, to sire, a new world, as if we are the loins of man.

I dream the dream of the crystalline-marble woman, twelve feet tall,
green-stained with intermingled serpentine. I alone find her, and consort
with her, in the dream. I combine my seed with her to give birth to the
future.

•

Mel would do small things to keep Wallis from drifting too far from her
— would perform small acts of kindness and warmth, if not reckless
passion, to try to keep, with some degree of tautness or tension, the
promise of a thing-beyond-friendship alive between them, like some
little fire of tended sparks. Candles at dinner one night, for no apparent
reason. A touch of her hand to his before going off to map the wolves.
She tried to keep him from sinking too deep (though neither would she

allow herself to be pulled down with him if he did descend to the bottom); she kept flexible the possibility of a future with him, as she considered Matthew's further disintegration.

Sometimes she watched Wallis map and would be struck by the fear that he, this one, would find oil where the others — even her father — had been unable to.

The wood in her woodshed was larch. Even after it had been sawed and stacked in the shed — rendered from the forest depths into neat stackings of sixteen-inch lengths — the bright orange wood still possessed a presence, as if it was not done living.

Wallis loved the weight, the density of it. He loved the sound it made when he split it with a single blow of the maul: iron cleaving tight wood, separating it cleanly down the grain. He learned to read the grains so that he knew beforehand how each piece was going to split. He loved the color of the wood when the sunlight was strafing bright upon it, the color of it when the snow was falling heavy upon it. And though the swinging of the sledge was easy — the wood desiring to be split, it seemed, when struck in the right place — he nonetheless would, after an hour or two, work up a sweat in the ferrying back and forth of the wheelbarrow from shed to porch, wearing a deep path of packed ice.

Taking one round log and splitting it in half, and then again to quarters, and then into eighths. Into sixteenths, after that, for kindling. The days falling away, uncounted, unmeasured, in like fashion.

A couple of hours of work would place a day and a night's worth of wood on the porch. He started to calculate the crude inefficiency of it, but then stopped, understanding that it was irrelevant, that he liked the work.

THE VALLEY WENT OUT TO SEE A COMET ONE NIGHT. IT WAS supposed to be the last significant comet visible in the century, and the last anyone would see of this particular comet for another two thousand years. They left the bar at midnight on a night when the temperature was falling like a stone dropped from a great height: fifteen below at sunset, with not a cloud or wisp of fog anywhere. By midnight it was thirty below, and before daylight it would fall to forty. Children were awakened by their parents (or stayed up late, so that they would better remember the evening), and they all met at the bar and then rode in horse-drawn sleighs across the frozen crust up one of the old narrow paths to the top of Hensley Mountain, where Dudley and Matthew had long ago drilled one of their dry holes. Brush and saplings crowded in from either side, and they traveled up the mountain in single file. It was so cold that despite their labors the horses did not sweat. There were three sleighs: a dozen adults, and half as many children. They carried stove-warmed rocks wrapped in hides in their laps and on the floorboard of the carriage. From time to time they could see the comet through the trees, but it was not until they reached the top of the mountain that it was in clearest evidence, lying not far over the horizon, due north.

They climbed out from beneath their hides and stood among the horses and watched the beauty of it. At that temperature, the snow was more like the color of mercury. It was so cold that the snow up top had not crusted but was as loose as sand; they stood knee-deep in it, picked it up with their gloved hands and tossed it into the sky toward the comet, and followed its glittering columns back to earth.

The comet's tail was clearly visible — it looked out of place amongst the star-multitude, blurry and restless, like a flashlight shining through a patch of fog — and it seemed that they could even see the slow fizz and sputter of sparks from its tail.

"Where did Dudley drill?" a woman asked Mel, and Mel looked around but could not place the exact spot. It made her uneasy knowing there was a hole in the ground somewhere just beneath her, only eight inches in diameter but almost twenty thousand feet deep. To seal it, they had pumped in a few sacks of cement, then welded a steel plate over the top, nothing more.

"Why did he drill on the top of a mountain?" someone asked.

"Because he's a numbnuts, is why," answered Colter.

"Colter!" Amy cried.

"Excuse me," he said, "but it's true."

"Apologize," said Amy.

"I'm sorry."

They moved in closer to the horses, pressing against them, shivering. There were no lights down in the valley, and the cold possessed such a weight that it seemed it might crack them all — as if they were each crystalline things of no substance or strength. It was frightening, being up high like that — up close to the comet.

"I can still smell the oil," Colter said. Mel knew what he meant; fifteen years later, it still lingered, faintly, emanating from the bark of the trees. Not any oil Dudley had discovered, but the rankness of diesel from the engines that had been running the search. That oil must be soaked into the ground all around them, too, and Mel wondered if Colter could be smelling it beneath the snow.

It was already time to leave; they could bear the cold no longer. "Look once more," the parents told their children. "Are you sure you see it?"

They all did; the children had seen it immediately, had easily picked it out from amidst all the other seeming star-sameness. Some of them even imagined they could see a grinning face and eyes on the head of the comet.

Mel marveled at how clearly the children could see it, and at how excited they were by it. She had thought they would consider it to be small and insignificant — a little blurrier than a true star, and not much larger — tiny against the whole sky — but they were carrying on as if it were one of the most exciting things they'd ever seen — like junior astronomers, every one of them. She felt deeper the suspicion that she was becoming jaded to life — that even out here, in the blood-and-guts middle of it, her crust was hardening. She felt wonder, and peace, even awe — but she could not summon the utter, reckless joy of the children.

Helen had come with them — piled beneath such a burden of coats and hides that she could barely stand — and she had begun to hack and cough; at one point she leaned over and ejected a launch of sputum that, when it landed against the snow, looked suspiciously dark, like blood.

They bundled back into their sleighs and settled in amongst one another for warmth. Though the rocks still retained some of their warmth, they could not feel any of it, and there never could be as many hides as they needed to stay warm. There was hay in the bottom of the sleighs for them to shove their feet into, and inside the sleighs they lit lanterns and took turns passing the hissing lanterns around, holding them up to their bare faces to warm frozen cheeks — each face illuminated orange gold for a moment, with shrouds of frost-breath puffing from colorless lips — and then the chattering of someone else's teeth would bear request for the lantern to be passed on. The horses made good time, heading down the mountain, plowing through their previous trail, so that there was only the sound of the sleigh skimming across the snow, and the jingle of the horses' harness bells, and the freezing trees exploding around them like cannons, while above, the silent comet was moving fast.

The snows returned two days later. The wolves were courting now — Mel had found blood in the urine of the alpha female, and had found the fresh tracks showing where the alpha male and alpha female had paired off — and she had known she was close to them, within hours. She'd looked into the curtain of swirling snow and had felt a deep loneliness, an exclusion that was almost bitter in its depth, as if the world were passing her by: a self-pitying bleakness made all the more bitter by the fact that she knew the passing-by to be false, but still, the emotion was in her, as she stared in the direction the wolves had gone . . .

By the time the snows stopped, a week later, the comet was gone, and for several days afterward, many people felt similarly passed by — all for different reasons specific to each of their lives, but all in the same manner — confused, abandoned, bereft — as if some potential had been unfulfilled.

"I don't remember seeing any when I was a kid," Artie said. "But now it seems like they're coming fast and furious — like there's one almost every year."

"Well, they say this is the last one for a long while," Danny said.

"What's the Bible got to say about all this, Amy?" Artie joked.

Amy, who was knitting, made a little humming sound, shook her head, then said, "Well, it's not good," and they all laughed.

Colter was practicing with his father's bow. He had set up a stuffed deer — burlap bags stitched and filled with hay — in front of the saloon, and had fastened a set of antlers to the dummy; while the adults visited, he would be out practicing, whether in the afternoon or by moonlight. He had an aptitude for it from the beginning, taking to it as naturally as some children do to a violin or fiddle, and within weeks, his aim was as close to perfect as could be imagined; he had riddled one deer's heart and had had to get Amy to sew him a new one.

He would shoot for hours, coming in only to warm his hands before going back out. He soon tired of hitting a motionless target and took an

interest in shooting at moving ones. He would toss things into the air
— hats, hubcaps, anything — and shoot at those. He usually missed,
and when anyone stepped out of the bar there would often be the risk
of arrows whizzing past like bullets — he had no concept of there being
a background behind anything he shot at: he saw only the object of his
intent — but at this too, his aim improved so quickly that it was clearly
not an acquired talent, but instead one of those rarest ones, a thing that
had been living within him nearly fully formed since birth, and which
only had to be revealed, not created.

"What would happen if he came back to the valley to stay?" Wallis
asked Mel one evening. "Would things between you two go back to
how they were? Would you try to get back to that point?" Wallis had
finished his new draft of the maps, another blind vision of how he
believed things to be.

Mel considered pretending not to know what he was talking about.
"You mean, what would happen to you and me?" she asked.

"Yes," said Wallis.

"He's not coming back," Mel said.

"But what if he did?"

"I would be happy to see him," Mel said, carefully, though unsure,
for the first time, if she meant it.

It went beyond fatigue. There was the awful feeling, the one worse
than burnout, that she had been on the wrong path all along and was
either going to have to find a new one, or just lie down and quit.

She looked at the man across the table from her. With all his wood
splitting and water hauling, he was starting to fill out wider, so that
more than ever he resembled Matthew. He wasn't, of course — he was
as mild and cautious as Matthew was impulsive and erratic — and Mel
felt disloyal and confused — not to Matthew, but to herself — for even
tolerating, much less liking and being attracted to, such a force, if one
could call Wallis a force.

It was like resting. She liked resting with him. She needed rest. But it
didn't seem fair to Wallis. If she rested with him, what would happen
then, after she had gotten enough and decided to get up and start moving again? It would be as unfair to Wallis, she thought, as what Matthew
was doing — had done — to her.

She tried to explain it to Wallis.

"So you have thought about us, a little," he said finally.

"A little," Mel said. "More than you, probably." She pushed her chair back from the table. "I think ahead to spring sometimes — late April, May, June. I imagine lying naked in a field of daffodils, with or without you. I think about black dirt. I'm going to take time to have a garden this year, which is a thing I've never done before. I'm slowing down. Yes, I've been thinking about it," Mel said. "Probably too much."

"That's a nice image," Wallis said.

"What?"

He turned his coffee cup in his hands. "The daffodils."

"You know Matthew comes back by himself in March, don't you?"

"No," Wallis said, "I didn't know that." He studied the fire. "I remember last year he got real blue, said he was depressed and was going to go to a beach somewhere. Said he needed some sunlight."

"Beach, hell," Mel said, "unless he means the one twenty thousand feet below. He comes up here and passes out. Helen and I have to tend to him for a week or two. We get him just recovered enough to go back to Old Dudley for one more year, and then one more after that one, and then one more . . . Anyway," she said, "you'll just go back to him too. I don't know why we're even talking about this."

Wallis shook his head. "It's different for me," he said. "I don't feel that allegiance to Dudley. I don't even *like* him."

Mel got up and began clearing the dishes, exasperated — remembering twenty years ago, when she had first found, and in that same year, first begun losing Matthew.

"That's how it starts out," she said. "You're too close in — you can't see it. But you'll have to have a thing only he can give you. You'll need him."

"I could quit," Wallis said. "I could quit any day — could just draw the maps. I wouldn't have to drill the wells."

"Bullshit," said Mel.

She left the dishes in the sink to wash later, or for Wallis to get, and went over to her desk and unrolled her own map. It was so different from his, in that it would never be finished — would never be right or wrong, but ongoing — and she wondered if part of her irritation with him that evening was simple jealousy.

They slept that night like strangers in a boarding house. Wallis wanted to open the windows to let all the tension out. He'd pushed too soon, he thought: wanting to define things.

He tried to remember his office in Houston, the smell and feel of it. The overhead lamp, the drafting table: electric eraser, pencil sharpener, file cabinets, desk, drafting stool. The view of the bayou below, twenty floors down. The way he had been able to stand by the plate glass window on a windy day and feel the building swaying — a terrible, exhilarating sensation of vertigo. Sometimes he would lean against the window to feel it tremble from the winds outside: a quarter-inch of glass separating him from all that was below. Once Old Dudley had come into his office and had seen him standing at the window like that, arms outstretched, and had smiled, not knowing whether to be pleased or worried, but all he'd said was, "Don't jump."

Mel dreamed that night of silt and mud — of brown swamps, heavy sediment moving in suspension. Water the color of chocolate milk baking sluggish in the sun — water moving so slowly that no direction of current could be discerned. Water acting lost, searching for a way out — a passage to continue toward the place it had long ago set out after, and still desired.

She tangled in her elk hides and perspired until her whole upper body was drenched with sweat, but still she did not awaken, only tossed and moaned; and in the next room, Wallis heard her, was kept awake by her, felt the air in the little cabin filling with her anguish — a thing like craziness — until finally he rose and threw open the window in his room.

He stood at the window and breathed deeply the scent of fir and pine, listened to the stillness. He stood there for a long time, until his own heart calmed, and he felt the bad air in the cabin flowing out the open window and being dispersed and broken apart by the forest and the beauty of silence. His heart calmed still further, and the sounds of Mel's moans quieted, then stopped, and after that, the cabin felt more like how it had earlier been. He imagined a single cut yellow flower.

The snow came down through the days and nights as if spilling uncontrolled from some wound in the sky, and further into the winter, various old buildings began collapsing beneath the weight of it. The snows were far beyond anything known or measured in the few decades that whites had lived in the valley, and every night people went to bed with the snow still falling, sometimes as much as an inch or two an hour, and wondered if their cabin would be the next to go. No residences had been crushed yet — just barns and outbuildings — but the snows kept coming, stacking and then compressing to become slabs of blue ice, dense as stone.

There was good work for Colter, and a few others, in the shoveling of roofs — though by February it had come to seem like a ceaseless work, with the shovelers spending more time on the roofs than on the ground, so that it was as if they were occupying some slightly elevated level beyond the town's strata. If people couldn't afford to pay, they bartered — meat, canned vegetables, antlers, hides, pelts, firewood — or traded services. It didn't really matter, in the end, who was holding the money at the end of the day; the same two or three hundred dollars would keep making the rounds, passing from hand to hand and becoming as thin and tattered as old brown leaves, until they were finally indistinguishable, worthless . . . The snow kept coming down, faster than anyone's ability to remove it, until most gave up and went inside, resigned to wait for spring, dependent now only upon mercy.

It looked increasingly as if the town had been bombed; so many buildings were crushed flat with nothing remaining but an erratic jumble of logs poking up out of the snow.

Wallis helped shovel, and in the evenings he would lie on his back in front of the fire and groan like a dog. He was becoming wider and even more muscular from all the labor, but the birthing pains of it were intense. He would roll over on his stomach and let Mel knead his back with her elbows and knees, trying to buffer the buildup of acid, and to keep the muscles from cramping and torquing, tugging at him in different places and intensities in such a way as to corkscrew him prematurely into some gnarled, bent-over crippled old thing. He imagined a hide stretched out on a rack to dry evenly. The heat from the fire, and the points of her elbows, quelled the rebellion in his muscles.

He would bathe, then crawl off to bed and sleep for twelve, sometimes fourteen hours. More than anything he wanted one day off. Just one day.

Mel made sure he kept eating, though he was too tired to have much of an appetite. She fed him the four basics: moose, deer, elk, grouse. He kept growing, and in his sleep, as his muscles swelled, it seemed that he would grow too large to fit in the cabin. Matthew's clothes fit Wallis perfectly now. And though he knew it was a dangerous and narrow path — slipping so easily into the groove cut by another — he would sometimes smell the old rock dust on Matthew's coats and shirts, from where Matthew had been working on the rock wall — wearing long sleeves and overalls even in summer to keep from tearing up his arms on the rough edges — and Wallis would feel the urge to use his new muscles, the great power and leverage of them. He would find himself craving to work on the wall himself — to haul and position and stack the dense blocks in their simple but unifying pattern — two on one, one on two. He found himself anxious for spring, so that maybe he could add to the rock wall.

His map was finished, or so he thought; he kept it rolled up, waiting for the master, and continued to read the master's notebooks.

"When was the last time you saw the wolves?" he asked Mel one night as they lay by the fire.

She had to look in her journal. She thumbed through it for a long time. "Two years ago last June," she said.

"What would you do if you didn't follow the wolves?" he asked.

"I don't follow them," she said. "I move away from them."

"What would you do?" he asked.

"What would you do, if you didn't map?"

"I can't imagine a damn thing," Wallis said. "I'd be lost."

"So he's got you," Mel said. "You're trapped."

"Except that I don't mind it."

"I snowshoed a long way today," Mel said. "Will you work on my back?"

He was surprised at the strength of it. It felt stronger than his. He tried to separate the muscles with his hands, with his thumbs, but couldn't. He leaned in with his elbows, but could find no yield.

"Try and relax," he said.

"I am relaxed," Mel said, then added, "That's okay. It feels good. You're warm. Just lie there, please."

He stretched out over her back, her skin warmed by the fire. He wondered if he smelled to her like Matthew, in Matthew's clothes, or like himself: or what, if any, difference there was.

After the fire burned out, and she was asleep, Wallis lifted himself from her back and lay down next to her and pulled a hide over them. She woke up once in the night and smiled at him, then went back to sleep.

They went out to backtrack the wolves together one day. He couldn't remember if it had been his idea, wanting to see how she spent her days, or if it had been her idea; wanting to show him.

They packed as if for a picnic. It had snowed several inches the night before, so that soon Wallis would have to get back to shoveling — it was time for him once more to shovel Helen's mercantile — but Mel said the wolves had been hunting not far from town, and that though they might not find any tracks in the new snow, it was also possible they would find some fresh ones. The wolves hadn't eaten in three days, she said, but she had seen long lines of ravens heading toward the river, and believed that the wolves were hunting again and would kill something soon.

They packed apples, oranges, boiled eggs, and venison sandwiches on thick bread. It seemed strange to Wallis that they were packing venison sandwiches in order to give them the fuel, the strength, to snowshoe into the woods to find where the wolves themselves had also killed and eaten a deer: as if the deer were a shared currency between two countries, or even a common language.

As ever, she skied too fast for him, so that often she had to stop and wait, though when going up steep hills, he would gain an advantage, so that it was she who had to work to stay up with him. She pointed out things for him to see — explained to him things it had taken her twenty years to learn, and which she was impatient for him to know.

Her mind that day was on snags, and diversity: on the different species of dead trees in a forest, and the different heights and ages and angles of them. Were they standing upright, were they leaning over at a forty-five degree angle, or were they parallel to the ground? Were they newly dead, not yet hollowed out and being used by woodpeckers, salamanders, beetles, martens, fishers, owls, brown creepers, and thrushes — or were they already rotting, being grubbed and gnawed by bears and giving sweet relief to the soil, and to the seething invertebrates that needed them?

The short, wide snags of ancient larch trees, their tops blown off by lightning or windstorms; the taller, more elegant snags of the cedar trees, in which were gouged out, in hieroglyphic patterns, the oval excavations from the giant pileated woodpeckers probing for insects . . . Mel said that cedar trees seemed to be the most valuable snags — that she believed the birds and mammals liked the way the cedar wood repelled mites and insects.

She pointed to a place where one tree died but remained standing, or fell only slightly — leaning, tipping — and explained that it braced the others around it, and it opened up new gaps of light that allowed different, smaller, younger trees to utilize that light which had previously been unavailable to them: allowed them to be "released," is what she called it; and how the leaning tree also cast new shadows, providing a cooler temperature in a certain spot and allowing the seedling of a shade- and cool-tolerant species — fir, spruce, cedar, hemlock — to germinate, and begin its slow journey to the canopy.

Following her, listening to her explain it in stream of consciousness — simply reacting to whatever she encountered — Wallis saw that it was like the workings of some engine, valves opening and closing, and with a power being generated from that compression and expansion.

It was similar to where Wallis went in his maps: the surface, the skin of the world, was no different from its depths. He had known that intuitively. But it was a source of great awe, to realize now that her forest above was like his subterranean oil fields.

He suspected the similarities did not stop there; that if one stretched the time scale out far enough — expanded it — all things, at one point or another — wolves and humans, forests and mountains, dead people and living ones — became similar, and that it was only in the compression of things — the moment — that there appeared to be any significant flutter of individuality.

He understood how such perceptions would lead one to shun, even fear, the future. Whatever peace or beauty existed in the moment would always be at risk — either attenuated, drawn out into nothingness by the future's assimilation, or compressed into the past, all massed into one forgotten gray block.

If he loved Mel, for instance — would it be like loving Susan? And if she loved him — would it not be the same as loving Matthew?

That day, however, they did not feel trapped by sameness, trend, recurrence. They heard the ravens not too far in the distance, sounding like roosters in a barnyard, and skied toward the sound of the kill. They drew nearer, and still had not crossed any wolf tracks, so that Mel wondered if the wolves were still feeding, and that perhaps that was what the raven furor was about: the wolves not letting the ravens join in the feast.

They crossed a marsh, so close now that they could hear wingbeats, could see the ravens circling just above the treetops. They could taste the excitement in the air, the pandemonium, and could smell the meat, too; and now finally they cut tracks and joined in on the trail, reading the wolves' tracks.

"A *moose*," Mel said, placing her hands in the tracks. There was blood everywhere, still bright crimson.

The troughed-up snow trail was as red with blood as if someone had been running down it with buckets of red paint, spilling it as they ran, and they saw now that the trunks of all the trees were sprayed bright red. There were craters in the snow where the moose had stumbled and gone down, but had then somehow managed to get up and go farther: though anyone could read the tracks and understand that it was futile — that the moose had never had any real hope of making it to a point beyond where the ravens were now calling.

There was so much blood. The alder bushes were bright red from where the moose had crashed, in her panic, over the tops of them — dragging her slickened body across the brush, painting the landscape as she crawled. Wolves hanging onto her, tearing at her.

She had broken free and gotten up and run again. More blood.

Now they could hear the wolves' snarls as they fed — fighting one another for a place at the carcass, a dominant wolf growling whenever a subordinate encroached too closely or bumped shoulders in the feeding process. Fifty yards away. The ravens spied Mel and Wallis and called out their alarms and flew away with heavy wingbeats and raucous shouts, bits of hide and flesh hanging from their thick beaks.

"Shouldn't we go back?" Wallis asked.

"We're already here," Mel said. She unclipped her skis and crawled forward on her belly — following the blood trough, the tracks, in that manner. Wallis lay down behind her and did the same.

More ravens flew away, startled by their approach. The wolves knew the humans were coming, could read the voices and movements of the ravens clearly, but were too intent upon feeding to run. They kept watch for whatever was coming, but continued to feed.

When they were thirty yards away, Mel and Wallis could see the wolves — five of them, two black and three gray, gathered around the bulk of the moose carcass; and behind the wolves, like attendants, stood two large bald eagles, fiercely yellow-eyed, and an even larger golden eagle: each awaiting their turn, should it come, but unwilling to challenge the wolves, with the wolves so hungry.

Now the wolves spied them, saw their plumes of breath rising, saw the round shapes of their heads amidst the trees, saw the tone of their eyes, though not the color — and the wolves saw that it was Mel and the stranger, whom they had known was in the valley; and for two or three seconds the wolves — faces masked red with moose blood — stared across the distance at them, evaluated them directly — surprised that Mel for once had not backtracked — then whirled and sprinted into the woods.

The three eagles hopped over to the carcass and began tearing at it. Mel and Wallis watched for a moment, hoping the wolves would circle back, but when they didn't, they crawled to their skis and turned back. For both of them it was the strangest feeling to be so willfully and intentionally moving away from the thing they were after — the thing they desired, and which they had, for a moment, tasted.

Neither of them spoke, feeling that to do so would tarnish or even betray that which they had seen and shared; and feeling, too, a slight guilt, as if they'd done something deceitful, but were thrilled by having done so.

Mel measured and recorded the chase — mapped the wolves' movements, estimated the blood loss from the moose, and counted the number of times the moose had gone down; and her notes reflected an unraveling, a widening, as they traveled away from the source — working all the way back to the point where the first blood had been drawn, and then even farther back, to where the moose had not even been running, had been unaware of the gathering wolves — but this time the map work felt hollow to Mel, as if she were working to phrase some useless question for which she already had the answer; and in the distance behind them, they could hear the ravens circling back in and calling to one another, as if laughing at her retreat.

THEY STOPPED BY THE BAR. COLTER CAME BY TO SHOW THEM the grouse he had shot that day. It was the first bird he had hit with an arrow in flight; it still had the arrow in it.

Everyone admired the bird and bragged on Colter, though even the praise seemed listless, sluggish, not commensurate with the accomplishment. Wallis handled the bird the longest, examining it more carefully than he would any work of art. The arrow had passed through both wings and the breast.

"That's fine," Mel said. "That's a good shot. But how's your reading and writing going?"

Colter looked to be sure Amy had not come in. "The hell with that," he said. He looked around the bar. "Who in here has it done any good for? My pop got by just fine without it. I know how to read. Too much of it makes you soft in the head."

Colter took his bird and went over by the fire. He pulled the arrow out of it, then began plucking feathers, dropping them in a paper sack to take back out into the woods. Wallis sat with him during the ritual. When he had the bird plucked, Colter cut open the bottom of the bird and pulled out the entrails, fed them to one of the dogs that was sitting at his feet, then rinsed his hands in the sink.

"What about Matthew?" Helen whispered to Mel while Wallis was busy with Colter. "What about my boy?"

Mel didn't answer; just set her lips and plucked at the label of her empty beer bottle.

By the fire, Colter had the grouse skewered on a branch and was roasting it over the open flames. Already it was making fat-sweat. Grease spattered into the fire, burst into flames. The scent of meat soon filled the bar, but even then, the bar's lethargy remained — seemed immovable, as if the world had slowed to a halt.

Wallis picked through the bag of feathers to find the bird's crop to see what it had been eating. Wet green fir needles, and snowberries like pearls. Wallis held the snowberries in his palm and studied them, thinking what a shame it was that they were of no use to humans: not as edible as domesticated berries, and ill-suited for necklaces of any durability. By firelight, he had never seen anything more beautiful.

They sat up visiting until midnight, unwilling to put a close on the day.

"I've been thinking about helping out at the school," Mel said.

Up until that moment, she had been thinking nothing of the sort — had only been considering the heaviness of all the sameness in her life. But now that she had said it, she liked the way it sounded. She could picture being of immediate, and daily, use.

Wallis was stricken. "What about your maps? Your data? Who would pick up where you left off?"

"Probably no one," Mel said. She shrugged. "Maybe that's not a bad thing. Maybe it's better if no one's really certain of where they go and what they do. Maybe it should just be like a secret."

She got up and poured a glass of wine: took a sip, then set the glass on the windowsill. She stood before Wallis then, not knowing what she wanted — whether she wanted to kiss him good night, or talk longer, or take his hand again for a moment — and so in the end all she could do was say "Good night" — the thinness of language like a mockery, the words being forced to substitute for all that she did not know — and she went down the hall to her room.

Wallis sat by the fire a bit longer, listening to the hammering of his heart — the terrifying lift and leap of it. A thing like the possibility of joy, which was almost like joy itself. He had never imagined such a race of heart could return — nor had he imagined he would ever go looking for such a return.

He slept hard. He woke only once in the night to the sound of the wine glass falling inexplicably from the window ledge — pushed over by a scampering night mouse, perhaps, or a barely felt earth tremor — a shifting or stretching below the snow — and he got a towel and cleaned up the spill, then went back to sleep, and was hopeful. He felt good things approaching, though he could not have said what they were.

In the morning, Mel did not go into the woods, but instead went to the school. She was unsure of how to go about presenting her offer, and when she arrived at the school early, the teachers — Belle and Ann, in their early fifties, were surprised to see her standing at the door. They invited her in for a cup of coffee — they lived in a cabin behind the school and had been up since four, grading papers and preparing lesson plans — and when Mel told them she wanted to teach the students about the woods they looked startled, as if a wolf or deer had come through the door and begun to speak.

"We'll have to reschedule things," Ann said. "What time of day would you like to teach?"

"Morning," she said. "First thing."

"All right," said Ann.

"After I'm done each day, can I stay?" Mel asked. "Can I sit in the back and watch, and listen, and see how you do it?"

"It might get awfully boring," Belle said. "Aren't you going to want to get on out into the woods after you're done? Won't you want to get back out to your tracking?"

"I'm going to take a break from it for a while," Mel said.

"All right," said Ann. "Do you want to start today or tomorrow?"

The first students were beginning to trickle in — some on skis, some on snowshoes, while others came riding in on ponies.

"Today," Mel said.

•

The Reptile Monarchies
Mesozoic Events

The storm is cleared, and a new sky overhangs the scene. We seem to be in another world. We glance over the territory lately covered by luxuriant coal vegetation, of which Cycads and Voltzias now hold possession. The Cycads are palmetto-like in form, fernlike in foliage, and pinelike in affinities; the Voltzias seem a progenitor of the cypress. No Lepidodendron or Sigillaria raises its green crown in all the wooded landscape. The reeking marsh has disappeared, and an undulating upland occupies the continent.

We glance over the great flat. Dark-wooded ranges of mountains frown down on us. We search for the old shoreline which had set the bounds to the empire of the sea, and see now that it is removed. Far southward it lies, within two hundred miles of the Gulf border of the human epoch — so much more of the ocean's domain has been wrested from his possession.

We range over this new bright landscape. All the old Paleozoic forms of animal life are displaced. Strange tenants have moved in. Instead of the feeble, lizard-shaped amphibians which housed themselves in a hollow stump, we find great quadruped-like labyrinthodonts crawling like enormous toads under shelter of a fringe of forest. Their ponderous bulk impresses deep footprints in the sand along the beach — four-toed and handlike — destined to remain and become a wonder for the human age.

But the amphibians have yielded empire to another dynasty. Great was Archegosaurus, but Deinosaur was greater. An extraordinary and amazing figure reveals itself stalking along over the beach. Evidently this monster, tall, scale-covered, erect, with diminutive head, swollen abdomen, and massive, trailing tail, is a representative of the ruling family. He reveals massiveness without elegance; strength without grace. He marches on two feet and leaves a footprint three-toed, like that of a bird. His jaws are armed with strong, sharp-edged, and pointed teeth. His long bones are hollow like those of birds; the pelvis, as well as the foot, is birdlike; and his lower jaw has lateral motion for triturating food, as in the ox. Shape like a frog; head, tail, and scales like a lizard; feet like a bird; sacrum like a mammal — what shall we call the creature?

We watch him through his seaside promenade, and follow him to the dank and peaty jungle where he finds his home. We see him browse from the lower tufts of foliage, and grind the fibrous twigs with the jaw movements of a herbivore, wearing away and blunting the crowns of his teeth. But he meets his enemy — another Deinosaur of blood-thirsty disposition, a flesh-eater, and armed with sharp and lacerating teeth.

Between the two a bitter feud exists, and they have, at former times, clenched in the struggle for prowess. The herbivore recognizes his superior; but unwillingly subject, fierce anger flashes from his dark eye, and with a defiant, unchristian growl, he makes room for the contemptuous and bloody, wolfish carnivore to pass.

We stand upon the slope of a western shore and survey the shining expanse. The tide is out, and the smooth sand beach is laid bare. Over its surface lie squirming and crawling and shrinking from exposure, the sundry forms of marine life which the last tide brought up. This is the opportunity for the land marauders. Now they hurry to the scene in search of a meal. There, most conspicuously, strides the tall uncouth Brontozóum, *a three-toed Deinosaur, standing fourteen feet high. Its foot is twenty-four inches long. At times it drops on four feet to seize a dainty morsel of crab, and leaves, for a space, the footprints of a quadruped. But the forward feet are comparatively diminutive in size. In the distance,* Otozóum *paces along the beach — another bipedal Deinosaur, but with four toes behind. With foot twenty inches in length, he has a stride of three feet, in a leisurely gait:* Otozóum *is partaking of his meal. Now and then he picks up a stranded fish. Among these gigantic figures more humble Deinosaurs are seen mingling. One of these leaves a footprint but three inches; and we notice one wee pet of a reptile which makes a track but a quarter of an inch in length. They are all engaged in refreshing themselves. This is the regular symposium of the reptiles.*

Let us wait here for the tide to come in. It is coming; and announces itself by its roar. The tide of the open sea is here augmented by the limits of the narrowing bay, and it swells into a terror-striking "bore." The Deinosaurs and Labyrinthodous hear the sound, raise higher their heads in listening attitudes, and scurry away to their retreats. The tide lingers awhile, dallying with the sands, and making advance to the shore. Now, at the appointed time, it presses a dewy parting kiss upon the beach which it fondled for an hour, then retires.

Where now, are the footprints, the tracks, of those gigantic saurians? Has the dallying tide erased them? No. It has covered them with a soft film of fine sand. They are not destroyed; they are preserved. The table is spread again with squirming viands, and the saurians recognize another call to refreshments. Again they range along the sand, and impress their tracks in the soft surface. Unconsciously, these creatures are inscribing their autographs on the pages of the world's history. By and by the tides will cease. This bay will be uplifted beyond their reach; these sands will become a solid brown sandstone. Quarrymen will ply their avocation along the walls of mountains and read these ancient texts with their hands like blindmen.

Stars tumble from the sky; comets swirl. The warm-blooded birds develop — now in this wonderful Mesozoic time, behold a real bird on the wing. Clothed with proper feathers and constituted a bird, it is yet reptilian. Its long and lizard-like tail, vertebrated to the extremity, is furnished with proper quills, but can not conceal its kinship with the reptiles. It comes out of the empire of reptiles and brings cellular reminiscences of the reptiles with it.

A higher type is now standing at the threshold of being. A knell is sounding the funeral of the reptilian dynasty. The saurian hordes shrink away before the approach of a superior being. After a splendid reign, the dynasty of reptiles crumbles to the ground, and we know it only from the history written in its ruins.

•

Wallis finished the chapter and watched the snow fall. The flakes were falling so thick and slow, and there were so many of them, and so large, that they obscured almost all vision. He was sick of them, and sick of the feeling that all he was doing was marking time, like a sleeping bear, until summer. He felt that he would be accomplishing more if he *were* hibernating — that at least he would be resting for his summer work, rather than arriving at it in such a bedraggled and confused state. He wondered for the hundredth time whether his new map had any worth whatsoever. It would be easy enough to find out — just spend a million dollars to drill yet another well, and let the question be answered. Wallis tried to imagine Dudley's scorn, or rage, at another dry hole. It was not a pleasant image. He tried to imagine the joy and pride of a colossal discovery. The crushing disappointment Matthew would probably feel, having failed nineteen times, while he, Wallis, had gotten it right on the twentieth try. The trucks roaring in and out of the valley, hauling oil over the summit hourly. They would probably keep the road plowed and open year-round for that. He imagined Mel's displeasure with the traffic and visitors.

He unscrolled his map once more. He had studied it so much that he knew every contour: knew where he was going to propose the well be drilled. Matthew had been close, but had still been wrong. He'd missed it by about ten miles.

Wallis pictured Old Dudley's jubilation at finally being able to crack open the valley like a nutmeat. Pictured the utter jig of victory Dudley would do. The old lecher would crouch down at the wellhead and lap the hot black oil straight from a puddle like an animal drinking from a creek.

Wallis wondered how long Old Dudley would live. He wondered if he would still be pounding away at the earth when he was a hundred; if he would be like one of those old Russian peasants who lived to be one hundred and thirty. He wondered who would take Dudley's place, after he was gone from the earth. Not so much who would take over the running of his operations — lawyers and accountants, he imagined; it occurred to him for the first time, and with a shock, that Mel would perhaps be his sole heiress — but rather, who would fill that niche, that void, of being the relentless pounder — the one who could never be sated, who had to soil or disassemble and alter all that was within reach.

Wallis stared at the wine stain from where it had spilled the night before. It had splashed onto one of the elk hides, and there was a puddle of it beneath one of Mel's filing cabinets. He went and got a rag and bucket of soapy water to clean the rest of it. He moved the file cabinet aside, and when he did so, he noticed that the floor had been cut and scored to make a trap door.

When he opened the door and peered down, he saw a full basement, without steps leading down. He could smell cooler, damper air below. He sat there on his knees for a moment, feeling foolish that he had literally been sleeping on top of a thing, another level, and hadn't known it existed. Then he went and got a lantern and climbed down into the basement. There was no ladder, but little toeholds had been carved into the bare earth walls. The basement was about ten feet deep.

It had an earthen floor, packed firm from decades of foot use, with river stones placed in the ground, so that a person could move around without getting his or her feet damp.

Old tables lined the earth-cut walls, and there were wooden crates and boxes piled on top of them. Children's leather ice skates, looking as if from the previous century, hung from posts, and there were bleached skulls and antlers stacked on the tables, as well as the specimens of beautiful gems and minerals. A glossy white quartz crystal as large as a wheelbarrow; a smoke-colored black one as large as a football. Amethysts and sapphires caught the lantern's glow and sparkled, sent the light skewing back in altered directions.

Old traps hung from the rafters, as did old rusting axes and adzes, their handles worn smooth by the hands of ghosts.

Some of the wooden crates had unknown handwriting on them — Matthew's parents, Wallis guessed — though on other crates he recognized Mel's handwriting. *Mama's wedding dress,* in a cedar chest. *Pictures, photographs. Old technical reports.*

One crate was marked *Skulls;* another, *Feathers;* still another, *Rocks.* Wallis opened that one, hoping and expecting to find old core samples that might be of use to him, along with data about the depths and locations from which they had been obtained, but found instead only more river stones, worn smooth and polished as if for no reason at all.

Wallis stared at the walls around him. It was good to see dirt again.

More of Mel's boxes: *Children's toys, children's books, Mama's doll furniture.* He smiled, thinking of her spartan life above, but of how she had yet been able to unburden the accumulations of her past.

A row of boxes on the far wall, all with Old Dudley's crude, boy-scrawl markings. *Notebooks,* one of them read, though the others bore only numbers: 1916, 1917, 1918, 1919. The latest was 1967: as if he had grown quiet after that — or as if he had been too busy eating the world to spend time discussing the hows and whys. Wallis pulled out the front crate and pried open the dust-sealed lid; lifted out the first ancient ledger. The dried leather spine cracked as he opened the June 1918 notebook.

The first page was torn out, as was part of the second page, but the text that remained read:

. . . after we had finished stoning him we trussed him with heavy rope and pulled him slowly through the furrows of his own field, fertilizing that already rich soil with his own blood. He protested thinly but was in no condition to offer resistance. We dragged him face down not at a fast pace for the mule would not gallop but at a steady trawl as if plowing. We were using his own mule to do the pulling while we stalked alongside giving encouragement to the mule. There seemed to have been some rift between the mule and farmer for now the mule pulled with grim pleasure and from time to time glanced back over his shoulder as if to be sure his master was still attached, or perhaps simply to better hear the insults the sorry old sodbuster was hurling at us — and at the mule — mixed with pleas and cries for mercy — as the mule trudged steadily on; and as we traveled farther across the field, the man's head bobbed less and less often, like some loose rolling pumpkin hitting a bump now and again, and the rest of his body, bound tight, was like nothing but a log. Through it all I felt nothing but an increasing desire or ambition to finish the task, and as we both sensed the old farmer was fading fast — he did not raise his head now — Pap would from time to time run back and stab and hack at the old cretin who had insulted him so grossly, and for some distance Pap even rode upon him, straddling him and riding him as one would a pony, holding his face down in the black dirt, but Pap soon tired of this fun, and when we reached the far end of the field there was not sufficient life in him to warrant any further response from Pap's ministrations and his was but a fading husk of a life. Johnny, upon awakening that dewy morn, would you have ever imagined such an adventure awaited you?

There lay behind us in wandering fashion and against the sunset a crimson sheen to the earth almost iridescent in nature, the spoor of where we had passed, along which crows now hopped in ragged skein, pecking at the red soil, and as old Pap was exhausted from the labors of his justice, I now had to do the digging.

We had brought no shovel so for a while I dug with my hands but it was slow going and so in due time I ran back across the soft field to the farmhouse and found a shovel in the barn. His family was off at the church social with Ma but I was still nervous and when the barn cat yowled and leapt out at me as I tried to wrestle the shovel from where it was stacked I shrieked and wet myself and did not feel sixteen . . .

I ran back across the field in the sunset, and when I got to the far side of the field Pap was sitting on a log still holding earnest conversation with Sodbuster, though Life had left him now, and he was naught but a warm mound cooling quickly in the twilight.

I did the digging — I wanted to set him deep — but Pap said no bother, it was all the same, and so we rolled him in and covered him back up when the trough was only three feet deep and patted the soil back in place, though it bothered me that he was only beneath the skin like that, and not deeper in soil's embrace.

Pap had no desire to commemorate or memorialize this day's passing, though I felt some urge to leave a mark, and so I gathered some stones from field's edge and made a small cairn of five or six stones which only I would recognize for a cairn, rather than mere happenstance assemblage.

The mule was reluctant to leave, as if now regretting its participation in earlier events, and not even by smacking its platy forehead with the shovel could Pap induce it to take one step from where it stood slump-shouldered, staring down at the fresh grave of its master, so Pap dipped the long handle of the shovel into the creek and then inserted it rudely and quickly into the mule's rectum, which got him moving briskly enough.

We walked home in darkness. Fireflies blinked peacefully, and an owl hooted down on the river. Heat lightning shimmered to the north, and a few faint fine mists of raindrops cooled our grimy faces. We could smell the coming thunderstorm that would later that night wash away most traces of our passage, so that in the next day's light all that would be visible would be the washed-out tracks of a man and a boy — any man, and any boy — and as we walked, Pap put his hand on my shoulder and said, "Nobody calls your father an old penny-pinching Jew, son."

•

Wallis stared at the youthful script for a long time. He looked up at the other crates and was almost afraid to read further, but he did — pulling down a volume from September 1919, and was relieved to find long pages of commentary on the weather — a drought year — and Dudley's surmisings on the effects this had had on vegetation, noting that native plants back in the woods had fared far better than the domesticated crops of man.

There was mention made of how much harder it was to work the larger field, now that old Pap had taken over his neighbor Jones's property, and was employing Jones's family to sharecrop the land they had previously owned.

But then in the November volume of the same year, Wallis read with sinking heart of how Dudley had landed in "the Home."

No sooner had I finished putting the final shovelful of dirt over the matted head of a Mister P. than did a figure appear from the gloom across the far side of the field, riding hard on horseback. We felt the percussions of his horse's hoofs drumming before we could spy him in that dimness. At first I thought it was P. himself somehow not yet dead and protesting his final resting place, but we saw then that it was P.'s brother, and that he had us sighted. It was June and there was a comet in the twilight sky and old Pap had been sitting there hunkered graveside like one of the Great Apes, resting from the ordeal and labors and contemplating, I suppose, the place to which he had sent the disrespecting Mr. P.

Pap had rolled and was smoking a cigarette and when we saw P.'s brother approaching hard, Pap ran and hid behind a tree as a child will do, but then realized the futility of that, and came back out into the field and with matches lit the dry standing cornstalks. They caught quickly on tongues of flame, but P.'s brother rode hard through them, scattering us in two directions. I went downstream and Pap upstream. P.'s brother turned his horse after Pap. I heard much splashing upstream and then silence. I lay down and hid in the water. Watched fireflies drifting along the stream edges and took note how they preferred not to cross the water proper. Luminescence around me on either side save for the winding ribbon of darkness ahead of me that was the river. After much time had passed I climbed out and went home, wondering what to tell Ma. Was surprised by the sight of a thoroughly drenched and bedraggled Pap sitting on front porch in darkness attempting to light a cigarette. How old he looked! Ma asleep in the house. Pap said he had escaped the wrath of P.'s brother by running back into the flames where the horse would not follow but that now the sheriff would be arriving any moment.

His gnarled hand on my shoulder. Said he had but a few bitter years left in the world but that all my time was still before me like green wood; that they would hang him, but would only send me to Reformatory until I came of age, at which point we could be reunited; I could be released back to the custody of my loving parents.

Car headlights appearing over the hill. Pap said, Tell them it was self-defense. I said, What about the bruises? Pap said, Tell them he fought hard, real hard. I'll tell 'em I tried to stop you. I'll tell 'em you were out of your mind — uncontrollable.

All those car headlights surrounding us. Swirling dust. Guns drawn. They took us out that night to dig him up. The cornfield was still smoldering in coals and stubbleflame and then the earth still loose upon him when we dug him up and pulled him back free of the soil.

That's him, Pap said, that's the one that hit my boy. Holy Mother of God, *another of them said,* he is still alive, but only barely.

They bathed him off in the creek and loaded him into the car and took him to the hospital in Smithville but he did not survive the journey, and our secret was safe.

Ma died several months later, believing I was guilty, and Pap passed two weeks before I got out on my eighteenth birthday.

The road ahead seemed long.

From there, it seemed, Dudley fell as if down a cleft in the earth. Surrounded by cretins and thugs he would have nothing to do with. He was kept chained to his bed at night — a twenty-foot length of chain around one wrist that would allow him, if he avoided tangling it, to reach the toilet, but no farther. The descent into dreamland deepened. Long hours in the library. Longer hours in solitude. Finally, with his good behavior, he was allowed to go back outside, though still shackled and manacled, and still within the fenced yard of the Home.

The Unstable Land
Phenomena and Causes of Earthquakes

When men feel the earth beneath their feet growing unstable, the most paralyzing sense of insecurity seizes them. The ground supports everything; and when it fails him, his dismay is complete.

Yet the solid earth has not only been shaken by throes which have engulfed cities and populations and mountains, but there is scarcely a moment when its movements or its tremblings may not be felt by the delicate means of modern science. The stability of the solid earth is instability masked.

The destructive shock lasts but a few minutes, or even seconds. The successive vibrations which devastated Calabria in 1783 were felt during barely two minutes. On the occasion of the destruction of the city of

Lisbon, in 1755 and the loss of sixty thousand lives, it was the first shock, lasting five or six seconds, which caused the greatest damage.

The motions which constitute an earthquake are various. Sometimes they are vertical. More commonly they are horizontal. The rate of transmission varies with the intensity of the shock and the nature of the rock materials. When mines of powder were exploded near Holyhead, in Wales, the waves of disturbance were propagated through wet sand at the rate of 951 feet a second; through friable granite 1,283 feet per second.

It is not supposable that the actual center of an earthquake disturbance is at the surface. It must exist at some considerable depth beneath the surface. According to Mr. Mallet, the center of disturbance of the Calabrian earthquake of 1857 was seven to eight miles below sea level. All perturbation lies at depth.

Sounds often accompany earthquakes. Sometimes they resemble explosions as of distant artillery; more frequently it is a rumbling sound as of heavy vehicles moving over a city pavement. I have myself experienced but one noteworthy earthquake, and that occurred only shortly after my arrival at the Home. I was not yet sunk into morosity, and was napping in the sun with my hands behind my head, iron manacles notwithstanding, feeling the warmth of midday sun on my closed eyelids, when the ground beneath me — limestone cap rock along the Balcones Escarpment — began to tremble, so that I dreamed I was falling, sliding down some abyss: that the earth herself was trying to shed herself of me, in due imitation of the pattern recently set forth by my parents, and mocking my loyalties.

It lasted about ten seconds. The bedrock on which I rested was very perceptibly vibrated, and a rumbling sound was audible, like that of a train of cars, with the beats quite rhythmical, as if, in those few moments, anyone who cared to listen could be made privy to some constant logic or rhythm always present beneath us, but never suspected, never even intimated — and yet one which powers everything.

Allow me to discuss the magnitude of this force.

Among the effects of earthquakes, though of a secondary character to the immediate destruction and turmoil, are the drying up of springs, or the sudden increase of their volume. Sometimes the occasion is signalized by the escape of mud, water, gas, or flames. Occasionally, as in the Andalusian earthquakes of 1884, the ground is rent open for considerable distances.

During the frightful disturbances of Calabria in 1783, the phenomena of ground ruptures ranked among the grandest and most fearful effects of the catastrophe. Whole mountainsides slid down in mass and tumbled into the plains below. Cliffs fell down and rocks opened, swallowing the houses which stood upon them. Entire villages of man were subsumed.

In one remarkable instance in the country of Cutch, the Great Runn sank down over an extent of some thousands of square miles, so that during a part of the year, it remained inundated by the sea, and during another part was a desert without water.

Earthquakes are found to occur most frequently at new and full moon; also, more frequently at perigee than at apogee; also, more frequently when the moon is on the meridian than when in the horizon; also, more frequently in winter than in summer; and finally, more frequently at night than during the day.

In subsequent days to the Balcones tremblings at the Home, I would conduct experiments upon the transmission of sound waves, both horizontal and vertical, through the strata. With a classmate I would take a hammer and would line him out at some great distance between us (as much as was permitted by the encircling of concertina wire), and would crouch with one ear to the ground and then signal him at his far and measured remove to strike the earth once with the hammer. I would make a visual note of the downward swing of his arm and then with stopwatch mark the first wave of sound, which would arrive slightly ahead of all others, traveling faster through the conduit of the rock; and then I would mark the second approach of sound — what we think of as 'true' sound, carried diffusely on the winds aloft, but in actuality slower and more sluggish than earth-sound — so that it was for me as if hearing two voices saying the same thing, not quite simultaneously. As if the sounds above were but wind-wavered, distorted echoes of the true stories being told below.

From my measurements of time and distance I could calculate the velocities of transmission for different mediums. The variability in these ratios would then illuminate for me the different porosities within each formation, and the ability then of each formation to retain within those porosities various fluids such as fresh water, salt water, oil, or even gas.

With the meager allowance given to me by the state for my labors — stripping the foil liners from the interior of cigarette packages — I subscribed to the Beaumont newspaper, which, though nearly three hun-

*dred miles from the Home, was but a short distance south of our farm;
and in that manner I was able to keep up with the news of each week's
subterranean developments: the dry holes and gushers, their depths and
locations, and the individuals involved in this titan play.*

*I learned intimately all the surface outcrops on the ten acres encir-
cled by the Home's perimeter. As my chains would permit me, I crawled
over every ledge, rill, gully and wash — handled every stone a hundred
times; as I similarly traveled, in my mind, to and fro in the great imagined oil fields of Spindletop, to the south.*

*In the evenings I would stay out as late as was permitted and would
not participate in the organized games, but would instead sit upon the
highest point and stare across the river to the distant stone building, two
miles away, that was the Home for girls. I would try to catch their scent
on the breezes: scent of garments, scent of hair, scent of underarms, scent
of anything.*

So went my sixteenth and seventeenth years.

•

Wallis put the journal up and was trying to decide whether to pull
down another.

He had no idea what time it was, and was startled to hear the
thumping of Mel's snowshoes against the porch.

The sound of the cabin door opening — an electric stillness, a tension he could feel even in the basement — and then the sight of her face
at the top of the cellar door.

She watched him for a moment before speaking. "How much did
you read?" she asked.

"Don't worry," Wallis said. "I won't tell. I have no reason to tell.
There is no one to tell it to." He gestured to the earthen walls. "It's all
over," he said. "It's almost all gone."

Mel sat down at the opening to the basement, framed in light. "It'll
be over after he's gone," she said. "Or rather, after you and I are gone."

"Does Matthew know?"

Mel shook her head.

The light from Wallis's lantern was fizzing, sputtering low on fuel.
To Mel, it looked as if he were disappearing. "Here," she said, reaching
a hand down, "come on up."

AT SCHOOL, SHE TAUGHT THE STUDENTS EACH DAY IN HER allotted thirty minutes about wolves and deer, and then from that — as if those stories were the base out of which could grow all other stories — she would inform them about other miracles of the woods. She told them of bulbs that lie dormant for decades, awaiting the breath of a forest fire that warms the soil in just a certain manner. She told them how the seeds of another plant might lie dormant for a thousand years, requiring precise factors before germinating. The seeds of such plants might then discover, upon blossoming, that their requisite pollinators — an insect, or even a bird or mammal — had gone extinct as the seed slept, so that those plants were also destined to fall into extinction, like an echo of the pollinator, and they would exist only a bit longer in the present, and seemed somehow less beautiful, not more, in that desperate isolation . . .

She told them about the sentences that the plants and animals wrote upon the land, and their invisible script in the sky — the way the ravens followed the wolves who followed the deer who followed the first edges of green growth at snow's edge in spring; and of the way the transcription was then reversed, in a blood tide pulled gently by star- and moon-spin: of how the wolves got the seeds tangled in their fur, as did the bears that came to eat in these green places, and to eat too upon the skeletons of the deer — dead deer lying along the edges of the wolf trails like salmon carcasses along a beach — and of how then the seeds were dispersed by the comings and goings of bears, wolves, and ravens, like some graceful net or ordered plan cast across a ragged surface of confusion.

There was a disparity, she said, a similiar confusion in our souls, and a sorrow in our blood, which occurred when the stars still ordered these movements and rhythms but when those orders could no longer be carried out, because of too many obstacles: dams, highways, cities; and when many of the principal characters in the plan were extinct, or of such reduced numbers as to now be insignificant.

The dread she felt in telling them such stories was balanced by the joy and hope she saw in their faces. She told them not to despair. She told them that the valley was like an island, still intact, and that those patterns of grace still operated fully in the valley; that that was why it was possible to feel such magic each day. She told them that what other people call "magic" was once a normal and everyday response to life everywhere else in the world.

The students wanted desperately to touch a wolf, see a wolf: to pet one, stroke one, gaze at one. Some mornings she would take them out in the yard and howl, trying to get the wolves to respond. The students would join in, as well: and sometimes the wolves would answer.

She would bring in samples of the wolves' fur; would bring old skulls and the plaster casts of their tracks, and the cracked-open bones of their prey, and their mummified scats full of deer hair, in her attempt to prove how a thing that was invisible could be understood to be as real as anything else.

The clock on the wall carved out her thirty-minute intervals, and then, after that, she sat in the back row, listening to Ann and Belle talk about Constantinople, Hannibal, addition and subtraction. *Jane Eyre*.

Colter asleep more often than not, with his head on the desk. The angle of sun growing slowly more direct. Some days the sunlight even carried with it — though only for a moment, felt through the glass windows — a thing like a trace of warmth. But most days, the snow kept falling, and the woods — save for a few of the starkest characters — kept sleeping.

The smell of paste, the clipping sound of scissors during art class. A sweet breathy stillness in the room, a laboring, as the students concentrated on their art projects like divers descending, and no world beyond the one which they held at that moment in both hands. Mel's attention would sometimes wander to the wolves — wondering what they were chasing, what they had killed that day — wondering if they missed or even noticed her absence from the woods.

The first gap, or arrhythmia, to her winter data in twenty years. Their stories being washed away to untold silence. At one point the wolves were silent for a week, and Mel had the thought, the fear, that because she had stopped pursuing them, they had left the valley: and when she finally heard them again — a single long, low howl, at first, but then the whole chorus of them — it was a sound that seemed to crack open all of winter's silence, and it took all the willpower Mel could muster to not go out to where they were calling.

It was still in the middle of the week, and the students were becoming accustomed to, even anticipating, her lectures. She could have taken a day off and gone out to meet the wolves, could have deceived herself that it was research for the students' sake — but she was honest enough with herself to realize the depth of her loneliness, and her homesickness for human company, and she knew that if she faltered and went back out to the wolves so soon after trying to turn back to the world of man, it would be for her as if she had leapt into some ever-deepening abyss; she would have no chance whatsoever. Irretrievable, she thought.

Nor did she shut her ears to the wolves, when they began calling again. She took the students back out on the porch, and they all listened. Everyone was surprised that she did not go to them. Even the two old teachers, Belle and Ann, were surprised; Belle encouraged her to go.

But Mel stood out there with them for a full five minutes, until the howls had ended — It will get easier after this, she told herself — and when they went back inside and the students wanted to know what the wolves had been saying, she had to tell them that she didn't know.

The snows kept piling higher. The sheer weight of the snows — twenty feet by February and still rising — was such that the weight of it was continually compressing, metamorphosing from white feathery stacked snow into thick blue waves of twisted ice, which draped themselves over whatever angularity lay below. Then the blue ice in turn compressed, so that the lower bands became a cobalt color, and below that, black: not from any impurities, but from a supercompression of whiteness.

The deer, with their hooves scarcely the size of coins, cut their trails deeper into the snow, packing their own trails tighter, while the snows on either side of their trails rose still higher, so that now it was as if they were living in tunnels; and always, they were having to climb up out of those chilled tunnels and strike off floundering toward some new tree, from which to chew the bark, or the twigs. And in this manner more trails would spread dendritic from the main trails, and these in turn would be cut deeper to form tunnels, and from them would spring new trails, wandering from tree to tree as the deer slowly girdled whatever soft tree they could reach or find, so that even in the deep heart of winter the deer were like a kind of fire, gnawing and consuming and burning, as the snows piled still deeper.

It was nothing for the wolves, with hearts of ice, to catch them now. It was as if the entire valley of deer had become like termites, writhing in logs. The deer were trapped in a maze, a labyrinth of box canyons; and one wolf would run along behind them, chasing them down the ice trail, while another approached from the other direction, and still others bounded along up above, huge-footed, as if flying across the new snow, until soon enough, all participants converged.

Things were different for the wolves now. They were still one organism — the pack comprised of five individuals, like the strands or fibers in a rope or a muscle — but now the alpha female carried a beaded chain of six tiny wolves — enough to double the size of their pack, if all survived — the embryos in February no larger than a string of pearls, but riding along on the rhythm of the hunt nonetheless, like a necklace, an umbilicus of tiny voyagers deep in their mother's belly, and warm, always as warm as a bed of coals, even amongst all that ice.

She was home well before dark each day. Often Colter would ski with her back to the cabin, asking her questions along the way, questions they had run out of time for during class, and which he had been holding cupped within him all day. Sometimes they would stop and search for antlers, though it was now all but impossible to find them, buried so deep in the snow, and embedded in those cobalt layers of ice. Usually, they just talked as they skied, though always their eyes were alert to the signs and presences around them — the markings of passages other than their own. Colter would ask questions about Wallis, too — a child's questions, such as what his favorite food was, and his favorite animal; his favorite color, his favorite book — as if molding or sculpting Wallis — for lack of anyone else — into some assemblage or approximation of a father, and Mel considered the buffering, calming effect Wallis might have on Colter, and then laughed out loud, considering the gas and fuel mixture that would have been Colter and Matthew together.

A thing could be either one way or another. There didn't need to be any more variance in the universe than that most basic rule of binary. A thing — glacier, fire, flood — happened or didn't. A thing came or it went. A thing was either being born and was growing, or was dying. And with only those two possibilities — the day and night of things — transcribed across every object of the world, came all the mystery and richness one could ever hope to seek. For even in the act of grasping one thing, and achieving knowledge, there was always somehow an inversion that occurred, where the thing that you grasped or knew revolved back to mystery. The pulse. Within this pulse, day was but a variation of night. The pulse was always moving back toward its other.

"Do you like Wallis?" Colter asked.

"I like him a lot," Mel said. "When I was younger, I wouldn't have paid the first bit of attention to him, but I like him a lot."

"I like how he listens to me," Colter said.

"I like how he doesn't knock things over," Mel said. "He's careful."

"Not boring, though," said Colter. "Just quiet, and careful."

"Right," said Mel.

The three of them made vanilla ice cream that night out on the front porch. There was a full moon low in the east, and as they were watching it, they saw that a lunar eclipse was occurring. At first they thought it was a shoal of dark clouds moving beneath the moon, and paid no attention to it. They commented instead on how odd it was that the wolves were howling so plaintively, and what a ruckus the coyotes and owls were making.

They then noticed the encroaching bulge of darkness, and were chilled by the beauty of it, and the singular shock of seeing one of the things most basic to their lives steadily disappearing. Even with the knowledge of what was happening, they felt an inexplicable quickening of their hearts, and a loneliness. They could not turn away from it, but stared in profound amazement: how could a thing be so frightening and beautiful both?

The shadow crawled deeper across the moon; the discomfort of the animals increased throughout the valley, so that it sounded now like some place of torture. Mel got her binoculars and they took turns watching. The curve of light, the last little glancing crescent of it, out on the far edge; all else was dim shadow.

"The Indians used to say that a frog was swallowing the moon," Mel said. "And you can bet they were scared shitless that they'd be next. You can bet they thought long and hard about mercy."

With the moon cloaked in reddish shadow, the constellations flamed brighter. Orion stood braced to the southwest, legs planted firmly, hunting forever. To the northwest, the comet continued to prowl, its tail more elongated than ever, so that it looked like the sweeping beam of a flashlight, or the headlights of some incredibly lost vehicle far back in the forest; or like some winter-lonely fire, burning so strangely out of season.

Not until the moon had been returned to them did they relax; and afterward, as the valley fell silent once more, they felt cleansed, even purged.

Colter had his bow with him, and they went out into the snowfield and tossed a target into the air for him to shoot at: a frozen grouse from the smokehouse, drawn but still fully feathered — and he hit it more often than not, and each time, they bragged on him.

The moon was brilliant upon them, as if the red cloud of dimness had never been there, and Wallis thought that Colter might be tempted to draw his bow and send an arrow at the great dish of moon, as boys and men have done for centuries, but Colter did not seem tempted by this suggestion, and said that it would seem disrespectful, that he had no cause to hurt the moon.

Later, after Colter had gone, Mel and Wallis fell asleep sitting on the couch — leaning into one another, and then lying down tangled and sleepy amongst each other. Sometime in the night Mel reached up and pulled a hide over them, and later in the night, still a long way from morning, Mel said, "Whatever is happening between us, we won't let him break us up, will we?"

Wallis, still half-asleep, said, "Who? Matthew?" and Mel touched the flannel of his shirt over his chest and said, "No, *him*," and Wallis said, "No, of course not," and then slept deeper, as if diving: but carrying her with him.

•

I dream of the malachite woman. I am out for a stroll, nineteen years old, watching the migration of hawks, when she steps into the corner of my vision. The eternal pulsing at my temples, the perpetual dull ache, clears for a moment. She has just stepped from out of the rain. She stands there watching me as if she has traveled so far — across aeons — but can proceed no further. There is mutual fascination. Her hair is long and black. Her green body has been smoothed by the rain and ten thousand pairs of hands. White swirls of marble run vertically through her, the color of cloud streaks.

I turn and stare at her. If I take one step, she disappears. But she will allow me to watch her, at that several-steps' distance, forever. The ring of fire encircling my brain is gone; the cauldron within subsides. For long hours I can stand there looking at her, knowing utter peace — appearing surely catatonic to anyone who passes by, but during that time so inwardly and passionately alive that all troubles become stilled — this is the rapture an emerging bulb must feel — but then as if through meta-chemical stirrings, as dusk seems to fall — the dimness at the perimeters

of my vision returning — I find that I must have and possess her — that
even if it were to mean the loss of my life, I must have her.

And even before I take the first step, she reads my intent, and dis-
solves. She does not take a step backward — this is how I know she is
real! She merely dissolves. I may not see her again for several years.

•

The map, to Wallis's thinking, was fully finished — fully imagined. He
split and stacked wood. He went for hikes while Mel was off at school.
He would surprise the snowshoe hares and follow their tracks in circles
for hours. They would run ahead of him and then stop and stare back
with only their black eyes visible amidst the field of snow.

There was nothing to do but wait for her to get home from school:
nothing to do but fall in love with her, like two ropes being braided. A
forced move in design space. He understood that it was impossible for
them to live together and not have it happen — that either they would
hate each other, or love each other. It seemed so basic and inescapable
that even Old Dudley and Matthew had predicted it.

What was unpredictable was how beautiful the specifics were. No
man or woman had ever fallen in love in *this* cabin, hauling *these* buckets of water from the creek, burning *this* firewood, and eating *this* meat;
and certainly never in this moment in time, never now. The act's mun-
daneness was balanced only by its outrageous specificity.

It is easy to fit together objects of ragged angularity to form some
kind of structural interlocking; how much stranger and rarer, Wallis
thought, if two objects of smoothness and roundness can be found to
form a fit that is pleasing to both the eye and the touch, and yet will also
provide support.

While he waited for her — puttering around the cabin and walking
around in the woods, and leafing through Dudley's old notebooks of
lust and desire — he thought about the difference between loneliness
and being alone. It was like walking on a journey, he thought, across a
landscape of varying terrain. You just kept walking. It changed, after a
while. After a long time the one would probably change to the other,
and then after still more distance it would change yet again. You just
kept walking. When you felt the peace of solitude, you lingered; when
it turned or scribed again to loneliness, then after a while you got up
and started walking again.

•

They were talking about the malachite woman one evening at dinner. She appeared less and less frequently in the journals, as Dudley had aged — appearing every two to three years in his youth, then five or six, and then finally only about every decade.

"He had one made," Mel said. "Maybe I shouldn't tell you. It was so sad. He had it sculpted and polished out of stone — malachite and jade. She couldn't have been anything like what he'd wanted. It was pathetic," she said, "heartsickening." She shook her head, remembering. "He had her made in India. She had black eyes — opals. She was, as they say, anatomically correct, to the extent that was possible. Every orifice was present, at least." She shivered and looked down at her arms as if trapped again by her own blood. "He kept it in one corner of his office, like a drugstore wooden Indian. Everyone who ever visited the office always thought it was *art*," she said. "Good God," she said.

"Where is it now?" Wallis asked.

"I haven't seen it in a long time. I think he got tired of it. I think he probably just threw it away somewhere."

Wallis pondered this for a moment: the notion of the jade and malachite statue lying in a forest somewhere beneath a few inches of leaves, or in a creek or stream somewhere, head tipped up out of the water, with the current slowly pressing subtle new curves and hollows into the stone woman. The surprise of some traveler happening upon the artifact in years distant.

"Hell, I don't know," Mel said, "there's no telling. Maybe he passed it on to Matthew, like some kind of damn heirloom."

"I'm surprised it's not in the basement, too," Wallis said.

"They're probably still using it," Mel said.

Another foot of snow fell that night. It draped over the cabin, draped over every object in the valley, and pressed down like thumbs or hands sculpting. Some people continued to accept it, receiving the blizzards fully into their hearts, still seeing the snow as the same unremitting beauty when it first began coming in late October; though now a few in the valley began to weaken beneath the psychology of it — bending to avoid snapping, like the trees they continued to hear breaking in the night; and the cold, sprucey scent of new-crushed boughs and trunks and branches continued to fill the valley at all hours, as if somewhere unbeknownst to any of them there was a silent sawmill, forever chewing up fresh fiber and flooding the valley with that scent.

The deer had herded into larger numbers than ever, and no longer possessed any discernible grace. Their ribs heaved gaunt as they limped along the narrow icy trails of their own making — they slipped often — and yet if they tried to venture off of those trails they would become even more exhausted. Sometimes they would do so, anyway — striking out through the drifts toward the top of some distant, unbrowsed bush, barely visible above the top of the snow — but they would not make it, and would instead simply disappear beneath, like a swimmer going down in heavy surf. They would not rise again, but would come to rest several feet below the surface, where they would remain for the rest of winter, perfectly preserved in the blue grip of ice; and only later, in the spring, would the tips of their ears, and then their heads and shoulders, and then the rest of them, become visible once more; and the coyotes, wolves, ravens, and eagles would gnaw on them as the snows receded, as if the wolves and coyotes were erasing them.

The rest of the herd would stand there and watch, whenever one of these voyaging deer panicked and struck out in its exhaustion for some new food-tree. If the deer made it and successfully broke a new trail, the others might follow cautiously; but if it disappeared, they might only watch a while longer — waiting for the deer to resurface — but then they would resume their slow procession down the old ice trail, walking with their heads down, relying only on mercy, and the fact that the wolves might recently have gorged and not be hungry. And the ravens would follow the deer wherever they went, always in attendance.

As winter deepened, Wallis saw people coming into the bar whom he had never met or even glimpsed before, so that it was to him as if the strangers were emerging from beneath the snow. Some of them came into the bar to drink beer, while others came only to stand by the stove and be warmed, and to stare at their neighbors. Wallis had presumed that these isolated holdouts would have possessed some great eccentricity, one which had sent them into the woods in the first place; but he was surprised to see that, if anything, the February and March stragglers were as normal, or more so, as anyone: more normal-seeming than any other random cross section from the outside world — and he wondered if they had come up to this country angular and eccentric, and had been smoothed and rounded, so that they were now somehow comfortable within themselves. They had about them the air of wild horses, or other wild animals, that had been gentled, if not tamed.

Some nights it seemed to Wallis and Mel that Danny was avoiding them; other nights, it seemed that he was avoiding everyone; he would not come out of his room. He was looking haggard and depressed, which they attributed to the winter sadness brought about by the short days — but one evening Helen came over to their table and told them that he was ill: that he had been having chest pains and nausea, pain in his shoulder and arm, and stiffness in his face, and that he had told her he didn't think he had long. His father had blinked out at forty-four; his father's father at forty-two.

Danny was forty-nine and had awakened the morning of his forty-fourth birthday from a dream of his father and had felt his own first angina. For the five years since he had been carrying it with him like an anchor that grew heavier with each passing day, until now, he told Helen, it felt like the wire was stretched trigger-taut: that he could feel the whole works straining to spill out; that no longer could any of the looseness, the sprawl, be held back.

"He just lies in bed a lot," Helen said. "Says he doesn't feel like seeing anyone."

"That's awful," Mel said, and rose to go in the back to see him, but Helen put a hand on her arm and stayed her.

"He means it," Helen said. "He doesn't want to see anyone, and doesn't want to talk about it with anyone."

"Well that's crazy," Mel said. "First off, he can't just cut himself off like that, like he's on some damn island or something, and second, it's not right to put all that weight on you. He expects you and only you to carry him through to the end, and listen to his tale of woe? Bullshit," Mel said, and started to the back again, but once more Helen stopped her and said, "Please. It is no burden at all." And Mel saw then that the shadow of Helen's own time had fallen across her — and the two women stared at each other for a moment, and Mel said, "All right. But what about you? How are you doing?"

"I'm just old, is all," Helen said. "It's not at all the same for me."

"But are you all right?" Mel asked.

"I'm old," Helen said. She watched the question in Mel's eyes — saw her doing the arithmetic, wondering who would leave first, Danny or Helen — and Helen said, "It's not good. He says you could thump him on the chest with your finger and that would be enough to make the whole thing go. He says it feels as if one icicle falls from the porch eave, his heart will follow." Helen shook her head. "He can't keep his food down. It's the end," she said. "He's a goner. We're looking at his ghost, even now."

Mel and Wallis skied home in silence, conscious of the rasping sounds of their skis, and of the heat and health of their own hearts. There was nothing that could be asked of their hearts, that evening, that would not be delivered. They had an excess. They skied in silence as a way of honoring that power, and the brevity of the moments in which they would be in possession of it.

A WOODCUTTER'S TRUCK WENT THROUGH THE ICE ON THE sixth of March, far too late to have been out driving on the frozen river. The mother and father and three sons on board had managed to swim to thicker ice and climb out. It had been a mild day, and though none of them had known how to swim before, they had learned fast.

They said afterward that the current beneath the ice had been strong. They said they didn't know how they got back up to the top, or how they'd stayed together: that some force had lifted them back to the top; though they remembered swimming, too — remembered holding their breath and kicking and clawing against the current.

The woodcutters showed up at the bar that evening to ask for help pulling the truck out. Wallis volunteered. The woodcutters looked at Mel to see what her thoughts were, but could discern nothing. Amy volunteered that she thought things would work out if he did attempt it, for she could tell that the Lord would be with him.

There were already lanterns burning on the shore and out onto the ice when they got there; perhaps twenty townspeople had gathered, and stood around waiting to help pull. There were four horses also, with harnesses being fastened — a busy, workmanlike rattle of chains, a hopefulness in the air — and there were dogs, whose nervousness out on the ice did not pass unnoticed. No one would hook their truck to the chain — there was the fear that the current might pull that truck down with it. The pulling would all have to be done from shore, where the traction was better, and by hand. Machines were too valuable to be risked.

Most everyone stood around on the shore at the woods' edge; only a few men stood with lanterns out on the ice, next to the fissure. They were roped together for safety, and though they joked among themselves as they looked to see if the truck was still down there, their jokes were brittle, and sometimes the joke-tellers would trail off in mid-joke.

A warming fire was built on shore, and everyone greeted Wallis with great friendliness, but with an odd hesitation, and Wallis realized they were frightened. He walked to the edge of the fissure, looked down, and thought that what he wanted was someone to tell him, *No, don't do it.*

Somebody handed him one of the horse's blankets to wrap around him as he undressed, and he crouched by the fire, warming himself as much as he could.

He could hear the torrent of current gurgling and splashing through the gash in the ice. He tried to find a way to say that he had changed his mind — that he wasn't ready to leave warmth.

There would be a rope fastened around him so that they could pull him out if he got in trouble, but he worried that the current would be too strong, or that he would slip free of the rope.

He was seized with the momentary, inexplicable fear that once he went beneath the ice, the entire town would simply let go of the rope, as if desiring or believing it proper that he should meet Zeke's fate, and that they would simply walk away — appearing to him then through the ice as distant stars.

Tent-winged caddis flies began appearing, clouds of them drawn to the lanterns. They fluttered against the lamps and burned themselves in such numbers that there was an acrid, smoky smell. Moths got caught in people's hair and brushed against their faces and arms.

Wallis wondered what would happen if he spoke out against the confines of what he had already agreed to. Could he ever be trusted again?

More moths sprung from the woods, from the rotting logs, and caddis flies emerged from the river — all of them spinning toward the lanterns.

Wallis roped up and walked over to the fissure. Steam rose from his bare skin. He could feel something welling up behind him, coming from the community — a fierce pride and wonder at what he was doing. He sat at the edge of the crevice and dangled his legs in the current.

The cold gnawed at his legs. He couldn't see the truck. He didn't know whether it lay below or had been carried downstream. For all he knew it could still be traveling.

There were two older men out on the ice with him — big-bearded men: not just winter beards, but lifetime beards. One of them was smoking a pipe, and Wallis wanted only to stay there and smell that pipe. The men looked huge and clumsy in their heavy clothes and coats. One of them handed Wallis the chain and then helped him twine it around his left arm to keep him from dropping it.

"Don't get your arm tangled in your rope," he said. "That would be bad. You'd have to stay down there with it," he said, and Wallis realized the older man was shaking — that he was terrified of water. Almost no one in the valley knew how to swim.

Moths continued to swarm the men's lanterns. Wallis turned for one last look back at the shore, but all he could see was an enormous cloud of caddis flies and moths. Some of the moths caught themselves against the lanterns and ignited to quick flashes of light.

Wallis stood up again, seized now with hard fear, with doubt. He could feel the water rushing beneath the ice, his bare feet growing quickly numb, even beside the fire. Naked before the village: the village watching him.

He knew suddenly, surely, that if he went in he would never come back out. He knew it with a certainty so strong it was as if he had already attempted it, and failed, and now was above, watching the subsequent replay of the same old pattern, same old attempt. A feeling stronger than déjà vu.

Mel, with the rest of the village, stood and watched him. More moth-singe around the lanterns.

"No," he said, "I'm sorry. I've changed my mind," and he stepped back into his clothes: and he could feel the villagers loosen with relief. They were not disappointed at all, but relieved and, it seemed to him, honored, that he had chosen to stay among them, rather than risk leaving.

The horses shifted in their traces, chains jingling, and nickered, their muscles tensed and ready to pull: all for naught, but no one minded. They trusted his decision. They shared his certainty — instinct a thing between them as real and physical, as tangible, as a stone that they might pass among them, from one hand to the next.

They walked home in a procession, steam rising from the untested, powerful flanks and haunches of the draft horses, horses' heavy hoofs shuffling through the deep powder. The lantern light shining on the horses made them look as if they were sculpted bright from ice. There was among them a feeling as if Wallis had already been rescued, or had chosen a new path. It was only a truck, they remembered.

Colter slept hard, like something sunken into the great depths of a place. Amy stayed awake through the night and watched him sleep, as she had when he was a baby. She felt utter serenity for his safety, if not his peace, in the coming world. He was strong and supple, and could manage whatever the Lord lay ahead of him. Zeke had been that way, but had not had luck or grace. Amy could feel that Colter had an excess of grace and luck, possessing both his own innate quantity plus the reservoir of another's; and for this, she thanked Zeke silently. She prayed through the night, though in the morning her chin tipped to her chest, and her thoughts drifted not toward God, but to the falconer.

It was the same night that Mel took Wallis inside her, and held him there at their cabin, on the bed of hides by the fire. That was the night that the past fell away, like gouts of bankside mud sloughing into fast waters.

She went to school the next morning feeling more like herself than she could remember feeling since she had been a much younger woman, or even a girl. The feeling of falling, or leaping, was similar — doubtless identical — for everyone, though she knew this love would play out differently, as all did: the specificity of each love unique, beneath the shield of the general, the familiar.

She stopped at an icy creek on her way to school, even though she knew she'd be late. The creek ran to the river, where it disappeared beneath ice, still feeding the dark river that ran so fast and far away. She pawed beneath the snow, found a dried strawberry blossom from the previous summer. She tossed it onto the creek, watched the little current whisk it. It had started snowing again, and was colder, too. In a day or so the new river ice would heal the gash where the woodcutters had plunged through.

She thought of how it had been, holding the rope. She remembered watching Wallis on the end of the rope by lampglow and firelight. She dwelt on the memories of the night before, back at the cabin.

Unavoidably, however, her thoughts turned to Matthew. If this year were like all others, he would be returning in a couple of weeks, coming back to be tended to, and to recover from his annual winter sickness. Her legs and heart felt quivery at the thought. She stood and said Wallis's name once, to the creek, then hurried on to school, feeling like a schoolteacher.

She tried to hold back. She had hoped to make it to April — to resolve things with Matthew in mid-March, and then move on, in one direction or another — but she found now that she had fallen several weeks shy of that goal, like the deer who did not carry quite enough reserves to take them across that last white expanse. She saw them every year by the hundreds: deer that were whittled down to next-to-nothing — brown tufts of hide stretched taut across knobby bones — deer that had plowed through five months of snow only to lie down at the edge of the end of snow, starving — lying with heads outstretched, no longer able to break through the shell of ice covering the world they'd known — only to have the bare brown ground begin opening up, revealing itself days after their death: bare earth, and then green shoots appearing right in front of the deer's unseeing, unmoving eyes.

Every year it was this way — as if spring could not occur without it; as if this falling just short were a pattern for most of the world: as if it took exceptional grace or strength or cunning to cross that last bridge.

Mel wondered what love would be like this time — if it would last long — longer even than the last — or if it would fizzle out in a matter of months, like tufts of hay tossed on a fire.

There was at first a bottomlessness to it, as well as an imbalance. They had been without each other's bodies for so long that now it was all they thought about. They stopped cooking, and nearly stopped eating. Their couplings traversed all rooms and corners of the cabin, at all hours of the day and night, as if they were in their lovemaking laying claim to new territory, or redefining old — and their hands and mouths and eyes on each other were a mapping, and a knowing.

One night during their passions the bed of snow that blanketed the roof of the cabin released, sending rafts of ice down the pitch of the roof and onto the snow below, where the slabs of ice shattered like crystal, a thunderous sound that surprised both of them; and under that new lightness they burrowed deeper into the hides, sleeping only occasionally, awakening often to further explore each other's bodies.

They were not thus engaged when Helen came over one night to tell them of Danny's most recent downturn, but the cabin nonetheless was dank and rich with the odor of their sex, and the air in the cabin was still charged with the electricity of its passage earlier in the day, so that Helen understood instantly what had been lost. She knew that when her son returned to the valley it would seem to him as if there had been a sudden shearing — as if a branch had snapped — and that he would be blind to how gradual it had been.

Helen wondered if Matthew would feel pain, or numbness. She could not decide which she would choose for him, were the choice hers to make.

For long moments she and Mel stared at each other — Mel's face pale with fear, and then blushing, as if with the shame of betrayal. Helen's face was hurt and puzzled, even grieving — but Mel regained her composure, and then, more slowly, so did Helen.

The news she had for them was that Danny had tried to hang himself; that he *had* hung himself, but that they had cut him down in time to save him.

There had only been a handful of them in the bar — Artie, Amy, Helen, and a couple of others — when they had noticed one of the rafters jiggling slightly. A bouquet of dried lupine hanging from the rafter had fallen to the counter, and they had all watched the rafter trembling for a while, and had believed it to be the echo of a faint earth tremor — but then Helen noticed that all the other rafters were motionless, and she'd jumped up and run into the back room, where she found Danny, blue-faced, kicking and gagging and clawing at his throat, looking for all the world as if he had changed his mind. He was all duded up in his rodeo clothes — boots, belt with trophy-buckle, crisp new jeans, pearl-buttoned shirt — though in the struggle, his hat had fallen off, and his feet were dancing light as a pair of mayflies three inches above the ground, seeking purchase but finding none.

In the furor no one had been able to find a knife with which to cut him down, so that finally Artie had had to climb up and use his cigarette lighter, snapping it repeatedly at the thick hemp rope, charring the fibers slowly as his friend's face blackened and his tongue protruded swollen and the gagging stopped, the kicking stopped, and a puddle of urine appeared below his boots, and Danny's eyes rolled back like the whites of boiled eggs.

Finally the rope burned thin enough that the deadweight of him snapped the remaining strands, and Danny fell to the floor. They got him going again, somehow — some half-assed version of CPR, Helen said — and he was in bed resting now, though he now complained of a continuous heat in his chest that felt, he said, like a waffle iron. He no longer had any feelings in his feet, either; but on the bright side, Helen said, his depression was gone.

"Who's with him now?" Wallis asked.

"Artie right now," Helen said. "But Amy's been sitting with him, reading him Bible verses."

"Shit," Mel said, and Wallis didn't know if she was more upset by the news of Danny hanging himself or by the fact that Amy was preaching to him, and Danny unable to escape.

"It's not so bad," Helen said. "He's listening to it, and it's doing him some good. He doesn't have long left. He's not even really Danny anymore."

Helen put her coat back on and was preparing to leave.

"You can stay tonight, if you'd like," Mel said. "Don't ski all the way home tonight. You can get up early in the morning."

"I'd like to," Helen said. "I'd like a little break from it." She glanced at Wallis. "But no, thank you. I'd better go check on Danny."

She went out and closed the door behind her. She fastened on her ancient wooden skis; felt the stiffness, the swelling, in her knees and back. She looked at the lit windows of her son's cabin and tried to feel anger at Mel, but couldn't summon it. She was sadder that Matthew would now have less incentive than ever to return than at the fact that he had lost Mel. Helen knew now that Matthew had probably lost her ten, maybe fifteen years ago. The news just traveled slower for some than others.

She looked up at the stars, then started off toward town, already making plans for Danny's funeral. She lamented that it was still too early for even the blossoms of the serviceberry, so called because they were the first flower to appear in the spring, and thus attended the spring burial services of those who had died in winter's depths and were kept stored in barns in coffins until the ground thawed and the earth's icy crust unlocked, and a true burial could finally be conducted.

She thought of her own dark cabin — the empty store, with the fire in the stove surely burned out. She thought of how tightly Danny would grip her wrist when she returned to check on him, and of how she would not turn away, but would sit there with him for as long as he wanted — for however long he had left — and of how, when she finally went back across the street to her mercantile for a brief nap before daylight, she would want more than almost anything in the world — even more, almost, than a visit from Matthew — a long hot bath; but how she would be too tired to haul and then heat that much water, and how instead she would curl up sore and aching beneath cold blankets and slip into her sleep that came easier and easier.

Her skis cut the snow like blades across the moonlight. Her muscles warmed and loosened yet again, as they had for the thirty thousand days before this one. She didn't resent Mel's choice, Mel's reaching out. She was happy for her. She was happy for both of them. She just missed her boy.

Mel and Wallis went by to see Danny before school. It was as Helen had said: he was living, but was already gone. Artie was sitting with him, reading a paperback detective novel from forty years ago.

Danny looked older than Helen. He wore a purple bandanna to cover the bruises and rope burn. His eyes looked lidded, like an old lizard's. He raised two pale fingers in greeting and then held them there, as if he had died in that position; only his eyes moved now. Mel leaned down against him and hugged him. She thought how if nothing else he should shave himself — his graying stubble made him look even older — and she said so.

With those same two fingers Danny gestured toward the bathroom, where Mel saw a bowl, a straight razor, and a shaving brush. She heated some water slowly on the stove. Then she poured it into the wash basin, put some shaving cream on the brush, and covered his cheeks and chin and upper lip with it, then wet the blade in the warm water and began stroking and scraping. Danny shut his eyes. The smell of steam from the hot water and the soap filled the little bedroom and pushed aside the odor of sickness and sorrow. The razor made a rasping sound not unlike the sound of skis across ice. When she was done, there were no nicks, only a clean-shaven face and throat. She had been heating a towel in the steaming water and she squeezed it out and wrapped it around his face and neck, scrubbed the soap and iron-colored flecks of whiskers away, and then left the steaming towel wrapped around his neck, and he smiled at her and then slept, and Mel hurried off to school, late again.

By early afternoon he was dead, dying in the space between Artie's and Helen's shifts of duty. He had started to scratch out a note to his children, but had not gotten beyond the salutation, "Dear," and their names. Helen came by the school to tell Mel and the others after class was out, and that night, everyone gathered at the bar for a wake. The bar had passed on to Artie, who was not only pouring drinks but tossing them down himself, and there was much wailing and keening, stories and testimonials, and in the woods, the coyotes and then the wolves began to answer the howls of the wake-goers; and in his cabin so far back in the woods, two ridges over, Joshua heard the cries — believing it at first to be the distant honking of geese returning to the valley a few weeks early, but then understanding, when the noise did not change locations, where it was coming from and what it was. He rose from bed and went out and unchained the black stallion, then took him down to the river and chopped a hole in the ice so that the horse could water. Then he put the coffin he'd made for Danny — at Danny's request, but which Danny had never seen — on a wooden sled and tugged it down to the ice.

Made of thin yellow pine and still smelling sweetly of fresh-cut wood, even beneath the glossy layers of paint, the coffin had been fashioned into the shape of a gleaming black saddle bronc with slanted red eyes and plumes of fire leaping from its mouth and nostrils. Its teeth were not the squared enamel of earthly horses, but fangs of varying lengths. The wooden horse had no tail — flames were painted across its rump — and its ears were folded back on themselves like a bat's. Gold streaks of lightning zagged across the horse's body in all directions. Barbed wire was coiled across the tiny bronc saddle, and there hung on the horse's flank a small deerskin saddlebag, into which some of Danny's possessions could be placed.

There was a panel, a hatch, in the horse's neck, through which Danny could be lowered. The horse was rearing up on its hind legs — purple stars and more gold lightning bolts decorated its belly — so that they would have to slide Danny in feet-first; and once inside, it would be as if he were leaning in tight against the big horse's neck with both arms wrapped around it — perhaps not the most glamorous riding style for an ex-rodeo star, but at least the horse was reared up and ascending, rather than plunging.

Joshua skidded his creation down to the river and pushed it onto the ice. The wooden stallion was half again as large as his black stallion. The days had warmed sufficiently to melt the crust of snow to water atop the ice, which froze at night, so that the entire river was now a glassine ribbon, black and shiny as obsidian and flecked with the reflection of each star above. Joshua wondered if there was a corresponding river, or echo, or memory of river, somehow working its path in similar fashion through the stars above.

He hitched the wooden horse to the stallion, then climbed on the stallion and clicked him forward. The big horse loved to run in the cold air, and soon he was trotting, with the larger horse sledding along behind, always at the same distance. The ice boomed and squeaked and creaked under the percussion of the stallion's steel hooves, and the waves of sound vibrated through the ice and traveled up the river as if along a quivering tuning fork. Anyone in town, miles ahead, who might have been near the river at that time, could easily have placed their ear against the ice and heard clearly the sound of their approach. Joshua nudged the stallion to a gallop now, exhilarated by the blur of stars hurtling past his cold-tearing eyes — frozen tears tumbled down his cheeks, and a shooting star melted from the sky just ahead of them, so that it appeared to have tumbled into the river just around the bend. The ice shuddered with each landing of the stallion's hooves, and the pinewood horse skimmed along behind, sending up a starlit spray of ice shavings. Joshua thought of all the fish sleeping beneath the river's ice: wondered if he was startling every fish in the river for a hundred miles in either direction. The sound of their passage reaching on up deep into Canada. Would the fish believe that spring had come early — that the river ice was breaking up a few weeks early, even when their bodies told them *No, it is still too early* . . . What would they think? That the rules had changed?

Joshua slowed the stallion to a canter, rounding a bend, to keep him from slipping on the ice. He was chilled from the wind of their speed and leaned in close against the horse for warmth, and wondered if indeed it was Danny for whom he had been hearing the sounds of mourning. In a strange way that he knew he would never be able to acknowledge to anybody — and stranger still for the lack of shame he felt, in thinking it — he hoped that it had been Danny, and not another, so that his trip would not have been wasted; and he wondered how it would make Danny feel, if it were indeed not Danny, but another who had passed, to see Danny's dark flame-breathing carriage come cantering up for him nonetheless.

The stallion slowed to a crisp walk now. White foam covered his mouth and nostrils, and he was lathered with sweat, steaming. A band of four coyotes trotted down the ice behind them. A lion crouched in the brush on the riverbank and watched, curled its tail slowly.

Closer to town the sounds of grieving, and laughter, grew louder, and the dull glow of lights from the village became visible over the trees. Joshua stopped and let the stallion rest. With his hatchet he chopped a hole in the river ice so that the stallion could drink again. After a great length the stallion lifted its head — water dripping from its lips — and then stared over its shoulder at the silhouette of the fire horse; watched it for a long time.

Joshua waited until the stallion had finally stopped steaming before brushing and currying him so that he would look his best. The coyotes stood motionless at a distance, curious.

Joshua walked back to his creation and examined it. It was still tight and intact, ready for use. He climbed up on it, opened the hatch, and slid down in it, then propped the hatch open so that he could see the stars.

He curled up inside the fire horse, smelling the odor of fresh-sawn pine, and gave the stallion the order to continue. They started forward again. Joshua watched the stars scroll past overhead and listened to the spray of ice against the belly of the coffin. Down in the horse's belly he could hear no mourning, but the stallion knew where he was going and stopped when he saw the lights of town clearly through the trees. Joshua climbed out, led the stallion up to shore, tied him to a tree — the fire horse remained hidden back in the woods — and went up the hill toward the sound of the wake.

It took a full day of bonfire to thaw enough ice and earth to create a place soft enough to dig, and then another two days of shoveling and pick-axing, working in shifts, to carve a hole deep enough for the fire horse. As the town worked, they tried to remember how many of Joshua's animals were already down there — five, they calculated, now six — a salmon, a bear, a bobcat, a goose, and an elk — and they commented on how they would soon have to expand the cemetery, and of how the occupants had to be spaced farther apart, like the giant trees in old-growth forest, with so much space between them. It wouldn't do to crowd big things together.

They finally had made the hole deep enough for the horse, but went deeper — and at dusk the next day they lowered the great horse into the hole and began filling in the loose soil, until it was up to the horse's back, at which point they slid Danny into the horse's neck. He had stiffened considerably, but they finally got him in, and knew that in the earth's warmth he would loosen soon to the desired fit.

They finished covering the hole, tamped the earth flat, piled flat stones over the spot to discourage the coyotes and wolves from digging, and retired to the bar to say their last good-byes. It snowed hard that night, so that the next day the signs of their recent labors were hidden.

In bed, Mel asked Wallis not to enter her, but to only hold her. She said that she felt weak and hollow inside, carved out, and frightened. Wallis asked if she wanted to go back to the wolves, but Mel said no, that she was just empty-feeling and frightened, was all — as if crossing a shaky rope bridge high above a gorge.

"When was the last time you were frightened?" she asked him.

The profiteers came a week later, on a Saturday. They came in a pack, half a dozen of them on snowmobiles straining to pull small trailers, and people in the valley heard the bee-buzz of their engines coming over the summit one morning and knew that they were back, and hurried toward town to be there when they arrived. Even before the profiteers got there, the townspeople could see the dense blue ribbons of smoke above the trees, ribbons of smoke glowing luminous in the sun and moving closer, as if a train were chugging through the woods, and they could smell the smoke long before the snow machines arrived, and when they came into town the sound seemed to saw winter in half in a way that was neither pleasing nor respectful.

The profiteers knew from past experience not to set up their trailers right away, but to settle in — to come into the bar and have a cup of coffee and maybe a shot of rum; to say hello, after a year's absence — to scope out new faces and take note of who was absent. Danny had always been one of their best customers, and they kept waiting for him to appear, before the silence of his absence finally sunk in on them. Artie explained that he would be taking care of the bar now.

The profiteers told how they had not been able to make it all the way in to the valley in a single day; how they had gotten only halfway the first day and had to set up a big wall tent on the summit and build a fire.

The profiteers were from Helena. One year there had been a woman among them, but this year they were all men. Coming down off the mountain like that, clad in their huge insulated snowsuits and bespectacled with goggles and helmets, they had appeared as an alien species; but now as they sat at the bar and chatted, with their helmets off and their snowsuits hung on the wall, they appeared human again, and benign, even friendly. They understood that their greatest asset was their rarity: that it was at first a simple enough pleasure for the towns-people merely to feast their eyes on the sight of someone new. In years past, depending on the winter, people had come up to them and had touched them as they spoke — strangers resting a hand on their backs or shoulders as if they had known them for a long time, or, more disturbingly, as they would rest a hand on the neck or flank of a domestic animal.

Typically, the profiteers stayed all day and then left at first darkness — wanting to take full advantage of that last diminishing wedge of snowy dusk, when they pulled in 75 percent of their business from the people who had had their eye on something all day but who had been unable to commit until night fell and the profiteers began loading their trailers, ready to disappear . . .

It was funny and touching, what sometimes happened in that last hour of light. One year a woman showed up wanting to buy a ride out of the valley — forever away from the valley. She was leaving her husband, and whether she left on foot or on the back of a snow machine, she was going that night. The one that gave her the ride out had ended up marrying her.

The profiteers had contracted with the postal service to bring in the last few months' mail, and now, as was their custom, they spread it out on the bar and let the villagers sift and paw through it: ancient, fermented fruitcakes from relatives back east; news of births and deaths, weddings and divorces; checks and bills; junk mail; catalogs; and long letters from old friends. Some of the mail was devoured right there in the bar, though most of it was stored away to take home to be read in privacy, and savored.

Sometimes it took half an hour to sort all the mail, and afterward, there was throughout the bar a tapering off of excitement, and a kind of crystalline silence that would creep in — there was never enough mail

— and after the pile of leftover mail had been double- and triple-checked (old newspapers held upside down and shaken for any stray postcards that might have been hidden) — a loneliness would settle, and the townspeople would feel colder, and unfulfilled, whereas the day before they might have been feeling just fine: durable, rugged, sturdy — square to the world, possessing neither hope nor despair.

Into this vacancy, this new loneliness, the profiteers moved. They began setting up their trailers, pitching awnings or tents over their wares if it was snowing or displaying them in the bright spring sunlight on nice days. The street became a small bazaar, and the townspeople strolled around each trailer, handling everything: touching things, sniffing them, consuming them with their eyes.

Old sports magazines. Fresh bacon, fresh lemons, fresh-cut flowers, fresh coffee beans. New books, spines uncracked, crisp as coins. Bathing suits, umbrellas, watermelons, pencils, necklaces, sugar, honey, salt, black pepper, red pepper, limes, oranges, apples, Bibles, records, cassettes, batteries. It always astounded the townspeople how much the profiteers could fit into their trailers, and how sharply even the most insipid junk spoke to their hearts. Teddy bears made in China by child slaves, toy dump trucks, brightly colored throw rugs, picture frames, potato chips, hot-pad holders, walkie-talkies, skillets, gloves, baseball caps, shirts, axes, saws.

They didn't need a damn bit of it, and they bought it all; and in the buying, they felt momentarily sated, though always, immediately afterward — and in the days that followed — they felt somehow weakened, hung-over and confused: as if they had blacked out, during the drinking of too much alcohol, and had, as they lay unconscious, been severely beaten.

Near dusk, Wallis and Mel walked with one of the profiteers down to the frozen river to look at the sunset's last red rays reflecting off the ice. It was going to be a cold night for snowmobiling, but that was how they did it; they had to be in and out that first night, before the next day dawned and people came back to them wanting refunds or exchanges, no longer pleased with the purchases and decisions they had made.

The man who went to the river with Wallis and Mel had worked on a couple of Dudley's and Matthew's wells. He asked when the next well would be drilled. Wallis allowed that he had finished a new map, and that he thought they might be ready as early as mid-summer. Mel said nothing, only watched the glimmering river of ice. She looked to the sky. Venus, above the trees.

The man nodded toward the sea of dark timber across the river — the velvet folds of it rising up to the edges of the mountains.

"You can bet we, or someone else, will be back for all that," he said, talking about the timber: speaking not maliciously, but instead with awe. "We won't forget this is here." He said it in almost a friendly way, like a kind of warning. "We, or someone else, will be back for that. The whole shittaree."

He turned and walked back up to the market by himself, ready for the last hour — the frantic hour. Mel and Wallis stayed by the river. They sat on a fallen tree and watched night swallow the valley, watched the stars appear. They listened to the dull voices above them as the profiteers weighed and measured antlers and hides the villagers had brought to trade — the profiteers paying them only a dime on the dollar, but in hard cash — and then with that new cash there was one more flurry of purchasing, and then the snowmobilers were packed up and heading out, their trailers filled on the outbound trip not with plastic and aluminum, but bone and hide. Mel and Wallis listened to the snarling cacophony of motor shrill as the profiteers left town.

Turning, they watched the beams of headlights ascending through the forest, climbing slowly toward the distant summit. Long after the sound was only a low buzz, and then nothing at all, they sat there, waiting for their hearts to calm.

Later in the night, the owls began to hoot. Mel and Wallis sat closer together, for warmth, and then closer still, for solace.

The river ice made feathery, whispering sounds — the faintest sounds of stretching, if not cracking. Not yet thawing, but beginning to consider it. A sound, to those who sat there and listened to it closely, like that of a bird wing brushing against snow.

The wolves had stopped howling. It was the time when they were digging a den — either excavating an old one or searching for a place in which to build a new one — and Mel would not have been out in the woods following them during this time, anyway — she would have been giving them space and privacy — and so the full weight of her letting go did not weigh quite so heavily upon her.

Wallis was torn between his dread of Matthew's March arrival and his eagerness to show him his latest map and its revisions. The specificity of each contour — all of it from his imagination. Four pounds of brainpan trapping, he hoped, upwards of 250 million barrels of oil.

There was a strange thing that happened, a kind of a leap or transformation, Wallis knew, when you tapped into that much power. Already, in the past year, he had found a few such fields down on the Gulf Coast, and he'd felt a cleaving inside him when this happened: an incandescence in which every fiber of him became part of something larger and heretofore buried.

In the days before Matthew's approach, Mel watched the moon's waxing, knowing that he would come shortly after its full crest. She began to suffer nausea and migraines. They were silent migraines at first, in which the vision in one and then both eyes blurred — but then the migraines would burst into true pain, expanding into her temples and the sides of her skull and behind her eyes as if taking root: and she would have the thought that she would be happy, would know complete peace, if only the headaches would go away; but she knew also that she was having the headaches precisely *because* she did not know peace or happiness. It was as if she'd allowed herself to fall or be shoved into a downward-spiraling funnel trap, like the doodlebug stumbling into the ant lion's lair.

She held close to Wallis on the nights when the migraines subsided. Who would ever have believed, setting out so long ago, that peace could be so difficult to obtain? They continued to love, in all different places, manners, positions, combinations, as if crafting the boundaries of some physical structure.

He asked her about conceiving — about how to avoid it. She told him that she didn't think it could happen — that if it was going to, it probably already would have.

"We used to try and avoid it," she said — speaking of her time with Matthew — "but sometimes we would make mistakes. At first we thought it was just good luck that I never got pregnant, but then we figured out that it wasn't going to happen anyway." She touched a hand to her bare stomach. "It's funny," she said. "Old Dudley's seed is bad — I'm the only thing that ever came out of him, and me just barely — I only weighed about three pounds when I was born — and now here I am, with my eggs no good."

"Sometimes I would miss a period or two," she said. "But I don't think I was ever really pregnant. I think it was just like a kind of a pause. I think my body took whatever Matthew and I made together and kind of absorbed it," she said. "*Consumed* it." She laughed dryly. "I'm sure it was me, not him. I'm Dudley's daughter. His flaws are mine, his blood is mine. Some of them, anyway. Most of them." She sat up and put her arms around Wallis. "It's a way the world has of keeping itself safe," she said. "What if I had a boy, and the cycle of Old Dudley started all over again?" She shook her head. "It's me. I'm the end of it, the last of it. And thank goodness. We don't need him procreating any further. It's something the world's done to protect itself."

She lay back down, her head on Wallis's chest. She remembered the first time she and Matthew had thought she might be pregnant, so long ago. The ambiguity of their response — the fear and joy both. That child would have been eighteen, now — a man, or a woman, on his or her own.

The moon was silver and swollen, just a day shy of full; in its irregularity, it seemed larger than full. They watched it through the window and lay in its light, bathing in the stream of it — as if it were not impersonal but had instead sought them out.

They heard a savage growling and thumping outside, and went to the window, and saw the humped, heavily furred silhouette of a wolverine on top of the smokehouse, tearing at the shingles. The moon was behind him, lighting the fine tips of his long fur so that they glowed like filaments, creating an aura of light that hovered around each of his movements.

The wolverine felt them watching him and turned to glare at them. He had a shingle in his mouth from where he had pulled it loose, and he chewed it up as if cracking the leg bone of an elk, then spat out the fragments and began clawing and ripping at the roof again. The sight of it made Wallis glad that the wolverine was trying to get into the smokehouse rather than the cabin.

"Don't worry," Mel said, "he can't get through. I've got it reinforced with steel plates and iron bars. He'll give up once he reaches those."

They went back to bed and lay there, drifting back down into sleep, arms around one another loosely, with the sounds of the wolverine outside falling over them in sheets and layers, sheathing around them as would the murmurs of some forever-trickling creek.

•

Solidified Sunlight
Coal and Coal Beds

I sit by my genial grate this pinching winter evening and watch the play of the flames leap from the coal and play with the draughts of air passing up the chimney. Here is comfort — here is peace. How the fierce wind howls about the windows while I enjoy this life-sustaining warmth. The other kids — the inmates — yonder at the Christmas play. The femmes — none to be found. Curious is this coal — this combustible rock, wonderful, and abounding in suggestions. This warmth is yielded by combustion. This rock burns. That which burns up is essentially carbon, or a hydrocarbon. It is so with petroleum; it is so with gas; it is so with coal. The source of uncombined carbon is in vegetation. Our carbonates, like limestone, contain carbon; but it is combined with oxygen; it is already appropriated, not free — not in a condition to be burned.

The coal must be composed of free carbon, to a large extent — mingled, probably with some hydrocarbon. Carbon, as we see in charcoal, burns without any brilliant flame, and without smoke. Hydrocarbon, as we see in kerosene and illuminating gas, burns with a bright flame. It is a mass of carbon saturated with some liquid or gaseous, or perhaps, bituminous, hydrocarbon. In any event, we are induced to trace its carbon to a vegetable origin.

Now, if we look over a pile of coal we shall probably detect some indications of vegetable tissue. In some of the shale attached to pieces of coal, or mingled with the coal, are some impressions like fern fronds. If we go to the mines, we even discover stems of moderate sized trees imbedded in the shales above the coal and occasionally in the coal itself. All these circumstances conspire to convince us that the coal is of vegetable origin. If we were to search further we should find traces of vegetation resembling our Horsetails and Ground Pines. So we may regard ourselves quite justified in concluding that the coal which blazes and cheers on the grate, was once in the condition of a flowerless tree, rooted in an ancient soil, spreading its green fronds to the sunlight, decomposing the carbonic acid of the atmosphere, fixing the carbon in its own tissues, and setting oxygen free.

So the sun was shining in the heavens a long time ago. The plans of vegetable structure were in existence, and the forces of vegetable growth. How long have those plans endured! How imperishable are the thoughts embodied in those plans! The tree stood upright in the soil; it drank in water by its roots and bathed its foliage in the primeval air. It built its stems and fronds with fibers and cells like the modern fern. The sun stimulated it into action. The sun's warmth imparted strength to discharge its functions. The sun's emanations of light and heat became transformed into stem and frond and tissue.

Whatever vicissitudes that growth may since have undergone, the same eliminated carbon is there; it is the same transformed sunlight that it was millions of years ago. It is ancient sunlight that has been locked up like a treasure and buried in the earth for ages. Here, in this flame, the tissue-substance goes back in its primeval condition — it becomes again carbonic acid, and mingles again in the atmosphere from which it was selected. Here, in this flame, the old warmth reappears; it is the warmth of the sun which shone in the Carboniferous Age. Here, in this flame, the old sunlight is regenerated; this is the very sunlight which became latent in vegetable cells so long ago. It is locked-up sunlight set free after a long imprisonment. It is the wasting sunlight of an age when its blessings were not appreciated, packed away and preserved to an age when man should dwell on the earth to appreciate its uses and make it an agent of exquisite comfort and high civilization.

There are several varieties of coal; let us look them over. Perhaps you will smile when I tell you that the plumbago of your pencil is essentially carbon. So it is. All your pencilings are strictly "charcoal sketches."

How long it takes, then — millennia! — to produce one good drawing by the hand of Man. Mountains rise and fall a thousand times to make one plumbago pencil, one pencil, the one in my hand. Why has the world been created but for us to eat it?

THE STONE WALL WAS BEGINNING TO EMERGE. IT WAS A treat to see the rocks again — to see anything of the earth, other than snow. Sometimes people would go down to the wall just to look at it, and if the sun was out they might stop and sit and stare at the beauty of the rocks — gray and red and yellow, and *rock*, by God, not snow — and they would watch as trickles of sun-water began to seep slowly from all the snow resting atop the wall. The wall would glitter. The seeps would freeze at night, casting the exposed rock in a thin glaze, but the next day if the sun was out, the wall would be glistening again, as if weeping, though to the townspeople in that bright March light it would seem as if surely the wall was crying for joy; and they would find themselves yearning for the time when the snow would go away so that they could resume work on the wall: patching the low places where frost-heaves, or the simple stretching and ripping of the earth's skin, had tipped it over.

The wall had long since stopped being for them the symbol or manifestation of any territorial urges. It set no boundaries, laid no claims. It was only an assemblage of order, a crafted thing of durability. A homage to the beauty just beyond and above the wall — the mountains themselves — and they found themselves barely able to wait for the opportunity to throw themselves at it, body and soul, one more season, one more year.

Though it had only been a little over thirty years since Matthew had first started fooling with it, the wall had now been worked on by three generations of families in the valley, and would, soon enough, be worked by a fourth, and then a fifth: for as long as people in the valley had eyes and hands and strong backs. One year, not so long ago, there had even been an old woman, older then than Helen was now, who had been blind in her last years but who had nonetheless participated.

She had enjoyed sitting on the porch of the saloon in the midday light, drinking a cold beer and listening to the sounds of the town, and to the summer swallows nesting in the eaves above her. A few trucks and jeeps passing by, and the taste, the scent, of road dust, afterward — and she would listen to the clacking sounds of the other townspeople wrestling with the rocks — the slam of tailgates being dropped, the grunting and clattering of slabs and wedges of rock — and she would wander across the street and through the woods toward wherever that sound was coming from.

They would see her coming, and would give her a pair of worn gloves to protect her arthritic hands and paper-dry skin, and would let her work amongst them, groping in the back of the truck for a squarish stone of proper size, one she could fit both arms around and give heft to; and then she would haul it toward the sound of the other rocks being stacked, wobbling as she walked, taking tiny steps.

When she reached the end of the line, she would set her stone down to rest — panting and scratched from hauling the stone — and then with her gloved hands she would feel the set-up before her — the types and shapes and densities of the stones already set in place, each resting bound not by any cement but by its own gravity and relation to the others — and after what seemed to the others a random examination, even a confused groping, she would pick up her rock again. Using her hips as a fulcrum, she would shove it into the place where she wanted it, and it was always a precise fit, supporting not just its own weight, but the rocks around it, and the other stoneworkers would always marvel at how she could find such a fit — not having had the seeming advantage, as they did, of knowing in advance what space was available.

One or two stones was all it took to please the old woman, and afterward she would go down to the river to bathe at some distance from the others, and then would head back up to the bar (her scraped arms stinging, but clean) for another beer. The sun would be lower and not as warm now, but she would wait until its last warmth had faded and the stoneworkers came back into the bar for their evening's drinking. That and the sound of the wolves howling, and other sounds and silences, other compressions, told her it was evening. She would listen to those sounds for a while and then walk home in darkness, bone-weary from hauling the big stones, but filled with something new and whole inside, and she would remember making the same walk down the same road as a child, also in the evening, running and skipping.

In the days that followed, the scratches on her arms would heal to tiny pinprick scabs, bumpy little tattings, and she would finger them in the warm sun and remember intimately the one or two stones she had placed in the wall, and their relation to the others.

No one had known how old she was — it was believed, when she died, that she was 108 — and she did not let Joshua put her in one of his craft, but instead asked to go up into the trees, like an Indian. They had obliged, and her bones were still out there somewhere, catching wind.

The sun caught the rocks, and the rocks caught the sun, and held within them a little more warmth each day, so that the sun became like a plant with roots, reaching horizontally into the wall and gripping it, clutching it, with tiny brushings of warmth. The patches of bare rock enlarged slowly, as if ignited, a few more inches each day.

Salamanders stirred between and beneath those rocks; they writhed within, on days when the sun struck the rocks squarely, and they peered out sluggishly. They crawled out of the damp crevices and blinked, then returned to the safety of the cracks and folds. Some were solid ebony; others possessed the fantastic markings of emerald swirls and fuchsia. Gold zags of light swathed their ribs, and some had red masks. In the winter, as they slept suspended, the moisture in their skin froze, then thawed out again in the spring. Even their blood formed ice crystals, as they slept: but now they yawned and stretched like little bears, purged, with their blood crimson and flowing again.

Young snowy owls, pushed across the border by snowstorms, began to work their way back north again. Occasionally a mature adult would show up, hunting the snowshoe hares, but for the most part they were accidental to the valley, and showed up only when they were lost or storm-driven down from the north.

Mel lifted one of the slabs of rock from the wall one day and scooped up a handful of the rainbow-colored salamanders to show Wallis. When he failed to express proper amazement at them, she remembered that he, like her father and Matthew, was color-blind. She wondered if in her next life she would be able to love a man who would have a proper appreciation of color. A landscape without color was still as beautiful to her as it had ever been — a snowy owl flying through falling snow carrying the limp body of a snowshoe hare, so that afterward the only thing one had been able to discern for sure was the owl's eyes and the drops of bright red blood on the hare's breast — all else soundless and colorless. The stands of white-barked aspen, leafless, also in the falling snow — or the memory of white swans passing overhead — black wolves, black ravens, black bears, and the charred stumps from the field of each summer's fires, waiting for the next cycle of winter's snow — the black seeming to summon the white, in that manner, or vice versa . . .

But those tiny handfuls of vibrant color — the stunning fluorescence of the salamanders, the electric blaze of a yellow tanager in summer — the wave of wildflowers that pulsed quickly across the land, then blinked out — the orange interior heartwood rot of logs, the brief incandescence of lichens following a rain — this transient, short-lived world of color just beneath the familiar tones of black and white — made Mel's mind feel, whenever she encountered such a shock of color, as if a part of her had been cleaved open, bringing a greater ability to sense things.

The reappearance of color was a feeling of refreshment, or purging, not unlike, she imagined, what the salamanders felt each spring when the ice crystals in their blood melted once again. A kind of a fizz, or carbonation, or brightness in her own blood — a feeling like youth, or health, or vigor, or love.

"You can't see *any* of it?" she asked Wallis, twisting one of the salamanders so that the sunlight flared off its ribs and illumined him differently.

Wallis shook his head. "I can see all the patterns," he said. "But not the colors."

Frustrated, even lonely, but determined to share that fizz with someone, she put all but one of the salamanders back under the rock and carried one to school, to show to the students.

T HE MOON FELL INTO ITS WANE. MATTHEW CROSSED THE summit on the seventeenth of March, just ahead of the geese. He got the rent car stuck several miles shy of the summit, but fashioned a crude pair of snowshoes out of the green limbs of fir and spruce, and with his pocketknife cut his briefcase to shreds to form bindings and webbing. In the night — the diminished moon appearing in fleeting glimpses from behind a light snowfall — he walked up and over the summit. Once back into the valley, he was able to follow the road into town by keeping to the side of the rock wall, feeling it in the night with his hands as if reading Braille.

He stopped to rest often, and to take scoops of snow into his mouth, for water — he was wearing socks for gloves — and he felt tired and even ignorant for having believed or assumed, as he once had, that his great strength and stamina would last him forever.

Now his knees hurt, his legs were tired, and there was a catch in his back, and worst of all, there was no longer the thing in his blood that had always made him want to push on. This, more than anything — the mental fatigue — he viewed as laziness, and the deepest of character flaws. One that like a strange contagion could lead to the unraveling of others.

All of his body was betraying him: not falling apart, but something more subtle and sinister. Calcium spurs in the joints of his toes. A fluttery heart, when climbing a hill, for the first time. Diminished near-vision. The usual litany of approaching middle age, and he was too tired to even be furious about it. He accepted it as had every other man before him — with a quiet, repressed rage — half ignoring it, as if it were not really happening — as if this diminishing were merely a dream, and any day now he would be restored to his full power.

A grouse burst from its snow-lodging before him, drumming away fast. The explosion of it so rattled Matthew that his heart would not stop racing for long moments afterward, nor would the adrenaline leave his throat, where it remained, bilious-tasting, and wasted. His legs felt quivery then, as the adrenaline finally drained back into his muscles, and he had to sit down on the rock wall and rest. He marveled at how a place that had once been so intimately his home could now surprise him with its strangeness, and how a thing once so familiar to him could now hold the ability to frighten him: as startling a revelation as if, in passing a mirror, he were to catch sight of his own image and cry out at first in unrecognizable, nameless fear.

Every March the pattern was the same, though with an increasing awfulness — a downward spiraling into despair, as Dudley worked him harder and harder, and as he worked himself harder, and drifted ever further from the valley. While conventional wisdom said it was a seasonal disorder, that he should flee farther south every March, he inevitably found himself drawn, in his last stages of consciousness, north to Mel, and the valley.

It was like a fever, when it came. His head seemed to swell, so that there was always a dull throbbing, and a pressure at the temples. All desires fled him — appetite, sex, pleasure, pain — and sadness would fill him: sadness entering him slowly, like a dark river. Sounds became muted, and sensitivity left his toes and fingertips, as did his once-keen sense of smell.

Later, as the depression deepened — dropping him mercifully from consciousness — he would lose even the ability to speak clearly, and then would be unable to speak or even think at all, so that anyone trying to carry on a conversation with him would be certain that he was a simpleton.

Just before he faded from consciousness (though sometimes he fell, crumpling as if knocked in the head with a sledgehammer), he would be filled with the most awful self-hatred: the seemingly sudden, illogical belief that all he had accomplished — the hundreds of oil fields he'd discovered — wasn't worth shit, was worth less than shit — *merde*, he thought, French for shit; *morir*, Spanish for death — *mordant* — languages and images and memories spilling from him as his brain shorted out as if with electrical skips, dropping him into that useless, resting fugue — and there just below the summit, sitting on the rock wall he had built so long ago, with his head bowed and the snow threatening to bury him, he had the epiphany in one of his last glimpses of lucidity that his life was getting away from him, that he really should try to patch things back together with Mel and find a way to live a life with her once more: and he raised his fevered face to the snow and felt a stirring of hope, even happiness, at the thought of her, and of reclaiming such a future.

One more well, he told himself — one more big field. Just one more, to purge it from his system.

He thought of how happy she would be to hear of his decision — his confession that he had been worn down beyond weariness: that her father had humbled him, tamed him, worn him smooth.

He rose stiffly from his wall and started down the mountain.

He arrived in town shortly before daylight, snow-clad, like the abominable snowman. He came in so silently that no dogs saw or heard him. He was anxious for the sight and touch of Mel — anxious to tell her the news — but could absolutely go no farther.

He clumped onto Helen's porch in his disintegrating, makeshift snowshoes. Helen had been dreaming of him, had been sitting in her rocking chair upstairs by her window watching for his passage; and when she heard the thump on the porch and the knock at the door, she knew who it was, and with great happiness she hurried down the stairs and opened the door to let him in, and hugged him silently, overjoyed that he had come to see her first.

He awakened to gray light and falling snow, and the scent of breakfast. Helen looked over at him and smiled, watching him. He knew he'd been lucky to awaken this time — that the next time he went to sleep, he would not wake until true spring — and like someone wearing a mask of another, he conversed with her, chatted about the way work was going, some of the places he'd been and things he'd seen, and all the while he felt his soul gushing away from him like smoke leaving a burnt-out match.

There seemed to be an extraordinary lag between the time he believed himself to be speaking the words and the time the sound of them reached his ears, so that there was often the impression that he was talking to himself, and he couldn't even be sure that the words he was speaking to her were in the English language. Only by the way Helen smiled and nodded could he have any assurance that he was still making sense to her.

When she excused herself to go upstairs to get the photo albums, he used the opportunity to carry his plate outside and scrape the leavings into the snow, on top of her garden plot. He scuffed snow over the top of the wasted food — elk sausage, fried venison, potatoes, toast, and eggs — and he stood there for a moment, strangely steadied and becalmed by his profligate waste. By the time the snow was gone — May or June — she would probably not recognize what he had done, and he thought of how the meat would help enrich the soil to help her vegetables grow, and of what an eerie metamorphosis that was — converting deer meat to plant matter, rather than the other way around. He wondered what the nature of vegetables from such a garden would be — fertilized with the flesh of deer and elk, rather than the compost of leaves.

He hurried back inside, put his plate in the sink, rinsed it, then sat by the fire and tried to focus on staying awake.

Helen came back downstairs with three big albums: infancy, childhood, and young manhood. He was terribly afraid he'd fall asleep midway through the viewing, and not wake up until April. The only thing he still knew, body and soul, was that he had to get home to Mel — had to lie down in her bed, in his cabin, as if fitting himself into some smooth cave of stone, in order to be healed; that it was the only place, the only thing, he still fit. If he did not make it to that place before his collapse, he was certain he would dissolve, and disappear.

He tried his hardest to stay awake as Helen thumbed through the pages. It was like shouldering a great weight — the burden of sleep crushing him down further. He tried touching the stove with his bare finger — tried to pull himself out of his descent and pay attention.

A page with some trimmings from his first haircut. Up until he had been five or six, his hair had been as white as Mel's was now. Cotton top.

Pictures of him fishing, swimming, canoeing; pictures of him down on all fours, eating strawberries in the garden, grazing them straight from the plants. Unfettered happiness. Helen's hand resting on his back now.

She said all the old things, the same things, that any mother has ever said. "You were such a sweet baby," she said. "I can't believe how *little* you were," she said. "It doesn't seem like that long ago at all."

Even in his delirium, Matthew saw how happy it made her to just be sitting there by the fire with him, living in both the past and the present. Her pleasure was an utter mystery to him.

He yawned, and reached his hand out to touch the stove again: held it there a moment before jerking it back.

After they had finished viewing the albums, she told him about Danny. He felt a twinge of distress, but no true or deep sorrow. He knew this would trouble her, so he told her a lie to hide his indifference, his numbness.

"I've been expecting it," he said, shaking his head — "I've been having these premonitions about it."

Helen told him about the burial and asked if he wanted to go across the street and visit the grave. "No," he said, or believed himself to say. "Later. It's too soon. I'm not ready." He tried to picture Danny's face and demeanor, but could summon nothing other than the fact that he was the one who had run the bar. Matthew knew he had to leave very soon, and that even if he did, he might not make it all the way to Mel's — only that he had to try.

Helen protested and tried to think of a way to detain him — wanting, somehow, to warn him of Mel's and Wallis's new bond, but unable to find the words — and trying to hold him back now would have been like trying to catch flowing water with one's bare hands. She loaned him her snowshoes and a coat, and he kissed her again and was out the door running, stumbling: and for a moment, just as he disappeared into the snow, she saw him for what he was — a middle-aged man, not quite a savage, not quite a businessman, not much of anything anymore — but then the snow swallowed him, and she was able, in his absence, to recast him once more into something strong and durable and heroic. She gathered the albums and carried them back upstairs, having to pause three times on the way up to catch her breath. Her own tattery heart hammering against her ribs like the drumming of a flicker against a rotting snag.

He went down not two hundred yards from the cabin: the cabin not yet in sight, though he recognized the trail, and could smell the wood smoke. With breathlessness and lightness he pitched forward. He knew utter weakness, utter helplessness, and felt a deep, abiding regret, as he sank facedown through the snow, knowing he would not be getting up again. He pissed in his pants, lay there motionless and warm for a while, and then the world went dark. But this time there was neither sorrow nor regret at his incompletion — only a darkness so total that there could not be a response to it. He was simply swallowed, and he tucked his head and slept, like a bird with its head beneath its wing.

Colter came across him two hours later; he had been out hunting for antlers and had cut Matthew's floundering new trail, had followed him to where the faint tracks ended. A couple of inches of snow lay atop Matthew's crumpled form, and Colter excavated him, wrestled his limp body up over his shoulders, and then managed to stagger those last couple hundred yards up to the cabin, falling several times but then rising again.

Mel and Wallis heard the commotion and ran to see what it was — believing at first that it was the wolverine again — and when Mel saw Matthew's frost-blued face and his whitened lips, she shrieked. Wallis's immediate reaction was one of relief, that Matthew was in such dire straits — so diminished. Wallis tried to stop himself from feeling that relief but was alarmed further when the relief spread to pleasure. He feared that such ungenerous feelings might be the result from having been studying Old Dudley's notebooks, or that the skull-grip of winter was altering his brain.

They dragged him in, foul-smelling as any wolverine, and laid him by the fire. They stripped his clothes from him, dried him and wrapped him in towels, and began rubbing his hands and feet, trying to get his blood circulating again. His pulse was down to thirty-two; his temperature, ninety-one. His eyes were catatonic. But slowly the fire warmed him, as did their ministrations, and his pulse rose to the low forties, and his pupils began to dilate. As his core temperature returned slowly, his breath began to form vapor clouds once again, and his fingers and eyelids twitched in dream state.

Later he sat up and looked around for a couple of seconds, then lay back down.

Mel sponged him clean and dressed him, and they carried him into the middle room where each year he took his convalescence. They pulled the shades, piled elk hides atop him for warmth, then went out into the bright sunlight to go skiing. Mel skied upvalley by herself, to be alone and think, and Colter and Wallis skied downvalley to look for more antlers. There was very much the feeling among them that Matthew had not returned on his own free will, but that instead they had captured a wild animal and brought it in from the woods: that they had altered some basic flow of nature, and that where he really belonged was down in the groove he had cut for himself: prone in the snow, two feet below the surface, and two hundred yards from the cabin.

M onsters of a Buried World
Valiant Behemoths Claimed by Ice

Some very remarkable facts have come to light from northern Siberia. That inhospitable region was once a home for tropic loving elephants. Only a hundred years ago, their carcasses were known to exist in Siberia imbedded in solid ice. The first discovery was on the borders of the Aleseia River, which flows into the Arctic Ocean. The body was still standing erect and perfect. The skin remained in place, and the hair and fur were still attached.

The most celebrated discovery was made in 1799. A Tungusian fisherman named Schumachoff was exploring along the coast of the frozen ocean for ivory. He noticed in a huge block of clear glacier ice a dark, strange object deeply imbedded. His savage curiosity was not strong enough to lead him to undertake the work of exploration. In 1801, however, the melting of the ice had exposed a portion of the carcass. It was a beast like those whose ivory lay strewn along those frozen shores. In 1804, the Tungusian was able to return and remove the tusks.

In 1806, Mr. Adams, who was collecting for the Imperial Museum at St. Petersburg, found the rest of the carcass still on the shore, but greatly mutilated. It appeared that the Yakutski had regaled their dogs upon the flesh; and bears, wolves, wolverines, and foxes had gladly feasted too. Thus this priceless relic of a prehistoric world was allowed to waste away. But it was not completely lost to science; the skeleton still remained. The tusks were repurchased, and the whole was transported to St. Petersburg, where the mounted specimen at present stands, in the Imperial Museum.

In 1843, a mammoth was found by Middendorf in so perfect a state that the bulb of the eye is still preserved in the museum at Moscow.

The same mammoth dwelt in our country, in Alaska. His tusks are *extensively sought and sold for ivory. This utilization of the ivory — products of an age in which civilization had not yet appeared to learn the value of the product — recalls our reflection on the fossilization of sunlight for a more suspicious period. All these things were wasted, before our grand arrival.*

The great original skeleton standing in the museum at St. Petersburg was duplicated at Stuttgart under the direction of Dr. Fraas, from various bones collected from different parts of Europe. Dr. Fraas, from samples of skin and hair still existing, ventured to give the extinct mammoth a complete restoration. Professor Ward, the great museum-builder of America, saw this monster of mammoths standing in the Museum at Stuttgart and purchased it.

Transporting it to Rochester, he reared a duplicate, which stood for months in the Ward Museum, where when I was twenty-two I had the opportunity of subjecting the creature to a careful study. Let us go back and repeat the visit.

As we enter the door of the building which has been erected for the beast, a dark mountain of flesh arises before us. We had gauged our apprehension to the familiar bulk of the elephant, but here the eye must be lifted to a higher altitude. The whole thought must swell to take in the idea of the towering form which looms above us and frowns darkly and severely down upon us. The monster's brow rises like some old granite dome, weather-beaten and darkened by the lapse of ages.

Two winding streams of ivory descend like glaciers from the base of the dome, while the corrugated and beetling proboscis swells between them. Serene and motionless this majestic form stands awaiting our wonder and adoration. No astonishment disconcerts it; no exclamations stir a feature.

Unlike the dumb mountain, however, this form seems in a mood of contemplation. All this dark and towering mass is conscious. There are eyes which take cognizance of our movements; there are ears which take in the sounds of our voice. This creature contemplates us; he throws a spell over us; he has us in his power.

The mammoth! Aye, the mammoth of mammoths! With long breath, after this suspense of amazement, we extricate ourselves from his spell, and meet his overpowering stare with the force of intelligent will. He is but a beast — let us analyze the sources of his power over us.

He stands sixteen feet in height. His extreme length is twenty-six feet, and the distance between the tips of his tusks is fourteen feet. The sole of his foot is three feet in diameter. His tusks are fourteen feet long and one foot in diameter.

Between his short, postlike forelegs a man can stand upright with his hat on, without touching the animal's body. The whole exterior is clothed with dark shaggy hair, quite unlike the modern elephants, and under the throat it attains a length of twelve to fifteen inches. The testicles weighing fifty pounds each.

Here the old Siberian mammoth enjoys his bodily resurrection. Dr. Fraas was the angel of the resurrection and has made him as nearly as possible like his ancient self. Dr. Fraas is an eminent anatomist and geologist, and we trust his judgment and his veracity.

•

Matthew slept, if it could be called sleep, in a perfect shell of stillness. At first they tiptoed past his room and were careful not to bang pots or pans, but gradually they became comfortable with his sleeping presence. Helen came by to check on him, and stayed with him for some time that first night, not even touching him — afraid of waking him and disrupting his rest. She sat there, watching, until her own head drooped, and she slept too. She slept upright next to him, wrapped in a bear robe that Mel came in and placed around her as she dozed, so that at a glance to anyone who did not know, it would have appeared that a bear was standing guard over Matthew — waiting for him to awaken.

Commerce blossomed; everyone could feel winter sliding away, could feel the mass of it behind them, perhaps vanished from all of the earth. It was still as snowy as ever, but the days were longer and brighter, so that they could feel winter pulled away, like the husk of one thing pulled back to reveal its true self.

The geese were funneling into the valley, and all kinds of ducks. Mergansers gabbled and dived; anywhere there was an open hole of water, the diving birds found it, exploited it, like roots trying to stretch open a fissure — as if the ducks and geese, with their energy alone, could crack open the winter and find spring beneath.

Human commerce blossomed, too, amongst the sound of dripping, and the goose music; more people began coming to town, and staying longer.

They shoveled away the snow and sat on the wooden steps in front of the saloon and drank mugs of beer and looked directly into the sun and rolled up their sleeves and tried to feel the sun on their arms. Some of them shut their eyes and sat very still, as if hoping the sun were some wild animal that would draw closer — as if they could better feel the faintest stirs of warmth by remaining motionless.

Always, they asked about Matthew. There was a wager on when he would awaken. Because the river was still frozen, families continued to drive up and down it in their trucks, scouting for fallen trees to cut into firewood, and to skid out for house logs with which to build new structures, or to repair the old ones. The trees grew largest right along the riverbanks, and each year a good number of them leaned out too far and finally crashed, making the ice shudder and split, though the trees would not break through. Their limbs would snap and skitter across the ice. The deer would hear the tree fall and turn and run toward it, to browse the black lichen that had been in the highest branches.

The trucks moved up and down the river like ships. The children rode in the back, so that if a mysterious weak spot should be encountered — one of the tires punching through the ice — the children could leap free — but almost always the river held, tight as cast concrete. The truck that had gone through the ice earlier was viewed to have been an anomaly, simple bad luck, rather than the pattern of anything to come. The drivers carried a bucket of gravel in the back to sprinkle under the tires for traction whenever they hit a slick spot and got stuck; but by and large the sleeping river was as well behaved as a freeway, and the mother and father, in the front, would scout for the new-fallen trees, and would stop next to one when they found it. Sometimes several trucks would be cruising the ice at any one time, and the river rang with the sound of chain saws, and there was the scent of freshly cut lumber. The families would picnic, with everyone doing a chore — gathering the lengths to cut into firewood, or splitting the firewood into stove-sized pieces. Sometimes one of the family members would cut a hole in the ice with the chain saw and ice-fish as the wood cutting continued. All manner of energy was returning — sexual, too, so that men and women — husbands and wives — seemed happier together.

And when the truck was full of split wood and a log had been chained to be skidded behind the truck, they would drive home — the children sitting high atop the mountain of wood, colder now in the wind, and with the gold sun falling behind the evergreen ridges — a corona from behind the ridge, and then the pulsing blue and pink light of dusk. The trucks drove with their headlights on, moving upstream now, and the ice cracked and groaned but did not break, and all across the river they saw the huge-footed paddings, the comings and goings of the wolves — each track so large that it looked as if the valley were filled with wolves; and yet no one ever saw them. They saw the wolves' deer kills out in the river's center and along its edges — the frozen mounds of hide and bones, with the ravens and bald eagles crowded around as if at a banquet — but the wolves were always gone by that time, and the coyotes would skitter away as the trucks went past, and some of the ravens would take flight while others remained on the frozen shells of carcasses. The bald eagles would turn and watch with snowy heads and fiery eyes, hooked beaks and bright yellow legs claiming the deer fiercely.

The river ice changed colors throughout the days, absorbing the various slants of sunlight — pink and then milky blue and then greenish and then bright white, then flame orange at sunset, as if something were alive beneath the river.

At night the warming fires that the families had built next to their work burned brightly long after the families had driven home — yellow flames sawing ragged against the darkness, and growing smaller quickly — and the silhouettes and moon shadows of deer came from out of the woods, passing in front of and between the fires to get to the limbs and brush piles — and the deer walked past and around the occasional remnant of carcass, and the river creaked as it froze tighter in the night after loosening a bit during the day: but whispered, too, as it began to consider its further release.

The northern lights swam silently above, rolling in sheets and waves across the sky — pulses of electric green and blood light reflected in the ice.

More wolves were now only days away from being born. Mel wondered how she would be able to resist going back into the woods to track the weave of their stories. She might just as well take her data from all the years previous and toss it over a cliff.

During the thirty minutes she taught each day, she sometimes took the students outside, and they went down to the river and listened to the faint crackings, and placed their hands on the thinning ice. They felt the tremblings of the river beneath.

With binoculars, they identified the birds coming into the valley now — the birds following the edges of the river, and filtering through the woods — crossbills, nuthatches, thrushes, kinglets — and she placed blindfolds over the students and taught them to identify birds by their music — taught sound as a kind of sight.

The ice continued to change colors. She cautioned them to stay off of it, and to keep their families off of it, no matter how badly they needed firewood.

They walked around the melting puddles and caught frogs and salamanders. They stood in the sunlight and examined them, learned their names and habits. Belle and Ann found that the students' increased knowledge of how things worked in their valley gave the students an increased confidence in the world, and a hunger, and that for the rest of the day they were better able to learn other lessons.

The geese kept arriving — noisy as trains, and in numbers so great that it gave the impression that all the land to the south was just as wild as the valley itself. As if the geese were sewing together places of similarity.

The children wanted to know when Matthew would awaken. They had never known him as anything other than someone their parents told stories about. They welcomed him each spring not as a native but as an odd visitor. They could see that Wallis was sweet on Mel now — many mornings he accompanied her to school and kissed her lightly before she went in the building — and they were not bothered by this shift in allegiance, not having the history against which to measure such a change in loyalty. They viewed it as no more spectacular or unusual than any other seasonal passing.

In the swamps and ponds the ice thinned and grew transparent. The sunlight passed through those opaque layers and became trapped beneath the ice, as if in a greenhouse, warming the waters so that in the muck and mire things were beginning to grow, and yet without oxygen, so that fetid, powerful gases strained against those ice caps; and whenever and wherever the sun's warmth could pierce a small hole in the ice, those gases would vent, sour and sulfuric — odors so dense it seemed they possessed colors — greens and golds, like the songbirds that would soon be returning from South America — and no one minded the powerful odors, but felt instead invigorated by them. The waters in the ponds and lakes and swamps began to turn over, recycling their layers of nutrients — bottom layers of water rising heat-stirred to the top, and upper ice-cooled layers sinking — and it was possible, in that growing sunlight, to believe that one could be similarly strengthened, just from breathing that air.

"This is water howellia," Mel said, holding a plant in her hands in the classroom — five minutes of her time left, before she had to lapse into silence. "It's not found anywhere else in the world. This valley created it." A glance at the clock. "Here's a sedge," she said, pulling another specimen from her bag. "This is what the grizzlies graze on in the spring to help purge their systems after the long winter's sleep. It helps clean out the toxins," she said.

"There are about twenty-five or thirty grizzlies living in this valley. Five wolves, though in a week, we might have ten or twelve. Maybe thirty or forty people," she said. "If we lost the wolves and grizzlies, this valley won't be worth a damn. Excuse my language."

"Lost them?" the students wanted to know. "How?"

The slowing days attenuated. The new light stirred the sludge in their blood. Colter chewing on a piece of sedge, sitting in the back of the classroom: pretending to listen, but the words not linking up and connecting in his mind. Adrift; one part of him drawn farther north, like needle and thread, while only a part of him remained anchored.

•

The Cemeteries of the Bad Lands
In Another Life, I Would Have Had No Love
   The wait for the Malachite Woman is interminable. I sit on the hill above the Home with my back to the fence for as long as they will allow me. My ankles are hobbled with iron shackles, as are my wrists. Even the once simple act of sketching in a notebook has now altered itself into a disagreeable task, so that the radial and brachial muscles of my arms and shoulders are swollen with muscle, as if I have been shoeing horses, rather than making these notes and guiding the reader through lands known only to me. From the ankle hobbles runs a span of chain a hundred feet long, welded to a stake driven deep into the caprock, around which my perambulations carry me like a badger defending his den; but of an evening, when day's work is done, I am content to sit on the hill and stare across the veld and forest-leafing below, to the Home for Girls, and contemplate the Malachite Woman, whom I know more surely than anything is there. I have never seen any of the girls from the Home — occasionally, after dusk, I can catch fragments of their songs,

and know again for certain that the Malachite Woman moves among them, as a deer moves among trees in the forest. Her movements and manners are inscribed perfectly in my mind, bounded and circumscribed by the places where I have not seen her.

I am too late in the hole, too firm in the trap; even were I to confess Old Pap as the sole participant, they would not let me out of here until my time is up, and would surely execute him.

Fireflies, like luminous spirits from the century before, at peace and immersed in beauty, prowl the riverbottom across the way, blinking serenely as if looking with lanterns for some lost something. The more desirable the Malachite Woman becomes to me — the more firmly I know and understand her — the more aware she becomes of my presence, and she disappears. Sometimes I fear she will vanish for two or three hundred years, such is the force of my desire: that though she would find me pleasing in every way, there is some rule of this upper universe not yet understood by me, which would require her to dissipate as if tatters of fog before the sun's rays, were I to draw too near her, with too much force.

Restraint is my only hope, and I have none.

I hold in my hand before me a pale stone gleaned from beneath another stone, here — tapped free of its chalky tomb with blows from my hammer (at the ringing sound of which, I am certain, the Malachite Woman turned her head and listened for some time, knowing it was me — me whom she has never seen) — imbedded in which lies the skeleton of no fish ever viewed alive by man, or even by the likes of man. It is like a useless puzzle piece, one which many would discard, not understanding that whatever story can be pieced together for it must also be applicable for us.

As the Malachite Woman stands there listening to the ringing of the hammer, not quite understanding what about the sound draws her interest, sparks emitted from the friction of steel against stone ignite briefly and tumble to the barren ground like melted or fallen fireflies. In breaking the rock open to discover the fossil trapped within, I smell the dust from civilizations that presided over life's beginnings. This fish, not man — not you or I — presided at the right hand of God, for the longest time.

The amphibian, the fish, the bird, the serpent, the mastodon are but a stage in the transformation of matter into mankind.

This dead stonefish could be but the lost soul of one of your great-

aunts, or even one of the Malachite Woman's progenitors. I grip the stone in both hands and sniff deeply, as if burrowing my face up into the clefts of the Malachite Woman herself. Which distance is greater — two miles, or two hundred and fifty million years?

This stonefish — this great-aunt, who did not quite reach the glory of you or I — died and floated down into the midst of a sleeping, dreamy Golgotha — descended into the dead past. How old are these graves, locked in stone? Through how many winter storms have these silent skeletons slept here? How they rise, story above story. These bottom tiers lay down to their long repose while the great lake flapped its waves above. Its fishes swam over cemeteries. Other mute remains came in, layer by layer, to the house of silence, and the hand of Nature carefully envaulted them. The receptacle was filled; the lake vanished; the continent was here.

Life once thrilled through all these torpid frames. These were conscious creatures. They were joyous creatures walking on the green earth. They were beings which inhaled the vital air and basked in the life-giving sunlight, and enjoyed each other's society. They fed on the productions of the forest and the glade. They slaked their thirst at the border of the wide lake; they cooled themselves in its waters, and sported with its waves. Death came to them, as to their thousands of predecessors — as it comes to us. They were mired in a slough; they were hunted in a jungle; they lay down in the shade of a friendly tree. Some force of nature bore them to their burial. The lake was their tomb, and the lake preserved its trust. It was a later vicissitude which opened their cemetery and exposed these testimonies of a vanished age to the curious and irreverent scrutiny of science.

I am nearer to this stonefish than to her, and, some days, anyone.

The clang of the iron triangle summoning me to the bunkhouse. I hide the stonefish in the bushes and trudge down the hill toward the Home, chain music around my ankles, where the lackey will unhinge me and allow me to prepare for my own nightly descent.

•

The longest Matthew had ever slept after one of his collapses had been five days and nights; and when the fifth night passed that year, and still he slept, Mel, as well as everyone else, was worried.

The children came to visit him. They brought presents — antlers, stones, drawings — and went into his room one by one and observed him sleeping, and left their gifts in a pile on the floor, where they would be the first thing he would see upon awakening. One girl, bolder than the rest, touched his hair. Mel had told them about him — how he became worn down at the end of each winter and never quite had the strength left to carry on over into spring — and they had wanted to come see what such a phenomenon looked like. There was almost nothing she knew that she did not find herself wanting to teach them. As one rope unraveled, another was being woven.

Helen came over to see him too, that fifth night, as she had every night. The river had finally begun to break up — great chunks of ice splitting and cleaving mid-river, shearing free with snaps of torque and cannon boom, which sounded like a sporadic, ongoing war — except that rather than strife, the valley was filled with excitement, as the river was free now to surge beneath the sun unhindered. It was joy in a language unknown to man, and all through the valley, the pleasure of that release could be felt, and the river broke off slabs of ice larger than buildings and tossed them to the side — raced them down river's center, then shoved them rudely onto the shores, where they ripped out limbs and even whole trees, plowing and scouring along the banks for hundreds of yards, like ten million years of glacial passage in a few moments. The rubble of ice, the strewn shards and edges, glinted in the sun like diamonds; and from a distance the sounds of the river flowing again was like a stirring in one's own blood — as if in this valley there could be no separation, no disconnection; that one thing could not move without the other feeling that movement intimately.

Each time a new ice floe snapped, the geese nesting on the river's islands and oxbows would begin shouting and honking, as if connected even more intimately — as if something in them had been tugged — and the people in the valley would feel their blood leap and surge yet again. And each of them marveled at how Matthew could keep sleeping through it. It was not the sound so much that should have awakened him, they supposed, as those leaps within the blood.

"He knows it's over between you and him," Helen said to Mel. "His body can smell the change. He doesn't want to wake up to that fact, is why he's sleeping so long this year."

The three of them were sitting on the porch watching the day's end and listening to the river's distant rush. Wallis tried not to think of old springtimes with Susan down in the green hill country. A snipe was making its wavery wing-song overhead, rising into the dusk and then plummeting — staking out its territory with a thing ephemeral, invisible, the song of wind rushing over its wings.

Wallis found himself once again daydreaming of his map: believing in it fully, despite the fact that he had never seen nor touched any of it. He held onto it as if to an anchor. It had to be right.

"Maybe," said Mel, talking about Helen's theory. "It could also be that Pop's taken the last bit of him there was left to take."

Mel washed Matthew's hair that night. He had turned over in his sleep shortly after dusk, and the elk hides were off him. She set a bowl of soapy water beside him, and another of warm rinse water, and by lantern light massaged his scalp. Wallis sat next to her, expecting him to wake up, and wanting to see the spectacle of it. She scratched his scalp and rinsed his hair, rubbing it with a damp towel, scrubbing the old week's worth of sleep away, but still he slumbered.

The lantern sputtered out of fuel. The soap suds came to her elbows, and she kept scrubbing: lightly, gently, but thoroughly. Starlight illumined the three of them.

Mel toweled his hair dry. If Matthew had felt it or even dreamed it he did nothing to show his appreciation. She tried to comb and straighten his hair without waking him. It was a mild enough night that she could leave the window open to dry it. It made Wallis a little sad to see someone so strong clinging, hanging by such threads, to the ghost of who he once was.

South winds blew all night, and Mel and Wallis slept lightly but without moving, as if on a beach listening to waves. Wallis dreamed or imagined he heard the faraway cracks of thunder, though there was no rain — only warm, incessant rivers of wind. It was a sound like the plates of the earth rifting apart — the river continuing to fracture — and rather than feeling loneliness at such a sound, Wallis felt a cleanliness; and all night they slept motionless, their bodies twined and lying loosely over one another.

When they awoke in the morning they could hear the geese coming up the valley in even greater numbers, and other birds — where had they come from? Had they emerged from the snow? Had they been blown in with that wind? — singing along the creek and fluttering around by the porch.

"Bohemian waxwings," Mel said, lying there with her eyes open, still not moving, and finally she sat up, saw Wallis looking at her, smiled, and for no reason known to her, covered herself.

They went to the window and looked out at the swirl of wings; a landscape of color. There was an insect hatch going on, mayflies with slow wings whirring, rising to the morning sun. The waxwings were all over them, dipping and darting, snatching them all — the world a cloud of glowing mayflies; and a cloud of waxwings equal to it. Birds swerved to avoid colliding with one another as they dived at the slow-moving, spinning, light-filled mayflies. It was an annihilation. Everywhere — on all branches, on the porch railings, and on the eaves of the cabin — waxwings were perched, gulping down the pale green mayflies; and the morning sun was behind them, illuminating the birds' flared combs and their bright eyes, and shooting light straight through their brilliant yellow tails, tails the color of sulphur. The sight of that color, the smudgings of yellow, and their furious activity after the long winter began to fill Wallis. He stared hungrily at the tails — yellow everywhere, a kaleidoscope — and felt tears welling in his eyes.

The light came in through the windows and, though it was only morning sun, warmed their bodies.

"Listen," Mel said, and at first Wallis thought she meant the chattering birdsong, but then he heard another sound above it, the steady streamings of the geese, and then above and beyond that, and all around it, another sound.

They went out into the sunlight.

It was the sound of running water — not just trickling water, but water gushing everywhere. The creek was making music again, and every little drainage, every little draw in the woods behind them, was gushing; and it was a sound that made them smile and then laugh, and they stood there flat-footed and bare-assed in the sun and laughed. Wallis had never thought of running water as a funny sound, but it made them laugh: the sound of the water, finally running free again, exciting the water in their own bodies, and they laughed, and held out their arms to feel the south wind on them, and watched the frenzy of the birds.

From farther down the valley, along the river, came the continued sound of explosions, and as the sun rose and spread warmth into new corners, warming new things, the explosions continued, a sound like the earth splitting. With each new crash they could feel things released, and they felt strongly now that they, as well as everything else, could get on with the business of living, and the business of growing.

In school that day, after her brief lesson, she sat in the back of class with Colter, while all the water in the world, it seemed, released and ran past them.

She skied home, believing for certain it was the day Matthew would awaken — the day she would have to crush him — but when she got home, Wallis was sitting out on the front porch, examining his map for the thousandth time, and Matthew was still sleeping.

They sat in the sunlight together for the rest of the afternoon, and were silent: both of them edgy and anxious now.

They slept wrapped in the same elk hide that night, warm together after having loved, and Mel dreamed several times of turning around and trying to go all the way back to the start, where Matthew was still waiting for her — but in the morning she had more resolve, and rose and dressed and went off to school again.

More and more of the rock wall was emerging, as were the tops of snow-buried bushes: as if the world were being created in a week. Colter had gone down to the river the first day of breakup to see if his father was still there, but one of the huge tongues of ice had carried him away, and had scoured clean the cairns as well.

The bears were tumbling from the earth — each day their tracks laced the slushy snow again, as if a tribe or nation of beings had come back into the valley with those south winds — and several of the black bears, gaunt and sleepy-looking, black as ravens, had been seen wandering through town as if lost. No grizzlies had been spotted yet, though some of their tracks were showing up along the river.

Each day in school the students asked Mel, "Is he awake yet?" and each day she had to tell them no, and had to just keep waiting, still trapped.

Some days they could hear, through the open windows, the sounds of Amy's singing — choirsong, joyous, carrying from half a mile away. Some of the students sitting closest to the window would grow drowsy and lay their heads down on the table for a few minutes. Mel remembered her school days in Houston thirty years earlier. Almost nothing had changed. There were still wars in Africa and Israel. The recent developments with Russia were different, but in Russia's formerly mysterious place now stood China. Central America was still in turmoil. The French were starting to act like Americans. The British were still the British. She stared down at her desk and ran her fingers over the scarred initials Matthew had whittled into the wood so long ago.

•

Earth's Deepest Graves
Where We Came From
    Attending carefully to the movements of Amoebae *beneath the hand lens, we discover that these movements have an end in view. The tentacles are extended in search of food. This animal is forever hungry. It is conscious of hunger. It knows how to secure food. It has a will which sets its organs in motion. It knows how to seize a particle of food. See! Its arm is wound about a minute animalcule; it holds it, but now it does not convey it to the mouth. Where is the mouth? In truth, there is none. The arm is absorbed — animalcule and all. It disappears in the common mass of jelly, and the animalcule is seen within it.*
    So this creature feeds. It gets around its food successfully; but it simply pours itself over it. What an amazing simplicity of structure is here! Indeed, there is no structure; we have little more than a shapeless particle of jelly. Whenever the animal takes breakfast, it extemporizes an arm for seizing it. Whenever it eats, a mouth is extemporized for admission of food, and a stomach is extemporized for receiving and digesting it. From all the ailments of hands, mouth, teeth, and stomach, this animal is happily free. Exempt from headache, sore eyes, ringing ears and heart flutterings, it still exercises all the functions requisite to make it an animal.
    This modern creature is the representative of Eozoön. *But* Eozoön *could not be placed defenseless in the sea. A little lump of jelly would be swept into annihilation by the waves.* Eozoön, *however, planted, held fast to its support, and immediately secreted a strong roof over him for protection. A thousand little holes through the roof allowed threads of its gelatinous substance to be protruded. These coalesced in a common film which spread over the roof like a coating of tar. This was unprotected, and a second and higher roof was built. The structure was now two stories high.*
    Through the upper roof innumerable minute perforations allowed the jelly of the second story to be protruded in fine threads, and these in turn coalesced, and a third roof was secreted. Thus the process continued, and the structure became many stories high.

Meantime other individuals were planted by this, or near this, and by and by, they were so enlarged that they grew together, and grew as one animal. So hundreds and thousands of animals grew together and continued to grow and enlarge the structure during probably a thousand years.

As time passed, this organism grew old and effete. The life-time of its species was drawing to a close. It was destined to be replaced by something better suited to the improved circumstances of the world.

All the time, however, the sediments had been gathering about the bases of the rising reef mass — as the dust of time accumulates about the temples of the ancient cities. As they become buried and forgotten — buried thousands of feet deep — buried in sea sediments which became stone. Then the aeons of the world continued to roll by. Oh, what a varied history was enacted while the tombs of Eozoö remained silent and undiscovered!

In the Age of Mind, a marble edifice was demanded to meet some want of civilization. The primeval tomb was opened by the quarryman, and there rested the relics of the first inhabitant of our globe. It is that of which we have been speaking. We are the quarrymen.

OLD DUDLEY ARRIVED LATE ONE AFTERNOON, WALKING UP the trail on flapping ancient beechwood snowshoes and wearing a parka lined with wolf fur. He was walking with a deer-antler walking stick and singing "The Eyes of Texas" at the top of his lungs. Mel ran down the trail to greet him and to quiet him, so that Matthew could still sleep.

"It's been too long," he said. "Has accident befallen my young man?" He patted Mel's flat belly. "Still unimpregnated, I see," and Wallis, who had gone down the trail also to meet him, marveled at how quickly the old man could take the wind out of any joy or peace: how he appropriated it, soiled it for the beholder, and in so doing made it perversely his own.

"Little namby-pamby crybaby was a bit woozy when he left," Dudley said. "He's not still sleeping, is he?" Mel nodded. *"Sissy,"* he hissed, and started to further enumerate Matthew's failings, but then noticed the bond between Mel and Wallis — a looseness of shoulder, a half-step closer to him on her part — a trace of odor, of comfort together — and he arched his eyebrows, was startled for a moment, but then said to Wallis, "Well, you must really be putting the wood to her. How many times a day, how many times a night, in love's first flush? Ah, but no matter, it will fade. Some day she will spurn you, twenty years hence, as she seems to have spurned my little man." He shook his head sadly, and for a brief moment his ice-blue eyes locked with the eyes of Mel's green fire, and Wallis could almost hear Dudley's brain gears spinning as he recalculated the lay of the land.

"Pop," Mel said, "you're the only other blood I've got left in the world, and it's good, as always, to see you, but you're going to have to cut the shit or leave. I don't have the time for it I used to. I can't shake it off like I used to. I used to be able to ignore it. But it bothers me now."

A sharpening of interest in Dudley's eyes — a glinting of pleasure. "You're getting older," he said.

"I've got a job," Mel said.

"Good God, girl," Dudley cried, "your first one! Congratulations!" He turned to evaluate Wallis anew.

Wallis took note of the old man's humped, still muscular shoulders — as if there were a young man beneath the parka, and wondered what it had been like for Dudley as a child — teased pitilessly about the tong marks, surely, and then to have to watch his father slaughter, for lack of a better word, a fellow countryman — as if he had been nothing more than meat — a hog or a cow waiting to be killed. As if in his old father's chest had beat some throwback heart, something not suitable to this civilized era but belonging more to the behavior of men from other, more savage times and places.

Wallis didn't care about any of that. It was interesting, but it was water under the bridge. He didn't care if Dudley had horns sprouting out of his head; he could find oil, and when he showed them how to draw the maps, and showed them things about the workings of the old earth below, there was such a muscular purity, a precision, to his teachings, that Wallis didn't care if it had been Dudley himself who had done the stabbing, burying, and burning: he would have listened anyway. He would have been unable to turn away. He wanted to know what lay below.

They walked up the path to the cabin. Now there were tiny patches of earth showing around the trunks of trees, and Mel and Wallis stopped at one of the larger patches to simply stare with awe at the beauty of the black dirt, and at a few sprigs of juniper and kinnikinnick.

Old Dudley watched them with fascination. "Why, y'all are *cripples,* is what you are," he said. "Your lives aren't worth a damn. You've got to add up both of y'all to even make a fraction of a normal, healthy, human being. Look at you poor fuckers, staring at dirt! You should both come back to Houston, where you can see all the dirt and grass you want. My *Lord,* children," he said, as Mel and Wallis stood there and admired the patch of bare ground, "what is wrong with you?"

They ignored him; they stood transfixed, unblinking, feeling a strength entering them, filling the fiber of their muscles with a power as had the sunlight and sound of flowing water stirred their blood earlier.

Old Dudley sensed it, and could sense also that it was not happening to him — a gulf, an absence — and he was jealous. "Hey," he said to Mel, tapping her on the shoulder with the back of his hand, "stop that."

Finally she looked up at him, her hypnosis broken, but her eyes seemed cloudy and distant, like those of a dreamer, or an old person, or one in love. Dudley waved his hand in front of her and said again, "Hey — stop that."

Dudley went straight to where Matthew was sleeping: gazed at him for a long while. Mel had been shaving him so that he did not grow a beard in his sleep, and Dudley commented, with some attempt at concern, on Matthew's jaundiced condition. "What I want to know is," he said, "how does he piss?"

"He doesn't," Mel said.

Dudley glanced at Wallis. "Does he still get boners?"

Mel went into the kitchen to begin supper.

Wallis watched as Old Dudley peered around the door to be sure she was gone, then gave Matthew a thumping kick to the ribs — not full force, but not a love tap, either. "Hey boy," Dudley whispered, "wake up. You're losing it. You're losing everything."

Matthew's mouth sagged open in unconscious protest, but then closed slowly — a movement that was strangely reptilian — and Dudley did not try to stir him again. Dudley frowned, then turned his attention to Wallis.

"You should come home," he said, and Wallis knew he meant immediately, rather than after the well was drilled.

"I finished the map," Wallis said.

Dudley stared at him, not knowing what he meant at first — thinking he was speaking of one of Mel's maps of wolf movements.

"How?" Dudley asked, incredulous. He gestured outside. "You couldn't have seen a fucking thing. It's all covered with snow."

For the first time, Wallis felt a twinge of doubt, but pushed it back. The accumulation of all the days of confidence held like a sea wall against ocean's breach. "I mapped the rivers," Wallis said. "And the slopes. And old samples. And some of Matthew's old maps . . ."

"The incorrect ones," Dudley said. "The ones down in the basement." He glanced at the cellar door, then back at Wallis, and saw that he knew.

"Yes," said Wallis.

"We'll look at it after supper," Dudley said. One more study of Wallis, to be sure that Wallis still belonged to him. "My old man was a corker, wasn't he?" he said.

"Yes," said Wallis, "he certainly was."

They went into the kitchen, where Mel was cooking venison backstrap in an iron skillet. She finished searing it, added salt and pepper, and put the meat on three plates. She added a little water and flour to the skillet to make a thin gravy, but that was it, for supper — the venison, and red wine.

Wallis tried to focus solely on the moment, and to enjoy the meal — no future, no past — and he glanced over at Mel by candlelight and smiled; tried to daydream for a moment, imagined loving her in the spring, and summer, and fall, if the well lasted that long, but then realized he was drifting again. He tried to plant his feet firmly in the moment: as if there might never be anything more than this evening — as if this could be the last of everything.

He had one more bite of venison. Old Dudley had finished his and was looking hungrily at Wallis's plate, but Wallis ate it quickly, before Dudley could steal it.

"How'd you get here?" Mel asked. "You're in pretty good shape, but you sure as hell didn't walk all the way."

"Dog sled," he said, proudly. "Dog fucking sled." He raised his sleeve to his nose to smell it. "They stopped and shat every quarter mile of the way," he said. "A green vitreous shit. Toxic. I couldn't hire a fucking snowplow — no one would take me. You live in a wicked place," he told Mel. "I tried to get here sooner. To wake Matthew and bring him back home before he enters fucking *hibernation*. But the young dogsled lady I contracted with — the lass — said her dogs were sick, and she had to rest them. Said she wouldn't run them any far- ther. We had to stop for the night." Dudley sniffed his sleeves. "The echoes of their putrescence bubblings rang all night. And the young lady would have nothing to do with me — spurned all of my advances, even those consisting of financial reimbursement. The stakes went quite high," he said, shaking his head. "She finally left the tent and slept out with the shitting dogs. But here I am."

"Oh, God," Mel said. "Where was she from — where did you hire her?" she asked, trying to think whether she knew anyone with a dog team.

"That little shitcan outpost," Dudley said. "The last place you come to. The other Swan. Anyway," he said, shrugging, "I got here."

There was a bumping sound from the bedroom — a weak coughing — and Dudley leapt from the table and ran to check on Matthew, and the others followed — but he had only been stirring, and now lay on his side, still sleeping.

They went back to the table. Wallis was eager to spread his map out and show it to Old Dudley, but Mel wanted to have a campfire.

"It's still winter!" Dudley cried, but Mel said, "No it's not, it's spring!" And they went out into the back yard, punching through the weakening snow in places and sinking to their waists. There were cav- erns of air beneath the snow all around them, but finally, by flounder- ing like deer, they got out to the campfire ring, and with a shovel Mel excavated enough snow to reveal the stone wall of the fire ring and the benches.

They went into the woods and began gathering fuel, snapping limbs and branches from the winter-tossed trees and carrying them back in armloads. They got the fire lit, then settled into the ice bowl Mel had carved out, as if into an amphitheater, and warmed themselves. Around them the snow and ice glazed, and they passed a bottle of wine back and forth; and to Wallis, in those moments, it was almost possible to believe that Old Dudley was normal, or at worst eccentric. Wallis was able to hold this illusion for about five minutes — until Mel got up and went off beyond the firelight to pee and Old Dudley leaned in and whis- pered, "She's playing you like a fish! She's committing a foul — rob- bing you from me, and from your work. She's doing to you what the *land* does — she's bending you, shaping you! Don't relent! Drill through her! Take the pussy and run! Don't let her trap you. You should maybe come back to Texas *now.*" He placed a veined old hand on Wallis's thigh and gripped it hard: the tong marks at his temple pulsing like the summertime tympanum of a bullfrog.

Mel returned and settled back into the ice cave. The light on their faces was orange, and at times the heat was intense, as if they were being roasted alive. "I see he's trying to trade Matthew in for a newer model," she said to Wallis, and Old Dudley grunted and said, "Same as you are, honey."

"Tell me about what it was like when you got out," Wallis said.

"You mean out of East Texas, or out of the Home?" Dudley asked. "The Home was the best thing that ever happened to me."

"The Home," Wallis said.

Dudley finished the last of the wine, tossed the bottle into the fire, and pulled another from beneath his coat. They began drinking anew.

"I escaped a few times," Dudley said.

"Where'd you go?" Wallis asked.

"The first time, I went all the way home," Dudley said. "Ma wasn't long for the world and Pap was looking pretty rough himself. Pap said I had a debt to society and had to finish paying it. He put me in his old shitcan truck and drove me straight back to the Home. Ma wanted to at least fix me dinner, and a pie to take with me, but Pap was going ape-shit. He'd gotten it into his loony old mind that I had gotten tired of taking the rap for him and that I'd come home to trade places with him. Shit," Dudley said, "I'm probably lucky he didn't *kill* me. He thought I was going to back out of my deal." He laughed, shook his head. "He questioned my *loyalty,*" Dudley said. "Dumb fucker."

"Did he have any loyalty?"

Dudley harumphed. "Obviously not." He looked up at the stars. "All of my sterling characteristics, I received from my mother."

"Me too," said Mel.

"I took a boxcar out there," Dudley said, "and got there damn quick — rode through the night and got there by daylight, just when the sun was coming up — but it took a lot longer, going back to the Home. I'll bet I hadn't been home thirty minutes before he was stuffing me in his old truck, taking me back.

"The damn thing kept overheating. We'd have to sit and wait for it to stop hissing, then bail creek water into it to try and cool it down. And he couldn't stand to just sit there and wait while it cooled — he had to keep moving forward, pushing forward, as if scared I would run away if we paused even long enough to sit beneath the shade of an oak tree. Instead, when the car was too hot to run, he'd push it by hand, with me at the steering wheel. Wiry little bastard would be huffing and puffing, sweating, about to pass out — we'd be rolling about one mile per hour, and even less than that, uphill — but he had to keep us moving. His soul was in torment," Dudley said. "Rage equals the mass of a thing times its acceleration.

"He'd huff and puff us up to the top of some little hill — I'd be worried that he would throw a clot, and I'd be stranded there — and finally we'd reach the crest, and he'd run around and get back in the truck, and we'd coast down the other side, wind rushing through the open windows, for a moment, until the hill bellied out and it was time to push again. I think that was when I first began to get the notion that he didn't care for me: that there was something wrong with him." Dudley touched one of his tong marks unconsciously. The fire had burned down to low coals and the three of them had edged in closer. "Oh, children," Dudley murmured, "what thin edge separates the world from true madness? Is it a weak or rotting floor through which any generation can crash? Do we not yet have the grace of the buteos, the accipiters, and the eagles?" He stared at his bare hands, seeming ill at ease on what to do with them.

"Later in the day, when it finally grew cooler, the shitcan started running again, and we drove on through the night. I was sleepy and lay down in the front seat. I watched the gas flares from the oil fields burning in the night — dozens, maybe hundreds of them, all around us. It was beautiful," Dudley said. "I sure didn't want to go back.

"We got there at daylight. I lost the privilege of going outside for a solid fucking month. *June.* At night I'd see lightning bugs out my window. Oh, I cried some bitter tears," he said.

He opened a third bottle of wine, but didn't pass this one around.

"What about the other times?" Wallis asked.

"I would only be gone for an hour or two," Dudley said. "I would be out and back before they ever knew I was gone."

"You went over to the girls' school," Wallis guessed.

"I would sit on their porch," Dudley said. "I never really went inside. I could have. But it was enough to just sit there in the night breezes and feel them sleeping: and to walk around the perimeter of their dorms, and take in all the different scents." Again, he touched his temples. "The calcium is slowly filling in my dents, over time. They're not so bad, now. They were really bad then. I didn't want to scare anyone."

"Is that where you met your wife?" Wallis asked.

Dudley laughed, glanced at Mel. "Oh, no," he said, "she was an angel. She had nothing to do with any of that. She was an angel," Dudley said.

"She was," Mel added.

"Then how — why —" Wallis began, and Dudley laughed, examined his big crooked hands again. They were the only thing about him that looked his age. "I don't know," he said. "I don't know."

They were silent for a while, after that. Later, Mel said, almost speaking to herself, "Sometimes I miss her so much that I still say her name out loud just to hear the sound of it."

The wind stirred the coals. Small flames leapt up and sucked at the cold air as if nursing. Dudley got up and put more wood on the fire. Pitched another empty wine bottle into the flames. The paper label on the bottle caught fire, so that it looked as if the bottle itself were burning. Old Dudley pointed to it and said to Wallis, "I suppose you want to know about epitheliality." Mel snorted.

She had heard Dudley lecture to, and capture, Matthew — had seen Dudley overtake and capture and absorb him like a glacier creeping down a hill that plucks a boulder from the hillside — but she didn't think he'd be able to get Wallis. He seemed to lie at deeper depth — or to have the ability, when threatened by Old Dudley's approach, to sink, like a fish that slowly lowers itself into deeper waters without seeming to move a fin — simply vanishing.

"We've got these tiny sheets or layers or wrappings of cells in our brains," Dudley said. "Each layer, each epithelium, is the thickness of only one cell. Same as rock formations in the earth. It's all electrical circuitry, of course, in our heads. And you can whip your head around real fast, and for a second — or for one cell's-width fraction of a second — you can see things that used to be on the landscape you're looking at — trees where now there are none, or buffalo, or Indians, or dinosaurs — but then your brain rights itself and the electricity flows back into its proper epithelial linings.

"You can see forward, too," he explained. "The residues of all things that ever happened — the memories of them — rest out on the land hundreds of layers deep — cell memories out there like the husks of autumn locusts. You can turn your head too quick in the other direction and sometimes gather enough data to understand what will happen in the future. But that," he said to Wallis, "is of no use to you or me.

"Now about hypercerebreality, and deep craniality," Dudley said — he was murmuring, almost crooning — "the electronics in your wiring can orbit round and round in your skullcap — that's the horizontal powers within you, the ones that permit you to walk around on the surface with your usual patterns of speech and locomotion — the ones that keep you from being too much of a numb-nuts — but then there's this state of deep craniality you can sink into it — a seam, a taproot of electricity that sends you several epithelial layers deep into your own mind. You get *below* the present," Dudley said. "What it's like actually, is a kind of orgasm. You get the root of your mind down into that one cleft and, my word, there's no telling what you might find."

"Where's Matthew?" Wallis asked.

"Well," Dudley said, glancing toward the cabin, "he's actually nowhere, right now. His power's off. His electricity's shut down. He's brain-dead. Burnt out." He cleared his throat and was somber, considering a future without Matthew. He'd certainly seen it before. After a while, they just didn't get better. The miracle of regeneration did not one day occur. The dry casings of insect shells scattered in the wind.

He turned his attention to Wallis. "It's getting cold," he said. "I guess we'd better look at your damn map."

Wallis was surprised by the trembling he felt. All winter he had been secure in the crafting, his dreaming of the document; but now as he rose from the stone bench and hurried back to the cabin to retrieve the map for the master, he felt as if he were climbing out of a dark and safe place below, up into the broad light of scrutiny: and it occurred to him for the first time that a work conceived and crafted in the darkness might not fare well under the examination of light.

He shook off these fears. It was his map, and he believed in it, as he had believed in half a hundred other maps he'd created, and which had found oil.

He carried it back to the campfire. Dudley and Mel had piled more branches on the coals so that the flames rose and were taller. They spread the map out and pinned it down with small stones.

Wallis watched as Dudley stared at the map. He saw the forward, expectant lean of Dudley's shoulders — like a man settling in to a great meal — loosen and dissolve into disappointment, even sorrow. He saw the brightness leave Dudley's eyes — saw a cloudiness enter them. "It's wrong," Dudley said. "It's just wrong."

Wallis felt his blood draining. "What part of it is wrong?" he asked.

"All of it," Dudley said, quietly, and by the way he did not rant or rave, Wallis knew that he must be right. Carefully — as one would pick up a dead fish — Dudley lifted the stones from the map, scrolled it up, and placed it in the fire, where it caught quickly, burning in a bright plume of flame that, for all its light, gave no warmth. The map faded then to a charcoal husk, and bits of it broke free and floated upward in sky-fragments.

"Listen," Dudley said, "it would have been asking a lot for you to get it right without even ever *seeing* it. Hell's sake, boy, I don't think anyone could be expected to produce a map like that. Everything's covered up with this nasty old snow," he said, and Wallis felt sickened by his kindness — realizing, by the degree of that kindness, so unnatural for Old Dudley, how dead wrong the map must have been. He realized too that Old Dudley was scared: that his best geologist was as if in a coma, and his second-best, his only other, had just crapped out spectacularly.

There would not be time to train a third. Dudley cut a glance at Mel, a look that implied he thought she might somehow be responsible.

"Maybe you should look farther in," he said. "When spring comes. Maybe you should cross the river."

Mel moved in close to comfort Wallis — she put her arm around him and said nothing — but Wallis needed no comfort, for there had been no ego in the drafting of the map, only pure and unfettered falling. He was unhappy, even sickened and amazed at how he had let himself believe so deeply in a thing that was so wrong, but there was no pain, and only the dullest sense of loss. Old Dudley and Mel were taking it far harder than he was.

Mel didn't see how he could stand to do it again. To her, this seemed as it would to pass through the long winter and come to the edge of spring only to turn around and head all the way back through winter. She twined her hand in his as if to hold him back.

There was a movement and a sound beyond the cast of firelight, back toward the cabin. At first their eyes wouldn't focus, and when they did their minds couldn't connect with what their eyes were telling them. Wallis believed it was a black wolf crawling across the snow, and

Mel believed it was a black bear, groggy from having just come out of hibernation. Old Dudley believed it was nothing of this earth but instead some manifestation of all his fears that had swelled up out of the earth like a crocus bulb and was now creeping across the snow toward him, seeking retribution — crawling slowly as if injured, but coming for him with unstoppable resolve. He screamed.

Matthew reached the edge of the orange light and lay there for a moment, breathing hard. His black hair was tangled but glossy, and his face had a sheen of sweat from the effort of pulling himself across the snow, but he looked younger, ten or fifteen years younger; and, having rested, he began crawling toward them once more, pulling himself across the crust of snow as if he had lost all use of his legs. He left behind him a yellow stream of incontinence so bright that it glowed orange green — so strong that they could smell it — and it was Old Dudley, not Mel, who went to comfort him, and gathered him in and brought him to the fire, where they saw now that their perception of his youth had been an illusion, and that if anything he looked ten or fifteen years older.

Matthew looked at Mel with great fondness, lying on his back with his head cradled in Dudley's lap. The reek of him was substantial. Matthew looked over at Wallis, smiled at him, then at Mel — at the two of them sitting so close together — and understood that he had been gone a long time. Mel blinked, reached out, took his hand — hers pale and long, slender; his dark and big and swollen and scarred from all the years of working with rock — and they stayed like that for a long time, Dudley, Mel, and Matthew linked as if in a chain, with Wallis sitting slightly outside of and unconnected to them. The ashes of his black map, the charcoal husk of it, stirred faintly as the coals shifted, and the fire grew lower, and the stars brighter, the night colder; and after a long while of just staring at Mel and smiling — not so much caring that he had lost her, but simply made happy by the sight of her — Matthew faded out again, as did Old Dudley — like two horses in harness — and Wallis and Mel lifted Matthew like a sack of dead weight and carried him back to the cabin, changed him into clean clothes, washed up, then went to bed themselves, leaving Dudley asleep by the dying fire.

The night cooled quickly, and though Dudley was warm in his parka, the soft snow into which he had settled froze hard in the night, so that by daylight it had him clutched as if in talons, and he woke up shouting, struggling to pull free — believing that the fur on his parka was a wolf, or wolves, who had him pinned, and that they were attacking him. And on the far side of the river, the real wolves heard him, and began answering with their own howls, a sound that echoed throughout the valley. And in his bed, Matthew's eyes fluttered, then blinked open, and with what little warmth was left in his cooling brain he considered the maps that lay ahead of him: considered future descents, future wrestlings with subterranean angels. A part of him missed Mel and was lonely for the immensity of that loss — but the loss had begun so long ago, and been compounded then daily, that this final loss in many ways seemed like only one more day's worth rather than the sum of all that had ever been.

They had a quiet breakfast. Matthew watched her often, as a visitor to a foreign country might watch the dining habits of a native. Several times Mel thought of what she wanted to say, but by the sleepy, dumbfounded way he was watching her, she didn't think it would matter: she would have to wait until his brain warmed fully. If she decided to ever speak of it at all.

She felt a huge weight of loss — almost as if he, or she, or both of them, had died — but there was also an incredible lightness and freedom, a giddiness. She had given up the wolves, and her old lover, and now she found herself wondering if there were anything else she could give up.

Old Dudley stared at his coffee. He wasn't concerned about Wallis's map not finding oil — he had known that there wouldn't be any, had simply turned Wallis loose into the rank wild valley as a lesson in wildcatting — to give Wallis a taste of what it had been like for Dudley when he had started out earlier in the century — back when nothing had been known about anything — but Dudley was morose at how spectacularly wrong the map had been. Dudley did not consider the failure to be Wallis's, but rather his own, for having picked Wallis in the first place.

By noon Old Dudley and Matthew were gone. Matthew still did not have the strength to stand for long periods of time, so Dudley pulled him across the snow in a child's sled, as if Matthew were some overgrown sauvant or prodigy. They stopped off at the mercantile to say good-bye to Helen — they lingered for only an hour — and then purchased an old snowmobile from Artie, one that hadn't been run in years. They were able to get it started after much effort, and it ran rough, but got them up and over the summit and out of the valley before nightfall, though the exhaust gave them both a headache; and to Matthew, as he rode behind Dudley, arms clutched around his waist, head bobbing weakly, the sound of the machine was as if a saw were ripping his brain open — and so sustained was their voyage, and the ceaseless roar of the machine, that he became convinced that that was what was happening, and that Old Dudley was running the controls, and he was puzzled as to why Old Dudley did not turn the machine off.

Back at the cabin, Mel and Wallis opened all the windows to let the south winds sweep through the cabin. The curtains blew steadily, and they shed their clothes and made love in a patch of sun on their rumpled bed, and whiled away the rest of the afternoon just lounging there, shifting or rotating around the bed, adjusting themselves occasionally to follow the clockwise rotation, the slant of that yellow warmth, and to bathe in those warm winds all through the rest of the lengthening afternoon. At dusk they rose without dressing, fixed supper, then loved again, and went to sleep early. They slept hard into the next day, with a feeling as sure and satisfying as if they had been constructing something real and physical and visible.

BOOK TWO

An Earlier Beginning
Intimations of a Fiery Aeon

We are searching for a beginning. We have followed down the succession of formations to what seems a foundation; but we perceive this must rest on something which already existed; it cannot be the beginning. It is an ocean-born mass of sediments. The ocean preceded the sediments. Something for the ocean to rest on preceded the ocean; what was that? Not something born of ocean. What existed before ocean and ocean sediments?

The deepest rocks are hard and crystalline. We have concluded that their condition has probably resulted largely from the action of pressure and heat. So the resulting state of the materials would be extremely different from that of the original sediments. This is called metamorphism.

An important point is the evidence of ancient heat universally extended. I do not suppose the metamorphism of the rocks has taken place at the surface. The heat engaged seems to have been interior heat. It was shut in and retained for ages by overlaying masses of strata.

That the heat was internal is evinced by many proofs of the continued existence of internal heat. You will recall the phenomena of geysers and hot springs. You will remember that lavas from volcanoes come from some heated interior. Your thoughts will again glance over the thousands of square miles of surface covered by lavas which issued through fissures in the Age preceding the present. You will be vividly impressed with the conviction that intense heat exists within the earth; and since all heat tends to waste away, you will conclude that the earth's surface temperature was much higher some millions of years ago than it is at present. The wastage of the earth's heat is proved by actual observation. Science has measured the amount of heat which arrives on the earth annually — that is, the amount on each square yard — and has also measured the amount which escapes annually. It is thus shown that the wastage exceeds the receipts. The earth is growing cold. This great fact is established by experiment, by observation on the escape of heat from within, and by the records of an ancient higher temperature than now exists at the surface.

Cooling off! That disclosure puts our minds in a new attitude toward the world's history. We have to contemplate the earth as a cooling globe. That points our thoughts backward, along a progress of cooling. That summons us to consider what conditions of the world must have been passed in the progress of cooling. By all the evidence that progressive cooling has been a fact.

This is the way reasoning leads us: Following the course of cooling backward, we arrive at a time such that water could not have existed on the earth. All the water of the earth must have been vapor or gas suspended in the atmosphere. At a time when no ocean had existed, no ocean-sediments had been deposited. All those rocks which have resulted from marine sedimentation were yet non-existent. The earth had probably a solid surface of some kind; but to emit heat sufficient to hold all the water of the world in an uncondensed state, the temperature of the surface must have been high — perhaps a glowing temperature.

We should distinguish between vapor and gas. Gas is dry, like atmospheric air — like the cloud of steam condensed in the air after escaping from the boiler. There may be mineral vapors as well as igneous vapors. Most mineral vapors must be intensely heated. We may call such a vapor "fire mist." If the earth were vaporized by heat, to what limits in space would the vapor extend? We must think of that. If the earth was ever a *fire-mist globe, its dimensions were vastly greater than at present. But now our world has shrunk to its final irrevocable being.*

There is another thought to be mentioned here. The earth is only one of a system of worlds. There is good reason for believing that any remote origin which we can establish for the earth must represent the remote origin of the other planets. In saying they are one system, I refer to their common motions and patterns about one sun: the common elliptic form of their orbits; the fact that all move from west to east; that all revolve nearly in one plane; that, so far as ascertained, they all rotate on their axes; from west to east; that the forms and movements of all, and of all the satellites, are conformed to one set of laws, and that all we know of other planets points to a fundamental correspondence and identity between them. So many patterns are unable to be altered, only discovered.

This conclusion vastly enlarges our field. We must think of each of the planets heated up to a fire-mist condition. It is easier to think the sun also heated to such condition, since he is at present not so far removed from it as the planets. Now, when all these bodies were in that heated condition which maintained them in a fire-mist state, the whole space of the solar system must have been filled with fire mist. These particles — some of which may even have been solid — would have weight smaller than imagination can conceive. So the mist particles were practically suspended in space and required no gaseous support.

The cooling history can be traced no farther back. Such, probably, was its beginning. I am perfectly prepared to admit that matter may have entered existence as a fire mist. However it originated, the temperature implied in fire mist is as inherently probable as any lower or higher temperature. Temperatures are merely circumstances. Whatever temperature prevails anywhere, things adjust themselves to it, and that is natural.

From this point a natural *process of cooling brings to pass all the events in our system's physical history — all the events in our world's history. We are proposing to show this, and trace our evolution in its general outlines. Now you shrink back and exclaim "Evolution? — Fate! Atheism!" That, my dear friend, shows your total ignorance of the nature of evolution.*

Be calm. God was in the beginning, is now, and ever will be. God originated; God controls; God is in the midst of his works. Suppose we call the fire mist the absolute beginning; there are certainly three things which are not fire mist, and require explanation infinitely more than a fire-mist condition of matter. Without these three things, there would never be a cooling history. These things are: 1. Matter — regardless of its condition. 2. Force — and that in its various forms. 3. Method — or everything would be plunged in chaos, and forever remain there. These things imply Power, Intelligence, Self-determination. Where self-determination is present, there is Personality. While the origination of Matter, Force, and Method remains, there is still need of a Creator. These three things originated, were the world to run down like a clock, we should be compelled in reason to ascribe its whole cycle of changes to the primordial activity of a Creative Being. For myself, this conclusion is infinitely short of satisfactory, as I shall explain in due time. But even this is a theistic view of the origin of the world.

·

It was not possible to quantify the happiness she felt. She had assumed the severance of Matthew would leave a scar, but she understood now that it was the wound itself which had been severed; failure had been excised. It was obvious to all — and now that the rift had been announced, all felt free to comment upon it — how Mel was helping sculpt Wallis into a citizen of the valley. Invisible or unnoticed by them all, however — except Helen — was the way Wallis was carving a new Mel. Not rubbing away old external trappings to help reveal the essence of who she had always been, but helping create an entirely new person: one who would fit the future, not the past. One who would fit happiness.

Anyone could have seen it. They could have followed her tracks in the disappearing snow and taken note of the length and briskness of her stride, including the long gaps where she appeared to have leapt, for no apparent reason.

She liked it when he dived. She was fascinated, watching him throw himself right back into his failure, his hands sculpting and sketching and erasing, reshaping each tiny contour on the map, working often by lantern light alone at her desk, in the manner that her father had so long ago worked late into the night beneath a single burning bulb. Some nights, as a child, Mel had awakened and looked down the hall — as if down a corridor or tunnel of light — and had seen him there at the end of the hallway, perched on his drafting stool, shoulders hunched forward, elbows on the table as he sketched and traced, drafting tiny worlds no larger than a desktop. Often she would go get in bed with her mother and press in against that warmth; and then, later, when there was just the two of them, she would go back to her room and would try to sleep, but would end up just lying there with her eyes open, staring at the ceiling.

She read quietly as Wallis dived deeper, wrestled further with the map — working the other side of the river, now. There was a tremor in her heart when she dared consider the possible consequences of his success, but such was the grace of his passion — the muscular immersion in it, to the point of near-hypnosis — as if he were a chrysalis struggling to crawl out of a death-husk — that she could not look away. She read, glancing up from time to time — his lone hand scribing one contour after another, altering hills and mountains, as if he were bound to a thing. Her captive. His own captive.

In the daytime he went out mapping on foot, gathering data, and working the south slopes first, where the sun had burned off the snow and the rock faces of bare earth were visible. He used a Brunton compass and measured strike and pitch and angle of dip — took note of each mountain's orientation, and the larger trends and patterns of the mountains as a complete range. In many places the exposed formations were so jumbled, so twisted and fractured, that they were like giant waves that had just passed their crest and broken into the surface below. It was as if he were standing ankle-deep in the backwash. He did the best he could amid such a landscape of chaos, and looked longingly across the canyons at the shady north slopes, dreaming ahead to July and August, when those slopes would be revealed to him.

Try as he might to dwell in the buried world, it was difficult not to become mesmerized by the beauty at the surface. A whole buried world of its own was emerging as the snow subsided, shrank from everything. The fallen tips of antlers, the tops of stones and boulders, ice-bent bushes, and burrows and crevices began to appear as the snow drew from the valley like the tide drawn by the moon.

More birds were being drawn up into the valley, as if sucked north into some vortex or gusted along by the south winds, though Wallis knew it was not entirely the lengthening light that was propelling them north (as it had sent them south), but some inner hardness, something more durable than even the seasons.

To ignore the essence and spirit of each individual arriving bird would be to subscribe to the view that they were mechanistic, nothing more than chips of color, feather-clad protoplasm hurled across the skies like tatters of bright cloth tossed on the winds aloft.

Wallis did not subscribe to this belief. One had only to look at a single blackbird perched triumphantly upon a slender green reed, eyes bright in the morning light and tilting his head back and trilling and cackling with an emotion, a pleasure at having arrived, that was nothing less than joy. If it were just about hormones, the birds could have stopped anywhere and sang and courted and staked out territories. They might or might not have been as successful, but they could have stopped anywhere — or could have decided not to leave at all.

But to live through the winter in the place of their absence, as Wallis had, and to be on hand to see them come back — filtering at first, then flooding — there was no way to deny that each bird's presence went beyond the mechanistic: that place, as well as season, played a part in it, and that in this particular place, they felt uncontrollable jubilation. Wallis had heard that sometimes they would sing with such vigor, and so unceasingly, that their vocal cords would burst, and still they would continue, so that the bird sang blood, sprays of it flashing through the air and coating the emerald reeds crimson, as if there were a flaw or leak in the system's design . . .

Wallis began carrying one of Mel's old bird books in his day pack, to identify the birds — to learn their names and where they had come from. He felt a strong affinity for them, and was surprised to read that many of them came from the country in which he had once lived. He had not paid much attention to them down there — the light was often bright and harsh, so that when he glanced up he saw only a colorless silhouette flashing against gunmetal sky, or flying into the radial spokes of sun-ray — but now, watching them return to a place of previous stillness and silence, coming back at first almost one by one, he could better understand and observe their differences.

He tried to focus on his maps, and on the stones beneath his feet — but it was increasingly hard to resist the temptation to lift the binoculars each time a whisk of bright feathers and joy rushed past, leaving behind an invisible, fast-dissipating trail of birdsong. He would raise his binoculars quickly and lean forward, almost with the anticipation of a hunter.

•

The first flowers were appearing — the first butterflies, amazingly, right behind them — their crooked, awkward flights stunning and their brilliant colors wandering as if lost across the snow fields. Sometimes he followed them to where, sure enough, there would be flowers, and often he would pick a cluster for Mel: trillium, serviceberry, and twin-flower — an elegant, simple bouquet of pink and white.

Some of the bouquets she took to school with her; others she dried and hung from the rafters in the cabin. A single vase of them sat on the table where they ate together. A loaf of new bread and two grouse for supper. Some daylight would still be left, afterward — a wedge of it, between dinner and darkness — and often they would fill it by cutting and splitting more wood.

The steady, rhythmic sounds of their working: the tight creak and then split of wood, with each swing of the ax. In some ways it was as if he — Matthew — had never left. As if Matthew had been transformed into Wallis, or Wallis into Matthew. Except that now she was happy again.

A slow afternoon at the mercantile. Blue-hazed sunlight from the ciga-rette smoke hung trapped in the high upper reaches of the store. Wallis had been out in the field all morning and had come in to dry his snow-drenched clothes by Helen's stove, and to wait for the school recess so that he could go see Mel, and maybe steal a kiss. It didn't hurt to try and patch things with Helen, either — to help her get used to the fact that it would be Wallis and Mel now, rather than Matthew and Mel — but he was surprised, as he spent time with Helen, by how little patching seemed necessary — as if Helen had other, far more important matters on her mind. Often she and Wallis visited with the ease of old friends.

Across the street, Wallis would hear the clang of the iron triangle signaling lunch and recess. Sometimes he would cross the street to have lunch with Mel; other times she would come over to the mercantile, where the three of them would sit on the steps in the bright sun.

Colter had been working out, doing exercises to strengthen himself for summer — performing pull-ups and push-ups, and lifting a single heavy slab of stone over his head repeatedly, as if it were a dumbbell — and it was a story as ancient as humankind, but no less amazing in its familiarity — the physical rise and development of an individual: like a blossoming. He was head and shoulders stronger now than any of his other classmates, and his accuracy with the bow had increased, as had his power, so that now he was hitting the bull's eye of whatever he aimed at, even from a distance of forty. He was whittling his arrows from cedar shafts and napping his points out of chert and obsidian — heating them in flames, then chipping at them with the tip of a deer antler — and his excellence at hitting flying objects had also improved. Mel forbade him to shoot at birds in the springtime, but he delighted in shooting flying insects — wing-whirring pine sawyer beetles, as well as butterflies and even the drifting flights of moths by moonlight. He would light a lantern against the backdrop of the saloon and then aim to pin the moths, sometimes still fluttering, against the wall with his finest, most delicate arrow points.

His back and shoulders were growing wider, his waist tapering, and his upper legs growing broader — as if the ceaseless pulling, the bow's resistance as the string was drawn, then released, was chipping away at him as surely as he chipped at the obsidian.

Anyone, everyone, could feel him ready to go — like a subterranean rumbling, a trembling: the landscape desiring to send him up and out into the other world. Helen, and others who were old enough to remember, said that he reminded them in that manner almost exactly of Matthew.

It was strange how Colter hitched his power to the rising springtime as if in lockstep harness with it. The force of his growth was so extraordinary and vital that it seemed as if he were neither a boy nor a young man, but instead a hard and wild creature living now in their midst — a trained dancing bear, or a coyote; a wolf, a wild boar, a swan, wearing only the skin or costume of a man. Pleasant among them, but always separate in some manner and not quite of them — and with a gulf between them that could never fully be crossed in life.

Coming back from a hike north of town, carrying another bouquet, Wallis heard the sound of someone crying as he passed near Colter's and Amy's cabin, where usually he heard singing. He moved through the woods toward the sound, and when he came to the edge of the woods he saw that Amy was standing in the little corral leaning against the pony with her arms around his neck. Her face was wet with tears, and Wallis was embarrassed to find her in that manner, but wanted to be sure that everything was all right. He stepped forward carefully. When she saw him she cried out, "He has gone!"

At first Wallis thought she meant that Colter had left on his trek prematurely. Amy started crying again, and Wallis led her over to the porch, where they sat down and rested in the blue lingering dusk. She sniffled, "He left without even saying good-bye — he didn't even come by to see me."

It took more crying, and several more teary statements before Wallis grew confused, and after one accusation — "He just wanted to *use* me. He's nothing but an old *miscreant!*" — Wallis said, incredulously, "Colter?" and Amy paused in her crying. *"No,"* she said, "Dudley."

"Oh, shit," Wallis said, before he could help himself, "that was weeks ago. You don't *like* him, do you?" But the look she gave him told him how far along it was, and he wondered if there was anyone Old Dudley could not snare. It was certainly not by charm that he captured any of them. As ever, he found instead the flaw in one's self and then widened it.

In the end, Wallis left the bouquet for Amy. At first she protested, knowing it had been picked for Mel, but when he offered them a second time, she said thank you. He walked on home, traveling not through the woods, but like a citizen of the town, hiking right down the muddy, snow-patched road, listening to the night mutterings of snipe and the riverine trilling of as many frogs, it seemed, as there were stars in the sky. Meteors tumbled in occasional cartwheels, and his peace at being settled in the world with Mel, and with so much newness before him, was tempered momentarily by the raw loneliness he had left behind: as if, this year at least, sorrow had avoided him and chosen another instead.

Trumpet vine crept along the stone walls, twining itself amongst the patterns of lichens, and the hummingbirds arrived from South and Central America, as powerful as small caps of dynamite, and regal as royalty: as if they had traveled all that way only to pollinate this one flower.

The first rains fell one weekend, a phenomenon so startling, after so much snow, that Mel and Wallis went out and stood in the light rain and rubbed it into their hair, into their scalps, and stood there washing in it; and afterward, they went back in, bone-chilled, to warm themselves by the fire.

Once the rains began, the valley snow slushed out and faded quickly — the creeks and river ran high — and the woods accepted both the sun and the rain with such intensity, such ravenousness, as to glow fluorescent with greenness. It seemed to Wallis that he could feel the land's energy, the turning over and stirring and stretching of it, even in his teeth.

Wallis moved farther into the high country, following the receding snow higher each day, mapping. This was where the grizzlies lived. The grizzlies had pretty much learned, in the last hundred years, to stay away from the river bottoms, where they could get into trouble with humans, and now the grizzlies spent more time up high, often hanging out at the edges of glaciers, and those receding snow lines, where the trickling melt-water kept a retreating strand line of vegetation always lush. Wallis watched the grizzlies browsing the sun-bright glacier lilies that grew in that wavering space between black earth and white glacier, and after the bears had passed on, he would go to that spot and gather several of the buttery blossoms to bring home for a salad each evening. He spent all of an afternoon watching a mother with three tiny cubs slide down an ice field, sliding several hundred feet on their backs with all four feet up in the air, whereupon reaching the bottom they would scramble back up to the top for another ride, again and again.

Wallis grew browned from his work in the high country, so tanned that someone who had known him before might not at first recognize him. Mel noted with pangs the browning of his skin and the increasing vigor surrounding him — the excitement with which he came down out of the mountains each evening — but she forced herself to remember her own burnout, and what a dead-end road that had been for her: twenty years of passion that had gotten her nowhere. Twenty years was not enough. It would take a hundred years of data to weave together any knowledge of significance; but now there was no one to pick up where she had left. It was the premature end of a pursuit: a thing not completed, not known.

Nearly every day Wallis would bring home a collection of various rocks he'd found, both for his own examination under hand lens and microscope, but also just to show her for their beauty: thirty, forty, sometimes fifty pounds of rocks each day — some glittering and sparkly, others colorful, and still others improbably dense and sullen — so heavy that it seemed they could not have come from this world, but were the clastic residue of exploded planets.

They stacked the rocks in a loose wall against one side of where the garden had once been. They were so beautiful that it was impossible to simply toss them out into the grass or cast them into a loose pile. Once discovered, they had to be somehow ordered and set apart from randomness.

One day in May a black wolf came trotting through town, cantering right down the center of the street without glancing left or right. It went right past the school — Belle and Ann and Mel and the students leapt up and went to the window to watch it — and it passed the mercantile, passed the saloon, and passed the cemetery, and continued on down the road in its easy, free-floating gait, as if merely traveling, and as if there were nothing remarkable in its passage.

She did not cut herself off from the woods entirely: not as Matthew had done. She still went out on hikes with Wallis on weekends, though they avoided the area where Colter said he believed the wolves were denning, to keep from bothering them.

Instead, they hiked north, working their way along the rocky south-facing slopes, hiking shirtless through bands of gold and copper light, with Wallis pointing out the fault striations on rocks — pointing out the direction each plate of earth had been moving, and which of the two had been the subsuming force. Mel continued to teach him about every living thing: the names and relationships of the lichens on the cliffs, and of ferns, back in the forest. The names of moths and butterflies. She weaved for him the stories of what ate what, which then was eaten by the next thing beyond that.

They lay on damp moss and sunned; they crawled on their hands and knees in the mosses at the edge of the snow line, the sun bright on their backs, and grazed the yellow lilies straight from the ground, while below them the valley glowed green, still whole and healthy.

Sometimes as they hiked back home their passage would intersect with the rutted paths to where Dudley and Matthew had drilled their dry holes. The little lanes ran seemingly indiscriminately through the old forest, as if they had been chasing something above the ground, rather than below — something elusive, erratic, and seemingly without logic. Old stumps — rotting, orange, crumbling moss-covered punkwood — lined the sides of the winding paths where bright light had been blazed into the forest. It was strange to think that each path led to a failure.

The roads had not been noticeable beneath the covering of snow, but now as more of them revealed themselves — the spoor of Dudley and Matthew — they became apparent: crude hackings and carvings into previously untouched places, as if rude wart-faced hogs had been snuffling in the soil. Mel said that eventually the forest would seal over the scars, in places where the soil had not washed away — as long as Dudley and Matthew remained satisfied they'd drilled dry holes, and did not come back, seeking to reenter those same old holes — but that, as the profiteers had warned, she was worried that the timber companies would soon come devouring, using the old roads as staging areas to launch their gnawing machines farther into the forest, in all directions.

Glissading snow-melt rushed down the rutted roads, carrying great scouring gouts of chocolate colored waters, spreading fans of silt into the creeks, which then discharged plumes of mud into the main river, covering the spawning beds of trout with sediment. "It's amazing what one man can do," Mel said, staring down at one of the roads as they stood ankle-deep in its rushing, muddy channel, as if crossing some new stream not on a map.

They stood a moment longer in the rushing mud, made dizzy by the incongruous sight of it — water the color of a bayou, gushing through such an otherwise sylvan forest — and then they stepped into the forest, as if trying to hide from the skein of roads scattered all about the woods.

"You should have seen it twenty years ago," Mel said.

"It's still pretty nice," Wallis said, thinking that she was half-joking.

"You should have seen it twenty years ago," she said.

B Y MID-MAY, THE SNOW WAS ALMOST ALL GONE; MORE AND more antlers were revealed, strewn up and down the slopes like bones, so that they were easy for the antler hunters to find. They gathered them in great numbers. The mountains were littered also with the skeletons of winter-killed deer, elk, and moose, the bones cast in hopeless disarray. Sometimes there were bones atop bones, from where one deer had died and gone down, and then a few feet of snow had fallen, and then another deer had died in that same spot. It seemed to Wallis that — as with the rocks — there were enough bones and antlers to build fences, walls, even houses from those white spars. He would spend some afternoons trying to reassemble the bones into working order, as if he were the curator of a great and vast museum.

Colter looked out the window constantly, watching the receding snowcaps, seeing them curl over the mountaintops like the sea foam of a retreating tide. Notches, crevices, and passes that had been obscured now became evident. He had picked one particular mountain, Dome Mountain, as his exit route, when it came time for him to leave the valley, and he carved the outline of it on his desk, so that each day with the tip of his knife blade he could etch into the desktop the contour of that day's shrinking snow line. The contours were pleasing to him, and in his boredom he soothed himself by running his fingers across the grooved cuts in the desk.

He was compiling a list, too, of what equipment to take with him — listing the advantages and disadvantages, the justification, of each item. As the afternoons lingered, he would trade notes with Mel, arguing or questioning the merits of each item, until it seemed to Mel that when he left, some part of her, invested in him, would also be leaving.

At lunch, Mel took the children down to the river, to the backwater sloughs and beaver ponds, where they caught the tadpoles of spring peepers and Pacific tree frogs and brought them back to the classroom in mayonnaise jars. They placed them on the windowsill in sunlight and fed them flakes of dry oatmeal and watched them through the hand lens daily, as the tiny nubs of legs began to sprout and the fatty tissue in their tails shrank.

Sometimes in the morning there would be a dead one resting turgid on the bottom — pale belly up, tiny mouth agape — and the students would want to fish it out and give it a burial, but Mel told them to leave it there to disintegrate into a milky blue drifting mass, upon which the other tadpoles would sometimes feed. Mel said that as each tadpole died, it released chemicals into the water that had been proven to accelerate the development of the surviving tadpoles.

The more that died in that puddle, the faster the survivors accelerated their rate of growth. The students puzzled at the mechanics, the consequences and logistics of such overcrowding.

They kept caterpillars, too, in mason jars, and fed them prodigious quantities of green leaves and grass, and performed crude experiments on their varying rates of growth and development based on different diets. The beautiful myth of the caterpillar spinning its cocoon and disappearing from the world. The leaf litter, stems gnawed bare, and tiny caterpillar droppings an inch deep on the bottom of the jar, and the jar itself (with holes punched in the lid to vent the air), a hothouse, a dynamo of heat, as the caterpillar slept; and in both instances, frog and butterfly, the students marveled at the high cost of metamorphosis. They placed a stone in with the tadpoles for the frogs to climb out on once the transformation was complete, and they hung little twigs and branches for the butterflies to cling to as they dried their wings.

The townspeople were beginning to move the rocks again, compelled in the sun's warmth and amidst the scent of blossoming lupine to carry the stones back and forth like ants, working on the wall yet another year, trudging up and down the road raising plumes of dust behind them. No rain had fallen, though there seemed to be enough snowmelt entering the creeks to keep the valley lush forever. Throughout the day, there was a pleasant harmony as the surging river beyond carried tumbling boulders along its bottom. The river's muted, subsonic clackings carried occasionally to the surface, mixing with the sharper sounds of their own work: one rock being stacked atop two others.

And in the lengthening evenings at the bar, there was the good smell of work-sweat and rock dust and cold beer. It was a clean odor, as if all angst or wretchedness had been purged from them. It was impossible to understand how anyone could consider ever leaving. They shook their heads over Matthew's defection, argued it round and round, before finally deciding that it must be extraordinarily fascinating down there where he spent his time, below the earth.

They discussed with increasing anticipation the preparations for Colter's trip, and imagined the things he might discover: gold, salmon, mastodons locked in ice, polar bears, echoes of white. They sat on the porch and drank and watched the sun set, watched the northern lights race and rill across the sky — images of green and red that seemed to be a form of communication they could not quite understand; and even though they might have seen the sight a hundred or even a thousand times in their lives, each time the lights emerged, the men and women fell silent in slack-jawed awe. Their faces relaxed — the furrows over their brows and the crows' feet around their eyes softened as the eerie lights passed over them, and there were none who did not feel cleansed and energized by the phenomenon. And the men all agreed that if they were Colter's age, they would do the same thing, with only a pack on their back, heading north until they came to the edge of the world; and they all agreed that they wished they had done so when they were younger, but that they had never gotten around to it.

The road over the summit opened sufficiently for a backhoe and snowplow to cut through the ice bridge connecting the valley to the rest of the world — though it was still like driving through a blue and white tunnel, with compressed walls of luminous ice twelve feet high on either side of the road — and the mail made its first delivery since the profiteers had been in, resuming its weekly run: a flood of mail, that first day, like the release of driftwood floes from behind the breakup of a river's logjam; and once more the town gathered at the saloon for the dissemination of the mail.

They stood in the glimmering puddles of snowmelt, hatless and in short sleeves, intoxicated by the sun — their blood leaping. From here on out — or for six more months, until the next November — their lives would have the potential to be as exotic as they wished or could afford. It might take two or three weeks, but they could place an order for mangoes, or coconuts, or fresh coffee beans from New Guinea. They could even order salmon — ordering the ghost of a taste that once ran strong through their valley, carving the river's heart.

They could, if they wished, gas up an old truck and set out south, up and over the pass — driving as far into the coming summer heat as they desired.

They didn't leave, of course. There was no place richer, nowhere any of them would rather be. Wild horses could not have dragged them away. It was simply an added feeling of freedom, knowing that they could now go if they wished. A power accrued in their restraint. They were no longer proud isolates, survivors, hangers-on; they could once again engage, and correspond, with the world.

There were drawbacks to this. The world could engage with and alter them — could come creeping in over the same road that offered that unaccepted freedom. But early in the spring, after so much seclusion, it never seemed a problem. It was impossible to imagine such hard-gotten integrity ever being altered or eroded.

Charlie cooked another deer in honor of the mail's arrival. They fell upon it quickly, craving red meat to nurture their day's labors. Charlie handed out the mail as he served the meat, and people delved in with equal intensity, tearing open letters and eating sometimes with their hands, then licking the grease from their fingers. Uncle Harold's garden in Alabama was already producing cucumbers. Sister Mary's floral shop in Michigan had gone out of business. Another grandfather had died.

Someone's relative in Philadelphia wanted to know if they could see the stars clearly, out in the country.

There was no mail from Old Dudley or Matthew. Mel had expected some letter of understanding from Matthew. She knew that none was needed, but still, she had been hoping for one — for the symbolism or ritual of the severance — but there was from both of them only silence, so that she knew they both had dived the moment they had gotten home, and were probably still diving.

The only mail she had was from an old college roommate, who'd been an ornithologist for the Fish and Wildlife Service for a while, but who was raising a family now, four girls in Tucson, divorced, working two part-time jobs, drowning a little more each day. Mel read the letter with a shiver, folded it, put it back in its envelope, and thought back to college. No one follows the course they chart out, she thought. No one.

There was no mail for Wallis — who had not been expecting or desiring any — nor for Amy, who had, and she took it hard, setting off into another round of weeping, so that Helen had to try to console her, leading her outside onto the porch and away from the curious stares of her neighbors, so that her shattered dignity might be reassembled.

One of the wolves passed through town again, a different wolf, silver gray, and larger, following the exact path of the black wolf. Unlike the other, it glanced sidelong at the school — again, the class and teachers hurried to the window — as if searching for Mel.

They saw that it had a face full of porcupine quills, an injury only recently inflicted, because the wolf's face had not yet begun to swell and fester. From time to time it would stop and sit down in the street and paw at its muzzle with both front feet. It would writhe and twist, smearing its face along the road in an effort to dislodge the quills, and each time it did that, one or two would snap off — sometimes the wolf would then get them stuck in its paws or in the roof of its mouth, and it would snap and bite at those, gagging — and then it would be up and trotting again, right on through town.

The children were horrified and wanted to know if the wolf would live. Mel said she didn't know: that it might starve to death, even if the other pack members brought it food — if it was even in a pack — or that the quills might cause such massive infections that the wolf's blood would be poisoned, and it would die of shock.

Colter couldn't stand it. Recess had come and gone, and they were mid-lesson in algebra, but he went out the door anyway, and into the street. Mel very nearly followed, but told herself that if she could let this go, she could pass through anything.

Colter knelt in the street and began gathering some of the quills that had fallen free and put them in the leather medicine bag he carried around his neck. He looked off in the direction the wolf had gone, and they thought he was going to follow it, but after a moment he came back to the schoolhouse, where he handed some of the quills to Mel without saying anything.

No one reprimanded him. There were only two weeks left in the semester, and everyone knew he would be going. He was already gone.

Wallis's map blossomed. This time he had it right. There were simply too much data now for it not to be accurate. So confident was he now that he was drawing the map directly onto a deer hide, sketching it with black ink. He took the information from all of Dudley's and Matthew's previous mistakes, wove that subsurface data in with what he was seeing above the ground — a slip-fault here, a sediment uncon-formity there — and now it was like pieces of a puzzle coming together on their own: as if the pieces desired to be reassembled and understood, and possessed a force of their own, propelling them toward that reas-sembly.

Amidst all the chaos and fracturing, the elusiveness, the oil was hiding. He had not been certain when he first arrived in the valley, but now he knew it for sure. He could smell it through microscopic vents and fissures in the soil and he could feel the liquid reservoirs miles below, as a man might feel the sleeping form or faint stirrings of his child, still in his wife's womb, through the drum-taut skin of her belly, halfway between the protruding navel and heavy breasts. He was going to find it, where they had not. Many nights he fell asleep on the skin of the hide, ink pen in hand, so that Mel would have to awaken him and lead him in to bed.

Sometimes she would stand over him for a moment, contemplating his sleeping descent, and wondering whether to wake him or to let him continue sinking.

It was a troubling proposition. Often she would sit in the chair and study him as he slept — his legs twisted beneath him, arms outstretched across the hide as if he had fallen and landed on it, or as if he were protecting it from something — and she would consider how much she loved that about him, when he was in that repose.

She was fully aware that with the last one, she had desired to rein him in — had wished for Matthew to love her as he had loved the maps and the world below — and that the guilt of desiring that same passion — of wanting it but not asking for it — had worn her thin as a scalloped seashell tumbled in the waves until translucent.

She was determined to neither ask nor even want that for herself, with Wallis. To love him as he was, when he dived — and to love him when he emerged — but to let go, and not try to control his descents.

She thought she had it right this time. She thought she loved him as much when he dived as when he ascended.

She studied Wallis's map as he slept atop it. She knew little about geology, but she understood maps, and the currents of deposition he had sketched showing the old ocean's tides and longshore currents and deltas and inlets were not so dissimilar from the movements of the creeks and rivers across that same stony, lithified land, millions of years later. She could read the contours, could read what it was he was tracking, and saw the logic he was applying. According to his map, there was not just one giant field lying on the other side of the river, but numerous smaller fields as well, scattered around the major field. Her father and Matthew would call it a bonanza. Mel wondered how Matthew had missed it.

Occasionally he would open his eyes to see her sitting there watching him, and such was the grace that was developing between them that he could tell when she was thinking such thoughts: and he would raise up on one elbow and watch her watching him by firelight, and he would wait for her to ask him to pull back or turn away, but she never did. She wanted it to be yet another dry hole, but she would not dream of asking him to turn away. It was the only recklessness left to her: the recklessness of love, after it had previously seemed that love had gone away.

They had made love on that map: it was not sacred; and afterward, sometimes, the sweat from the backs, and the warming drain of their fluids, would darken the hide in places, as if in blasphemy: the map Wallis would be presenting to Old Dudley, when Dudley returned for his bounty.

"Will you go with him?" Mel asked. It was not too early to begin asking that question.

"I don't know," Wallis said. "I would like to find a way not to."

The world had broken open; the mountains had split to reveal a living world that had been lying beneath, raucous and seething green. The din was as startling. It took some time before their ears could sort out the sounds and their meanings — sounds arriving seemingly overnight, on the south winds. Blackbird trill, snipe wing-mutter, goose-honk, duck wing-whistle at dusk, frog-song, thrush-squeal, wrens and chickadees courting, raven laughter, hawk-shriek, rain on the tin roofs; and mixed in with it all, the land reawakening: water dripping, running every-where, and the wind propelling warm air through the valley, with the days climbing now toward the solstice.

It was the time of year when rain should have been falling every day — brief intense showers after which the trees sparkled with water drops on their needles and the forest was illuminated with a gold light, steam rising. Few rains fell however — though when they did, the vil-lagers would go into the woods to search for the false morel and shaggy mane mushrooms that popped up immediately.

Walking home from school after such a rain, Wallis and Mel would keep an eye out for the emergent dark shapes of the mushrooms, and would race each other to get to them first. And again, as with the glacier lilies, they would crawl amongst the rain-washed mushrooms on all fours, browsing them straight from the ground like bears, with a light mist falling on their backs and muggy steam rising all around them.

On the last day of school the children released the oxygen-starved butterflies and the writhing little frogs and toads — some still bearing the nubs of tadpole tails — and the children cheered as their captives hopped or flew off in all directions, though they were quickly mortified as swarms of birds — how could they have known? — gathered and began picking off the clumsy butterflies mid-flight and chasing and pecking at the terrified tiny toads and frogs. A few escaped, but not many, and the children stared in disbelief, stunned and chastened by the difficulty of releasing something created into the world. After some milling around, they went back into the classroom somberly for their last lesson of the day, though soon enough their spirits brightened, made joyous again by the thought of summer vacation.

Colter's going-away party was that evening. He had planned to leave that afternoon — the moment school was out — but Amy had talked him into staying one last night.

Everyone gathered at the bar. Colter was as quiet as always, though they could all feel his stored tension, could smell the adrenaline coming off of him.

The men all wanted to buy him drinks, kept sliding them down the bar to him, but after his first tentative sip — touching his tongue to the suds at the top of a beer mug — he decided that he did not care for it, and passed each beer down to Amy, who drank them.

"My strength is as that of ten men," Amy quoted, "because I am pure."

This started the men wondering how strong Colter was, and they ventured drunkenly out into the moonlight, to where the rock wall ran past the rusting wrought-iron spires of the cemetery's gate. They pointed out different rocks for him to heft. The exercise soon turned into a contest, and Colter sat back and watched the men grunt and groan and strain. He did not participate, but saved his energy for his trip. The men stumbled and staggered beneath the residue of Matthew's work, his dry masonry — some of the slabs they could not even budge, a failing which they discounted as "not being able to get a good grip" — and sometimes they dropped the boulders on each other's feet or hands, so that they yowled in the night, and the damp earth shook with the thumps of the dropped stones.

Colter slipped away without their noticing. His pack was on the front porch. He was gone before anyone knew it, gone without a word to anyone. He had taken care of his good-byes earlier in the afternoon. When the men realized this, they returned to the bar and washed the blood and mud off their bruised fingers. Artie went to the porch with the camera to get one last picture of Colter, but had to settle for taking one of Amy, Mel, and Wallis standing together, looking out into the darkness after him.

There was a small comet to the north, and that showed up in the photo, too, as a smear of light, like a firefly. They watched the comet, knowing that as Colter hiked north he would be watching it too, and in that manner they were connected a bit longer, though tenuously now. They ransacked their minds, trying to remember if they had taught him everything he needed to know. It seemed to each of them that they must have forgotten something, though no one could think of what it might have been.

•

Historical Glimpses;
Or,
The Story of the World Set In Order
Wandering Germs of Worlds

It will be interesting to inquire what matter was before it became fire mist.

Comets are facts of observation; there is no mistake as to the real existence of such bodies, whatever they be. They excite our admiration. They are full of wonder. They come from the unsearchable depths of space and, after shining in our heavens a few weeks, disappear back into the unsearchable depths. What is their origin? What their end? Think of the approach of one of these mysterious messengers from the infinite. Before discernible to unaided eyes, the astronomer with his instrument detects it as a faint luminosity just appeared. For weeks he watches its changes. Nightly it grows brighter. It is approaching; it will arrive. Like the headlight of a locomotive seen at first as a luminous point in the far distance over some miles of track, gradually growing brighter — with no other evidence of motion — with brightness at length increasing in accelerated ratio, then dazzling us by its glare, and finally thundering past with a velocity which appalls, and retiring into the night that reigns in the opposite direction — so comes the headlight of a train of cosmic matter; so grows its luminosity; with such a stunning demonstration of physical power it rushes past us, then sinks into that infinite distance in another quarter of the heavens. I confess it is impossible to contemplate all this without a feeling of awe.

Would that the mystery of the comet were once unfolded to us! It tantalizes us by its near approach and its undiminished inscrutability. But, thanks to intelligence — thanks to the spirit of science — thanks to that beneficent constitution of the universe by which it gives up its secrets one by one, to the demands of intelligent inquiry such as my own, we have found out something. We have seen comets torn to pieces by the power of attraction — without a collision — by the attractions of the satellites of Jupiter. This was Bi-é-la's [Be-ála] comet, and each fragment thenceforward pursued its separate path. We have seen comets so shat-

tered and disintegrated by the pulls and strains to which they were subjected in our system — in making their circuit about our sun, in getting through the entanglements of Jupiter's and Saturn's attractions, that they appeared literally to be going to pieces and dividing up their remains among the planetary masses of the system.

The comet, in short, appears to be essentially a flying train of stones traveling with three thousand times the velocity of our own "railroad express." The smaller stones, more resistant than the larger ones, by other matter disseminated through space, slacken their motion slightly, and are struck by the larger, causing ignition. The harder, rounder, little stones consume the larger, more angular ones. They possess some irreducible essence.

We have seen the meteor ignited in the upper air. We have seen its bright streak vanish while we gazed. But finally even the little stones were melted — were vaporized. While passing through the space measured by its line, the comet changed from a cold stone to shining dust, and then a darkened dust left floating in the upper strata of the atmosphere.

But though unseen, the meteoric dust still exists. It now belongs to the earth. It will be wafted to and fro by the winds; it will come down, after some months, and contribute some new material to the earth. It will fill our lungs, our blood. Some of these atoms will fall on the ocean; most of them will fall there; and after other months they will settle to the bottom and mingle with the ooze which is there accumulating. You will remember our walk under the sea and the comet dust which we found. It is an impressive thought. This black particle now resting through an eternity on the midnight-shrouded ocean bed, shone lately in a star. These are greater changes of fortune than any suffered by us.

The point which we have reached reveals the boundless space around us well stocked with material particles. They are not uniformly distributed; by their mutual attractions they are gathered into swarms. By degrees, each swarm grows as long as it has a separate existence, by the accession of other swarms. As these swarms sail majestically through the ocean of immensity, some are brought under the control of distant suns, and start on long journeys to pay their flying visits.

They approach now as comets. If they are induced to circle perpetually about given suns, they finally go to pieces again, and the parts are either drawn to their central suns, or distributed among the planets. If they escape from the systems entered, they steady themselves across the gulfs of space that separate systems, and in the progress of centuries, float into other ports and new excitements, new lives.

But some of these swarms remain floating in the depths of extra-firmamental space and gather to themselves, by their increasing power of attraction, all other swarms and particles from their region of immensity. They become Nebulae. *They are luminous because, pounded by the fall of other swarms, and lighted by the collisions of their internal parts, they glow. They are composed of matters solid, liquid, and gaseous. They rotate. Poised in space, the impacts of gathering matters have started them on their axes of motion. The background of the heavens is phosphorescent with the glow of these distant fields of world-stuff. Each is a living picture of that primordial state in which we fancy the matter of the solar system existed when that history of cooling began, which we endeavored to trace to a starting point.*

All of the rest of the world must follow them.

THE FIRST DAY AFTER SCHOOL LET OUT, AND AFTER COLTER had struck out north in search of all the disappeared things, Mel faltered and slipped back into the woods, searching for the wolves and their pups, who would be between six and eight weeks old. She didn't tell Wallis where she was going — if he had asked, she would tell him she was going to the school to take care of some paperwork, and to then maybe take a little hike alone — but he didn't ask.

She went past the school and up the ridge above town and then toward the river, toward the place where Colter said he had seen the wolves' sign. The snow was almost gone, and she watched the sky and listened for the sound of ravens. There was a warm breeze and it felt good to be back among the woods, as if waist-deep amidst an excess of the senses — but she wondered at the uneasy feeling of betrayal in her heart; at the difficulty, the compromise of spirit that would be involved in trying to have both: a life of anchored domesticity, surrounded by one of unfettered wildness.

She saw ravens drifting in purposeful circles ahead, and began to notice wolf fur caught here and there in the bushes. A red-eyed vireo flew past with a twist of silver fur in its beak: cushioning for its nest. Wolf scats began to litter the trail, scats of meat and bone wrapped in loose deer hair. She heard the growling sounds of the pups and crept to a vantage behind a log, where she could see them in the clearing below.

Four adults were lying in the sun, basking like dogs: two big gray wolves, two smaller black wolves. She imagined how warm the sun must be on the black wolves' fur. Their hocks were muddy from where they had been chasing deer. There were six gangly pups — five gray pups, one black — wrestling and tearing at a deer's hindquarter. Bones lay scattered around them, and the grass was flattened from their games.

Mel watched as the pups played and fought hard for half an hour — yipping, growling, snarling, and chasing each other around the clearing in manic games of tag — before they suddenly tired and went over to collapse against the adults, where they all then slept in the sun. The wind ruffled their fur and likewise swirled Mel's hair around her face, carrying her scent away from them. She lay her head down behind the log and napped, also in a patch of sun, saddened without knowing why, and when she awakened and looked out in the clearing, the wolves and the deer leg were gone, though the grass was still flattened.

She walked home to Wallis. When she got home, she did not enter what she had seen into her journals, nor did she tell Wallis, or anyone, of what she had seen.

She spent two restless days around the house, snapping at Wallis, considering running as Colter had — running from something, rather than to something — before finally finding some solace in the old garden, which she had not tended in years, and whose soil was rich and black from a decade of fallow compost. She had driven Wallis from the cabin with her surliness — distant toward him, suddenly, certain that he was only using her, that he would abandon her any day to resume life with Old Dudley and Matthew — "Three fucking peas in a pod," she had shouted as he went up into the mountains with his compass that day — but now she found release in kneeling in the garden and pawing at the black dirt with her bare hands — digging up pink earthworms as thick as her little finger and as muscular as snakes. Robins and hermit thrushes surrounded her as she worked shirtless in the warm sun, the birds chirping in excitement and hopping on the writhing earthworms, so that if anyone had seen her, they might have mistaken her for a saint, of whom animals were unafraid, and to whom they were drawn.

When she had the garden furrowed and ready for seed later in the afternoon, she lay down in the earth and napped until long shadows crept in from out of the woods and bats flitted overhead in ragged pursuit of insects. She awoke craving vegetables, but meat was all there was, and she went down to the smokehouse to select a venison ham to fix for supper, and told herself to remember to apologize to Wallis for being so rude. She felt fairly certain that the soil had absorbed her venom — that the toxins had drained from her, had leaked into the soil like something spilled — but she was mildly troubled by the sensation that, as she'd napped, the earth had carried her farther along toward some destination, and she was not altogether comfortable in not knowing where or what that destination might be.

Mel's fears faded when Wallis returned home. They had a candlelight dinner, and wine, and made up. The distance before them lengthened once more — stretched back toward infinity.

Throughout the valley, people — mostly women — were planting, and with a wild zeal, a purity of passion, unlike that of any gardeners Wallis had ever seen.

The tender plants — peas, tomatoes — were started indoors from seed on windowsills or in small greenhouses. No one had ever gotten a tomato to turn red in the valley, but still they tried, every year — the northern limit of successful tomato growing lay about forty miles to the south, like the strand line of rich sea-wrack — and all they ever ended up with were little testicle-sized clusters of green fruits, with a subtle failure of temperature and sunlight always conspiring to fall a few days short of redness. Occasionally one of the tomatoes would blush with a few sundial streaks of pink, or would fade to some metallic noncolor in a strange band of the spectrum between green and red — and such a fruit would be hailed as a champion and displayed at the bar — though when they cut into it and ate it, it still tasted like shit. "Next year," they would say, "maybe next year it will be warmer," and they would purchase canned tomatoes, or one of them might drive to a distant valley and purchase several bushels of tomatoes — marveling at the excess, the bounty, elsewhere — and bring them back for canning.

The rest of the crops, however, they planted with a recklessness, secure in the knowledge that those crops would flourish. Root crops, warm beneath the skin of the earth and growing even through the light summer frosts, did best: carrots, potatoes, radishes. Lettuce did well, for a brief period in July, and they planted vast amounts of it, and ate as much as they could during that time.

They traded seeds, and gathered wildflower seeds to plant around the borders of their gardens and walkways: bear grass, lupine, paintbrush, phlox. The blossoms seared their winter-tired retinas, charged their souls, with a higher voltage that allowed them to live more fully and deeply. The blossoms also attracted the jeweled hummingbirds — glittering colors they had not seen in a year — and now the transformation seemed complete. The shimmering indigo on the head of a mallard drake. The ruby eyes of a loon. The pollen yellow chest of a tanager.

·

Mind In Matter
The Interpretation of Nature

Two little round seeds lie on the table before me. They seem to be exactly alike in every respect; but they came from two different packages, and were labeled by different names. What is there about them which makes them different? I plant the two seeds, and one grows to a stout "mustard tree," and the other to a field turnip. Assuredly, with this difference of outcome, there was an original, fundamental, internal difference in their natures.

The ova of two animals — say the elephant and the rhinoceros — are both simple nucleated cells. To the unaided eye, no difference is discoverable. Subject them to chemical analysis, and they are found composed of the same elements combined in the same way. Treat them with reagents and put them under the compound microscope, and nothing is seen in one which does not appear in the other. Materially they are the same. But one develops, out of itself, the embryo of an elephant, and the other, out of itself, the embryo of a rhinoceros.

On these two different embryonic foundations the two different animals in their completeness are built up. With no difference in the matter, there nonetheless existed in the two germs a profound difference in nature and destiny. Beyond anything scrutable existed something inscrutable. That which was not matter gave to matter a destination from which it could not swerve.

A human organism with all its parts perfect and all its parts in harmonious action is a splendid mechanism which can never cease to awaken admiration and wonder. But while we contemplate it alas, its activities cease. A powerful current of electricity has passed through the frame, and life is extinct. The change which we witness is appalling. The eye has lost its light; the voice gives forth no more intelligence; the muscles cease to grasp the implement; the fabric of a man now lies prone, motionless, speechless, insensible, dead — a stupendous and total change. But what is changed? Not the mechanism. The heart is still in its place, with all its valves; the brain shows no lesion; the muscles are all ready to act. Every part remains as it was in life. Neither chemistry nor the microscope detects, as yet, a material change. But something has gone out of the mechanism, for it is not as it was — something inscrutable, but yet something which ruled the mechanism — sustaining its action, lighting the eye, giving information to the tongue, making of this machinery absolutely all that which led us to say, "Here is a man." The man has gone out and left only his silent workshop behind.

Consider the life powers in action. The organism is in process of growth. A common fund of assimilative material is provided by the digestive organs. Out of this, atom by atom is selected and built into the various tissue fabrics. Here such atoms are selected as the formation of bone requires; there, the atoms suited for nerve or brain structure; in another place, the material of which muscles are made. Nice selection of material is indispensable.

Then notice the building of the bones. In one place the framework is so laid that the filling up will result in a flat bone. It is to be a shoulder blade, or a portion of the skull. In another place the framework is elongated; it is to be a long bone. Every bone is constructed for its place and its function. The whole system of bones, moreover, is conformed to a definite fundamental plan of structure — it is according to the plan of a vertebrate.

Selection of appropriate material is an act of intelligence. The determination of one form of structure rather than another implies discriminating intelligence and executive will! The conformation of the total system to an ideal plan implies first a conception of the plan. Certainly, we must say that here mind is at work. But is it the mind of the animal or plant? Every person can answer for himself whether he made his own bones. The question is absurd. Is the mind evinced possessed by the matter? Do these atoms and molecules move and arrange themselves by an intelligence and choice of their own? Do they intelligently maintain *the processes of digestion, blood purification, assimilation, and tissue building? How do they conceive, think, and will without brain? How select without eyes or hands? But, it is conceivable, you say.*

There is intelligence acting in the organism, which does not belong to the matter or the individual; whose intelligence is it? Intelligence is an attribute; it belongs to being; it does not act abstracted from being. What being then, acts in the living organism?

You say you will admit that the earth exerts an active power through a medium. What ground have you to claim that any active power is possessed by the earth? Have you ever known a stone or a stick or a chunk of ice to exert any active agency — except this hypothetical agency of attraction? You think you have often seen matter put forth activities of its own; but really you have only seen activities exerted in connection with matter — just as you observe selection and choice in the working organism. Now in reality, all you know about the origin of efficient power is given you in your own consciousness when you exert power; and what you infer from analogy when power seems to be exerted by other persons. That is, you only know that efficiency originates in will *— your own will; and when you see efficiency exerted anywhere, you can only affirm that* some will *is acting.*

Now, are you prepared to ascribe such will to the earth, to stones and mud and chunks of ice, when the so-called attraction seems to be exerted by them? This is the same question which has settled itself in the negative. The downward pull on the apple comes, then, from some other source. This is the other alternative. It means that power is exerted on the apple, and on all things, causing them to tend together in a certain fashion which we call the law of gravitation. Now, power is an attribute. It belongs to something; as it proceeds from will, power and will together are attributes of being. Manifestly, that being is omnipresent, for attraction is omnipresent. It is the Omnipresent Being. We can achieve this power.

Glance next at the prevalence of patterns and plans in the world. There is the plan of vertebrate structure; I have often made mention of it. In the modification of the plan for beings so diverse, it is wonderful that a simple conception should persist through all the ages of vertebrate history. It is an imperishable thought. The Articulates present us another plan persistent for even a longer period. The earth grew and attained completeness according to a method.

Out of the infinite storehouse of possible plans under which the Su-

preme Power might have proceeded in the origination of things, he has chosen the method which we call evolution. This is a divine choice. This sets forth a divine and eternal thought. This embraces the world, the heavens, the universe, and everywhere proclaims the Mind which instituted it. This great all-embracing, all-enduring fact inspires our souls with awe; it illuminates the dark realm of matter with the sunlight of a divine revelation.

Nonetheless, we are ourselves amazing, and massive — of utmost significance.

Be still! Do not say this doctrine displaces the doctrine of divine creation; for it proclaims a perpetual creation according to an intelligible, God-chosen method. Do not say that in recognizing the "reign of law" we displace personal divine agency; for the first principle in an intelligent divine government must be order, regularity, uniformity.

Do not say on the other hand, that the ascription of world-regulating law to a personal Will is the delivery of the world to the government of caprice. Caprice results only from the absence of mind.

I must not claim your attention longer. Perhaps I have penned some sentences which might seem difficult; but I hope you will all treasure the truth in these sentences, and ponder over it; then, when a little older, you will be enraptured, as I have been, with the richness and depth and grandeur of the meaning which the divine hand has written in the rocks and in the stars. It is all there, only for us to take.

The babies of prey were born in the first week of June. The predators had had their babies early — the wolves and coyotes and even the owls birthing in April, and the bears, gentle omnivores for the most part, also crawling up out of the earth in April with their cubs — so that by June, when the rest of the world was born — the deer fawns, the elk and moose calves — the young predators would be ready and waiting for them. Only the caribou, giving birth on the highest, snowiest ridges, were safe; down below, it was carnage.

Mostly it was the deer fawns that paid the price. For a week or so the woods would echo with their bleats and squeals as the lions, bears, coyotes, and wolves pulled them down and ate them before they were even a day old. The scats of the predators littered the trails, and in those scats could be seen the telltale little black hooves, no larger than a thumbnail — the only thing indigestible about the fawns — and the fawns were to the young predators what the blossoms of color were to the winter-tired humans: a burst of energy that got them over a hump and kept them going.

It was Artie who discovered that Amy was pregnant. She had lost her taste for alcohol of any kind, for the time being, and now that the warmer weather had returned, it could be seen that she had gained some weight. Everyone else thought she was just looking a little heavier, but Artie understood and, when they were alone in the bar one afternoon, had the nerve to ask. He asked shyly, as if she herself might not yet be aware of her condition, and she smiled, relieved that her secret was over, and said that yes, she was in her sixth month.

Artie counted backward, started to ask "Who?" now that the initial breach of intimacy had occurred, but when he settled on New Year's, he raised his eyebrows but said nothing, unwilling to utter the name, and Amy nodded, with a strange mix of embarrassment and pride.

What she did not tell Artie, but told the women in the valley (telling it to them when Mel was not around), was what a miraculous conception it had been: that they had not been coupled, and that although they had both been undressed, Old Dudley had been standing a good six feet away from her when he had gone off. It was almost like a spray, she said, and only a little bit had gotten on her. He had gone off just looking at her, she said.

"Are you sure?" they asked.

"I'm certain," she said. She lifted her shirt and let them feel her stomach.

It had been over a year since a baby had been born in the valley. The women smiled, then laughed. "I thought his seed was bad," Charlie's wife, Linda, said.

A woman named Jeanette had had three husbands in her life. "Maybe it has turned good in his old age," she said.

"Old pine trees start producing excessive seed crops in the last year or two before they die, or when they're injured," Helen said. "It's nature's way."

"We probably shouldn't tell Mel," one woman said. "It'll just upset her."

"She has to know sometime," Helen said. "Does Old Dudley know?"

Amy shook her head, and her face fell. "And no way is he going to believe it," she said.

"Not to worry," said Linda. "They can do tests, and stuff like that, now."

"Can you imagine," said Jeanette. "You've got a little *heir* in there."

Amy frowned, then started to cry. "I just want him to love me," she said. The other women fell around her with support. Helen went outside to smoke a cigarette. "Good luck, honey," she said, on her way out the door. She stood there in solitude for a long time, curious about the terror she felt — like a chasm opening below her — and she was mesmerized by both the beauty of the scene before her and the dread welling strangely within her, total and absolute.

She forced herself to stay calm. She finished her cigarette; coughed twice. A taste of blood — more than usual. Another little vessel rupturing in her throat. She massaged it lightly.

She went back into the bar to gather her sweater and say good-bye. She coughed once more, by accident, and sent a projectile of blood, a spray of it, across the room. The mist of it settled on the wall as if sprayed from an aerosol can of paint. The other women stared at her in horror, and then sorrow. Helen sneezed another spray across the room. Someone handed her a scarf, but then she leaned forward and vomited a bright red half-pint of blood into an empty beer mug.

They carried her across the street to her store. They took her upstairs, built a fire in the stove, and took turns sitting with her.

In the morning she was better. The little fissures and ruptures in her throat and lungs sealed off tenuously.

Linda helped her downstairs to open the store and start the day. Helen lit another cigarette. The road was open, but Helen chose not to go see a doctor. "I'm seventy-eight," she told Linda. The blue smoke filling her lungs. "I hope it goes fast," she said. "I would like to see my boy. And I would like to see that baby."

Venus, still bright in the morning sky. "I hope it doesn't hurt," she said.

The year's first lost tourists filtered in one weekend, in their bright clothing and their shiny rental cars. They usually came as young couples, just married or recently engaged. Something about the blank spot on the map drew them, made them want to see what was up in that corner of the world: as if that blank spot were the closest they could come to seeing into the future. They never came to backpack — the dense, brambly jungle was alien to their learned patterns of recreation.

But they would stand and gaze at the rushing river and at the distant mountains for hours. Sometimes they would set up a tent by the side of the river a mile or two outside of town, and in the evenings after making a little fire on which to cook, they would extinguish their fire — blue smoke hissing as it filtered upward through the old cedars and green cottonwoods — and they would walk hand in hand down the road to town, where they would enter the bar shyly and spend the evening sipping beer or something stronger and listening to Artie's wonderful bullshit.

Later, further into darkness, they might sit on the porch — surprised by the night's coldness — to look at one of the comets that seemed to always be circling overhead, and to listen to the trilling of the frogs.

They would visit the cemetery; would lean against the wrought-iron fence, resting their hands on the stone wall, and would stare at the graves — some old, some new — and would feel the gulf of knowledge that lay between them and this place: all those buried lives of which they would never know anything; and so much peace overhead, like the weight of night itself. The hooting of owls; the river's roar. The howls of the wolves.

They might step back into the bar for one more nightcap, but then they would walk up the road to their tent, where they would build a new fire and sit by it, watching the stars and talking quietly about the future.

Later in the night, chilled, they would crawl into their sleeping bags and hold each other, more certain than ever that the fit of one to the other was nothing less than a miracle, and they would fall asleep to the lull of the river's steady thunder.

They might stay another day or two, taking short walks up and down the river, and going back to the bar each evening for drinks. They would buy a few items from Helen's store — lingering, as if stunned by the peace of things, the lack of confusion they felt, which was so prevalent wherever they had come from. In the bar, they were impeccably polite — aware somehow, strangely, of an inner softness; they were now acutely conscious of it, being in the company of those so hardened and integral to a place.

With their subdued, respectful manners and their quiet absorption with each other, they were no bother, really. Sometimes they stared a bit too much, but beyond that, they altered nothing, interrupted little.

They usually came on weekends, so that it was possible for the shyer hermits to avoid coming to town then.

The pilgrims came with respect. The land lured it out of them, from the first moment they crossed over the summit and stared down at the green valley below.

Joshua was working on Helen's coffin, working on it diligently and with her blessing. She and Mel hiked over there one afternoon. Helen had tired after only the first ridge, so that Mel had had to carry her in her arms the rest of the way — amazed at how light Helen had grown — and when they came over the last ridge, they could hear the hammering and sawing and drilling and sanding. As they drew closer they could see Joshua standing at the side of his creation with fresh-cut wood shavings piled around his feet, bright in the sunlight.

Helen wanted a bird. She had vacillated between a golden eagle and a raven, believing the former to be more beautiful, but the latter wiser, and had finally chosen the raven: not so much for its wisdom, but for all the various voices it possessed. She still believed that Matthew might be returning to the valley someday, and the way she imagined it, if she chose to be buried in a raven, then every time that he heard a raven caw, croak, or purr, he would be reminded of her, and might remember how she had loved him, and how she would always love him.

The women admired the craftsmanship. They ran their hands over it. For eyes, the bird would use two black river stones. It was still rough-cut, unfinished — not yet recognizable as a raven — but the wood was beautiful, and they ran their hands over it again and again, and breathed in its scent.

"It may take me all summer," Joshua cautioned.

"Oh, I'm good for it," Helen said. "No way I'm leaving til Matthew comes back." But even as she spoke, another vessel pulled loose in her throat, and once more bright blood leapt from her mouth — a clenching in her lungs — and Joshua and Mel waited as she turned away and dabbed at her chin with a handkerchief. They stared at the spatter of it on the ground. Helen turned back to face them, embarrassed.

"Dry, this year," Joshua said. "Could be fires, by August."

"I don't have a spot picked out yet," Helen said. "Maybe Matthew can help me pick one out when he comes back. Some place close to town, along the river."

She turned to watch it flowing past Joshua's house. His black stallion was standing in the shade of a tree at water's edge. Helen was struck hard and sudden by the eerie thought that there was something she had forgotten to do.

"I'd better get back to work," Joshua said. "If I'm going to finish."

Mel and Helen stepped back into the shade and watched Joshua work for a while; then Mel picked Helen up and carried her back up the ridge and through the woods.

"What do you want?" Helen asked, as they passed the cemetery.

"I haven't thought about it yet," Mel said.

By mid-June, when all the flowers were blooming, it was impossible to measure anyone's happiness. People laughed out loud at any moment. The sound of Amy's singing carried through the woods at all hours — hymns, mostly — and in her garden, Mel found herself humming. She wanted Wallis to stay, but had decided that even if he left, she was going to stay happy this time — in this new, second life. That she would chase nothing.

She could not work in the garden long enough. Because no rain fell now, the garden needed watering in the mornings as well as evenings, and she and Wallis hauled bucket after bucket of cold creek water. The days kept expanding as the solstice approached, so that it seemed there could be very little darkness in the world anywhere. They enjoyed making love in the garden, in the evenings, in the black soil before any plants came up, and anyplace else where they found intense patches of sunlight: the simple light so sensual, so arousing, after so much deprivation, that it was as if they could not help themselves, nor did they wish to.

The stones in the rock wall absorbed the day's heat and held it far into the evening, so that sometimes after loving, they would not dress but would move in closer to the rock wall and press themselves against it as if against a warm stove, while the rest of the forest cooled slowly and the wind stirred in the treetops. Wallis wondered if there was something about the valley, the landscape of it, that summoned the physical act of love.

On the solstice they went camping. They hiked into the high country, into a stony basin, and camped below a cirque by the edge of a small lake. The twin humps of Roderick Buttes descended from the skyline above them like steps in a staircase, and that night they watched as the sun settled slowly toward the horizon, following the silhouette of the mountain, perfectly tracing the outline of Roderick Buttes with a corona of fiery gold light — refusing to set, skimming the earth perfectly — and it was impossible to watch its passage without believing that, through the millennia, the sun had cut and etched as if with a laser that outline against the sky: that those humps against the sky were the pattern of the sun's desire.

Finally the sun reached the end of the buttes and now it descended below the earth, and the alpenglow cooled slowly from the high country, though they could still feel the sun's warmth below them.

The lake was still frozen with milky ice. A pair of ducks whistled overhead, flying fast and hard into the gathering stars. The country smelled different up high: sprucier, colder. Mel ran her hands over the smooth white limestone on which they were sitting. She rubbed her finger on the embedded fossils of crinoids and brachiopods. A band of mountain goats, white as cotton, had been standing motionless on the icy ridge above them, and now, as darkness fell, they began walking across a stretch of stony cliff.

"It's lonely up here," Mel said. "I like it better down along the river. But I wanted you to see this."

A star melted from the sky; it fell as slowly as a tear. It fizzed, then disappeared. The sun had set so far west as to be almost north. "Can you imagine what Colter's seeing?" Mel said.

Later, with each of them wrapped up in their sleeping bags, Mel said, "It's as if there are all these different layers: like the same world exists beneath this one. It's as if were you to scrape away the crust, you'd find a whole new world just below, but it would be almost just like this one."

But Wallis was already asleep, dreaming of nothing, hearing nothing — only resting atop a fast-cooling slab of rock, and she was alone, much as she had always been. She was just learning what Colter might take twenty or thirty years to learn — that pure beauty held no company, no companionship.

In the morning on the hike out, they veered toward the sky language of ravens and came across a fresh-killed deer, a big doe, with wolf tracks splattering the mud, and bloody wolf prints drying on the stones.

They walked around the edge of the disemboweled carcass, then continued down the mountain, hearing the ravens behind them settle back onto the kill; and they knew that the wolves would be slipping back to the kill also, emerging from hiding. Mel was glad she didn't feel the compulsion, the obsession, to take notes and gather data. To let it all be forgotten.

Closer to home, they stopped and gathered wildflowers for a bouquet to put on the kitchen table.

The ascendancy was already over — it was all downhill now, until December's dark solstice, and yet spring had not even fully occurred in places, or was only just now on the verge of occurring. What power could be achieved by such compression — fitting so much growth into such a small amount of time and space?

Unbidden, the villagers began coming to Wallis, asking him to withdraw or withhold his map from Old Dudley: first Artie, then Charlie, and even Joshua, as well as others he did not know. Word had gotten out that he believed deeply in his map; that this map was different, and that it would open up a valuable new world below them: one in which they would share little if any part.

They were hard-pressed to say what precise thing accounted for their change of heart, unless it was the simple brute proximity of the thing: the understanding that whereas the previous explorations had been speculative, cushioned by the possibility of failure, this one was different. Like Wallis, they could feel the certainty of this one, and so one by one they trudged up the trail to his and Mel's cabin, past where Mel was working in the garden — nodding hello and commenting on how lovely the sun felt — but then they would continue to the porch and would tap lightly at the open door, and peer inside to where Wallis would be sitting shirtless at the desk with the map spread before him, windows open and curtains billowing, studying the map so as to memorize every bump and fold below, or rereading Old Dudley's journals, or working up reserve calculations of just how much oil and gas might be recovered, based on all the different variables.

After the second or third visitor, he had come to expect them, and he would push his chair back from the desk when they came, and they would visit quietly, explaining to him what their fears were, and the reasons they had changed their mind: and that they did not necessarily want him to go away, but that neither did they want him to drill, now that they understood — now that they believed with great faith — that he was going to find oil.

Artie came closest to being able to explain it. "It was like a game, before," he said. "It was kind of fun, watching Old Dudley and Matthew root around for it. But it's not that way, with you," he said. "It seems too final."

Many of them had been having dreams about it, they said — dreams of the future, in which their valley was altered savagely, irreparably.

At first Wallis countered with the defense that if he didn't find it, somebody else would. That they could not stop progress. But this explanation held no sway over them. His success, his certainty, had become like a strange creature in the valley — one which they were increasingly realizing did not fit. Wallis didn't know how to answer them, beyond that; he felt betrayed by their changes of heart. He felt alone, stranded, like a dinosaur, continuing to believe in a thing steadfastly, while all around him other things dissolved, altered, shifted.

He and Mel talked about it in the evenings.

"I can feel it too," Mel said. "How close it is. It scares me, too."

"You've changed your mind also," Wallis said, looking out at the lingering dusk. Adrift: as alone as he had been when Susan had died. He had gotten nowhere; had traveled no distance, in all that time.

"Yes," said Mel, "I guess I have. I'm not going to ask you to turn away — I'm not going to try to change you — but yes, I've changed my mind, too. I don't want you to drill the well."

•

The World Without a Backbone

Here were banks of polyp corals — each little creature planted in his cup and expanding his petal-like tentacles in the life-giving sunlight. Over this slope of animated stone crawled lazy sea snails grazing on the tentacled growths then beginning a work of coral building which the Florida reefs still witness.

The cycles of Cambrian and Silurian time swept on and came to an end. The history of life showed no departure from the fundamental types with which that history was inaugurated. There were new species, new genera, some new families, sometimes a new order or class. The changes were so slow that the world seemed finished for these happy creatures that held possession of it. Yet an occasional visitor from another world would have noted changes. The Cordilleran Land had sunken step by step, and was even now reduced to an archipelago. These lands were the empire of silence and desolation. Populous as were the waters, here was no motion or sound of animated creature. Sparse tree growths fringed

the bleak horizon, but flower and fruit, grass and herb, were yet un-
known. The sea, always jealous of the conquests made from his domain,
continued to growl around the borders of the land, and pursued indus-
triously the work of reclamation of his ancient slime. The wandering
winds finding no fertile isle to fan or sail to waft, confederated with the
destroying waves to wreak their anger on the crumbling shores and
howled sullenly through the vistas of the sparsely wooded plain.

D REAMS ENTERED ALL OF THEM, THROUGH THE HEART OF
summer, so that the time and difference between waking and sleeping became less noticeable. They dreamed of people in the outside
world whom they had not seen in twenty years, then received a letter in
the mail from that person the next day, or the next. Amy dreamed that
Colter was fine, three hundred miles north, and enjoying new sights,
new marvels: fine and safe and healthy.

Mel dreamed that her father was beginning to grow older: that
Wallis somehow had her father under control, rather than the other
way around.

She dreamed that Matthew was vanishing: that he was losing body,
soul, and mind, and was becoming distributed like sand or dust by the
four winds.

Helen dreamed that a man had been spying on her, lusting for her
old body. The dream was troubling, though it also had strange moments of pleasure — and when she awoke in the morning she found
nose- and paw-prints against her windows where a black bear had been
standing up, trying to peer in. She told no one of the dream, and, lonely,
began setting out food on the picnic table behind her store, preparing a
place setting for the bear as a child would make a tea party for an
imaginary guest. It was not imaginary, though, because each morning
when she went to the window, the food was gone, taken neatly from the
plate, and she found herself lying awake at night listening and waiting
for the bear — straining to hear the clink of the china cup and saucer as
he lapped from his bowl of milk — but he was always stealthy, and
never came until he heard the rasp of her snores, with his arrival noticed
therefore only by her dreams; and she would awaken earlier and earlier
each morning, hoping to catch a glimpse of him, but always failing, and

marveling yet at the resilience of hope and longing beneath even a skin as ancient as hers.

Heat came in a way that they could never have imagined back in the whiteness of winter. Hawks and eagles soared above on the convective currents of breath rising from the stone lungs of the mountains. Some days, with his work largely done, Wallis would lie across one of the hot slabs and absorb the radiant heat below as well as that from above. He would lie there as if he had the oil pinned — knowing that he had it pinned — and that as soon as the master showed back up and gave permission, he could drill it.

The heat was so different from any he had known. It was more intimate, and briefer. There was no cooling sweat — nothing but dry heat turning the skin papery.

The rhythm of it was different, too. Back in Texas, the heat had fed on itself, and on the Gulf's sea mass, climbing through the day toward a crest that did not usually occur until shortly before dark; and the echo or shadow of that crest fell over into the night, slicing down into what otherwise would have been the night's coolness.

This heat, however, had a more gentle swell — not like tall breaker waves crashing at the shore, but like waves farther out at sea. Some mornings there was still a shimmering frost, but the sun, rising so early — clear of the horizon by five o'clock — would brush away that silver velvet and climb quickly, steadily, toward a crest around one or two o'clock — but then just as steadily, it would descend, cooling in the same trajectory with which it had risen.

Such steadiness, day after day, seemed to imbue a power, and a peace. Wallis wondered if some landscapes were violent, while others gave peace. He knew it didn't matter — that his business, his attention, needed to rest below, where there were no emotions of man, and never had been — but lying there stretched out on the rocks, it was hard to pretend that he still had the same allegiance to that cold world below. It was hard to pretend that he was doing anything other now than worshiping the sun, and the earth, and his brief place caught between the two.

His neighbors kept coming to him: petitioning him to turn away. Even Helen came, which pained him — pained them both — but she had to say what she had to say. "You found it," she told him. "That's the main thing. You found it, where Matthew and Old Dudley couldn't. But you don't have to suck it out. You can leave it there. Think of it like this," she said, "it has more power if you leave it there."

Out of respect, he did not argue, only listened — but he knew that they had never been out on the rigs down on the coast, had never watched the mud-gleaming steel pipe come out of the hole, had never seen the heavy casing set back into that tiny hole, cemented and then perforated — had never set a wellhead on the casing, opened the valve, and waited, watching and listening as the blood of the ancient world, green-black and bearing an odor not known to this world, gushed steaming up that pipe and into the new world: powerful not for the uses it would be put to, but powerful in itself, in its integrity, before it was broken apart, refined, and ignited.

Powerful in its having been discovered; powerful in its having escaped its entrapment.

"We need wood; we need meat," Mel said. There still seemed to him to be plenty of wood left, and plenty of meat, too, and moreover, plenty of time to get more, if necessary. The next winter seemed like a far shore. But he obeyed her. Though there was nothing he could do about red meat until hunting season, he caught fish from the river, and in the mornings and evenings he sawed and split and stacked wood ceaselessly.

His physical strength continued to grow through the summer, so that it seemed to be almost past measure. Strangely, though, while all the others around him were working on extending the rock wall, and glorying in that work, he felt no desire to join them — knowing instead that the rocks he would be moving soon would be on a scale so much more vast and fulfilling.

He felt ready for the task of summoning the oil. He wondered when the falconer would return. Some days Wallis felt antsy — as if, were the master not to return soon, a thing might be lost, might slip away — while other days he felt great serenity.

The two emotions rose and fell, advanced and retreated gently in him. He kept doing as Mel had told him: splitting and stacking wood. Growing stronger, like a tree putting on growth rings. Most days, he felt that he could eat the world.

Breakfast, work, lunch, work, dinner, rest; begin the day again. Mel had forgotten how one fell into the mash of love — the dailiness of it stretching out into whiteness, the dailiness of it stretching out to form a firmament of comfort, and peace. Of how days of doing nothing really of substance added up into a thing that had substance.

Falling asleep with her hand lightly across his. Nothing more, nothing less. The scent of the garden earth upon her.

He was starting to learn the value of a day, as opposed to the millennia.

The rains would not come; they passed to the south, isolating the valley, stranding it in heat. The creek had gotten shallower, so that to bathe in it in the evenings they had to lie down on their backs and splash water over themselves. The creek ran higher at night, carrying the echo of the day's snowmelt up in the high country; but the snow in the high country was fast disappearing, and though the woods were still bursting with growth and vigor, there was often a stillness to the days, and the old-timers, such as Helen, said that fire was coming for sure, that year; that it was already a done deal. She said you could feel it in the rocks.

Wallis was surprised by how brief and quiet the Fourth of July was. There was a pig roast — the fire was dug in a pit in the center of the road and buried in coals, and there were perhaps as many as twenty tourists — ten of whom had attempted to ride their bikes into the valley, but who had had so many flat tires that they had ended up carrying their bikes on their backs like crucifixes, vowing never to return — but still, the celebration was quiet. People ate and drank and rested in corners of shadows, out of the day's heat, and at dusk the children ran up and down the street holding smoking sparklers, bright fizzes of silent light, waving them in graceful tracings and etchings, running ceaselessly; and all the women, even the tourist women, gathered around Amy, and the residents discussed plans for a shower. They traded recipes, cures — remedies for the rigor not so much of the birthing but of the hauling around of the child for nine months within. Many of the women seemed to have forgotten that Amy had already been through it with Colter, while others remembered, and asked if Colter would be back in time for the birth, and Amy said, "I don't know."

There was the usual testing to see if it was a boy or a girl — analysis of urine color, profile of the belly, reaction of hemp rope held over the belly — and the usual inconclusive disparities.

"Will you go to a hospital or have the baby at home?" one of the bike riders asked.

"I aim to have it at home," Amy said, "but I know I should go in and get a checkup first." She sighed, and looked up over the mountain. "It's a long way, and I don't like to leave."

"Oh, you should go," one of the riders said. "You have to get a checkup."

"I know," Amy said. "I know I need to."

"How much time do you have?"

"Seven weeks," Amy said.

The women all made clucking sounds.

"Where is the father?" one of the tourists asked, with fierce indignation, looking around at the crowd of men who were gathered around the charred hulk of smoldering pig. They were endeavoring to lift it from the pit using pitchforks, and the pig kept slipping and tumbling back into the coals.

"In Houston," said Amy, looking at Mel directly, neither apologetic nor prideful, and Mel stopped, knowing instinctively that it was the truth, but nonetheless trying to count backward and deny it; and when she could not, she lingered with the women for as long as she could, to show that she was not bruised — she gave Amy one last quick look — and then she left, went down to the river by herself. Wallis saw her and went to join her, though the men were about to cut into the pig, and everyone was assembling for the feast.

Wallis sat down next to Mel at water's edge. They sat with their backs against a big aspen tree whose bark was white as a deer's belly, smooth as a young woman's skin. From back up at the bar there came the solitary sound of a banjo being tuned and then played slowly, tentatively. Mel listened to the fluttering of the green and silver leaves above and then laid her head in Wallis's lap. She was quiet for a long time. They listened to the river and the leaves, and farther up the hill, the banjo, and now a fiddle, still quiet and slow, but growing a bit louder, a bit more confident — and after some time she told him, and asked if he had known.

"No," Wallis said, not believing it at first, either. "I didn't ever hear anything like that."

"God help the child if it's a boy," Mel said. Then later, "God help her if it's a girl."

"I thought his seed was bad," Wallis said.

"That's the story I always heard," Mel said. "And God knows if it hadn't been, there would have been by now ample evidence supporting the contrary."

They lay silent a while longer. There was a pause in the music, in which the leaves seemed to speak louder. "I guess something in him changed," she said.

"If it changed in him, maybe it changed in you," Wallis said — an observation; as if star alignments had shifted, like the tumblers of lock and key.

"No," she said. "I'm different from him."

They rolled over and made love, pale as the aspen trees that stood guarding them. Afterward, they fell asleep in the grass, and later awoke chilled. They dressed and went back up the hill, where the music was still playing.

Amy was lying on the porch, stretching her back; Mel sat down next to her. "I was taken a little aback," Mel said, and put her hand on Amy's knee. "I'm happy for you. Are you happy?"

"Yes," Amy replied.

The pig was eaten; only bright bones remained. Artie set off the grand fireworks display, flowering Roman candles and pinwheels and rockets that launched into the night with shrieks and whooshes, flowering in fountains of sparks high over their heads, but which did not explode or crackle. He had bought the silent ones for that purpose, not caring for the sound of gunfire — though downriver, the wolves saw the sky lighting up with showers of fire and smoke, and began howling anyway.

The pig had come from Idaho, the fireworks from China, the tourists from Missoula. The wolves, frightened by the fireworks, huddled, nestled, deeper into their den. The pups wrinkled their noses, tried to learn the world in a night.

As the heat continued to suck moisture and nutrients from the once-lush roots and grasses, the bears began to feed instead on ants, as they waited for the huckleberries to ripen. They prowled the trails with their big heads hung low, searching for a bite to eat — a mushroom, or a slow squirrel — and turned over nearly every heavy stone they passed, looking beneath for swarming ants with eggs, which they would then lick up with gusto, smacking them as if they were sugar, ignoring the tiny stings. In some ways it was as if they were farming the ants, for after the bears had upturned a stone or boulder, the surviving ants would recolonize — would shift camp a few inches to hide once more beneath the safety of the rock in its new location — and the next year, walking down the same trail, the same bear would turn the same rock over and once again lick up as many ants as possible, before continuing down the trail to the next rock.

The bears had begun disassembling Matthew's wall in places, too, searching for the ants that had taken refuge beneath it, flipping the flat stones over — more and more such disassemblings each summer, so that it was as if the rock wall were unraveling, and as if the glaciers were coming back through the valley again, giving slow drift to the massive rocks, spreading rubble and disorder where once grace had existed. Or rather, bringing a different kind of grace, not clearly visible at first.

Several of the villagers began to have troubling, unspecified dreams about Old Dudley. None of them mentioned the strange dreams to anyone else, and so the braid of his appearance among them, as they slept, passed unremarked upon — though he was present in bits and pieces.

The heat grew closer to brutal, further into July. The lichens on rocks were the first to show the stress, drying out and curling until they fragmented at the slightest touch like an old yellow newspaper. The brown leaf-litter of pine needles seemed to ache for ignition; and curiously, people found themselves tempted to light those fires: felt an inexplicable desire to hold a match to that which desired to burn, as if to aid in fulfilling some larger plan. But they resisted.

Helen took short walks whenever she could, looking for her bear friend and searching for the right tree in which to be buried. Often Mel went with her, offering to carry her whenever she tired, but Helen preferred to walk, and when she grew too weak and tired to go any farther, she would stop and rest. Mel was curious about what it felt like, and Helen said it felt like she was old dirt — not good rich young black earth, but old gray leached-out powder dirt.

"Dust," Mel said.

"Almost," Helen said. She held out a hand to test it for steadiness. It trembled.

"Do you have any idea how long?" Mel asked.

Helen shook her head, pulled out a cigarette, lit it. "Soon," she said.

Mel was still curious, almost pushy. Less than a month? More than three months? Half a year? A week?

Helen sucked on her cigarette. "It's not something I've ever done before," she said calmly. "I just don't know. I don't have anything to gauge it against." She leaned forward, coughed up another spray of blood across the leaves. "I need to rest for a little while," she said, and lay down with her head in Mel's lap. "I'd sure like to see him one more time," she said, and Mel stroked what was left of her old gray hair.

They were eating from the garden now: mixing their meals of meat with squash, lettuce, spinach, carrots, potatoes, strawberries. As the food grew, it seemed that Mel could not spend enough time in the garden, keeping it watered and weeded: especially the weeds. They grew so much faster and more vigorously than did the crops that she had little time for anything else. Harvesting and washing the food, weeding, watering again — time for a nap, an hour or two spent with Wallis on the porch, or in the cool of the back bedroom — time to prepare supper, time to read poetry, and suddenly the day was gone, though there was always another one just like it.

The antlers of the deer, elk, and moose were growing at the same pace as the garden, and were covered with velvet that glowed like candles when the sun hit it, though already some of the antlered creatures were rubbing their antlers against the bark of saplings, anxious to scrape away the loose tissue to reveal the hardened material below with which to conquer and claim and dominate territories.

Of all the antlered creatures, only the caribou were outside of this cycle of antler growth. Because they occupied country that was uncontested by other ungulates, their antlers served a different purpose — scraping or shoveling away deep snow to find food in winter, rather than fighting for territory in summer. It struck Wallis as odd that the same basic instrument could be used for two such separate purposes. The caribou antlers were like a combination of elk and moose antlers, rotated sideways and lengthened slightly for leverage and balance: as fine-tuned as the whorls of a seashell, specific to one particular beach's rhythm of tides, so that while the deer and elk and moose were growing their antlers for war, the caribou, two thousand feet above, and back in the shadowy woods, were shedding theirs.

It pleased Wallis to consider these things — how a thing could be twisted or flexed only slightly to become totally different.

Still no rain fell. People began to be cautious with matches.

Mel took a day off from gardening to carry Helen back over to Joshua's to view the progress of his work. They stopped near a marsh and watched a golden eagle, bronzed as if in armor, chase a pair of mallards around the pond fruitlessly — not diving on them from above, but flying after them, following them as a wolf might lope behind a deer: chasing them, it seemed, only for entertainment, a slow game of tag. The sun lit all the hues of gold in the eagle's feathers, and the sight was so peaceful, so strange — the eagle flying around and around the marsh, with the ducks also flying in circles, unwilling to abandon their brood — that Helen changed her mind about what kind of bird she wanted to be buried in.

They continued on. A black bear rose up out of a swamp, blinked owlishly, grunted at them, and moved slowly away, mud-crusted, swarmed by a cloud of swirling mosquitoes. The midday light illuminated that cloud of insects like a corona; a wavering shadow-shape that followed his rough outline wherever he went; there could be no escape from his torment. He went only a short distance before lying back down in a shallow pool of black water and covering his eyes with both paws as if to say, *Have at me, I can offer no more resistance.* Helen and Mel watched the bear for a while with sympathy, and Helen said, "Brother, I know how you feel."

They passed through columns of sun, columns of shadow. The woods were hot even in the shadows, and because Mel was not in as good shape as she'd been when she backtracked the wolves, she had to stop often and rest. The two women would sit beneath the dark green fronds of an old cedar and wave lightly at the gnats and black flies and mosquitoes, waiting for their strength to return. And after some time, as they moved closer to Joshua's, they could hear the distant sounds of hammering and sawing, the dentistlike sound of a battery drill. The squeak of wood planks being bent and torqued, twisted to yield to a new purpose.

When they came over the last ridge and saw Joshua at work in the clearing below, they were startled by the immensity of the project, and by the stage of its progression.

Though there were not yet wings, the body, the undercarriage, was complete, as was the tail and, most alarmingly, the head and beak. The massive coffin was up on sawhorses, and Joshua was up on a ladder with a hammer and chisel, working on the eyes. A great gray owl perched on a broad stump in the clearing not far from where Joshua was working, observing Joshua's creation with great interest. The owl had a dead mouse clutched in each of its talons and was snacking on them, tearing alternately at one and then the other. Joshua greeted them as they came down the hill — knowing he should be more somber, not so cheery, but unable to help himself, so long had he been without company and so pleased was he with his work.

"What do you think?" he asked.

Helen sat down on one of the sawhorses in the shade of the great creation, breathless. Mel spoke for her.

"You've worked so hard on it," she said. "I know it means a lot to you."

Joshua nodded, barely hearing her: watching Helen, wanting words.

"It's gorgeous," Helen said finally, when she could speak again, and when her heart had slowed from its initial leaping of panic — though by no means was it calm. "It's absolutely beautiful," she said, and instead of noticing the coffin, she tried to pay attention to how Joshua received her words: the warmth, the relief, in which he basked. She allowed him his pleasure for a few moments, then said, "Though I have changed my mind."

"About dying?" he asked, incredulous.

"No," she said, "about this," and nodded toward the coffin. "I want it to be part raven and part golden eagle." She looked at what was still left unfinished. "The wings and legs, anyway," she said.

Joshua stared at her, hammer and chisel still in hand. His vision blurred, so that green floaters of rage swam before him; he felt light, dizzy — tricked, manipulated: as if beauty were being wrested from him. He forced himself to say nothing — only stood there breathing hard, waiting in vain for the frantic rage to seep out of him. He remembered what it was about humans that he didn't like — their malleability, their confusing unpredictability. He stood there blinking and fought hard to regain his composure: to bid farewell to the vision of a thing that had existed only in his mind, and would now always exist only in his mind — the pure black raven holding Helen in its belly.

When he could speak, he did so carefully: his hands still white-knuckled on the tools. "I'll have to make it even bigger," he said. "To balance the wings in proportion to the body. Jesus God, Helen, it'll be big." He glanced out at his stallion, which was thrashing in the river, rolling on its back. "Each wing will have to be twelve, maybe fourteen feet long," he said.

"I'll try and hold on," Helen said. "I'll try and wait. If I have to leave early, you can just put me in it and add the wings on later."

Joshua winced at the unprofessionalism of it. He looked ready to cry. "Okay," he said. He looked his age, then, with curls of wood-plane shavings caught in his silver hair, and motes of yellow sawdust trapped in the hair on his arms and at the base of his throat. He looked back at the river, wanting a bath — a purging of the old vision. That night he would have to begin dreaming a new one. When he had been a boy, sixty years ago, had he dreamed he would build boxes in which to put the dead? What curve of earth had moved him toward that purpose?

Mel and Helen thanked Joshua and left. He sat his tools down and walked slowly toward the river, undressing after they were gone. The owl had vanished.

When he was naked, Joshua stood in the sun for a moment — chagrined by the looseness of his skin, the dried wrinklings, the sagging, shrinking muscles — and then gathered his breath and dived into the river.

Mel carried Helen all the way home, helped put her to bed — it was still light out — and then, rather than heading home to see Wallis, she took off running in the other direction, running up the road that led out of the valley — running hard and strong for hours: running through the moonlight, carving back the years and cutting through the plaque of some awful accumulation; running late into the night, until finally panic was gone, and peace had returned, at which point she slowed to a walk — the moon upon her wet skin like silver — and she turned back, taking her time, cooling gradually, and refreshed: encouraged to know that she could still run if she had to.

Some nights the bear did not come to Helen's offerings. Other nights it came but did not eat what she had left on the table — the scraps of a small meal she had been unable to finish — a bowl of oatmeal, a dry biscuit — and so she found herself cooking for the bear, though the effort tired her.

In the daytime, when she was feeling up to it, she would go into the woods searching for him — hoping to sneak up on him in the heat of the day while he napped, as he had been sneaking up on her in the night. She would find his enormous scats everywhere, and his tracks anyplace there was a little dampness; and she could smell him, too, though she couldn't see him. She never got close enough to him to surprise him; he always heard or smelled her coming, and would slip away silently on his big padded feet, stepping from stone to stone to avoid crunching twigs.

Sometimes Helen could take only ten or twelve steps before she ran out of breath, and she would have to sit down quickly and rest. If she breathed in too deeply, breathed as hard as she wanted, she ran the risk of starting up the bleeding again. But if she didn't breathe deeply, she couldn't get the air she needed, and she would pass out, which happened with increasing frequency.

So she would sit and wait, poised as if balanced atop a high fence; and when the fluttering in her throat and the pain in her chest had passed, she would light a cigarette, and would sit there smoking it, amazed that she had lived so long — knowing that there had been a mistake somewhere, a broken cog or gear-tooth that had allowed her to make it this far.

Occasionally she would pass out as she smoked the cigarette, the smoke robbing the oxygen from her blood and brain, and she would topple over on her side, where the cigarette would start a small fire in the dry grass and leaves. The flames would run quickly for a short distance, burning up whatever tinder-dry material they could reach, casting sometimes for ten or fifteen feet before encountering a patch of lush vegetation, which slowed the flames to a creep; and in her unconsciousness, Helen would take in the scent of the burning grass, and would relax, would know peace: and in so doing, her lungs would open and her muscles would begin carrying oxygen again.

She would sit up and stare at the blackened, smoldering ring around her — her clothes and hair scorched — and at the bright ball of the sun above — and she would not always be convinced, in those first few moments, that she had not already passed on to another place in which time disappeared. Perhaps it is not the flesh that is mortal, she would think, but time. Perhaps time moves in cycles — is born, lives, then dies — while the physical materials are constant, like some residue of time's passage.

The thought would invariably make her feel small, strangely unclean, insignificant: as if she were merely the spoor of some mindless thing.

Her breath would try to leave her again.

In early August, Mel missed her first cycle — she, who had usually been as steady as the moon — steady and fruitless.

She knew instantly. She could feel it as if already the presence of another person was fully in the room — a person unknown to them, but a third presence — a triangulation.

She did not feel her old life being whisked or drawn away, like something glissading down a snow slope. She did not think to look back. Instead she turned and looked forward, as if into a breeze bringing them both a fresh scent — doing so unconsciously, so that that which was being carried away by that same breeze went unconsidered. She told Wallis, and they both felt that the change in Mel's blood, and the new fullness in the cabin between them, was nothing but good.

"Are you certain?" Wallis asked.

"Pretty sure," Mel said. "Yes."

"I thought you were infertile," he said.

"I guess something changed."

They went for a walk up into the woods behind the house. Everything looked slightly different: every leaf, every species of tree, every stone — sharper, clearer, as if before they had not really been looking at these things, but somehow past or around them. The new view was startling.

In those next several days, he often asked her if she had started her period yet. He examined her, then tasted her, to see if there was a difference, and he imagined that there was, though in no way that he could have described. The moon melted from its fullness back toward a diminished shape, and they felt as if they had struck out on a new long journey, one for which they had ample reserves and infinite patience.

They agreed not to tell anyone. They decided to hold it secret between them — to treasure the solitariness.

They walked upstream along the creek that ran past the cabin, following one of the low wandering rock walls Matthew had built. Wallis stopped by a trickling spring and picked up a damp stone, jeweled emerald with spongy moss. A tiny salamander, red with a green blaze down its back, curled into a reflexive, defensive posture. A wood frog leapt into the creek and splashed across. A thrush warbled. Wallis imagined the bulldozers treading across the back of the frogs and salamanders. He touched the tiny salamander with the tip of his little finger.

"I won't give him the map," he told Mel.

"He'll be mad," Mel said, and then, "Are you sure?"

"I'm done with him," Wallis said. "I'm done with all that. Yes, I'm sure," he said.

A hot breeze stirred the treetops, brought summer scents to them. "Are you sure?" Mel asked again. "You can't change your mind, with him — you can't betray him, then go back and apologize. Are you absolutely sure?"

"It was nice," Wallis said. "I liked it. But it's all behind me now. I don't want the well drilled here. Not in this valley."

"He'll say you're being selfish," Mel said. "He'll say you're being a hypocrite."

Wallis laughed. "He'll say worse things than that."

"Yes, he will."

Because he could not bear to destroy the map, he hid it in the basement: rolled it up and placed it in a cedar chest to show his daughter or son, forty or fifty years distant, perhaps. It took all the resolve he could summon to separate himself from it.

He rolled the hide within a decoy of other blank hides and furs, locked the chest, moved it into a corner, piled empty cardboard boxes over it, then placed a shelf of canned goods in front of it.

He imagined the cabin crumbling in a hundred years or more; imagined the basement filling with sediment and the forest growing in across the spot, swallowing the map in that cedar chest. He thought how strange it was that he could accept the notion of it rotting, but that he couldn't burn it, even though the two processes were basically the same, and only a matter of time's scale: that rotting was nothing but a very slow burning.

Helen selected her tree. It was the one she had known she would select all along, one she had walked down to visit the first day she had got it in her mind that she needed to be making such a decision — a great cottonwood, towering above the aspen at the edge of a marsh behind her house.

She kept looking for others, but that was the one against which she had measured all the others in her searching, and the time had come for her to be grateful for that one rather than to squander any more time or energy wishing for something beyond it.

She now spent time in the tree's company, and was increasingly glad she had chosen it. It was a short walk from her cabin. She could walk down there at any time of day and nap in the green grass beneath its broad lattices of shade, breathing the punky moldering scent from the leaves of years past. It had been such a dry year that the marsh was a scorched field of umber sedge and sawgrass, possessing no mosquitoes, in mid-August, so that she was able to sleep peacefully, and it seemed to her as she slept that she was beginning to understand some things about her tree.

Occasionally when she woke there would be the impression that she heard the sound of voices: voices that had fallen silent just as her eyes fluttered open, so that it was more the sharp edge or echo of their silence than the sound itself that had awakened her.

Often they would be the voices of people she had known but who were now dead — her mother, father, aunts, brothers, sisters, usually — and other times she woke thinking of men she had loved long ago with a clarity and longing she had not known in many years, and she would feel both hopeful and refreshed.

She lay on her stomach in the cool grass, face turned to one side, a trickle of drool falling from the corner of her mouth, saliva sometimes flecked with blood, but feeling only comfort and peace. The day's currents of heated air moved just above her as if searching for her; but she kept sleeping, down in the cool grass, as if already buried.

In her sleep she could smell the fresh-peeled bark of young cottonwoods, trees scribed and even toppled by the toothy workings of beavers. It was a syrupy odor, like sassafras, clean and sharp to the nostrils, the palate, the mind. She heard from a farther distance the barely audible sounds of axes ringing and saws buzzing as people began to go about the business of gathering firewood in earnest; and these steady, lulling sounds reassured her. There were certain things in which economy was grace, but the gathering of firewood was not one of them. It was one of the rare things for which excess was best.

Sleeping beneath her tree was the only peace left to her. All other waking moments were dominated by an awareness of the rudeness with which her body was betraying her, with farts and whistles and other leakages escaping from her without warning or control: imbalances, rumblings, intestinal flutings; lungy gags and mutters, even in the midst of the once-simple act of breathing. The heart's riddled erratica: she had had enough. No rhythms remained in her possession. She belonged to the stars already.

Things began to move fast for her now. As one thing fell away, it carried with it ten other things: plunging. The townspeople had been honoring her struggle, yet now that she had chosen her tree, they couldn't help but feel some small sense of betrayal. How could the valley still be the valley without Helen? What tree could take her place?

The little green globes of huckleberries blushed pink, then swelled and sugared toward purple, converting sunlight to sparkling sugar, in one of the sun's last acts of magic before it was lured south in its own migration. The days were dryer than ever, and the heated breezes stirred and circled the valley, bathing and ripening the berries, passing across them like the warm breath of animals.

People prowled the sunny hillsides with buckets, gathering the berries in great quantities, eating them as they picked, but still managing to fill their buckets. Their hands, arms, and faces were stained purple from eating the berries, as were their clothes from where they had passed through the shrubbery. Birds and bears also moved across the mountains in these same berry fields, browsing and grazing, so that their faces and muzzles, their chests and legs, were purpled, and it made it seem as if they were all of a brother- or sisterhood, in that last part of August. Even the creatures that did not eat the berries had parts of their bodies painted from where they had passed through the berry fields on their way to other comings and goings.

The larch trees began to burn orange gold, changing at their tips first — the coned crown of the tree turning amber while the needles below remained green, so that in that first week, a forested mountainside looked as if ten million matches had been struck; and then in the days that passed, as the gold coloration crept slowly down the tree, the trees looked like candles with flames that grew longer each day, so that the mountains looked as if they were already burning. The shape and essence of a thing is responsible for the shadow it casts: can a shadow reverse this, and create something real? By what process can a dream become reality? Could a dream of earth create stone, landscape, lives?

Wallis had no regrets about burying his map. As the animals began to stir and consider leaving the mountains, preparing for the journey south, he felt that the life that was leaving the landscape was somehow finding its way into his heart. And he felt as if Mel were holding his heart; holding it with great care, soothing it. Not even the old buried earth had owned him as she did now.

A mother, he thought, and then almost as if in indulgence — a father. Such new land, so close — so imminently touchable.

Amy visited often. She and Mel canned jam together at the cabin: stoked the fire up for boiling water with which to sterilize the jars, poured in more sugar, then sealed them and set them on the table in the window's sunlight and waited out on the porch, drenched with sweat, listening to the *pop!* of each lid flexing as the jam expanded in the jars to form a seal: dozens of jars popping, a percussive chorus of security: food through the winter, bounty carried forward, protection against austerity.

After each batch of jam had sealed, they would make their way down to the creek and undress and lie in the shallows, hanging their sweat-soaked clothes over the bushes, and would let the creek cool them as a bucket of water cools the horseshoe taken from the blacksmith's anvil. Nude, Amy looked as big as a horse, lying in the shallows, and both women would watch as the baby within stirred and flexed: moving with such animation, such stretchings, that they could see the tidal rolls of knees and elbows.

Each night, frosts cut the leaves as if to draw blood, burning them red at the edges and drawing more moisture from the drying land. The wind rubbed the dry tips of branches against other branches, a ceaseless scraping, the friction of which often kindled small flames that burned for a few minutes before petering out. Crystals of quartz up in the high country caught and bent sunlight, focused and magnified it into flame whenever the concentrated light fell upon the proper medium: a patch of duff, a clump of lichen — and these little fires, too, burned bright for a few moments before extinguishing themselves, so that there was now the far scent of smoke and wisps of gray thread rising from the forest, so tiny as to look like ropes dropped from heaven.

Mel held both hands to her still-flat stomach and thought of how much Matthew would have enjoyed this year had he still been living in the valley.

The garden was producing. Each night she laid light sheets over the plants to protect them from the frost, and in the day she gathered more harvest: peas, carrots, potatoes. She stacked the bushels on the porch and felt for a moment like her father, glorying in the number of barrels of oil a certain well might have brought forth. She touched her hands to her belly again and tried to pooch it out round: tried to imagine it swollen as huge as Amy's, but couldn't.

She sat on the porch barefooted, hot and dusty, and ate a carrot. She could smell the smoke from the little fires, could hear the tiny gnawings of distant axes and saws as villagers continued to gather wood. Wallis was off fishing.

She decided to go for a walk. Each new time she went into the woods without paper and pen and returned without data — or rather, with secret data held only in her mind, unrecorded to the rest of the world — she felt stronger and fresher, and found that she enjoyed each walk more than the last. It was like seeing the world anew. Twenty years' data were enough; it was time to rest and to marvel, but not count. Her scientific walks had once been a kind of work; now, her entries into the woods were like a kind of prayer. Many days, early into the autumn, she would find herself so happy while on a walk, or working in her garden, that she would find herself crying.

One afternoon she came across the carcass of the wolf she'd seen late in the spring with the porcupine quills in its face and muzzle. It had died only recently — it still had all its fur on it, and had not been touched by other animals — only by the indiscriminating lusts of flies, ants, worms, and beetles — and in the heat the wolf had swollen and bloated to twice its normal size, so that it looked like some kind of monster. Mel stopped instinctively when she saw it, believing it at first to be a sleeping white bear.

Mel approached the dead wolf and its stench with a deep mix of sadness, revulsion, and curiosity. She stopped when she was ten feet away and crouched and studied its swollen, barely recognizable face. A thousand putrescent infections had set in, rendering the flesh pulpy and in that manner finally releasing the barbed quills from the sodden medium in which they had once found firm purchase. Mel could see that the wolf had been blind for some time before his death — perhaps all through the summer.

As she studied the wolf, she read the signs now, her eyes casting upslope of where the wolf's final death throes had occurred: the torn-up duff where it had careered down the slope, cartwheeling to its final resting place — black dirt and drying strawberry vines and porcupine quills caught between the wolf's toes from where it had been digging mindlessly in its agony, building its own grave — and, studying further, she saw too where other wolves had been visiting the quilled wolf in its last days. She read their tracks, and the multitude of their scats — farther up the incline, some castings of old deer bones — and realized that the wolf pack had been tending to the wolf as it died — feeding it, and keeping vigil.

She remembered now the howls of a week, two weeks, three weeks ago, and was surprised and slightly ashamed that she had not been able to interpret them: that she had been living so totally in another world, with other concerns — so disassociated from that to which she had previously been so deeply attached.

She squatted there a while longer — "Poor wolf," she said — and watched the wind stir the woolly underfur of its belly. The hair was beginning to pull loose in clumps. Mel watched the dead wolf a few more moments — as if still not quite understanding it would not at any second get up and walk away — before a thing relaxed inside her, and she understood that it already was getting up and walking away.

Mel moved closer and touched the wolf's ear. Another tuft of fur fell free. She put her hand to its muddied chest and wondered, What kind of tree, what spirit and nature of a tree grows out of a dead wolf's chest?

She said a prayer for Matthew, and a prayer for the wolf, and turned and went back down the mountain. She came out onto the road below town at dusk, where she saw a figure walking ahead of her. She ran to catch up. It was Wallis, walking home from the river with a stringer of fish. She admired the fish, kissed him. They walked hand in hand home.

•

The Dynasty of Fishes
Devonian and Carboniferous Times

When the morning of the Devonian Age dawned, a new form was seen moving in the populous sea. It was a vertebrate form. Without a bony skeleton, its cartilaginous framework and general plan embodied a new conception. Among vertebrates its organization was decidedly low. It was not a fish in any ordinary acceptance of the term, though we shall have to call it a fish. There were other vertebrate forms more clearly fishlike, but all widely separated from modern fishes. One could easily distinguish three types of these archaic vertebrates. They are known among us as E-las'-mo-branchs, Plaé-o-derms *and* Gan'-oids. *The Elasmobranchs are a group which still survives. They are all sharklike.* Cestraeion, *the Port Jackson shark, has spines in front of both the dorsal fins; the nostrils unite in the cavity of the mouth, and the upper lip is divided into seven lobes. The teeth along the middle of the mouth are small. External to these are large flat teeth twice as broad as long, arranged in oblique series so as to form a sort of tessellated crushing surface.*

Among the very earliest American fishes were some of these spine-bearing sharks. The spines are flattened, two-edged like a bayonet, and curved as if one had belonged to the right side and the other to the left. Some of them were more than a foot in length. Being two-edged and very sharp, they must have been very powerful weapons. These cestracionts were numerous during the Corniferous period. Their smooth brown spines are very often found in the Corniferous limestone of New York, Canada, Ohio, and Michigan. If you wish the name, here it is: Machaeracanthus, *or "dagger-spine."*

Another of the most common and most striking fishes of the same age appears to have been a relative of the modern sturgeons — a family of plated ganoids. Our American geologists have almost buried it under a pile of nomenclature, which they have finished in the following shape: Mae-ro-pet-al-ich'-thys, *or "big-plated fish." These fishes were of large size. The cranium was composed of large polygonal plates, united by double sutures which are nearly concealed by the tubercled enameled surface; the tubercles are stellate; the surface is ornamented by double rows of porea and single thread lines, forming a pattern which does not correspond with the plates below. These large, geometrically formed plates often attract the attention of quarrymen, since they are sometimes fifteen inches in length.*

These relations enable us to contemplate with new interest some of the despised fishes which live in our time. Our sturgeons, garpikes, and sharks are the sparse representatives of those ancient families which once sustained alone the dignity of the vertebrate type. In their forms was first enshrined the conception of the vertebrate plan of structure that was destined to remain on the earth under its various modifications, until man, the thinking and ruling vertebrate, should arrive. In modern times, our familiar bony-scaled garpike haunts the freshened waters of river and lake — the poor degenerate descendant of ancestors which once dominated over the world. Venerable relic of a mighty empire! Were the lineal descendant of Menes or Nebuchadnezzar II to stand before me, the antiquity of his lineage would inspire my interest and veneration, but it would be as yesterday compared with the lineage of this poor garpike.

Why have these creatures been preserved in existence so long? The march of organic improvement has advanced for thousands of centuries, and left them far in the rear. These forms are misplaced in the modern world. They constitute an anachronism, which is either an absurdity, or a phenomenon too full of meaning for ordinary comprehension.

The garpike destroys our game fish and our market fish — as he ravaged neighboring kingdoms while he ruled an empire of his own. He tangles and tears the nets of the fishermen, who visit their execration upon him. His flesh is unpalatable for food. The mud-loving sturgeon, less destructive in his nature, brings no utility into the modern world. The fierce shark, equally unfit for fuel, is the freebooter of the ocean. Other fishes furnish aliment to man. They come from unknown realms to meet man and serve his ends. But these archaic types linger from a time when human wants had as yet no existence, when human food was not demanded. They were never intended for food, since they made food of every other creature. These useless and destructive beings are out of joint with the world and with history. Why are they here?

Why? They come to import ideas into the modern world. They bring down to us living illustrations of faunas passed away. The plates of Cephalaspis and the spines of Machaeracanthus quarried from the rock might pique our curiosity and distress us by their mystery; but they would not instruct. It was intended that the intelligence of the being which always stood as the finality of organic improvement should grasp the conception of the world and reproduce the grand history of departed cycles. Why? It was an act of beneficence which saved these relics of ancient dynasty from total destruction. There was purpose, not accident, in the failure of their complete extinction, and the assignment of the world exclusively to more modern creatures. These freaks are precious examples preserved in a museum. These are caskets filled with documents from an olden time. The garpike and the sturgeon and the shark are missionaries from the past to the present. Hear them. They are preaching to man's intelligence. They are unfolding the plans of Infinite Wisdom. "He that hath ears to hear, let him hear."

Nothing exists but for the benefit of Man. Beauty is for us alone.

•

One day the geese got up from the river and left. There was an excitement in their leaving, all through the day; but that night there was a loneliness, and people gathered at the bar to shore one another up, and to make brave jokes about the coming winter. It was the finest time of year — the days suspended in hazy gold light, the daytime temperatures mild, the nights starry and crisp — the leaves turning color, the scent of wood smoke pleasing in the air, and the cabinets in all homes filling with bounty — but for those who had lived through it in the past — this sweetest time of year — it was burnished with the knowledge, the forethought, of its brevity, and of the coming price to be paid yet again. The departure of the geese was the first indicator of that marker coming due.

Artie came up to Wallis that night and set a beer before him, on the house, and said, "Thanks for not drilling the well." It was the only thanks he'd received from anyone following his decision to bail out of that old life, but he understood that no thanks were needed — that it was simply the only thing, the right thing. Still, he was glad for it, and he smiled at Artie, lifted the mug to him in a silent toast.

"How's Helen?" Artie asked. Mel was across the street, seeing if she needed anything.

"Not good," Wallis said.

"I can't believe she's leaving," Artie said.

Mel and Helen came in the door — Helen rallying, a good night, leaning on Mel's arm, and immediately, all bittersweetness left the room, all sense of abandonment, as they realized Helen had outlasted the geese one more year.

"Has Joshua been in?" she wanted to know. No one had seen him for some time — a sign that he was hard at work. Helen went over to Amy and lifted up her maternity dress and put her hand on Amy's belly. "I sure would like to see that baby," she said.

The baby stirred, seemed to jump, then kicked. "I think you're going to," Amy said, looking straight into Helen's eyes. What she saw there was fright — a flightiness, a worry — her old blue eyes like small gems seen underwater in sunlight. Any hour. Any second. "I'm sure you'll see it," Amy said, taking Helen's hand in hers.

Mel wanted to tell Helen her own news, yet hoped also she would not have to.

Later that evening, Mel carried Helen back across the street. Wallis went with them. Helen fell asleep in Mel's arms, but woke once more inside her own home, and insisted on fussing about in the kitchen and preparing a dinner for the bear, who had not been back for three nights in a row. She scrambled some eggs and mixed pancake batter; when the pancakes were made, she spread huckleberry jam on them and set them on two plates. Mel and Wallis thought she had prepared the meal for them, but then she told them they would have to leave now, or the bear would not come.

They didn't know what to say — feeling the edges of a sorrow that was nearly infinite, believing that Helen's mind was being taken from them before the earth took her body.

They watched her carry the plates of steaming food out into the cold night; watched her sit down at the picnic table and light two candles; watched her wrap the elk hide around her and hunch forward, nodding off, settling in to wait.

"We can't leave her out there on a night this cold," Mel said. "It would finish her off."

"She's got to go sometime," Wallis said.

"We can't," Mel said. "Not before the baby. And not before Matthew..."

The candles wavered wilder in the breeze; one tipped over and snuffed out. They thought she was asleep, and were about to go back out and get her, but she lifted her head, picked up the fallen candle, and relit it, then sat there, waiting, while the flames fluttered.

The bear — a big one, black as the starry night itself — appeared so gradually, so slowly — blackness appearing from out of blackness — that at first they did not understand what they were seeing: the bear moving so carefully, so stealthily, as to seem like a man in the costume of a bear. Helen had drifted back into sleep for a moment, but she awakened when she felt the bear settle his heft so gently onto the seat across from her.

The bear watched Helen intently for long moments, perfectly motionless, so that now it seemed like a stuffed bear — Mel and Wallis could see that beneath the elk hide Helen was shivering, and whether with fear or cold, they could not tell — and then slowly, the bear lowered his head to the plate and began to eat.

With her hands trembling, Helen took up her fork and picked at her own food.

The bear finished his — a few crumbles of egg fell from his mouth, and cautiously, he licked them from the table — and Helen blew out the candles and pushed her plate with the remaining food across the table for the bear to eat too, which he did.

When it had finished, it looked at her a moment longer — woman and bear illumined in blue starlight; the bear's damp eyes and nose gleaming, and its claws shining at the table like silverware — and Mel whispered "We should go," as the bear turned and climbed down from the table and went back off into the darkness.

Mel and Wallis were out the front door and walking down the dusty road by the time Helen gathered the candles and empty plates and went back inside.

They all three slept hard that night, dreamless.

W ALLIS WAS OUT IN THE GARDEN ONE DAY, WHILE MEL had gone to town to check in on Helen, when he felt the ground trembling. He looked up to see a horse gallop through the yard, followed closely by a silver wolf.

For a second, as the horse raced by, Wallis focused solely on the percussive sound of steel-shod hoofs clipping and clattering occasional stones. Such was the horse's speed that the hoofs made sparks against the stones, and so dry was the tall autumn grass that many of these sparks found flame, flaring into smoking bright wisps of orange that raced outward; and after each spark-fire burned out it left behind a smoldering black scorch ring in the same shape as a horse's hoofprint, only larger — as if something giant had just passed through, and the horse and wolf were following that.

The wolf struck the horse hard with his teeth in the horse's haunches and sheared off a slab of muscle. The horse snorted and bucked but made no other sound, and kept running as if nothing had happened. The wolf rolled, dropped, and was up and running again: racing low through the hoof-struck patches of burning grass. Blood gushed bright from where the horse's haunch had been. The horse was almost to the trees — almost into the woods. Wallis could see that was where the wolf wanted the horse to go, to tangle it amongst fallen logs; but the horse in its panic could not know that.

The wolf closed the distance and moved in for another strike — this time leaping high, whether for the thick neck or the face, Wallis couldn't tell — and just as the wolf lunged, the horse ducked his head and skidded to a stop, then reared up and kicked the wolf as the wolf went sailing in front of it. There was the sound of steel hoof against bone, and the brittle sound of bone snapping.

The wolf yelped, and then the horse was rising and striking again, trampling the wolf as it tried to crawl away. Blood gushed from the horse's haunch each time it reared.

Before Wallis could get there and try to calm the horse, the horse went suddenly weak. It stopped its trampling, stared at the ground as if it had forgotten where it was or what it was doing, and then collapsed, the back half going down first, sinking, and then the front half followed.

The horse's ribs were heaving, but otherwise it looked calm. Wallis went past it and into the timber, searching for the remains of the wolf. Everywhere at the woods' edge the grass was trampled, but he could not find the wolf. He found fur, but no blood.

Wallis went back into the grass, thinking he must have stepped right over it. The horse watched him, docile. Wallis walked around the horse, searching. There was blood back in the grass, lots of it, wet and red, but it seemed to be the horse's blood.

He walked into the woods a short distance and found more fur; then he saw a line of blood smeared on a log where the wolf had slithered across it.

Wallis turned and went back out into the bright heat of the field to examine the horse. The little fires were still crackling but had nearly burned themselves out. The smoke drifted past Wallis and the horse in thin threads. The horse flicked her ears, turned and looked back at the smoke, and laid her head down.

Wallis ran to the cabin for a bucket of water. He found a piece of straight wire to use as a needle and some string for catgut. He went back to where the horse lay, its head outstretched, and washed the massive wound. Then he began sewing as best as he could. The horse sighed and made nickering sounds as Wallis worked the wire and string through the flesh.

The sun blazed directly overhead. Flies landed in the wound and bit at it, and they bit at the blood that was smeared on Wallis's hands and arms. He swatted at them, crumpled them, but there were always more.

When he finished stitching, Wallis went back up the hill, searching for the dropped haunch. He found it lying in the sweet green bunchgrass next to a hoofprint-shaped ring of ashes. The meat was partially cooked, seared gray by the flames. He picked it up, took it to the creek, rinsed the grass and twigs off of it, and hung it from a hook in the smokehouse. Then he got a cotton sheet from the cabin and went back to the horse. She was now thrashing her head and trying to get up, as if believing the wolf was coming back.

Wallis erected a tent over the horse to give it shade, then poured water over the wound. He left a large bucket of water by the horse, and a note for Mel, and walked away, to try to clear the trouble from his mind. He got Matthew's fly rod and took off through the woods. All his life he had cared for horses, had slept in the barn with them whenever one was sick or giving birth. He had handled, shoed, and trimmed ten thousand hoofs. He had wormed them, pierced them with trochars, and even killed them to put them out of their misery, but he had never walked away from one — had never left one to the wolves.

He was pretty sure that while he was gone the rest of the wolves would find and finish off the horse.

Deeper in the woods Wallis came upon a speck of dried brown blood on a kinnikinnick leaf. No hair, no fur, no feathers, and no more blood — just the one mysterious drop. It could have come from a marten catching a squirrel, or from a hawk hitting a grouse; from a wounded deer, lynx, or hare, or wounded wolf. It could have come from the cough of an aging bear. Anything.

He fished upstream, fishing into new country. Before the sun had gone beyond the cliffs, dropping the canyon into an early twilight, he had caught half a dozen trout, and he kept them all, thinking, Another three days' worth. He cleaned them, put them in his pack, and headed home.

Once he was out of the canyon, he came back into the sunlight, but he could see that the quality of light was changing, compressing and becoming enriched as more and more minutes were being stolen away. He quickened his pace as if suddenly believing he was running late. A feeling like having overslept.

When he got back to the cabin, he found that the horse had managed to stand up and had pulled against the lead rope, broken it, and hobbled over to the creek, and now she lay collapsed in the creek with the blood-soaked sheets furled around her like Japanese flags. Minnows darted in and out of the cavern of the wound. The horse's eyes were closed, her face half beneath the water, the creek riffling past and around her.

Wallis walked to the creek's edge, wondering how he was ever going to get the horse out of the creek if it was dead. I'll have to pull her with another horse, he thought — but then he saw bubbles coming from her half-submerged nostrils. Wallis waded out and lifted the horse's head, rolled a boulder beneath her chin, and propped her head up above the current. He untangled the sheets and hung them around the cabin to dry.

Wallis worked in the garden, waiting for Mel. Some carrots were ready; he picked and washed them. His thoughts turned to Helen; he hoped that she had not died that day.

In the creek, over the light sound of the drought-stretched riffles, the horse moaned occasionally. Wallis wondered if the wolf was dead.

He was just breaking time down into smaller units until Mel returned. He could sense how it was weakening him, and yet how wonderful that weakening was, and he wondered, Is this how it is for the wolves? How sometimes desire can make you weak, instead of strong?

There was still a little sunlight. It had been one of the warmest days all week. Wallis decided that at dusk he would build a fire next to the horse and sleep outside to keep the coyotes away.

In the yard, where the wolf had caught, and then been kicked by, the horse, the ashes were cold and blue. He gathered them in a bucket and spread them across the garden soil. He wondered how it would look to Mel when she got home: scorched-earth pockmarks running in a trail down through her yard, and a bloating horse sprawled in her creek, and blood flags bannered around her house, stirring and furling in the breeze.

He went inside and thumbed through more of Old Dudley's journals.

> . . . Each phase is derived from the preceding phase through a material continuity. The developed embryo is made of the very yolk-stuff which existed in the beginning. If the living gradation is derived from the embryonic, there must be a material continuity or relationship among

living animals — as we already inferred from their resemblances. If the palaeontological gradation is derived from or determined by the embryonic, so there must have been a material continuity running through the palaeontological series, as we could easily infer from their successional resemblances. Each new species is derived from a predecessor. The highest and the living forms are only the last terms of a long series of generations. It took us a long time to get here, nearer the crown.

Do not be alarmed at the conclusion. If it is true, it is precisely what we are interested in finding out. If it is not true, then science himself will disprove it. Our fears of consequences, our unscientific objections and prejudices count for nothing, except as complaints against God's method in the world, and our own God-likeness.

•

Wallis leaned back and watched the sun set below the mountains, the cool purple light of dusk rolling in like a tide.

The horse had moved again — had gotten up and walked out of the creek — had gotten halfway down toward the smokehouse, as if trying to save Wallis the trouble of hauling it there when it died. A trail of blood ran from the creek to where the horse lay. It was hard to believe there could be any more blood left inside it.

Wallis built a fire to keep the horse warm, laid an elk hide over it, and spread one for himself to lie on as he waited for the horse to die, and for Mel to come home.

Further into the night — Orion had crossed half the sky — Wallis awoke to a faint splashing, something crossing the creek, and then a few moments later, Mel was back, and she said that Helen was all right, or rather, was still alive, and that after visiting Helen she had gone for a long walk in the woods to look at the little fires. She asked what had happened in the yard.

Wallis sat up and explained about the wolf and the horse, but was surprised to see that the horse was gone; that it had gotten up and walked off as he slept (carrying the elk hide still on its back). They could find no further sign of it, nor did they ever see it again, and never knew whether it — or the wolf — had lived or died.

Everyone was waiting for the fires, now. Sometimes the firewood that men and women were cutting with their chain saws would ignite simply from the heat of friction. But none of the fires ever went anywhere.

A branch rubbing against the eave of Helen's store caught fire and burned a hole in her ceiling, but Charlie, drinking on the porch across the street, saw it, and was able to run over with a bucket of water and put it out: though now as Helen lay in her bed she could see the stars through the hole in the roof.

·

The Human Factor in the World's Vicissitudes
Man in the Light of Science

Now that we have traveled over the entire course of terrestrial history, we seem to have attained an eminence from which we can take some comprehensive glimpses of the whole in its relations. Now that we find man to stand at the end of that history, we are able to comprehend the relation which he sustains to its successive steps. Let us look over the fields and see what it suggests.

We learn, first of all, that man is the fulfillment of the prophecies of the ages. The first step of organic progress led toward man. It determined the direction of the course of organization, and now that we know man was destined to stand at the end of that progress, we understand that the law of progress contemplated man. Striking illustrations of progress are distinctly traceable in the history of vertebrates. Even the first vertebrate was but a prophecy of man. In the skeletal structure of the humble Devonian fish, man existed in potentiality. The whole general plan was destined to endure through the history of life and unfold in man. The amphibian, the reptile, the bird, and the quadruped are only successive modifications of the vertebrate conception embodied in On'chus and Onych'odus.

Still more striking are the successive modifications of vertebrate limbs. In the pectoral fin of the fish, we have a number of bony, articulated rays, which answer to digits; and above, are carpal and metacarpal bones, and finally, radius and ulna, humerus and scapula, exactly as in all other vertebrates. When, with the commencement of the purification of the air, the situation was suited to low air-breathers, the pectoral fin was modified into a five-toed forefoot. When, later, the situation demanded a more perfect air-breather, the reptilian limb appeared. If the reptile was appointed to swim in the sea, its hand was shaped into a paddle, sometimes with six digits and many phalanges, as in the fish. If it was destined to fly, a finger was enormously elongated and a skinny membrane was stretched from finger to hind limb and tail. When the time came for the fitting of a vertebrate to make its home in the air, the bones were made hollow, to combine lightness and strength. The hand and fingers were abbreviated and consolidated; cartilage was attached alongside, and in this were inserted the broad light quills which form the expansion of the wing. But here we find all the structures contained in the reptilian foot, except so far as changed function demanded modification.

The paddle of the whale, the shovel of the mole, the clawed foot of the cat, the cloven hoof of the ox, the solid hoof of the horse, the wing frame of the bat — all are but modifications of the same bony elements, adjusted in the same way, but modified in relative development. All this was prophetic of man. When an animal was to appear whose forward extremity should rise above the simple function of locomotion and seizing of prey — an animal that should swing an implement of civilization, ply an oar, wield a pen, manipulate a needle, make a watch, play a violin, emphasize thought by a gesture, or execute the behests of intelligence rather than of appetite and passion — then, assuredly, a different and nobler plan of structure had to be devised.

No, it was and is the same old plan. All these resources existed potentially even then in the clumsy fin of the fish. Thus is man related to the plans of the present; thus, to a plan which has persisted for millions of years; and thus, was man all the time anticipated and approached, during the progress of the transformations wrought by the ages. Man was anticipated even in the stone before life: the earth and rock beneath our feet.

I will simply recall here what has been said about the anticipation of man in the provision of beds of oil or coal laid by from the poison which once infected the atmosphere, and which temporarily barred the march of progress. No other corporeal being has been capable of comprehending the uses of oil; no incorporeal being had need of oil. It is something which stands in relation only to man; for man it was designed. We may say the same of iron, silver, and the other useful products of the mineral kingdom. It is only to man that they are useful. Again I must tell you, man is the fulfillment of the prophecies of the ages.

We understand now that man's birth was foreshadowed. It was expressed in the formal gradation of the continents. They are graded, in the present epoch. The mammalian fauna of Australia is almost exclusively marsupial; that of South America is characterized by abundance of edentates; that of North America is predominantly herbivorous, while carnivores take the lead on the eastern continent. A similar gradation existed in the age before man. The mammalian fossils of the Tertiary are, in Australia, predominantly marsupial; in South America, edentate; in North America, herbivorous; in the Orient, carnivorous. The apex of organization in the age before man, was located in the Orient. It might have been anticipated, therefore, that when the apex should rise to the grade of man, the Orient would be the theater of its display.

Man seems signalized as the last term in the series of organic improvements. His erect attitude gives us an intimation. The first vertebrate, the amphibian, could slightly elevate his head. The reptilian head could be raised to a higher angle; and the highest reptiles could rise on four feet, or even ambulate as bipeds — though withal, in an awkward way; but all reptiles dragged a cumbrous tail prone on the ground. The bird perched in an oblique attitude and raised the head for an outlook; but when he flew through the air, he took the attitude of a swimming fish.

The ape could clumsily stand on two feet and wield a weapon with his hands; but the very shape of the foot, and the unmuscular legs show that Nature never designed him for a habitual biped. Man alone finds the upright attitude quite natural and comfortable. Here has been a progressive upward inclination of the spinal axis. Vertical in man, the progress comes to a limit. This criterion is not suited to index any further improvement. We infer that no further improvement will present itself to be indexed. We have achieved already our perfection.

The same inference is sustained by man's cosmopolite adaptations. From the beginning of life on the earth, the range of individual species had been narrowing. The brachiopods and trilobites of the Cambrian ranged through wider seas than those of the Carboniferous. Land animals, when they appeared, were fenced within still stricter limits; and when the mammals came upon the theater of being, each species was assigned to a particular corner of one continent. Under this law of progressive restriction of faunal range, man should have been shut in a narrower field than any of his predecessors. His is not. On the contrary, all restrictions are removed. Man ranges over every continent and through every clime. No conditions are too hard; no difficulties insurmountable. Nature seems to have reached a point where a new policy is inaugurated.

The shackles are removed. Man is free to possess the earth. With man in possession of the earth there is room for no wider-ranging animal. There is place for no successor.

Nature in man seems to have reached a period. While other animals rise in steady gradation from lower to higher, man proceeds by one grand leap to possess a rank and dignity unapproached by his best predecessors. In intelligence, in aesthetic perceptions, in moral sense, in religious susceptibility, in theistic apperceptions, he stands separated by an unbridged gulf from his mammalian fellows. Man is the capital and completion of the long-rising column of organic life.

The structure is finished.

•

Old Dudley came creeping in the next day, right at dusk: crawling on his hands and knees, dressed in his black suit and covered with charcoal. He had come alone — had come to claim his map and his falcon — and his car had broken down on the summit. Trees blown over by the autumn winds were falling across the road, and because there was no traffic for days at a time, the logs blockaded the road. Some had caught fire, as the little fires began to pop up with greater frequency, like small campfires being lit by invisible campers, or invisible tribes, so that often Dudley had had to scramble over and under burning logs, coughing, his old eyes watering like a hound's, his nose runny with black-crusted mucous, and his hands and arms and knees blistered with dozens of small burns from where he had touched live coals. He crawled up onto the porch of the mercantile and crept inside, to where Mel and Wallis and Helen were having dinner. At first they thought he was a black bear or a black wolf that had nosed his way inside, but then he stood up on his hind legs and, as if he had been invited, began to tell them his story. Mel went over and hugged him; Wallis and Helen greeted him less warmly.

It had taken him three days and he had had no water until he reached the first creek on the Swan side, coming down off the summit. Coyotes had followed him for the first two days, and on the third day — when he had done most of the crawling — ravens had circled him, laughing, all day long. All he had for a weapon, he said, was a ballpoint pen; and when he reached that first creek and crawled into it, and had drunk deeply, wallowing in it, he had looked up to see a huge fire-blackened mountain lion crouched at the water's edge, watching him. Dudley said he froze, and that he and the lion stared at each other — it waved its tail like a snake, once — but that then the lion lowered its head, took a quick sip of water, and bounded away.

"I shit my britches," he said. "I had to rinse off in the creek. Then it was off on my journey again, with those gott-damn coyotes walking right behind me, like some mongrel dogs down in Zacatecas or Durango."

Mel got him a damp towel with which to clean off, and fixed him a plate of supper, but Dudley rejected it, and instead prowled the aisles of the mercantile, finding and opening cans of Spam and deviled ham and Vienna sausages, for which he had developed a fondness long ago while working on the drilling rigs in West Texas. He licked the potted meats straight out of the can, cursing whenever he cut his tongue on the can's edges — blood trickled from his tongue, ran from the corner of his mouth — and with his fingers he scooped out the slushy gray meat.

Helen was too tired to stand up. "What's wrong with you?" Dudley asked.

"Did Matthew come with you?" Helen asked, ignoring the question. Dudley licked his fingers, greasy-white with gelatinous slime, and said, "No, he's a goner, he hasn't been worth a damn in over three months. He's all burnt out. I got to get a new one," he said, and glanced at Wallis, still licking his fingers.

He sat down by the stove to warm himself, his charred, damp clothes steaming and giving rise to an unmistakable series of odors — mildew, shit, sweat, and ash. Mel went upstairs and looked through Helen's closet to find something that he might wear. Helen had never been big on dresses, though inexplicably, in her closet, there was a shimmering emerald-green saffron one, an evening dress, covered with decades of dust.

Mel found an old pair of bib overalls, a T-shirt, and an oversized sweater. She slit the overalls wider with her knife as if slitting the belly of a fish, and took the clothes down to Old Dudley. He examined them, frowned.

"You can't smell yourself, can you?" she asked. "You don't have any idea how rank you are, do you?"

He looked hurt. "Hey," he said, "I got here, didn't I?"

While Dudley showered, Mel took his clothes out into the woods and set them on fire: just a little fire, a cautious one. When the fire was out, she came back inside and made a pot of tea.

Helen, who had not spoken since Old Dudley had told her that Matthew had not come with him, said that she was tired, and asked

Wallis to carry her upstairs to bed. She was pale, and lighter than ever — as close to weightlessness, it seemed, as a person could be and still be alive. She was asleep even before Wallis ascended the stairs.

When Dudley came out of the bathroom, looking unavoidably strange in the altered overalls — like a circus animal dressed as a human, yet unwilling to perform — he looked around for his old foul clothes, almost frantically.

"I burned them," Mel said. "You'll thank me for it. They were deathly."

"Did you get the money clip out?" he asked.

Mel held her breath for a minute. "How much was in it?"

He stared at her. "What there always is — as much as it'll hold. Shit, I don't know," he said. "Ten, maybe fifteen thousand."

"Was it a nice money clip?"

Dudley shrugged — not heartsick, only annoyed. "Fuck, I don't know," he said. "Some asshole gave it to me — some friend, a long damn time ago. It was probably silver or some bullshit thing like that. Shit, it doesn't matter. I can't even remember the asshole's name, or why he gave it to me. Probably some dirt farmer whose land I found oil on," he said. "They get pretty excited, when it happens the first time. They think you're doing them a favor — they think you found the oil on their land because you *like* them." He shook his head. He seemed already to have forgotten about the money. "Confused little bastards," he said. "Poor bastards — so gott-damn hungry for love they try and recreate the world to make there be some in it for them." He shook his head again. "Fuck-heads," he said. "Fakers, liars, desperadoes. If it ain't there, it ain't there. But you can't tell them that."

Mel pressed her hands to her stomach, tried not to laugh. "Pop, I'm sorry. I'm really sorry" — but then she could not hold it back, and burst out laughing.

"Very funny, missy," Dudley said, "but some people have to *work* for a living." He stalked out the door and went over to the bar.

"Will you tell him this trip?" Mel asked, and Wallis said, "Yes, I have to." He waited a moment, then asked, "And will you tell him?"

"About us?" Mel said. "Yes. About the baby? Maybe."

They went down to the river, to the place where they had lain before, on the Fourth of July, and loved again, as if to lay some final bulwark of resistance against the past; and afterward they lay in the cool night, watching the same stars they had watched that night of conception; and they could see, up on the mountainsides, one or two blinkings from the little spot-fires that were cropping up.

They did not see or hear Old Dudley in the bar, when he met up with Amy. "Been up to the devil's work, I see," he told her, and she told him that yes, she had.

They did not hear him tell Amy — pleased as he was with this strange phenomenon — as he put it, this "unstoppering of his sperm" — that only if it were a boy, he would claim it, as he had just lost one, and needed a new one.

Amy was disgusted, but didn't believe he meant it. They went out onto the porch and sat there with their feet hanging over the edge, watching the same stars and the same fires as were Mel and Wallis.

Amy, in her maternity dress — short of breath — slipped off her sandals and twined her bare feet with Dudley's. He tried to remember the joy he might have felt with his wife just before, and after, Mel was born, so long ago, but he could remember nothing.

Amy was talking about God, and heaven — asking if he believed in a Supreme Being. He nodded, gripped her hand tighter, smiled grimly, and said, "You bet." Amy was asking if he would help raise the child to believe in the power of a Supreme Being, and Dudley laughed, nodded, and said again, "You bet."

"You can read my old journal," he told her, "back at the kids' cabin. It tells about all that stuff. It's kind of like the Bible."

"Mmm," Amy said, and held his hand tighter. They watched the stars. Amy gave a silent prayer of thanks, for having been given a second chance.

"The Berkutsk," he told her dreamily — slipping, falling, into the dream state of lust that was all he knew, anymore. "That giant golden eagle they hunt with over in the Middle East. I was over there doing business with the Arabs one time. They liked me. They wanted to give me another one to take back to the States, but the namby-pamby Fish and Wildlife folks confiscated him when I got off the plane in Los Angeles. I miss that bird," Dudley said. "He rode all the way back with me, sat in the seat next to me, never bothered the stewardesses or anyone. Slept almost the whole way. Crapped once on the newspaper I had beneath him. Shat out the perfect single foreleg of a desert kit fox, clean as a whistle. So clean you could put it on a necklace and wear it around your neck.

"They thought I was a movie star," he said, "riding up there first class with that big golden bastard, with a permit that one of the princes had given me. Damn thing didn't mean anything when I landed, though. Damn bird was eight feet wide, when he stretched his wings. Had to give him an aisle seat.

"You should have seen that bird kill things," Dudley said. "They used to hunt men with them, in the ancient wars — a scene like something from Revelations, is how I like to imagine it, with maybe the whole sky filled with these Berkutsk eagles, routing the opposing army — diving from the sky, their talons ripping through the flimsy metal and leather armor of the fleeing soldiers. A sky full of harpies, is how it must have looked, and maybe they thought it was the end of the world, but shit, look, that was over seven hundred fucking years ago, and the world's still going.

"The Arabs took me up into the mountains one day. We rode on camels, for Chrissakes. We were hunting wolves. The wolves were up high that time of year, hunting these big-horned sheep. The kings and princes enjoyed hunting the sheep, and didn't want the wolves killing any of them, was the official reason for the hunt. But I knew, we all knew, it was just to be hunting wolves, period. To see that big fucking Berkutsk in action.

"Where they hunted them was in country so steep you couldn't fire a gun: the echo would have started an avalanche. They'd spot the wolf running from them, and turn the eagle loose. The guy who carried the eagle was always a big sonofabitch.

"The wolf, or wolves, almost always seemed to know what was going on. They'd break off their chase of the sheep and head up a canyon, trying to stay in the rocks. But the eagle got them every time — or every time I saw it hunt, anyway. It would come down from the sky like a hammer and take just one, while all the others kept running. Sometimes the wolf pack would turn and try and fight the eagle after it had nailed one of the pack, but usually they just kept running.

"The eagle would have his talons locked through the wolf's back, or through its skull, and sometimes we'd have to ride over there and unfasten the eagle — it would get those long fucking talons tangled up and wouldn't be able to get free of the dead wolf. In the wild when it happened like that, they'd sometimes die, death-anchored to their victim. Only the falconer could get near the eagle. It wouldn't let anyone else get close, and it didn't even really like the falconer being there. The eagle would spread its tail like a fan to hide the prey, covering it like a blanket, and would hunch up over the wolf, obscuring it.

"The falconer would hood the eagle then, and finally, once the eagle had relaxed, the falconer could pry open those clutched hooks, could retrieve the bloody wolf, which he would throw over the back of a camel.

"You could feel something circulating in the eagle," Dudley said. "Something like the crackle in a neon light bulb. Even though the eagle was hooded and calm, its blood would still be revved up, and I swear to God you could hear the noise of its blood like electricity in those God-awful stony mountains, and you could feel it. It raised the hair on your arms, and on the back of your neck, even on a warm day."

Artie came out on the porch with another pitcher of beer, a bottle of tequila, and a bottle of dark rum. "On the house," he said, resting his hand on Dudley's shoulder, and asked, "How's it going, big fella?"

"Ahh," said Old Dudley, "I'm gonna die." Artie smiled, patted him on the shoulder.

"I'm glad you and Wallis decided not to drill," Artie said. He looked out at the stars. "The place needs a rest. It's changing too fast."

Dudley's tong marks rippled — like a fish breaking the surface — and his eyes narrowed, but he said nothing.

"What'd they do with your eagle?" Amy asked. "In Los Angeles — when you landed, and they confiscated it — what'd they do with it?"

"Fuck," Old Dudley said. "Shit. Hell if I know," he said. "It's just gone, is all." He shrugged. "Maybe it got away," he said. "Maybe it's still out there." Dudley poured half a glass of beer, then filled the rest of the glass with tequila and rum — a hideous caramel mixture. He drank deeply from it. "I want it all," he said. "I want it all, at once." He poured more tequila to replace the gulp he'd taken. "It's good," he said, wiping his lips. "Do you want any?"

Amy shook her head. Artie went back inside to tend to his customers.

"I've said it before," Old Dudley said dreamily, massaging Amy's thigh now. "To break them, you just have to wear them down. You have to stay up with them for two or three nights, when you first get them. They'll fight you with every ounce they've got. You have to fight them physically. And even though they're stronger than you, you can outlast them. After a day or two, they start to get tired. They need to sleep, to rest. And you keep waking them up. It's just you and them, alone in a padded room — you've got on a helmet, a flak jacket, and leather gloves — and every time the bird's head droops to take a nap, you wake it up and make it fight you again.

"Finally it gets tired. It gets so tired that something happens in its hot little brain, where this time when it looks at you — they think with their eyes, same as a man thinks with his dick — they understand that you are the Supreme Manipulator, the Supreme Being — and forever after, you own them.

"It's really nice," Dudley said. "You can hold them on your arm, after that." He lifted his arm at cross-brace to demonstrate. "There is this lightness they have on your arm when it finally happens. You can feel that something has left them: something dense and dark and unmanageable."

"You already told me that part," Amy said.

"Yeah, well, listen again," he said. His hand had paused on her thigh, but now it began working farther up under her dress, so that she had to grip his hand with both of hers to stop him.

"Please," she said.

"Come on," Dudley said, hopping down from the porch; and holding out his arms to catch her, as if she were a girl. "I'll show you my Bible."

She lowered herself carefully into his arms. They set off down the road in starlight, he in wide-gapped overalls, she in her new bulk, feeling special and pretty. They moved slowly, and she held onto his arm for balance, walking barefooted.

When they got to the cabin, Amy was tired, and she collapsed onto the couch. Dudley went to get her a glass of water, and she was surprised by his thoughtfulness, but then understood that he wanted something in return.

Wearily, she sat up and brushed her hair back from her dampened brow and tried to postpone it. She saw him but once or twice a year and since he was to be the father, it was important to bond with him — but what she wanted, what she needed, more than anything in the world — even for only a moment or two — was rest, and peace, and space.

"Can I see that Bible of yours?"

Dudley had had a hand on each of her bare knees, but now he paused, considering it: knowing that it was the last and only obstacle.

"All right," he said. He got up and went over to Mel's desk — now

Wallis's desk — and began rummaging. He found his charred journal, the one the binoculars had ignited, and cursed profoundly.

"Excuse me," he said, "I've got to go into the basement." He lifted the rug, lit a candle, opened the trap door, and descended into the earthen dark, while Amy — feeling guilt at suddenly wanting to be alone for a moment — thanked God.

Down in the basement, Dudley could feel that the pages of all his journals had been opened, read, and learned; he knew it, could sense it, as surely as if Wallis were down in the basement with him; and he would not have minded it all, but for Artie's revelation that Wallis had abandoned him.

Such was the earthen hole, the subterranean maw, his domain, that he could sense from the gravity of things — minor dislocations, tiny adjustments — things that had been one certain way for decades now being slightly altered, repositioned by even an inch or two — a discordant feeling, as if one were to awaken in one's home one night to the sound of someone downstairs playing the piano.

Dudley's eyes narrowed. He moved to the seemingly casual jumble of empty cardboard boxes and let his brute senses take in what information they could. He closed his eyes and smiled, went back to the shelf, pulled down the last journal from his boyhood, snuffed out the candle, and went back upstairs, where Amy, still confused, felt like weeping when she saw him: troubled by how strong she had felt in his absence, and how weakened now by his return.

He thumbed the last brittle journal open to the last page, sat down on the couch next to her, and read to her out loud:

One Empire
The Unity of Nature

Through my window I watch the paling of the evening twilight, till a mild ray from a little star meets my eye. The pensive hour awakens a train of thought. A tiny ray of starlight — whence comes it? What is it? What does it say to me? My soul listens, and I hear starry responses: "I am a tremor in the universal ether. I am the throb of a world in flames. I swing on the farther verge of the abyss of space, and launched years ago on a wave of ether to be floated down to your dark planet and whisper a sublime truth to your understanding.

"I have traveled ten score thousand miles a second, but since I started

your grandparents first saw the day. They have spent their useless, toil-
some lives, and the third generation now meets me at the window. I am
a flash of divine intelligence. I am a messenger from the Infinite. I bring
tidings of the immensity of creation, of the recognition of one supreme
authority among all the constellations — the unity of the vast empire
which stretches as far as light of star has flown or electric thought has
pierced."

So I listened to the message of the starlight, and my thoughts were
stirred. They wandered through the vast spaces of the silent worlds, and
I saw them all balanced on the invisible threads of gravitation — the
same gravitation which drags the sands of the Cordilleras down to the
Gulf. I saw worlds in pairs and triples, waltzing about a common center
of gravity.

The unity of the physical world is as vast and as wonderful viewed in
its historical relations as in its spatial extent. Down through all the cycles
— through all the burnings and freezings — through disruptions and
collisions — through cataclysms of fire and flood, one hand has steadied
the grand movement, and held it close to the plan which One Intelli-
gence ordained and One Will perpetuated. I too know and possess this
Power.

We have seen how man's organization is bound up with the constitu-
tion and the history of the world. We know that man, in his own person,
is the link which binds together the beginning and the end of geological
history. In his material substance, he is a part of the material world. In
his plan of structure he is brother of the entire subkingdom of verte-
brates. In the basis of his life he asserts kinship with all that lives or has
ever lived. He can stand erect in the vast and majestic realm of nature
and say, I am the king of it. I am bound up with it — not with the earth
and moon alone, but with the stars. Their vicissitudes are my personal
concern. I am made of world-stuff.

We note another aspect of the unity of nature. Not alone the unity of
things in themselves, but the unity of things with each other. Plant life
dawned as soon as the turmoil of the primitive ocean had subsided.
Humble animal forms rose above the horizon of being as soon as a place
in the world had been prepared for them. As conditions improved or-
ganization slowly climbed the ladder of gradations, on whose topmost a
round man such as myself stands erect and regal.

Throughout the history of life, the relations between organic and inorganic nature have been reciprocal and responsive — insomuch that a careless logic has held the organism to be the result of its environment. The earth was given to us to eat. When it's gone, another will arise.

Observe also the correlation between the world and intelligence. The capacity of knowledge exists in the presence of something to know. With the knowable and the knowing faculty confronting each other, the pleasure of knowing also stimulates the knowing faculty to exercise, and thus fulfills the manifest end of its existence, and fulfills a clear mandate incorporated in the being of man to seek for knowledge.

How true are the instincts of men and animals to something which is real. The tadpole absorbs its gills and pushes out upon the shore — taking advantage of a fall of rain — and ventures trustfully on the land, believing that a suitable home will be found. Nor is the trust betrayed. The mother fowl calls her newborn chicks, and they already know her voice. The hungry babe cries out in the night, and Nature has responded beforehand to the call by filling a mother's milk-breast. The intellectual instincts find the realities of nature equally responsive. Whatever intuition of a master tells us may be trusted. It is a voice implanted in my nature; it speaks for the author of my being; it is the voice of God, and Man. There is no difference.

One kind of intelligence takes hold of knowledge. In the mind which conceived the plan and frame of the universe was an apprehension of the mathematical relations of the magnitudes involved. The plan of the solar system in its co-existent parts and in its progressive creation was a thought in the mind of the Originator. Man, so far as he grasps it, rethinks the thoughts of the Supreme Thinker! So far as man thinks the divine thoughts, he possesses a faculty akin to the divine intelligence; so far he partakes of the divine nature; so far he comes into a sympathetic union with the Being whose existence is before all and beyond all. In the unity of our massive intelligence we find a bond of brotherhood and sympathy between the dwellers in distant worlds and between all and the Supreme Intelligence.

I shall continue.

One common aspiration stirs every human soul — to accommodate itself to the Supreme Being whose existence it feels, or more explicitly understands, and whose authority it unhesitatingly recognizes. While this common religious nature expresses the unity of mankind, it has also a higher significance. The correlative of the religious consciousness is

God. Man and his Creator, therefore, constitute one system — a complete system, the unity of which is expressed in a body of reciprocal relations between God and Man. As the demonstrated unity of nature implies one original Planner and one Supreme Ruler, so this truth, here made known as an inference from facts of observation, is identical with the intuition of the Unity of God revealed in the universal consciousness of Man. Man is God!

Only a parting word now remains to speak to the kind reader who has followed thus far. These geological talks must not be further extended. I fear that several of the last ones have been rather abstruse; but my thoughts are too grand to level down. I could never forgive myself had I omitted them, for they seem to me to be the ripe fruit, while all the rest is the mere stem and dry branches on which the crop of fruit is developed. I am sure my maturer reader will be glad to get this fruit, and I am equally confident that even the youngest ones will keenly relish it as soon as their appetites are a little more matured.

•

Old Dudley's lust had subsided, through his narrative — he had half-submerged into that time, over fifty years distant, when he had first set out to learn about, and consume, the buried worlds — and he felt relaxed and soothed, as if all were right with the world again, though when he looked over to see what Amy thought about his spirituality, his feelings were hurt to see that she had fallen asleep, and he wondered at what point in his narrative.

He woke her gently, and lifted her dress up over her head and arms. He undressed himself and helped her down to the floor, as if lifting a boulder from some precarious position. He was greatly pleased by the immensity of her.

Too tired to protest, she accepted him, though without pleasure. When the pain began — she was afraid he would injure the baby — she told him to be easy, that it hurt, but she might as well have been speaking to a boar, or a bull, and she tried to pull away from him, but he stayed with her, the two of them linked: she like a wounded animal trying to escape, and he like an awful, mindless machine — a metronome. He finished his task, finished it in a manner so that it seemed not to be his task, but the urgings of some force below.

Spent, he collapsed and pulled free of her, still alternately spurting and leaking — his sign on her like a signature — and he lay on his back like some bear in a zoo, breathing hard, while Amy, sore, and with the baby discomforted and alarmed, found a washcloth and cleaned herself up and dressed. She was alarmed to find a bit of blood spotting the washcloth, and she curled up on the couch beneath an elk hide and lay very still, holding her stomach, listening to the internal rumblings. She knew she should get up and cover Dudley — he was snoring — but she didn't feel like it, anymore than she would have felt like putting a blanket over an old hound sleeping by the fire.

She didn't take it personally. She knew that the weak flesh shrouded a great mind. Still, she hoped he hadn't hurt the baby. She felt terribly responsible, for having let him inside her in the first place.

She dreamed that it was late autumn, and that the baby was already born, and was two years old, playing in the sunlight. She dreamed that Colter came home — a grown man, in the dream — and did not recognize his brother.

Dudley did not sleep long. He ascended back into consciousness as if shedding the dead skin of sleep, or as if dressing in a newer, cleaner suit of clothes. He did not pull on a shirt but merely pulled on the saggy overalls as if stepping into a sack. He lit a lantern and, feeling his age — his knees raw from his calisthenics with Amy, his back aching — he descended into the basement again and began unpiling the empty boxes, ferreting out the map. He knocked a can of flour over, and because he was hungry, and too sore to climb back up, he ate cupped handfuls of that as he worked, digging deeper.

He found the cedar chest and broke the little lock with one of the specimen stones, bloodying his knuckles as he did so. He unrolled the hides; found Wallis's map at the bottom, and rolled it out and studied it, read it, recognizing its authority immediately.

And that was how Wallis and Mel found him, when they got back, hours later, and went down into the basement to see what was sending up the lantern glow. Dudley was still seated there, reading and studying the map — committing it to memory, every roll and swale, cliff and crevice — reading it as if the stone below were still moving — reading it as a sailor might watch waves at sea. He was coated with white flour, and his knuckles were smeared with a cakey mix of blood and flour, and when he heard them enter his lair he looked up slowly, like a Buddha — his face white and round and as serene as the moon's — and smiled.

WALLIS AND MEL HAD TROUBLE BELIEVING THE FORCE-
fulness with which he moved. It was not with spendthrift panic,
nor impulsiveness, but rather, a steady accruing of power. Wallis could
not help but think that it was as when a hawk folds its wing and
falls — no longer a hawk, but rather a falling instrument of geometry,
mathematics, and gravity, with only the faintest resistance of friction
separating it from purity: falling faster and faster, as impersonal as
death.

Without rushing, he took a warm bath, chatted a while, never men-
tioning the map, or even geology. Then he walked off into the night,
toward town — he'd left the map in the basement, and for a while Mel
and Wallis held out hope that he had not believed the map, or had not
read it correctly, or had simply flagged in his desire to drill the valley
again — but before dusk of the next day, the tractor-trailers came rolling in over the summit, bringing a barge for crossing the river, and
construction workers and equipment for building a new road on the
other side of the river — a road that would lead them and give them
access to the heart of the well.

Amy had limped home that morning, holding her back, saying only
that she had slept wrong, and Mel and Wallis were out in the garden, picking beans, when they heard the rumbles of the machines' entry, and felt the vibrations: bulldozers, backhoes, hydraulic drills, and
wrenches.

"I didn't think he'd do it," Wallis said.

"You thought he'd stop with nineteen, and change his mind on
twenty?" Mel said.

They went into town to see the spectacle, and when they got there,
they found that the hiring was already going on. The foremen were all
friendly, smiling.

They weren't in a hurry; they moved slowly. They kept an engine or
two running on their diesel rigs, as if to begin lulling and acclimating
the villagers to the low purr of the engines.

They almost pretended to be lost — almost, but not quite. They
scuffed at the dirt and admired the scenery. They leaned back, crossed
their legs, put their hands in their pockets.

"Is anybody here good with a saw?" the foreman asked. "Me, I'm
frightened of falling trees."

"What do you pay?" someone asked, and that was that.

Helen came outside — Wallis and Mel could tell it had been a rough night for her — and she looked as if she were still partly asleep. She went over to a bulldozer and climbed up on one of its huge tires so she could reach up and feel the blade's shiny curved steel. The blade itself was as big as the side of a small house. She touched the rock-dulled teeth of the blade. Each tooth was the size of a man's head. She stroked the teeth — those she could reach — as she would the flank of a wild horse: as if trying to calm it, even change its essence.

Some of the road crew was watching her — she was so tiny — and Wallis and Mel heard the main foreman asking around, casually, "Does anyone need any backhoe work done, while we're up here? We'd be happy to help out. Hell, we came all this way, we might as well. Just don't tell the boss," he said, and there was a new quickening in the air, a stirring of interests. Each machine was viewed in a new way: in terms of horsepower, in terms of muscle harnessed. A month's work able to be done in a day. No one stepped forward with requests, but all eyes glanced at the waiting machines, evaluating them. A stock tank dammed, a diversion canal dug. A pit for a foundation. A basement, a new septic tank.

"We'll need cooks," the foreman said, slapping his flat belly. He laughed, then caught Mel's eye, and finished his laugh, his eyes hooding.

Charlie stepped up, raised a tentative hand: a cook. The foreman — the noonday sun caught his short trimmed hair, caught the red filaments in it, and that was how Wallis would think of him, as Red — evaluated Charlie's heft with pleasure. Amy stepped up, also. Red eyed her stomach. Two cooks.

"We don't want the well drilled," Amy said. "But if you're going to drill it, we should have the jobs."

A few people glanced in Wallis's direction. He felt sick to his stomach.

There was a wind, up in the tallest trees. It already felt like fall.

A man spoke up from the back of the small, curious crowd — one of the more reclusive residents from the north end of the valley. He would be living within six or seven miles of the construction.

"Whose idea is it to drill on the other side? Is it Old Dudley's?"

Red nodded. "He said one of his geologists worked the prospect up. Said it was a fella who used to live here — his name was Matthew, or something like that."

Someone laughed. "Another dry hole," someone said, and Helen turned fiercely to see who had said it.

"Where are you thinking about putting the road?" a woodcutter asked, and everyone saw what he was thinking: that there would be a fifty- or sixty-foot wide swath of piled timber wherever the road went, and that it would be available for firewood.

"Well, I can show you where the old man was talking about," Red said. He called to one of his helpers, who brought over a map. "Here's roughly where we're thinking about," Red said, spreading the map out and pausing, then following the river's curve with his finger. Pretending he did not know every contour on the map. Wallis and Mel looked at him and could tell that he would not be content to just blade a path through the forest: that he would want to build a road that would last forever. He'd scrape all the soil away and pack the glacial cobble down with air compressors; he'd blast bedrock, if need be, would carve not just the skin and meat from the earth, but would go deeper, would cut and smash the bones, trying to get to the soft organs beneath.

"I thought we'd go up somewhere along this side," he said, pointing on the map. "I think somewhere up in here is where the old man and — what's his name? — Matthew — have in mind." Red fell silent and sat there, holding his hunger: trying not to disappear beneath the hugeness of it.

It didn't have to be roads. It could have been anything. Timber. Love. Money. Meat.

"Oil," someone said. "Old Dudley and Matthew think there's oil there."

"Yeah," said Red. "I don't know." He shrugged. "I get paid whether it's there or not." He gestured toward the man who'd just made the connection. "What do you think?" Red asked. "Do you think it's there?"

The man seemed uncomfortable with this responsibility. "Hell," he said, "I wouldn't know anything about it." He backed a bit farther into the small crowd.

A small girl spoke up — Suzie, one of the schoolchildren.

"You don't need to be drilling here," she said angrily. "It's not right. It'll upset the way things are — the way the animals are — their lives, their . . ." She looked around helplessly. "Their *cultures*," she said. "Their relationships to the land." Red smiled, listened patiently.

Wallis thought of Colter.

It was just a four-mile strip, Wallis told himself. Just fifty or sixty feet wide. Suzie turned to her father, who tried to comfort her. There were tears in her eyes.

"I'm sorry," Red said. "We have a permit. It's public land. I'm just doing my job."

The herd of people moved in closer, made indecisive by her tears. Some of the boys were beginning to climb up on the giant machines now, sitting in the seats and working the levers.

"You guys are lucky," Red said, looking around at the forest. His crew wandered over and sat idly next to him. "One day you're just living here, kind of having a hard go of it, and the next day — bing! — we find an oil field for you, and you wake up and your roads are going to be better." He nodded toward the pay phone. "They'll have to put in phone lines — your phone'll be upgraded — shit, you might even end up with some in your houses — and hell, who knows, before it's all over, you might even have electricity. Building codes," he said, then chuckled before anyone could take him seriously. "Just kidding about that one. Funds for the school. Oil and gas royalties for the educational system. Computers. Field trips. Stuff like that."

"Clearcuts for kids," Belle said, unsmiling.

Suzie turned and began to walk away, her back to them. She started to run.

"A new playground," Red said, nodding across to the school. "Maybe even better teacher salaries."

"You came all this way to give us these things," Belle said.

Red smiled. A bolt of hunger leaping from the pit of his stomach. "No," he said, "I came here to build a road."

People stared blankly across the river at the dense forest beyond, unable to see into the future — unable to imagine anything beyond that which they had always known. What was the difference, after all, between nineteen wells and twenty? They began to drift away, save for those who wanted to volunteer for a month's work.

Red began speaking in a more comfortable, less salesman-like voice as Mel and Wallis were leaving — now that the herd, it seemed, had been winnowed down to true believers.

"This fucking stone wall," he was saying. "Who the fuck built this rock wall?"

·

Another hot day of late August strained past, like a woman giving birth: the sweat streaming down the side of her face, the earth grimacing and shuddering — one more day, the easiest thing in the world — a sunrise and a moonrise — and yet the hardest thing, too.

The apples were falling to the ground, the branches of the tree in the schoolyard bending with their weight. Belle went around picking them up and putting them in baskets to store in the school's root cellar. The south wind would bring fire, which would collide with brief autumn, and then the long winter. The fire had to come.

Once they began — once people's hearts had settled so easily back into defeat — the road crew worked quickly. All day and night their saws buzzed as they cut a straight wide line through the wilderness. The diesel engines of the barge growled, sending up ebony plumes of smoke as it ferried men and machines across the river. Iridescent rainbow ribbons of fuel and exhaust drifted downstream, shimmering in the sunlight, and Wallis was glad that the geese were gone, glad that Colter was gone.

The workers lived in a tent-camp by the river, sharing twelve-hour shifts, so that they were continuously gnawing at the road. They shot deer out of season, as if helping themselves to the pantry of the un-locked house of a stranger. They were loud and slovenly and their camp soon took on a stench.

People in the village continued, however, to be unalarmed by the road. It seemed only what it was — a strip, a lane. They could not grasp it as a thing larger than itself.

They swam in the river to escape the maddening heat, and often to go examine the road's progress. Wallis and Mel summoned the courage after a few days to paddle across in a canoe and inspect the finishing stages of the road.

The dust on it was already ankle-deep. The fronds of ferns and cedars on either side were coated with dust. There was the asphaltic smell of diesel everywhere. Mel remembered the last time she had been there, and had smelled the thick scent of a herd of elk. Neither Mel nor Wallis could avoid feeling revulsion at the uprooted stumps, the giant ruined spruce, the huge slash piles of dirt and moss and fern and timber, and yet they were confused by how strangely satisfying they found the beam of light through the darkness: the light-filled tunnel of the road.

They canoed home.

"It's all going to burn anyway," Wallis said.

The valley was now so primed for fire, so hot and still, that it seemed the simple friction of one's movement against the air — the raising of one's arm, the tilt of a jaw — would be sufficient to set off sparks, which would then ignite the rest.

Soon Red had the length of the road cut and was laying in culverts, hauling gravel across on a small barge and sending road graders up and down the lane, compacting gravel over gravel: doing his best to make a road that would last forever. There was only one horse left in the valley, Amy's pony, and he had rented it, and rode it up and down the road, inspecting everything; and sometimes when he was riding hard, the steel hoofs of the pony struck pieces of flint in the gravel and the sparks skittered into the drying grasses and ignited brush fires, which splayed like fingers for short distances into the old forest before extinguishing themselves in the deep mosses and shady rot farther in. Some of the slash piles on the edges of the road were ignited in this manner, and they blinked into life in a trail behind Red's hard rush, the flames crackling sometimes to heights of fifteen and twenty feet.

The workers would hurry along in Red's burning wake, breaking up the fires with shovels and axes — Red cursing at them over his shoulder, as if the fires were their fault — Red turning savage, almost crazed, for if the fires burned up the forest that was now the road's border, there would be no borders, hence no road — and everyone now, even the outsiders, the road-builders, could feel the forest drying and the south slopes baking and asking for more heat, and for sparks, and for fire.

He finished the road. He took pictures of it with a little video camera. He rode the gravel-packed lane — as tight and planar as if he had poured concrete — and from the back of Amy's little pony (the hoofs clopping gently) he filmed it to take home with him. He took pictures of both himself and the crew standing on it, not like artisans but conquerors.

There was a going-away party for the crew — a gathering at the bar, and a feeling of relief on both sides — the villagers happy to be getting their town back, and the workers, ready to flee this dark land — and Wallis went into town for the celebration, and to be sure they were really leaving. Mel was gone — had carried Helen back over to Joshua's to view the finishing touches to the eagle-raven. The woodworking was finished, and now it was being painted — coat after coat of glossy black and gold paint. Yellow eyes, now, rather than opal.

Several of the men were sitting on the porch, having already packed. They were drinking beer, while down in the camp below, others gathered their cookware and folded their tents and cots. It was dusk.

There was the blast of a shotgun, followed by an animal moaning and squalling — Wallis thought at first one of the workers had shot himself — but then he saw the shape of a black bear, Helen's big bear, running awkwardly through the brush, dragging a bloody hind leg and roaring. A man shouted, "I got 'im!" and ran behind the bear with a gun, too excited to reload and shoot again.

The bear went right through what was left of the workers' camp. It ran through their midst, knocking over skillets and pans, and straight down the dock and out into the river.

The bear did not linger in the river, but kept swimming, his broad head striking a hard and resolute V through the dark water of nightfall.

Wallis had thought and hoped it would end there. But even as the ashes were settling from where the bear had run through the fire, the men were dragging their canoes and drift-boats into the water, and they set out paddling after the bear. One of the men pulled an iron surveyor's rod out of the sand, more of a pike than a rod — it was six feet long, like a spear, but solid iron — it weighed forty pounds — and he rode in the bow of one of the boats, while another man paddled.

The men on shore cheered.

For a few moments it looked like the bear might make it. He was about halfway across even before the men launched their boats; but the bear was tiring, and the men were eager, and the distance closed quickly. Wallis wished the bear would dive, like a duck or an otter, but the bear kept swimming. The men circled him with the boats; forced him to swim in circles. They slapped at him with paddles; sometimes they would hit him, and the sound of the flat wood against his skull carried across the water. Wallis shouted at them to leave the bear alone, but now the man with the pike moved in closer, the pike raised high in both hands as a man might harpoon a whale, or perhaps as men had surrounded mastodons and mammoths, in this same country, only a few thousand years ago.

The first blow drove the bear underwater. The pike stuck him in his thick neck, and the sound of it — deeper and different from the paddles

— reverberated not through the air, but underwater, and through the water: perhaps to the sea.

For a long time the bear did not come up, and the men began to curse, thinking they had lost it — they all stood up in their boats, waiting — and finally the bear surfaced, fought his way back to the top as if summoned, and the man with the pike wasted no time, struck him again almost immediately, and this time the pike's tip penetrated the bear, rode down between his shoulder blades and lodged at a depth sufficient, Wallis gauged, to have reached his heart, and Wallis turned away, sickened.

The bear sank quickly now, despite the men's attempts to hold on to the heavy pike; and there was a ring in the water, a wake in the center of their boats, where the bear had been, and then nothing, only calm water.

The men did not know how to react at first. But soon it was as if they reached a consensus, as if they had had a communication between themselves without speaking, and they began to cheer, a little halfheartedly at first, but then with real enthusiasm, as if having bluffed themselves into believing, in their own hearts, that loss was instead victory.

Red and his crew had not been gone for more than a few hours before townspeople began paddling over to the other side, that same night, in canoes and rafts and drift-boats, to examine the road. Many of those who did not have boats swam. They carried their drinks with them, swimming sidestroke with one arm held above the water, gripping an open bottle of beer, while those in boats paddled with their drinks resting on their bow — an open bottle of wine, or some sweetened fruit drink — a margarita, green as a meadow, or a daiquiri, or some cool blue drink, glowing in the moonlight like a beacon.

They walked the new road, then — walked it like a city street, claiming it, up and down most of its four-mile length — Amy swam her pony over there, and rode sitting sidesaddle — still sore from Dudley's visitation, and looking as if she were about to give birth any minute — and Wallis went over there and walked with them.

They walked it in wonder, marveling at the edges of the great subdued beauty. They strolled, sipping their drinks in that moonlight, all the way to the end, where they milled, trying to sense the oil they had been told was beneath them.

Later they headed home, strung out in small straggling groups, talking among themselves. There was a consensus to bring a picnic table over, or two or three: to set them up along the river for evenings such as these. Some of the townspeople admitted that they wouldn't mind living over there. The road was still immaculate — it could be walked on barefoot — and Wallis knew someday there would be a store over there, too, and roads branching off of the main one, and that soon the weeds of the world would come somehow drifting over the high valley pass and find purchase in the disturbed soil, the arid gravel and dust of the roadbeds.

If the well discovered oil, there would be pipelines and perhaps a small sulphur refinery; but even if it found nothing, the cut had been made, the slash to wildness: and they walked it flat-footed, all of them, admiring it and smelling it and breathing in deeply, always so hungry for the last of the new, and unable to help themselves, unable to turn away.

No one told Helen about the bear. When Wallis got home that night, and settled in to the fit of Mel's arms, he saw that she had black and gold paint on her.

The rig, and rig workers, came next. They came like a wave, crossing over the summit and descending into the valley even as the road builders were leaving. The trucks and tractor-trailers came creeping into town as if in a parade: a slow chain of large and small trucks, with the barge immense among them, barely able to negotiate the bends in the road — crushing branches and saplings on either side — and behind it all crept the lying-down framework for the drilling rig itself, being pulled slowly down the road like the deposed king in a funeral procession.

The drilling crew — roughnecks, tool pushers, drillers, and roustabouts — seemed coarser, happier than the road builders, and as they set up camp by the river, where the road builders had also stayed — the sound of hammers striking steel tent stakes — it was as if a circus had come to town.

Wallis and Mel, along with several others from town, walked down to the river and watched them set up. Helen, too tired to walk, watched from her upstairs window. Already a dented mobile home was being set up, with generators and a satellite dish to transmit and receive information. Workers with saws were felling new trees to make more room for the many tractor-trailers that were gridlocked by the river, and they had a big fire going in the center of the camp, though the day was hot as iron and the danger of fires was present in everyone's mind.

Already they were shoving the barge into the river and loading the first of the rig's framework onto it, along with a bulldozer and winch for muscling the iron and steel onto and off the barge.

There were great ropes and chains, huge tanks to act as mud pits, reservoirs for the drilling fluid — the lubricant with which they would enter the earth — and floodlamps too, so that they could work at night.

Amid the din and motion of the machinery and the heat of the bonfire, it seemed to the townspeople that the rig workers had come here to hunt a thing — some huge beast that was moving away from them; and yet it seemed too that the workers had already trapped it, captured it, and that they were here now only to clean and quarter it. Some of the villagers expected to see giant saws and axes, as if to be used in dismembering their quarry.

Mel gripped Wallis's hand tightly, forgiving him. Wallis watched them with fascination and horror: feeling strongly the desire, the urge, to step across and join them in his project. He didn't want them in the valley, but he had summoned them, and now that they were here it seemed false to turn away. He wanted it to be a dry hole, and yet he knew it would not be.

He wanted to be there to touch the oil, when it was found: to smell it, hold the oil in his hands, touch it to his cheeks: oil that was 500 million years old.

The wolves had fallen silent.

Even back in their cabin, Mel and Wallis could hear the sounds, carried on the hot breezes, of the workers and their engines — the barges running ceaselessly, carrying equipment back and forth across the river, and the sounds of the rig being assembled: shrill screechings and clanging of pipe, motor-roar, torque of steel, diesel smoke. And when the rig was assembled and began drilling — when the diamond-studded bit first began chewing at the earth — they could hear that too, and could feel it — the dissolution of a tautness whose existence could never be proven. And still Mel forgave Wallis — massaged his neck and shoulders and tried to ease the tensions out of them, understanding the weight of his guilt — though not knowing the confusion of attraction he was feeling, the curiosity and mounting excitement, as the drill bit ate its way deeper and deeper.

She thought that because he lived in a pure landscape he had become pure.

She forgave him and prepared her lesson plans for the coming school year. Fire would come in September, and snow in October. She would have liked to have had a few more days of summer — there were a few more things she would have liked to have done — but they would have to wait until the next cycle.

The younger rocks were softer; the drill bit gouged down through them, plunging, as if in free fall, making a thousand feet a day. The harder rocks of the older formations would soon be encountered, and the drilling would slow — Wallis had mapped the oil lying down around seventeen thousand feet — but for now the bit went almost unimpeded through the sands and gravels of the not-too-distant past.

Wallis could not keep away. Some nights as Mel slept he would slip out of bed and go down toward the rig — crossing the river by canoe, other times swimming, and still other times getting a ride across on the barge.

He would travel Red's fine new road until he saw the glow of the rig, the dome of yellow light above the horizon.

Both repelled and attracted by the thunder of the drilling, he would move closer, to the first rig he'd seen in almost a year.

He would come around the corner and stand there just outside the ring of light, watching the tiny figures working high up on the drilling platform, illuminated by the incandescence of halogen lights — a light so intense and all-reaching that it seemed they were searching for the oil with that light rather than with the drill bit: as if the oil had already come to the surface, but had escaped.

The brilliant blue sparks tumbling from the work of a hooded welder below the rig hypnotized him, as did the rawness of the sound: the roaring of the pneumatic drills, and the slamming of metal against metal.

Finally he would pull himself away and walk home. He would bathe in the river so that Mel wouldn't smell the scent of the rig upon him, and back at the cabin he would roll in the dry soil of the garden, then rinse off again in the creek, and sit for a while on the porch, and let the breezes carry from him more of the scents of his infidelity.

He would watch the heat lightning in the distance, would feel the drying forest's ache for fire, and would wonder why it had not come yet.

It was almost maddening: almost too much to take, in the daily waiting. There were none of them who would not have forgiven another, were one of them to snap under the tension and run out into the woods with a match and start it all, to get it over with.

But each small fire ran its course, up in the mountains. A hundred, and then a thousand fires started up, then blinked out. The right place — the one that would allow widespread transmission — had just not been touched yet.

Always, a thin creek here, a mossy cliff there — a shady old grove or a stretch of barren rock — blocked the fires' runs; and each night they blinked on and off on the mountainsides like candles. But as the moisture continued to leave the land, that was all about to change, and everyone knew it.

It was Helen who told them the night it was coming. She had lived through all the other fires, and knew their language. She came across the street and told people in the bar that it was coming that night.

People began running back to their homes, frightened but almost invigorated, to pour buckets of water onto their shingled roofs, to dampen them against the coming breath of the fire. Wallis hurried across the street and climbed up on Helen's roof and accepted bucket after bucket from Mel as she handed them up to him. The water ran off the roof in sheets as he emptied the buckets over the cedar-shake shingles. Mel passed the buckets up to him until he had all of the roof wetted.

When he was done he stood resting, watching and waiting. In the corner of his eye he caught a distant pulse of heat lightning, though it could also have been a wash of aurora. He climbed down, believing. He and Mel asked if Helen would be all right for a while — they needed to go wet their roof — and she said that she would be. They told her they would be back as quick as they could — to not worry — and she laughed at their concern and tried to imagine what there might possibly be to worry about.

They ran down the road to their cabin, running like deer. Once there, they passed buckets back and forth, wetting the roofs of both the smokehouse and the cabin. They could hear the cracking of lightning off the tops of the mountains to the west now, a sound like artillery. Their breath came fast and shallow, and their hearts beat weak and nervous.

They finished wetting down their cabins — there was nothing more they could do — and ran back to town. They could taste the fire in the woods and could see shudders of light, cracks of lightning, drifting their way with the wind — the vertical jags of streak lightning moving like the long legs of something striding toward them. There was no rain — only fire and wind, and thunder so loud as to ignite the woods simply from the sound of it.

They reached the mercantile just as blazing pins of light — burning pine needles — were blowing in tracers down the street. Helen had fallen asleep in her rocking chair, and they carried her upstairs to wait out the storm; to be prepared to evacuate to the river, if necessary.

From Helen's porch they could see the whole street illumined with gold and orange tracings of light, and as the windswept pine needles landed they began setting spot fires wherever they could find tinder. Across the street, through the smoke, Wallis and Mel could see Artie sitting on the porch in a rocking chair, drinking a beer.

It was only an hour or two before daylight, but now the sky opened with crevices of brighter light. The winds were so strong and swirling that they were extinguishing the grass fires, and now whiptail pine and larch trees were being blown over, crashing across the road, and the shakings and crackings of thunder were superimposed over each fork of lightning, each clutching finger of fire, so that the noise and light came not from any one direction but from all directions, and all known order seemed to be rendered meaningless.

The lightning was both horizontal and vertical, and though Wallis knew he and the town itself were insignificant, and though he felt things were relatively safe in the greener strip along the river, it was still hard to throw off the old beliefs, the old notions of self's center, and not believe that they were the object of the storm: that it had come hunting for them, and had found them.

Mel thought, Helen has to see this, has to smell this, even if she has to be carried in the rocking chair and set out in the middle of the street. She could wet her hair and put a baseball cap over it to keep the sparks from finding a nest in it. The winds, the heated gusts, would rock her chair with no effort by her. She could glory in the smoke. She could smoke a cigarette, if she wished. One more. One more day. One more event, one more hour, one more anything.

Mel and Wallis hurried upstairs to get her.

When they reached the top of the stairs and went into her loft bedroom, they thought at first that she wasn't in there, even though they were looking right at her. She was sitting up in the corner of the bed with the hides around her, and her head was tilted forward — as if still sleeping; as if exhausted — but they knew by the way there was no feel of her in the room, no essence, that she had gone on.

The thunder and lightning continued to explode, lightning without rain, just outside the window, but it seemed as far away as if on another planet, and they kept staring at the husk of Helen — of who she had been.

"Shit," Mel said, angry that Helen had missed it — the fire's drama — and frustrated that there was no way to slow the earth down enough, or halt it in its tumble, to turn it back even one small click, to the point where Helen could see it and feel it — what it was like out there on the street.

They carried her down anyway — loaded her into the rocking chair and carried her out into the dry firestorm and set her in the road, facing the wind: but it wasn't the same, wasn't even remotely the same as life.

Once or twice — as the ferocious wind howled past her, rocking her chair, making it seem as if she were back in the world — Mel felt pulses in her own blood that hinted to her that Helen's still-warm brain was registering, even if only through brute friction, the mildest of sensations — but then that feeling was gone, and as the forest and the mountains flamed, Helen grew cooler, and her memory settled down inside Mel like an animal turning round and round, arranging itself for a winter's sleep.

There was still one thing they needed to do for her, in the echo of her living. She had died in fright and they could only hope that after she crossed over there was less of it.

They carried her and the rocking chair around to the back — amazed at the radiant nothingness that was coming from her — and left her on the back porch, staring shut-eyed out at the smoke, and went upstairs to hide the proof of her terror from those who had loved her.

The lightning had captured her fear at the moment she'd sat up in bed and stared out the window; the ancient dusty glass, and the super-brilliance of the lightning — a flash of immense light through some shifting peephole of total darkness — branches waving, back in the forest, in the rainless storm — had acted as camera and flash; had etched her likeness, her moment of maximum terror, into the window glass, as if onto a photographic plate.

Wallis and Mel went over to the window, lit a candle, and studied it. Helen's mouth was wide open in protest, her eyes bulging, her gray hair frayed and wild. They told themselves it was over — that she wasn't feeling that anymore.

The bursts of lightning that were still torching the sky kept illuminating the window visage like the candle behind a jack-o'-lantern, and in those moments, the terror still seemed to have a pulse to it: but it was the pulse of the sky, not Helen.

Mel took a pocketknife and began prying out the ancient molding that held the windowpane in place. The nails were rusty, and the wood pulled free easily. They popped the windowpane out and held it as one would some portrait that revealed a terrible truth about one's self: a failure of courage, an inability to be alive to the world, or an inability to be loved.

The storm was winding down — the lightning exploding only every half-minute or so. They could feel the storm passing over as one feels the shadow of a hawk passing between the sun and one's self, drifting. They could feel the fires up in the mountains sawing hungrily at the dead and dry rotting wood and boiling the sap within the living trees. They could feel the winds' fingers shaping and sculpting the directions of the fires, sending them this way and that, laying down ash and coals.

They carried the pane downstairs and took it into the woods and placed it under a rotting log, giving it a head start on being absorbed back into the knowledge of the world. They mounded orange log mulch around it. Let creeper vines grow over it, Mel thought, and kinnikinnick. Let grouse feed on the berries, and let falcons smash the grouse into explosions of loose feathers. Let it all start over again.

It was hard to breathe. They walked down through the woods toward the river. Occasionally they would come across little candles of flame burning in the underbrush, but there was still just enough moisture, just enough life, held in the forest along the river to keep those fires from spreading and running; they blinked out after a short while on their own. Mel and Wallis passed through them as if walking through a dark woods lit with tiny lanterns, and after a while they didn't even bother trying to snuff them out with their feet.

When they got down to the river, they undressed and waded out. Occasional streamers of flame drifted past — burning wisps of lichen and floating leaves — but the winds had dwindled with the storm's passage — the strange electricity had departed — and now there was only thick smoke as the forest burned. It smelled good and they had faith that the fires would braid themselves around them, weaving and running like rivers themselves: that a mosaic would be cast across the valley, and they could both feel the richness the fire was imparting — all the locked-up nutrients it was releasing from trees and logs that would have taken centuries to rot, now being made available to the soil, and to life's use, in a single night, as if in the ultimate gluttony.

They floated out into the river's center. Sometimes a particular dead tree lining the river's edge would catch a spark and ignite quickly into incandescence before dying out — trees leaping into flame in this manner on either side of the river for as far as they could see — but those fires died out quickly, and there was only more smoke. Sometimes branches and limbs and whole tree trunks would fall into the river, and their flames would change from red to yellow as they drifted slowly downstream before sputtering into hiss.

Wallis and Mel swam out to the center and treaded water and watched the burning trees drift past. The river was still cold, as if the world's fires could never touch it.

They were not the only ones in the river. Deer were standing ankle-deep in the water, peering nervously over their shoulders. Scent was the way they saw the world and with everything smelling of smoke they were blind. Elk were easing into the river too, the bulls with their great racks of antlers held high, as were other animals whose dim shapes could not quite be identified as they swam laboriously for the other side, as if it would be safer: and perhaps it was. Coyote, black bear, fox, badger — they were all crossing the river, not noticing Wallis or Mel, or if so, taking them as one of their own, and Wallis and Mel could feel at a distance the turmoil in the hearts of the wolverines and the grizzlies. Mel thought of the wolves as she might a lover of twenty-five years ago, whom she had not seen in all that time.

Through the smoke they saw and then heard the barge crossing the river as the crew's second shift abandoned the drilling rig. Trees had fallen across their new road, some burning and others wind-thrown, so that they had not been able to drive, and they had run the whole four miles down the dusty new road, as panicked as horses.

Lanterns lined the edges of the barge, and Mel and Wallis could see human shapes standing out on the bow, peering nervously ahead — as if not believing the other shore lay right in front of them — and Mel and Wallis could hear their frightened curses. Wallis wondered if any others had been left behind, or lost. He wondered if they had shut the rig down or had just abandoned it and run for their lives, leaving the pipe spinning in the hole, still bearing down and searching for the bottom.

When the barge found the dock, the men leapt from it like rats; didn't bother to moor the barge but simply leapt to shore and climbed into their trucks and drove off, abandoning their campsite; and the barge, unfastened and with lanterns still burning, swung in the current and began floating downriver.

Wallis and Mel watched the dark shapes of swimming animals veer slightly to accommodate it. As it drifted past them, they were tempted to climb on board and ride it downriver to wherever the current would take it: the river gripping the barge as a hand would a pen, writing a script with its passage in the same manner that the fire was writing its way through the forest.

Instead they let it pass, lamps sputtering, its eerie glow dimming in the smoke as it moved farther away. Mice swam toward it, and small birds were landing on it too, drawn to its lanterns amidst all the darkness: understanding somehow that the fires in the lanterns were safe.

In the last light that was visible to them, they saw a coyote swim quickly out to the barge, scrabble up over its edge, and immediately — the last image they could discern — it began snapping at mice and birds, gulping them down. There were no sounds from the barge; and slowly the barge disappeared into the darkness and smoke.

They were getting chilled, treading water in the river's center. They swam to shore and climbed out, clean as fish.

"What should we name him, if it's a boy?" Mel asked. "What should we name her, if it's a girl?"

The crew was gone, their camp fully abandoned, and the people of Swan had gathered at the saloon. Charlie was on the phone to the outside world, reporting the fires and trying to learn if all of the Northwest was aflame, or only their valley — and a telephone operator in

Spokane, the direction from which the winds were blowing, said that no, she knew nothing of any fires, nor had they had any bad weather.

Ash began floating down on them as they walked. It coated them like snow, and landed on the backs of the caribou, who lifted their heads and stared straight up into the sky.

The sun began to filter orange through the smoke. People went down to the river to wash charcoal off their faces. They waded into the river, and into the smoke, as if for baptizing. Mel and Wallis began telling people about Helen, and one by one, they went up onto the back porch to pay their respects, and to gaze at her, as if a century had fallen away, and there were none among them who did not grieve.

Though the fires were still burning in the mountains, the valley was relatively calm — only random spot fires — and people began to go back to their homes, reassured, for a while. It was hard to breathe the smoke, and hotter than ever, but they understood now that most of the burning was going on up in the high country. A group of women gathered to go check on Amy, who had not shown up. Mel and Wallis went with them.

As they drew nearer to the cabin they hurried, half-fearing that they would hear the cries and even screams of childbirth, and abandonment — and hearing nothing, they hurried faster, fearing trouble — but when they went up onto the porch they heard Amy call to them to come in, and they saw that the blood-drenched nightgown was hanging still damp over the porch railing, and inside she was dressed in a clean one and was holding and rocking a sleeping little girl baby who had a thatch of orange hair as bright as the rising sun.

"Close the door, you'll let the smoke in," Amy said, and they all stood close to her, breathing in, and worshiping, that special grace of the newborn. They all wanted to hold her, but no one asked — not yet. She was still too new. She was still all Amy's. Mel crouched and touched the baby's downy hair. Amy smiled.

"Was it hard?" someone asked.

"Like pushing out a piano," Amy said.

The baby, still asleep, grasped Mel's finger. Wallis thought ahead to the spring. *March.* The geese would be back. The frogs would be calling again.

Mel and Wallis gathered volunteers later that afternoon to get the pieces for Helen's coffin. It was dusk by the time they got there, having had to detour around some small fires while walking carefully across the smoldering ashes of where others had already passed through — certain aspects of the forest looking barely recognizable, with the slopes and shape of the ground below more revealed, with its shield of vegetation scorched free — and when they got to Joshua's cabin, he was already asleep, so that they had to awaken him.

The stallion would not go into the woods while the woods were still burning, so the mourners had to carry all of the burden themselves. Joshua helped them, and cautioned them continuously to avoid scraping any part of the coffin against a branch, which would mar the finish.

They carried the work in pieces: Wallis and Mel each carrying a glossy wing, larger than a surfboard. Others took turns ferrying the body of the coffin, while Charlie and Artie toted the fierce head. They hurried across steaming orange coals, hopping from rock to rock to avoid searing the bottoms of their boots.

"Don't drop it," Joshua kept saying, "please don't drop it."

They lifted her, light as a tissue, and placed her in the elongated body of the raven as if to sleep for the night, so that the tautening of her body wouldn't make it more difficult to load her into it the next day. Then most of them went back across the street to drink, carrying her with them to set on the porch of the saloon so that she would not be alone.

Mel and Wallis went home to see what, if anything, remained of their cabin. They walked in silence, each feeling strange, as if they were walking three or four steps ahead of themselves: as if they had already stepped into the future.

When they got to the cabin they saw that it had not burned, though the smokehouse was partially charred and still smoldering, and they could smell the odor of fresh-cooked meat where the last of their supply had sizzled in its own juices. Runnels of fat had oozed steaming beneath the logs and ran in trickles across the yard downslope from the smokehouse, and already the wolves and coyotes had been in the yard, eating the fat-soaked dirt and clawing at the smoking timbers, driven nearly crazy by the odors so close yet unattainable.

There was no need to conserve. Mel and Wallis went straight to the best of the meat, the remaining elk backstrap, and ate some of it straight off the bone; and finding that it was cooked to perfection, they cut it down and carried it up to the house and sat on the porch and ate it with their fingers, and the smoke was still so dense in the valley that they could see no stars. The night was hot, though they could feel occasional rivers of coolness, and autumn coming on, autumn sliding southward at a rate of several miles each day, like a traveler whose mission even death will not deter.

The town buried her in the cottonwood tree the next afternoon. Wallis climbed up into the highest fork of the tree and they hoisted the box up with her in it, using ropes and pulleys. Joshua wanted to do the finishing work — the fastening of wings and beaked skull-head, with dowels and pegs and a wooden mallet — but was too old to climb the tree, and so he had to settle for calling out instructions to Wallis aloft. It felt to Wallis as if he were assembling something which, when finished, would assume life and fly away. He was sorry Helen was not around to see how handsome the thunderbird was.

The leaves of the cottonwood were beginning to blush yellow. He knew she had seen that plenty of times in her life, though surely not enough. He searched for Mel below, found her, and smiled as she signaled to him, as she mouthed the words "Be careful."

At the bar that night the entire valley gathered for the final sendoff — the drinking, the story-telling of Helen's life. They sat on the porch and watched the fires. The smoke was clearing and now they could see the ragged waves of orange light gnawing across and through the forest. Some crept while others raced. They seemed as ripples on the surface of previously still waters.

Mel wondered what the faces of the mountains would look like after the fires had swept across: which trees would be killed, which ones would be injured, and which ones would be strengthened. The wash of green, wave of green, that would follow in the fire's wake in the next spring, and for so many years subsequent.

"You could never figure it all out," Mel said, watching the blinkings of orange. "The closest you could come is to learning a small thing really well, and then hoping that big things run pretty much the same way."

"What small thing would you learn?" Wallis asked, and Mel laughed.

"You're right," she said. "There's probably nothing that small."

THE FALCONER RETURNED WITH HIS INJURED BIRD THAT evening. Dudley and Matthew had passed the rig workers in their exodus, had ordered them to turn around and go back into the fire, but they would not; and soon the burning timbers had criss-crossed the road in such numbers that it stalled Dudley's and Matthew's progress yet again — as if the valley were doing all that it could to repel them — but once more they abandoned their rental car, the black limousine, and Dudley had Matthew fashion a travois out of lodgepoles, and Matthew pulled Dudley the rest of the way down into town in that manner, as if dragging a rickshaw. He pulled him under and over the flaming timbers, both men gagging and coughing on smoke, eyes watering and noses running crusty black, ashy-haired, with their skin blistering and their suits charring from the radiant heat as they passed through the more intense fire zones. Often they would stop and lie down in the creeks that crossed beneath the road, in the backwater sloughs and marshes in which stood already the panting herds of deer and elk, as well as the solitary moose. Badgers, bears, porcupines — all eyes gathered around these deep ponds, glinting red in the firelight, and observed the two men as they lay belly-down in the ashy water and cooled their blistered pink skin.

"Pussies," Old Dudley said, speaking of the rig workers who had abandoned the valley. Matthew said nothing, only hitched up the travois when Dudley told him to and began pulling again, descending deeper into the flames. He remembered the first year that he had started working for Old Dudley. They had drilled over five hundred wells that year, and had hit on almost three hundred of them.

Flaming trees and burning snags and limbs fell toward them from all directions, falling like swords with whiffs of sound like the cutting of paper with sharp scissors. Some of the snags and timbers were immense and shattered into millions of bright coals like rubies and garnets and glowing sapphires when they hit. "Pussies," Old Dudley said again, though with less resolve.

Finally they were through the worst of it, and had descended into a relatively green zone of calm and peace, closer to the river and town. Old Dudley's suit coat had been charred loose from his back, and he had dipped his white dress-shirt in a creek and then wrapped it turban-like around his balding, silvery head, so that now he was shirtless, and both his tong marks as well as the crescent welded scar across his breast pulsed pink in the hot night.

They came across a bull elk that had fallen in the forest, having succumbed to smoke, and whose hide was now burning. Matthew, unable to pass up meat, built an extension to the travois, skinned and gutted the bull, rolled it over onto the sled behind Old Dudley, and continued on toward town.

They skid-dragged right past Amy's cabin, and though a lantern was lit inside, they did not think to visit or even stop, but pushed on.

People out on the porch of the bar heard them coming from a long way off: heard the raspy scraping of the travois, then saw the dim silhouettes, like that of plowhorse and strange potentates approaching.

Mel and Wallis did not get up from the porch but others greeted them more warmly, as if the two men had come to rescue them, and were amazed that Dudley and Matthew had made it in. No one told Matthew about Helen, though they could all see him looking around for her. Finally Mel said, "I'd better go deal with that," and she went over to meet them. Old Dudley hugged her and looked past her into the darkness and said, "Where's that traitor boy?"

Mel and Matthew neither embraced nor even shook hands, only stood there — and the people from the bar came down behind them to gather around and examine the elk. Some of them began picking at the blackened crust of its hulk, tentatively at first, but then one of the men called out, "It's pretty good if you just eat the part on the outside," and soon a dozen of them were cutting at it with their knives and eating it in that manner.

"What would you say if I told you I changed my mind?" Matthew said, reaching for her hands. She pulled them free.

"I'd say you've always only wanted what you can't have," she said. "Come on, there's something you need to see."

She had no patience for his self-pity, when he saw the giant raven-eagle perched in the cottonwood against the spark-drifting, smoky sky — he who had ignored Helen, had ignored everything, for the last quarter-century — and she left him crying there in the grass beneath the cotton-wood tree and went back to the bar. Charlie had dug another pit in the road and was building a fire in whose coals he would bury the elk up to its antlers.

Mel went to Old Dudley and told him about Helen. He was eating some of the elk and seemed preoccupied with that; he merely nodded, licked his fingers, and said, "She was old."

"You're old," Mel said.

"But it's not my time to go," he said. "I have not given the Grim Reaper my permission."

"You should go see Amy and the baby," Mel said. "The baby was born."

"Boy or girl?"

Mel started not to tell him. "Girl," she said.

"Shit."

"Does it bother you," Mel asked, "that I'm free?" She looked out at the burning mountains, the burning night, and lifted her arms to it all. "Does it bother you that I escaped?"

Old Dudley shook his head, and plucked more meat from the carcass. "Nope," he said, "you're a girl, a woman. I let you go. If you'd been a boy, I wouldn't have let you go."

"Bullshit," Mel said. "I'd have gone anyway. You couldn't have stopped me."

"Maybe," said Dudley, licking his fingers again.

Matthew came walking up from out of the woods, his tearstains making charcoal runs down his face, and anyone who knew him, who had loved him, could see that there was even less of him than before: that in fact, perhaps now there was next to nothing.

The others saw only the husk, and perceived that he was all still there. As if the ancient stories would be resurrected.

Charlie began filling dirt back in over the coals of the elk's fire: buried it up to its neck, so that it appeared that the elk was drowning in earth. Its antlers rose six feet into the air, like a gleaming double tree in the center of the road.

The townspeople began walking down the road toward Mel's and Wallis's cabin. Many of them had had their watches stop, they noticed, around the time that they had been burying Helen, and this unnerved them, so that they walked closer together through the burning darkness like a herd. Burning logs continued to float down the river like ghost ships. Dudley walked with his arm around Matthew's shoulders, Dudley's chest and back pale as marble in the night. "Cheer up, boy," he said, "she's probably happier now."

The village ate far into the night. Mel fixed benches in the smokehouse, like seats of bleachers, by placing boards atop planks, and many of the villagers sat on the benches facing each other and gnawed at the grouse and trout, while others took sections of deer and elk up onto the porch. They smelled strongly of smoke, as if they themselves had been aging in the smokehouse for months, and a certain psychological duress was beginning to accrue. They all sought isolation, but under their own terms. This was more like a siege, and the continued absence of daylight — the unceasing smokiness — was as if winter had come two months early; as if they had been deprived of the most basic cycle of their lives.

Matthew and Wallis sat next to each other on the porch and ate ribs. Daylight was beginning to glow through the smoke.

"They say you really used to be something," Wallis said, not unkindly. They had been friends once but if there was anything left within the husk of the man sitting next to him, Wallis could not feel it. It seemed strange to him that they were only months apart in age.

Matthew said nothing, just kept gnawing at the rib. He felt a vague bitterness and confusion at Wallis's success. How strange it seemed to succeed at a thing by turning away from it rather than hurling one's self at it.

When Old Dudley — still shirtless, his stomach distended, meat-drunk — had gorged his fill, he came limping around, looking for Matthew — and he told Matthew to hitch up, that it was time to go see the baby.

Without a word — making it clear that this was all but an inconvenience, a waking dream to endure between the drilling of one well and then the next — Matthew rose and picked up the long handles of the travois and, with Dudley settled into it, set off scraping down the trail with his head down, leaning forward, and they were soon swallowed by the smoke.

The rest of the villagers ate a while longer — ate until the meat was gone — and then they carried all the bones and carcasses off into the woods for the ravens and coyotes to help themselves to — and after that, they headed off into the smoke also, and after they were gone the smokehouse was entirely empty, four walls and a roof bereft of anything.

As the villagers disappeared like wolves into the smoke, Mel thought how even if one day the wolves were gone from the valley there would still for some short time afterward be the echo or shape of a thing like wolves.

·

School started the next day. Mel was sleepless that night, in a good way, thinking ahead to the future: to her child, to the hunt in the coming weeks, to the next day's lesson plan. She knew her first impulse would be to try to tell the students everything in a day, all at once, and that she might have to work against her instincts, and instead move carefully, steadily.

She lay there awake while Wallis slept. She felt more than ever that she was two or three steps out in front of herself, for the first time in a long time, and it was not a bad feeling.

She arose near what she believed was dawn and fixed a cup of tea, being careful not to awaken Wallis. She sat there for an hour: not reading, not thinking ahead, not looking back: not doing or thinking anything. Then she dressed and went to school, walking slowly. When she got to town and went into the schoolhouse, where there was a battery-clock that worked, she saw that it was 3:00 A.M., and she laughed, fixed a fire to begin warming the room up, then lay down on the floor and napped for another couple of hours, until the world began to glow dully with daylight, and she was awakened by the laughs of children.

Old Dudley and Matthew kept waiting for the rig crew to return. Dudley stayed at Amy's the first couple of nights, but said that the baby's cries kept him awake at night, and so he moved over to the mercantile, where Matthew was staying.

The two men spent large amounts of time skulking around the rig, impatient to begin again; and though the well had only drilled down through about four thousand feet of glacial dust and cobble, the two men amused themselves by wading out into the mud pit and straining out and examining the ground-up drill cuttings from that insignificant passage: studying the powdery remains intently, as if trying to fool themselves into believing that some great treasure lay right beneath their feet, rather than so many miles down.

They prowled and paced, waiting. They were deeper into the forest, closer to the fires, and sometimes they would look up from their examinations and watch a flame leap from treetop to treetop; and in the evenings, as dusk settled onto the layers of smoke below, they would watch the floating traces of sparks overhead, sparks following currents of heat as if riding along the borders of an invisible river of fire, lighting the banks of the river above them like blinking lanterns set along that shore.

Matthew rowed Dudley back and forth across the river several times each day to check on the well — as if the old man believed that the well might have resumed drilling on its own, according to his passion.

In the afternoons, Dudley often napped, and Matthew had time on his hands. He would usually spend those afternoons hanging around beneath Helen's tree, like an old hound. On more than one occasion he climbed up into the top of the cottonwood and opened the hatch of the great thunderbird and peered in at her, and was each time afterward sorry that he had, though still, he could not keep from wanting one last look.

Other afternoons he would rise from the tall grass beneath the cottonwood, would rouse himself from his funk, and would set off down the river to search for fish, to help replenish Mel's empty smokehouse.

Some afternoons he would catch some, and would gut them and carry them on a stringer thrown over his shoulder, would take them back to the school, where, if school were still in session, he would peer in at Mel through the window, as if a drunkard, and would gesture to the fish he had caught for her.

He would remember his own days in the little schoolroom, not so long ago, but seeming as if centuries past. Mel ignored him.

The woods kept burning, though the main teeth of the fire had passed through the valley, and now there were only the steady, random creepings of fire, like a dog clacking and grinding on the same bone for days on end. Old Dudley had been trying, with the satellite phone, to find a new rig crew — calling contractors in Louisiana, Texas, Oklahoma, Wyoming, even Russia and China — but none were available immediately, so that finally he stopped calling, and announced one evening at the bar — baby Mary on his knee, as he warmed to her slowly — that he was going to drill the well himself, he and Matthew, and that they were going to start the next day. "We'll need a third hand," Dudley said, casting around the room for Wallis, and whether Wallis was recruited or volunteered, he could not really say.

Later that night, in bed, he talked it over with Mel — told her how it would probably be his last prospect, and how it felt like that whole part of his life was slipping away, as if sealed beneath ice, and how he wanted one more glimpse. He told her how he wanted it to be a dry hole —

though he knew it wouldn't be — and how he wanted to be out on the rig — wanted to be among the first to know, one of the first to see what he had discovered.

He told her the money gotten from two weeks of work on the rig would be enough to carry them, and the baby, through whole other years.

"It's okay," she said. "You don't have to explain."

"This will be the last one," he said.

"Shhh," she whispered. She didn't want him to tell her something that might later turn into a lie. Then she realized what a peculiar thought that was, as if a mountain could turn into a sea, or a desert into a forest.

Slowly the valley was being revealed and returned to them as the smoke pulled away, leaving patches of blue sky above. The wolves had left the valley, so that there was a silence, but the autumn nights grew frostier by a degree or two each night, and the leaves of cottonwood and aspen, as well as the needles of larch trees, burned gold amidst the partially blackened landscape — though as the smoke cleared in tatters and streamings, the villagers could see that there was still much among the forest — the deep green-blues of spruce and fir — untouched.

The gold cottonwoods and aspen, as well as the gold candles of the larch, had grown brighter during the last week, though they had a peculiar timeless, burnished look, as if the smoke had softened them, like scraps of hide or leather worked by hand. The yellow sunlight of late September struck them as if it had come to rescue them, but still they began falling from the trees, falling in the least breeze and landing on the blackened landscape like golden coins or needles. They cast a net, a mesh, across the charred land, and held the coals and ashes in place, as if claiming those ashes, not wanting to let them be blown or washed away. Tumblewheels and dervishes of yellow leaves skittered in front of the tongues of any breeze, and the winds were colder now, though still the sun in the middle of the day carried warmth. The fires up in the mountains had for the most part stopped their runs, and had boxed themselves into corners and were trapped, dying out, gnawing at nothing.

"Don't let him hurt you," was the last thing Mel said to Wallis before he went off to work that first day. She fixed two lunches: one for herself to take to school, and one for him to take to the rig. Cheese sandwiches, and an apple. They were out of meat. "Be careful," she said. "Don't let them hurt you."

They rowed Dudley across the river in a high wooden dory. They took a wheelbarrow with them, with which to transport Old Dudley, once on the other side: to save his old energy, he said, for the task at hand. There wasn't room in the dory for the wheelbarrow and the three of them, so Matthew swam, slowly, crossways to the current.

Once across, Matthew lay in the sun spitting out river water while Dudley sat in the shade and waited for him to recover. It was already warm and there were no morning clouds. Old Dudley, who had been studying Matthew the way a fisherman might view a beached and rot-bloating mullet or suckerfish, tapped his watch and said that it was only a ten-year lease they had from the government, and that if they didn't hurry up someone else was going to go in there and take it and drill it themselves.

Matthew rolled over onto his hands and knees, then rose stiffly. He pulled down fresh fir limbs and placed them in the wheelbarrow to form a seat, to give padding for Old Dudley, and then helped him in.

Once Dudley was situated — sitting cross-legged like a swami — they set off down Red's new road.

Old Dudley was heavy — like unnumbered sacks of wet concrete. They took turns pushing him. His face was serene as he tried to get a feel for the thing he would begin destroying in a few days. His face was at times slightly expectant, too, like a well-behaved child at Christmas anticipating the possibility of a gift. He looked around at the cathedral shafts of light coming down through the trees, and at the soft flutter and sound and movements of birds in the canopy high above — the lime-green and coal-black wispy lichens hanging above like seaweed — and he was calm, and rode like a dignitary. Occasionally they would pass a gravelly creek flecked with nuggets of pyrite and shiny wafers of mica, like children's glitter poured into the stream, which caught Dudley's eye with a far keener interest than did the birds or trees; and as they crossed these shallow creeks, moving their way upstream along the big river, he would stare up each little creek-canyon and sniff, flaring his nostrils, would glare unblinking up toward each creek's source, scowling, and Wallis could almost see his mind working things out, evaluating the lithology of source rock above and weaving out in his mind the story of its slow destruction, dissipation, and redistribution below — the ongoing web of mountain death that was gushing down the creeks at the rate of a millimeter per year.

They pushed on. When it was Wallis's turn to push him, Dudley would twist and look back at Wallis balefully, as if distrustful of Wallis not to dump him — but when finally he had made his point clear, he would twist back in his perch and continue his survey, voiceless all the while.

A large bird, the dark shape of a raptor, flew through the trees. Dudley twisted to follow the bird's quick flight. "Goshawk," he said. "Northern goshawk." He stared in the direction the goshawk had flown. "Male," he said finally, "immature male."

After two miles, they stopped for water. Matthew and Wallis crouched at the river and drank from it like lions; Dudley, though thirsty — his balding head gleaming — remained in the wheelbarrow. When they resumed their journey and came around the last bend and saw the rig erect amidst the forest, untouched by the fires, it was to all three of them as if they had come upon an altar, some shrine built by souls more kindly and intelligent and worshipful of beauty than their own.

"Sweet motherfucker," Dudley said, and climbed out of the wheelbarrow. He ascended the hinged steel ladderworks as if going up the outside fire escape of an abandoned office building. The rig's motors had run dry after the crew had fled the fires, but Dudley found some drums of diesel and got the engines going again with no more trouble than a man starting a garden tractor or a chain saw. The noise, after so much silence, fractured the quietness like an exploding tree.

Old Dudley and Matthew climbed up into the crow's nest and as the sluggish drilling fluid began circulating into the hole again, Dudley wrestled another stand of pipe into position and called down to Wallis, explaining to Wallis how to set the tongs to hold the pipe in the hole and then break the thread in order to screw in a new stand of pipe.

Wallis did as he was told. All his work before had been in the office, on the maps, in the abstract, and this was not an unpleasant feeling — leaning in against the force of the tongs, wrapping the chain around the new pipe and then leaning back with the huge wrench to fasten in the new pipe, and feeling in that moment the precision fit of the threads. The earth seeming to accept another length of pipe.

Matthew climbed down from the crow's nest and told Wallis he was a natural. He and Wallis stood there on the derrick floor, watching the shining steel pipe disappear so slowly, an inch every few minutes, into the hole.

Dudley, dressed in a pair of Matthew's old overalls, hosed down the drill pipe as Matthew and Wallis lowered it into the hole, and Wallis thought how it must seem to Dudley as if he had gone back in time half a century: as if he were roughnecking, working so long ago on one of his first rigs out in West Texas, and how too it must have seemed to him as if there were a fault or fissure in time, a setting-back of things, in a way that was vital and necessary — and Wallis thought that it must have been pleasing, even heady, for Dudley to feel so young and strong again.

It took about half an hour for each new length of pipe to chew down to its full length — about a foot a minute. The noise was deafening, so that it precluded all daydreaming, though in its own brute way it was hypnotic. Often, that first day, Wallis found himself staring down at the earthen tank of drilling mud next to the rig, sloppy and frothy. It seemed to him like some artificial pond or aquarium in which dwelt the most hideous creature, so awful that it could never be seen by humanity.

"How deep will you go?" Matthew shouted to Dudley, over the diesel roar. Dudley was up in the crow's nest again, swinging the pipe into position, while the two younger men below worked the tongs. "How deep will we go?"

"To the bottom of the fucking world," Dudley brayed, "to the United fucking States of China." He kept hosing the pipe, which was shiny and silver. Mud and river water dripped in sheets from up on the rig floor, a sound like rain, though it was a bright blue day. It was a messy operation, Wallis thought — like cleaning and butchering a deer, or an elk, or a moose.

There wasn't time for daydreaming: Wallis could see that right away. It was different from his old life — the days he'd been spending with Mel. If you took your eyes off what you were doing or allowed your mind to wander even a slight distance, you'd get your ass kicked; you'd have five hundred pounds of pipe fall on you, or you'd get a hand, even an arm, wrapped up in things, and lose it. It was all chain-rattle and torque, all wrench and clatter.

The wind gushed a curtain of gold leaves down past them and onto the ground, the riverside aspen leaves showering the forest floor again, and Wallis paused and stared at their beauty for a moment.

"*Hey!*" Old Dudley shouted, "hey, *numb-nuts!*" Wallis jumped back just as a twenty-foot length of chain, thick as a snake, fell from up in the crow's nest and crashed onto the rig floor where he'd been standing. Sparks bounced from where it hit the steel grid of the deck. Wallis remembered — in that half-instant when he'd leapt back — only speed, and force, and the slightest, sickest whisper of sound — the limp chain unfolding only a little, as it fell — and now, seconds later, it lay there totally motionless, totally harmless. Matthew, who had been standing a few steps back, out of harm's way, stepped over to where the chain lay and moved it out of the way.

"Would've tore your head clean off," Dudley was bellowing. "Would've snapped it off your neck like wet toilet paper. Ninety per-cent of rig fatalities occur right there where you're standing, numb-nuts — the combat zone, inside that three-foot radius right where you were standing with your head up your ass. Jesus God," he said, "be careful. You would've made a hell of a mess."

Wallis said nothing, only looked up at the image of Dudley aloft, silhouetted against the sky, and moved back in and unhooked the pipe tongs. Dudley laughed and released the drilling brake. The diamond bit bounced and shuddered, trying to get a bite on the new rocks far below. There was a horrible caterwauling that resonated throughout the rig's frame, and through the men, a metal against metal sound, as the pipe torqued and spun and bit and fought, settling back to its duty. Dudley revved the throttle. Black smoke coughed into the blue sky, and the pipe's squalling quieted to a steady clattering purr. It would be an hour or so before the first drill cuttings would begin circulating back up on the current of drilling mud, which was cycling back into the mud pit. They would catch the cuttings with a strainer — like netting salmon leaping up the falls, Wallis thought — and examine the cuttings to see what kind of old earth they were piercing, down there. To begin — to continue — putting the story together: as if it were any different from the one going on up above.

The day passed quickly; it melted into work, passed like a muscle's contraction: there was little thinking, only brute effort and rhythmic, mechanical repetition. They stopped working at dusk, weary and sore, Dudley and Matthew unaccustomed to the consequences of physical labor, and as the engines sputtered back down into silence, the quiet came washing in over them as if cleansing them.

Old Dudley slept in the wheelbarrow, exhausted: rode in it as if in a nest, like some enormous fledgling, and he did not wake even as they loaded him into the dory and paddled across in the clearing night crispness, with all the fires on the mountainside visible now, though much reduced, and dying out, with fewer and fewer each night.

Amy would be waiting for him with a lantern on the other shore, with the baby Mary in a little pouch hung around her chest. They would awaken him by splashing water on his face. He would blink slowly, ascending from dreams of nothingness — would blink at the distant mountainside fires and the stars — the woman and her baby standing in the lantern's glow — and the group of them would walk slowly home.

There would be no one waiting for Matthew. Sometimes Wallis and Matthew would go get a beer at the bar, as if trying in some faint way to honor the past, and each other, but more often than not, Matthew would go into the mercantile to get ready for bed and Wallis would go straight home, where Mel would be waiting.

They met each morning before daylight in front of the mercantile, and one morning there was a sheet of white cast over the world — not snow yet, but frost; and as the sun rose the frost turned from silver to fractured diamonds: the world melting back into the birthing colors of autumn: red, gold, yellow, blood brown. Dudley had started out in a foul mood, sore and weary, ranting once again at the drilling crew's cowardice, but after they had rowed across the river, and as they began pushing him down the road in the wheelbarrow toward the rig, his mood improved, until he was well on his way to a thing that could almost be called good cheer. It felt to Wallis almost as if they were a family, walking down that leaf-strewn road in the fall, and it felt as if Dudley's mood, the risings and fallings of it, had enough power and force to be cutting or scoring little striations upon the landscape, shaping in some way the face of the earth itself.

Often Matthew worked the crow's nest now while Wallis and Dudley stayed below on the rig floor, fastening pipe and monitoring the drill rate and pump pressure. There was always the danger of drilling into a cavern, which would swallow all the lubricating mud and then twist the pipe. Or the drill bit could strike a pocket of gas, which might blow all the heavy mud — and the flammable gas, in addition to all the steel pipe — back up out of the hole. Anything could happen. There was always a tenseness, a vigilance, up on the rig.

Dudley worked the drilling brake through the soft stretches to keep the pipe from descending too fast — to keep it from twisting and getting stuck. He seemed to Wallis to be inflating with power and happiness as he rode the drilling brake, leaning his whole body against the long-handled lever. It was something someone in a rest home could have done, if they knew how — something subtle but also imprecise, like the occasional flex of a paddle as one rudders a canoe down a small stream — but he was enjoying it, so hopped up and anticipatory — always eager to let the bit down farther — that Wallis believed at any second a trickle of drool might escape his mouth. The rig's throbbings and tremblings shook Dudley around as he leaned the upper half of his body against the drilling brake. It had a safety chain fastened to it to keep the entire pipe string from falling down into the void, should any be encountered.

From time to time Dudley would twist and look up at Matthew, would stare at him impassively a moment or two, but there was nothing that could be shouted over the roar of the rig, and Dudley would just stare, curious as to why such a strong man was unable to endure. Pleased but disappointed both, that he had finally worn him down.

Often Wallis could feel Dudley's eyes on him. For long stretches of time Dudley's hand would be steady on the brake, but then he would bump the throttle up a bit, impatient. Wallis could feel that Dudley was just about to call out another warning — a call for Wallis to pay attention. A mile and a half of rock still separating them from the oil. Old Dudley ignored Matthew and Wallis, now. He shifted his attention to the pressure scale — the great clock-face dial, the red needle leaping and trembling — the slow etch of the geolograph scribbling like an EKG the drill rate below — the brute story of endurance and resistance versus weakness and fatigue — the drill rates transcribing the story of which layers of earth were easy to drill through, and which, more resistant.

Later in the afternoon Dudley put the drilling brake on automatic and took Wallis down to the mud pit to strain for samples. It was far too early to be thinking about oil or gas, but he examined them anyway: rinsed the mud from them, sniffed them, rolled them around in the palm of his hand, looked at them with a hand lens, then put them in his mouth and tasted them, sized them for grain dimensions, clay content, and grittiness, and tried to taste any oil or gas that might be in them.

He gave Wallis a clean handful with which to do the same. It felt to

Wallis like taking communion. The sun was level with the trees now and it was orange from the fire's smoke. It seemed strangely as if the sun were descending to the same place they were drilling into. Wallis tasted the grains of rock: tried to taste where they had once lain on the surface, and tried to taste the sunlight that had once shone on them.

The shorter the days became, the more beautiful they were. Some days the men stopped working late in the afternoon so that they could walk home in the long light — still pushing Old Dudley in the wheelbarrow — and to give Dudley a rest. Wallis didn't see how the old man could keep going, but he knew that neither could Dudley turn away, and let Mel be even temporarily victorious.

The light passed through the drought-thin leaves of the cotton-woods and aspens as if through yellow parchment, giving a glow of that same color to everything — yellow from the sun and the leaves, gold from the sepia of the smoke.

Dudley's blisters were suppurating from where he had walked and then crawled through the fire. He had new blisters, too, from where he'd been leaning on the brake. His back was hurting him, as were his old knees, but he was happy, as close to peace as he could get.

They always crossed the river before dusk, in the laying-down slant of sunlight: back into the quiet village. A few students were hanging around the school picking apples. Every day, they could see the occasional gray threads of chimney smoke rising through the trees in the unburned, rotting sanctuary along the river, and could smell pies baking: apple and huckleberry. The muffled gurgle of a chain saw could be heard on one of the hills above town, and the ring of axes and mauls, a tiny wooden symphony conducted by the cooling nights. Old Dudley nodded off on the river crossing each day, falling asleep to the sound of river water trickling off the oars, but would awaken again upon reaching the near shore.

Some evenings the three of them would go up the hill to the mercantile to eat supper together. One day a man had killed a doe with his bow and arrow — archery season was open, with rifle season not too distant — and he had her hanging from a tree by the neck and was skinning her. A raven had already found the man — or perhaps followed him in from the woods — and strutted boldly down the road toward him, like a sailor. The three men went over to examine the doe — a clean lung shot

— and the man gave them one of the shoulders. He simply folded the shoulder back, made one curved knife stroke along the inside to separate the ligaments that held the shoulder in place, and it was theirs. They put salt, pepper, garlic on the roast and grilled it.

The meal revived Dudley somewhat and he said that he was going to go see his daughter, his new daughter. Matthew said that he was going to bed. The bare shoulderbone gleamed a pearl color, resting on the grill by the side of the fire. Wallis was still strangely hungry: as if no amount of meat could fill him. He could feel not just the length of the nights increasing, but their weight. He could feel his old hunger returning.

Matthew was quiet each day as he worked: as if the fires once within him were now only smoldering, slowly gutting him as they would hollow out an old tree. But even as his interior became more brittle, the labor was hardening and chiseling him again, melting his city life from him, so that it gave the illusion that what they were now seeing was his muscular core beneath; that there was no hollowing within.

But Wallis could see it, and Old Dudley could see it. Mel had known it for a long time, but now Wallis was noticing it; and it was becoming, finally, self-evident to Matthew: that the shell of his muscles was returning, like rock armature, but that this time, his endurance and stamina were not. That finally there was nothing beneath the surface. Old Dudley had gotten it all.

With his body chiseled back down to old iron, he grew colder more easily. Several times, late in the afternoons, he would have to take a break and go stand by the warmth of the motor to get himself back up to operating temperature. He would stand there shivering — anxious to get back into the hunt — but knowing that he had to pace himself, that he could not allow himself to get burned down before the oil was reached.

Old Dudley watched him with a thing that was as close to sympathy as he was capable of feeling, and cursed yet again the rig workers who had fled, saying that he could train a gorilla to do what Matthew and Wallis were doing — that Matthew's talents these days were in the office — and finally they had to quit even earlier and go home to warm up and dry out, though Wallis knew Dudley did it to rest the machine as much as Matthew. Some days it was so cold that they breathed clouds with each word.

Dudley was ass-whipped: there was no other word for it. Still, he kept going. But now it was as if he were eating himself, not the world.

The children wanted to visit the rig on a field trip, but Mel counseled against it, saying that the roar of the rig might damage their hearing, and the sight of it might damage their spirits. She said her father might say inappropriate things. But the students lobbied her hard, and in the end she saw that they were right — if nothing else, they needed to cross the river to go watch the drilling so that when they were older, they could help bear testimony to the before and after of a place — though Mel also understood as well as anyone that the before and after of things was always a moving target, slightly different with each day's sunrise.

They made a picnic of it. They crossed the river in canoes and life jackets. They ran eagerly up the road toward the sound of the rig. Wallis took them on a tour of the giant machinery, while Dudley and Matthew kept working. Old Dudley eyed the larger children as if evaluating them for labor.

"How deep is it?" a boy wanted to know.

"Eleven thousand feet," Matthew said, glancing at the dial. "About two-thirds of the way there. But it gets hard, from here on. It gets real hard."

They could feel in their bones the caterwauling of the bit as it jumped up and down, torquing, trying to scratch its way through denser, older rock. What they were looking for, Wallis told them, was new rock beneath the old rock. They were looking for a place where the layers of earth had been swirled, bent, folded, and flexed back on themselves, so as to provide layers of repetition. The rig would in essence keep drilling through the same formations, again and again, but at greater depths each time, until finally, near the bottom, they would find younger rocks trapped far beneath the older rocks — as if youth were tucked below age, far beneath the curl of a towering wave.

And the story of the drill bit already reflected that this was what they were finding. The drill would go fast for a while, as the bit ate its way down quickly through the younger, softer rock; then it would slow down almost to a halt as it encountered the older, more resistant formations.

It was kicking Old Dudley's ass. He would lean down on the drilling brakes, then let up, then lean down again, as if trying to tap or chisel at the formations using an eleven-thousand-foot awl. Every shudder and torque below passed up the drill string and into his old body like a conduit. His old eyes would drift crookedly, by day's end. His teeth ached, as did his feet and shoulders from the constant vibrations.

He felt trapped. He knew he should walk away from this one — abandon it, for the time being, to the coming winter, and let Mel have another year of peace. But he kept drilling, even as he felt his life, his reserves, draining from him: as he found himself doing the work he had always hired others to do for him.

The students went back down to where Mel was waiting for them. They set out a picnic blanket in the drying yellow autumn grass and ate cold grouse and apples and watched the men up on the rig. The children seemed impervious to the noise, and after their meal, lulled by the mild sun, lay in the grass and napped.

Wallis looked down at them from the rig floor: watched Mel's hair, white and sunlit, almost incandescent, catching and absorbing, altering, the light. He wondered if the baby could feel the sunlight.

THE FIRES NOW SEEMED NO MORE HARMLESS THAN ARTESIAN fountains — like water that burbled continuously from some cleft of a rock, growing neither larger nor shrinking, but always flickering. The villagers, spurred by autumn, resumed the cutting of firewood, even in the midst of the fires. They began clearing the road to the summit, cutting and sawing those fallen, charred logs into firewood. The chinking sound their axes made against the burned wood was different from the sound it usually made striking green or cured wood. It was more metallic, and the sound had less resonance, and died away more quickly. It was like the sound of railroad workers driving iron spikes, or like the sound in the blacksmith's shop during the shoeing of horses. It was as if the sound of iron were everywhere — as if the woods had been altered — and as if all softness had been lost to the valley for some indeterminate time.

Sometimes from the rig floor, through a gap in the trees, Wallis could look out across the river and see the figures of the townspeople removing the logs. It was strange to see how quickly everyone adapted.

It looked like some scene from hell, and yet the villagers were moving around as if already accepting the near-total transformation: flames licking all around them, ash covering everything like snow, and rocks and trees split open from the heat as if from bombs.

They went about their work methodically, chopping and rolling the logs to one side, as if this were the same world they had been born into: or as if they could not see the difference.

Each night Wallis bathed in the creek, then bathed again in the tub before coming to bed; and each night, Mel's hands and arms accepted him, pulled him close to her. She sniffed his body for scent from the rig, but he made sure he had it cleansed from him, and she was satisfied.

The garden was now a fallow frost-sheared rubble of dead brown leaves, though there were jars and cans of its residue, its bounty, stored in the basement.

He felt her bare belly with his hands: traced the slope of it, as if trying to map any subtle changes. How strange again it was to know a thing was there without seeing any evidence of it.

Matthew usually stayed up in the crow's nest all day, dreamily swinging a new stand of pipe into position whenever it was required of him. Wallis and Old Dudley spent much of their time between pipe connections crouched at the mud pits, catching the recirculating drill cuttings with a strainer and examining those fragments, and plotting and replotting the drill rates. They were beginning to notice thinning layers of rock, as if the sheets of earth below had undergone vast stretchings and alterations, and daily they found themselves amending and revising Wallis's map slightly, as their drilling revealed more tortuous swirlings than even what Wallis had predicted: the legacy of ancient, massive pressures applied from several directions, and forever unyielding, like giant hands squeezing wet clay, shaping and smearing it across a crooked landscape.

Belle and Ann had left Mel in charge of class for a full day, had made the six-hour roundtrip run down into the other village of Swan — had cleared the rest of the way with a chain saw — and had come back with a truckload of pumpkins, which they stacked on the porch of the saloon for anyone who wanted them; and now at night there were pumpkins, carved and glowing, in the windows and on the front porches of all the cabins, as if mirroring the image of the burning woods just beyond.

A school play; *Romeo and Juliet*. The villagers sat in the bar and watched it. Old Dudley sat in the front row with Amy and the baby. The play was eerie by lanternlight.

The older students helped the younger ones recite their lines. The villagers clapped at the end of each act. Amy had made pumpkin pies and cider for refreshments. Dudley sat with a pie resting on each knee and a third in his hands, eating it as he would a giant sandwich. The ash from the fires was still falling like snow, and there was the heaviness, the compression, of that silence, like a blanket being laid over the world.

It amazed Mel that the students were in class each day: amazed her that none of them skittered away. They showed up every day. They listened to what she had to say; they drank it in. After so many years of silence, it felt strange to be speaking, as the woods poured out of her.

The children took what they needed, drinking it in like water, and let the rest go past. It was as if she were a river. They stood at the edges and watched, and listened. They took from her what they needed, and listened to her voice.

The three men had dinner together at the mercantile again: twelve thousand feet. Dudley, looking emaciated, ate the last three cans of Spam with both hands and then opened a can of lemon pie filling and ate that with a spoon. As lean as he was, he looked like a young man by candlelight. The fires glimmered, up in the mountains. A bat flew in through Helen's open window upstairs and flitted wildly around the candles, looking for moths. They kept eating, untroubled by the bat. Wallis felt another weakening within, like the falling-through of rotten planks below, as he realized that he wanted there to be oil or gas down below: a great sprawling reservoir of oil, black as night and flammable, sweet and clean. He wanted to pump it up, suck it up out of that old trapped ocean that lay beneath them.

It would just be a little hole in the ground. It wouldn't change things much.

Dudley finished his meal and got up and opened the front door to let the bat out, and went out on the porch. "Gonna rain tonight," he said. "I can feel it in my dick."

Wallis and Matthew didn't believe him but they got up and went out on the porch anyway. He was right, though. Wallis remembered the feel of it. The wind was from the south and the rain was very near, though where it had come from they did not know — only that it was coming in from the south like an animal. There would be no wavering left or right; it had them in its sights, and already, the valley was taking the leading edge of it, the south wind entering and funneling into the canyon like a tongue, and there was no lightning, only damp wind. They sat out on the porch and rolled up their sleeves and waited to receive it. Dry leaves tumbled down the street in advance of it, leaves hopping and skipping.

The rain came in a spray at first — as if the wind that drove the rain had outrun it and carried with it, at its front, only the lightest drops — but still these were appreciated, savored, and the speed of the spray stung their faces and arms, and even Matthew laughed. Old Dudley was wearing a straw hat and the wind blew it off his head and blew the mercantile door open, and the hat, with a funneling of leaves, blew into the mercantile — the hat leading the way like a magic trick — and the curtains inside swirled and flapped as if something wild had gotten inside. Jars were knocked from the shelves and broke when they fell, and the fires out in the mountains flared brightly, quickly, enriched by that first gust of air, but then they disappeared completely as the night-purple wall of rain passed over them. The heavy drops slammed into them now, rain lash coming like an attack.

The scent of steam, of fire hiss and water-splashed coals and ashes, was everywhere, and with the torrent also came mud, floating ash mixing with the rain to streak and coat them, but it didn't matter. The three men went out into the street, and people came from out of the bar, and stood in the ash rain as if having believed, for a little while, that it would never rain again; and after a short while Wallis hurried home, to share the excitement with Mel.

In the morning, the mountains above them were white. There was over a foot of snow up in the high mountains and the sky was purple with more storm clouds, and the larch trees' gold needles blew through the sky in currents, and though it was not raining at the moment, they could feel another wave of it coming: the specificity of the air's moisture as heavy as a wet burlap bag with stones in it. Sunlight poured down through breaks and openings in the clouds, but more rain was coming, and behind it, in the coming days, snow.

Matthew fell from the rig that afternoon, under that purple sky — flurries beginning to stir once more, laying down yet another coat of snow — and he bounced off of a support girder and then tumbled into the engineworks below. There were abandoned tools and tool boxes down there, steel clutter and ragged pieces of iron, and when he landed he was still for a long time. Dudley and Wallis hurried down to check on him — it seemed to have been an inexplicable fall; he had been working the chains, swinging the next stand of pipe into position, and had just taken one step too many — had walked right over the edge as if forgetting where he was — and when they got to him, they saw that all was not well. He was starting to sit up, but had landed on a greasy screwdriver with a blade a foot long, and the blade had passed just beneath his ribs. They could see the black oil on the end of the screwdriver, could see the beginnings of blood spreading around it. The blood had not yet gotten into the new snow; it was still gathering around Matthew's stomach.

He was groggy from the fall. There were a few scrapes on his head and face, from where he'd bounced around on the girder, but they were inconsequential. Wallis was strangely as aware of Old Dudley's reaction — or nonreaction — as he was of his own concern.

Old Dudley might have appeared to have been in shock as well, but Wallis knew better. Dudley just didn't care. He stared blankly at the scene — the red soaking wider around Matthew's ribs, now — and if he looked faintly troubled, it seemed to be more because he realized he was being called upon to respond with an emotion that he just didn't have.

It was guilt, which Wallis saw on Dudley's face — different from a land- or greed-guilt. It was the guilt of not-loving, and the shame of not being able to love.

Finally Dudley forced himself to say something — "Jesus," he said — and the sound of Dudley's voice seemed to draw Matthew up out of his shock and back among them. He sat up this time, pronounced that he was all right, and pulled himself free of the screwdriver. There was a sucking *pop* as he did so, a small sound, like a fish rising to sip at some delicate mayfly.

"It didn't get anything," Matthew said, holding his gloved hands over the wound. "I know it didn't. I'd feel it, if it got something important." Steam rose from his breath, and from the wound. It was beginning to snow harder. The engine was running rough, so that Matthew was having to shout. Dudley reached down and shut the engine off.

"Just flesh and muscle," Matthew said. Now he might have noticed the strange stillness on Dudley's face — the nothingness — because he said, "Honest." He held his gloved hand out — the falling snow sticking like feathers to the bright red blood on the glove. "Lookit," he said. "Liver blood would be darker. The stomach and intestines would have some green in 'em. Just blood," he said. "It's nothing. It's just a hole."

Still Dudley was silent, nearly expressionless, and unmoving: as if worried that it was he, Dudley, who was in danger of being betrayed.

Matthew went over to one of the empty jerry cans and shook from it the last sips of gas, directly onto both the entrance and exit wounds. Then he tore his shirttail into strips and rolled them up into little balls and plugged the wounds.

"Let's go," Matthew said. "Sixteen thousand feet. The home stretch. We've still got a couple of hours of light left."

Old Dudley's legs were buckling. His face still had that strange mask of nothingness to it, but now his legs were quivering. He sat straight down in the snow and waited for his nausea, or his weakness, to pass.

The snow was piling up on all of them — on their shoulders, on their backs.

"I'm fine," Matthew said. "I shouldn't be, but I am." He started climbing up the steep steps, back up to the rig floor.

But the engine wouldn't start, when they tried it again. Dudley fooled with it — his hands shaking — and got the engine to run for a minute or two, enough to get the mud circulating again, but then the engine began to clatter, and shut down again.

They went up on the rig floor to where Matthew was sitting. He was looking out at the river and at the woods. Wallis thought with a shock that he looked like what Old Dudley must have looked like, thirty-five or forty years ago.

The three of them sat on the silent rig floor with their legs dangling over the edge as if sitting on a dock. The scent of the gasoline Matthew had swabbed on his wounds was strong, though Wallis worried not so much about it as he did about the grime that had been on the screw-driver.

It kept snowing. One last flock of geese, coming down from Canada, flew down the river, silent through the falling snow. The men could see the snow on the geese's broad backs as they flew, so that it was as if they had hatched full-grown from the snow — had been born in winter. Another smaller band of geese came flying in at a tangent and joined the main flock, like two streams coming together to form a larger stream. They continued their flight down the river.

"I could have kept going," Matthew said.

"Maybe you should go in and get it looked at," Wallis said.

Matthew scowled. "Go in where?" he said.

"What will happen to the hole?" Wallis asked.

Old Dudley shook his head and looked up at the snow. "Six county fairs and a goat roping," he said, "and I never fuckin' saw anything like it." He glanced at Matthew's wound, then looked up at the snow again.

"The pipe's going to get stuck, without the mud circulating," Matthew said. "Same as if your blood stopped moving. We're going to lose the hole. We're almost there, and we're going to lose it."

"You don't know if we're almost there or not," Dudley said. "You just know it's down there. But you don't know exactly where. It could be another hundred feet, or it could be another five thousand."

Matthew swung his feet lightly, like a child. "We're going to lose it," he said matter-of-factly. "Will you start over again, when we do?"

"Hell yes," Dudley said. "But we ain't going to lose it." He patted the rig floor. "You probably think the hole goes straight down, don't you?" he said to Wallis. "Well it doesn't. It's torqued way the fuck out there, somewhere." He pointed out to the river. "It could be on the other side of that river. It could be under that island. It could be back up under that snaggley-ass forest, over a quarter mile away. It's like a big boner," he said, "and a woman — the way it bends way around, once you get up inside her. It can bend way left, or way right — can go way up, too. There's no way in hell sixteen thousand feet of hungry pipe is going to go straight down, like a plumb-bob. The earth has her desires, her muscles, too — she's going to take and bend that steel pipe and guide it in to the oil."

"You're a sick motherfucker," Matthew said. "You ought not to talk that way."

"What do you know about it?" Dudley asked. "You haven't learned shit yet. I've lost more holes than you'll ever drill."

Wallis had thought at first that they were joking with each other, but it seemed that for some unknowable reason they had both crossed some invisible line, a line which had moved or been pushed closer by frustration and fatigue.

"You don't know shit," Old Dudley continued. He was talking like an old man now — as if now that the well's drilling was suspended, he was losing any remaining traces of vitality he might have been conserving — as if it were draining back down the hole. "Look at you," he scoffed. "When are you ever going to be anything other than a fucking hayseed? Plugging yourself up with a wad of cloth." He snorted. "I tell you what," he said, "I should have known something like this would happen. I had a nightmare last night. I dreamed I was fucking a woman and all of a sudden my dick went soft, and I was just humping away with a big old soft bunch of *nothing*. It was a damn bad dream," he said. "I thought maybe I'd already come, is why it had all gone soft, but no, it had just gone soft. A fucking nightmare," he said. "Let me tell you, I knew it was one bad-ass omen."

They sat a while longer. "Good," Dudley groused, "a blizzard. Lovely. A gott-damn blizzard. Fucking nature. Fucking evil bitch. Come on," he said, "let's get out of this shit."

By the time they got to the drift-boat, the snow was up over their ankles. Matthew was moving easily, as if nothing had happened: just a flesh wound, and as if the screwdriver's blade had purposely sought the one path through his body that would avoid piercing anything vital. He waded out into the river and held the boat steady while the others climbed in. Old Dudley was a bit tottery, like someone's grandfather.

As ever, Dudley slept, crossing the river — slept on the bottom of the boat with the snow falling all around them and the night coming in fast, as if made bolder by the falling snow.

For two days Dudley cursed into the telephone, trying to find someone he could pay to come into the dark wilderness, while Matthew hung around the schoolyard or, feeling increasingly unwelcome, unfitted to his own town, camped in the snow beneath a little tarp under Helen's tree.

On the third day the rig workers came back into the valley, bold and brazen as ravens, searching out Old Dudley, looking for work, even as he was still on the phone, cursing. All the things that had been said between them on their way out, their exodus from the fire, were forgotten, or ignored. They needed the money.

Next came the hunters, two days later — the opening weekend of rifle season. They surged over the snowy pass in big trucks with snow tires and chains. They loved their vehicles and stayed in them constantly, cruising the road back and forth, hoping for a lucky shot at some roadside creature.

The workers repaired the engine, jury-rigged it, and resumed drilling the well, carving away only a hundred feet a day now. Wallis could not help but think of a big cat nearing its final stalk on its prey, sinking to its belly in the last distance and creeping. Mel kept right on teaching, one day after another, as if disregarding the fact that her world was only inches away from being cracked open. She taught one day at a time, until it seemed almost to her that the cumulative sum of her work, and the dispersal of it among those students, was in some way, subtle at first but then stronger, disempowering the rig and the three men's desires. Or if not that, disempowering her own terror.

For Dudley it was as when a woman he was with was almost undressed: almost.

For Matthew it was as when one has a headache or fever, but is finally almost ready to drift off into sleep.

For Wallis it was like a huge luxury, a curiosity. After this well was over, he knew he could turn his back and walk away. He just knew it.

The rig workers came and went, with their barge running again. And the road hunters continued to prowl, so that now there was sporadically through the day the sound of gunfire, bursts of three and four and five shots at a time. Some days Mel would stare out her window from the schoolhouse and think, You should have seen it twenty years ago. And when the road hunters went home with their bounty and lied to their wives about the circumstances in which it had been procured, they said, "It's like stepping back in time a hundred years."

Mel and Wallis went out into the charred smokehouse, as if believing they might have overlooked some scrap of meat. It was time to shoot a deer and, if possible, an elk. They stood in the total emptiness of the smokehouse: nothing left but a few dark spots of blood-drip on the bare soil. They wanted meat so badly, were sick of beans and squash —

Mel wanted it more than ever, and imagined that she could feel the tiny one inside her desiring it — but she knew that Wallis did not want to be gone far from the rig when the oil was found.

Matthew had volunteered to help get her meat again this year, as he had every year, and, not knowing how to reject his offer, she had accepted. It had occurred to her that perhaps getting back out into the woods would help halt his errant arc; this soul-jettisoning plummet he insisted on completing — but that was no longer any real business of hers, and she knew in her heart Old Dudley would never let him leave the earth alive.

Still, even in his diminished state, he was a far better hunter than Wallis, and she thought it kind of him to offer; both for the getting of the meat itself, and for the instruction he could give Wallis.

The well snapped a leg; a cross-brace broke its weld, tipping the whole rig fifteen degrees toward earth one night. Miraculously, the pipe did not get stuck, but there was a two-day delay while they waited for giant hydraulic jacks to come and erect the tower once more. Dudley fumed and howled, swore he should go back to Houston and check in on all his other prospects, but could not tear himself away from this one. They were down below sixteen thousand feet and the pay could come at any minute. They got the well drilling again but had not been running for more than a few hours before the weld on another leg snapped, tipping the rig fifteen degrees in the other direction.

The hydraulic jacks had just left and could not get back for another two days. Finally they came and made those repairs, but a day later — the first of November — the engine broke again, meaning a week's delay.

Old Dudley was so mad that he was biting the insides of his own cheeks until blood trickled from the pulpy wounds inside. His rheumy eyes leaked tears of self-pity. He believed sincerely they were only inches away. Mel laughed, feeling a secret power surging within her. She knew it was not her desire, her wishes alone, that were toppling the rig, any more than it was Dudley's or Matthew's desires that had torched the woods. But still she felt pleasure, and a silent strength.

A man was dispatched, like a messenger from ancient times, to get the required parts. He would drive out of the valley. A day later he would catch a flight, then fly all day. He would drive to the rig yards in Louisiana and spend a day or more searching among hulking, rusting giants for the right parts. He would fly back north — another day. Then he would drive back to the valley, if the roads were not snowed out. Another day would be spent repairing the engine and replacing the broken parts. Perhaps they would get it right the first time, and the engine would start again. If they did, Wallis and Matthew would be able to hear the drumming of engine, the squeal and torque and clatter of pipe, and could turn around and head back in. It would take another full day or two to circulate out the old mud and fill the hole with clean new mud, and so there would be time for Wallis and Matthew to get back before the truth was reached.

They packed lightly: a hatchet, a bone saw, and a tarp to use as a tent; matches, knives, a compass for blizzards. Two sleeping bags. One rifle, for Matthew; Wallis's responsibility would be to pack and to learn. The plan was to shoot a giant bull up high, where the bulls had gone to isolate themselves, and then to pack it down in stages — four loads of a hundred and twenty-five pounds each, plus the antlers and hide. They would also shoot a big deer on the way out, down near the valley floor, so they wouldn't have to carry it as far. They would try to accumulate a bounty of grouse, as well, though they'd have to kill them silently, by throwing stones or catching them with their bare hands; they couldn't risk shooting and scaring off the elk. They would catch and kill ruffed grouse down in the pine bottoms, and spruce grouse in the cedar jungles, and finally the enormous blue grouse up on the snowy ridges.

Later in the season, Mel could shoot another deer, if they thought they needed more meat.

They all had dinner over at Mel's the night before they left. Amy and the baby rode over on the pony and brought a deer roast to cook. Dudley walked in front of them, holding the pony's halter. Mel was happy to see them, and glad for the meat. She began seasoning it and basting it with butter and brown sugar, to bake in the wood stove; lining it with small potatoes and onions from the garden. She still had told no one of her pregnancy, though she longed to share the news with Amy, with anyone.

They ate by firelight and candlelight, and afterward, Mel got a book of poems from the bookshelf and settled back on the couch, lean as a cat. She began to read out loud.

"Aww, fuck," Dudley complained, but Amy hushed him and said she wanted to listen.

Matthew listened to the poems for a while but then got up and went over to his rifle and took it apart and began oiling it, and checking and rechecking the packs.

Dudley crept a couple of laps around the cabin — the baby awoke when he passed her, and she eyed him intently — and then he dressed in a parka and high boots and went outside to lead the pony down to the smokehouse, so that it wouldn't have to spend the night standing in the snow.

"If he lives long enough, he'll be a decent human being by the time he dies," Mel said, amazed.

"I have been talking to him about the golden rule," Amy confided.

"Not a chance," Matthew said, reassembling his rifle. He yawned, then started down the hall toward Mel's room before stopping, remembering, and for a long moment he stood there, captured in his mistake. Finally he turned and came back into the main room, gathered a couple of elk hides, and went into the kitchen, where he prepared a pallet. Soon he was snoring, and Mel thought, with some surprise, He doesn't miss me at all. Even with no one to replace me, he is not lonely.

Dudley came back inside. He stamped the snow from his boots, awakening the baby, who began to cry. Amy gathered her up and the three of them — father, mother, daughter — sat on the couch, and the baby calmed again.

"If I leave, I might not be able to get back in," he said. "If I stay, I might not be able to get back out. Gott-damn, I've got my dick in a wringer."

"Teat in a wringer," Amy corrected him.

"That too," Dudley said. "The whole shittaree."

Amy lay down on the couch with the baby. Dudley lay down on the floor next to them, after covering Amy and Mary with a hide, and then himself.

Mel and Wallis went to their room, where they looked out the tiny window at the falling snow.

"I'll be glad when they're all gone," Mel said.

"They'll always keep coming back," Wallis said.

"It's scary, all this snow falling, and us not having any meat," Mel said.

"Do we have enough wood?"

"You can never have enough wood," Mel said.

They undressed and made love quietly, slowly, on the floor, not the jouncy bed, feeling like thieves: trying to match the snow's silence.

Four hours later they were up and fixing breakfast. Wallis kissed Mel good-bye; Matthew nodded to her — she smiled, thanked him, reached out and squeezed his hand — and they stepped out into the snow, which was still falling hard.

They snowshoed down the trail and then turned up a side canyon of leafless aspen, heading into the mountains above them, silent on their snowshoes. They breathed heavily at first, unaccustomed to the rhythm of that particular labor, but moved strongly, their lungs filling easily in the cold air.

They crossed no tracks that day: the snow was still too fresh, the storm ongoing: all the animals were bedded down, waiting it out. For a while a pair of ravens followed them silently through the woods, through the falling snow, but they never made a sound, called out neither encouragement nor warning.

"What are you thinking about?" Matthew asked suddenly, when they stopped to rest. The sweat was pouring down them, and though Wallis was overheated, he knew he would grow quickly cold when they stopped moving.

Wallis started to tell him the truth — about Mel being pregnant — but instead said "Nothing," and Matthew stared at him — the ends of his hair beginning to freeze with small icicles. Matthew grunted and said, "Good, because there are elk just over this next rise."

There were no tracks, and the rise was too high for him to have seen over it, but now the swirling winds brought their scent to Wallis, so strong and unmistakable that he didn't see how he could have missed it, and Matthew said, "Get your head out of your ass. Hunting's the one thing you can't fuck up at. You owe it to the animal you're about to kill" — and they crept up over the ridge. The elk were about fifty yards in front of them, bedded down in the snow beneath some scattered lodgepoles, a different elk beneath each tree. Some elk were bunched up together out in the open, as if in a barnyard, snow covering their backs as they lay resting. Their yellow hides seemed to glow, the only color in the storm, and Wallis and Matthew scanned the herd quickly, searching for antlers. There were a few spike bulls and rag-horns in the herd — their antlers rising above them like small nests — and still the elk did not see or notice them, though Wallis could feel that he and Matthew were being watched, and that time was moving away quickly now — that they had only a few seconds left in which to study and analyze the situation, and then to choose whether to act.

"There she is," Matthew whispered, pointing to their left, to the lead cow, the matriarch, who stood watching them. She had been posted as the lookout while the herd rested, and she stood there staring at the two men, trying to decide whether to sound the alarm. It was an awful responsibility for her. The cost of alarm — of two dozen cows, calves, and young bulls leaping to their feet — over ten thousand pounds of elk — and asking them to surge with adrenaline, to sprint away in belly-deep snow — was not a cost to be weighed lightly in the winter.

Wallis and Matthew knew the decision she was going to make before she made it — could feel it traveling in the air between them — and they scanned the herd quickly one last time for the outside chance of a hidden giant bull. The lead cow barked her alarm, whirled and ran toward the herd, and now they were all leaping to their feet and galloping with her, not even bothering to look back to see what had caused her to sound the alarm.

It was a feeling like having broken something: like having stepped on and shattered something. Divots of black earth flew in all directions, and rocks and stones clattered beneath the snow. There was the scent of elk urine and torn earth, a violence against the sky and the snow as they ran away, deeper into the forest.

The snow continued to fall steadily, as if already assuming its responsibility of filling in and smoothing over some wound. Wallis and Matthew went to look at the depressions in the snow where the elk had been resting. The heat of their huge bodies, though insulated by the hollow hairs of their coats, had finally melted the snow — they'd been resting there a long time — so that it had yielded to accept their shapes. But their bodies had cooled, over time, nestled in the damp snow, and the snow had begun to freeze again, to a watery, smoke-colored ice, clutching them. And still they had rested, had waited.

Only their scent remained. An inch of snow covered their beds. Already the black earth of their hoof-flight was hidden beneath snow.

"We'll follow them to the bull," Matthew said. "We'll let them calm down a little. We'll let them slow to a walk and get back in single file. Then we'll follow them. They'll know we're behind them. They'll hear us, and sometimes catch a glimpse of us. Sometimes the wind will swirl and they'll catch a brief scent of us. They'll notice how the ravens look down on us as they fly past; they'll *feel* us behind them — and they'll keep moving — not at a run, but at a steady walk. They won't stop to rest again.

"We'll keep pushing them," Matthew said. "We'll keep just the right amount of pressure on them, until they start to crack. They'll stop trying to outdistance us; they'll try and lose us. They'll go down steep ravines and then turn right back around and head straight up the steepest slopes. They'll disappear into the thicker timber, trying to wear us out and make us give up and turn around and go home. But we'll stay with them, always keeping the same amount of pressure on them: not too much, but not too little.

"Finally, they'll panic. They'll start running. They'll run to the biggest bull they can find — they'll head for whatever ridge he's hanging out on, in the hopes that he can help defend them, one more time. They'll lead us straight to him. They'll betray him."

"That's not nice," Wallis said.

"No," he agreed, "it's not."

They sat there in the echo of the herd's flight and waited for them to calm down, somewhere out beyond. Their own snow beds began to form around them. They waited for an hour — Matthew was motionless, as if in a trance — and then set out after the elk, barely able to follow the faint sign of their passage.

Later in the afternoon the elk understood that they were being followed and ascended into an alder jungle at dusk. But even in the dim light, and then the darkness, it was impossible to lose their trail, for there were so many of them.

The elk led them through one of the burns. The snow had extinguished all but the largest smoldering logs, around which they could still see glimpses of soil and rock — and some of the standing snags still glowed orange, sometimes breaking into sputtering flames when a breeze passed. At one point they got too close to the elk — the elk had slowed at the other end of the burn to look back and determine whether they were still being followed — and Wallis and Matthew saw them standing just back in the shadows: the faint light of a handful of lantern snags flickering through the snow against their yellow hides, and the firelight dull against the polished antlers of the young bulls.

Wallis and Matthew stepped into the clearing of the burn, and across a distance of a hundred yards the elk watched for only a moment, as if to understand fully who and what the men were, and then they whirled once more and ran, disappearing into the night.

Wallis and Matthew set out after them.

Even without the tracks in the new snow, they could have followed them by scent alone. The odor was like a river winding through the woods, head-high at first, but then settling as it cooled, so that it was as if they were wading into that river of scent.

On through the night they traveled, crossing over north into Canada. Later in the night the elk descended and turned back south, unwilling to leave their home. Now, however, the wind was at their backs, and they couldn't tell what scents lay ahead of them; and so they had to be prudent — could no longer afford the luxury of all-out flight. Matthew felt their increased discomfort, and backed off accordingly. If he and Wallis pushed the elk too hard — if they made them panic — they might leave the area completely. They had to push them to the edge of despair, but not beyond.

Wallis knew that at dawn the ravens would start following them, wanting to see how it would turn out: having a stake in the matter. They would follow the men for a while, and then they would fly ahead and follow the elk herd for a while — democratic, ambiguous, reading the paths of both predator and prey, waiting to see.

The elk climbed back to a ridge before daylight. As the sky paled and a gold bow of light appeared beneath the purple-gray snow clouds, the elk descended again into the deep timber, and Wallis saw how completely they were in control. They had stranded Wallis and Matthew on that bare ridge at daylight — had put them up there to be illuminated by the rising sun as neatly as if tying off a knot. There wasn't anything to do but laugh. Wallis and Matthew could hear their barks of alarm down in the dense timber as they sighted the men and fled once more.

The sky was breaking into light — the cumulus clouds still spitting snow pellets — but a drying north wind was following the mountain's spine now, and there was going to be a lot of sun, at least in the first part of the day. River fog still covered the valley below — hid everything beneath a glowing blue cloud.

About twenty yards downslope, two blue grouse, camouflaged against wind-scoured rocks, grew nervous at the men's pause, and tried to sneak away. Wallis and Matthew would never have seen them otherwise — the grouse had a ten-thousand-year head start, using all the time since the last glaciation to paint their feathers to the same hue as the rocks that remained.

"Now's your chance," Matthew said. "If you're hungry — if you want anything."

Wallis found a rock and hurled it at the closest one. Blue feathers flew, and the rock-struck grouse tumbled crippled down the slope, while the other one leapt untouched and sailed away down the mountain.

Wallis scrambled downslope after the injured one. It was a big strong bird — he had only stunned it — and he caught it with both hands just as it was sorting itself out and about to take flight. He pinched off its head, then plucked the feathers in the north wind.

Matthew gathered some dry grasses and juniper and made a small fire. They seared the bird, ate it rare. Afterward, when they resumed their chase, Wallis was strengthened by the meat.

He hurried to stay up with Matthew, but whenever he could he stopped and quickly made small cairns of stones to mark the mountain where he had taken the grouse as well as to mark the path of the chase.

"Hurry up," Matthew said once. "Stop fucking with those rocks."

For a while, the tracks split in different directions through lodgepole blowdown, where the slender trees, having put all their energy not into root production or thick trunks, but into a quick ascent to the canopy, had drunk in all the light for a few years before growing sunscalded, weak, and wobbly, and falling, one over the other, like matchsticks in the first strong wind.

They crawled over and through and under this chaotic spill of timber. It was a horizontal forest; sometimes the trees were stacked atop each other higher than their heads, a wooden gridlock through which they slithered. It would have been a sight to see the elk herd doing the same — to see the seven-hundred-pound animals flowing through this near-impossible maze, gangly legs pulling themselves over the blowdown — but they were fifteen minutes too late. The elk had already passed.

B Y EVENING THEY HAD COVERED ANOTHER FIFTEEN MILES, and had swung back around to the south end of the valley. Sometimes it seemed the elk knew what the men were attempting to do, and would never lead them to the bull, would never betray him: he who had doubtless given creation to so many of the herd who now wandered the mountains below.

Wallis and Matthew stopped and drank from a creek. They passed by numerous herds of mule deer and whitetails. Often they came across the tracks of lynx, bobcats, and mountain lions. It was already a severe enough winter that some of the moose were shedding their antlers, which rested upturned and palmlike on the ground, gathering the falling snow as if with outstretched mahogany hands. Sometimes when Matthew found such an antler — the hair and blood still ringing it at the base — he would pick one up and hang it in a tree, would wedge it between branches. He would even pause to carve his initials and the date in some of the larger ones, before moving on; and as they traveled, Wallis would occasionally make small stone cairns, markers of their passage.

Because it was a clear night, they stopped to rest on the ridge where the herd had led them that evening. There was no bull on it, and the elk had immediately gone back down into more lodgepole blowdown. The sunset was lurid red, and Wallis and Matthew broke boughs to form brief napping spots at the base of a great fir. They could see the valley some twenty miles to the north.

Matthew no longer worried about alarming the elk: the elk knew where and what the men were and what they were after. Wallis and Matthew could hear them resting down in the lodgepole, grunting and barking as they settled cautiously, distrusting, into new snow beds beneath the frigid stars. As if wondering whether they would live another day; see the next night's stars.

Sometimes one of the young bulls, feeling both the pressure of pursuit and the anger of being pushed and cornered, would respond with coughs and high-pitched bugles. Wallis and Matthew knew that up on whatever mountain the bull was on — and it could have been any of a hundred — the big bull, the largest bull, could hear the younger bulls, and was made aware that something was going on below, though it also seemed likely that he could have no idea that it was humans: that perhaps it had not happened this way enough times in his genetic history — men chasing elk through waist-deep snow, instead of giving up — for him to even register concern.

Perhaps he thought simply that a lion or wolf was skulking around. Perhaps he put his head back down, laid it gracefully against his flank — the tall antlers rising above him to catch the stars — and slept.

In the blue snowlight of the evening, Matthew went off to try to find a grouse, a rabbit, or anything; the carcass of a lion-killed deer. Wallis stayed on the ridge and tended the fire, imagining sleep, rest, and peace.

Matthew soon returned with two blue grouse. He had seen them roosting in a fir tree downslope, silhouetted against the stars, and had climbed up and caught them as they slept. To Wallis it didn't seem fair, but they plucked them anyway, feathers swirling by the fire, rising on the fire-warmed currents, and then roasted them over the flames.

They let the fire go out but were asleep before it faded to water, and steam rose to the stars. They slept in the ice and it was a sleep that Wallis did not want to come up out of, not until the long days and scent of growing things returned.

They awoke deeper into the night — the stars had changed completely, a whole different landscape of them above, as if the men had traveled to another place; and the new stars seemed closer. Matthew knew that the elk were gone: that they had moved on.

Matthew and Wallis dropped farther downslope, following the tracks. The snow was frozen to a crust, the temperature below zero. Their steps were cannonlike in that stillness, so they had to give even more space to the elk. Behind them, on the ridge, a few wisps of steam still rose from their dying fire.

Wallis thought of the faint black mark the fire would leave on the stones after the ashes were blown away in the spring. The fire and boiling water from snowmelt and steam would have cracked some of the rock substrate. A juniper berry would one day get caught in one of those cracks, or a penstemmon seed. It would lie dormant in that crack, awaiting soil; or perhaps it would blossom into life, and with the brute desire of its own roots break the rock a bit farther apart, creating its own soil; and then fail and wither, having created not quite enough.

Another seed would be carried in — perhaps in the excrement of a grouse or other passing animal, like words moving across the rocks — and perhaps there would still be some ash from the fire, down in some of those cracks, though surely the rains and snows would have scrubbed clean all trace of the faint smudge on the stone's surface. One of the new seeds would eventually take. It would break the crack open wider. It would live, grow, and die. If a juniper, it would drop needles. It might live a few hundred years, never growing more than a couple of feet high, but spreading tenacious roots, until its success killed it as it got too large for the austere land in which it lived. The cracks would be several inches wide now, and as the juniper died and crumbled, a fir seedling would take over, able to send its roots deeper, now that the rock had been sufficiently fragmented: a fir tree blossom from the dying juniper's heart.

It would grow slow and wide, thick-trunked, in the near-constant winds at the top of the world. It might grow for five hundred years. Green lichens would shroud it; grouse would roost in it. One cold night two thousand years from now, an animal — a lynx, bobcat, marten, or wolverine — might creep up into the fir tree and catch one, or even two, of those roosting grouse. Feathers would float up into the stars.

Wallis thought how his bones would be nothing more than salt in some distant ocean. Someone wrote or told the story a long time ago and will always be telling it, then erasing it — telling it, then erasing it, giving and then taking. The wide horizontal roots of the juniper read the sentences already written in the stone, Wallis thought — the roots clutching the rock, feeling it, as if reading Braille — while the vertical roots of the fir trees plunge as deep and far as they can, like reading the same words, or sentences, backward.

It was very hard for him to accept such a thing: that a story is already written. He laughed out loud, thinking of what Old Dudley would say to such a thought.

They followed the single-file tracks of the elk lower and lower, back down into a dark creek bottom. It snowed all day. Wallis was beginning to see green floaters in his vision. Their clothes were wet again and Wallis could feel the weight dropping from him already; could feel his body once more beginning to devour muscle and organ. It hit Matthew, too — the steep hills and unending travel, as well as the psychological weight of holding that herd in their mind, nothing but the image of that herd — and though Matthew wasn't as trembly and weakened as Wallis, neither did he seem to have any excess left.

In the buffered silence of the falling snow they were able to get in closer to the elk, though still the elk knew they were behind them.

They found a spruce grouse. It too was easy to catch; again Matthew walked up to it and lifted it from the branch as if taking a bird from a cage. They made another fire down in an old cedar bottom. A cow moose walked past, paying little attention to them or to the small crackling fire. The hugeness of the animal — like a mastodon — and the blackness of the coat, to absorb solar radiation in winter: everything about it had been sculpted to fit the far north, and to fit this one season more than any other.

On the next day Wallis's tremblings got worse again, so that he was frightened. He did not see how, if they even found the bull, they would be able to pack it out. The elk were climbing again, and Matthew said he thought this might be it — that the elk might be getting tired. It was the only thing he said all day. He touched his ribs once, carefully — the wound where he had fallen from the rig.

They spent the day climbing. It turned colder again that night — the cold rolling across the landscape like a wave — and that night, Wallis was torn between wanting to dry his clothes by the fire and going directly to sleep. In the end he settled for merely warming them — melting the crusty ice-shroud of them back into dampness — and then crawled into his sleeping bag and slept once more as if falling. He slept leaden, willing to let the elk herd get away, to empty his mind of them. He did not even think the words *I quit*, but simply slept.

He grew cold further into the night and was conscious of his damp clothes freezing around him, even in the sleeping bag, but still he could not surface. The elk slept, too. If they had gotten up and moved on, Wallis would have let them, but as he slept he could feel them sleeping, as if balanced by his own sleep, and that was when he knew they would get the bull.

He awoke at daylight to snow falling on his upturned face. On the other side of the tree, Matthew was still asleep, or perhaps dead. Wallis had a craving for pancakes, honey, bacon, black coffee. He broke off a piece of bark from the tree they were sleeping beneath and examined it, smelled it, pretended it was a piece of food: a hot biscuit with butter melting over it. He put it to his mouth and chewed slowly. His eyes watered.

Wallis sat up, and clumsily, with frost-stiff hands, made another fire: and even after he got it going, it was a long time before he could feel warmth from it. He ate a couple of handfuls of snow, pretending they were ice cream, or frozen melons in the summertime, and lay back down to rest. The snow was landing on Matthew's face and not melting, so Wallis reached up and snapped some boughs from the tree and laid them over Matthew's face like a screen. After a time the fire burned down and Wallis let it go. He was thinking about rotting logs: about how rich the soil was in a forest where old trees toppled over and were then eaten by the soil. It was nice to lie there on the mountainside with his body consuming itself and the snow burying them, and burying also the jagged, random trail of blackened campfires they had left behind them.

It was later in the day — early afternoon — when Wallis awoke again. There was a foot of new snow down, and it was still snowing. He felt better — light and empty, but better — as if the mountain had taken away some of his weakness. He went up the hill toward the ridge to see if the elk were still bedded down above them.

He came over a ridge and at first did not recognize them, covered with snow. Only their heads were visible, seeming suspended like puppets, in that world of white. Some of them were looking down the hill in his direction, but Wallis realized that in the falling snow they could not see him. Or perhaps they too were giving up. They were huddled together, twenty or more of them, looking shell-shocked, and the bull was with them.

The bull looked like something from the imagination: as if he did not belong in this world. His antlers rose six feet above and behind his head. He looked weary, but at peace. He looked almost glad that the rest of the herd had come to see him.

Wallis went back down the hill to wake Matthew. There was a moment of panic when at first Wallis could not find his tracks back, but then his eyes adjusted to the whiteness and he was able to tell, faintly, where he had been.

It was hard to wake him. Matthew appeared confused by the whiteness of sky and whiteness of the mountain, and he seemed longer in coming up out of it than Wallis had been. Finally, however, he sat up. Wallis told him the bull was just up the hill.

Matthew held his gloved hands under his armpits to warm them and looked uphill into the snow. When his hands were warm he took his knife out and began carving on the tree they were camped beneath. He carved a picture of an elk — a bull. When Matthew was done he sheathed the knife, warmed his hands again, then rose stiffly. His clothes had frozen and he twisted and stretched, bending them back to the shape of his body. He picked up his rifle, tapped the snow from it, cleaned the scope, opened the bolt, and blew through the barrel, covering it with his hand so that the flesh of his lips did not freeze against the metal. Then he started up the hill, tracing Wallis's old tracks. It was still snowing hard. Wallis followed.

It was strange to Wallis how the idea of killing had been kept focused and separate in his mind; how there were no thoughts of what might need to come afterward: no thoughts of the work of gutting and cleaning the elk, or the long pack out. There were not even any thoughts of the coming moment, the coming first moment after the killing when all the other elk would leap up in alarm, spraying snow everywhere, and run off into the snow, into the storm, as if forever pursued. The disruption of beauty.

There was only the thought of the immediate killing. Beyond that was nothing. There was only the image of the bull.

They stopped below the ridge and peered over. There was nothing in sight and at first Wallis thought the elk had moved — had heard or sensed or smelled the men coming — but then he realized it was only snowing harder. Matthew looked at Wallis with doubt and Wallis held his hand up for him to wait.

They stared back out into the snow and now sometimes through the swirls they could pick out a glimpse of ear, or the darkness of a muzzle. A spike's antler. The bull's antlers, briefly, like a ghost, quickly hidden by the storm.

"Yes," Matthew whispered.

There was no way to get closer. They were already too close. There could be other elk, sleeping cows, all around them; if they spooked even one of them, the whole herd would explode.

They had to pick out the one thread — the bull — without disrupting any of the others. Wallis shuddered from the cold and the anticipation as the bull's antlers appeared against the sky briefly, then shrouded out again. There was the momentary temptation — if Wallis had had the rifle — to measure down blindly below where the antlers disappeared, and to shoot at nothing, on faith.

Matthew crouched lower into the snow. He laid the rifle beneath him to keep the snow from it and lowered his head like an animal and waited. It started to snow harder. Wallis burrowed down too. They could see nothing now. Forty yards up the ridge, on the flat, the elk rested. Wallis emptied his mind of them, as he knew he must, so they would not know he was among them.

It was warm down in the snow. After an hour or so, he slept.

When they awoke it was late afternoon and the storm was clearing. There was patchy fog, spits of snow still falling, but milky blue above them, and a new sound in the world, the loud sound of snow-not-falling: a brittleness.

Another half-foot had fallen and as they sat up from their snow caves they saw that the elk were gone. Wallis felt despair and failure — felt that the elk had cast a spell on them, to send them down into sleep, when they had been so close to killing — but Matthew held a hand up to caution him, to tell him to keep hunting.

They eased up to where the elk had left their snow-beds. The ice sculptures of where they had been had six inches of snow in them, indicating the elk had gotten up and moved out just as the men had gone to sleep. Wallis wanted to go back down to their camp and gather their packs and sleeping bags and snowshoes, if they were going to follow them, rather than wandering blindly off into the mountains — the elk's tracks were sealed over and hidden by the new snow, as were the men's own tracks leading back to camp. It would be night soon, and seemed a recipe for disaster, a kind of willful death, to go pushing off into the late afternoon, directionless and unequipped — but Matthew said that he thought he could smell them, that they would be just a little ways upslope, and feeding, because they'd be hungry after having bedded for so long. He started up the mountain, with each step punching through up to his waist.

Wallis turned and started to go back down to camp. But the lure was too strong. He followed in Matthew's snow-churned wake. More clouds were breaking apart; an immense sky was opening above. The sun was striking the new blue and white world but gave no warmth, and Wallis knew how cold it would be when the sun went down.

Matthew cast slowly up the hill. After half an hour they had finally broken a sweat. He paused at another ridge, having lost the scent, and looked up the hill, which led toward nothing but blue sky. Wallis turned and looked below and saw the elk moving slowly and in single file through some timber below. The bull was still with them, but was so much larger that he looked like some kind of monster. They had seen the men and smelled them, and were trying to sneak away. Wallis didn't see how the bull could move so much mass through such timber without getting tangled. He pointed them out to Matthew, who had already seen them and was raising his rifle. There was a lot of timber below and Wallis thought that if Matthew did not get a clear shot he would rather die than spend another week chasing the elk.

The bull was at the back of the herd. All the elk knew the men had spotted them now and they picked up their pace, accelerating to a trot: leaping over logs like show horses, the whole herd moving into that powerful, flowing motion. Some of the cows and calves were already out of sight, disappearing to safety, and still Matthew did not shoot, waiting for the perfect chance.

Finally, long after Wallis thought it was too late, Matthew fired. The sound of it seemed to break the mountain open, and the bull made only a small stumble, as if he had tripped over a stone, and then moved more quickly, broke into a run, as did the rest of the herd ahead of him. They all disappeared.

Wallis felt an immense emptiness.

"I got him," Matthew said, though his voice had a bit of doubt in it. "You'll see. I got him."

They sat down and waited. If the bull was dead or mortally injured, their pursuing him wouldn't change what had already happened; and if he were untouched, there would be no rush either, because it would be a long time — the middle of the night, perhaps, or the next day — before the herd calmed down again.

It was too cold to sit still. Wallis and Matthew dug through the snow, pawing like horses, until they found some grasses and twigs. They built a tiny fire, trying to warm themselves, but it was useless, and they began to shiver. The sun went behind the mountain and the light turned orange. The grass and twig fire burned out and now only the lichens on the rock burned, flaming briefly then glowing incandescent in the dusk.

"Okay," Matthew said. "He's dead now. We can go get him. It won't be but a couple hundred yards at the most."

They went down to the spot where the bull had been when Matthew shot. At first they couldn't find any blood and Wallis thought it had been a clean miss, but then Matthew found a spray of blood farther off the trail where the bullet had passed through, and a few hairs that had been cut during the bullet's exit.

They followed the herd's tracks through the timber in the dimming orange light. About every twenty or thirty yards they would find a drop or two of blood, but it wasn't enough to kill a mouse, much less an elk.

"I hit him in the lungs," Matthew said. "In a minute his lungs will collapse, and he'll go down."

After a couple hundred yards, the herd's tracks continued parallel across the mountain, but the bull's veered suddenly, sharply, downhill, and for the first time Wallis believed that they were going to find him.

They came across a tangle of fallen and leaning timber. Now there was more blood: some was smeared against the fallen logs.

"I got him in the heart, too," Matthew said with satisfaction. "The heart and the lungs." He was not excited, only pleased.

The elk traveled another three hundred yards before dying. They found him by a little creek, hung up in a jumble of blown-down timber that he'd tried to leap. He was caught in the nest of it, the latticework of it supporting his huge body above the ground so that it looked as if he were still alive, and only in mid-leap. There was more of him, it seemed, than there had been when Matthew had shot, and even the antlers seemed larger, so that for a second Wallis wondered if there had been some mistake: if this were not their giant elk, but some even greater creature that had died of natural causes, and which they had merely stumbled across.

The blue light of snow at night began to glow. They went up to the elk and touched it — leaned in against it. It was warm and unmovable. It floated above the ground, suspended by the latticework. Wallis started to laugh, not knowing why. Matthew smiled. Years, and all errant choices, seemed to vanish.

The bull had a ripe smell that reminded Wallis of horses, of dark cool stables — the kind barn cats like to nap in in the summertime. The odor was rich enough and strong enough that it seemed you could ignite it: could strike a match and have the air all around leap into blue flame. It was a good smell. Wallis laughed again — took a glove off and pressed a bare hand to the elk's warm side — and did not know why he laughed, only that he wanted to. It was a feeling to him like standing in a garden in the spring, with the earth all turned and ready. "Shit almighty," Matthew said, still grinning.

"What?" Wallis asked. He wanted to know the name for this happiness. That incredible scent of musk, down in the woods.

"I forgot my pulleys," Matthew said. "We'd never have been able to budge him — wouldn't have even been able to turn him over to clean him. But this way" — he laughed — "this way I can just crawl under him, open him up, and let it all fall out."

They lingered, not yet wanting to leave the elk and go get their packs and equipment. It was getting colder quickly under the clearing skies, but the elk was warm, like a stove with a bed of coals still inside it, and they were reluctant to depart, to leave that brush of air against them, which was the space, the distance, between body and spirit. It wouldn't last — or rather, they wouldn't be able to discern it much longer — and they sat there and waited for it to leave, or for the point where they could no longer feel it. It was gone soon enough — quickly — and only when the woods grew still and lonely again did they go up to their camp and pack up without saying anything.

They built a fire down in the woods next to the elk to warm them as they worked. There was plenty of dry wood and it was easy to make a roaring fire with flames that lit the woods for some distance. The orange light danced slowly against the elk's hide and faster against his antlers, which made it seem as if he had come back to life again. Matthew crawled under the suspended bull — if it fell it would crush him — and began cutting. Hair drifted upward on the fire's currents as he cut. The knife made a rasping sound against the coarse hair and thick skin and cartilage. From time to time Matthew would have to stop and sharpen his knife with a whetstone.

"Nothing in the world dulls a steel blade like elk hair," he said. He was doing a neat job and no blood had touched him yet, though that would soon change. "I'd like a stone knife someday. Black obsidian," he said. He went back to cutting. Wallis added wood to the fire. He would not have believed he could skin such an animal. It seemed like surely enough meat for the coming year.

By morning they had the hide and antlers sawed off — Matthew had brought a small wood-handled folding saw, whose blade was now ruined, and which he tossed in the fire — and they had the hindquarters and shoulders cut and hanging from trees.

Their packs were filled with the loose meat — the roasts, tenderloins, and lengths of backstrap like anacondas. They were covered with blood from where they had labored to lift the hindquarters and shoulders into the trees and Wallis was glad that the bears were sleeping.

The fire had sprawled and wandered through the night. Ashes, and charred half-lengths of timber, lay in a circle thirty feet across. They roasted some of the ribs over the coals of the fire and ate on them for a long time. They ate one whole side of the trimmings — stripped the bones clean and gleaming — and the other side they broke in half with the hatchet and tied to their packs like a frame, to help hold in place the ponderous shifting weight of all the other meat, which was still warm against their backs.

Matthew carried the antlers — settled them over his shoulders upside down, with their long tips and tines furrowing the snow behind him as if he were in a yoke — and Wallis carried the wet hide atop his pack of meat, sending the weight of his pack up to around a hundred and thirty pounds.

It began to snow again. Wallis wondered where the other elk were: if they knew that the chase was over, and if they were glad that it was over.

They stayed on the ridges when they could. They had to take small, slow steps under such a load. They would travel a mile, drop their weight, then backtrack to where they'd left the other meat, then pack the second load back to that point — each of them carrying a hindquarter on their back, and dragging an elk shoulder behind them like a sled across the snow.

In that manner they moved across the valley, continuously giving up all progress that they'd made, working hours to move the first load only one mile, at which point they were then ready to start all over again with the second — and the winter-short days passed quickly, and they slept soundly through the nights, though in their dreams they were still walking, forever hauling the meat across the frozen landscape.

Ravens followed them, after the second or third day, even through the falling snow. Wallis and Matthew dropped off one ridge down into a creek, ascended another, and Matthew said he knew where they were. The ravens landed in front of them and strutted with outstretched wings, drawing little tracings in the snow, barking and cawing in voices that alternated shrill and hoarse, as if they were hurling different languages at the men. Sometimes the ravens would dart in and peck at whatever elk quarter they dragged, but usually they pecked only at the fragments that were left behind. There was a moment of startling beauty on the third day. Wallis and Matthew were walking on the lee side of a wind-sculpted snow spine, the storm's fog so thick they could see no more than a few feet. Four ravens followed them, walking behind them in their penguin strut, as if grounded by all the snowy weather. Wallis and Matthew continued along the ridge.

To their left — to the west — a slot appeared in the fog. They could see pale blue sky above, and gold light fell through the slot and illuminated with ancient copper light the forested canyon below. The lens of gold light fell through that slot — the only thing they could see, in any direction — then traveled north, tracing itself down the canyon, paralleling them. As the cloud rent moved away from them — as it passed over the dense forest far below — it kept revealing more of the uncut, untouched forest. The impression it gave was that the uncut forest would never end — that the light could travel forever and always stay above uncut forest.

In less than a minute the gold light had moved out of sight — the wind was blowing thirty miles an hour — and neither Matthew nor Wallis said anything about it to each other, though they did stop and watch it, as it was leaving, as if unsure of what they had just seen.

It had turned cold again. They ate on the elk as they traveled. Wallis wanted bread, or potatoes; he was tired of all the meat. He wanted an apple pie, dense with sugar, and a hot bath. He wondered if the parts for the rig had arrived; if Dudley was drilling again — if even, perhaps, the oil had been reached, and the hot scented steam of its success would be waiting for them when they returned.

The antlers had sunk lower on Matthew's shoulders, so that the yoke of them was cutting deeper in the snow. Sometimes the heavy tips of them would strike a rock far beneath the snow and make a clinking sound. Matthew had cut a small strip of hide to use as a cushion over his shoulders, but the length of the journey and the weight of the antlers had worn his skin raw and then bloody, so that a thin red Y ran down his back.

The furrows in the snow behind him, wide as the antlers were, looked like the narrow borders for a small road, and within them were the tracks of the creatures that were following them: ravens, coyotes, and lions. The wolves still had not come back.

Wallis and Matthew moved down out of the high country and into the trees again. It was growing warmer at the lower elevation, so that rather than snow there was sleeting drizzle, which chilled them worse. They came across a dropped moose antler, resting upright on the snow — they could read the moose's tracks leading to it, and leading away from it — and the upturned antler was full of water and slush from the sleet. They knelt and took turns drinking from it. They were almost home. One more night, and the next day. A year's worth of meat, put away for good.

The Y on Matthew's back widened, but he was moving stronger again. Wallis was shivering hard. For a long time the effort of hauling and skidding the meat had been enough to keep him warm, but now that that balance had been lost, he needed help from the outside; his body could no longer hold off the mass of winter.

"Do you want to stop and light a fire?" Matthew asked, watching Wallis's slowing movements as the clumsiness of hypothermia came hurrying in. Wallis nodded, lucid enough to know that it had arrived. He felt as if Matthew were some great distance away watching him, now — evaluating him as Dudley sometimes did. Wallis no longer felt that they were brothers in the hunt, or brothers in anything, and as his mind began to close down, with even the hot chambers of the brain beginning to chill, he had the feeling that Matthew was going to let him freeze: that he had run Wallis into the ground, had let him haul out half the elk, and now, only a day's journey from town, he was going to let winter have him; that Matthew would carry the rest of the meat out himself on this final leg of the journey, leaving Wallis to disappear beneath the snow.

Matthew waited as Wallis knelt and slipped out of his pack. Wallis lost his balance once and tipped over in the snow. Not thinking clearly — not thinking at all — Wallis searched through his pack for matches, shivering. He found them, held the small box of them tight in his gloved hands, then remembered that he needed wood.

Matthew just stood there, watching; he hadn't taken his pack off. Wallis moved into the trees and began fumbling with branches, snapping and gathering twigs indiscriminately, dropping some while holding onto others. Matthew was drenched — and the antlers were covered with ice — but he was different: he had a fire in him that Wallis could see he himself did not have.

Wallis heaped the branches, some green and some dry, into a small pile, and began striking matches, barely able to light them; and the sodden pile of wood would not light. He tried until he was out of matches, then rose and went back to his pack to look for more. He was moving slow and was to the point where he wanted to lie down. He knew he had to keep going, but knowing it and doing it seemed vast distances apart.

At first Matthew didn't say anything. It was evident as Wallis rooted through his pack that he wasn't going to find any more matches; and that even if he did, the results would be the same.

"Watch," Matthew said, taking a cigarette lighter out of his pack. "Look," he said. He walked over to the nearest dead tree, an old fir, shrouded dense with black hanging lichens. "This is what you do," he said. His words were breaths of steam rising into the rain. He stood under the tree's branches and snapped the lighter a couple of times. On the third snap the lichens caught, burned blue for a moment, then leapt into quick orange flame.

The whole tree, or the shell of lichens around it, metamorphosed into crackling fire: the lichens burning explosively, and the sudden shock of heat, the updraft, in turn lighting those lichens above, accelerating the rush of flame as if climbing a ladder. It was a forty-foot tree, on fire from top to bottom in about three seconds.

"That's how you do it," Matthew said, stepping back. Wallis had stopped shivering, his blood heated by one last squeeze of adrenaline at the sight, but now even as he watched the flames, the chill, and then the shivering, returned.

"You'd better get on over there," Matthew said. "They don't burn long."

Wallis walked over to the burning tree. There was a lot of heat — the snow in all directions around it was searing and then glazing — but Wallis knew it wasn't a heat that would last long, and so he sat under the tree, as much to get out of the rain as to feel warmth.

Flaming wisps of lichen floated upward in curls and then descended; by the time they were landing on him they were almost out — and a few of the tree's branches burned and crackled, but then the fire was gone.

"Come on," Matthew said. "Let's go find another one." He set off into the rain, the antlers behind him plowing a path.

That was how they came out of the mountains and back into town, in that last night and the next day: going from tree to tree, looking for the right one, properly dead and set off a ways from the others. They moved through the drizzle, from one tower of flame to the next — Matthew probing the dead trees with his cigarette lighter, testing them.

They went on through the dark night — the trees sizzling and steaming after they were done — and on into the gray rainy day. They were into country that Wallis recognized and knew well now, even beneath the snow, and they were back among the deer. They were seeing lion tracks, finding lion kills. They cast their way down the mountain, bearing left and right, left and right, correcting their path each time back toward the valley's center.

The rut was on as they approached town the next day — the giant bucks chasing any receptive doe — and though they were exhausted there was still more work to be done; they still had to shoot a deer.

As they drew nearer the village — the scent of the forest ripe with musk — they could hear that the rig was running again, could hear the groan and clatter of it — could see the black clouds of diesel against the rainy skies — and they quickened their pace, as if afraid of being abandoned.

They saw dozens of bucks prowling the woods, some bucks larger than others — a swarm of antlers moving through the forest, with all the bucks mesmerized by sex — and they were almost to Helen's burial site when they saw the buck they wanted.

They saw him because he had seen them and was coming up the hill toward them. The buck was watching the giant antlers strapped to Matthew's back, and came forward with aggression. He was wet from the rain, and with every step twin streams of fog-vapor trailed from his nostrils. His antlers were black brown from his having lived in a dark forest and not having ventured out in the daytime, and they rose three feet above his head and extended a foot on either side beyond the tips of his outstretched ears. It did not seem possible he could carry such a weight on his head.

Matthew dropped to his knees. The deer stopped, then came closer, still entranced only with the antlers, and ignoring the man underneath them. Matthew raised his rifle and shot the deer through the neck as it faced them directly, not twenty yards away.

They saw a thin pattern of blood spray across the snow behind the deer — saw the deer's head and antlers snap back — but the deer did not buckle or drop. Instead it whirled and ran down the hill, running hard and strong.

Other deer — smaller deer — stood around watching them. It

started to rain harder. Wallis and Matthew stood in the hissing, steady rain, breathing their own milky vapors. Wallis knew in his heart that he was almost ready to quit, and that, strangely, Matthew was too — as strange a thought as if a stone were to quit being a stone.

The snow was deep and slushy. There was little, if any, blood trail to follow, and the big buck's tracks merged with hundreds of others: the carnival of the rut.

Looking down toward the river in the direction the buck had run, Matthew dropped his pack in the snow — the bloody Y on his back identical to the one on his chest, like the delicate, perfect, world-shaped markings on the wings of some obscure tropical butterfly — and Wallis did the same. A blood trail was beginning to form on Wallis's own back and chest in a pattern not that different from Matthew's.

They carried the antlers through the woods toward Helen's tree. To not be wearing the packs after having carried them for so long was a feeling like flight; as if now they could have gone another hundred miles.

That feeling soon left them. The rain and slush beat them down again. They began lighting trees once more — moving from tree to tree.

Ahead of them, through the drizzle, they saw Helen's tree. Wallis let Matthew carry the antlers by himself, from that point; he stood beneath a burning tree and watched Matthew labor the large antlers through the woods toward Helen's shrine. He had begun building a rock wall around her. How long would her markers last? He had not gotten very far on it and he might not have enough years left in him to do it the way he wanted — to build one as he had for Mel. Wallis wondered: *How many chances do we get?*

Matthew knelt beneath her tree and positioned the elk antlers against the base of it. He stayed there praying, or thinking, for a long time. Wallis took a few steps forward and lit another tree, which roared; a twist, a crack in it, resin-rich, able to catch the lichen-flames and spread the fire throughout its core, throughout the rotting heartwood — and that tree burned until it was a charcoal spar, smoldering, and then tipped over, snapping about halfway up and falling to the ground to form a leaning awkward letter A.

The sound of it brought Matthew out of his reverie, and he looked over at Wallis as if not recognizing him at first — but then he rose and made his way slowly back to where Wallis was waiting.

They went back up through the woods. Already the ravens had

found their meat and were resting atop it. A coyote stood next to the cache, but turned and ran when it saw them.

Matthew shooed the ravens away with waves of his arms — at first Wallis thought they were not going to leave — and as they finally flew off, they croaked and grunted not as if with laughter, but as if with encouragement, urging the men to go on, to never quit.

Wallis and Matthew loaded up and pushed on down the hill, trying to sort the wounded buck's tracks from all the others. A drop of blood here; a loose hair there. Wallis very much believed the deer could run to the horizon: that he was only nicked.

They found him down near the river in a backwater slough, thrashing around in six feet of water, having broken through a skim of thawing ice as he tried to cross; but even if he had succeeded in crossing, where would he have gone? Out into the river itself, and downstream, then, like a log? It seemed to Wallis as fair, as fitting, for him to die in this pond as in the river, fifty yards farther. They watched him for a moment as he swam in circles with only his head and the tower of antlers above the water. The deer was choking on his blood, coughing sprays of it across the water with each exhalation and swallowing blood with each breath. The bullet had missed an artery but severed a vessel. His face was a red mask of blood.

The buck glared at them as he swam — a red king, defiant. Matthew raised his rifle, waited for the deer to swim back around — waited until it was closest to them.

The deer continued to watch them as it swam toward them — head held high, drowning in blood. Matthew shot it in the neck again, breaking the neck this time, and the deer stopped swimming immediately. The antlers sank.

They sat and stared at it for a long time — watching it motionless through the refraction of water — as if expecting it to come back to life.

Another buck, following the scent trail of the giant's musk, appeared on the other side of the pond: lowered its head, trying to decipher the cone of scent that had drifted its way — wondering, perhaps, where the deer had gone.

Rain was dimpling the surface of the pond. It was now more than ever like a dream and Wallis felt as if he had to come back up into the real world or be lost. They could hear the steady pounding of the rig in the distance. They left the elk meat by the pond and traveled upriver to where they'd left the canoe; pulled it out from under its shell of snow, and paddled downriver to the slough. They loaded the elk meat into the canoe until the canoe was low in the water. Dusk was coming on and they could see a few lights across the river. Wallis stayed on the far shore while Matthew made two crossings with the meat; then Matthew came back for Wallis. The rain had stopped and the sky was clearing to stars and Matthew said they had to go back and get the deer out now as the pond would freeze thick if they waited until the next day.

They waded out into the pond together. The water was warmer than the air around them. The deer was lighter underwater and they were able to muscle him to the shore. Then they scrambled out and dragged him over to the canoe — gutted him quickly — and trembling, they loaded him into the canoe and set out across the river one more time, riding lower than ever. It did not matter to Wallis whether they tipped over or not, for freezing was more imminent than drowning; but they reached the other shore, sledded the canoe up onto the gravel, and finally they quit; abandoned the meat, hundreds of pounds of it, only a short distance from home, and ran stumbling and falling up the hill toward town. There was a fire burning in the rig workers' camp but they did not veer that way, wanting to make it all the way home rather than to yet one more temporary place among strangers; and they knew also that no fire would warm them — that they had to be dry, and enclosed by four walls.

Lights were on in the bar. They went straight in and lay down next to the wood stove, shivering. Artie and Charlie brought them blankets and hides, and he helped them out of their wet clothes and wrapped hides around them. They heated water on the stove for baths and for hot tea for them to drink; the first fluid they'd had in days that was neither snow nor cold creek water. The heat of it made them vomit as the tea hit their stomachs. Artie looked at what they had spat up, and at the blood stains on their shirts. "They got an elk," he said.

Matthew tried to stay awake — tried to head back out to find Old Dudley — but he had not gone ten steps before he lay down exhausted, in the middle of the street, and fell hard asleep, with the evening's sleet turning to slow-falling snow. Steam rose anew from his wound. The men from the bar went and lifted him up and carried him back inside and laid him down by the fire again.

Wallis left for Mel's, carrying a load of meat on his back. She was still awake as he drew near — he saw her lantern through the window — but she had turned the lights out for bed when he was still some distance from the cabin, so that falling snow and darkness suddenly separated him from her. It was a sight so startling, after so long an absence from her, that his legs buckled, and he felt tears leap to his eyes.

He hurried the last hundred yards to her cabin and dropped the meat on the porch and, not wanting to alarm her, knocked on the door.

She came out and held him for a long time. "I've gotten so weak," was all she said. "I missed you," she said. "I've been waiting for you to come back."

They spent the rest of the night hauling the rest of the meat home and hanging all the quarters from the rafters. When it was finally done they stood there amongst the chilled mass of meat, and felt as rich as pirates.

"Another day and you'd have been snowed out," Mel said.

"We cut it pretty close," he agreed. "No kicks from the baby yet?"

Mel laughed. "Two more months for that."

"January," said Wallis, and they both stood there, imagining it.

"I guess y'all will go out to the well in the morning," Mel said. "He's been getting really anxious for y'all to get back. *Really* anxious," she said. "He hasn't been acting right," she said, and Wallis laughed out loud. He said, "How would you know?"

"No," Mel said, "he's been different. I'm worried."

"Churchy-different?" Wallis asked. "You mean that golden rule stuff?"

"No," Mel said. "Unhappy, maybe even frightened."

"Shit," Wallis said, trying to imagine it. "He's not sick, is he?"

"No," Mel said, "he just looks weak."

"He'll perk up when he sees Matthew," Wallis said.

Mel slept. Wallis went back to town in the snowy dawn and began fixing breakfast over at Helen's. He went across the street and woke Artie and asked Artie to help carry Matthew over to the mercantile, so that Wallis could feed him and get him lucid and presentable before Old Dudley showed up. They hauled him through that falling snow as if rescuing him from a burning building — though it felt strange to Wallis as if there could be no rescuing of him, that they might as well have been carrying him out of one burning building and into another.

They sat him up in a chair by the fire, and Wallis fed him bites of pancake as one would feed a baby. Matthew's eyes kept rolling to their whites and his chin kept tipping down to his chest, but slowly, they summoned him from his depth. Artie had three plates of pancakes and asked all about the hunt.

They stared across at the bar through the falling snow. Artie had strung Christmas lights in candy-cane striping all around the porch. He said that it was the first time there had ever been Christmas lights in the valley and that Dudley had said Artie was turning into a sissy and that the valley was going to hell.

Artie said maybe not; that he had seen two swans earlier that day, flying downriver right before dusk. He said he hadn't realized what they were for a moment — that with their seven-foot wingspans, and their solid white bodies, he had thought they were angels, or ghosts. He said it had been almost thirty years since he'd seen a pair in the valley.

Matthew roused — surfaced a little higher; found himself capable of speech.

"Helen said there used to be a shitload of them come through here," Matthew said. "They'd pass through late in the autumn, then come back in the spring on their way back to the Arctic. They'd raise their young here." He began to eat from his plate — eating on his own, now. "Helen said the wolves would lie in wait all along the shores of the little ponds and lakes, and watch the swans. The wolves would kill them one by one — would grab them by the neck whenever the swans came too close to shore."

"They don't make any sound, do they?" Artie asked. "They're not like geese."

"No," Matthew said. "Except once. Right before they die. It's the only sound they make in their whole life. That's why they call it a swan song. They lie down and stretch out their neck and whistle. It's not a pretty sound — not at all like you'd think. It's horrible."

"Did you ever hear one?" Wallis asked. "A dying swan?"

"Sure," Matthew said. He shrugged. "When I was a kid I roped one from the dock. I baited it into a snare and threw the rope over its neck. Somehow I got it dragged up on the shore before it could take off flying. It might have carried me off with it. I tied the rope around a tree and then killed it."

"How did you kill it?" Artie asked.

"Stones," said Matthew — as if in a trance, now. "It took so many of them."

"Did the swan do it?" Wallis asked. "Did it sing?"

"Yes," said Matthew.

Old Dudley came riding in on Amy's pony, layered in coats and furs, so that he looked like some creature from the forest. The pony was plowing through snow up to its belly. Anyone who was going to get out of the valley needed to do so soon, and he knew it.

He saw the smoke rising from the mercantile's chimney and with his heels prodded the pony into a trot. He rode right up onto the porch, and might have ridden the pony through the door had they not heard him coming and gone out to meet him.

Old Dudley's face was cherry-red, and the tong marks were betraying his mood, pulsing reptilian. "Care for a pancake?" Matthew asked.

"If you two are through with fun and games," Dudley said, "we're drilling below eighteen thousand." He turned to Wallis. "I want you to look at it and see what you think," he said, "but it looks like we're into basement rock, and have been for a motherfucking week. It looks like there's not a gott-damn thing there. It looks like another motherfucking dry hole."

"Are you sure you don't want a pancake?" Matthew asked. "They're really good this morning."

It was the closest Wallis had seen Dudley come to striking Matthew. Artie excused himself, made a silent wish that Old Dudley would not be wintering in the valley.

They walked down to the river to catch a ride over on the barge with the day shift. The day shift's fire had only recently been extinguished, so that steam still rose from its blackened coals. Severed deer heads, shrouded in snow, hung from a pole lashed between two trees, and the scent of venison was all around.

"They're going native," Matthew said. "Good. We can use them on the next well." Again Dudley looked ready to strike Matthew, and even raised his hand.

It was a thing Dudley might have said, twenty years earlier. Wallis glanced at Matthew and tried to imagine him standing out in an oil field somewhere, in a Louisiana bayou, or a Kansas wheatfield — one of Old Dudley's many other operations — and, bent over and crooked and aching and hungry, announcing that he was going to drill to the bottom of the fucking world.

The barge pilot let them off on the other shore. They crowded into a truck and drove toward the distant noise of the rig. The road was snow-rutted, frozen into a violent crust that boomed as they walked across it. It was a landscape of jagged teeth, as if the ocean had been frozen in a moment, with all whitecaps and waves halted. In the truck, the men asked if they would be going home soon.

When they got to the rig — the high-intensity halogen lights flooding the wilderness, washing out all shadows — Dudley and Wallis and Matthew got out and stood there for a moment, watching the drill pipe spin, gleaming in the hole. The immensity of their failure. It felt to Wallis for the first time as if they had traveled a long way.

Over the din of the rig, it seemed to Wallis that he could hear the metal of the rig contracting, groaning against the cold as the temperature sank like some weighted thing no longer able to stay above the surface. It had stopped snowing and the forest was glazed beneath mounds of new snow. In other places the crescent moon's light cast a gleam over blue ice and silver ice, and there was a riot of wild stars.

They went up on the rig floor and began examining the little bags of ground-up cuttings that Old Dudley had been saving for them in their absence. He was certain they held nothing but the Cambrian basement rock — the cold, sterile, igneous foundation of the crust, across which no life had ever traveled, and where there could hence be no oil — but Dudley wanted to see Matthew and Wallis acknowledge this — wanted to watch them fully examine and observe and hold their failure in their hands, as if to humiliate them.

They looked at the dry cuttings for two hours — emptying out one little sample bag after another, as if emptying tiny bags of treasure: but it was all igneous, they had passed through any chance at all for life, and were deep into the basement — the useless, barren basement.

"You vile little twat," Old Dudley said to Wallis. "Eight million dollars, and the ridicule of my peers. Oh you little fucker. You come up here and take my boy's girl from him and con us into believing your gott-damn stupid map . . . Oh you fuck-faced little *rodent*," he said.

Old Dudley's eyes were starting to drift and cross, and he appeared dizzy. He sat down, steadied himself. He was panting, as he often did following his creeping, and the rank odor often associated with that began to arise from him. His face was gray. He looked down at his boots. A single teardrop fell on his boots. "Send them home," he told Matthew. "Get me out of here," he said. "Boy, get me out of here."

The river was beginning to freeze on either side of its banks, though it still ran dark and strong and deep through the center. They drove back to the river and signaled for the barge to come get them; and even before the barge reached them, Old Dudley went out onto the ice and swung feebly at it with an ax, as if to clear a lane for the huge ship. Wallis thought for sure he would punch through the ice and disappear, and be swept away from them. He kept flailing at the ice even after the barge had arrived, as if he had forgotten for what purpose he had been swinging the ax. He looked like a mortally injured animal in its death throes; and the barge slipped in through the crust of ice like a Russian ice-breaker, and Matthew went out on the ice and gently took the ax from Old Dudley, and lifted him up onto the barge.

On the other shore, he said he was going to Amy's to pack up, and for Matthew to be ready to leave in two hours. Matthew nodded, said he would be napping in the mercantile, and to come and wake him when they were ready. Wallis said he didn't guess he would be seeing him again for a while, and reached out his hand to shake, but Old Dudley ignored it, climbed up on Amy's pony, and set off up the road slump-shouldered. Matthew watched him leave, then went inside the mercantile to finish the leftover pancakes, and to sleep the sleep of the dead. Wallis went home to do the same.

When Wallis awoke a day and a half later, and went back into town, the rig was gone, as was the barge, and the workers. It was snowing again. Wallis knocked at the mercantile door, went inside, where it was ice-cold, and found that Matthew was still sleeping. He went across the street. No one had seen Old Dudley or Amy, and they assumed he had left with the rig.

Wallis went up the road to Amy's. He saw the pony in its corral, and smoke from the chimney, but when he knocked at Amy's door she said that no, she hadn't seen him in two days, and had assumed that he had been staying out at the rig, or over at Mel's, without having told her his plans.

The town went searching for him. It was easy to cut transects on either side of the road between town and Amy's cabin. Their only fear was that he might have stumbled into the river, and they would never find him. Mel was crying, as they searched. The snow was falling so heavily now that it was sealing off even the tracks of the searchers behind them. They poked and prodded beneath the snow with sticks and branches, feeling for a frozen arm, a frozen leg.

They found him shortly before dusk. He was sitting under a spruce tree in a jumble of boughs and branches, with a sheet of snow over him, blue but alive, barely. He was not conscious. He had not made it two hundred yards past the spot where he had left Matthew and Wallis, upon returning from the dry hole.

They carried him in to the mercantile, took him upstairs, and laid him in Helen's old bed and warmed the store up as hot as they could get it.

He roused to consciousness, pained, shortly before midnight. Mel knew if he survived he would probably lose both arms and legs to frostbite, and was praying for him not to make it.

He was coughing, as pneumonia set in — drowning in his own lungs; and in a delirium he muttered words that at first she could not understand, but which upon leaning closer, she heard clearly: "Hungry. I'm so *hungry.*"

There were candles lit all around his bed. He didn't recognize her, didn't recognize anyone or anything. Amy was asleep with the baby downstairs. Matthew was asleep downstairs, snoring. Wallis was sitting up with Mel, rocking in a rocking chair. Old Dudley's breath came harder, in rattles and wheezes: he coughed, hacked, struggled to suck in enough air to breathe, to live, as if sucking in air through the tiniest of straws. They could both see and feel his life leaving him now like an upturned leaf floating down a river.

He roused once to lucidity. His tong marks lay smooth and flat, looking by some trick of candlelight to have almost disappeared, so that to Mel it was shocking — as if she were seeing a glimpse of who he might have been, had he been normal. He sat up and looked at her impassively, then over at Wallis in the corner, in his rocking chair, and scowled. He raised a crooked finger and pointed to Wallis, started to say something, but was seized by more death-coughing.

Mel went to him and took him by both shoulders. She shook him lightly but firmly. Her last chance to say it. "What," she said, "*what* do you have to recommend you?"

Anything. She wanted him to say anything — even to utter indecipherable gibberish. She couldn't think of a thing, but believed that he, surely now, if never before, could answer it.

He lay back in the deathbed, turned his face away from her, and said, "Nothing," and died.

Amy had heard Mel's hissed whisperings and had hurried up the steps with the baby Mary, for Dudley to hold one last time. She wept at having missed him and placed the baby on the dead man's chest, and laid her own head down on his chest and cried sobs of frustration and loneliness. Mel sat stony. Wallis went over and stood behind her with both hands on her shoulders.

After some time, Amy lifted her teary face and asked Mel, "What did he say? I missed it. What were his last words?"

Mel stared at her blankly, as if through the vast clear waters of a deep lake. Her mind did not seem to want to stir, but finally the words came to her, and she told Amy, "He said to tell you and Mary that there is great glory in life."

Amy began to cry again, and picked up the baby and held her close to her, and whispered in the baby's ear, "Did you hear that, little girl? Your daddy said that there is great glory in life."

EPILOGUE

THEY KEPT HIM ON BLOCKS OF ICE IN AN EMPTY GARAGE while Joshua worked on his coffin, working furiously to beat the freeze-up. Mel had given Matthew charge of all Dudley's properties, and Matthew had gone home to Houston, saying that he did not want to see the burial: that he wanted to believe the old man had not been found in the snow, but was instead still out there somewhere, wandering, and that he might yet show up again someday.

They kept him stiff on blocks of ice set atop boards laid across sawhorses, and kept little fires burning in a ring around him to keep the wild animals from breaking in and bothering him.

Joshua worked fast, working day and night in the same garage in which Dudley lay in repose, withering in the great cold. Joshua warmed his hands by the little fires as he worked, and when he had the ship finished, a twenty-foot scow in the shape of the full bare body of a woman, everyone came over from the bar and helped sand it and then paint it green. The woman in whose body he rode, the Malachite Woman, had long black hair carved back from the brow, and full bared breasts that would ride just above the water line. Her green eyes were haunting, as real as anything Joshua had ever done: as if the ship yet might come to life, or as if a soul inhabited it.

On ice, Old Dudley had shrunk to half his normal size, like some desiccated salamander. They gave the green paint a full night and day to dry and on the next night carried the ship down to the freezing river with him in it.

There was a brief debate about whether to set the ship afire or not, but Mel, after considering it, said no; just send him on down with a lantern in the bow.

The lantern was lit and placed. Dudley was lying on his back staring up at the sky, with his hands folded peacefully over his chest, and a bear hide draped over him for warmth. A light snow was falling.

They shoved the boat out across the ice and slipped it into the dark fast flowing water, then stepped back wordlessly as the boat was taken quickly from them.

The town watched through the curtain of falling snow as the boat, lit by its one lantern as if up on a stage amidst all-else-darkness, bobbed in the current, hurrying south between the snowy shores. The Malachite Woman's head, immense, like that of a dragon, rose high above the water. She stared resolutely, eagerly, downstream. The ship moved quickly away, riding and pitching on the little waves. It began to snow harder. The lantern disappeared.

Mel was crying, squeezing Wallis's hand. People stared into the darkness where he had gone — where the Malachite Woman had taken him — and then started trudging up the hill through knee-deep snow, back toward the bar.

"Why are you crying?" Wallis asked. "What's the matter? He couldn't live forever."

The snow was pressing down on them. They could barely hear the river's gurgling against the muffled silence of the snow.

"I'm so happy," Mel said.

They headed home on snowshoes. She wanted to be sure the boat was leaving the valley, so they climbed a ridge and followed the river south for a ways, until they caught back up with the dim sight of the boat: the lantern still glowing.

There they, and only they, watched it disappear a second time. Nothing else was moving; no other animals were about. They went home to their cabin. In bed, Mel took Wallis's hands and pressed them to the warm small mound of her stomach. It would be a thousand years, she hoped, before the valley saw anyone like Old Dudley again. Ten thousand years.

They awoke in the morning to blue sky and a world of deep white silence. They fixed breakfast and then struck out on snowshoes across the smoothness of untouched snow.

Acknowledgments

I am extremely grateful to James Linville and George Plimpton of the *Paris Review,* who first expressed confidence in this story, and to Houghton Mifflin, and to the late Sam Lawrence, who asked for this book, and to Joan Williams, who first brought it to his attention. I am grateful to Harry Foster, who has helped it through various drafts, and to Camille Hykes, who has also been working closely with the story for many years. I'm grateful also to Dorothy Henderson, for extraordinarily generous editorial help, and to *The New Yorker* and *Bomb,* in which sections of this book appeared in different form.

I am grateful for the support and advice from my agent, Bob Dattila, and to my friends and family and community. I'm grateful as ever to Russell Chatham, for the cover's painting, and to Stuart Klipper, for the interior photographs; to the James Jones Society, for the support and encouragement offered by the James Jones First Novel Fellowship; to Melodie Wertelet and Michaela Sullivan for the book's design; to Donna de La Perriere and Katie Dillin for production assistance; to my typist, Angi Young; to Tom Jenks, for editorial direction; and for use, in part, of the old Chautauqua papers by Alexander Winchell: his *Walks and Talks in the Geological Field.* I am grateful to the Guggenheim Foundation for the gift of a fiction fellowship.

I cannot thank my editors enough for help with this story. Finally, I am indebted to the vanishing wild landscape of northwest Montana itself. There still exists a health and strength — a magic — in its last vital cores. Whether these cores can be protected for the future or not, I do not know; but I hope for their continued existence and am grateful for having known them.